TURNING TOGETHER

Lara Zielinsky

Supposed Crimes LLC • Matthews, North Carolina

All Rights Reserved

Copyright © 2007, 2013, 2023 Lara Zielinsky

Published in the United States.

ISBN: 978-1-952150-41-8

Cover art by Somewillwin

Cover design by Geonn Cannon

www.supposedcrimes.com

This book is typeset in Goudy Old Style.

For subtext fans everywhere who love to parse looks and words and read between the lines to find a slow-burn love story.

TURNING POINT

CHAPTER ONE

PARKING HER Mercury Mountaineer beside the mailbox at 134 Alaca Drive in Altadena, Brenna Lanigan pensively studied the cream-colored brick home trimmed in earthy dark brown. Nothing special indicated that one of television's most popular stars lived there. Set on a large corner lot, it was typical of the surrounding homes. Six-foot-high privacy fencing enclosed the back yard. The red and white "Beware of Dog" sign nailed to the fencing gave her pause. Tidy beds of annuals lined the stepping stone walk to the front stoop. Somebody in the house obviously gardened. Brenna thought of her own gardens. She could be pulling the weeds on her dahlias.

She realigned her hands on the driving wheel and considered leaving. She could forget about putting herself in this awkward situation entirely. It was Saturday afternoon. She should be grocery shopping. She could be visiting Kevin in Michigan.

She wished her sons had not had dates last night.

She wished...for an excuse.

There was none. One by one, her castmates had accepted their invitations to this party for the son of another member of their ensemble. As the "lead" on the television series *Time Trails*, she could not be the only absent figure.

She sighed and checked her appearance once more in the rear-view mirror, not sure what to expect of a party at the home of Cassidy Hyland. She had only appeared with the woman at official Pinnacle public relations events, and even then, she interacted with her as little as possible. She tugged nervously at the short blue ribbon holding her auburn hair away from her face, her frown deepening. *What if I took "Dress: casual" wrong?* She looked critically over her short-sleeved jersey, dark blue jeans, and cross-trainers.

Looking again at the handwritten script on the party invitation, Brenna recalled her frustration at learning the woman had a son, much less one turning five on this early autumn day. She could not picture Cassidy Hyland tending a bloody knee or wiping a child's runny nose. The image did not fit with her first impression. Since Cassidy's arrival, Brenna had tried to learn as little about the woman as possible. Clearly she had succeeded.

She had been furious when the producers at Pinnacle Pictures decided the series could use an injection of pure sex appeal, thereby implying she herself had none. Hyland was thirty years old, long-legged, thin and blond, the epitome of the Hollywood starlet. She was in demand for high-value movie scripts and celebrity appearances, while Brenna was five foot five, forty-one years old, and hadn't had a big-budget movie project offered to her in two years. Following a supposed one-time appearance in a double-episode arc in April of 1999, Hyland joined the *Time Trails* cast full time. The costumers and the directors made the most of her "assets" by giving the younger actress a figure-hugging uniform that was slightly different from that of the rest of the cast, explaining she had come from a different branch of the new military structure.

From her first set call, Hyland had displayed almost inhuman poise. Incisive ice-blue eyes pinned Brenna in the scenes they shared. She stood regally tall, stalked with the sleek grace of a panther, and looked unaffected by the hours and hours under the stage lights. Flawless honey-blond hair framed her cream complexioned face. By the end of a twelve- or fourteen-hour shooting day, Brenna was tired and worn, disarrayed in body as well as mind. She felt like a wrinkled old woman next to the golden glory of Hyland, a veritable angel...

Brought to earth to make my life a living hell. Brenna sighed. The writing staff loved the sparks of tension as the two characters set out in very different ways to get things done, and they constantly staged them in close, tense exchanges.

Resolutely, Brenna gave the blond bombshell who had exploded into her life as cold a shoulder as possible. However, ignoring that statuesque frame standing less than an arm's length away in most of their scenes was impossible. She found herself tongue-tied or abruptly turning away to avoid her. Early morning one month ago, Brenna found the party invitation tucked in the edge of her makeup mirror. She was not over her feelings of resentment toward the producers, but she suddenly realized she was being unfair to the woman when she overheard the rest of the cast cheerfully accepting their invitations.

So why am I here, almost an hour late, just staring at the house? Her hesitation smacked of fear, and Brenna despised being afraid of anything. She gripped the door handle and shoved it open, stepping out onto the grass easement. *So what if it's the first non-production-related event where you're going to be in the same room with her? Suck it up.* Hurrying up the walk, she rang the bell before she could change her mind.

She remembered leaving the child's gift on her front seat at the same instant the door opened.

Cassidy Hyland's small home buzzed with the joyful laughter of children; adult voices filled her living room. She smiled with pleasure at her success. Her castmates did not seem put off by the number of her neighbors, parents of Ryan's playmates, also attending the party. Though, she sighed, one important face was still missing. She had tried several times to break through the ice that existed even off camera between herself and Brenna Lanigan, nominal leader of the *Time Trails* actors. She had understood from the beginning that Brenna's opinion mattered to most of the other actors and that they were only following her lead in leaving Cassidy mostly shut out of whatever socializing they did away from the set. She'd hoped that a birthday party for a child would be something so non-studio that everyone would see her as just another person.

Rachelle Cheron had been the first to arrive, with her daughter and husband, then Rich Paulson, along with Sean Durham with his son, followed quickly by Terry Brown and his daughter. Each had accepted enthusiastically while between takes at various times in the past month. With everyone else here, Cassidy hoped that she could be an accepted member of the troupe now. It had been more than a year, after all.

There was a light tap on the window separating the kitchen from the screen porch. Cassidy looked up to see her neighbor, Gwen Talbot, mouthing the word, "Cake?"

Realizing she was holding up things over a clearly false hope, Cassidy put down the tray of juice cups and turned to a nearby drawer to withdraw the cake knife.

"Can I carry something?"

Startled by the warm, rich voice that reminded her of smoky jazz clubs, Cassidy spun, knife still in hand. "Brenna?"

"Um, hi. Rich let me in." Brenna backed up and gestured toward Paulson, just closing the refrigerator door, beer in hand. "I hope I'm not too late."

With a tap of the bottle's neck to his receding hairline, a twinkle in his brown eyes, and a grin in salute, Rich was gone. Cassidy took the opportunity to watch him go and spend the few seconds collecting herself. Lowering the knife, she took a step back and slowly turned to Brenna.

Brenna Lanigan, swirls of gray in otherwise midnight blue eyes, was a beautiful, petite woman. She had brown hair pulled back in a low ponytail, but if Cassidy wasn't mistaken, the red highlighting was from the woman's Irish-American heritage, natural, rather than from a bottle. She had always appreciated genetics over Hollywood facade.

Taking in the other woman's attire, she was pleased Brenna had understood this was an informal party. She wore a sweatshirt with cropped sleeves bearing a New York University logo. One smooth, slender hand rested against the kitchen's island countertop. The fingertips of Brenna's other hand were tucked into the front pocket of figure-hugging, stone-washed jeans. "You look like you had a good night's sleep."

"I...yes, I did. Thank you."

The woman displayed a slow, surprised smile that Cassidy appreciated after being served up a year of cold shoulder. Perhaps this could be the start of a change between them. "You're just in time for cake," she said genially. She recalled the woman's two teenage sons. "Did Thomas and James come with you?"

"I had to start them cleaning the gutters," Brenna replied.

"Is that a normal chore?"

Brenna shook her head. "Punishment. They missed curfew last night."

Cassidy absorbed the information with surprise. "That's pretty rough. Didn't you miss any curfews as a teen?" Brenna frowned at her. *Oops, too familiar*, Cassidy thought. In an attempt to recover the situation, she pointed to the kitchen doorway. "Um, cake?"

Brenna gestured for Cassidy to go first, then picked up the tray of juice cups and followed.

"Bren!" Rachelle Cheron came to her feet from the couch. A woman of exotic almond coloring and angular features framed with ebony, short-styled loose curls, Chelle smiled widely and easily. "So you didn't go to Michigan this weekend."

Brenna shook her head. "The boys had dates last night." She accepted a one-armed hug and inhaled the scent of baby powder from Rose, the eight-month-old in Chelle's arms.

"I don't envy you. Girls today can be predatory," Rachelle said. "After all, your boys are related to a *star*."

At the emphasis on the label, Brenna shook her head with chagrin. "I don't remind them." Studying Rachelle and Rose, Brenna wondered how the little girl would grow up to view her mother's job. Thomas and James certainly were not shy about sharing their negative views.

Brenna pinched a smile on her features and turned away, taking in the whole of the living room space as she looked for a place to sit. There was the brown stuffed leather couch where Rachelle sat with Rose. Behind her were two stuffed chairs in matching brown leather, one occupied by another woman ~ a brunette unfamiliar to Brenna ~ holding a cup of punch.

She caught the soft sound of music and noticed the entertainment center set off to the side behind the couch. A shadowbox on the wall held several figurines ~ some Disney characters and others clearly Hummel or similar. Brenna reached up toward a beautiful figurine of dancing children wearing homespun overalls. The effect of bare feet and heads tipped back in open laughter was enchanting. A hand brushed Brenna's shoulder. Startled, she looked back into Cassidy's pale blue eyes capturing her with curiosity.

"Cake?" Cassidy asked.

Brenna looked around to realize they were alone. Everyone else had already left the living room for the porch. "Yes. I'm sorry."

"It's all right. I don't have time for a proper tour, but perhaps another time?"

Tongue-tied, Brenna could only silently follow her hostess out to the porch, stepping through the sliding glass door. Out in the fenced yard, Brenna spotted Terry Brown following Rich Paulson toward the porch.

The dark-skinned Terry was another actor from *Time Trails*. He played Creighton, Susan Jakes' hatchet man. He was an expert at killing people ~ not in the traditional sense, though he could do that in a pinch ~ but as a computer expert who could wipe away records, making someone disappear from history before they took him or her out physically as well. He was also their "cover" man, inserting their impersonations into databases so that their presence would not upset the timeline while they were trying to restore it.

Paulson's character, Dr. Pryor, handled the team's medical needs. Both men were as level-headed and personable as their characters, with lengthy résumés as character actors.

Jacques Cheron, Rachelle's husband, brought up the rear, along with a man Brenna did not recognize. She was surprised to realize that it was probably someone from the neighborhood. All talked easily and looked comfortable, dressed in jeans and pullover shirts or sweatshirts. The atmosphere reminded Brenna of her own large family gatherings as a child. Again she marveled at the simplicity. She had never expected to find Cassidy like this.

Looking at her hostess, she noted the woman's soft, grass-green, scoop-neck cotton blouse as she talked quietly with a portly woman standing beside her. What Brenna had thought were slacks were actually dark green jeans. Knife in hand, Cassidy stepped up to the other end of a wooden picnic table covered in drawing paper where some of the children were drawing with crayons on the space in front of them. The half-sheet cake in front of her on the table was decorated with colorful handmade whorls and a stick-figure boy and dog. A boy with blond hair climbed onto the bench at the end and leaned on thin arms over the cake.

"Time for cake?" he asked.

"Yes." Cassidy tucked his shirt in where the tail of it was dangerously close to the icing. Brenna was surprised to realize that he was Cassidy's son. He looked small for five years old.

A dark-haired boy built considerably thicker than Ryan climbed up next to him and yelled, "Sing!"

Brenna smiled and joined in a discordant, yet joyful rendition of "Happy Birthday" to Ryan.

Cassidy cut the cake, occasionally nudging her son's hands away from the blade as he reached to move pieces by hand. Paper plates began to circulate.

Ryan scooped ice cream rather messily, though Cassidy did not appear to mind. She handed Ryan his plate, then another to the boy next to him. The two jumped off the bench and pushed their way out into the yard to sit on the grass and eat. After being served, many of the other children followed.

Brenna stepped up for her piece of cake and overheard the portly woman speaking to Cassidy. "The cake's a hit. That recipe I gave you turned out really well. And I love the decorations."

"Thanks, Gwen." With a warm smile that crinkled the skin at the corner of her eyes and lips, Cassidy leaned forward and pressed her lips briefly to Gwen's cheek. Brenna wondered who this neighbor was to be treated with such casual intimacy.

"Brenna?" Cassidy's voice brought her eyes back up. "Do you want ice cream?"

Jerking her head up as she tried to formulate a response, the first thought Brenna had was that Cassidy's eyes looked different in the sunlight. *Softer*, Brenna thought. She was more used to the defiant expressions she encountered when they were in character. She reminded herself, *Cassidy is not Chris Hanssen, and I'm not Susan Jakes.* Brenna tried to remember that she was here because Cassidy had invited her. It was time she related to the woman on a personal level. She cleared her throat. "Yes, thank you."

Passing a paper plate of cake and ice cream, Cassidy made introductions. "Brenna, this is my neighbor, Gwen Talbot. Gwen, this is Brenna Lanigan, from *Time Trails.*"

"Hello. My son, Chance, is Ryan's shadow there." Gwen pointed out the boy next to Ryan where they sat in the grass. The bigger boy was swiping a finger of icing from the top of Ryan's slice. Beside them, Sean had his son, Kieran, sitting next to him and was supervising the messy consumption of cake and ice cream by the two-year-old.

"It's very nice to meet you, Gwen." Brenna stepped back, looking around for a place to sit.

"Sit here," Cassidy suggested, pointing to the bench opposite Rachelle, Jacques, and Rose. "The kids seem to prefer the grass."

"I can see that," she said with a half smile. Clearing aside a few crayons, she settled onto the bench, looking up to see Rachelle sharing small bits of cake and the occasional smear of ice cream with Rose.

Brenna moved aside as Gwen settled to her right, then was unsure where to go when Cassidy settled to her left, having at last served herself a piece of cake. Cassidy's thigh was firm and warm against hers. She resolutely ducked her head to her food.

Always to be counted on for livening up a social occasion, Rachelle started small talk about the L.A. County park system. Cassidy joined in as she described the new installation of fitness stations at her own neighborhood park. Feeling the body moving against her own, Brenna considered getting up, but she became entranced by the voice and the long fingered hands with which Cassidy was illustrating her points.

"You don't work out at a gym?" Rachelle sounded as surprised as Brenna felt.

"Ryan and I can go through the park together. At a gym I have to leave him with the sitting service. I try to limit that."

Brenna asked, "What do you do with him while you're at work?"

"Ryan's in preschool at Gwen's elementary school, so she keeps him with her until I get home."

Quite neighborly, Brenna thought, aware she'd had no such offers from her neighbors. Then again, she tried to keep to herself, and her neighbors in Pacific Palisades, many of them in the business like she was, did the same. Cassidy, it seemed, lived in a more working-class neighborhood. She studied Gwen again and watched the woman respond, "Chance gets time to play with Ryan, so it works out for everyone." The dark-haired woman shrugged as her voice trailed off.

Glancing over her shoulder back to Cassidy, Brenna ducked away from the intense smile Cassidy beamed at her neighbor. "I couldn't have done this without her," Cassidy said.

A small clock on the fireplace mantle chimed the hour, drawing everyone's attention. "Time to send the children home," Cassidy murmured as she extracted herself from the picnic table bench. At the sound of the doorbell, Cassidy went to let in the first of the other children's parents. For a while the house filled with the commotion of greetings and farewells tossed among the adults and eager children showing off their prizes from the party.

Terry straightened from dusting grass cuttings off his daughter's jeans. "Great party, Cass. I had a good time."

"Glad you could come," Cassidy said with a smile. "Nice to meet you, Becca." She offered her hand to the young girl.

Becca's brown eyes widened, and she blinked, hiding her face before turning to grin up at her. "Can I come back?" The girl's eyes followed when Cassidy raised her face to Terry's.

Cassidy directed her question to him. "Perhaps we can all get together sometime?"

Terry nodded as he warmly held both Cassidy's hands in his dark ones and then turned to Brenna. "It was good to see you, Bren." She nodded. Terry prodded his daughter out, though she tried to cling to Ryan. Cassidy, Brenna, Rachelle, and Jacques, holding Rose, remained in the foyer.

"Thanks for a great party," Rachelle said, adjusting the shoulder strap of her baby bag. "I'll see you both Monday morning." She looked first at Cassidy, then Brenna, and nodded at some personal thought before she stepped out, followed by her husband.

Brenna stood alone with Cassidy on the front step. Ryan hugged his mother's hip and waved goodbye to the guests.

The sound of a car door opening and slamming shut caught Cassidy off guard. She had been trying to think of something to say, something that would convey how much she appreciated Brenna's attendance at the party. The other woman, also startled by the sound, spun around, turning her back toward Cassidy to assess the new arrival.

Stepping out of the house to stand behind Cassidy, Gwen grasped her arm, tense and alarmed, but Cassidy patted the hand and Gwen withdrew. She frowned at the tall man with conservatively trimmed blond hair. "Mitch," Cassidy said, "what are you doing here?"

He nodded curtly to Brenna as she passed him going to her car, then snapped his attention back to his ex-wife. "I came to see my *son*."

Cassidy saw Brenna hesitate, look back, then resume her walk to the curb. She said quietly but forcefully, "You're supposed to call first."

"You're not alone." Crouching, Mitch pulled his left hand from behind his back, revealing the wrapped present he had been concealing. Ryan let go of his mother's leg and sprinted to his father's open arms.

Damn, she thought with heartfelt disappointment, both for Brenna's departure and her ex-husband's arrival. Familiar wariness rose like bile in her throat as Mitch pulled Ryan to him in a tight hug. Then Mitch's green eyes fixed on her.

Chapter Two

Script pages turned amid the group of actors seated casually on the floor of a set sparsely decorated and liberally painted in green tones. The Vortex room.

"All right. Let's try the basic marks." Director Mike Malley, his own script copy in hand, started pointing out places. "Bren, here. Will, out of frame. Terry, you're starting here. And Rich, you're there."

Rising to her feet from downstage left, Brenna shrugged her shoulders at Will Chapman as the actor folded up his script and stalked off stage right, pushing past Cassidy as the blonde unfolded from her Indian-style position downstage right.

Brenna saw Cassidy absently rub and rotate the shoulder Will had knocked into. Will, she recalled, had not been at Cassidy's home the other afternoon. Clearly he was ticked off about something. Brenna was surprised to see him taking it out on Cassidy.

Mike wasn't done with his stage directions. "Chelle, you cross front, but let's have you coming left instead of right." Chelle took her position. "All right, lighting check."

A scurry of technicians with light meters stepped into everyone's space, positioning their meters as needed, shouting notes to the overhead lighting grips. The walk-through would allow the light team to take their readings and check for any overt glare or bad shadows caused by the actors' relative heights and the lamp positions. The cast, used to the routine by now, stood quietly, glancing over the current script page.

When the stage was cleared, Mike called, "Begin."

"All right, everyone. You know the mission. Lieutenant Raycreek's made the calculations. We're going in, making the correction, and getting back out again. Is that clear?"

Time Squad Commander Susan Jakes looked in turn at each of her team, dressed in their Time Squad jumpsuits, a sleek, futuristic black with colored armbands denoting their respective ranks.

The camera and lighting grips measured distances and took notes for the framed close-ups, each actor taking a moment to nod as he or she would when the cameras rolled.

Trailed by a grip, Rachelle crossed the stage reciting her line. She held out her right hand. Empty now, during filming it would hold a remote-control-like prop. On cue she now "handed" that to Brenna.

Time Agent Luria Dewitt reported, "I've set the circuits, Commander."

Sean Durham dusted his hand through his blond hair and tapped his script, which would be replaced by another prop, an information disk, during shooting.

Time Agent Jeremy Dewitt questioned, "Are you sure this is the right place? It doesn't look like one of Heatherly's usual hits."

Susan's reply was confident. "Mark did the calculations himself. I had him check them after Robinson's last orders."

Luria nodded. "Well, good thing I packed my dancing shoes. Looks like our target location is a rock 'n' roll club."

Rich smiled at Cassidy as the woman stepped up next to him, reaching out for his "file copy," looking down at the script.

Time Agent Chris Hanssen asked brusquely, "Has CE Creighton completed the insert?"

"Yes."

"What's our cover?"

"Lu," Susan said, nodding toward Luria, "and Jeremy are a couple looking for good games. You and Doc will 'fleece' them to make them look inviting to Baxley. Be sure to do it where he can see you."

"Who's our target? What did he do?" She lifted a file photo, a grainy black and white of a man in a

1950s-era suit and fedora.
      "Baxley's your basic time jumper, an opportunist.
We've traced his interruptions through two time
streams. Mostly gambling scams. We've gotten the
warrant, so it's time to bring him in." She looked
around at the others. "Any other questions?"
      There was no reply. Chris continued to look
pensively at the rather handsome face.
      "All right. I'll be site coordinator. We have 72
hours."

Rachelle, Sean, Cassidy, Rich, and Brenna stepped around an "X" on the floor by the shadows of the crossbeams of an overhead lamp.

"Mark?"

Followed by a lighting grip, Will Chapman stepped up to a mocked-up panel, his back to the other actors.

Lieutenant Mark Raycreek cast a silent look over his shoulder, turned away from the team, and pushed forward on a handlebar-style switch.

"And...break!"
Libby, the lead grip, pulled her luminosity meter from around her neck. "We got all our reads."
"Great. We'll set up for the transmission site on the alley set next door." Mike looked at his watch. "Well, maybe we'll do it after lunch. Take an hour, folks."
Brenna started off the stage, walking past Will's position just as the huge man turned. As she bounced off his shoulder, she looked up at him, catching a sour expression. "Something wrong, Will?"
"Would be nice to get something to do for a change. I flip switches and read off-screen quite a lot."
"The nature of the beast, right? You'll get another episode."
"I damn well plan on it."
Surprised at his vehemence, Brenna turned to watch him storm off in the other direction. He sidestepped Rich, but though there was plenty of room to go around Cassidy, who was next to him, Will clipped her right shoulder. Rich grasped Cassidy's other shoulder to steady her and guided her as they turned behind Sean and Rachelle.
"You coming, Bren?" Rich asked. "We're off to the catering table."
Brenna declined automatically. "No. I've got a few calls to make." She saw his lips quirk in dismay as his eyes darted to Cassidy. She reluctantly turned around. "Never mind. They'll wait until the dinner break." Rich's

smile reappeared as she came alongside them.

Listening to the other cast over their sandwiches thank Cassidy again for the weekend party, Brenna joined in with, "How long have you lived there?"

"Just this last year."

"It's very homey."

There was a brief silence as the rest of the cast, Cassidy, and finally Brenna, realized how atypical such a civil comment was between the two women. "Thank you," Cassidy said quietly.

Following lunch break, the crew and cast were back on the sets, breaking off into rehearsal pairs as the main set was configured for the first full scenes to be shot that night. Taking this first day to rehearse by herself, memorizing lines away from the distractions of the set, Brenna started for her trailer. Cassidy's voice interrupted her.

"Brenna?" When Brenna turned and Cassidy saw her frown, she took a step back. "I'm sorry. I forgot you had some calls."

"Actually, I'm just going to rehearse."

Cassidy pursed her lips; Brenna fidgeted with the script pages in her hands. "Would...would you like to rehearse together?"

From the venturing tone, Brenna knew that Cassidy had worked herself up to ask. A month ago she would have not even tried to meet the woman halfway. Something felt different though; Brenna found she was actually curious to see how Cassidy rehearsed. She nodded. "All right. Where would you like to start?"

"I thought, maybe, well, the argument we have in scene 7B about really having to take in Baxley."

"What's wrong with it?"

"There's not a lot of room for understanding in the dialogue."

"They're not supposed to understand each other. Susan's by the book. They get in, they get the guy, and they get out."

"But Chris wants her to think about it. She's emotionally involved."

"Susan isn't. So she'll ask 'Why?'"

"Because the world isn't all black and white," Cassidy snapped. She swallowed and took a step back. Brenna realized only then herself that the taller woman had invaded her personal space. "Um, sorry."

"Don't be. Characters get carried away."

"Do you think we could shade the argument a little differently?"

Brenna was intrigued. This was perhaps an opportunity to reveal more of Susan's layers to the audience too. "If we don't change dialogue; we'll have to do it all in the blocking."

Cassidy smiled. "Let's go to the set then."

Brenna found herself eagerly following.

Commander Susan Jakes paced, occasionally looking at the junior officer, Lieutenant Chris Hanssen, who stood stiffly beside a craps table. It was the middle of the night, and the two women were alone in the community dance hall.

"Commander," Chris started.
Susan spun, slapping her right hand at the air. "No!"
"He wants to stay here."
"That's what he tells you. He's playing you."
"Just put a tracker on him."
"And let him keep amassing his private little fortune? No."
"It isn't a fortune. And he doesn't want to go back to work for Heatherly."
"What the hell makes you believe him? We've seen more than our share of turncoats, Hanssen. The minute the Squad lets this one get away-"
"I believe him. Have you talked to him?"
"No. And I'm not going to. You're going to bring him to the recovery coordinates tomorrow on time."
"Heatherly has an assassin waiting for him if he comes out in the open."
"Damn it, Hanssen, I should have recommended you for the records department instead of reconnaissance when you first came on. You're not seasoned enough. You're not seeing clear-"
"Then why didn't you?"
Susan blinked. The quiet interruption stymied her a moment.
"You had full control over my assignment to this squad. So why didn't you put me in Creighton's place? My tech skills are equal to his."
"Creighton thought you'd make a versatile member of the on-site team."
"You didn't trust me."
"No, I didn't."
"But you gave me a chance." Susan frowned. "Give him a chance to prove himself."
"Why does he want to stay here? This is ancient history."
"He likes it."
"He likes it?"
"Actually, he said he'd rather die among friends than people he's never known."

```
    "We can't make a judgment on that here. That's for
others to do."
    "Is there nothing I can say?"
    When Commander Jakes shook her head, there was a
sadness about it. Chris Hanssen straightened up.
Brusquely the commander issued her final order, "Be at
the rendezvous spot. With Baxley in custody."
```

Brenna turned and walked away from Cassidy. As she reached the edge of the set, she turned back. "We ad-libbed in the middle there."

"It was easy because the emotional arc rings true. They do disagree." Cassidy crossed to her. "But the lines suggest that Chris is turning Susan's opinion, just a little."

"We can't ad-lib for shooting without approval."

"I know. So, how can we convey some of the lines without words?"

The two women sat down in a pair of chairs near the camera lines and pulled out their scripts to consult and scribble.

Brenna walked past the central sets of *Time Trails*, headed for her trailer to relax until her after-dinner shoot of several C.U.s, or close-ups. She had just finished an interview about her upcoming fan convention appearance with Terry. She reflected on the give-and-take she had experienced while rehearsing with Cassidy. She felt like she had stretched muscles she hadn't used in years. It was a tiring, but good feeling. She smiled.

"Ms. Lanigan?"

Am I ever going to get to my trailer today? Irritated, Brenna rolled her script in her hands. "Yes?" But when she turned and saw a pre-teen boy standing nervously about four feet away, she forcibly relaxed. "Oh, hello." He scuffed a foot against the floor. She affected Jakes' patented glare and stern tone, forcing down her smile as he squirmed. "Did you sneak away from a tour?"

He straightened like a green military recruit. "Ah, uh...No. I mean, NO, Ma'am! I'm here with my Uncle Bill. He...William Doherty...um...he wrote the script, and he thought I'd like to see it being made while he's in another story meeting."

Brenna grinned and put a reassuring hand on his shoulder. "That's okay. I've brought my sons once or twice. You're all right back here as long as you stay out of the way." She started to turn away but stopped when he spoke again.

"Would you...please?"

The boy presented her with a small book pulled from his back pants pocket. He wiped his hands on his jeans ~ no doubt to wipe away the sweat ~ before passing her the small notepad-sized autograph book.

"All right." She smiled as he fumbled with a pen, then passed it to her. His shyness was endearing.

"You...you said you have sons?"

She pursed her lips to stifle a chuckle. Apparently he was bold enough to start small talk with her. "Yes, two. Thomas is seventeen and James is fifteen. What's your name?"

"I'm..." He swallowed. She patiently waited. "My name's Ricky. I mean...could you make it to 'Rick'?"

"Sure." She signed, "To Rick, love, Commander Jakes" and passed it back. "Here you go."

"Oh, man! I can't believe...Yes!" Rick whooped and was quickly shushed by a dozen people nearby. He lowered his voice and finished, "Thanks, Commander!"

As the boy bounced away, Brenna wondered who else he would sneak up on before the end of the day. She looked forward to listening for the random whoops and hollers from distant parts of the soundstage.

"That was sweet."

"Hmm?" Brenna looked up from the pen still in her hand. In his excitement, the boy had forgotten to reclaim it. Over her left shoulder, she saw Cassidy step around the edge of a temporary wall. Unnerved by the idea of Cassidy watching her, she explained, "The writer brought his nephew to the set."

"I heard."

"You didn't come out."

"He'll find me later."

"I was just thinking about that."

"I wonder who else he's gotten today."

Brenna shrugged as Cassidy walked up next to her. "I didn't see him around before lunch, so...maybe I was the first."

"Appropriate," Cassidy said with a smile. She nodded toward the set where several of the actors and the director were going back over their placements and working through the apprehension scene again. "Are you going to your trailer? I just spent twenty minutes repeatedly darting after our 'bad guy' for a one-minute fifteen-second onscreen result."

"Yes, I was. So, did the-"

To Brenna's surprise, Cassidy sighed and rubbed her feet, releasing them from a pair of dress heels as soon as she sat down in a nearby canvas chair. "I wish I had a longer dinner break. I could really use my foot bath. But I'm first up for the C.U.s."

Brenna could not recall Cassidy expressing any discomfort before and wondered if it was because she had not bothered to notice or if the woman was in an atypical amount of pain. Cassidy continued massaging her stocking-covered foot. *Well, there's time enough to correct that now.* Brenna rolled up her script and patted it against her own thigh, snapping her gaze up to Cassidy's face. "I might have something to help there. Why don't you come to my trailer to sit for a few minutes? Besides, I forgot to leave Ryan's present on Saturday, so I can give you that, too."

"You don't have to."

"I do. I had it with me, but in...I left it in the car."

"Oh." After another brief hesitation, Cassidy nodded. "All right." She bent over to put the heels back on. With a sigh, she stopped. "Forget it. I'll walk in stockings."

"I think I have a spare pair of slippers."

Cassidy's head snapped up in surprise. "I...thanks."

Brenna realized where Cassidy's eyes were staring ~ at the casual hand she had put on the other woman's arm, which she quickly withdrew. She covered her quandary about why she had done something so intimate with a quipped, "Sure."

Brenna in her boots and Cassidy in her stocking feet walked around to the back of the soundstage and out the door to a line of trailers. Each cast member had one. They walked to the second to last one on the left.

"I don't think I've been in here." Cassidy took the last step up into the cozy trailer. She eyed a refrigerator and Formica-topped folding table. Brenna's "home away from home" was littered with photographs and books. A hand-crocheted afghan lay haphazardly over the back and arm of a small recliner. She noticed a book half-tucked under the old beige version of a script page and picked it up as Brenna disappeared into the second half of the trailer, tossing over her shoulder, "Have a seat."

When Brenna returned, Cassidy held up the book with a questioning look. "You read this?"

Brenna laughed. "I have to know a little bit about the science of some of this stuff or I'll never say it right." She took the book from Cassidy's hands and laid it aside, glancing at the star-speckled cover of Hawking's *A Brief History of Time.*

"Yeah, but him? Seems a little dry. I read Feynman myself." She offered a wry smile. "You're right, though. We've got to sound somewhat convincing when we do this."

Brenna presented her with two pairs of slippers. "Go on. Blue cotton or Bullwinkle J. Moose?" Cassidy hesitated, then reached for the brown character slippers. "I figured you for a Bullwinkle fan," Brenna added as Cassidy dropped to the couch to place them on her feet.

"You did?" She sighed in relief as the thickly padded interior hugged her aching feet.

"I just took one look at you and said, 'Bullwinkle.' Though as you can see, I brought the blue ones in case I was wrong."

"Always prepared? I find it odder that you would like Bullwinkle," Cassidy admitted.

Brenna shrugged. "I grew up watching this earnest moose that seemed to mess everything up."

"Though things usually came out right in the end."

"Serendipity." Brenna smiled.

"Or his buddy Rocky." Cassidy chuckled. The two women fell silent for a moment.

"Oh, mmm...Here." Brenna reached around behind the edge of the couch, just out of Cassidy's line of sight, and withdrew a wrapped box. About twice the size of a shoe box, it was covered in paper printed with party hats in a menagerie of colors. "For Ryan."

Taking it, Cassidy nodded and set it beside her on the couch. "I'll give it to him tonight."

Brenna shifted. "I can rewrap it, if...would you just tell me?" She leaned against the arm of the small stuffed chair where she sat across from Cassidy.

"What? You want me to open it? I'm sure he'll love it."

"I haven't bought for that age in years, Cass."

Cassidy hesitated at the woman's earnest expression, surprised by the unexpectedly vulnerable admission and the way Brenna had shortened her name. Since she did not want to ruin the cute paper, Cassidy asked, "What is it?"

"A stuffed animal."

She considered that. Her son did sleep with a worn stuffed crocodile.

Brenna went on with a tone that sounded abashed. "I saw it at a specialty toy shop when I was in Mount Clemens."

"What kind of animal?"

"Well, really a...a monster." Brenna shifted and crossed her left leg over her right and steepled her fingers together over the knee. "There's this story...I've always loved it. About a boy and the monsters he meets in a land of make-believe. Maurice Sendak wrote it."

Cassidy smiled. "I know that one. *Where the Wild Things Are*," she identified. "Right?"

Brenna grinned. "Yeah. This was a handmade toy modeled after the cover illustration." She shrugged. "I wasn't sure you'd think it appropriate. I did include a copy of the book, if you don't already have one."

Cassidy picked up the wrapped box and studied it. "Ryan doesn't have it." She set it down. "I know what I'll be reading to him next." She smiled at Brenna and saw the woman exhale.

"If we get out of here at a reasonable hour," Brenna said.

"You mean midnight isn't reasonable?" Cassidy's gamble at making a joke paid off. Brenna tipped her head back and laughed until tears appeared in her eyes.

"Oh God. I'm sorry. You're right. Midnight is not reasonable. So, when do you read to him?"

"I try to read to him at least twice a week. Sometimes it's just Saturday and Sunday afternoons. Sometimes it's after getting a lucky break here and being home around ten."

"It is hard to have a young child and work these hours."

"And teenagers are better? I seem to remember you saying that yours were out past curfew. The anxiety would kill me."

"Thomas and James are generally pretty good ~ and helpful now that Thomas also drives."

Cassidy nodded. There did not seem to be much to add. They fell into silence, and she ran her hand over the couch cushion, tracing the simple maroon linear print, unable to avoid contemplating a nap. She even yawned. Quickly she stifled it, as she was quite sure the change in Brenna's attitude toward her was not yet up to offering to let Cassidy nap on her couch

Brenna suddenly moved, jerking Cassidy's attention to her. "We had better head back." Cassidy bent over to remove the slippers. "Keep them."

"All right," she accepted and stood. Collecting the wrapped present and the costume boots in her arms, she stepped back as Brenna held open the door. As she stepped into the daylight, she came close to Brenna, acutely aware of the other woman watching her pass.

Brenna waited at the bottom of the steps to Cassidy's trailer while she dropped off the gift and slippers and put her boots back on, though Cassidy had invited her to enter. But it was together that they walked back to the soundstage.

CHAPTER THREE

IT WAS late Friday, near the end of their last scheduled day of shooting the season's tenth episode, *Crap Shoot*. After a late dinner break watching the stars come out and eating a snack on her trailer steps, Brenna was back on the soundstage. She looked over to where Cassidy worked with Will Chapman in a concluding scene. She and Cassidy would have the next one.

The rehearsal for the scene was still fresh in her mind, practiced Wednesday morning with Cassidy after the woman had been to costuming for her shooting of two stunt scenes with the B camera team.

Previously Brenna would have only done the rehearsal with Cassidy with the other actors and the director for the regularly scheduled run-throughs. But Cassidy had approached her with an idea, and they followed through the rest of the week, consulting together on several scenes. The episode had finally come together with a fabulous amount of character development, prime among them the relationship between Chris and Susan.

In the plot, Baxley had taken advantage of Hanssen's mixed feelings about bringing him in, building an elaborate story. When the time came to take him in, there was a firefight. Jeremy Dewitt had to shoot Baxley, who was holding Chris hostage in a room filled with "normals," their term for those living in the timeline they had intercepted. Dozens of people could have died. Chris' fight with Susan now proved that the commander had been right. Regulations also meant that the young officer had to be reprimanded for her misjudgment.

In the end, they didn't rewrite a single word in their four scenes together. To Brenna's surprise, they managed to convey all of the nuance with simple body language. All it took was simply letting herself react to Cassidy's very mobile features ~ letting herself see, for the first time, the skill and knowledge with which Cassidy Hyland played her character. When they had played this final scene through at the pre-shoot rehearsal, the director had been very pleased and congratulated them both on the development.

Having finally recognized Cass as a member of the *Time Trails* team, both on- and off-camera, it felt right to Brenna that their arguments came out with a softer edge. Cassidy's smiles off-camera were more frequent now, and Brenna realized that the other woman also had been unhappy. While her presence could still have negative repercussions for Brenna's career, she recognized that it was not Cassidy's fault. Letting that go made her feel as if a weight had been lifted from her own shoulders.

The director's call for action drew Brenna's attention from her thoughts to the unfolding scene. On stage, Will Chapman portrayed Lieutenant Raycreek. As the second-ranking officer in Susan's Time Squad, it was his job to inform Chris Hanssen of the punishment Susan had devised for her disobedience.

Raycreek slammed the ball around the court walls, forcing Chris to chase it. When she stopped to catch her breath, he continued to drill: "You disobeyed her, Chris. You'll be on restricted duty until she thinks she can trust you again. You knew that going in. Why did you do it?"

"I believed it was the right thing to do," Chris replied defensively, panting.

"Sometimes it's not right or wrong that you should be concerned about, it's doing the prudent thing," Raycreek countered, starting another round of the game. "Rules and regs protect everyone."

"It's prudent to stand by and let someone die?" Chris sneered. She missed another shot. "Your game," she conceded sullenly.

"He played you for a fool, Chris. If you had listened to your commanding officer, you wouldn't be in this situation right now," he offered coolly, then walked toward the doors.

The stagehands used a pulley to open the doors, and Chapman walked out of camera view.

"Cut. Excellent."

Chapman spun his racket in his fist and strode quickly off the other side.

It was clear to Brenna that Cassidy's energy was flagging. Will had taken her all over the court with his shots, certainly more than was required for the cameras. Inhaling, Brenna started for the doorway to take her place for the next sequence. Around her, the camera crew, microphone, and lighting grips adjusted their equipment for the closer up angles coming in her one-on-one scene with Cassidy.

Concentrate, she prodded herself, hoping to finish this in just the necessary number of takes required to get all the right angles. She felt the telltale warmth of nerves dampening her palms, so she paced, trying to shake it off.

Cassidy had a moment to breathe as well. Since she would not be required to be in exactly the same position for the opening of the next scene, no one jumped to chalk the floor as she stepped away. She joined Brenna behind the doorway for a few moments of respite from the hot lights. "Brenna?"

"Ready to get off your feet?" Brenna asked.

Cassidy drew closer, decreasing their visibility to the others as she gave a tired smile and sighed. "Absolutely."

Her voice, soft as it was, drew the attention of another actor. Jeff Liverpool, the now dead Baxley, walked up and interposed himself. "Hey, Cassidy, it's been great. Thanks." He cast a look over her costume once, then offered his hand.

"Mmm hmm," she replied, forcing a smile as she looked away from Brenna. Patiently she shook the hand of the man she had spent the most camera time with over the previous week.

Brenna caught Cassidy's shake of her head as the actor turned away. She thought she also heard a breath of relief. When Jeff was out of earshot, headed for costuming to get out of his clothes, she nudged Cassidy's arm. "Trouble?"

"Not any more."

"What happened?"

"Oh, that's right," Cassidy started wryly. "You had that interview with *TV Cult Times,* so you missed the fifteen takes it took to convince him not to pinch my butt when he was holding me hostage."

Brenna bit her lip to hold back a laugh and shook her head. "It's such a cute butt, though."

Cassidy blinked. *Where on earth did that come from? Exhaustion?* When she opened her eyes again, she saw Brenna sauntering away to the water cooler tucked against the wall of the soundstage. Deciding to extend the joking, Cassidy called, "So's yours." Brenna spun around and shook a finger at her while sipping from her paper cup, barely hiding a grin. Even though she wondered why Brenna had bantered with her in such a teasing way, Cassidy could not deny she was relaxed again by the time the director's voice reached them both.

"All right, last one of the day, folks."

Cassidy stepped out onto the gym set again, and he looked over at her. "Let's see how few takes we can do, hmm?"

She displayed a thumbs up and stood on her mark at the service line, stretching to loosen her body.

"Action!"

The stagehands used pulleys to open the doors, and Brenna swept inside, racket in hand.

Commander Jakes hesitated when she saw the room was already occupied. The blond head swiveled toward her. When the azure eyes fell on her, Jakes straightened her uniform, a telltale "I'm not sure what I'm doing here" sign.

"Commander?" Chris Hanssen's voice was low, a little tired but clearly questioning. She straightened from the beginning of a solo game. Considering she might be in for another reprimand, Chris drew herself up into an "at attention" posture, tucking her hands behind her back.

"I didn't expect to find anyone here." Jakes swallowed.

"I'm working some of the stiffness out of my arm."

That drew Jakes' attention to the bandage on Hanssen's left arm. "Are you all right?"

"Yeah. The doctor patched me up."

The women were silent, looking at anything other than each other. Something occurred to Susan and she finally, reluctantly looked at Chris, "Did Lieutenant Raycreek deliver my decision?"

"I am relieved of duty for one month."

"Do you understand why? You could've been killed, Lieutenant, many of the non-coms as well. We cannot reverse the orders once we're on the ground. I thought you understood that. When I said no, I meant it."

"What if his story had been true?" Hanssen bristled. "It would be an innocent man that is now dead. We still don't really know. We'll never really know."

"You've got time on your hands. Read his file again, Chris. He lied to you."

"So he lied to me. Don't tell me you haven't believed a lie once or twice," Hanssen shot back.

"You don't know anything about my service record." Jakes stepped forward and glared hard at the woman whose gaze was just a bit higher than hers. "When you're in command, you can give the orders. In the meantime, I'm in charge here."

"You don't give a damn about the fact that a man died."

Jakes snatched the ball from Chris' fingers, and Chris flinched. "Everyone's life matters to me." Catching her breath and trying to diffuse her frustration with the younger officer, she repeated softly, "Every life." There was a quality of regret.

Chris' body language softened slightly, but she still barked, "Second thoughts, Commander?"

"Cut." The director interposed himself loudly, drawing both women's attention. "Too angry. More contrite. Remember you're inviting a connection here."

Cassidy nodded. "Sorry."

Brenna's hand slipped over hers with a squeeze. "Where from?" she asked Mike, stepping back from her mark.

"Let's start at the service line. Start your marks there."

"Okay." Brenna took several steps back while Cassidy adjusted her position as well. She looked over Cassidy's form and, catching blue eyes on her, she smiled briefly. "I'm ready whenever you are."

Cassidy nodded and turned away. Mike stepped off the stage and slipped back behind the number one camera. "Action!"

"You don't know anything about my service record." Jakes stepped forward and glared hard at the woman whose gaze was just a bit higher than hers. "When you're in command, you can give the orders. In the meantime, you follow orders."

"You don't give a damn about the fact that a man died."

Jakes snatched the ball from Chris' fingers, and Chris flinched. "Everyone's life matters to me." Catching her breath and trying to diffuse her frustration with the younger officer, she repeated softly, "Every life." There was a quality of regret.

Chris' body language softened slightly, and her tone was conciliatory. "Second thoughts, Commander?"

Jakes' voice also softened. "I know you won't believe this, but I was almost willing to give Baxley that chance." She came back alongside Chris. "Until he took you hostage." She exhaled.

The two women stood side by side for a long moment, each counting two beats. Cassidy jumped when Brenna's hand landed on her shoulder. Their gazes met across that shoulder.

"I told Jeremy to shoot."

Cassidy's stomach quivered, and she could not look away from Brenna's very direct, very blue gaze. She could not remember her line and backed away from Brenna abruptly.

"Cut!"

Mike's voice swiveled her head around sharply; Brenna's hand squeezed her shoulder, then dropped and skimmed along her spine.

"Bren, too soon. Cass, why so jumpy?"

Brenna shook her head. "It's my fault. You're right, it was too early." Cassidy looked to her questioningly.

The director seemed uninterested in placing blame. "Whatever." Mike turned away, stepping back down. "Let's just do it again. From 'Second thoughts.' And, action!"

```
     Chris' body language softened slightly, and her
tone was conciliatory. "Second thoughts, Commander?"
     Jakes' voice also softened. "I know you won't
believe this, but I was almost willing to give Baxley
that chance." She came back alongside Chris. "Until he
took you hostage." She exhaled. "I told Jeremy to
shoot."
     "There wasn't any other way?" Chris sounded
confused.
     Jakes shook her head. "It was up to Baxley to trust
you, or us, to get him that hearing. If he had...maybe
we wouldn't be here right now." She lifted her hand to
the woman's shoulder. After a moment, her hand slid
away. Hanssen looked up toward the blank gym wall as
Jakes walked out.
```

Cassidy finally took a breath when she heard the doors slide open and then shut again. She poised herself and studied the ball for a long moment before serving it against the wall with a resounding thud.

"Cut! And print!" Cass watched Mike turn to the crew and wave his hands. When she turned back to talk to Brenna, the other woman had already disappeared. Taking a steadying breath, she walked gingerly on aching legs to her trailer to clean up.

Brenna stepped from her trailer, still wiping a towel over her chin and cheeks, removing the last remnants of the thick stage makeup. "God, I need a shower," she groaned. As was typical, she could feel the ache in her legs and back, not to mention her feet, now that being "on" had been turned off for the day. Stopping on the pavement, she rubbed the back of her calf through the loose tan cotton pants. Relief spread into her sneaker-covered foot, and she lifted the other to rub at her ankle.

"Looks like you need your slippers back."

Cassidy walked up stiffly, obviously still aching from the shoot as well. Brenna noted the loose pale green cardigan over a white cotton tee shirt and jeans and the white cross-trainers she held in her left hand. Looking down at the woman's feet, she chuckled. "Seems you're wearing them."

The taller actress lifted a foot and balanced, removed one slipper, and held it out. "A compromise," she proposed. "You get one. I get one."

Brenna shook her head and waved it off. "I'm glad you've enjoyed them. What's on tap for your weekend?"

"Time with Ryan. I have tickets to the A's game tomorrow."

"He likes baseball?"

Cassidy put the absurd slipper back on her foot and nodded. "Loves it."

"Maybe you can bring Ryan to one of Thomas' high school games." That earned Brenna a smile.

"Sounds nice. What about you?"

"Me? I'm headed out tomorrow for Mount Clemens."

"Family?"

"My husband, Kevin," Brenna confirmed, "is attending a charity fundraiser."

"Are you going to appear as the Commander?"

"No. It's hard enough..." She shook her head. "Just me." The blonde nodded. Brenna sensed they shared an acute understanding about the line drawn between family and screen ~ and about how it sometimes just didn't seem to separate the two worlds enough.

Before she could respond, they were distracted by a car peeling across the lot. A brown LTD jerked to a halt, and the tinted passenger window rolled down. "Cass?"

Recognizing the voice of Cameron Palassis, one of the show's writers, from inside the shadowed recess, Brenna nodded, looking from Cassidy to her boyfriend. "Hello, Cameron."

Leaning out, he offered her a nod. "Brenna." He tilted his head again toward the blonde. "Are we going out tonight?"

"Cameron, I said..." Apparently sensing a conversation coming that she should not overhear, Brenna started to retreat. "Wait," Cassidy called after her. "Please?"

Brenna was pinned in place by blue eyes and nodded tightly, remaining still. She watched the younger woman step off the curb and lean into the car window. Unintentionally, Brenna overheard the tense exchange.

"Cam, I'm tired. I haven't spent time with Ryan all week. Not tonight."

"I could come by...We'll...put him to bed and go out?"

"No." Cassidy stepped back onto the curb. "I'll call you tomorrow."

Brenna saw Cameron's baffled expression, but as he drove away she watched Cassidy instead. The woman's posture was hunched, but she quickly recovered with a shrug of her shoulders before turning back to face

Brenna.

"I'm sorry."

Brenna shook her head. "It's not my business."

"I just..." Cassidy fell silent again. "I don't know. Maybe I am too tired." She brushed her long fingers through her loose, straight locks and rubbed the back of her neck.

Worried that the other woman might fall asleep at the wheel or something equally dangerous, Brenna asked, "Would you like to get a coffee before heading home?"

"No." Cassidy shook her head. "I'll be fine. Go on. Have a good weekend."

Brenna nodded. "All right." Stymied as to how, or if, to help further, she turned and walked into the parking lot. She unlocked the door to her SUV and opened it, leaning on the frame for a moment, watching as Cassidy crossed the dark empty lot and got into her blue compact. Once behind her own wheel, Brenna sat a few minutes quietly pondering her day before turning the ignition over and driving the forty-five minutes along L.A.'s dark surface roads toward home.

CHAPTER FOUR

THE WOMAN half-asleep on the couch stirred as Cassidy stepped inside her door. "Cass?" She rubbed the head of the sleepy Dalmatian next to her feet.

"Yeah, it's me, Gwen." Cassidy took off her sweater, hung it over a hanger, and tucked it back into the small closet by the door. "Sorry to be so late. We lost a lot of time with reshoots today."

"Hey, no problem. Ryan's a great kid. I fed him with mine and then brought him over here, leaving Lou to watch ours. He's bathed and been in bed since eight-thirty."

Sitting next to Gwen on the couch, Cassidy looked at the clock over the mantle and winced. It was after ten o'clock. *Where did the time go?* She leaned back and pressed the heels of her palms against her eyes.

Gwen noticed her footwear. "What on earth have you got on your feet?"

"Huh?" Cassidy sat up and looked down, unfocused, and then she blinked, bringing the furry brown blots into focus. "Oh, yeah. Slippers. I was on my feet in every scene. I didn't feel like even wearing sneakers after I finished today."

"Since when do you own a pair of slippers sporting a moose head?"

Rubbing her eyes tiredly, Cassidy said, "They're not mine. Brenna gave them to me."

"No kidding? Is that finally smoothed over?"

"I guess so. You remember she was here at Ryan's party last Saturday." Cassidy slipped off one of the Bullwinkles, curled her foot under herself, and studied the wide-eyed simpleton face. "We're getting a chance to talk more between takes since we aren't up to our necks in stunt shoots. We've been rehearsing together, too. There was this scene we did~"

Interrupting with a yawn, Gwen patted Cassidy's knee and stood up. "Well, that's as much as I've heard you talk about work right after you come home. Though it's incredibly fascinating, I've gotta go."

"Thanks again." Cassidy reclined against the arm of the couch as she watched her friend leave. Once the door was closed, she sighed and propped her chin on a fist. Her body began to relax into the cushions, and she reluctantly pushed off. *I better check on Ryan. Then,* she promised her muscles, *bed will follow.*

Rubbing Ranger's head as the Dalmatian walked alongside, Cassidy went to her son's bedroom and nudged the door wider. The night light next to his bed illuminated his face. Leaving the dog in the hall, she crossed to the bed and crouched, brushing away the long bangs from Ryan's forehead.

"You need a haircut, buddy," she whispered with a smile before kissing his cheek. "Maybe tomorrow before the game, hmm?" She adjusted the stuffed animal in his haphazard grip and then backed away, firmly closing the door.

Cassidy made a brief stop in the bathroom, changing out of her clothes into a roomy oversized tee emblazoned with the St. Louis Arch, a present from the city's mayor when she went back to her hometown to be the marshal of the Independence Day parade. The gold-painted, six-inch-long stainless steel Key to the City was tucked under her winter sweaters in a bottom dresser drawer. She had been flattered to be honored by the city, but she wondered why, when she had been a National Merit Scholar as a senior in high school, that accomplishment had not been worthy of the same attention.

She flossed and brushed her teeth, then worked a densely bristled brush through her hair. Though she had removed her stage makeup at work, Cassidy gently washed her face again and applied moisturizer. In her bedroom, she pulled down the covers and crawled between the sheets. Consciously relaxing her back, she stretched up over her head and turned on the radio. Rachmaninoff played as she drifted to sleep.

"Hey, Mom." Thomas Lanigan, Brenna's oldest son, looked up from the couch as his mother stepped inside. He crunched a few chips and took a sip from the soda perched on the side table. "How'd it go?"

"Pretty good. Is James still up?"

"Yeah, playing Playstation in the game room."

She heard a guttural yell and glanced at the television in front of him. "Off." He gave her a sheepish look as he tapped the remote sitting next to him. The offensive wrestling program vanished. "Please tell me you've eaten dinner." She leaned over the side of the couch and snatched up a chip with a grin. "It's been a long week. I won't find just chips and soda in those veins, will I?"

"Nope. We had the leftover penne from Tuesday. James scarfed the leftover casserole from Wednesday night."

"Anything left in the fridge for me?" She walked into the kitchen, and Thomas followed, leaning on the counter as she ducked her head inside the refrigerator. "Oh hey, not crazy about my quiche?" She pulled out the aluminum pie pan filled with half a quiche.

Thomas shook his head. "Figured you'd prefer it."

"You're right. It's light enough for this late." She cut herself a slice of the vegetable and cheese dish and took the refrigerator chill off with a few seconds in the microwave. Grabbing a fork, she returned to the living room, Thomas tagging behind. She kissed his cheek as he sat on the couch next to her.

James stepped in from the bedroom wing. "Glad you're home, Mom." He patted her shoulders as he leaned over and kissed her cheek. "Can I go over to Marcie's?"

Brenna laughed. "You've got to be kidding. It's after ten. We've got a plane at eight."

James frowned but nodded. "Well then, I guess I'll hit the sack. See you in the morning."

Watching Thomas flip on the television again, she called over her shoulder to James, "No telephone, either."

Her younger son groaned but called back wanly, "Yes, Mom."

"Good." She kicked off her shoes and tucked her feet under her on the couch, nibbling on her quiche. "Video games, huh?"

Thomas lifted his shoulders and looked away. "He's really nuts over her."

She reached over and rubbed her knuckles over the strong line of his neck. "How are you and Cheryl doing?"

"Fine. There's a dance I'm taking her to at school next weekend."

"I've got a convention appearance."

Thomas frowned. "Can't you just leave us here?"

"Alone?"

"Yeah. C'mon, Mom. We're old enough to watch ourselves for a weekend."

She pursed her lips, chewing her quiche while she considered. "I'll think about it."

"Thanks." She ruffled his hair as he shut off the TV and sprang up from the couch. "I'll get some sleep now."

Brenna finished her dinner quickly. Returning to the kitchen, she cleared the dishes from the sink into the dishwasher and set it to run. Then she ducked into her bedroom and the master bathroom, scrubbed her face, and brushed her teeth.

Changed into a slip gown, the slim straps faintly caressing her shoulders, Brenna curled up under the covers, adjusted pillows behind her back as a support, and flipped on the television. She paused with a finger over the channel-up button as she recognized the set on the screen. She laughed when she recognized it as an episode of a sitcom she had guest-starred on several years earlier. Her character swept into the scene, startling the principals out of a heated kiss. Brenna critically observed that she might have smirked a little too much at them. She sighed. More than twenty years in acting, and she was still uncomfortable and self-critical. She wondered if she would ever get over watching herself. Mercifully it was the last scene, just before the news.

The news report was depressing, and she was about to switch off the set when the sports preview mentioned the Oakland A's baseball game. She waited through the evaluation of the team's chances and hoped, for Cassidy and Ryan's sake, that the game would be enjoyable. Turning off the set, Brenna cross her arms over the top of the covers and studied the ceiling, replaying the week in her head.

You should have held those slippers for her birthday. Yeah, but she looked so miserable. Okay, but now you're going to have to come up with another present.

She wondered how Cassidy's son had liked his gift, then decided wryly that she must be turning sentimental. Maybe it was the fact that *Time Trails* was supposed to end in April. It was the longest running set she had worked continuously since *Lantry Place*, the soap opera where she had started her career at age eighteen.

She closed her eyes and rolled onto her side, curling around a pillow. Parades of co-stars followed her into sleep.

Phhhffffft. Phhhhffffft. Looking around, disoriented for a moment, Cassidy finally reached for the cell phone vibrating on her belt. Beside her, as she flipped open the phone, Ryan jumped up excitedly as the batter stepped up to the plate, yelling, "Home run! Home run!"

Patting his back, she spoke into the phone. "Hello?"

"Cass?"

When the batter connected, the shouts around her drowned out anything further that was said. She glanced toward the field and saw the runner skidding safely into first base. As the cheering dwindled, she heard, "Where the hell are you?"

Cameron, she identified. "At a baseball game," she explained patiently in the break in the noise.

"I thought we were going out."

"Tonight." She tucked the phone against her ear more tightly. "Cam, this is my time with Ryan."

"Then we won't go out. Or we'll take him with us. Where would he like to go? I haven't seen you in nearly two weeks, Cass. I miss you."

"You see me every day on the lot."

"C'mon, Cass. I mean *see* you."

She placed her hand over the phone and glanced toward Ryan, who was oblivious, bouncing excitedly and wildly cheering the game action. "All right. After the game, I'll talk to Gwen and see if she can watch him for a couple of hours. Movie?"

"Dancing," he countered.

"I've been on my feet all week." She sighed. They constantly had the same argument, and she was tired of it.

"Just as a prelude. Then we can go back to my place...take a dip in the Jacuzzi?"

Cassidy pondered the invitation and brushed her fingers over her son's freshly cut mop of hair. She relented. "All right."

"Great. I'll pick you up at seven?"

"Okay. See you then." Before he could add anything, she flipped the phone closed and slowly replaced it in her belt pouch, snapping the cover shut.

"Mommy?"

She looked down to see her son looking up. "Mmm hmm?"

"Can I have a cotton candy?"

Following his finger-pointing, Cassidy spotted the pink and blue swirls of spun sugar parading toward them up the near aisle. Feeling bad that she was going to leave him alone for another evening, she nodded. "Sure." She stood and called out, "Over here," to get the hawker's attention. He smiled, and she waved a bill, flashing a single finger. He nodded back, and soon a blue swirl of cotton candy was being passed along the row toward her.

She had not settled to the bench before Ryan was leaping on her, giggling and hugging. "Thank you!" Encouraging him to sit, she smiled and kissed his head as he tore off a large chunk and stuffed it into his mouth, instantly staining his lips and tongue blue.

"I love you, Ryan." With another brush of her hand over his head and a pat on his shoulder, Cassidy turned back to the game.

The trio from California stepped out of the flow of humanity off the gangway and fell into a cluster with two teenaged girls and a well-dressed older man in a dark blue sport coat, matching trousers, white shirt, and tie. Brenna threw him a playful smile and then turned to the girls. "So, how's life?"

From behind, her husband of fourteen months, Kevin, swept her up in a hug, kissing her cheek. "Ignoring me already?" He chuckled. She turned in his embrace and kissed his cheek. "That's better."

"Good to see you again," said Eleanor, at fifteen the elder of the two brunettes.

"You, too." She reached out and grasped the girls' hands. "So, what's on the agenda?" She looked from father to daughters.

"You two can bum." Marie pushed at her father's arm. "We're taking Thomas and James to Toppers."

The park name sounded familiar, but Brenna had not been since childhood. "Is that the amusement park on the north side?"

"Yeah. You've been?"

"A few times." She passed her boys each a twenty. "Have fun. Be careful on the transit."

"We'll be fine, Mom."

"Meet back at the house at eight."

"Aren't you two going out tonight?" Thomas asked.

Kevin placed a hand on Brenna's shoulder. "Charity dinner and auction, over near the college."

"Well, we'll see you tomorrow, then," Eleanor said cheekily, earning herself a laugh and a kiss on the cheek from Brenna.

The two adults accepted the bags and watched the kids leave, as only teens can ~ helter-skelter, half-chasing one another and leaping for the escalators and the exit. "So," she said at last, "to the home front?"

"Looking to put your feet up already? I thought we'd check out the new artist showing at the Guggenheim Gallery."

Brenna pursed her lips and then shrugged. "Can we at least get a good Irish before we set out?"

Offering his elbow, he waited for her small hand to tuck into the crook, then patted it. "I think I know just the spot."

She smiled winsomely. "I was hoping you'd say that."

Twenty minutes later, ensconced in a car headed to downtown Mount Clemens, Brenna leaned on the open window and rested her temple in her palm.

"It's good to see you," he said. His right hand found her left on the side of her seat. She looked over to see him focusing on the road. "Missed you."

"What's been happening?"

"Ellie broke up with Kyle, I think. I couldn't get more than two words out of her about it, though."

"Just give it time," she suggested. "She looked in good spirits. Maybe she's adjusting."

"Yeah, but you can talk to them."

She patted his arm and laughed. "Just get in touch with your feminine side."

Kevin parked behind a small pub painted green and dubbed "Biscuit and Jug." Brenna grinned widely. "I don't think you've brought me here before."

He chuckled. "There's a pub in Mount Clemens you haven't been to?"

"At least with you, farmer's boy," she shot back with a saucy smile.

"Ah, really, Brenna m'dear, ye wound me." He pantomimed an arrow shot to the heart and then tucked her against his side and entered the pub.

She liked the smells immediately, detecting both hops and cue chalk. "A finger of the Irish," she said to the bartender, who sported a scruffy face of whiskers. "On ice."

"Two," Kevin said when the bartender's eye turned to him settling onto the neighboring barstool.

When they received their drinks, she clinked her liquor glass against Kevin's. "To time off."

"Time off," he echoed.

She rotated around, scanning the room, locating the dartboard and the pool table nestled in the back corner. "Indulge me?" she asked over her shoulder.

"You'll whip me."

"Saying I haven't already? Come on. Get out of that stuffy jacket and give me a game."

"Isn't that...?"

The sharply whispered phrase caught her attention.

"Nah, it couldn't be. This is Mount Clemens."

"I heard she's married to some fellow here. You think that's him?"

"She wouldn't go for him. Must be some bigwig giving her the city keys or something."

Brenna suppressed a wince on Kevin's behalf and turned around. The speakers, a couple of college-age young men, stood before her.

"Hey..."

"Hello," she offered back politely.

"You're Commander Su...I mean, Brenna Lanigan, aren't you?"

It was useless to deny it. "Yes."

"Oh, man. Yes! The guys will never believe this!" The dusky blond, who reminded Brenna a lot of Sean Durham, snatched a napkin off their table and dug in his pocket for a pen. "Would you sign this?"

She signed quickly and passed it back.

"So, is that guy your husband?"

"Yes," she said. "Kevin?" She looked back, and finally Kevin stepped forward, looking the younger men up and down.

"Hello," he said slowly, offering a hand. One took it. "Kevin Shea, running for councilman," her husband said.

"Ah, geez." The young man pulled his hand away fast. "Politics? So geek, man." Brenna watched his expression change when he looked back to her. "Well...nice to meet you," he said, nudging his buddy past them to the door.

When they were alone again, Kevin looked at her. "Now, did I just throw a damper on that or what?"

"Don't mind them," she said, though she was disturbed by their reaction. "Come on. Table's open. Let's play one game, and then we'll go."

"All right."

CHAPTER FIVE

"CAMERON! CASSIDY!"

Turning in Cameron's embrace, Cassidy spotted a bearded male waving his sport cap from a table just beyond the edge of the busy dance floor. Hanging on the man's arm was a giggling brunette, also waving. "It's Angel and Lynn." Angel and Lynnette Corteñas were a couple she and Cameron frequently paired up with for dates on the town.

Cameron brushed his hand down her back as she stepped away from him. "We only just got here," he said with a frown, scanning the room.

She nodded. The blues beat of the music was pleasant, but she preferred to just sit down and have an evening of good conversation rather than dancing. "We haven't seen them in weeks, though."

"He lost his job out at Viacom two weeks ago."

"Has he found anything new yet?" she asked, leading him in the general direction of the Corteñas. When Cameron shrugged, Cassidy said, "Then we definitely have to spend some time with them." She spun away from him and moved quickly up the two steps to the table where Lynn was standing to greet them.

"Cass!"

"Good to see you." Cassidy smiled, and the two women shared an embrace. Turning, she accepted a warm hug from Angel. "Angel." She kissed his cheek with a grin.

Cameron stepped up next to her and clasped both of Lynn's hands in his own. "So, what brings you two out tonight?"

"A little change of pace from the house," Lynn said, glancing significantly toward Angel. Cassidy realized that meant that he had yet to find work. "We've been renovating," the brunette said.

"Renovating? Now?"

Angel nodded, sitting down as he gestured for Cassidy and Cameron to join them. "A few adjustments were necessary."

"Tightening the belt already?" Cameron asked. "I heard Viacom's severance packages were pretty good."

"Not that...well, not just that," he corrected. "It's...Lynn's pregnant."

Cassidy watched the look of anxiety and pleasure fill the expectant father's face. She caught Lynn's nod and wan smile. Reassuringly, Cassidy reached across the table and grasped her friend's hand. "That's wonderful." Lynn looked up, and Cassidy squeezed her friend's hand again. When Lynn blushed, Cassidy leaned close and whispered, "It really is. If you need something, call."

The brunette nodded before turning back to her drink ~ a sparkling cider. "Angel's got a lead at Tri-Star."

"Something will come up." Cameron looked away and waved at a waiter. "Molson Ice," he requested. The waiter nodded. "Thanks." He turned back. "Movement is the nature of the business. No worries."

Sipping at her ice water, Cassidy thought about her own situation. She wondered where she would be in a year when *Time Trails* was finished. Musing her way through the regular cast, she wondered where everyone else would go as well.

"Cass?"

She looked up to find all three of her tablemates studying her. Cameron had spoken.

"Just listening to the music," she said, noting the tune currently filling the club.

"Want to get back out there and dance?" Cameron asked.

She shook her head, running a finger in the top of her water. "It's late. I'd like..."

While she spoke, Cameron had turned around and straightened, wrapping his fingers around the back of her chair. "Oh, hey, someone I was hoping to see. Cass, come on." He grasped her arm and stood, pulling her up with him. "Hey, Angel, buck up, buddy. Lynn, it's great about the baby. Call sometime."

"Cameron," Cassidy said as they stepped away, "you didn't have to be so abrupt. Who'd you see?"

"Griffin Torend. Come on." He waved at someone as they moved through the throng on the dance floor. "Hey, Griff!"

"Cam!" Griffin Torend was forty-something, wearing clothes meant for a much younger and trimmer man. His gray khakis were tight around his waist, and the cotton blend shirt with breast pockets stretched tightly around his torso. They stopped next to him. "So this is your girl, eh? Nice. Mmm. Nice to meet you." He offered a hand.

She nodded. "Hello."

Cameron slid his arm around her waist and patted her hip. "Cassidy Hyland, my gem on *Time Trails*. Cass, this is Griffin Torend, casting agent for dozens of startups."

"Right now I'm looking into the cast for the next series," Torend said, "and a few more conventional projects for J-TV."

Wanting to return to Angel and Lynn rather than spend time talking business, Cassidy tried to bow out of the meeting graciously. "Well–"

"Got anything new lined up yet?" Griffin asked, cutting her off.

Despite having been thinking about that very thing, Cassidy stepped back. She had a gut feeling she did not want to discuss her future with this man. "I'm too busy doing my best in my current role."

"Business mind, my dear."

Cassidy felt her molars compress together in the back of her mouth. *God, I hate people treating me as though I have "dumb blonde – handle with care" stamped on my forehead.* She quickly doused the anger boiling up inside her.

"Thank you. I already have an agent." She disengaged from Cameron's elbow and excused herself. "I'll be right back." Though Cameron frowned at her, she shook her head and headed for the restroom corridor, tired and feeling a distinct itch from being around Torend.

With a sigh, she sank onto the small couch in the outer lounge of the ladies' restroom. *Come on, Cass. Cam obviously thought you'd appreciate a contact.* She had never expected to encounter someone who actually made her jaw hurt from restraint. She rubbed the sore muscles in her cheeks and dropped her head into her palms. "I haven't hidden out in a restroom since I started on *Time Trails*," she lamented softly.

Right after her introduction in the series, she abhorred going out because of the mob scenes her appearance generated. However, she had done it, knowing the consequences if she did not. Suddenly lonely, all Cassidy wanted to do was curl up under a blanket with Ryan and a good book. She stood up, turning directly into a pair of young women who were leaving the restroom. "Excuse me."

"Oh my God!" one of the two women squealed, and Cassidy swallowed, freezing in place. On Cassidy's left, hands wrapped around her upper arm in a vise-like grip; a blonde whose hair was liberally streaked purple went wide-eyed. Reflexively, Cassidy grabbed for her slender shoulders as her brown eyes rolled back in a faint.

The girl's friend hovered as Cassidy carefully moved the limp woman to the couch. "You're so cool. So normal," she gushed.

Cassidy didn't make any acknowledgment, concentrating instead on assuring herself that the fainter had regained her senses. Deciding to forestall another attack, she apologized. "I should have been looking where I was going. Are you all right?" The woman ~ whom Cassidy judged to be in senior high or college ~ nodded.

"Yeah. Hey, look, I'm sorry. Karen and I just moved into the neighborhood to go to school. I didn't expect...*You!* You're probably my favorite person on TV, y'know?"

Cassidy pulled her wrists from the woman's urgent grip and swallowed again. "Really?" She forced her tone to sound interested.

"Oh yeah. I just loved the poignancy of the ending scene between you and Commander Jakes in *Conspiracy of One!*"

Cassidy blinked. That episode must have aired just recently, she realized, probably in reruns. It had been her first episode, a two-parter, when she had not yet known that the *Time Trails* assignment was going to pan into a full-time part. Her character, Chris Hanssen, had lost everyone in her air squadron in a massive dogfight. Headquarters had ordered her reassigned to Jakes' unit. She had been a fighter and now was out of her depth, cast among what was supposedly a group of desk jockeys. But when she discovered they were really a group of Time Marshals, she had wanted to go back in time to stop the deaths of her squadron mates. Jakes had firmly stood in the way. Their first moments on screen together were nothing but fighting.

Ultimately, at the memorial service at the end of the two-parter, Jakes had looked as devastated as Hanssen. Hanssen, the character, had not yet learned the reason for that, though Cassidy knew it had to do with Jakes having been a peer of the air squad's commander. The toe-to-toe between Jakes and Hanssen, both hurting and angry, had bristled. They hissed and circled like a snake tangling with a mongoose. The process had both energized and unnerved Cassidy for hours on end.

The women in the restroom grinned at her, bringing her back to the present. "You are so cool."

"So, you ever kissed her? Bet she's hot."

"Kissed?"

"Yeah. You mean that isn't where all that tension is going?"

Cassidy blinked. "No."

"Damn waste then. Lots of rumors have Sue and Chris in liplocks after hours."

Taken by surprise, Cassidy sat down on the couch. "Well, it's not in the script, as far as I know."

"Oh, okay. Even if it were, you probably couldn't tell us. Gotcha." Karen fished around in her small handbag for a moment, coming up with a pen and a scrap of paper. "Would you sign this?"

Frowning at the pad, Cassidy hesitated. Her policy was to not sign autographs during her off-time. However, she needed to let the women go, realizing she could not ask any questions about their assumptions or she'd seem to be fishing. Which she would be, but she wouldn't want to seem to be naïve about her own character. She took the paper and qualified her actions even as she signed, "I don't usually do this."

"Gotcha." Karen took back the pen and paper and studied it. "'Thanks for the chat. Cassidy Hyland. Damn, this is so cool!" The two women, deep in hushed conversation, quickly left the restroom.

A few minutes later, Cassidy returned to the dance floor. She found Cameron and tapped his shoulder. "Time to go," she said firmly, loud enough to bring his head around. "It's late."

Cameron nodded. "I'm done here." He had apparently sat down for a deeper conversation with Torend. Reaching across the table, he shook the man's beefy hand and stood. "I'll call you next week, Griff."

"Right. Nice to meet you, kid."

She nodded politely but turned away quickly and followed Cameron to the exit. Stepping into the brisk night air, she rubbed her arms to warm up. Out at the car, he unlocked her door, pulling it open for her. His hand brushed her arm, but she did not move. "Something wrong?" he asked, when she brushed the hand away.

"I want to go home, Cam."

"Sure. Some music on the couch..."

Feeling disquieted and restless for no reason she could pinpoint, she shook her head. "No. Take me home. My home."

"I thought you didn't like to do anything in the house with Ryan?"

She swallowed. "I don't."

He dropped his gaze away from her, but when he looked up she could see he had come to a decision. "Fine. Go on. Get in."

He ducked into the driver's seat, and she breathed out slowly. She had never before felt the need to cut a date short. She sighed. Maybe she was PMSing or something.

"...welcome to Mister Kevin Shea!"

Applause filled the gymnasium of the brand new Milburn County Boys and Girls Club. For the dedication celebration, the sports space had been set up as a dining hall. Brenna looked up as Kevin's hand slipped over her bare shoulder as he passed behind her to the podium. While he adjusted the microphone, his brown eyes searched hers out, and she offered an encouraging smile. He turned back to the crowd and waved at a few people in the front tables, as he waited for quiet. Finally the last few handclaps died away.

He grinned at the gathering. "Ladies and gentlemen, eighteen months ago a group of students from Tillek College came to my office and told me stories of collecting children after school and trying to find them a safe place to play and study. They had a proposal, and my business agreed to sponsor the project. But, eh...I just got the building permits; *they* got the place built." He pointed to a packed table near the front and gestured for them to stand.

The applause resumed as the young adults rose slowly to their feet, the Greek letters proclaiming their sororities and fraternities on the front of shirts emblazoned with the words "Tillek College Greek Council." Some looked unsure, and Brenna's heart went out to them. She too liked public service work, but moments in the spotlight unnerved her, as it was doing to them right now. The thought made her smile wistfully as she thought how she had deliberately stepped on stage time and time again. Despite the butterflies. Her reverie was interrupted by the call of her name.

"...Brenna Lanigan." Kevin had continued his remarks and somehow worked his way around to introducing her. She started to rise to acknowledge him when he turned to the audience and added, "You might know her better as Susan Jakes, the commander in *Time Trails!*"

The college students stood and howled, clapping and stomping loudly. Only by the grace of God, she thought, was she able to keep the mortification from her face. She painted on a thin-lipped smile before quickly sitting again. She grasped her napkin and pinched it between her hands and then held it over her mouth. When Kevin moved behind her, she remained seated, despite his hand on her back, the signal to rise again. She dropped her head and barely shook it.

"Bren?" he whispered, leaning over and pressing a hand to each shoulder, before kissing her left cheek.

She carefully held her hands together on the tabletop, wishing she could defuse her temper but knowing she did not have that luxury while in public. Finally the applause died away and the emcee stepped back up as Kevin returned to his seat.

"Thank you, everyone, for joining us for this dinner. Now, if you've stuffed yourselves enough," a low trickle of laughter started at the college students' table, "it's time to pick up the cards for the auction. We've got it built, but now we've got a mortgage to pay," he added.

As the auction items were dragged out, Brenna stood up from the table. Stepping backward, she turned into her husband directly behind her. Looking up at Kevin's sport-jacketed frame, she realized she was glaring only when he ducked his head to the side.

"What's that for?" he asked.

"When can we go?" she said by way of answer, catching a curious look from a young man walking toward them and schooling her features carefully.

"It's a chance for us to socialize. Forget about the week. Spend a little time with friends."

"Friends of whom?" she asked grimly. She turned away from him as the young man from Sigma Chi stopped about four feet away. "Hello," she greeted, showing her teeth with a brief smile.

"Hello, Ms. Lanigan." He looked over his shoulder, apparently seeking encouragement from his friends. She glanced past him and watched several of the students nod briskly and offer nudging gestures. She tracked to his eyes as he turned back to her, and she waited patiently for the request she could sense coming. "I...well, my friends and I would like to say thank you for coming. Many of us are avid fans of your show."

He offered a sheepish grin; she took a deep breath and refreshed her smile. Kevin remained at her back, and with that acute awareness she had developed on stage, she realized he was focused on her young admirer even more than she was. She reached out and put a hand on the young man's arm. "What's your name?"

"Me? I..." He stumbled over his own tongue, and Brenna would have laughed if she were not so upset. "Mike...I mean, Michael Turncot." He let out a nervous laugh as she took his hand and shook it. "I'm with the Greek Council."

She nodded. "I can see that, Mike." *Time to put on a good show, Brenna.* "You did a lot of work here. Why don't you introduce me?" she offered, loud enough to draw the attention of the other young adults. "Congratulations."

"Thank you." A young woman dusted her hands on her Delta Delta Delta shirt tail, before offering it. "With all the work you do, this must seem like such a small project."

"Small projects make the biggest differences, I've found," Brenna said sincerely.

Kevin remained close by, but her irritation ebbed as she focused on the volunteers. They relaxed around her when it was clear she admired them in return. She walked through the facility with them, talking about the work itself, the setbacks, and the time they thought they had lost their grant. She commiserated about the time an entire corner of the infant structure had collapsed under an unexpected snowfall the previous November.

"Thank goodness no one was hurt," she exclaimed. "Really, what you've accomplished is remarkable."

"Your husband had a lot to do with our success. He donated the supplies and kept up with the permits," someone said. "Kept telling us the project was important enough to keep going."

"He's right. So, tell me more about the programs you're going to run here."

The students answered all at once, and Brenna heard a cacophony of responses. "After-school studying and activities for school age children. Athletic clubs. Basketball, soccer in the field out back, and a day camp program in the summers."

"How are admissions handled?" she asked.

"Parents are referred by the local public aid office. We've already got forty-five children in the borrowed office space near the sports center at the college."

Someone offered her a drink, and Brenna took it with a nod of appreciation. Sipping briefly, she identified it as clear soda. "I'm really impressed. I'll keep an eye on your progress. If you'll excuse me, though, I should find my husband." She brushed a hand through the fall of her hair against her shoulders and stepped backward.

Mike, who had brought her into the small group, led her out, and up to Kevin, who was chatting with a slim man in pinstripe pants and a double-breasted, blue-black vest smoothed over a crisp, white cotton shirt. The gentleman nodded past Kevin, acknowledging Brenna's arrival.

Kevin turned and smiled, holding out a hand. She put hers into it and allowed herself to be drawn forward and introduced. "This is my wife, Brenna Lanigan. Bren, this is Senator Josiah Birmingham, chairman of Michigan's Democratic Party."

"Senator Birmingham." She held out her hand, and the senator bent over it and squeezed lightly. "A pleasure."

"My pleasure," he said. "And who's this?"

She introduced her young escort with a genuine smile. "Mike Turncot, Tillek Greek Council president."

"Senator." Mike turned to Kevin, who smiled. "Mr. Shea, the council would like to invite you to speak at our Pan-Political Rally on the twenty-fourth. Would you consider it?"

Kevin smiled. Brenna could tell he was quite pleased with the invitation, though he sounded terribly formal when he shook Mike's hand and said, "I'd be delighted, young man."

Brenna felt a chill go through her as Kevin leaned forward, shaking Mike's hand again. "Very delighted."

"That's was some fun, right?"

Brenna sighed. "No, I was very uncomfortable."

"You seemed to be having a good time with the students. The senator thought you were perfect."

"Perfect? Was I being sized up for something? Kevin, this was supposed to be just a social outing, with a bit of charity benefit." She could feel her face growing hot with anger.

"It was."

As the car idled at a stop light, she looked at him. He looked straight ahead. She noticed his fingertips tapping on the steering wheel. "But that wasn't all. What is it?"

"The party money is being spread around. They've been talking to me."

With foreboding she asked, "About what?" Kevin didn't answer. "What did they want you to do with your *celebrity* wife?"

"It wasn't like that. They want me."

"But I'm a particularly sweet bonus? For what?"

Kevin turned into the driveway and shut off the engine. "I don't know yet." She narrowed her gaze at him. "I don't!" She pushed her way out of the car, entering the house quickly. Kevin followed in her wake. "Bren," he started.

She turned around a few steps away from James and Ellie rising from a checkerboard. "Good night, Kevin."

The children left their game. Brenna stepped into the hall bathroom, staring her own anger down in the mirror. Kevin was out of sight when she emerged again, and she heard the telltale noises that said he was in the bedroom. She settled on the couch, grabbing a magazine from the coffee table while waiting for him to return to the living room. When he did come out, it was to offer her a brief kiss and remind her to turn out the light when she came to bed.

"Kevin." Her voice stopped him in the corridor.

"Yes?"

She looked up at him as he paused in the doorway. "Please don't do that again."

"Darling, I didn't..."

"You did." She kept her voice even. "You have me, not a fictional character."

"Someone was bound to mention it. Consider it diffusing the tension."

"Whatever you might have thought, it made *me* tense, Kevin. I'm not going to be Susan Jakes forever. We've talked about this. I thought you understood."

He leaned against the wall, bracing his frame against that of the hallway. "Derek thought it would be a good idea."

Now it comes out, she thought with a sigh. "And you went along with it to get that invitation to the Pan-Political Rally?"

"That segment is important."

"I won't go with you to the rally," she said quietly.

"Your father is coming."

"He'll be all the support you need. You'll be fine."

"Are we?"

She fingered the magazine in her lap. "Yes," she said, not looking up at him.

He stepped close, put his big hand on her shoulder, and bent to kiss her cheek. She accepted it and pressed into it briefly before he pulled away. "Coming to bed?"

She rubbed her hand over his before it left her shoulder. "You go. I'll be in later."

CHAPTER SIX

GREETED BY Peter, the north entrance guard, Cassidy Hyland drove through the gate and pulled to a stop in a space near the far end of the Pinnacle cast lot. The sun was already breaking through the Los Angeles smog. She should have been there almost two hours earlier. As she pressed the remote lock on her key chain, she spun round and bolted for the support trailers where her makeup awaited.

The crunch of gravel under the tires of another vehicle turned her head as she hit the sidewalk with full-length strides. She was stunned to see Brenna Lanigan stepping out of a taxicab. She waited for the compact woman to reach the sidewalk. Jogging toward her trailer, Brenna did not look up until the last second before they collided. Cassidy grasped Brenna's arm to steady them both, letting go when Brenna's gaze darted to her face. "Are you all right?"

"Plane was late," Brenna mumbled. She started past Cassidy, then stopped and turned around. "You didn't come looking for me, did you?"

"No. I'm late, too," Cassidy explained. "I couldn't drag myself from bed this morning. Then Ryan didn't feel well, so I had to take him to the sick care arrangements I have."

"I hope he gets well soon," Brenna offered.

"Thanks." They strode toward the studio set together, almost perfectly in step. "How was Michigan?"

"Cold." Brenna shook her head as she pulled open the door. Cassidy grasped the side, gesturing for Brenna to enter first. "My flight was postponed because the overnight temp was twenty-eight with freezing rain."

"I'm sorry."

"You can't control the weather." Brenna shrugged. "I wanted coffee on the plane, but because of the delay, they weren't serving."

Cassidy watched her uneasily run her fingers through her hair, presumably fixing it. Though if she'd been asked, Cassidy would have said that even tired, Brenna looked good. She exhaled and felt her cheeks. They seemed too hot, probably with Ryan's fever.

"Did I hear someone asking for coffee?"

Cassidy turned to the approaching voice. "Morning, Cam."

Beside her, Brenna hesitated, then offered, "Cameron."

"You two are awfully late for your calls, aren't you?"

"I had a flight delay," Brenna responded. "And apparently Ryan is sick," she added, to Cassidy's surprise.

"Well, Sean's been looking for you both for thirty minutes. The gang's all here."

"Thanks." Brenna turned away.

Cass began to follow her, when Cameron touched her arm. "Yes?" There was deliberate coolness in her voice.

Cameron had the grace to look sheepish, then his expression cleared. "Would you like to try doing something tonight?"

"No. I'm going to talk to Sean about going home early so I can take care of Ryan."

"Awful short notice."

"I'll talk to Sean about it," she repeated, turning away and feeling better for having asserted her parenting above other things. The image of Ryan crying and rubbing his runny nose and coughing through a sore throat that morning flashed through her mind. It made it easy to ignore Cameron's grumbling as he walked toward the executive offices.

"You're going home?"

She had forgotten Brenna's presence. Turning now to the other woman, she saw that Brenna had moved off a few feet but still waited. The unconsciously supportive gesture warmed her. She nodded. "Ryan is really sick."

"I'm sure Sean can rearrange things. We can just do our scenes later in the week."

Brenna's lips pursed together in a tight line, but then she smiled gently, again warming Cassidy with the sense that an understanding was passing between them. Cassidy rubbed her throat as she cleared it.

Brenna stepped closer. "Are you sure you're okay?" She held the door for Cassidy to enter the soundstage area first.

"Yeah, I'll be fine." Cassidy wiped her brow.

Brenna pulled her toward the coffee pot. "Here." Pouring two, she fixed hers with sweetener. When she held up the fixings, Cassidy said, "Cream only."

Coffees in hand, the two settled in chairs near the set. After a fortifying sip which soothed her throat, Cassidy asked, "Did you have a good time Saturday?" When Brenna did not immediately answer, Cassidy figured she was debating whether or not to share. "It didn't go as you had hoped?" she guessed,

"Forget it. How did baseball go?"

"Oakland lost."

"Was Ryan upset?"

"No. He was already blue by then," she replied. Brenna gave her a look of confusion. "He was stained blue from the cotton candy. He was so amused by that, he forgot about the game."

Brenna giggled, surprised by the mental imagery. *Oh, it feels so good to laugh.* "I remember when mine would do things like that."

"Are you two ready to get down to this week's episode?"

They both turned to see Sean Durham with a sneaker-clad foot propped on another nearby chair. He queried them both with a raised eyebrow. His green eyes crinkled over a suppressed smile as he crossed his hands over his bent knee and studied them.

"Sorry, Sean. We ran into each other running late," Brenna said easily.

They both glanced toward the soundstage. Behind Sean, Cassidy could see the other actors walking through a blocking sequence on the medical bay set.

"I wouldn't have even noticed you except Rachelle kept stopping her dialogue, wondering what you two could be discussing so intently."

Cassidy took the opportunity to make her request. "I need to ask for the day off, Sean. Ryan was sick this morning."

"Do you have temporary arrangements so that you can stay at least until first break? If we get through the read-through, I can rearrange the shoot a little. Maybe you could come back early tomorrow for most of your close-up work? Shooting those out of order won't make much difference." He looked away, obviously already mentally rearranging things. He even grabbed at the pen tucked behind his ear and the script in his hands, thumbing through already-tagged pages.

Left alone, though the man was still standing right in front of them, Brenna smiled at Cassidy and patted her arm. The blonde exhaled in relief. "Told you it could happen." Brenna looked at Sean and grinned.

"Well, come on. Let's get you two your script copies. No filming until after lunch, so you can skip costuming." Sean dropped his foot from the seat of the chair and stepped back, spun around, and headed back to the set.

Cassidy stood. "I'm ready."

Brenna came up behind her and idly patted Cassidy's shoulder. "All right, let's get the job done so you can get out of here."

As Brenna walked ahead, Cass felt the residual warmth on her shoulder. She watched Brenna walk confidently onto the set, take a script copy from Durham, and give Rachelle a warm hug.

"So, Ryan is sick?" Rachelle asked as Cassidy walked up. "I'm sorry. You should be home to take care of him."

Cassidy knew that Brenna had already updated the other two on the situation. "Where are Will and Terry?" Cass asked.

"Working with the stunt team. They've got a full-fledged B plot this time, an explosion in the Vortex lab."

"Inside intrigue," Brenna mused before she realized what Rachelle's explanation meant. "You've read already?" She flipped ahead through the pages.

"Some," Chelle admitted to Brenna. "We were beginning to think something had happened to you."

Brenna ducked her head, pleased to have been worried about but quick with assurances. "Delayed flight. I had planned to leave last night, but freezing rain grounded flights until morning."

Joining them, Rich interjected, "You haven't even been home, have you?"

Brenna shook her head. "I gave Thomas the keys and took a cab here."

"God," Chelle commiserated. "You should go home and get some sleep."

Cassidy silently echoed that thought. She found traveling difficult. Brenna had to have been up continually since Sunday morning. When her flight was grounded, she likely stayed up waiting for the first flight out, just to be here for a six a.m. set call. Her respect for Brenna rose another notch.

Sean appeared again, mercifully offering a tray with juice and sweet rolls. "Now do you think we can do some full read-throughs?"

"Food? God, I'm yours!" Brenna scanned her script pages as she sipped. "From the top?"

"From the top," Sean confirmed. "And, Cass, listen close. In this one, you're going to spend a lot of time being me."

Cassidy's face paled. "What?"

"Yep. It's called *Brains and Brawn*. We get knocked through a vortex and end up with our bodies switched."

"So you're me?" Cassidy asked. "And I'm going to be you?" Chris Hanssen might not like being part of Susan Jakes' Time Squad, but she was the antithesis of Jeremy Dewitt. The guy loved the role of card sharp, or gunslinger, or sports figure. Whatever action was to be had in a particular case, he wanted to be in the thick of it. Cassidy was uncertain she could carry off the swagger of someone so confident.

"And you get to kiss me." Rachelle took Cassidy's hand to hop off the exam bed.

"I what?" Cassidy just stared around at the other actors, digesting the situation.

Sean cleared his throat, drawing all attention back to him. "All right, let's read scene 4 B."

It was the middle of the last day of filming *Brains and Brawn*, the gender-bending body switch episode. Most of the major work had been done over the last five days.

Though Chris and Jeremy had been sent to handle an extraction, that mission had been abandoned as soon as they discovered they'd swapped bodies. Dr. Pryor had gone after them and had been working on unswitching the pair in the rudimentary medical facility they had located. When there was an accident with the Vortex equipment, Susan risked herself to get the data to the doctor. They conjectured that perhaps something in the circuits had reversed the bodies, but the doctor had determined that the two incidents were unrelated. The vortex Chris and Jeremy had been sent through had coincided with a storm at their destination. Creighton had determined that the explosion, occurring when the vortex equipment was offline, had been a local electrical short. Chris and Jeremy had traveled back to the Time Squad's headquarters to await the doctor's remedy.

Out of consideration, Sean held the "big" scene until last, rightly figuring Rachelle and Cassidy's ease with each other would increase over the week's work. But right now, standing outside the set of Commander Jakes' office, Cassidy was pacing to try and shake off her nervousness. Her palms were soaked with sweat. She had called her agent and asked about the possible angles, fallout, or benefits, of the kiss.

"Coudreau gets great work."

Great, I'm being compared to a character on Friends. *Lisa Coudreau's kiss, though, had been a stunt kiss ~ the actress in her own character.*

This would be Chris' body, but supposedly with Jeremy's will inside it. The way Sean and Rachelle portrayed Jeremy and Luria, the couple's relationship was deep and solid. There was nothing timid in their touches, no hesitation as they went from moment to moment.

Cassidy wasn't a novice, but kissing Rachelle or being kissed by her ~ they had tried it twice ~ had set her head swimming. She had been unable to complete her lines in fourteen rehearsals.

There was a buzzer. Time was up.

A buzzer sounded. Anxiety making her run her fingers through her hair, Commander Jakes looked up from the pile of papers on her desk of papers. "Come."

The doors opened to reveal Chris Hanssen attired as Jeremy Dewitt, a lost look on the blonde's usually self-assured features. Beside Jakes, Luria, who had obviously been crying, turned. "Chris?"

Controlled by Dewitt's thoughts, Hanssen's body jerked at the misidentification. "The test didn't work."

Cass delivered the line dryly and dejectedly, obviously pushing forward Dewitt's depression at the situation.

"We will keep trying, Jeremy," Jakes assured, rounding the desk with a purposeful stride. She stopped at the slouched shoulder and tried to get "him" to look at her. She started to reach for the shoulder, paused. "I..." She dropped her hand. "Would you like to sit down?"

When "he" wouldn't, Jakes led the way over to the leather-padded bench against the view port wall. "Don't give up hope. There is a way."

Luria walked up. "Jer?" She used her husband's nickname. "It will work."

"I hope so." "Jeremy" looked at her, pained.

One second Cassidy was staring at Rachelle's full, dark lips, watching her speak, and the next second, Rachelle's hands were on her cheeks. Rachelle's chocolate brown eyes swept her face before she moved to meet Cassidy's lips with her own.

Luria gave her husband a reassuring, even desperate kiss.

Cassidy's grip reflexively tightened on Rachelle, as she felt she was going to fall.

"Now, let's go try again." Commander Jakes put a hand on "Jeremy's" back and propelled "him" out the door. "I want my officers back." Luria was close on their heels.

"Cut, and print that." Assistant director Kim Swanson ducked out from behind camera one and waved the two women over. "That's a wrap."

Having been in an earlier scene, the "test" Chris/Jeremy had referred to, Rich Paulson walked up. "That was fantastic. And perfectly timed," he complimented.

"Thanks for the shove," Cassidy said to Brenna.

"No problem. We worked it out in blocking while you were back getting reset in makeup."

"I'm sorry."

"It was a gamble. I'm sorry that we couldn't get it changed. Network floated the idea, and the demographic seemed to love it."

"So it was a stunt."

Sean stepped out from behind the camera. "Yeah, I'm sorry. I didn't think you'd have a block about a five-second kiss."

Next to Cassidy, Rich looked at the time on a nearby wall. "Bren, are we seeing your kids tonight for the Halloween party?"

"Yes. I'm on my way out to meet them."

"This will definitely end the day on an up note." Rachelle turned. "Cass, are you coming?"

Cassidy shook herself and answered quickly, "I have to grab Ryan. I'll be back in a little over an hour."

"Are you going to be in costume tonight?" Brenna asked.

Cassidy nodded. "I'm switching to my own instead of staying in this one. But it is Halloween, so I thought it best. What about you?"

"I'm staying in costume, too." Brenna hesitated, then added, "What you did was just an amazing performance, Cass. Even with the blocking changes."

"Rachelle, too."

"Mmm hmm." Brenna ducked her head and walked off set. Cassidy turned in the other direction, headed for wardrobe.

CHAPTER SEVEN

A LITTLE more than an hour later, Brenna led a band of children from the front gate to the Pinnacle offices. Guardians and other volunteers from the Los Angeles Kids Experience (LAKE) trailed behind. She guided them to the offices first.

Time Trails producer Victor Branch had been alerted by the gate guard and stood at his office doorway. In a gray business suit, he was dressed typically except for a plastic tiger face mask pulled down over his features. He growled impressively. "I see you brought my dinner, Commander."

Several of the youngest children cowered, some older ones laughed. He tipped up his mask and dropped to a crouch, drawing a bag of candy out from behind his door. The children spotted it, and small plastic orange bags were presented in short order. Giggles of delight filled the corridor as the youngest opened their bags to "Aunt Brenna" and yelled, "See what I got!" before dancing out of the doorway to let others partake of Branch's bounty.

Hands resting lightly on her upper arms, Brenna smiled, occasionally brushing fingers over soft cheeks and kissing others until the candy distribution was complete.

"What do we say to Mr. Branch?"

"Thank you, Mr. Branch!"

Victor laughed, ruffled the hair of a few of the nearest children, and waved Brenna to him as she gestured for the other adults to lead the children down to the next office area. "Nice group of kids," he said. "These are the ones you work with?"

"One weekend a month, I help out with their fundraising," she answered quietly. "I'm glad you agreed to host the Halloween party. They'll enjoy themselves in a safe place."

"No problem. I'll trail with you down to the soundstages."

"Who's still on set?" Brenna asked.

"Rich has been helping the props guys. Cassidy just got back with her son. Chapman was here earlier. Interview, I think." They walked behind the group as the children were greeted by more executives and writers in partial costume. Then Ginger Vitano appeared. Victor's personal secretary had dressed as a fairy godmother, complete with wings. Waving her wand, she helped lead the tour to the party area on the other side, collecting actors from several of the soundstages along the way.

Victor and Brenna chuckled as the wide-eyed youngsters listened to the few rules: no touching props, no straying from the group, and absolutely no stepping through a closed doorway.

"Aunt Brenna, does she mean it? She'll turn us into frogs if we do bad?"

Brenna washed the smile from her face. A look of disapproval shaped her features as she affected Susan Jakes' sharpest tone. "Regulations must be followed at all times."

"Well?" asked Ginger. "You already have pretty full bags of candy, but are you ready to get to the fun?"

"Yes! Yes!" The children bounced up and down, their costumed feet padding over the floor with a rustling sound.

"All right. Commander Jakes," Ginger waved her wand, "would you lead the way?"

"This way," Brenna said, pushing wide the double doors that led out of the administrative building to the rows of large soundstages. She strode firmly, listening to the chatter of the children behind her, unable to keep from smiling.

She checked the light above the door before entering *Time Trails'* primary soundstage. On the far side a tent had been set up covering tables of food. However, a trip through an area filled with gory games and Halloween decorations was part of the treat before the tricks she knew her castmates were planning for the children.

Hearing Rich's easy lilt rather than the Doctor's brusque tone and seeing fewer lights on, Brenna knew that they were having a post-shooting discussion, not a filming moment. She rounded the corner of a set wall and grinned as she found Rich and Cassidy, Ryan in her lap, seated casually on the edges of one of the exam tables, sharing a laugh. She caught the punch line to Rich's joke.

"With a gleam in its eye, the cat said, 'I'm no mouse.'"

Cassidy and Ryan both laughed. Just then Cassidy caught sight of Brenna and the collection of children staring at her from around the black-clad legs. The children's wide eyes made her consider putting on her character's austere expression, but then she caught Brenna's smile and let her own smile come back.

Children suddenly swarmed in, in a chorus of "Hi!", "Cool!" and "Got any candy?"

Brenna was dragged forward until she was almost on top of both Rich and Cassidy. "Hi, guys," she said simply.

"Looks like you brought the whole L.A. school district with you," Rich said.

"Just half," she replied. "Think you can handle them?"

"Yep." He grinned, tight-lipped, lifting a prop. "Have you had your shots?" he asked the children.

Screeches and giggles greeted his mock threat, and he swept one of the kids up onto the exam table, pretending to scan her pixie tails with a wand-shaped prop. "These growths out of your head, are they normal?"

"Yes!" She put her hands on her hips and glared at him as he tugged one.

He lifted the girl down, and Cassidy set Ryan down, issuing an invitation. "Who's ready to bob for apples? Or paint a pumpkin face?"

Hands went up, and voices cried out, "Me!"

"Commander Jakes?"

"Lead the way," she said, patting Ryan on the back as he stared at the large group of kids.

The two women fell into step side by side, with Rich behind. A figure suddenly sprang from behind a wall, arms outspread, a black cape over his shoulders and arms, face covered by a bat mask. "I've got you now!" issued forth in an impressive Dracula imitation. Not expecting it, Brenna squealed and leaped sideways, stumbling into Cassidy as the children behind them screamed and fell into each other.

"Hey! Hey!" The mask came off revealing Sean Durham's surfer-dude good looks. "It's okay. Just me."

One of the kids asked, "Who're you?"

The actresses righted themselves, helping each other. Cassidy's hand remained on Brenna's arm as they listened to the children's reactions.

Another child elbowed the questioner and loudly whispered, "He's a vampire!"

Cassidy laughed and patted Sean's shoulder as the now foursome of actors led their merry troupe to the far side of the soundstage and out into the lantern-lit tent where the rest of the cast had assembled.

The main attraction was the center table, laden with soda, punch, and barbecue foods. Over at the far edge of the tent, Cameron and Victor sported aprons and spatulas and stood over grilling meat. The children swarmed the table, with some of the younger ones getting help from a cast member in filling their plates with hot dogs, hamburgers, and potato salad.

Nearly everyone picked up a candied apple from the bin at the end of the table.

The group settled on the ground, devouring their food. Brenna circulated a few minutes, checking on everyone. Rachelle waved her over.

"How's things?"

"Fine. You're in costume, too." Brenna crouched next to her. "You didn't have to do this."

"The kids are worth it." Rachelle smiled and accepted another shy, but interested study of her costume from a curious child. "I'm surprised you haven't brought them through before."

"Trying to keep some of my life separate, I guess."

Rachelle chided, "These kids are great." She finished off the last of her potato salad, scrambled to her feet, and trashed the paper wares. She smiled and patted Brenna's shoulder, then turned away and announced that her "booth" was open. "Who's ready for the haunted tent?" Cheers went up. "Everyone grab a buddy."

Children scampered about, seizing hands. As Brenna watched, Will Chapman was surrounded by half-pint admirers. Four grabbed his hands and arms, and he laughed. As sour as he had been lately, the laughter was quite a shock. Terry Brown and the two guest actors from the current script were soon dragged toward the decked out entrance to an adjoining tent.

Thrust into the lead, Brenna was the first to step into the dark opening, followed by her collection of children. Halloween decorations leaped out at her, and props rounded out the garish appearance. A sharp-looking weapon danced in mid-air, and someone piped in non-English language chant music. Several children screamed when stagehands, sporting alien makeup courtesy of the set's makeup artists, burst through openings and scowled in the red and ultraviolet lighting.

Brenna was laughing when she emerged from the other side, having had to pick up one of the smaller ones who had gotten frightened. Child in her arms, she turned to watch the rest emerging.

"That was so great!"

"Too cool! Can we do it again?"

Brenna shook her head. "There are other games."

"All right!" As a pack, the children raced into the main tent again, sizing up the carnival games.

Stagehands and cast members manned the booths, handing out bean bags and baseballs and fishing poles for carnival-style games. Props had been stacked into pyramids for several knockdown-type games.

There was face painting by the makeup crew and miniature pumpkin painting. Brenna took out a pile of Vordt statuettes with several baseballs, then slipped off to the side and sipped a soda while watching the happy melee. Sensing someone at her shoulder, she turned to find Cassidy. "Hi."

She scanned down the still-costumed woman. "I think you can take off the boots."

Cassidy shook her head. "It's all right." She carefully leaned against the tent pole. "Nice thing you have here." She glanced away.

Following the other woman's gaze, Brenna noticed Ryan at a booth fishing a prize from the murky Vortex pool. "The guys in Props are gods," she responded. She leaned closer to Cassidy and pointed out Chelle passing out the stuffed animals and other toy prizes for winning at the games. "Look at all that stuff."

Smiling, Cassidy pointed toward the apple-bobbing cauldron where a line of children waited their turn at the wet game. As they watched, a ten-year-old boy came up with a mouthful of apple. One of the volunteers offered him a towel and sent him with a ticket to Chelle's booth to claim a prize. "Where are Thomas and James?"

"They'll be here in about twenty minutes. Thomas had weight training, then he was going to drive them over."

"I'd be white as a sheet letting them drive alone," Cassidy admitted.

Smiling, Brenna made a show of patting her cheeks. "I use heavy makeup."

A little girl rushed toward them. Brenna caught her before she could run into Cassidy. "Hi!" the girl enthused.

Brenna crouched to be at eye level. "Hello there. Having a good time?"

"The best!" The girl's arms flung around her neck, and she felt the fluffiness of a stuffed toy on one cheek just as a wet kiss pressed against her other cheek. "Thank you!" the girl gushed before running off again.

Brenna put her hands to her face, hiding the heat, and nodded after the girl was gone. A hand moved softly across her back, and she dropped her hands hastily.

Cassidy observed, "These kids mean a lot to you."

"Yes." She glanced up nervously only to find comprehension. Inhaling, she stepped away. "Sorry."

"Nothing to be sorry for."

Their gazes met, and suddenly the noise around her muted to the borders of Brenna's awareness. "All right," she said, startling herself with her own voice.

Cassidy smiled slowly, holding Brenna's gaze.

"Mom!"

Brenna's head jerked around, and she spotted her sons standing at the entrance to the tent. Thomas wore his baseball uniform, and James wore a biker's leather jacket and black leather pants. He even had a metal-studded black leather cap pulled cockeyed on his head.

"Yours?" Cassidy asked quietly. "I like the leather look."

"My rebel with a cause," Brenna offered cheerfully. She left Cassidy's side to greet her sons. All three were swarmed when she wrapped an arm around each and kissed their cheeks.

"Kisses for me, too!" yelled the children.

Brenna distributed her kisses judiciously, making sure she caught each cheek once before sending the children off to more games. Sean Durham waved at her, but children still swamped her. "Thomas, would you go take over at the slot track? Sean's got a plane to catch."

Thomas went over to the slot racing table where Sean had been directing the various racing heats of wooden track cars. Brenna had promised to find a stand-in for him so he could head out early for his flight to Boston and the convention there.

Thomas lined up the cars, and Brenna kept an eye on him while she relieved Rachelle at the prize table. Two circuits of the track later, the blue car had won. Thomas passed a prize claim ticket to the winner, lined up the cars again, and started the next round.

Handing fishing poles to the youngest children so they could catch prizes from the Vortex pool, Cassidy scanned the cheerful tableau, confused by her emotions. Her eyes strayed frequently to Brenna. She was witnessing a side of Brenna that she'd suspected had existed, but which had been held secret. Judging by Rachelle's surprise, Cassidy realized that it was something Brenna had hidden from the entire cast, not just her. She wondered why. Most of them had a charity or two that they spoke for or worked with. Brenna seemed particularly watchful and engaged with this group, she realized, observing as the other woman accepted another hug from a little girl as she gave her a prize in exchange for her winning ticket. She had a distant, wistful look on her face as she closed her eyes and wrapped her arms around the smaller body.

Out of the corner of her eye, Cassidy saw one of the volunteers look at his watch and set down his ticket bucket. He stepped from behind the table and strode across the tent. Her heart sank as she realized the evening was about to end.

Brenna knew it too. Noting his approach, she stepped from behind the prize table and listened as he spoke to her quietly. She frowned but nodded, then stepped to the center of the room and stood by the decimated food table. "Could I have everyone's attention?"

Cassidy smiled painfully. It wasn't Jakes' voice, but Brenna's own rich contralto that quelled the mayhem of the room. The effect, however, was the same: All stopped and turned their eyes toward their leader.

"Has everyone been having fun?" Cheers from the children filled the room. "I'm glad. But now, it's time to say goodbye." Moans and groans and some tears came.

A pair of arms slipped around Cassidy's thighs. A young boy had latched on. She dropped a gentle hand to his dark hair and brushed the tight curls, causing him look up. His chin pressed into her thigh muscle as he hugged more tightly. She asked, "Would you like a buddy to walk with you to the bus?"

He nodded but said nothing. Cassidy guessed he was just about Ryan's age and took his hand in hers, separating him from her legs so she could move. "Come on, Ryan," she called out, drawing her son away from the abandoned game tables. He ran up and caught her other hand. The boys eyed each other around her hips. "This is my son, Ryan," she said. "What's your name?"

"Isaiah."

She smiled and patted his shoulder. "Nice to meet you, Isaiah."

Walking toward the exit, she noticed all the others in the cast and even the executives found themselves in similar situations. She shrugged at Cameron, who was trying to prevent a little girl from climbing into his arms. One of the guest actors swung a boy onto his back, and Cassidy shook her head in amusement. Terry had a boy on the end of each arm. Both looked to be about eight and wore glasses, clearly very taken by the brainy member of the Time Squad. Finishing her survey, she turned her gaze to Brenna, who had a boy and a girl clasping each hand.

The auburn-haired woman smiled back and started to lead the way out. "All right, everyone, to the bus."

Filled with sugar, the children skipped and dragged their companions along the set interiors. They bounced with enthusiasm through the Vortex set and scampered about, shouting to one another as they separated into a "good guys" and "bad guys" game.

Cassidy stood amid the rest of the cast, arms crossed over her chest, watching the children run around, laughing and even cheering on her own son, as Ryan stood in the middle of the transversal platform and, clearly mimicking Susan Jakes, ordered, "Go!" She felt eyes on her and looked to the side to find Brenna studying her, a puzzled look on her face. Raising her eyebrows and nodding toward the melee, Cassidy expressed her amusement without words.

Brenna shifted, and Cassidy, thinking she was going to push through the crowd toward her, felt a rush of anticipation. However, the other woman did not join her. Instead Brenna grinned and turned away. Holding her hands like a megaphone around her mouth, she ordered in a perfect "Jakes" voice, "At-TEN-SHUN!"

Forty-three children ground to an instant halt.

"Time's up. Move 'em out."

Their wide eyes fixed on the transformed Lanigan, who suddenly appeared, with every gesture, to be the *Time Trails* leader. It startled Cassidy, who was surprised to realize that before now she was not sure she could have told the difference between the two. She was really getting to know the actress separate from her character. The revelation made her smile.

The children quickly lined up and began marching like a drunken military platoon out the doors held open by Terry and Will. The line broke when the children spotted the bus idling. They raced to get seats.

Snagging Ryan, who tried to follow the other children onto the bus, Cassidy spun around with him in her arms and almost slammed into Brenna. The other woman caught her before either of them could stumble. Cassidy complimented her restoration of order. "I've never seen anything like that."

"Commander's skill," Brenna said with a grin. Cassidy felt the woman's hand just barely brushing her own arm where she held Ryan securely against her hip. Looking at Ryan, Brenna added, "Jakes has taught me a few things over the years."

"You, too, hmm?" Cassidy smiled. She turned around to watch the last of the children escorted onto the bus by the volunteers. After passing blown kisses and hand slaps through the open windows, the cast members slowly trailed back toward the soundstages. Cassidy squared her shoulders and turned around.

"Where are you going?" Brenna asked.

"To help clean up."

"I can do that. You should change and take Ryan home."

"We're a team," Terry said, coming up within earshot. "Besides, more hands get it done faster."

Brenna looked from Terry to Cassidy and back, then over his shoulder to Rachelle, Will, and Rich standing around expectantly. "Well, I guess that settles that."

"Commander's overruled," Rich Paulson teased with a grin.

The actors and Brenna's sons trooped back to the tent, grabbing trash cans from behind the set walls along the way.

Cassidy set Ryan down next to the food. The tired boy was asleep before the group finished. Within an hour, the grounds behind the soundstage looked as though the party had never taken place. Props had been returned to the Property Department, and the tents were pulled down, bundled, and delivered to the catering truck. Tied trash bags stuffed the bins outside against the walls of the building in wait for the night cleaning crew. The tables ~ folded up, thanks to Rich and Terry ~ were stacked inside the soundstage against an interior wall, and everyone was given an assortment of the leftovers.

Balancing Ryan on her left hip, Cassidy stepped into her trailer and put the bagged leftovers into her mini-fridge, keeping one caramel apple out for Ryan. Carefully she set the boy, still sleeping, on the far cushion of the couch. Then, with relief, she sat next to him and propped her feet over the arm, preparing to push off her shoes.

"I told you that you should have taken them off."

The voice startled Cassidy. She hadn't known anyone else had walked to the trailers. She distinctly remembered Terry and Rachelle heading for the makeup room. Brenna had not only come out to the trailers, however, but she now stood silhouetted in Cassidy's open doorway. Surprising her further, Brenna reached out and, wrapping warm fingers around her ankle, tugged off Cassidy's shoe.

"I'm sorry. I didn't mean to startle you."

Cassidy reflexively caught first one tossed shoe, then the other, as Brenna quickly removed them. Dropping her feet to the floor and flexing them, Cassidy bent over and rubbed her toes. "Thank you. Did you need something?" She started to rise.

Brenna noticed Ryan on the couch then. She seemed to catch herself before bending over and stroking his hair. Cassidy froze, warily watching the other woman's manner with her son and wondering what had Brenna so preoccupied. It seemed she might never learn when Brenna abruptly straightened and fidgeted.

"You're probably anxious to get home. It can wait." Brenna turned to the door.

"No. Go ahead and sit. I just need to put this up and change into something else."

"But...?" She glanced pointedly at Ryan.

"I doubt he'll wake up," she assured.

"All right." Brenna stepped back into Cassidy's trailer and closed the door. "I wanted to ask you something."

"Go ahead. Ask." Brenna moved to the couch, and Cassidy watched her drape an idle hand over Ryan's back. Ducking away to change, she heard the question, "Would you be interested in joining me at the next event?"

Popping her head back out, she asked, "What?"

"Well, I was just...You looked like you had a good time tonight. We...I thought..." She finished in a rush, "There's an overnight camping trip in the mountains the weekend before Thanksgiving."

Turning away to finish changing, Cassidy collected her thoughts. When she reappeared, she wore a gray pullover sweater, jeans, and Nikes. "Don't you have enough chaperones?"

Brenna shook her head. "It's not that. Not just that," she corrected. "I...thought you and Ryan might enjoy yourselves." At his name, Ryan stirred slightly. Brenna missed Cassidy's surprised reaction as she concentrated for a moment on gently rubbing circles over the small boy's back. "He's sweet, Cass."

"Ryan could come?"

Cassidy's response drew Brenna's eyes back to her. She sounded shocked. "Of course." *What was so odd about inviting her son along on a camping trip?* Cassidy continued to study her. Brenna had felt less scrutiny from the children patting her hips and asking why her pants didn't have pockets. She shifted self-consciously and cleared her throat. "Um. Well?"

Cassidy straightened her shoulders and leaned back on her palms on her writing desk. Brenna likened the posture to surrender. "Sure, we'd like to join the trip."

Brenna exhaled in relief, suddenly aware how much she had hoped for a positive response. "It'll be fun and relaxing. We're planning s'mores, campfire songs, and storytelling."

"Singing, hmm?" Cass smiled.

"You have not lived until you've heard all fourteen verses to 'I lost my poor meatball' sung by a group of sleep-deprived kids." Brenna chuckled.

"Sounds like fun. It's settled then."

Brenna opened the door as Cassidy lifted Ryan. The boy settled against his mother's generous chest with a mumbled grunt. *Positively endearing,* Brenna thought.

CHAPTER EIGHT

THOMAS WATCHED his mother at the stove stirring a saucepan of sizzling chicken strips. When the phone rang on the wall next to her, startling her, she stepped away from the food, caught his eye, and gestured for him to continue with the preparation while she grabbed the cordless handset.

"Oh, Kevin. How's Mount Clemens?"

Recognizing his mom was speaking to her husband, Thomas glanced over his shoulder and watched her. She tucked the receiver between her ear and shoulder and fished in the silverware drawer for the flatware.

"No," she said into the phone. "You caught us at lunch." There was a pause as she listened, fishing for the butter knife. Coming up with it, she spoke again into the receiver. "Yes, I know it's late, but I had gardening to do."

She moved out of earshot to the dining room table, circling it and laying the settings while still talking. Thomas studied the chicken, moved it off the burner, and stirred the stewed tomatoes, checking the pasta with a quick taste. He moved to the cutting board, intermittently watching his mother while he chopped the salad ingredients. His mom suddenly sat down at the table and grabbed the handset firmly off her shoulder. The raised volume of her voice made it possible for him to hear.

"No. I told you I wouldn't."

Uncomfortable, Thomas concentrated on his task, trying to ignore the conversation even as his mother's voice lowered in volume but intensified in emotion. He stopped cutting and looked at the salad ingredients. The cucumber, his mother's favorite addition, was missing. Leaning into the refrigerator, he found the hydrator empty. "Hey, Mom, there's no cukes."

Silence greeted his statement. Returning to the cutting board, he looked into the dining room and saw her still sitting. The phone was on the table; it was her face that concerned him. She had it covered with one hand. The other hand rested against the tablecloth in a balled fist. "Mom? Are you okay?"

She was still for a breath, then moved her hand away from her face and quickly stood, turning her back on him and walking down the corridor toward her bedroom.

In that split second, Thomas realized his mother had been crying. He looked down at the phone she had abandoned on the tabletop. Picking it up, he found it had been turned off. A sizzling sound caught his ear. He returned the phone to the wall before finishing the meal prep. Just as he was placing the salad and three bowls on the table, James wandered in from the driveway, carrying his basketball under his arm.

"Hey, bro. Where's Mom?"

"Her room. Help me finish here?"

"Sure thing. She reading?"

Thomas shrugged. He did not think so, but he decided against sharing his suppositions. James set the basketball down and collected the pasta bowl, taking it out to the table. When he returned to the kitchen, Thomas was pouring sodas. "Take the other two bowls. I've got the drinks."

James looked toward the bedroom hall. "Aren't you going to call her?"

Thomas shook his head. "I don't think she's too hungry." Though James was only two years younger, Thomas recalled their parents' divorce more vividly. The phone call worried him. When the three of them had left Mount Clemens two weeks earlier, he sensed something had changed between his mother and Kevin but had thought little of it. Now he was concerned. His mom did not cry.

His silence tipped James. "Okay, so tell me what happened?"

With a sigh, Thomas confided, "Kevin called. I think they had a fight."

\#

Tucked where they were in the kitchen talking, Thomas and James did not see their mother return to the dining room. Settling into her chair at the table, she heard the end of their conversation. She acted surprised, though, when they came out with the glasses and the pasta dish.

"Mom?" James sat in his seat on her right against the sideboard. Thomas took the seat to her left.

She grasped their hands, smiled, and dropped her head. "Grace?" Thomas offered the prayer, though she could tell he was still studying her.

"Thank you, Lord, for the fullness of your bounty. Amen."

"Amen," she echoed, as James did the same. Thomas did not let go of her hand immediately. Brenna squeezed his hand, then tugged hers free, picking up her fork. "Thank you," she said quietly.

"Anytime, Mom."

"Were you planning to go out tonight?" She looked from one to the other, wondering what they would say.

As James started to respond, Brenna caught a quick head shake from Thomas that silenced him. Thomas drew her attention and filled in quickly, "No, Mom. What would you like to do?"

Touched, Brenna almost relented and excused the boys to their own fun, but then she remembered the upcoming camping trip. "Why don't we go get some more things for the campout?"

"Hey, that would be cool," Thomas agreed.

She smiled. He had been excited about the trip since agreeing to take some of the adults and older kids up into the ridge for a guided climb.

"So where do you want to go?" Thomas asked. "I need a few more things for the climb anyway."

"There's a new warehouse-style store on Riordan Avenue."

James was surprised. "That's all the way into Alameda."

"I know."

"Oh, okay. Sure, whatever," James recovered.

"You don't have to go," she allowed.

"Maybe we can take you out to the movies on the way back," Thomas suggested.

Brenna smiled tightly at Thomas' concern. He had obviously overheard more than she'd thought. No typical teen would offer to take his mother out to a movie. She grasped his hand. "Maybe we'll just rent something."

Lunch was finished quickly, and the dishes put in the dishwasher before the trio piled into the SUV. Thomas asked to drive. Brenna kissed him and laughed. "Not on my life."

Thomas was smiling as he slid into the front passenger seat and buckled up. Clearly he thought his mission had been accomplished.

"So what stuff do you think we ought to get for the kids to do?" she asked as they left the neighborhood and merged onto the highway toward Alameda.

Cassidy studied her son, asleep beside her, as they lay on her bed for his afternoon nap. The radio played softly as she lightly rubbed his back with one hand and read script pages in the lamplight. His copy of *Where the Wild Things Are* lay across the covers just beyond her right hand. Putting down her script, she reached for the colorfully illustrated book, lifted it, and studied the cover for a long moment.

Opening the pages, she perused the pictures, but her mind wouldn't stay on the fanciful monsters, instead drifting constantly to the woman who had presented the gift. Then there was last night's unexpected invitation to go camping.

Lightly brushing her fingers through Ryan's hair, she murmured, "Camping, huh? I think you'll like it. Certainly you'll have a lot of fun with the other kids." She leaned back, looking at the ceiling. "I wonder if Brenna will bring her sons."

She wondered if the teenagers found camping fun. She thought about the last time she had ventured into the mountains. About eight years earlier she had gone on a winter ski trip to a Denver cabin with a group of college friends. She remembered spending most of the slope time on her rear end, pride damaged more than anything else. The nights had consisted of keeping warm under blankets that barely covered anything. Efforts to keep warm had led to other interesting pastimes.

Maybe she ought to call Misty and catch up.

Mentally cataloging her camping supplies, Cassidy realized she would need several things. A glance toward the clock revealed that it was only one-thirty. Maybe she could cut Ryan's nap short at two, drive to the new Sports Warehouse on Riordan, and pick up what they needed. Until then, she decided, she could read the latest script. She wasn't in any frame of mind to memorize lines, but at least she could give it a read-through and get a feel for the overall picture. After last week's surprise, Cassidy was leery of her character taking on anything else right away.

A while later, satisfied that Chris Hanssen was back in the realm of standard sci-fi fare, she reached the closing scene and set the script aside. A glance at the clock prompted her to wake Ryan. "Come on, buddy," she whispered. "We're going to get you some camping things."

"Camping?"

His green eyes blinked open, and she smiled, kissing his cheek. "Yes. Do you remember Ms. Lanigan?"

"Mmm hmm."

"She invited us to go with the bunch of kids from the Halloween party up into the mountains in a couple of weeks."

"So why we gotta go shopping now?"

"Because I've got the time." She coaxed him with a bribe. "If you behave, we'll go for ice cream afterward."

"Ice cream? Mmm." He sat up and rubbed his eyes. "Can I have chocolate? Two scoops?"

Cassidy stifled her laugh. *Bribery works.* "We'll see, after we go shopping."

"Okay." He scrambled off the bed, stood there in his sock-covered feet, and declared, "I'm ready to go. Come on!"

"Put on your shoes. I'll be right out." She stepped into her bathroom, ran a quick brush through her hair, and slipped her feet into a pair of sandals. Stepping back out, she asked, "All right, ready?"

Ryan looked up from the floor where he was tying his shoes and nodded.

"Come on." On the way to the front door, she snapped up her purse from the side table. She buckled him into his booster seat in the back before getting behind the wheel. After allowing a jogger to pass behind the car, she pulled out of the driveway.

CHAPTER NINE

GRAND OPENING banners were displayed all around the large store. The aisles were crowded. Cassidy grasped Ryan's hand firmly in her own. *Most of the county must be here.* Her son was captivated by the displays. She repeatedly had to tug him back against her side while reading the aisle listings to find their particular objectives.

Buffeted as she moved into the appropriate aisle, Cassidy searched the shelves until she found the lanterns. She found battery-operated, gas, and candle lanterns, all rated by lumen output and designed for different conditions. Checking that Ryan remained at her side, she pulled down a boxed gas powered light to read the labeling more closely. She scooted closer to the shelving and grasped her son's shoulder as a family with a cart tried to maneuver past.

"Excuse us," the man said, shifting the front end of the cart away from her feet.

His gaze stopped on her briefly, and Cassidy watched a puzzled half-recognition flash in his brown eyes. She smiled faintly, and he nodded, taking his family past without any further exchange. Cassidy lifted the box back to eye level and continued reading. The lantern's bowl was open at the top without a guard screen. She shook her head and replaced it on the shelf. She wasn't going to risk Ryan sticking his hand inside out of curiosity. She liked the idea of the gas over the batteries though, for longevity, and continued searching for another model.

"Mommy?"

She felt a tug on her jeans and looked down into Ryan's upturned smile. "Yes?"

"Can I see the animals?"

"Animals? Where?" She looked around. He tugged her pant leg again, and she followed his outstretched arm. At the end of the aisle, just visible through the throngs of people, was a display of woodland animals. Cassidy suspected it was the entrance to the hunting section and shook her head. "No, Ryan."

"Mommy, please?"

She crouched and rubbed his shoulder. "They're not real, honey."

His eyes gleamed with excitement. "Toys!" Tugging on the hand holding his, he pleaded, "I'll just look. I promise."

Cassidy shook her head and stood. "No, now wait." She fished behind the front row of the display and withdrew an unbattered box containing the lantern she had selected. "All right. Now let's go find you a sleeping bag."

She tucked the box under her left arm and reached down to take Ryan's hand in her right. They navigated the aisle and emerged near the display that had caught his attention.

Pausing for a moment, Cassidy studied the animals and realized the animal carcasses were real, preserved, and posed. Glass eyes seemed to follow her as she looked away. "Come on," she said to Ryan, who was transfixed. She scanned the aisle labels and moved two down against the wall of the warehouse building, which proclaimed "sleeping bags."

The crowd was thinner there, and Cassidy breathed a little easier, scanning the labels of the bags for something warm enough for a mountain winter night. Ryan pointed out a sleeping bag covered in Rugrats figures. The fleece was too thin, though, more suited for a summer than a winter trip, and she shook her head. Ryan pouted. She pointed out one which advertised a thicker woolen lining covered in Barney renderings. He turned up his nose at the purple dinosaur, and Cassidy continued looking. A plain blue one received the same disdain.

Ryan sat down on the bottom shelf as she moved away a little to look at others. *At least he isn't throwing a tantrum,* she thought, counting her blessings and continuing to look along the shelves for something that would suit her requirements and his. She tried very hard to compromise where it was reasonable to do so. Her mother had always told her to pick her fights carefully. So far the advice had proven sound. Ryan was well-mannered and generally aware of the feelings of others and did not cry out for every trendy thing.

She found a Disney Dalmatians bag with enough lining and turned to suggest it to him, figuring he would like it because it looked like their dog, Ranger.

Ryan was no longer seated on the shelf.

The aisle was nearly empty. One bearded man in fatigues was looking at the tarps, and a pair of teenaged boys checked out the waterproofing sprays, but no Ryan.

"Ryan?" Calling out as she went, she hurried down the aisle to one end and looked among the throngs for her son's three-foot-tall form. There were children everywhere, but each was attached to a parent or seated in a cart. Quickly she moved toward the other end of the aisle. "Ryan!" Stumbling into another patron, she dropped her lantern.

"Oh, I'm sorry." The speaker, a woman, leaned over to pick up the fallen box. "Let me help you get that."

The voice? Cassidy stopped and focused on the person in front of her. "Brenna?" She met curious blue eyes as delicately strong hands closed around her forearms.

"Cassidy?"

"I'm...Excuse me. I have to find Ryan." Cassidy looked past her castmate and scanned the aisle, dimly noting Brenna's sons straightening up behind their mother.

"Ryan is missing?" Brenna questioned sharply. Cassidy's gaze jerked back to hers. "How long ago?"

"A few minutes, maybe. I don't know," Cassidy admitted.

"Thomas, James, fan out. You both know what he looks like."

"No problem, Mom." Cassidy caught a nod from the lankier Thomas. "We'll find him," he assured her. She nodded back.

The teens spread out, each taking an aisle and calling out the boy's name. Brenna drew Cassidy back into the quieter aisle. "Cass? Where did you last see him?"

Her heart was pounding, and she fisted her hands together to focus. "We were here looking at sleeping bags." She took a deep breath. "He didn't like what I'd chosen, so he sat down to sulk."

Brenna nodded. "Okay, was there something that caught his attention?" Cassidy shook her head. "Anywhere in the store?"

Cassidy paused. "The animals."

"The what?"

"The animals displayed in the hunting section." Cassidy strode away quickly; Brenna kept up. "The taxidermy display," Cassidy clarified.

"Oh." Cassidy had stopped in front of it. Brenna was confronted by a ten-point buck and, on faux wood set at various levels, raccoons, and birds, even a rabbit. "Oh," she said again in a faint voice. She swallowed against her suddenly queasy stomach. "Let's take a look through here," she went on quickly.

Their search turned up no sign of Cassidy's son.

Meeting back at the animal display, Brenna asked, "Okay, do you have a picture?"

"What?" Events were eroding Cassidy's control. The blonde's voice was curt and distracted as she continued scanning their immediate area.

Brenna spoke with quiet, calm direction. "You need a picture of Ryan. We're going to the management."

As Brenna's hand rubbed lightly on her back, Cassidy took a deep breath and let it out slowly. She searched through her purse for her wallet and Ryan's birthday picture. Shaking fingers pulled it out of the plastic, and Brenna's hand closed over hers.

"All right. Let's find the office."

Cassidy looked up hopefully as Thomas jogged toward them. He shook his head, admitting defeat. She stopped. "Do you think..."

Brenna met her gaze with determination. "No, it's just a big place. We need more people to help look." Looking around, she spotted the office sign behind the Customer Service desk. "Over there. Let's go."

"All right." Cassidy admitted to herself that she felt infinitely calmer with Brenna beside her.

Brenna tugged Cassidy forward through the service line. "We have a missing child to report."

The clerk, whose name tag identified her as "Jessie," looked over from the customer she was helping with a catalog and brushed her braided bangs out of her face. "We don't have any kids here."

"My son's missing," Cassidy supplied.

"We need to see the manager," Brenna insisted. "Now."

"Okay. Just hold on." Jessie went into the back. Brenna watched her enter a doorway down the short corridor.

Brenna's hand closed over Cassidy's again as the blonde patted the counter surface impatiently. "Relax. You're going to have to remember what he was wearing."

Cassidy blanched. Had it been a red shirt or tan? Was he in his blue jeans or black ones? She looked away from Brenna's face to see a thick-waisted man in short shirtsleeves and a red tie step out of the office and walk out behind Jessie.

"Here's the manager, Mr. Dunwald."

"Mr. Dunwald, my friend's son is missing. If we give you a picture, could you ask your staff to help us look for him?"

He held out his hand. Brenna placed the picture in it. While looking it over, he asked, "How long has he been missing?"

Cassidy looked to Brenna, finding her encouragement calming. "About...um, a...half hour I think."

"What's his name?"

"Ryan Hyland."

"How old?"

"He just turned five."

"How tall?"

She breathed slowly. "Thirty-nine inches at his last checkup." She hesitated. "I think."

"All right. We'll go call for him over the intercom. Does he know enough to report to a clerk?"

"We've never been here before."

He shook his head. The clerks, Brenna noted, were all wearing green vests. She squeezed Cassidy's hand again, drawing her attention. "What if he tells Ryan to go to someone in a green vest," she whispered.

Cassidy nodded. "That'll work."

The manager asked one more thing before turning around to catch up the intercom microphone. "How long do you want to wait before we call the police and report a kidnapping?"

Cassidy's face went pale at the blunt question. Supportively, Brenna wrapped her arm around the taller woman's lower back. "Make the announcement," she ordered him sharply. The manager shrugged and turned around.

"Attention, customers. Would Ryan Hyland report to a clerk in a green vest please?"

He turned back to the two women. "Why don't you sit in my office until we have word?"

Brenna nodded to Thomas, who disappeared back into the aisles to continue looking. "Come on," she said to Cassidy. "Thomas will go and keep looking. We'll sit down for just a couple minutes. That's all it will take." The manager opened the counter door and gestured them back to his office.

Thomas skidded to a stop in another aisle and pushed his hair from his face. "Hey." He drew the attention of a skinny man in overalls balancing two oars in each hand. "Have you seen a kid about this tall?" He held out his hand waist high. "Blond hair? Looking a little lost?"

The man shook his head. "Nope."

"If you do, would you please take him to the front desk?"

"Sure thing. What's the kid's name?"

"Ryan."

"Okay."

"Thanks." Thomas dodged around another patron and found himself near the back of the store. A layaway area was there, along with the restrooms. There was not much else there, and the area was empty of people. He turned around, starting back, when he looked left, then right, and spotted his brother, hands on his hips and looking up a ladder laid against a set of shelves, leading to the top. "James!"

His brother brushed a hand across his freckled cheeks and then waved Thomas over. "Any luck?"

"Nothing. You?"

"Do you remember that time I was, oh heck, I must've been about Ryan's age? I followed Dad up onto the roof when he was cleaning the gutters?"

"Shit. Yes. You think he went up there?"

"We won't know until we get up there and look around. He could be stuck on top of one of these things."

"So why isn't he hollering?"

"Come on. I had the idea. Let's give it a shot first, then think about the logic. This is a five-year-old we're talking about."

Thomas sighed, pushing his fingers through his hair. He was tired, but his mother clearly wanted them to do as much as possible to help. Looking for Mrs. Hyland's son was the least they could do. Certainly she wasn't in any shape to do it herself, he thought, remembering the fear he'd read in her face at the manager's suggestion that they place a kidnapping report. "All right. Let's go." He grabbed the base of the ladder, steadying it as his brother climbed up quickly.

"Hey! You kids get down from there!"

Thomas turned around to see a freckle-faced clerk who looked about his age jogging toward them. "We need to get up there and take a look around."

"You could get hurt. And it'd be my neck in a sling."

"Well, listen. We're looking for a little boy. Maybe you've seen him?"

"That the 'Ryan Hyland' they called for over the intercom?"

"Yes."

"We've got a policy not to let on that the person being sought is underage. Predators, y'know?"

Thomas nodded quickly, waving off the protocol talk. "Yeah. Sure. Fine. Have you seen him or not?"

"He wasn't around when the announcement came in, or I'd have called in. He was climbing the ladder earlier. I shooed him away. Told him to go back to his parents. He looked at me, cried and ran off."

"Which way did he go?"

The clerk pointed back over his shoulder. "That way."

Thomas and James exchanged hopeful looks and dashed away. "Do you think it could be that simple? We're just a few steps behind a five-year-old wandering the store?" James asked.

"We'd better hope so."

"I wonder how Mrs. Hyland's doing," James said, as they rounded the nearest corner and drew up short on the rear loading dock. "Whoa!"

Thomas grabbed his brother's arm and prevented him from falling off the edge. They looked down. No Ryan on the outside asphalt. Looking around, they tried to figure out where to go next. Thomas spotted a dark opening to the side of the dock. "Look, over there!"

James scrambled over to the hole first and looked inside. There was a notice on the wall, which he read aloud. "'Stand clear ~ compactor.' Where the heck's the safety stuff they always have around?"

"I don't know." Thomas leaned against the side and looked down. "Ryan!" he called into the opening. "Ryan, can you hear me?"

There was no answer. James grabbed his brother's shoulder and tugged him backward. "I think we'd better report to Mom," he said worriedly.

Thomas considered. Whether Ryan was down that shaft or not, they needed help to look. Big help. "Yeah, let's go."

CHAPTER TEN

IN THE manager's office, Cassidy fretted. "What's taking so long?"

Brenna laid her right hand over Cassidy's. "They're looking for him. Thomas and James are, too. We will find him."

"It's been over an hour. Maybe the manager's right. He didn't run off; someone kidnapped him."

Aware of the tension in the taller woman, Brenna sympathetically rubbed her shoulder. "I won't lie to you. The longer he's missing, yes, the more likely it is that someone coaxed him away. But you have to have faith."

"Ryan knows not to go off with strangers," Cassidy reasoned, finding some measure of calm. In the next moment, though, she recalled, "We haven't practiced his safe word in a while. What if he doesn't remember it?"

Brenna's expression told Cassidy that she wanted to give the reassurances she sought. The door of the manager's office started inward. She pushed abruptly to her feet, Brenna immediately doing the same in front of her, standing between her and the doorway. The manager's head appeared around the door frame. "Ms. Hyland?"

She answered quickly. "Yes."

Dunwald stepped all the way inside and closed the door. Something in the careful way he shut the door and the way the latch resounded in the silence made Cassidy bite her bottom lip nervously.

"I am sorry. We haven't located your son. I just called the police. We will have to file a missing child report." He moved around and sat down behind his desk. "Since your son disappeared from our store, I'm going to ask you to fill out an incident report here before the police arrive."

"Why?" Brenna asked sharply. "She's going to have to tell the police the exact same thing."

"You can use it to write your statement for the police. Our headquarters requires their own on file." He fished a form from the low filing cabinet drawer behind his desk and slid it across the table along with a pen. "Here you are."

Cassidy reached for the pen; Brenna snapped up the paper and scanned it. "We'll just fill them both out at the same time, all right? Show the police in when they get here."

The manager looked from Brenna to Cassidy and then frowned. "Of course," he agreed stiffly before withdrawing.

He was gone only a few seconds when there was another knock. Leaving the form on the desk, Brenna stood quickly and opened the door. Jessie stood outside. "Yes?"

"There are two boys at the desk who say that their mom's back here."

"That'd be my sons."

"I don't want to let them back here," Jessie explained. "Could you come out front?"

"All right. Just a minute." Brenna closed the door and turned around. Cassidy's forehead rested in her left palm as she bent her elbow against the wood laminate surface. "Cassidy, I'm going out to talk to Thomas and James. Maybe they've found something."

The blonde stopped in the midst of lifting the form to read it over. Brenna could tell from the line of tension in Cassidy's back that the other woman was barely holding herself together. Tears of empathy pricked her eyes. Not questioning, just knowing she needed to do so, Brenna tucked her arms around the younger woman's shoulders and pressed her cheek against the top of the blond head. "I'm sorry," she murmured.

Cassidy turned in her arms suddenly and wrapped her arms around Brenna's waist, startling her when Brenna felt a cheek press against her breasts. "Oh God..." Tears dampened Brenna's stomach through her thin shirt.

"I know. Oh, I know." Brenna spoke against Cassidy's hair and brushed her fingers through the soft locks. Instinctively, she pressed a kiss to the top of Cassidy's head and then reluctantly pulled away, crouching a little to catch Cassidy's gaze. "I'll be right back. I promise."

"Thank you." Cassidy wrapped her arms around the back of the chair, resting her chin on the top edge for a moment before drawing a deep breath and turning back to the form. "I'd better look at this."

"You might want to wait," Brenna suggested ruefully. "It's probably more of a liability protection for the store than an incident statement for the police report." She left Cassidy looking at the form, her gaze scanning the text dubiously.

Brenna found her sons pacing at the service desk. "Hey," she drew their attention.

"Mom!" James rushed up as she stepped from behind the counter. "We've got to get the police."

"They've already been called," she assured him. "What'd you find?" she asked, dropping her voice as she caught glances from other patrons around them.

"We don't know. Out back there's a loading dock, and a big hole compacting the boxes and stuff."

Brenna drew a deep breath. "Any signs that Ryan was there?"

"Not that we can tell." Thomas shook his head when she shot her gaze up to his. "I called for him, but we can't see anything."

A commotion drew Brenna's attention to the store entrance. "Good, they're here. I want you to show the police where you were. We only need one to talk to Cassidy in the office." She nudged both boys over to the officers and introduced herself.

"We're here about a missing child report. Where's the mother?"

Brenna checked the officer's badge. "Lieutenant Taylor, the mother is in the manager's office. My boys have been looking for her son and have a place they'd like your men to check first."

"We need a statement from the mother."

"Listen, it's a trash compactor that's open in the back," she said firmly. "I'll take one of you to meet with Ms. Hyland, but I want someone to check out that compactor."

The officer waved over his partner. "Murph, you, Jefferson, and Maxwell go with these kids. I'm going to talk to the mother."

Murph, whose badge read "Sgt. Murphy," nodded his dark head. "Got it. Okay, boys, lead the way."

Thomas and James guided Sergeant Murphy through the store. When curious onlookers started crowding them, the other two officers behind started running interference, urging people back from the threesome.

"So, how long has the kid been missing?" Murphy asked.

"We've been looking for at least an hour," Thomas supplied. "This way." He turned at the end of an aisle and stopped at the back storage area. "The loading dock is through here."

With Murphy, the two boys stepped out onto to the loading dock, and Thomas pointed to the left. "You think he might've fallen down there?" the sergeant asked.

"We couldn't see anything," Thomas said. His brother pressed up against his back and peered over his shoulder.

"We'll check it out. Now, get back. Maxwell," he called to one of the other officers. "I need your light."

"Yes, Sergeant." Immediately one of the officers stripped a long black tube flashlight off his belt and crossed to where Murphy was dropping to his stomach. "What'cha got?"

"Kid maybe fell in here." He waved the light to his right. "Shine it down there. Straight down."

The tube was long, going deeper into the ground than the four-foot drop to the surface of the truck driveway. The light only bit faintly at the shadows, illuminating not much more than nothing. Murphy rolled over and sat up. "We're going to have to get down to the other end of this thing. Open it up where they pick out the pieces for the trash pickup."

"I'll find a clerk who knows the way." James was off and running before any of the officers could stop him.

Murphy wiped his hands on his uniform pants as he stood. "Let's take the stairs down. Maybe we can get to the room without a clerk's help."

Thomas tagged along because frankly he did not want to face his mother without the officers, especially if the news wasn't going to be good. He was tired enough to contemplate the worst.

They found a set of short stairs that led to the basement level and a series of storage rooms. Pressing his ear to one, Officer Murphy heard the whir of gears and immediately stepped back. The doorknob turned in his hand, and he shoved inward, shining Maxwell's flashlight around the dark room.

The far wall was dominated by a set of metal doors. Another officer behind him located a light switch. Flipping off the flashlight, Murphy tossed it back to Maxwell, who returned it to his belt. "All right, let's open it up."

They checked the latch mechanism and slipped the restraining pole from the catches. The doors swung wide. The officers jumped back out of the way as bits of boxes spilled out, littering the floor around their feet.

"Okay, start digging around."

Thomas looked at the mess. "He can't be in there, can he?"

Murphy, who had begun digging in the darkness of the bin's interior, looked over at him suddenly. "Kid, you better get out. We'll do this." The teen's shoulders slumped. Murphy left off his task for just a moment, crossing the room. He laid a big hand on the slender shoulder. "You did a hell of a job. You don't have any worries. You did everything right."

"Well, I...I'll just be outside then."

"Go on back to your mom. Catch that brother of yours if you run across him and sit tight."

He opened the door to show Thomas out and glanced out into the corridor. "On second thought, make sure no one else comes down here 'cept the ambulance when it arrives."

"You're calling one? Even if..." Thomas blinked. "I know. I know. Think positive."

The officer thumped Thomas across the shoulder. "Got the right attitude. Now, go on."

Thomas ran to the stairs and halfway up before he just stopped, sat down, and took a deep breath to calm himself.

On the first floor, another pair of patrolmen worked to clear the store before the ambulance team arrived. "All right, everyone, time to go. Sorry for the inconvenience, but we need order here."

"KTLA News." A middle-aged man in a staid suit and tie, microphone in hand, pressed forward through the crowd. "We heard on the scanner there's a missing kid. Possible accident?"

The officer right next to him groaned and turned his back. Over his shoulder, he ordered, "Outside. You'll have an update as soon as we do."

The reporter shrugged off the hands of the crowd pushing at his shoulders. "Just point out the manager."

The manager, with Cassidy and Brenna, stepped out of his office at that moment, with Officer Taylor.

Yelling past the policeman's blocking shoulder, the reporter announced, "Don Deering, KTLA News! Which of you is the mother of the missing boy?"

Cassidy's head shot toward the voice when she heard "mother," though she had been talking to Officer Taylor. Brenna beside her, grabbed her arm in warning. She turned toward her.

"Ma'am, I want to talk to you!" Deering, his cameraman, and another reporter whose shirt was imprinted "KRDV Radio 940" shoved their way through the crowd.

Lieutenant Taylor stepped in front of them. "You were ordered outside, gentlemen. Now move."

"How long has the child been missing? Do you suspect foul play? What's the expectation here?" Both reporters peppered Taylor with questions, occasionally glancing toward the two women making their way with the manager back into the safety of his office.

Taylor grabbed the radio reporter's lapels and picked him up. "No questions until this situation reaches a resolution. Now," addressing both reporters he added, "do I move you, or you remove yourselves?"

The reporters and cameraman retreated to the open doorway of the store, camera lenses trained on the interior, focused on the back of the retreating officer.

"We're here at Sports Warehouse where the grand opening celebration has been marred by the disappearance of a child. More details as they unfold. Stay with KTLA, your team in the city." He motioned to his cameraman. "All right, Randy. Cut. Let's check the crowd and see if anyone's seen anything."

The reporter and cameraman mingled, chatting up the gathering crowd. "Anyone know what's up inside?" Deering asked nonchalantly.

"Missing kid got himself stuck in a hole out back of the store, I heard. Saw the cops heading out that way as we were coming out."

"Out back, you say?"

"Yep, I was by the service desk when the redhead told that officer to check out the trash compactor."

"A trash compactor?"

"Yeah."

"No kidding." Deering got a gleam in his eyes.

"What's the press doing here?" Cassidy whispered to Brenna as they grasped hands, stepping back into the manager's office.

"You can always count on them showing up." Brenna studied Cassidy's face with concern. "How are you doing?"

"Tired. Worried. No, scratch that. Scared to death. I'm really glad I've got a friendly face in all this." Cassidy gave her hand a quick squeeze. "Thank you. The officer's questions were unnerving."

"Just remember, you didn't do anything wrong."

"I let him out of my sight in a crowded store. Whatever happens is my fault."

Brenna patted Cassidy's shoulder. Leaving her hand there a moment, she spoke softly into Cassidy's ear. "We're parents, Cass. We're not perfect. Just keep positive. We'll hear something soon."

The musical interlude from *Eine Kleine Nachtmusik* suddenly erupted between them, scaring both women into jerking apart. The refrain sounded again, and Cassidy reached for her belt and the cell phone attached there. "Hello?" she said timidly into the mouthpiece. "Cameron?" she said faintly, then looked at Brenna. "I...hold on." She covered the receiver with her hand. "Brenna?"

"Do you want me to talk to him?"

Lieutenant Taylor saw her with the phone. "Who is that?"

"A friend of hers," Brenna answered.

"We're having enough trouble with the crowds here. Don't bring anybody else onto the property."

"But..."

"No. Tell whoever whatever you want, but we've got enough problems. Already we're having trouble bringing up the ambulance."

Brenna frowned. "Where is Cameron? I could go get him."

Cassidy's "He's at my house" was almost lost under the policeman's emphatic words, "If you leave, you're not coming back inside, lady."

Brenna pursed her lips, itching to retort. She left the choice up to the person who mattered most at the center of this fiasco. She grasped the other woman's arm, holding her attention. "What do you want to do, Cassidy?"

"Don't go. I'll...he shouldn't worry. I'd like you to stay." Brenna nodded. Cassidy returned to the phone. "Cam, I got held up at the store for a bit longer than I thought. I'll be there soon, I hope." She absently shook her head at the phone; Brenna felt her hand gently squeezed as Cassidy continued to talk. "No. No, just wait there for me."

There was a long silence while Cassidy obviously listened to Cameron. Finally she murmured, "Bye," cutting the connection with a firm snap of the receiver.

There was a knock at the door, and Taylor opened it. "Murph."

The officer sent with her boys walked in, and Brenna stood up. "Sergeant?"

"Your boys are resourceful," he complimented. "We checked the compactor."

Cassidy rose quickly behind Brenna, her hand planting itself on the shorter woman's shoulder. "Compactor? Just what exactly do you think happened to my son?"

"Ma'am?"

Lieutenant Taylor made the introductions. "Sergeant Donald Murphy, this is the boy's mother, Ms. Cassidy Hyland. She and her friend and those boys looked for Ryan before we were called in."

"Well, Ms. Hyland, we were checking out the back loading area and the compactor. We went down to open it up~"

"Trash compactor? Show me."

Cassidy's grip on Brenna's shoulder started to hurt. Though understanding her friend's anxiety, she peeled the long smooth fingers from her collarbone and grasped them, meeting scared blue eyes. Brenna spoke for them both. "Can we go with you to the area?"

"Nothing there. That's good news."

Sharply, she corrected him. "The boy is still missing. Good news will be when he's found."

"I...well, yeah, of course, I just meant..."

"Come on, Cassidy."

Sergeant Murphy looked to his superior, who shrugged. "I...It can't hurt, I guess. All right." He watched the blonde straighten her shoulders, and he stepped back, half into the hallway. "You know. You're familiar somehow. I..." He caught a glint of steel in the redhead's eyes as he tried to recall. The two of them together clicked in his head. He looked back at the missing child's mother. "Shit, you're from the television."

The two women were just passing him, entering the corridor to leave the Customer Service desk. The blurted words drew significant attention from the photographers gathered outside, being held back physically by other officers. The two women dropped their eyes away from the burst of shouted questions and distant flashes.

"Are we looking at a kidnapping, sir?" Murphy asked his superior. "We didn't find any sign that the kid had been near the compactor."

Taylor shook his head. "I honestly don't know. But I didn't expect we'd be dealing with celebrities," he confided as the women moved quickly, now with a pair of officers ahead and behind, toward the back of the mostly empty store.

CHAPTER ELEVEN

BRENNA FOLLOWED a step behind, letting Cassidy work out some of her anxiety as they strode quickly through the store. Still, she cautioned, "We don't have to do this."

Cassidy turned and stopped. "I have to know. I have to see it for myself."

"They said he wasn't there."

"Maybe he was...for a moment. I just have to look."

It was the anguish plainly shown that made Brenna concede. "All right."

They entered the loading dock with the officers who pointed out the compactor shaft. Cassidy stepped close but stopped just before she could look down. "Bren."

Brenna was instantly at the other woman's side, her hand reaching out as Cassidy's reached back. "I'm here."

As their fingers slid together, Cassidy took a steadying breath. "Thank you."

"I told you he wasn't in there," Murphy said, coming up beside them.

Still holding Brenna's hand, Cassidy looked around the floor and noticed a small red object. She bent and picked it up. It was a small Lego piece, like the ones her son kept in his pockets despite her attempts to get him to leave them in the car or in the house.

"What'd you find?" Brenna asked, peering around Cassidy's shoulder.

"It's a Lego," she said quietly. "He was here." She squeezed the plastic bit hard in her hand and closed her eyes. "He was here."

Looking down the shaft, she shivered. Her eyes scanned the edge of the loading dock, and she backed up suddenly. Brenna grasped her hand, trying to stop her.

"He isn't down there, Cassidy. Have faith."

Cassidy stumbled into a pile of boxes along the back wall of the loading dock. The stack was upset when she tried to right herself. A childish yell sounded from elsewhere in the pyramid of cardboard. The officers leaped together into the debris before Cassidy or Brenna could scramble to their feet.

Boxes flew everywhere. Someone hollered, "Got him!" One of the officers rose from the floor, kicking away cardboard and holding Ryan aloft. He was mussed and crying.

She dropped to her knees weakly. "Ryan!"

They brought him over to her, and she sat with him on the floor, hugging him and crying. Brenna crouched over her shoulder, steadily rubbing it. Ryan tried to pull free, at the same time pulling at his mother's neck and hair and crying. Brenna's hand brushed over his head soothingly. She brushed at her own wet cheeks and leaned in, pressing a kiss to Cassidy's cheek in her relief.

Thomas and James raced up, and the officers let them through. In aggravation, Thomas started, "Where in the hell~" A sharp look from his mother tempered his tongue, and he finished more calmly, "Where'd you find him?"

"Playing among the boxes," Brenna said.

"We checked here, I swear we did. Called for him." Thomas crouched down next to Ryan, who was finally beginning to snuffle in his mother's arms, both of them calming. "Why didn't you answer us?"

The boy's blue eyes looked up owlishly, and he pouted. "You didn't use the secret word," Ryan said plaintively. Cassidy's tears renewed against his head on a choked-off laugh.

Brenna, brushing at her own tears, gave a watery laugh as well. She dusted her fingers through the mop of blond hair that looked so much like his mother's. "Honey, I think Mommy's going to refresh your memory how that all works." She offered to take Ryan so that Cassidy could stand. The younger woman took her hand instead of passing over her son, and Brenna found herself lifting both from the floor. The effort resulted in Cassidy steadying herself against Brenna for several seconds.

The police escorted Brenna, Cassidy, and their sons back to the office. Cassidy apologized profusely for making such a stir, still holding Ryan like she would never let him go.

Brenna finally coaxed Cassidy into giving Ryan to her boys for the moment. "We ought to get the report done quickly so you two can get home." Passing Ryan to her sons along with her car keys, she warned them, "Go directly to the car. Don't talk to anyone."

"We'll escort them, ma'am." Maxwell and Murphy, who was throwing an arm around Thomas' shoulders, pulled them together as they guided the boys out of the store.

Twenty minutes later, with most everyone dispersed except a few diehard reporters, Cassidy and Brenna emerged. Cassidy shook Lieutenant Taylor's hand. "Thank you," she said with a weak smile.

"You're welcome, ma'am. Just glad there was a happy ending."

Cassidy was too relieved to speak. She followed Brenna to the parking lot.

"KTLA TV." A reporter approached them. "Don Deering here. So, Ms. Hyland, isn't it?" She nodded absently. "Your boy's all right?"

"Yes," she said, accepting Ryan back from James. Deering reached out and rubbed the fur of the stuffed raccoon Ryan clutched to his chest.

"Don't you think safety measures in the store should have been more stringent? Certainly there was a real danger he could have fallen into that trash compactor?"

Cassidy blanched as the vivid fears resurfaced. Brenna stepped forward, taking Deering's hand off Ryan. "He wasn't hurt, and everyone's fine. I suggest you go back to your station and leave the two of them alone. Now."

Deering shrugged but persisted even as Cassidy was opening her back door and securing Ryan in his car seat. "She ought to decide that, don't you think?"

Brenna, who had a hand on Cassidy's back, felt it stiffen. She patted the muscles and stepped away from the car, drawing Deering's eyes to her. "Mr. Deering, I'm going to say this once: We don't need your attention or the attention of your camera. Now get out of here before I have the police remove you."

Deering looked her up and down, and she was never more thankful for her alter ego: A quick placement of her hands on her hips and a glare made him reconsider pushing the issue. With a dispirited wave of his hand in front of the camera lens, the reporter turned his back and walked over to the closest police officer, his cameraman following.

Brenna caught a grimace from Taylor, but the officer quickly straightened up and delivered a summary which was probably considerably dryer than the reporter would have liked. Taking a deep breath, Brenna finally released her own tension. She turned around to see Cassidy slipping into her driver's seat. There was a tug on her shirt.

James whispered, "Mom, she's in no shape to drive."

Brenna looked more closely and saw that Cassidy's hands were shaking. Bending to the window, she knocked on the glass. Cassidy jumped. James was right. She motioned for Cassidy to roll down the window. "Hey, listen. Why don't I drive? Thomas can follow us."

Hands squeezing the wheel, Cassidy nodded reluctantly and got out, moving around to the passenger seat. Brenna waved to Thomas, who jogged over. "I'm going to drive them."

"Where to?"

Brenna slid into the driver's seat and gently touched Cassidy's arm. "Do you want to go home?"

"Please."

"All right. Thomas, follow me." She reached out the window and patted his cheek. "Be careful. I love you."

"See you in a few minutes," he said confidently, turning away.

With Cassidy collecting herself en route, Brenna soon pulled into the Hyland driveway. Thomas pulled in behind. Cameron was just getting out of his car at the curb. "What the hell happened to you? I heard a report over the radio that Ryan was missing."

"He was," Brenna confirmed. "But we found him." She pointed to the back seat. Cassidy had gone around to the other side and let Ryan out of his car seat, taking him inside.

Watching Cassidy disappear inside her home with Ryan, Cameron asked, "How'd you get caught up in all this?"

Brenna shrugged. "I was there."

"You and Cassidy were shopping together?"

"We happened to be at the same store."

"You live on the other side of town."

Cassidy emerged from the house. "Cam, leave her alone. She was there, and I'm glad for it." She turned to her friend. "Thanks, Bren. I've sent him to his room. I'll talk to him later, when we're both a little less traumatized," she explained when they both looked at her. "Cam, I know you wanted to go out tonight, but I'm not good company right now. Call tomorrow?"

"I'll make you some dinner."

"I can't. I have to talk to Ryan."

"All right," he conceded. He looked toward Brenna and frowned. Turning back to Cassidy, he leaned in and took her elbows in his hands, pressing a kiss on her cheek.

The teenaged boys walked up. "Well, Mom, ready to go?"

Intent on Cassidy as the blonde stepped away from Cameron, Brenna offered, "Don't be too upset with Ryan, Cass."

Cameron got into his car. Brenna saw him watch them for a long moment before driving away. She turned back to Cassidy, who was looking at the ground, rubbing her hands over her face.

Brenna took a deep breath, reached out, and clasped the other woman's hands between her own. Their eyes met, and Brenna felt her stomach twist. Seeing Cassidy so exhausted, she wanted to offer to do something more ~ like watch Ryan while the young woman slept. She stifled the offer before it could reach her lips; Cassidy had requested to be alone. "Call me if you need to talk."

Impulsively, Cassidy embraced her, and Brenna felt the warmth as their cheeks touched. They separated slowly before relinquishing their mutual grip.

Cassidy turned and entered her home, while Brenna followed her boys back to their car. Still pensive, she leaned against the passenger window and quietly thought over the afternoon's events, while Thomas drove home.

CHAPTER TWELVE

ARMS CROSSED over her chest and leaning against the open glass door, Cassidy watched Ryan run in the backyard with Ranger. The dog was chasing the unexpected "prize" of her son's afternoon escapade ~ a taxidermy raccoon from the sports store's display. Though he had scared her and several L.A. police officers, Ryan appeared unaffected after being missing for more than an hour.

She watched him stop and turn, catching sight of her in the doorway. He waved and smiled, falling down as the dog leaped at the toy. He laughed as the dog licked his face and then the stuffed animal. She wasn't sure about the sanitary implications, but clearly there was no way she would be able to get the "toy" away from the pair any time soon. Cassidy shook her head.

Thinking about the afternoon quickly took Cassidy's mind down paths she felt better forgotten. Looking into that compactor had scared her nearly witless, despite Brenna's hand in her own to steady her. She closed her eyes and offered up silent thanks that they had found Ryan among a collection of boxes rather than at the bottom of that shaft.

I should have kept a hold on his hand, she berated herself. If she had, he wouldn't have gotten away from her to go look at the animals and consequently gotten lost. Brenna had pointed out that holding on wasn't always possible. She sagged. As the sunset lent an orange haze to the day's end, Cassidy wished for some of that confidence now.

Abruptly she sat up. "I could just call her." She realized that just speaking with Brenna would probably cheer her up. "Ryan!" she called. "Time to come in for dinner."

He ran toward her, and she had to sidestep him and the dog as they barreled through the doorway as a pair. She stepped into the kitchen, sending him to the bathroom to wash up while she put on a couple of hot dogs to boil and retrieved the bag of chips she kept rolled up on the top of the refrigerator. Warming the buns in the microwave, she had a hot dog, complete with ketchup, ready as Ryan slid into his chair at their small kitchen table.

He dug in immediately. She reached for the phone, going so far as to pick up the receiver before scanning her phone list and realizing that she did not have Brenna's home number. Undeterred, Cassidy dialed Information, her hip resting against the counter as she waited for the recording. "Los Angeles," she responded to the prompt. "Lanigan, Brenna." The computer reported the entry as unlisted and disconnected her. Looking at the phone, she muttered, "What now?"

She considered who might know the number and realized that there were very few options: the studio, which was closed, or someone on the coordinating production staff. She blinked. *Of course. Cameron.* She wondered why she had not thought of him first but chalked it up to stress. *Except you saw him just a few hours ago,* memory prompted. Quickly she punched up his number.

"Hello?"

He sounded tired. "Cameron. Hi." She settled to the table, brushing her fingers over the surface. "I have a request."

"You need a day off? No problem. I'll arrange it."

"No, I...I'm okay. I just need a phone number."

"Okay. Sure. Who?"

"Brenna's."

"Lanigan? Why?"

"I need to talk to her."

"Something wrong?"

"I'm sorry, but I really just...Brenna'll understand." There was a long pause before she heard the flutter of papers being turned.

"I...I'm sorry I couldn't help you today. All right. Here's the number..."

She copied it to her list and initialed the entry: BL. "Thanks, Cam. I really appreciate it."

"Ryan is all right, though?"

"Yeah. I'm just..." Cassidy couldn't explain it. Instinct told her Brenna was the only one she could talk to about this. "Sort of a 'you had to be there' thing."

"All right. Well, I...I'll see you at work on Monday?"

"Catch me at the lunch break?"

"Will do." In the silence, Cassidy could hear his breathing over the line. "Well, um, have a good night."

"Thanks." She pressed the disconnect button and immediately dialed the number. Disappointment filled her. The line was busy.

Script loose in her palm, Brenna curled up on her couch, throw pillow against her stomach as she tucked up her bare feet. She could still hear James cleaning the pots from their dinner and filling the dishwasher. Thomas had excused himself to his bedroom to call his girlfriend. She looked at the clock. Twenty minutes already. She sighed, wondering what they could possibly be talking about after spending a whole week together at school.

She acknowledged that she wanted to use the phone and that probably also explained her own distraction. For the last hour she had repeatedly reached for the phone to call Cassidy, only to pull back. Certainly the woman had had a trying enough day; she wouldn't want to bring it up again. But Brenna couldn't get it out of her mind. She kept thinking about just how bad things could have been and wondered at the fate that had put her at the store just in time to help.

Thomas came in and sat down, flipping on the television. As he settled back, he looked over at his mother at the other end of the couch. "Mom?"

"Hmm?"

"Do you mind?"

She shook her head, then straightened a bit. "I just can't seem to get today out of my mind."

"It was totally weird, but everything turned out cool."

"Yes, I know." She leaned over and rubbed his shoulder. "I'm really proud of how quickly you jumped in to help."

"She's a friend of yours." He shrugged as if that explained all.

"She's different from other women I've had as friends," she answered, wondering exactly what she meant by that ~ and exactly when she had decided Cassidy was someone she could call "friend." She did not have many of them. She shook herself. "I'm just really glad nothing serious happened to Ryan."

"Now that's a cute kid," Thomas agreed.

"He is." Brenna laughed. "I wonder if Cassidy was able to clear things up with him about the 'secret word'."

James came in, drying his hands on a towel. "That was the weirdest thing I think I'd ever heard."

"He is only five," Brenna reminded her son, reaching up and extending her hand for him to grasp. "I remember you at that age. Remember when you climbed up on the porch railing, convinced if you just spread your arms, you could fly?" She covered her face. "Luckily you only sprained an ankle instead of something more serious." James rolled his eyes, and she chuckled. "See. Kids and risks ~ natural companions."

"Thanks, Mom," he groaned and left.

Thomas stood. "Are you deserting me, too?" she teased.

"I've got *Hamlet* to read for school."

She nodded. "All right."

"See you in the morning." He kissed her cheek.

"Good night."

After Thomas left, Brenna found her thoughts drifting back to Cassidy and their last moment together on the woman's front lawn. "I'm going to call her," she resolved, reaching for the portable phone on the table. Looking at the keypad, she paused. *What's her number?* Brenna couldn't recall, though she thought the invitation from Ryan's birthday party had it for the RSVP. Of course, after the party, Brenna had tossed the card. She sighed. *Who else would know the number?*

"Cameron!" Hopping up, she checked her desk and pulled the writer's number from her Rolodex. Quickly she punched in the sequence and put the phone to her ear, walking back to the living room couch. Halfway there, she pulled it away and disconnected. *Busy.*

He's probably talking with Cassidy, she reasoned, trying hard to ignore the disappointment coiling in her stomach as she sat down with the script and tried to concentrate.

Stepping out of the bathroom where she had just turned off her son's bathwater, Cassidy looked at the script on her bedside table. *I should work,* she thought, picking up the pages. Reclining on the bed and trying to focus, she rehearsed the dialogue different ways in her head.

Giving up because she was too distracted, she reached for the remote and turned on her TV, keeping the volume low. The background noise frequently helped her concentrate.

"New at 10 o'clock, it was a busy day for a grand opening. It all went awry for a local celebrity and her son when crowds spelled a danger every parent fears."

Cassidy set aside her script and turned up the sound. She caught a piece of news clip ~ her carrying Ryan, flanked by Lieutenant Taylor and Brenna. "God, I thought this was over," she groaned, reaching for the phone to call the station and request the story editor.

It rang before she could start dialing. After a moment to collect herself, Cassidy picked up the receiver. "Hello?"

"Hey, Cassidy."

"Rich?" Surprised by Rich Paulson's voice, Cassidy blinked, then put the receiver back to her ear. "What's up?"

"That's my question. Just heard a news brief. You had a little excitement this afternoon? Everything all right?"

Cassidy brushed her fingers through her bangs and pulled them back from her face. "Yeah. We're both fine. It was nothing really."

"Not what the news said. Ryan almost fell into a trash compactor?"

"There was an open one near him, but no...he didn't."

"Well, that's good news. I wanted to check on you, I guess."

"Might've been different if Brenna hadn't been there," she said.

"Brenna? Our Brenna?"

"Yeah, we were both shopping for camping equipment when we ran into each other."

"How's she doing?"

"Fine. She was great. Her boys, too."

"I'm glad you had some help." There was a long pause. "Well, I just wanted to call. Guess I'll let you go."

"Thanks. Really."

"Good night."

"Good night." With a half smile, she set down the phone, wondering who else would call. Slipping from the bed, Cassidy returned to the bathroom.

"All right, Mr. Prune. Bedtime." She pulled Ryan from the tub and wrapped a thick towel around him. Perched on the toilet, she rubbed him down and patted his face dry. He rubbed his eyes tiredly. "So, did you have enough fun for one day?"

"Mmm hmm."

"All right. Can we have a better day tomorrow?"

"Mmm hmm."

She picked him up and brushed her nose against his cheek. "I love you."

His arms wrapped around her neck. "I love you, too, Mommy."

She carried him into his bedroom and helped him into his pajamas. Tucking him under his covers, she knelt by his bed. "Please don't run off again, okay?"

He put his arms over the top of the covers and nodded emphatically. "Okay."

She stifled a chuckle and ruffled his hair. "Sweet dreams."

Retreating to the door, she turned off his light. He turned on his side, and she paused for a lingering look. *Thank God for you, Brenna.* Any longer and Ryan might have come looking for her. He might have actually fallen into that compactor. Her need to talk to the other woman suddenly acute, Cass returned to the bedroom and dialed the number Cameron had given her. "Hello? Brenna?"

Across town, phone to her ear, Brenna unfolded suddenly on the couch with a huge exhalation of relief. "Cass, are...is everything all right?"

Cassidy took a deep breath, feeling real relief flood her for the first time in hours. "Yeah, I just...It's okay that I called?"

"Absolutely." The redhead curled back in the cushions and pulled the pillow into her lap as she spoke. "How's Ryan? Any lingering effects from his adventure today?"

"Not a thing. I think he's still unaware just how much trouble he caused."

"Did you try to explain it to him?"

"Yes."

"Well, you'll just have to watch him more closely for a while. You've got an adventurer, like James was. Still is, really," Brenna mused.

"Really?" Cassidy curled up on her bed and relaxed into the pillows. "Tell me about it?"

"When he was about Ryan's age, he tried to fly off a porch railing," Brenna reminisced. "He was always the one halfway down the street when I called them in for dinner." She chuckled. "Thank God, he doesn't drive yet. I'll never see him once he does." She choked up a bit. "But," she suddenly sounded more assuring than reminiscent, "that's what we raise them up to do ~ be able to walk away from us, hmm?"

"And be safe," Cassidy agreed. "Yeah. So why is it so damn scary when it happens?"

Hearing the other woman's exasperation and completely understanding its source, Brenna hugged her pillow tighter, let out a half-chuckle, and sighed, feeling better than she had in hours. "I don't know," she admitted ruefully.

Cassidy felt warmed beyond belief. "You were so positive for me today. I...don't know if I'll ever be able to thank you."

"You needed someone," Brenna offered quietly.

The line was silent between them for several breaths. Cassidy closed her eyes and inhaled as the unexpected connection soothed her. "You were perfect for the job." She heard Brenna's soft intake of breath.

For her part, Brenna didn't want the call to end. She looked around the couch and table, spying her dog-eared script. "Well, so...um, you want to practice a few pages?"

"Over the phone?" Cassidy turned the receiver and put her hand over her mouth to quash the laugh bubbling up. The idea of reading script pages at one another over the phone in the middle of the night was absurd. However, she didn't want to hang up, either. "All right." She reached for her script and heard through the line as Brenna did the same. "Where do you want to start?"

Brenna started reading; Cassidy recognized the section and flipped there, picking up her response.

A long, strange day came to an end on a high note.

CHAPTER THIRTEEN

SCRIPT UNDER his arm, Sean Durham trotted onto the set and settled at one of the round tables where several other cast members already sat. The new script called for a bar setting, and the props people had recreated a speakeasy from the 1920s. "They're about to break," he said. "Who's going with me to get the trays?"

"You want to eat here?" Terry Brown raised an eyebrow.

Cassidy elbowed him. "I'm partial to this place. Cozy." She looked to her right and smiled at Brenna, just sitting down. "Don't you think so?"

"Yep." Brenna grinned back, looking around at the atypically costumed group. Many of them wore Prohibition-era, semi-formal attire. "Wonder if we could convince the writers to let us stay here. I like the change of clothes."

She laughed, running her fingers over the jacket line of her blue skirt suit. She cast a sidelong glance at Cassidy, who wore a torch singer's elbow-length gloves and long, slinky white dress, complete with sequins. With the woman's blond hair pulled up off her cheeks but falling down her back, the effect was stunning, like looking at an alabaster or marble statue, despite the rouge defining her cheekbones. "Hmm?" She caught Cassidy's eye and cocked her head.

The blonde nodded. "I'd go for it."

Rachelle Cheron paused as she was settling onto a chair. "Oh, um, Cass, didn't see you this morning, but I wanted to say how glad I am that everything is okay with Ryan."

Cassidy nodded sheepishly, tracing idly on the table with her sequin-gloved hand before intertwining her fingers and looking toward Brenna. "Thanks to Brenna, I didn't go nuts."

"Brenna?" About half the table, unaware Brenna had anything to do with the situation, looked straight at the compact woman.

"I was just in the right place at the right time." She looked at Cassidy, then ducked her head. Taking the attention off both of them, she pointed to Sean. "I think that's enough. Engage your afterburners and get us our lunches. Best speed," Brenna said with a tossed thumb over her shoulder. "I'm hungry." She winked at him.

"Aye, aye, Ma'am!" He stood and saluted before leaving.

In their *Time Squad* uniforms, Rich Paulson and Will Chapman finally stepped up to the bar set, leaning on the table sections between the others. "So, how's it going?" Will asked.

"Not bad," Brenna said. "How's shooting?"

Rich grinned. "Four more scenes."

Thinking quickly, Brenna calculated. "What, then? Another five hours or so? You might make it home for dinner."

"If we can get through everything in a minimum of takes," he said with a nod.

Curious, Cassidy asked, "What's tonight?"

"My anniversary." Rich smiled.

"Congratulations," Cassidy said. "How many years? Are you doing dinner?"

"Twenty-nine years. And yes, we're going to dinner. Then dancing. And a play at L.A. Playhouse. I don't have to be here tomorrow. I checked." He grinned.

"Nice to see someone having some fun," Will added.

Just as Sean reappeared, his arms weighted with trays and a collection of juice and soda cans, a stagehand appeared. "Ms. Hyland?"

Cassidy, who had just taken her choices from the pile, turned around. "Yes?"

"Phone call for you. You can take it over there."

"Who is it?"

"Wouldn't say. Said it was important, though."

"All right." She stood, catching Brenna looking at her while nibbling on the corner of her tuna fish sandwich. "I'll be right back."

Will dropped into the chair Cassidy had vacated and dug into his meal. Looking briefly at Brenna, between bites he said, "So, part of the weekend had some excitement for you?"

"Yes." She sipped her Diet Coke. "How about you? What'd you do this weekend?"

Around them, other conversations started up.

Will shrugged. "I flew out to Phoenix and visited my sister."

"Family event?"

"Nah, just a visit. Haven't seen her much. She's expecting her first baby in a couple of months. We haven't had a chance to talk."

Brenna nodded. "Sounds nice. How's the weather out that way?"

"Nice." They fell silent. He studied her for a moment longer before turning back to his meal.

Brenna glanced up at Cassidy, just at the edge of the set wall, as she talked on the phone. Looking agitated by the conversation, the blonde paced. Brenna continued to eat but kept an eye on her, her own stomach twisting in concern. She considered that it must be a reaction from the weekend. She had become deeply involved in a very private pain with the younger woman. The connection lingered a little bit, she supposed. When she looked at Cassidy again, her heart constricted.

Cassidy's face was ashen. She had covered her mouth to prevent whatever she was feeling from coming out. Brenna snapped to her feet as Cassidy hung up. Intercepting her at the far edge of the stage, she put a hand on her arm. "What's up? You're white as a sheet."

"It's the makeup," Cassidy joked, with obvious forced effort.

Unexpectedly hurt by the dismissal, Brenna realized that was also why Cassidy had tried the joke. The blonde had been hurt by the phone caller. "What is it?" she coaxed. With a glance over her shoulder toward the others, she nudged Cassidy behind the stage wall.

Taking a deep breath, Cassidy searched Brenna's face before finally deciding to share. "Mitch heard," she said briefly. "He wants to see Ryan."

Brenna shook her head and leaned against the wall carefully. "Mitch? That's your ex, isn't it? He has visitation, right?"

"Yes."

"Nothing happened. Ryan is fine. I'm sure he just wants to see that."

"He's never agreed with my having custody," Cassidy explained. "All he needs is a good reason to challenge."

"This isn't a good reason," Brenna assured her.

"What isn't a good reason?"

Brenna and Cassidy, who had huddled close to talk, looked outward, startled. Cameron and producer Victor Branch had wandered over from their offices. "Hello," Branch said when their gazes fell on him.

"Hi," Brenna returned.

"What's up?" Cameron queried again.

Cassidy's answer was unexpectedly short. "Nothing." She moved quickly away from the group.

Brenna could not stifle her surprise.

Cameron posed his question again directly to Brenna. "What's happened?"

"Cameron, I shouldn't get in the middle of things."

"You seem to be doing that lately anyway. Why stop now?"

Brenna was stung by the cutting remark. She pushed aside the wave of indignation with a deep breath and turned away. "Nice to see you, Victor," she offered in parting.

"Um, yeah. Bye." Victor looked from Cameron to Brenna, then back to his writer. "What the hell was that all about?"

Cameron watched Brenna settle next to Cassidy. The women resumed eating in silence while the rest of the cast animatedly conversed around them. "I wish to hell I knew."

"Cameron."

The two men looked up to see Will Chapman coming toward them. "Hello, Will." Cameron became even more uneasy; conversations with the actor seldom went well lately. "What's up?" he said carefully.

"I wanted to talk about a scene coming up. Instead of sending Pryor out again, I can recover the team this time. I've got an idea to restage it," Will suggested. "It'll give more punch to the action, an undercurrent I think the fans will appreciate."

"No," Cameron said sharply. "The story stays as is."

"So you'd rather write flat shit than build a story with some character, Cam?"

"You're the flat one, Chapman. Dull as a board. Your dailies put half the exec team to sleep."

"Then give me something to do!"

"You get what you can handle."

"Cam," Branch interrupted. "We'll discuss it later." He saw the director come around the edge of the set. "We'd better go."

"All right, everyone," Gerry Hifer, the new episode's director, addressed the group at the table. "Break's over." Cameron and Victor left, the latter dragging the former away with a bit of effort, and the cast cleared away their lunch mess, quickly sweeping everything into the trash cans.

Brenna stepped out of her uniform with relief and pulled on her thick robe. Hanging the costume carefully, she sat at the small mirror and brushed her hair, loosening the spray's hold on it. There was a knock at her trailer door. "Come in."

"Ms. Lanigan?"

"Kyle?" She turned around to face the guest actor, Kyle Masters, cast to play her office boss. It was strange for her to be playing a secretary in the current episode's pre-women's lib era. Playing the demure was tough; Susan's in-charge attitude was part of her nature. It did not vanish overnight. "What's up?"

"We didn't get a chance to talk today. I was wondering if you'd like to go to dinner. Read a few lines," he offered hesitantly. "Work on our rapport?"

"I can't do dinner," she said, "but I'll read with you for a little while."

"Thanks. You all are a pretty tight-knit bunch," he said. "Saw you during the lunch break."

She nodded sagely. "It's hard to come into that, I know. I've had to do it myself a few times."

"And...Cassidy, is it? She's a bit of a chilly personality."

"Not really. You just caught her on an off day. By the end of the week, you'll see." Cassidy's performance had been rougher than usual during their run-throughs after lunch. *Mitch's call really rattled her.* Brenna resolved to find out more, to see if she could help at all. She shook the other woman's troubles out of her head and returned her attention to Kyle. "Well, ready to read?"

Cassidy stepped into her trailer just as the phone rang. Picking it up, she answered, "Hello?"

"Hello."

Recognizing her ex-husband's voice, Cassidy sat down hard. "Um...hello, Mitch." Distracting herself, she slipped off the high heels. Reaching for the Bullwinkle slippers, she held them in her lap for a long moment, the soft fluff comforting. "I'm sorry about earlier. I...You just caught me in the middle of working. Came out of left field."

"I still want to see Ryan."

"Nothing happened."

"This time. What about next time?"

"There won't be a next time," she insisted.

"You can't know that. Who's with him right now?"

"Gwen. You know her."

"Yeah, and I know she's got three of her own to look after."

"Mitch, don't. Please."

There was a knock at her trailer door. "Come in."

Cameron stepped up and stood in the doorway. "Hi, Cass."

She held up a hand, motioning him to silence. "I'll have to talk to you later," she said into the phone. "A writer just walked in." She hung up, took a deep breath, and turned to Cameron. "Hi."

"Just wanted to come by and see how you were doing. Who was the phone call?"

"Mitch heard about this weekend. He wants to visit Ryan."

"So he wants to visit with his kid. About time he shared some of the responsibility. As long as he stays away from you." He moved toward her.

That Cameron could suggest letting Mitch have Ryan for any time filled Cassidy with so much anger and fear it made her curt. She stepped out of his reach. "I'm still in costume. Excuse me." She slipped into the second room of her trailer, emerging a few minutes later, straightening a pullover sweater over her worn jeans.

He smiled and held out a hand. "Dinner?"

"I'm going home." The flat statement was not an invitation to join her.

Cameron overlooked her coolness. "I'll meet you there."

"Mmm hmm." She walked out of her trailer before he could say anything more.

The parking lot was almost empty when Cassidy reached her car. She was still trying to calm herself as well as to understand why she had gotten so upset with Cameron. Noise a few spaces away drew her gaze up from the pavement. Brenn was getting in her car. She called out, "Good night!"

The other woman turned from pulling her car door closed. "Cass? I didn't think you were still here."

"And you..." Cassidy noted how tired the other woman looked and regretted bothering her. "What kept you late?"

Stepping out of her SUV as Cassidy came closer, Brenna pointed toward another section of the lot. "He did." Cassidy glanced over and saw a silver car driving away. "Kyle wanted to practice our scenes again."

"So, is Jakes getting along with her boss?" Cassidy asked with a twinkle in her eye. "Should Chris offer you a love song the next time you come into the club?"

"No. Please don't." For a moment, Brenna wondered about Cassidy's singing voice. She had not had a chance to see the woman rehearsing the numbers she was doing in the episode. Brenna shook it off. "Did you resolve things with Mitch?"

"Not yet. I'll call him tonight after Cameron leaves."

"Entertaining tonight?" Brenna's voice was uneasy.

"I need to find a balance between spending time with Ryan and with Cameron."

"I know the feeling."

Cassidy nodded. "I guess you do."

"Well," Brenna said quietly, reaching out a hand, "good night."

When their palms touched, both stepped forward. Cassidy suddenly threw her arms around Brenna. "Thanks for everything," she whispered in Brenna's hair, inhaling the distinct scent of muscle ointment. She closed her eyes and squeezed lightly. Happiness tingled along the nerves in her back as Brenna's hands moved lightly up her spine before the two pulled apart. When she met Brenna's eyes again, they were lightly crinkled by an uncertain, but pleased smile. She felt a similar one shape her own lips. The change in their relationship felt incredibly good.

"You...you're welcome," Brenna said, and Cassidy was surprised to hear a mild huskiness in the voice.

Cassidy could say nothing, being caught up in the depth and breadth of swirling cobalt. Following a deep breath, Brenna slipped from Cassidy's arms. She clasped Brenna's hand for a moment longer, suddenly reluctant to let the other woman leave.

Brenna's voice was soft in protest. "I...should go." Cassidy released her hand. Brenna looked up and nodded. "Take care of yourself."

"I will." Cassidy stood in silence, watching Brenna slip behind the wheel and drive off the lot.

CHAPTER FOURTEEN

"COME ON, Cass. Sit down. Relax." Cameron patted the couch where he'd sat after turning on her stereo with an easy-listening CD.

Cassidy finished up the last dish and dried her hands. "Something to drink?" she asked.

"Sure."

She fished in the refrigerator and discovered the remnants of a bottle of white wine. She was moving it to the counter when Cameron entered the kitchen. Stepping aside when he reached into an upper cabinet for a pair of glasses, she felt his hand slip over her upper back. "Sorry," she said, moving away.

"No, I was just getting the glasses." Cameron turned to her. "What's wrong? You've been jumpy all night."

Cassidy shook her head and shrugged. She was both keyed up and exhausted, her mind filled with thoughts she could not seem to put in order. "Tired, I guess."

He poured and handed her a glass, then guided her to the couch, kissing the back of her neck before she sat down. "Well, day's over now." After setting his wine on the low table, he turned her around and put his hands on her shoulders. "Massage?"

"No, it's okay." She sipped the wine and tried to focus on the evening. Unfortunately, the only thing she kept thinking about was her conversation with Brenna in the parking lot after work. And the hug. She wondered what the other woman had thought of her at that moment ~ and just when she had realized Brenna needed that hug as much as she had.

She leaned into Cameron's body reluctantly and wondered why. With a rueful sigh, she sat up straight. "Thanks," she said politely as his hands slipped from her shoulders.

"Is it the call from Mitch?" he asked. "Why didn't you tell me when he first called?"

"What?" Cassidy, who had not been focusing, looked at him in confusion.

"At the studio, during lunch. That call you got ~ it was from Mitch, wasn't it?"

Her forehead briefly furrowed. "Oh. Mmm hmm."

"You said it was nothing."

"I couldn't deal with it then," she said. "We were heading back into shooting."

"You told Lanigan about it."

"She asked."

"So did I."

"Mommy?"

Cameron and Cassidy turned to see Ryan in his footed pajamas, peering at them from the bedroom hall, his stuffed monster doll hugged to his chest.

"What is it?" Cassidy held out her hand to her son.

"Can't sleep. Can you tell me a story?"

Cassidy looked over her shoulder at Cameron, then back at her son. "Not tonight, buddy," she said quietly. "I'll give you a hug, though."

"Okay." Ryan climbed onto her lap and turned into her chest. She closed her eyes and reveled in the sensation as she wrapped him securely in her arms and kissed his hair.

Cameron's hand moved between her arms, and he patted her son's back. "There you go, guy," he said. "One bona fide Mom hug."

Cassidy loosened her grasp but was pleased when her son did not immediately get down from her lap. She absently stroked the monster toy, thinking of the woman who had given it to him, while her other hand lightly drew circles on Ryan's lower back. Looking up, she saw Cameron looking pensive.

"Back to bed," she said, keeping her mouth from showing the regret she felt as her son left her lap. She stood and walked him back to his bedroom. Pulling the covers to his chin, she kissed him again. "Good night."

When she returned to the living room, Cameron was sitting back against the couch sipping his wine. "So, are you ever going to tell me what happened Saturday?"

"I told you," she said, resuming her seat. "Ryan got away from me, and it took a while to find him."

"Somebody take him?"

"No. Cam, I got the third degree from Mitch; I don't need you to cross examine me, too."

Cameron eased back and lifted his hands in the universal symbol of surrender. But he couldn't resist one last question. "How'd Lanigan get involved?"

Ruminating, Cassidy leaned back. She remembered the wariness on Brenna's face when they ran into one another in the store aisle and how it was just as quickly set aside when Cassidy revealed her problem. Brenna had taken thorough command of the situation, dispatching her sons. Cassidy smiled. "After the Halloween party at the studio, she invited me to go camping with her charity group. Saturday, I realized there were still a few things I'd need. It seems we both had the same idea to check out the new warehouse store. She was there to pick up a few things for the trip herself."

"She invited you on a camping trip?"

"Yes. Next weekend."

"That was nice of her."

Cassidy thought Cameron's tone didn't sound like he thought it had been. Her response was defensive as a result. "Yes, it was. We haven't talked much~"

"She's done her best to *ignore* you. You've~"

"But that's been changing. We've become friends."

He scoffed. "Since Saturday?"

"You don't think it could be that simple?"

"Nothing with that woman is *that* simple. What's she getting out of it?"

"She said she thought Ryan and I would have some fun."

"Press gonna be there?"

"No, a bunch of underprivileged kids. Damn, Cameron, can't you just be happy for me?"

Cameron shifted on the couch and even pulled his arms down from around the back of the cushion as he rubbed the knees of his trousers. "She's never made a gesture like this before. Doesn't that just seem...weird to you?"

"I'm flattered she wants to spend time with me *and* Ryan," she responded pointedly.

Cameron straightened and shot back, "Don't start. I like Ryan just fine, but I'm dating you, not him."

"Cameron, we're a package deal."

"Why are you picking a fight with me?"

"I'm not picking a fight."

"Speaking of picking a fight...You should thank me. Today, Chapman wanted to rewrite a scene. Branch got him to cut our 'discussion' short at lunch, but I still found a sheaf of script pages on my desk. After one look, I ripped them up."

"Why? Maybe Will had an interesting idea. You let Rich pitch you ideas all the time."

"Paulson doesn't want to write scenes where he's kissing you," Cameron replied.

"Chapman wants to kiss— But Raycreek and Hanssen have nothing in common."

"He doesn't care about that. He knows you're the ratings grabber, and he wants in on the action."

Cassidy sighed. "I really thought I was beginning to be part of the team. Brenna—"

"Brenna's been all over you lately."

"I worked hard to get her to acknowledge me," Cassidy objected. "That's why I appreciated the invitation to go camping."

"We could've gone to Napa or something."

"But Ryan couldn't come along on a winery tour."

Cameron stood abruptly. "Fine. Forget it. Go camping."

Cassidy said nothing. Leaning on the arm of the couch, she rested her head on her crossed wrists, watching as he collected his coat. "Will I see you tomorrow?" she asked to his back as the door opened.

"Maybe." Cameron's terse response followed him out.

Worn emotionally, Cassidy rose from the couch and went to her bedroom, stopping at Ryan's door with a quick glance inside to see that he was safely asleep.

She decided to unwind in the bathtub. Opening the taps to the clawfoot tub in the master bathroom, she returned to her bedside table and picked up the script. She shook her head and put it down. *You want to unwind.* Pinning up her hair, she stepped out of her clothes, slid into the warm water, and stretched out in lavender bubbles.

Breathing deeply, she ignored the phone when it suddenly rang in the bedroom. Whoever it was, however, disconnected as soon as her answering machine picked up. A beat later, she remembered she had wanted to call Mitch. Shaking her head, she closed her eyes resolutely. *Tomorrow. From work. Maybe Brenna would be willing to sit with me while I try to reason with him.*

The thought of Brenna brought Cassidy back to their hug. Her body flushed at the memory. In that instant, when Brenna had presented her hand, Cassidy had seen the same "this is absurd" expression on Brenna's face that she figured she'd had on her own. When she initiated a hug instead, Brenna had leaned into the embrace. Remembering the contact, Cassidy crossed her arms over her chest and submerged in the water. The warmth soothed her prickling skin. *What an incredible feeling of belonging.*

Cameron's words bubbled to the surface along with her released breath. *"Brenna's been all over you lately."*

What did he mean by that? Was it just a professional thing, some form of manipulation, or something more personal? When she surfaced, she scolded herself for being fanciful. "Ridiculous. You are overanalyzing again, Ms. Cancer Ascendant. It was just a hug." She grabbed her sponge and scrubbed her skin until it held a rosy glow.

When the water had cooled, she pulled the plug, stepped out of the tub, and dried. After pulling on a night shirt, she pulled up her bed covers and curled around a pillow. Sleep claimed her quickly.

Inside her front door, Brenna was surprised from behind with a hug from Thomas as she turned around to put up her coat and keys. She jumped, then returned the embrace. "Good to see you, too," she said with a chuckle. "What's up? Besides you, that is?"

"I thought you were stuck at another all-nighter."

"No. I ended up in a conversation in the parking lot, then took surface roads instead of the highway." Putting her purse down, Brenna thought back to the hug. *And I needed time alone to think.*

Thomas nodded. "Sure. Are you hungry?"

"No. I'm just going to bed. You should, too," she told him with a kiss. "Why are you always up waiting for me?"

Thomas shrugged. "I'm usually still doing homework." She looked askance at him. "Well, okay. It'll sound kind of stupid, but sometimes I think you could use someone to talk to. I like being that someone," he added sheepishly.

Moved by her son's admission, Brenna patted his arm. "You're going to make some young lady very lucky, Thomas. Thank you."

"Mom," he groaned as she leaned against him and hugged him.

"Where's James?"

"Right here."

She hugged her younger son, who appeared at her shoulder from the bedroom hallway. "I missed you guys," she said. "Are you looking forward to our weekend away?" They both nodded.

"Good night, Mom."

"Good night." Brenna entered her room and flipped on the late news to watch as she changed. The reminder to vote in the elections the next day brought Kevin to mind. She had already sent in her absentee ballot, but she ought to encourage him on his important night. She reached for the phone, then remembered it was going to be two a.m. in Mount Clemens. She arranged her pillows and curled up, hoping the bed would warm quickly as she snuggled deeper into the mattress.

"Thanks for everything," Cassidy whispered in Brenna's hair.

Brenna's eyes opened as the soft voice played in her head. She had been looking at her own hand, wondering why a handshake was not what she wanted to offer, and then suddenly they were hugging. Awash with pleasure, Brenna realized she had not wanted to say goodbye in the first place.

She took a quick breath of relief and met Cassidy's gaze. Surprise and curiosity were mirrored there. Stepping closer to the other woman, Brenna felt Cassidy's arm brush against her hand as she lifted it to waist height. She remembered how warm the skin of Cassidy's cheek felt as it lightly touched her own. She could smell the scent of lavender caught in Cassidy's hair, present even after a long day. Her arms went around Cassidy's back; Cassidy's fingers spread and slid up Brenna's back. She closed her own eyes and moved her hands up a little. Cassidy's arms squeezed briefly before the two pulled apart.

When she met the blue gaze again, there was a faint smile. She felt a similar one shaping her own lips. The change in their relationship felt incredibly good. "How was that?" Brenna asked. She was surprised to hear a mild huskiness in her own voice.

"Perfect," Cassidy said absently.

She backed reluctantly from Cassidy's hands and their grasp lingered for a long moment. She hesitated. "I...should go. Take care of yourself."

"I will."

Brenna's heart had been pounding so hard afterward that she needed the extra drive time to relax. Just the memory now sharply raised her heart rate. Closing her eyes tightly and balling her hands against her chest, she wondered what the next day would bring in her changed friendship with Cassidy.

CHAPTER FIFTEEN

"ACTION!"

Brenna and Kyle were ushered inside by the doorman, and Brenna gave up her rain slicker and hat, revealing a ladies' skirt suit in a very flattering dark blue.

With her boss, Virgil, Susan Jakes entered the nightclub set in this altered timeline. He had coaxed her to dinner while they worked on an office project. "Are you sure we can spare the time away from this project?" she asked.

"I appreciate that you want to get it finished, but taking a break isn't a crime," he answered, taking her coat.

"How can we talk in this noise?" Susan asked.

He smiled at her. "Don't you like the music?"

Susan studied the woman crooning into a microphone and swaying to the pianist's music as she sang. When she didn't answer, her escort shrugged. "Something to drink?"

Jakes shook her head. "No. It's all right. Should we sit?"

"Perfect." He smiled.

Surreptitiously Susan kept track of the other Time Squad operatives. Chris was the singer, Creighton kept the liquor flowing behind the bar. Their waiter, Jeremy Dewitt, showed them to a table near the stage.

Chris' blue eyes brushed over them as she moved across the stage, beginning another song:

> *No, you don't know the one*
> *who dreams of you at night,*
> *and longs to kiss your lips*
> *and longs to hold you tight...*

Finishing the stanza, she paused, turned back, and found Susan Jakes studying her. "You, you just don't know me," she crooned, watching as Jakes' escort grasped her hand where it rested on the table. "You'll never ever know, the girl who loves you so..." Chris dropped her gaze back to the couple in the front row, finding Susan's eyes. *Mind on the mission*, she reminded herself. She paused for the handful of beats between the stanza and the next refrain, looked at Virgil, and then growled seductively.

"Cut!"

Cassidy immediately softened the line of her shoulders and laughed. Brenna reached over and tapped her on the arm, and she turned to the Commander. "Yes?"

"Don't do that!" Brenna said with mock distress. "You're acting like a jealous lover."

"Just trying to distract him from guessing we know each other already." She laughed again. "But I could do jealous, if you like."

Kyle Masters stood. Half a day with the blond actress he had thought was ice cool had quickly shown him her playful side, which, as the day wore on, she had thrown his way once or twice. "I'll flip you for her. Someone have a quarter?" He caught one tossed from off set. "Heads she stays in this time frame with me; tails she goes back with you."

Cassidy nodded, catching Brenna's shoulder in a quick hug. "You have to come back! What would I ever do without you!"

Brenna laughed uneasily, and Cassidy felt the other woman tug away gently. Reluctantly she let go, watching Brenna move away with her head down. She was obviously thinking very hard about something as the post-camera smile had evaporated, replaced by...*Anxiety?* "Bren?"

Brenna turned at the soft call, but just then, Hifer walked up. "Are you three finished?" He chuckled. The trio suddenly looked up and laughed, separating. "Go on, back to your marks."

"Scene 18 B. Take 12." On their cue, the trio replayed the scene, finally finishing it to Hifer's satisfaction.

"All right, everyone. Take five. We're going to set up for the scene with Terry." The dark-skinned actor stepped up. "Ready, Terry?"

Terry nodded, and Brenna watched him sink into character; it was a palpable change. His eyes went shallow and dark, and the musculature and veins in his neck and arms became more pronounced. *Damn,* she thought. *He's going for scary.*

Cassidy stopped at her shoulder on her way off to the side. "What's up?" the blonde asked against her head.

"Look at Terry," Brenna said softly. Her head close to Brenna's, Cassidy turned and caught sight of Brown, pacing the portion of the set where his character worked. He was so caught up in character that he was muttering to himself and stalking, ignoring the lighting and sound grips moving the booms around to illuminate the area properly.

"Damn. That'll give me nightmares," Cassidy remarked. "He should've worked on my last movie. I didn't have anything on him as a vampire."

Brenna chuckled at the image of Cassidy as a vampire. "I'll have to go to the opening of that now," she teased.

"It was fun." Curious about Brenna's earlier withdrawal, Cassidy slipped an arm over the smaller woman's shoulder and watched gray-blue eyes look uneasily at the hand trailing over her costume. "I liked the fangs," she said.

"Cass, I..." Brenna eased out from under the touch.

"Horror movies scare you?" Cass asked in a playfully low voice. "Look. No sharp teeth." Brenna's eyes met hers, and Cassidy gave her a full grin, showing her very white, very straight teeth. Cass released Brenna as Hifer stepped toward them.

"All right, everyone. Places."

Brenna went over to her mark with Kyle, and they leaned across the table toward one another; Cassidy returned to her mark, and Terry stood behind the bar. "Action!"

The dark-skinned actor became frenetic; Brenna was transfixed. Standing behind the bar, he smashed a bottle against the bar. With an animal-like growl, he jumped onto the bar surface and began raving, then he leaped onto the stage and grabbed Cassidy.

Brenna started toward him.

"Let her go!"
Creighton lunged away from her, dragging Chris with him. He grabbed the microphone and held it like a knife against her throat. Chris' face filled with fear when Creighton held her close with one hand and growled his lines into her face. "Stop singing!"
"Would you prefer a different song?" Chris' voice was a weak, breathless plea.
Jakes was only a step away when Chris pulled free of Creighton, who was restrained by several patrons. Creighton's strength gained him his freedom, however.

Suddenly a real knife was in his hands, and then, just as suddenly, he plunged it into the chest of another patron. He started shaking and then turned and rushed headlong through the gathering crowd and into the night.

Jakes grabbed Chris' upper arms as the singer backed up into her. Tension rippled through the muscles under her hands and just as suddenly, Hanssen turned into her shoulder, grasping Jakes' left arm with her own right hand. They both knelt to see to the murdered man. "Are you all right?" Jakes asked Chris.

"Yes. I...Thank you." Hanssen and Jakes huddled close for a long beat. Chris reached out and checked the man's throat for a pulse. "He's dead."

"What the hell happened? We were supposed to stop a murder, not cause one."

"I'll go check behind the bar, see if I can find any clues."

Susan patted her back. "Go on. I'll cover for you." She stood and steered her "date" away from the dead man.

"Cut!" Hifer ended the scene.

Terry stepped out and took a bow to the applause of the camera crew, then looked toward Brenna and Cassidy, offering a wide smile. "Ladies, my Hyde imitation."

Glad to have a diversion from her still-racing heart, Brenna threw a prop to Terry.

He caught it, raising it in an exultant fist. "I would like to thank the Academy," he began.

Cassidy leaned against a console, laughing.

"One take, and damn, I'll take it. Next scene up," the director said. "Terry, go take a break. Everyone else...let's belly up to the bar."

"Does he do that often?" Kyle asked as Brenna, he, and Cassidy fell into step together on the walk over to the second soundstage.

"Nail a scene in one take? Not on your life." Brenna laughed. "But damn, he did, didn't he, Cass?"

The blonde nodded. "I'll give his name to my last movie director. Terry's got the sequel locked up." She shook her head and took a deep breath. "I thought I was the only horror film vet."

Brenna shook her head with appreciation. "Terry's gotta have a few on his résumé somewhere."

They sat at a bar table and worked into the short filler scenes, bantering with Sean Durham for a few minutes. They talked about their later scenes, relaxing with sips from their stage drinks ~ filtered water. The lighting and sound crews climbed around the set like flies on a screened porch.

The sound of flipping script pages brought their attention back to Hifer, who was going over the planned angles with the camera crew. One of the extras playing a bar patron came up. "Hey, George." Cassidy waved him over to the empty fourth seat at their table.

He sank into the chair. Gratefully he sipped at the cup at his place. "Man, this is great."

"The water or the job?" Brenna asked.

"Both."

Shaking off the energy lingering from the shoot, Brenna settled back and watched the two men chat quietly. She looked over at Cassidy, whom she found looking back, over the rim of her water cup. Her blue eyes really were very pale, almost clear. "How'd it go with Mitch last night?"

"I, uh, actually...didn't call him yet. I'm going to at the dinner break." Cassidy hesitated, then stirred her water idly with a finger as she spoke softly, "Would you consider being there?"

Brenna startled. "Me? Why?"

"Well, you were there Saturday. I...Mitch might want to ask you a few questions."

Nodding, Brenna sipped her drink while thinking. "All right." She wanted to ask about Cassidy's evening with Cameron but wasn't sure it would be appropriate, so she chose a safer topic. "How's Ryan?"

"Doing fine. He had a little trouble going to sleep last night, but your birthday gift is his favorite toy at the moment, and he cuddled in with that."

Brenna smiled, remembering the *Wild Things* monster she had picked out. "I'm glad." She slid her hand across the tabletop and squeezed Cassidy's.

The director stepped up to the table. "Just business," he said. "Without the sound I could've shot the last five minutes. Keep it up, just put the dialogue in."

Brenna looked up at him and nodded, withdrawing her hand from the tabletop. "Will do." She caught Cassidy's nod at the director out of the corner of her eye, and Kyle and George's as well.

"All right." He stepped back to the camera line. After a few checks on the lenses, he called, "Action."

"We can't let them lynch Creighton," Jakes said. "We all have to get out of here together."

Hanssen considered aloud, "I'm a co-worker at the club. What if I asked to see him?"

"You...you show up from the hiring agency and tell me you're my new secretary," Virgil said. Jakes reached over and squeezed his hand. He squeezed back. "Now, you tell me you're not even from here."

Jakes looked at Hanssen. "Are you certain you can

do this?"

Hanssen looked back with firm determination. "We all go, or no one, isn't that what you said? I can do this." Their gazes held for several beats.

Susan nodded. "All right. You know when we'll intercept the line. I expect to see you there, Lieutenant."

"Cut!"

Brenna leaned back and smiled. *Nothing like having a good rapport with the people you work with.* That had been devastatingly simple.

The director looked at his watch. "Well done. That's dinner, folks. It's five o'clock. Keep this up and we'll be out of here by nine."

"Are you going to make that call?" Cassidy stopped walking, and Brenna caught up to her in the back lot near their trailers. The evening lighting bathed them each in separate pools of lamplight.

"Yes," she replied. "Thought I'd call Gwen then and check on Ryan."

"Missing him?"

"Yeah."

Brenna shrugged. "Do you have to stay?"

"I have a scene over at the warehouse set after dinner."

"I've got mine with Kyle." They stepped up into Cassidy's trailer, and the blonde offered a bottle of fruit juice. "Thanks." Brenna sat down on the small couch. "Are you sure you want me here?"

"It won't take long. Then I thought maybe we could talk about the camping trip."

"All right."

Cassidy set aside her own fruit juice. She sat at the desk, picked up the phone, and punched in her ex-husband's number. "You know," she said while waiting for the call to ring through, "I don't ever remember a day going this easily."

"Me neither," Brenna admitted. "Nice, though."

"Hello, Mitch. It's Cassidy."

Brenna saw Cassidy's shoulders stiffen. What was it about Mitch Hyland that got his ex-wife so nervous? Offering encouragement, she reached out and squeezed Cassidy's knee.

"Yeah," the blonde continued. "I guess you could come for a visit. This weekend okay?" She nodded at the receiver. "That'll work. Do you want to meet at the house?" She nodded again.

Brenna leaned back and smiled when Cassidy looked toward her. "Well, no, I don't think we should do Disneyland." Cassidy shook her head. "It's too much of a day. Ryan will just get overexcited." Another pause. "The park with Ranger would be better." Finally the conversation was coming to an end. Cassidy said, "Yeah, see you Saturday," and pulled the receiver away from her ear, straightening her hair and disconnecting the call.

"So, Saturday in the park. Good. Mitch'll get a chance to see Ryan, and you can show him things are fine. Why didn't you want to do Disneyland?"

"Nothing really against it, but Disneyland...well, it's where we used to go on our dates."

"Afraid of seduction?" Brenna asked with a half-serious questioning tone in her voice.

"No. Afraid of losing Ryan in a crowd again," she admitted.

Brenna sobered. "True. I think you've had enough excitement in that department to last a while."

"That's why I'm looking forward to the camping trip," Cassidy said. "It'll be fun, but no crowds. And I think Ryan will enjoy the outdoors."

Brenna smiled. "We've done this about three times a year since coming to L.A. Just a chance to get out of the city for a weekend. When I started working with these kids, taking them on a camping trip once in winter and once in late spring was my first suggestion. Thomas is quite the mountain climber."

"Mountain climbing? I haven't even been camping in years. I'm looking forward to it." Cassidy shifted from the chair to the couch, settling next to Brenna.

"Have you been in the mountains at all?"

"A couple of ski trips to Denver when I was in college."

"We won't see any snow this time out."

"Yeah. Now when the snow hits, I like a fireplace and an endless supply of Irish coffee or mulled wine," Cassidy mused. "How about you?"

"The same."

They were interrupted by a knock. "Yes?" Cassidy got to her feet and opened the door.

"Ms. Hyland, have you-" The stagehand looked past Cassidy. "Ms. Lanigan? Mr. Hifer says you're needed on set."

"All right." Brenna rose from the couch as the young man dashed away. "I'd better go."

"I'll come watch until I get my call."

"I thought you were going to call Gwen, check on Ryan."

"Oh, right. I'll be there in a minute, then."

Brenna stopped at the door. "Don't you dare make faces at me," she warned.

"Would I ruin a love scene?" Cassidy grinned.

"Speaking of...What was that business singing to Virgil and me? It wasn't in the original blocking."

Cassidy held her door open. "I know."

Brenna stopped on the stoop and looked up. "What is it?"

Cassidy smiled. "I like the way our characters are connecting. I thought

I could extend it a bit. Do you mind?"

"The characters," Brenna echoed. "Um, no. That's...that's fine. I probably should, too." *What is going on?* She felt like something was changing ~ too fast or in a direction she could not determine.

```
    The lighting in the alley was very low.
    Susan Jakes moved closer to Virgil and stroked a
hand across his chest. He smiled, and she looked into
his features. "I'll miss you," she said, a little
bewildered.
    "Are you sure you have to go?" he asked.
```

Cassidy watched from the side of the stage, arms crossed over her chest pensively. Despite knowing she had a job to do in another time and place, it was clear Susan was strongly drawn to the man the team had come to save. *Damn*, Cassidy thought. She felt her cheeks heat as the two actors kissed. *She's good at this.*

CHAPTER SIXTEEN

BRENNA CAUGHT the phone in her trailer as it rang mid-morning. "Hello?" She tucked the receiver between her ear and shoulder as she settled on the couch and pulled off her costume boots. "Kevin?" Leaning back, she briefly pulled the phone away, studied it, and then tucked it back under her ear. "You've never called me on set. What's wrong?"

"It's official. After a very close recount, I won the election," he said.

She could hear the smile in his voice. She smiled genuinely. "Congratulations." He had worked hard on the campaign. She heard music in the background. "Celebrating?"

"Yes." There was a long pause. "I miss you."

Wriggling her toes in relief at their release from the tight confines of the boots, she massaged them distractedly. "Miss you, too," she replied automatically.

"Could you fly out here this weekend?" he asked. "For a private celebration."

His voice had dropped, and she felt an expectant shiver. "I have a convention appearance. ...It's in Vegas....I know," she added quickly. "You're not crazy about that, but we could have some time together."

The line between them was silent for a long time. "I fired Derek."

The name did not ring a bell for Brenna. "Who?"

"The staffer who suggested I take advantage of your celebrity. I was stupid to listen to him."

"Yes," she said. She closed her eyes and felt the hot sting of tears. "You were." The feelings of betrayal hit her hard again.

"It won't happen again."

"It won't?" Brenna whispered to keep her tears from him.

"Bren, I love you. Please come to Mount Clemens."

She covered the receiver and breathed deep and slow. Pained, she said, "No."

He did not answer immediately. "I need to make it up to you." His voice was quiet, regretful.

She drew a short breath. *An apology?* "It hurt," she admitted. "Still does. Tom did the same thing to me. Tried to make me choose," she told him honestly. "I need my work, but I need to be me, too."

"I know you like the work."

"I *love* the work. But I won't be used to get you votes, or favors, or anything else."

"I was losing in that district. I lost the demographic vote at the university in the end anyway. Made up for it in the retired–"

"Kevin!" She wiped her face, aware that she was smearing the heavy makeup. "Polls aren't everything. I have to mean more to you than a few votes."

"You do," he protested.

Awash in emotion, she sucked in a deep breath. "Then," she said on a watery inhale, "how could you hurt me like that?"

She ignored the knock at her door, waiting, wanting him to answer so she could heal. The slight in Mount Clemens had, she thought, been resolved. Brought up again, she realized how, left untouched, it had only festered.

"Bren, come home. Please?"

She shook her head. "I can't. Not right now." She took a deep breath, trying to collect herself. "I'm sorry. I have to go." Taking a deeper breath as she pulled the phone away from her ear, she tapped the button and set the cordless receiver back in its cradle. Standing, she turned to find the door already open and the doorway occupied. Cassidy stood there, backlit by the sun, and Brenna felt tears prick at the back of her eyes. *Damn.*

"Bren? Are you all right?"

Sidestepping the question, Brenna asked, "Something up on the set?" She had to close her eyes when Cassidy's shadowed with concern. She raised her hands as the blonde came closer, taking the final step into the trailer. "No."

Cassidy's concern deepened. Long fingers slipped over Brenna's wrist and pulled her hand away from her cheek. "I'm sorry about this. Gerry needs you back on set."

Brenna nodded, trying to put her smile back in place as she moved toward the door. Cassidy's hand caressed her shoulder. Drawn by the touch, Brenna looked up into a face that showed understanding.

"You'll need a quick run through makeup." Fingertips traced Brenna's cheekbone.

Two new tears tracked down Brenna's cheeks before she could turn away. Quickly she left Cassidy alone in her trailer.

Not seeing anyone in Makeup, Brenna slid in front of a mirror in the corner and repaired her face herself. Voices reached her from next door.

"Chapman still wants this?" The voice belonged to Cameron Palassis; his voice was hard.

Picking up the cake of base, Brenna was surprised to hear Victor Branch respond, "He will want to be written out if he doesn't get more to do."

"How are we supposed to explain this to the audience?" Cameron shot back.

"He doesn't care. It's just the one scene for now, anyway."

"You damn well know he'll want a whole script on the subject later."

"Demographics might like it. They liked Raycreek and Jakes for quite a while."

"Until their off-screen breakup soured the on-screen chemistry. Chapman doesn't get along with anyone now, especially Cassidy."

Brenna was shocked. *Will is demanding a script change or he'll walk? God, we're only a few episodes from the whole thing being over anyway. And he wants to be written in with Cassidy?*

Brenna admitted to herself that she had not been an advocate of focusing so much attention on Chris Hanssen at first, but after a year and after all the plot lines which had seen them thrown together, Jakes had a stake in this, too. From Branch's words, though, it didn't sound like Chapman wanted more professional interaction between his character and the lieutenant. They had specifically mentioned Jakes and Raycreek's affair. She sighed. *And how badly that went.* She frowned. *Is Will angling for a romance with Cassidy?*

Palassis was right. Other than the odd scene here and there, Chapman's Mark Raycreek barely spoke to Cassidy's Chris Hanssen. There were very few grounds to support a closer relationship.

The two men moved away from where she sat. She finished reapplying her makeup and went out to her soundstage, her mind still reeling with questions. *What scene does Will want changed?* she wondered. Then she wondered how, or even if, she could or should stop it.

Terry Brown and Will Chapman were conferring at a cafeteria table when Brenna arrived for her own dinner break. "Mind if I join you?" she asked, looking between the two as she held her tray.

Terry gestured to the seat across from him. "Of course." Will's gaze was polite as she settled.

"Terry," she started easily, hoping to feel Chapman out. "How's the shooting?"

"Coming along."

She looked at Will, who had turned to his meal. Uneasy, she wondered what to say. An imp prompted her to joke. "How's the base line coming, Lieutenant?" she asked with a light smile.

"Just a few minor rewrites to the history books, Commander," he replied in kind, after a hesitation. Brenna nodded. "Something on your mind?" he asked.

"I've just been thinking about the end of everything," she said quietly, projecting a vague note of melancholy. "This will all be over sooner than we think."

"I keep trying not to consider it," Terry said honestly. "I've enjoyed myself."

"We certainly have been through a lot together."

"I think about it all the time," Will added. "Where everything could've gone, what's next."

"Do you really? I'm going to miss the entire company," Brenna said, biting into a sandwich. "We've done something special here."

"It's just a job, especially now," Will countered. "Certainly the writers have squandered the real possibilities."

"What possibilities?"

"Storylines that matter to the social conscience or the science conscience. For crying out loud, we're a science fiction program. Where's the 'out there' stories? Instead we get–"

"We have social commentaries," Brenna interrupted. "That's the whole premise behind changing history."

"Today's issues are so much more personal ~ cultural but impacting on the individual," Will insisted.

"What are you talking about?"

"Situational ethics; conservative, liberal; inclusion, exclusion; love's many forms."

Brenna frowned. "We're not *West Wing*."

"No. With our science-fiction setting, we could be a lot less threatening than something like that."

"Is that what you would suggest to Cameron or Victor?"

Will shook his head. "No, I didn't suggest a political storyline."

"What did you suggest?" she prodded pointedly.

"Some changes."

"What would piss Cameron off so much?" Brenna asked. "I...overheard him talking with Victor."

Terry looked askance at Will.

"I thought a scene we're doing could use a little emotional punch."

"That doesn't sound so bad," Brenna said.

"Cameron didn't like it. But don't worry, I have other ideas." He tapped her plate. "You should get back to eating. Don't you have more shooting?"

Realizing he wasn't going to share anything further, Brenna returned her attention to her meal. She only vaguely heard the cafeteria doors open. A prickling sensation caused her to straighten and rub the back of her neck, drawing her gaze toward the doors.

Stepping in with Cameron at her side and out of costume, Cassidy entered the cafeteria. The blonde's hair was loose against her sweatshirt-covered shoulders. Brenna noted the college logo ~ University of Missouri. Light eyes swept the room and found hers, the smooth chin dipping in acknowledgment. She nodded in return greeting. Terry turned to observe where she was looking.

Cassidy took a couple of steps toward them before Cameron's hand on her arm stopped her. The two then turned into the buffet line, collecting up trays and utensils.

"Looks like she's done for the day," Will observed.

"It'll give her a chance to get home and see Ryan before bed," Brenna commented idly. She lifted a hand and gestured the two toward the table as the cashier handed them their change. Her gaze continued to follow the tall woman as Cassidy smiled and sat down in the chair to her left. "Going home?" Brenna asked.

"After this." Cassidy nodded to both men across the table. "Terry. Will." Cameron settled next to her. She shifted toward Brenna to make room at the table that normally seated only four. Their hips touched. Brenna inhaled sharply, drawing Cassidy's eyes to her face. "How much longer do you have?"

"I should make it out of here by nine," Brenna guessed, "if everything goes according to schedule."

Cameron leaned forward, looking around Cassidy toward Brenna. "Shooting going well?" He directed his inquiry to Brenna as well as Terry and Will.

Terry replied with a brief nod, "The usual."

"That's great." He looked at his food, then up at Cassidy for a moment.

Cassidy addressed Terry. "Aren't you going to the Vegas convention this weekend?"

"Yes. So's Brenna."

Brenna met Cassidy's questioning look. "We're flying out together. Friday night."

"What are you planning to do with Thomas and James?"

Brenna shrugged. "I'm going to give them a chance to spend the weekend alone. They asked for it."

"Did you set down the rules yet?" Cassidy teased.

"That's planned for tomorrow." Brenna chuckled. The two women shared an understanding grin that excluded the men, something they knew ~ strictly one mother to another.

In the brief silence that saw everyone return to eating, Will and Terry exchanged nods that made Brenna uneasy. "Well," she said, standing and briefly dropping her hand over Cassidy's to draw the other woman's attention. "I have to get back. Have a good night."

"Take care," Cassidy replied.

The look they exchanged warmed Brenna, reminding her of Cassidy's concern in her trailer earlier. She nodded at the others, then discarded her tray and left the cafeteria, very aware of blue eyes on her back.

CHAPTER SEVENTEEN

ADVENTUROUSLY, RYAN hauled himself around a wood-and-steel frame jungle gym on the north side of Constance Park. Ranger leaped beneath him, barking enthusiastically.

"So, things are going well?"

Cassidy tore her watchful gaze from her son to meet the hazel green eyes of her ex-husband. "Yeah." They sat together on a gray steel bench set in the sand nearby. Her eyes swept his frame, realizing he had not changed much in the year since their divorce. He was still the physical fitness hound she had met at a beach bar when she first arrived in Los Angeles. Most people would never think he was a paper-pusher for one of the largest investment firms on the West Coast. His eyes settled on her, as if questioning her answer. "And Ryan likes the neighborhood," she added.

Mitch nodded and pressed his hands against the seat, flexing his arms. He released the tension and sat back again. "You and that writer fellow still getting along?"

Cassidy hesitated, surprised to hear her ex-husband talk of Cameron when he had been adamant that the man's name never be mentioned in his presence. Trying to hide her hesitation and cover her surprise, she added quickly, "It's been busy lately, with lots of stuff to do as the series closes down."

"Really? Not seeing much of each other?" Mitch crossed his arms over his chest and nodded toward the playground. "So when you do get together, you get sidetracked? Is that how you lost track of Ryan in the store?"

"Cameron was not at the store." Cassidy shook her head and set her jaw. *Okay, so we're finally going to get to it.* The few pleasantries they had exchanged on the walk out from the car had just been a lull. She squared her shoulders and wished Brenna was there. She envisioned the compact woman as she had confronted the nosy reporter at Sports Warehouse. She smiled at the memory and then asked the question that had been bothering her. "How did you hear about it?"

"You remember Booker?" Cassidy nodded, recalling Mitch's college roommate. He had spent a lot of time in their home while Cassidy and Mitch were married. "He caught the newscast. Thought I should know." He flexed his shoulders, and Cassidy moved a few inches away on the bench. He grasped her right wrist. "I should've heard it from you."

Cassidy shook her hand from his grasp. "Nothing happened!"

"A hell of a lot could've happened. What if he'd been kidnapped or really fallen down that compactor?"

Cassidy winced. She had envisioned many horrifying scenarios, only holding the inner demons at bay with Brenna's help. Brenna had been so convincing that it was just a minor mishap; her faith had held Cassidy's world together. She nodded toward the play equipment. "Ryan is fine. He's the first thing I think about every day."

The green eyes searched her face. "Are you going to take up another project when you finish *Time Trails?*"

"Something will come up."

"Can you really provide for him the way he deserves?"

"We settled this in the court hearing. I'm not giving Ryan to you. He needs his mother, not a nanny. My life is stable enough, thanks."

Mitch shook his head. "When you don't know where your next gig is? So what happens in a year when you're yesterday's news?"

Cassidy exploded. "And you're better? Never home as you check out corporations for other people's investment? Can you take a five-year-old on a business trip, Mitch?"

"I can provide for him."

"With a nanny," Cassidy jabbed.

Mitch laughed. "You're crazy. He's my son."

"I won't give him up."

"I'll take you to court again."

Cassidy wasn't cowed. "I'll win...again. Don't threaten me."

His voice dropped as he stood up. "I can do as I damn well please."

Cassidy felt his big frame towering over her five-feet-eight inches like a boom about to fall from set rigging. She watched his eyes go dark and started to take a step backward, then realized that was exactly what he wanted ~ to prove he still had the control. *Damn, and I lived with this man for five years!* She shook her head at how blind she had been. "I am not coming back to you, Mitch. It's over."

"It's never going to be over. We will always have Ryan," he shot back. "I will always have a place in your life." He cursed. "We had a nice life going until that writer of yours gave you some backbone."

"He helped me see what I was too close to see. You're arrogant and possessive, and I would've seen it sooner or later without Cameron's help."

"The minute that man is out of the picture and you're nobody, you're both mine again," Mitch challenged. "All I gotta do is wait, and you'll crawl back." He stepped back, relaxing out of the menacing stance and chuckling at her wide eyes. "I see I've made my point."

Cassidy swallowed, consciously slowed her heart rate, and licked her suddenly dry lips. "You've made your point."

She caught movement out of the corner of her eye and looked toward a jogger moving past their location. The line of Mitch's shoulders softened further as the jogger gave them a curious glance. Gaining several steps away from her ex-husband, Cassidy crossed the path and searched the jungle gym. "Ryan!" she called, finding him hanging upside down on the monkey bars, knees bent around the cross-beam. "Hey, buddy, are you ready for some lunch?"

"Is Daddy coming with us?" Ryan asked. He rolled himself over and, while his mother reached out to spot him, dropped to the ground.

Mitch strode up behind Cassidy as she dusted Ryan's pants free of sand. "Absolutely, wouldn't think to miss it. Do you want hot dogs and ice cream?"

"Ice cream! Yay!" Ryan sprang past his mother and leaped into his father's outstretched arms. Green eyes shot her an unmistakable message over Ryan's head: *I got him.*

With a shaky hand, she patted Ryan's back and encouraged him to get down and walk between them. Ryan reached out and grasped one parent's hand in each of his own, looking up at them as they exchanged looks with him and with each other.

"Lunch!" he yelled happily, skipping briskly and gleefully dragging his parents along.

Cassidy's heart skipped several beats. She held on as firmly as she dared without hurting Ryan or letting Mitch's grip take him from her.

The cacophony that met their entrance made Brenna jump a little as she and Terry Brown were announced onto the stage at the Vegas convention. The two were in street clothes. Terry wore a black tee shirt with the show's tagline, "All time stops here," and a pair of blue denim pants. Brenna had opted for black slacks and a hunter green silk blouse, very different from the black jumpsuit uniform with purple armbands she regularly wore on the set. The convention hall was packed, standing room only, and the two actors were the center of attention.

Terry took the microphone from the emcee and passed it to Brenna. She grinned as a bouquet of roses was thrust up from the foot of the stage, and she bent over to accept them. On the other side of the bouquet, she found the face of a boy who looked to be about twelve. He flushed bright red when she passed a kiss to his cheek with her fingers before taking the roses with a mic-enhanced, "Thank you." She straightened to more cheers and stepped back, handing over the microphone to let Terry speak first.

"It's great to be here," he said. "Just caught a vortex for a short stay. You know how much our commander likes tunnel travel."

That raised a laugh, and Brenna grinned, then put her hands on her hips in her favorite Jakes pose and gave Terry a glare. "Creighton should be careful. He might just find himself dropped in The Lost World instead of the tunnel home," she joked to applause.

They hugged, and Terry gave her a kiss on the cheek. He stepped back and gestured at the audience. The emcee waved at them from what was now the front of the question line, a queue of hopefuls who had questions at the ready for them. "Looks like it's time for questions."

First up was a girl with a round face, big blue eyes, and tied-back blond hair. She asked Commander Jakes if she missed her mom because she traveled so much.

With a reassuring smile, Brenna said, "Someday I hope to get everything just right and see her again." She nodded to the mother who patted her daughter on the shoulder before drawing her away from the line. For the benefit of the rest of the audience, Brenna added, "Changing official time has left me very little *personal* time." There was a roll of knowing laughter, and she stepped back, watching the next questioner come forward.

Terry answered a question about why he didn't take the second spot when Chapman's character Raycreek had mutinied in an episode two years earlier. "You want me to face off with her?" He hooked a thumb toward Brenna. "I don't have a death wish. She's tough."

"Is Commander Jakes going to find a new romance?"

Brenna answered lightly. "Isn't she still smarting over Raycreek?" she asked. Two years ago while she was briefly involved with Chapman, they had taken it on-screen for a few episodes. The storyline had sizzled, then fizzled. The arc that brought Cassidy in had fractured the team, ending the relationship both on- and off-screen. She'd married Kevin just four months later, in August.

Turning more serious, she asked, "Besides, who else is there?"

A cacophony of suggestions rose up. She heard several people suggest she give Raycreek another chance. *Nope,* she thought. *That boat has sailed.* She raised her eyebrow in shock at Terry when his character, Creighton, was suggested. "But he's married!"

"So what?" someone shouted back. "Maybe you'd rather she get with

Hanssen?"

That rattled Brenna. *Where would they get that idea? Susan in love with Chris? What will these fans think of next?*

"I think maybe Jakes is just a little busy running from crisis to crisis to settle down," she responded finally. *How about that?* She covered her eyes. Factions of the audience began arguing among themselves.

Searching for serenity, she pictured Cassidy, out of costume, the blonde's hair loose around her cheeks, and her face filled with the concerned expression she'd worn when she inadvertently overheard Brenna's conversation with her husband.

That brought to mind Mitch, Cassidy's ex-husband. She wondered how the woman's meeting in the park had gone. Distracted, Brenna did not focus on the next several questions addressed to her. She only hoped the answers she gave made some kind of sense.

Finally the organizers brought the audience under control. There were more questions asking for spoilers. They didn't have information themselves, so Terry and Brenna truthfully shrugged. "Your guess is as good as ours. Maybe better." Before long, Brenna and Terry were taking their last questions to repeated standing ovations.

When they were motioned off, Terry and Brenna stepped into the wings. Inhaling and exhaling to dispel her tensions, Brenna looked up at a pat on the shoulder from Liza Garnet. She played one of the big-wig types on the show, returning from time to time with dire pronouncements about the future of the Time Squad. The dark eyes smiled back. "Don't let 'em shake you. Remember, it's just a role."

Terry's hand on her shoulder drew Brenna's attention away as Liza walked out on stage to thunderous applause. "What did I say?" Brenna asked him. "Was it bad?" *Maybe I was more disconnected than I thought.*

"Not bad at all," Terry said without elaborating. "Come on. Let me take you to dinner."

Brenna frowned but nodded. "All right."

They entered the elevator and slipped up to their adjoining rooms. Brenna washed up but decided against changing. Terry knocked a few minutes later and presented himself in a black leather jacket pulled over a yellow polo shirt and black slacks. She reached over and grabbed her own soft black leather jacket and stepped into the corridor, locking her door behind herself and tucking the key card into her purse. "Ready?"

"Ready," he said, offering her an elbow. "What are you interested in?"

Brenna considered that. "How about something fun? Fondue?"

He laughed. "Messy. I like it."

Contemplating the cheese melts and the bits of beef, an indulgence she rarely allowed herself, Brenna led the way out to the curb and hailed a cab.

"I've never seen anything like it," Brenna praised, lifting a forkful of sizzling steak from the boiling oil. Dipping it in a bowl of spicy steak sauce, she let the excess drip before popping it in her mouth. She regarded Terry across the table. "You can do scary really well. Cassidy was shaking."

"I had a chance to play Jack the Ripper on stage two years ago during the hiatus. Enjoyed it," he said with a smile, dipping a chicken strip in a béchamel sauce. "You've got a theater background, too, but you haven't done anything on the breaks. Why not?"

"Between spending time here and in Mount Clemens, my boys' schedules, and trying to hold it all together, who has time?"

"Would you be interested if there was, say, a local playhouse production to do?"

"How local?"

Terry smiled. "Mine."

She laughed. "Yours?" He frowned. "I didn't mean it like that," she assured him. "Just, I didn't know you owned a playhouse."

"Part owner. I went into it with some friends."

"That's great. What's the playbill this season?"

"We're currently casting for *Juniper Falls*, a locally written play." He paused to drop a vegetable piece into some melted cheese. "I could pass you the script if you want."

"Oh, I couldn't. Where would I find the time?"

"You ought to consider what you're going to do after we wrap," he prompted.

Brenna speared another strip of steak and dropped it in the sizzling oil. "Kevin wants me to come to Mount Clemens."

After a telling pause during which she felt her cheeks warm, dark eyes met hers across the table. "You don't sound like that's what you want."

"I should," she said, finding it convenient to check on her steak and then changing the subject. "So, tell me more? Where is it? Who are your partners?"

Terry bit into another piece, but otherwise did not seem fazed by her topic shift. "It's in Fullerton. We converted a vineyard press house about three years ago. We've had a few nice reviews. Small company, pretty stable. We like local writers over getting name projects. A labor of love," he finished with a smile.

Brenna smiled warmly, pausing as she contemplated the memories she had of theater life. Starting out in New York, at nineteen, those days had been scary and exciting. "Sounds wonderful."

"Will you consider coming out? At least see a performance? Meet the company?"

"All right. Just one night. Sometime." She speared a strip of meat and settled it against the hot rock. "You'd make a good salesman." She laughed lightly.

"My wife will appreciate knowing I have another occupation to fall back on," he joked, making her chuckle deepen with genuine pleasure. "You'd like the work."

"I'd love the work," she acknowledged finally. "I miss live performance."

"You did have fun on stage today." Terry paused. "You...were relaxed for a change."

"Are you saying I'm not usually?" Brenna speared a strip of yellow pepper, sinking it in the bowl of oil. "Tell me more about your playhouse."

"So you are interested?" He reached over and picked up his drink.

"Maybe," she granted with a nod, sipping from her own glass.

"Well, that's one down, one to go," he said idly.

"Who else are you asking?"

"I'd like to get Cass before she gets another offer." Terry shrugged. "Her range is impressive. Like her singing last episode."

Brenna remembered she had not had to work hard to remember to stare at Cassidy. The woman's voice had been mesmerizing. Brenna paused with her fork in her mouth, then slowly chewed and swallowed. "She surprised me."

"Why?"

"Well, we all know why she was brought on board," Brenna said frankly.

"We've had some good moments together," Terry observed. "Off-screen as well as on."

"Until recently I haven't seen her much away from the set," Brenna said. "I enjoyed the birthday party she hosted."

"My wife and I have gone over a couple of times now. One time the power went out. We walked over to a corner hot dog stand. Ryan ate himself silly with hot dogs, soda, and chips while playing with my daughter in the yard with that Dalmatian of theirs. Cass even got down on the ground and rolled around some herself."

Brenna imagined Cassidy wrestling with her son on the ground. She was suddenly unable to speak as the image of Cassidy "letting go" blew coherent thought away.

"I understand she had quite a fight to keep him," Terry went on, drawing her attention. "That's why I'd love to see her stay in town and work at the playhouse. I doubt she really wants to uproot and move somewhere else."

Brenna nodded. "Mitch, her ex, was planning to visit this weekend. He heard about the incident at the store."

Terry steepled his hands, then folded one over the other. "Was she upset?"

"Shaking like a leaf. Do you know why?"

He pursed his lips, clearly withholding something. "Maybe on Monday we can ask how things went." He waved over a waiter and requested a refill on his beer. When he turned back, he asked, "So, what do you want to do for our entrance on stage tomorrow?"

Brenna shook her head. While Terry had shrugged off the concern about Cassidy, she found herself unable to do the same. "I think I'm a little tired. How about we wing it? I'd like to get back to the hotel. Get some sleep."

"Sure."

She finished a last bite of fondue, then laid a credit card over the check the waiter brought with Terry's beer before he could. "Thanks for the conversation and the company," she offered in explanation.

While he drained the beer, she sat quietly pondering their conversation. When he set the empty glass down, they gathered their coats and wended their way out of the restaurant.

Blasted by the chill of the open refrigerator, Cassidy searched for something for Ryan's bedtime snack. She tried to shake off the afternoon's unease but found it impossible. Each time she closed her eyes she saw Mitch playing with Ryan, tossing a baseball with him, or helping him drink from the park fountain or Ryan laughing as Daddy jogged with him through the sprinklers. Every time it happened and the boy raced back breathlessly to her side giggling, she would catch Mitch's significant look, and her heart sank a little further.

Finally she had been able to call a halt by pointing out that Ryan had to bathe and get to bed. Her son had been upset, but Mitch did not have any argument he could offer up without making himself look foolish. They had driven back to the house, and Mitch had let Cassidy and Ryan off in the driveway. Then he pulled out and drove away.

"Mommy?"

"Ready for bath time?" She turned to see her son coming off the porch where he had taken the dog into the yard.

"Okay." He headed for the bathroom, and she followed.

She swallowed as she asked, "Did you have fun today?"

"Yeah." He grinned, pulling off his shirt as she bent past him and twisted the water spigot. "Daddy's a lot of fun."

"Don't we have fun?" she asked uneasily.

Ryan tried to explain himself. "Sure, but...he's...Daddy."

Now nude, Ryan stepped into the warm bubbles, holding her hand so he wouldn't slip. It was an unconscious request for support, and after the emotional rollercoaster of the afternoon it warmed Cassidy's heart. She reached for the washcloth and soaped it, then washed his back and chest. She splashed him lightly, and they both giggled when bubbles covered his nose. He wiped them away with wet hands and then patted her cheeks with his bubble-covered palms.

Once she had his hair washed, she stood. "Play for a little while, then after snack and story, I'll tuck you in bed."

He immediately grabbed for the collection of toys in a bucket by the side of the tub and splashed them noisily into the water. Smiling, she stepped out of the bathroom and returned to the kitchen. She poured out two small glasses of milk and set a plate of chocolate chip cookies between them on the table before returning to the bathroom. "Snack time."

Ryan stepped out of the tub and wrapped up in a fluffy dark green towel. She lifted a corner of it over his hair and dried vigorously, to his delighted giggles. "What's for snack?"

"Cookies and milk," she answered. He pushed past her. Only with quick hands did she grab him and pull on his pajama top and bottoms. "Now, you're ready," she said with a laugh. Scrambling back to her feet, Cassidy followed her son to the table .

An hour later Ryan was fed, his teeth brushed, a story read, and covers tucked to his chin. Cassidy retreated to her room and lay across her bed. Tension formed in her neck and shoulders as she tried to dispel her anxieties.

Mitch was just playing on your fear, she told herself. *It's a bluff because he knows you get like this.* Deciding a bath might help, she checked on Ryan once more and then went into the bathroom. Adding salts instead of bubbles, she leaned back and closed her eyes, letting the aromas soothe her while she concentrated on pleasant thoughts.

Next weekend will be fun, she told herself. She immediately smiled, thinking of the hiking and campfire fun. Mountain climbing, she recalled, was also on the agenda. She shrugged. She had never climbed, but she was in good shape. She had really enjoyed the children at the Halloween party and looked forward to more time with them. Ryan would enjoy the time with other children, as well. She welcomed the opportunity to chat with other adults about things which had nothing to do with work. Particularly, she looked forward to getting to know Brenna with both of them letting their hair down.

Despite the times they had recently shared, Cassidy knew there were more depths to discover in the intriguing woman. She closed her eyes and pictured Brenna's tear-stained face two days earlier in the woman's trailer. At the sight of Brenna's pain, Cassidy's protective instincts had flared sharply. Her fingers tingled in memory of the briefly comforting touch she had offered.

"Good night, Brenna."

"Sleep well. See you in the morning." Closing her door, Brenna hung her jacket and sat down on one of the beds. Eyeing the phone, she thought, *Should I?* She shook her head against the sharp tang of concern that dampened her palms. *This is so weird. She's a grown woman, able to take care of herself. You're getting too involved, Bren.*

"Oh hell." She reached for the phone and dialed quickly before she could change her mind.

"Hello?"

She hurriedly identified herself when she heard Cassidy's voice on the line, sounding soft and tired. "It's Brenna. I didn't call at a bad time, did I?"

"Brenna?" Cass' voice was light, incredulous.

Leaning back against her pillows, Brenna smiled. "Yeah. You sound good."

"So do you."

There was silence, and Brenna just listened, intent on the other woman's breathing for some sign that she really was okay.

Finally Cassidy asked, "What's on your mind?"

Brenna temporized. "I was...Terry and I were talking and I remembered you were supposed to see Mitch today. I...How did it go?" Cassidy exhaled, and Brenna's throat clenched.

"It went." Now Cassidy's voice was flat.

"Not good?"

"I was reminded of why I left him," Cassidy said. "He's...scary when he wants to be."

Brenna felt her heart rate speed up slightly, remembering the feel of Cassidy shaking in her grasp during filming. To have access to that sort of fear...Anger on Cassidy's behalf burned behind her eyes. Rubbing at them, she offered, "I'm sorry I couldn't be there. How's Ryan?"

"He loves his dad."

"How are you?"

"I just finished a bath to unwind."

"Good."

Both women fell silent, trying to figure out what to say. Cassidy finally prompted, "This is long distance. How's the convention going?"

"Makes me wish we had another year at this. The fans are really into it."

"Yeah, I know. So what questions did you get?"

"Standard fare." Brenna thought a moment. "I did get one new one, though."

"Yeah?" Cassidy had not done a con in about eight months and wondered what the fans were thinking up now.

"There's a group that wants Jakes to have another romance." Brenna wondered why she was having such a hard time with that. Liza was right; it was just a role. "Some want her to go back to Raycreek. A few...want y–Hanssen."

"That's new." Cassidy's voice was playful. Brenna pictured her relaxing, phone pressed to her ear, and waited for more. "What does Commander Jakes think?"

"I haven't..." Curled on her bed, Brenna pulled her knees up and pondered the question. "It's pretty ludicrous."

"I don't know. We have a strong enough friendship for it to make sense," Cassidy pointed out. "And the audience obviously has fewer biases than the studio would credit them with. There won't be a ripple, I think, when Luria kisses Chris in *Brains and Brawn*."

"Susan couldn't do that," Brenna said quickly. She passed her hand over the bed covers to still the tingling in her fingertips and quickly changed the subject. "I'm glad you're all right."

"Bren?" There was a long pause before Cass spoke again. When she did, she had apparently changed her mind about what she wanted to say. "Never mind. See you Monday."

"Yes. Sleep well." Brenna held the phone listening as Cassidy broke the connection first. Setting the receiver back on its cradle, she rolled onto her stomach, fisting her hands under her chin and wondering why she was so unsettled. *Cassidy's all right. So's Ryan. Now,* she sternly told herself, *call your sons and then go to sleep. You've got a long day tomorrow.*

She called her home number and waited two rings for it to pick up. She recognized the "hello" from her youngest. "James?"

"Hi, Mom. How's Vegas?"

"Fine. How are you two?"

"Thomas is out with Cheryl at the dance."

"Not back yet?"

"Curfew's not for another hour."

"Oh, that's right," Brenna said, checking the bedside clock. "Well, you get some sleep. I'll be back by dinner tomorrow night."

"Having a good time?"

Brenna thought about the day's events. "Yeah, it's been a good day. Next weekend ought to be even more fun, though."

"Yeah. You know...Did Ms. Hyland ever get what she needed from that store?"

Brenna frowned. "I have no idea."

"Well, we've got lots of stuff. If she needs something, she can just borrow it."

"They could share with us." Her lips quirked in a smile. "Always room for one more in a tent."

"Yeah."

"You get some sleep. I love you," she told him. "Tell Thomas I called."

"I will. We're fine. Really. Stop worrying."

"Don't deny me my ulcer, okay?" she said with a laugh, hearing him laugh in return. "Better. Now, good night."

Still chuckling, he replied, "Good night," and disconnected.

Energized, Brenna rolled onto her back and sat up. *It's too cool for a swim, but maybe...Yeah.* On light feet, Brenna left the bed, changed into a pair of shorts and tee shirt, and headed downstairs to hunt up the rec room. Maybe after a light workout she could get some sleep.

CHAPTER EIGHTEEN

ON MONDAY the set overflowed with activity. Pinnacle had granted press passes to dozens of media outlets for interviews with the cast and crew about the final season of *Time Trails*. Seeing that everyone on the set for the morning shooting was already present amid the chaos, Brenna Lanigan strode into the menagerie with an undaunted smile. She waved to Terry Brown, already in full costume and makeup. He was being questioned by a bored-looking interviewer, and Brenna hoped the copy eventually proved kinder than the reporter's expression portended. She caught Terry's eye and offered a thumbs up before ducking around the corner.

"You look like you already had your morning coffee," Will Chapman commented, slipping into his chair as the head of makeup, Brent Eastland, shook out a hairdresser's cape and secured it around his neck.

Brenna shook her head and laughed. "I had a chance to eat with Thomas and James this morning before taking them to school."

Will nodded and closed his eyes. Eastland applied his base and watched carefully as Brenna applied her own. "You don't have many scenes to run through today."

"Stunts with the second unit, then interviews." In the mirror, she saw a reporter peering in the doorway, an elaborate 35mm slung over her shoulder. "And here's the first one," she said softly. She turned in the chair and greeted the woman by rising slightly and holding out her hand.

"Melissa Peregrine, *Sci-Fi* magazine. Ms. Lanigan?"

"We can talk as long as you can keep up," she allowed, using Jakes' all-business inflection. "I have thirty minutes before I'm due on set."

"Yes, ma'am."

She caught the younger woman's straightening shoulders behind her in the mirror and touched up her base to hide her amusement. *God, I do love making them jump.*

Peregrine started off with a question that Brenna expected. "You're coming to the end of five years with your character. What's changed most about Susan Jakes?"

"You have to know where she started. I think initially the producers were concerned whether the show would fly with the commander being a woman. They were concerned about a woman being able to project authority," Brenna mused. "Once I was established, I think they took a deep breath and, after watching the dailies and watching this character evolve through me, they have pretty much entrusted her to me. They've let the woman in the commander come out, more fully integrating her. I think they discovered women really do lead differently than men."

Will nodded as he pulled off his smock. "In the long run, we've benefited from having a female in charge. The dynamic has been risky, but it paid off, I think. Brenna's a big reason why."

Brenna flushed, and when Will leaned over, she kissed his cheek. "Jakes is philosophical, but she's also capable of taking great ~ and occasionally questionable ~ risks."

"Only occasionally?" Will quipped. "I don't know about that. But questionable? I'll certainly second that." He was laughing as he left.

Brenna turned back to Peregrine. "While she has always been a devoted commander, over the five seasons Jakes has evolved. I think she's more relaxed, more confident. I don't think that confidence was really there at the start, just the potential for it. However, she's seen her toughest decisions result in incredible goodness. Her team is a family, with her as the matriarch, with all that entails about mutual respect and love. Regarding the 'dangers' of time, she's more thoughtful, more reflective."

"Will Jakes go down in history as one of the greats?"

"Unquestionably, she will. It has taken me a long time to understand her influence, and mine, as a role model."

"Is that the biggest achievement of Brenna Lanigan ~ to let people know that women can do anything they set their mind to?"

"I've taken my influence on young women seriously. I've tried to be vigilant about it, to share as much as I can of myself and my philosophy with them so that they understand that the sky's the limit."

The two left Makeup; their voices softened as they neared one of the soundstages. Peregrine prodded, "How has it been as an actor? Seventeen-hour days for the birds?"

"The work has clearly been a once-in-a-lifetime opportunity. I will always treasure the relationships I've developed in this foxhole."

"That sounds like you've been in the trenches of a war zone."

"Trenches?" She contemplated the intensities of filming. "That's a good metaphor."

"So when the series is over, do you expect to suffer post-traumatic stress?"

"That kind of let-down is very specialized, so I'd have to say no. I've left other jobs before..." Brenna gave her answer some thought. "But this one is special."

The reporter looked at her in puzzlement. "Aren't all roles 'special' until the next one comes along? What do you see happening after this?"

Passing the warehouse set, Brenna did not answer the question but stopped and listened to the actors' exchange.

Chris was trying to get Creighton to believe he wasn't insane and that she would get him out before the lynch mob got there. Brenna listened to Cassidy's voice, rounded by Hanssen's careful diction ~ caring while being simultaneously urgent. Mindful of the fact that sound levels were very sensitive, Brenna caught Cassidy's eye across the distance and mouthed, "Nice job," and smiled broadly before ducking her head and walking out of view.

The action surprised Cassidy and she stumbled over her next line, causing a break in the action. A grip checked their poses, and Cassidy once again grasped Creighton's arm and delivered her line. As soon as the director called cut, she left the set and followed Brenna. She held her breath, watching Brenna perform her own stunt for a chase through a darkened building.

Standing next to Peregrine, Cassidy focused her eyes on a catwalk over the stage. Rushing forward, Brenna limberly vaulted the railing and dropped about eight feet, the fall being filmed in front of an aqua green screen. Post-production would make the drop look like a considerably greater distance. When Brenna finally rolled to her feet and Cassidy could draw breath, the young woman flashed a thumbs up before ducking away.

Brenna chuckled as she caught her breath. She looked up at the collection of stunt actors that had been chasing her and flashed them the same thumbs up. "Good work, Brenna," called the second unit director. "Ready to do it again for the reverse shot?"

"Again?" She groaned in disbelief. The evil look she shot at the director prompted laughter from somewhere beyond the lights. Shielding her eyes, Brenna identified Rachelle leaning casually against a set wall . "You want to do this?" She gestured to her position. "Come on. I'm sure a wig'll be enough to let you pass as me from behind!"

"I'm smaller than you," Rachelle shot back, chuckling.

"Not many people can say that." Brenna laughed and stepped off the soundstage toward Rachelle. She found herself next to Cassidy, who had returned with a bottle of water she offered to Brenna. With a grin she took a healthy gulp just as they were cornered by the *Sci-Fi* reporter.

"Are you hoping for any particular developments before things completely wrap?" Peregrine asked, catching Brenna's attention again.

Brenna passed back the water bottle with a mouthed "thank you" to Cassidy before answering. "I'd like to see some of the interpersonal stories wrapped up." She nodded toward the nearby set. "I think we've certainly discovered that messing around with time, even if you have completely altruistic reasons, doesn't let people really *live*. I mean if someone can come along, a grandchild maybe, and arrange it so that his grandfather doesn't just not die in the battle but becomes a decorated hero, it diminishes the sense of success in the ordinary trials of life. That young man isn't living *his* life, he's living someone else's."

"So you don't think Susan Jakes has been one of the good gals?" Peregrine asked.

"Oh, undoubtedly, but it hasn't been because of things she's done with the timeline. Her real contribution has been how she's affected the people she met."

"Jakes certainly did a lot to reshape Chris' outlook on both the Time Squad's mission and her own life," Cassidy interjected. "She was not exactly a fan when they first met."

"And vice versa. Susan likes a tight team, and Chris did her best to be outside of that most of the time," Brenna pointed out, catching Cassidy's hand as it swept across her shoulder.

Looking up from her pad, Peregrine asked, "What are biggest issues that remain for Commander Jakes?"

"The characters have grown, but we haven't managed to reveal much of that in close scenes. There's always so much action..." Brenna hesitated, trying to find the best way to explain. The squeeze of Cassidy's hand on her shoulder gave her a moment of peaceful clarity. She smiled and looked back at Peregrine. "It's hard to say, other than Luria and Jeremy, whether any of these characters would want to stay together if the Time Squad were to lose its mandate."

Cameron Palassis leaned in around a corner. "Heard chatter. Interview?"

"Mr. Palassis, I'm Melissa Peregrine, *Sci-Fi* magazine. What sort of stories do you have on tap? The kind Ms. Lanigan was describing?"

"It's an action show. There's at least one last big showdown coming. A familiar enemy will reappear." Cameron shook his finger at Brenna, and she frowned.

Peregrine caught the reaction and jumped on it. "Not thrilled?"

"If the action has a science fiction heart, it's all right. But stories have to have emotional connection to the audience. And the characters have to mean something to each other. We have what amounts to six lonely characters. A few recent episodes explore what they are like inside when they are out of the uniforms. I like Susan. I think we should give the audience a sense that these characters will live beyond 'the end'."

Cassidy pressed Brenna's shoulder and grinned toward Peregrine. "Triumphant into the sunset."

"With a threat or an unsettlement looming."

"In other words, an opening for a movie plot." With another grin, the tall blonde squeezed Brenna's shoulder, and the smaller woman reached up and squeezed back.

Clearly sensing something from the two women, Peregrine asked a more directly pertinent question. "What of Hanssen's dedication to Time Squad? From rogue ne'er-do-well to respected officer. Jakes has had a definite hand in that."

"Hanssen's almost all the way in, I think," Cassidy said quickly. "All that remains, I guess, is for her to believe in the value of her own life as much as she has believed in that of others."

"Jakes could help her with that," Brenna added. "It's one way to show how their relationship has matured ~ her progression from stern leader to friend."

Peregrine tapped her pad with her pen. "I'm seeing a friendship between the two of you. Which, if rumor is to be believed, is quite a change. Things weren't easy on the set when you first arrived, Ms. Hyland."

"No," Brenna admitted before Cassidy could speak. "It was...a very uncertain time." She cast a wry glance at the blonde, who nodded in understanding. "As actors, we're thrown together in many situations that can force revelations of ourselves, maybe even parts we don't like and never share with anyone else willingly. It's a pressure cooker. Adding new ingredients upset the whole balance."

"And now?"

"From the beginning, Chris and Susan weren't set to be friends." Brenna looked at Cassidy, recalling some of their conflicts. She wondered if she could ever make up for some of it. She felt she wanted to say more as her gaze intersected Cassidy's. Hesitating over exactly what to say, she suddenly heard Peregrine's pen scratching on pad. Brenna jerked back to the reporter. "But that's the nature of the beast," Brenna concluded quickly. She disregarded the shiver that ran down her spine at Cassidy's smile.

Clearly frustrated by the half-response, Peregrine asked a more direct question. "Would you work together again?"

"I'm game." Cassidy smiled.

"Maybe after a *short* break." Brenna shook her head. "I need to find more time for my personal life. I haven't managed it very well."

"Do you like Ms. Hyland's suggestion about a movie?"

"Not right away. I'd like to do a play, maybe. But I want to just take some time. I'd like to give my time, my heart, and my life to my loved ones." She looked toward Cassidy, who slowly let out a breath.

"We'd all like that, I think," Cassidy said. She nodded and left for her set.

"I'd like to be little Brenna Lanigan for a while, remember who she was. Jakes has become bigger than life. At least bigger than my life."

"Everyone's smaller than the bigger-than-life Commander Jakes," Will said, stepping out from behind the opposite wall from where he apparently had been watching. Surprised, Brenna caught the teasing in his tone and put her hands on her hips, smiling as she saw another camera flash go off.

The interview was concluded when the director called Brenna back for a second take. Pulling herself up an access ladder behind the set wall, she stepped back out onto the catwalk. The stunt actors crowded just off the walk behind her, and the second unit director called, "Action!"

One breath, then a second, and Brenna bounded forward, grasped the railing, and threw herself over. She was thankful for her rock-climbing experience, which had cleared her of any inhibitions or vertigo. Once down on the ground, she remained sacked out on the air mattress, arms splayed and eyes closed, waiting until her heart started again and the director called, "Cut."

Stagehands pulled away the mattress, and she took her mark directly beneath her jump point and completed filming the end of the jump. On cue, she crouched, then stood. Spinning clockwise, she ran off stage left, ducking imaginary attacks from above.

She ran into Cameron coming around a corner of the soundstage. The two tumbled together until she could recover her feet. "Sorry," she said, reaching down and grasping his hand to haul him up. More flashes went off, and she sighed.

Cameron dusted himself off and straightened his pants and oxford shirt. "Having a good time?"

"Just dandy," she drawled. "If you have a chance later, maybe you could explain about the big returning enemy you dropped like a rock in my interview."

"The ideas are only just beginning to form. A lot of the staff is working on it." He glanced up and spied Branch, who was also mingling with off-set cast and crew. He waved to him. "Victor?"

"Yeah?" The producer offered Brenna a smile; she nodded back. "What's up?" He directed the question at Palassis.

"Are we set with the finale yet?" Cameron asked.

"Of course not."

Cameron turned back to Brenna. "We'll cover a lot of ground over the next several episodes, Brenna. Those interpersonal relationships you were talking about? They'll get covered."

"Ms. Lanigan?" A set grip located her standing between the two taller men. "You're needed on your mark."

"Thanks." She glanced at Cameron, offering a final word concerning the one thing that had continued to bother her since the previous week. "Listen, I don't know what Chapman asked you to do, but I want you to reconsider. For Cassidy's sake." She returned to the soundstage, setting for another angle on the stunt shot.

Cameron frowned and then sighed. "I guess she overheard."

"Funny that she'd come to Hyland's defense like that, though," Victor commented. "Certainly a lot of changes in the last several weeks."

"Yeah." Cameron ruminated on it for a moment longer and then looked around. "Have you seen Cass?"

"Just came from there. She's back on the set. She was in Lanigan's interview for a while," Victor said with a shrug. "You sure you want to talk to her right now?"

"Damn straight."

As Branch watched Palassis stalk off, Will Chapman walked up, patting his sweating face carefully with a soft towel. "What's with him?"

Branch shook his head. "Brenna and he squared off about something. Finale, I think. But there's something else going on with him. I wish to hell I knew what. He can't even manage to concentrate on the new series pilot at the moment."

"Really?" Will raised an eyebrow in question.

Seeing Cameron leaning against a set break watching the soundstage where Cassidy was among the filming cast, Branch confided, "Cassidy's got him not knowing if he's coming or going, and I don't think she knows it."

"She doesn't," Will said, patting Branch on the shoulder. "But I'll change that."

CHAPTER NINETEEN

CASSIDY COMPLETED her stunt and heard the second unit director call, "Cut." She stood and stretched to the little extent she could. Though the dress was less binding than her Time Squad jumpsuit, it was still a dress. *Like those women detectives in the TV shows in the 80s who ran after crooks in high heels because some studio execs felt that sneakers were too "manly."* She sighed.

Despite the wall of activity that separated her senses from what was happening in the off-stage area, Cassidy got the distinct impression she was being watched. She tried to shrug it off. It was a curious reporter, perhaps. But the sensation persisted, and she turned, aware of a flutter as she hoped to see a specific face. She stifled a surprisingly strong wave of disappointment when she spied Cameron leaning against a set wall. Hoping the lighting angle concealed her response, Cassidy looked around once, still hoping to spy Brenna. She slowly stepped down from the slightly elevated decking of the soundstage.

"Hi, Cass." Cameron crossed the three steps separating them and grasped her arms just above the elbows, leaning forward with obvious intent to kiss her.

Cassidy could not put her finger on why the attention felt wrong, but she was uneasy as she broke off the touch of their lips.

Cameron lightly squeezed her elbows ~ *a warning?* ~ then dropped his hands. His smile was forced, surprising her and causing her a little alarm. His voice came over the uneven thudding of her heart.

"I thought we could talk over a late lunch," he said. "You don't have another set call today. Wanna go someplace off site?"

"I have interviews." She intently watched his expression, which only twitched briefly, adding to her confusion.

His composure broke slightly as they moved aside to allow a stagehand bearing props to pass. Struggling to regroup, he smiled suddenly. "What about this weekend? We could take Ryan and go up the coast, maybe to Napa. I..." His voice trailed off as he shrugged.

Cassidy sipped in a breath slowly and let it out just as carefully. Cameron took a step back. "It sounds like that would be a nice trip." She had a previous commitment which she preferred to keep. "But Ryan and I already have plans."

Cameron straightened and, though he wasn't an imposing figure, she had to quell the dismay roiling in her stomach. His gaze narrowed, and she fought her impulse to look away. Cameron seldom was ever truly angry with her, an appealing trait after the white-hot flash point that had been Mitch.

Cameron's voice was low and deliberate. "Where?"

"I told you we had a camping trip."

"When?"

"This weekend."

"No. When did you tell me?"

She searched her mind for a date reference, then answered, "Two, maybe three weeks ago. Do you remember when Mitch called me at work? That night."

He looked puzzled for a long moment, then shook his head. "Well, would you like some company? Maybe I could go with you."

Cassidy shook her head. "Cameron, you couldn't stand having that many kids around."

After a moment, he nodded. "When do you leave?" His tone was flat.

"Saturday at dawn."

"Dawn. When will you be back?" Cameron was squeezing his hands repeatedly.

"Look, I have to go." Filled with unease, Cassidy backed away. When he remained focused on her, she looked away, ostensibly adjusting the fit of her costume. She spotted a reporter standing about five feet away, patiently waiting for his interview. Thankful for a reason to cut short their exchange, Cassidy called, "I'm ready."

The reporter was a thin man in his mid- to late-thirties, with dark hair; his smile was clearly admiring. "Any place you'd prefer to do this?" He stepped back to let her move away first. As she passed Cameron, she felt the reporter's notepad gently touch against her lower back.

Behind her, Cameron stalked away.

Cassidy tried to relax, but Will was edging into her personal space at the conference table. Still, she had to admit he was interjecting supportive additions to her answers to the reporter's questions. The reporter had already, in her opinion, covered the typical questions. The appearance of her co-star fueled a change in the direction. One she hadn't expected.

"Do you think your character has made any connections with the other team members? Do they still resent being bunked with a screw-up?"

"Resentment? No, I...think we've gotten past that." Cassidy caught a raised eyebrow from Will and added, "With most of them."

"Definitely with Commander Jakes," Will injected.

He caught her eye, and Cassidy thought there was a message there she was supposed to catch. She frowned and dropped her head briefly, aware of a heat in her cheeks. When she had controlled it, she looked up. "There has been a different edge between Jakes and Hanssen as they're working out their differences or at least coming to an understanding. I've learned a lot working with everyone, but Brenna in particular. She's ~"

The reporter's follow up interrupted Cassidy's thought. "Why do you think that is?"

Will supplied the answer. "Female bonding. Audiences eat it up. It's closed out nearly all the males."

He shoved off the table, the intensity of the maneuver startling Cassidy. Her chest tightened at his abrupt and dismissive tone. *Damn.* She had finally begun to feel part of the company, with the banter, the lunches, and the clincher, Brenna's openness in talking with her. She didn't want to lose that.

"Will, wait." She pushed to her feet, waving the reporter to stay seated. "Wait here," she commanded sharply. Will turned. She looked into his features. In a low voice she asked, "What is wrong with you?"

"What?"

His exclamation was muted, in deference to her own lowered voice, she guessed. "I..." She searched for words. "Why are you being like this?" It sounded petulant even to her ears, but she hoped for an answer.

"It's no secret."

"I can't change the scripts," she replied sharply. "I try to be part of the team, but you're making no effort at all."

"You can't change things, but he can." Will's accusation accompanied a glare directed somewhere over Cassidy's left shoulder. Turning, she jumped when she saw Cameron only a few feet away. "Right, Cameron?" Will's tone was baiting.

"What?"

"Hanssen and Raycreek would make a good match, don't you think?"

Though the question had been posed casually, Cassidy could see Will's eyes harden. A focused glare nailed Cameron as he walked up.

Cameron did not look away from the challenge. He snapped, "No, I don't think so."

Cassidy flinched. "Cam, I ~"

"Stay out of this," he told her sharply. He turned back to Chapman, shoving a finger in the bigger man's face. "Stop your bellyaching. There's auditions going on right down the street." He waved in a gesture of "out there." "You can walk away anytime."

Stung by Cameron's sharp dismissal, Cassidy watched silently as Will straightened to his full height and crossed his arms over his chest. His expression was supremely confident.. Standing firm in the face of Cameron's fury, which was washing off the writer in almost visible waves, Chapman suddenly appeared mountain-like. Immovable. Granite hard. The smile he wore promised unpleasantness. She tried again. "Will..."

He glanced at her briefly, only shaking his head before returning his gaze to Palassis. "I don't like being window dressing," he said. "Scenes with Cassidy could change that."

"You will never touch her," Cameron shot back. "Never."

Suddenly Brenna was pushing between the two men. She did not touch either one, but awareness of her presence diverted them from their enmity.

Looking up at one then the other, Brenna warned, "Not here. Not now." The rest of the reporters swung their attentions toward the tense group. "I don't give a damn what your differences are, but you can't do this here!"

"Did you know they're saying you're gay, Cassidy?" Will blurted. "They say you'd rather have Jakes than Raycreek."

Cameron became incensed. "The fans are always making up some kind of crap. Fuck that and fuck you. Come on. Let's get out of here." He stepped toward Cassidy, his body rigid, angry. Brenna stepped back to remain between them.

Thanks to Cameron's own talks with her about Mitch's behavior, Cassidy recognized the signs of impending violence. "No," she said sharply. Thanks to her restroom encounter, she had an idea of what was fueling the rumors, but she wanted to hear more. "I want to know why they're saying I'm gay. Just because Luria kissed what appeared to be Chris?"

"Even before that."

Cameron fumed. "Come on."

"Because the number of scenes you have with any male can be counted on one hand. Or they're your father figure, like Dr. Pryor."

"But the storylines..."

"And who do you think writes the damn storylines? This jackass who thinks you're too hot to be on the same set with most of us. Who thinks we'd lust after you."

"Cameron?"

"I am not letting him get his hands on you."

"Excuse me? Cameron, they're co-workers. I...What's wrong with..." Cassidy found no words to express herself, leaning into Brenna, looking from one man to another as if both had escaped from an asylum.

"I'm protecting you!"

Cassidy recoiled from his vehemence. Clearly defeated by that single reaction, Cameron threw up his hands, then shoved a finger into Chapman's chest. "Fine. You want scenes, Mr. Macho, you got 'em." He cursed and pushed through several reporters on his way out.

Cassidy and Brenna held their breath as Cameron stormed off. Abruptly, and still keyed for violence, Cassidy sank into the nearest chair and dropped her head into her hands.

Brenna pushed into Chapman's personal space. "I never figured you for such a bastard," she said harshly. "That was completely uncalled for."

He pursed his lips, looking in the direction Cameron had gone before responding coolly, "It was a bit more of a dust-up than I had figured on, but it worked. He showed his true colors." Turning away, he strode toward the edge of the set.

Hurting for Cassidy, Brenna spat after him, "So did you." Will paused at the edge of the set and gave her a look she could not interpret, eyes narrowing almost angrily, then just as abruptly he shrugged and resumed walking away.

Confused but pushing him from her mind for the moment, Brenna turned and grasped Cassidy's shoulder. Rich, who had walked into the mess without warning, now stood absolutely frozen. Converging from the other direction was a sea of reporters, microphones, pads, and pens at the ready and asking loud questions.

"Rich, run interference." Brenna nodded toward the press.

He looked from her to Cassidy, who was trying to hide her face in her hands. "Uh. Sure." He drew the reporters after him with promises of sneak previews. Smartly he played off the entire scene as a rehearsal, insisting it was all part of the storylines coming up. "If you'll come with me, there's more on another set for you to see."

There were grumbles as Brenna continued to "act" concerned over Cassidy who had seemingly withdrawn in shock. Finally when the reporters were on the other side of a closed door, she squeezed Cassidy's shoulder. The blonde started.

Brenna kept her voice low, to soothe Cassidy as well as not be overheard. "It's all right. You needed an out. I just made you one."

Rising to her feet, Cassidy inhaled shakily. "I have never been so humiliated." Her baffled voice caught on the question. "He's demanding I do a scene with him just to prove Chris isn't gay?"

"I used to think Will was just a harmless, bored actor," Brenna admitted as Cassidy eased out of the chair. "But that was purely self-serving."

"It's not really like it is even today's news. I had heard rumors; I just didn't put a lot of stock in them." Cassidy reminded, "You also mentioned something from the convention in Vegas."

Brenna flushed. "I...Well, how would Chapman have heard? I...didn't talk about it."

Cassidy shrugged and exhaled. "I don't know. I don't want to think about the numbers game, politics, any of it. I wish I wasn't here right now."

Brenna caught Cassidy's shoulders and ushered her gently toward the exit. "Let's get you out of here, at least." They walked together out the back of the soundstage, looking around cautiously for unwelcome press before they locked themselves in Cassidy's trailer.

Anxious to be gone, Cassidy pushed the gown off one shoulder and struggled to pull it off. She had trouble with a catch and tried to force it. Brenna's hands closed over her fidgeting ones. Cassidy met a sympathetic expression, and her adrenaline shock faded, giving way to tears.

"Relax," Brenna whispered. "You'll need that costume for the scenes you have to shoot tomorrow. It's not the dress that you're mad at."

Cassidy drew a ragged breath. She finished the buttons and turned around. Brenna tugged the bodice off her other shoulder, and her fingers momentarily touched bare skin. Cassidy shivered and dropped her head. "Thank you." She hoped Brenna understood her gratitude was not only for the help with her costume.

"You're welcome."

The inflection promised Cassidy that Brenna knew what she had meant. She lifted her eyes in time to see Brenna lean away and snap up a loose tee shirt.

"Here."

With a quick pull, Cassidy was covered again. Then she dropped to her couch, laid back, and covered her face to compose herself. Brenna perched on the edge of the cushion next to her, resting a hand on Cassidy's thigh. "Take a deep breath. It's over."

Dropping her hands and opening her eyes, Cassidy looked for forgiveness. "Brenna, I'm so sorry. I hate scenes. I can't believe he did that. I should tell Cameron—"

"Don't take any of this on yourself. Cameron is the one who should apologize. Instead he stormed off to do God knows what. Hell, for that matter, Will needs to make a trip to a confessional," she said quietly. "All you've ever done is your best with what we're given ~ Cameron's writing, whatever motivates it. You've done a remarkable job, making what could have been a flat character very appealing." Cassidy was silent, but Brenna easily read surprise on the expressive features.

"Do you think so?"

"Yeah, I do." Brenna smiled gently and patted her leg. Registering warm skin beneath her palm, she realized that Cassidy was not fully dressed. Moving her hand reluctantly away from the smooth muscle, she spoke quickly to cover the moment. "You'd better finish getting dressed."

"Brenna, I..." As she started to her feet again, Cassidy's face loomed close, her eyes filling Brenna's world for a long and breathless moment. "Cameron and I are through." She had no idea why she felt the need to say it, but she knew she wanted Brenna to know.

Brenna abruptly turned away. "Go home. Get some distance from this. Get some sleep."

"What about the reporters?" Cassidy pushed to her feet.

Despite the butterflies flying through her stomach, Brenna was calmly reassuring. "Check the *Variety* copy in the morning." She brushed Cassidy's arm. Brenna drew Cassidy's warm hand to her chest. "There won't be a word about this." Cassidy looked dubiously at the door. "I promise," Brenna said, drawing the woman against her. She put her arm around Cassidy's back. "I don't want dozens of reporters following us into the mountains this weekend." She leaned back and smiled uncertainly into turbulent green-blue. "That is...if you still want to go."

Cassidy took a deep breath and smiled back. "Yes, I still do."

CHAPTER TWENTY

THE SUNRISE was a sea of golds and reds on the eastern horizon when Cassidy pulled into Brenna's driveway Saturday morning. Her headlights illuminated the other woman, flanked by her sons. All three wore jeans and hiking boots. Brenna had her hands on her hips and a welcoming smile on her face. It was a unique sensation Cassidy felt, as though the rest of the world were already far away. As soon as she turned off her engine, Brenna was at her door, grasping the handle, and looking down at her over the side. The expectant expression made her concerned. "I'm not late, am I?"

"Not too bad," Brenna replied, closing the door after Cassidy emerged. She glanced into the back seat. Soundly sleeping, Ryan was tucked among the bags in the back. "Why don't you get a cup of coffee? I'll move Ryan, and Thomas'll put your stuff into the back."

"Thanks." Wearing her own jeans and trailblazer boots, Cassidy stretched and then rubbed her face tiredly. "You mentioned coffee?"

"On the kitchen counter. Go on inside." Brenna gestured to the house, then leaned into the car.

Cassidy did not move immediately for the house. She watched nervously as Brenna pulled Ryan's limp form against her chest. Absently, Brenna pressed her lips to his hair, and Cassidy swallowed, aware of a surge of warmth that washed through her. Undoubtedly thinking herself unseen, Brenna allowed a fond smile to brighten her expressive face as she moved Cassidy's son to the backseat of her own vehicle.

The emphatic sense of caring from her friend warmed Cassidy immensely. She had done the same with Cassidy over the last week. Not a whiff of the confrontation had appeared in any news source. At work Brenna kept close tabs on her and even listened in on interviews, ready to provide a diversion if the subject arose.

For her part, Cassidy had spent much of the week evaluating a variety of things. Her relationship with Cameron was at an end. She had not seen him once on the set since the mid-morning break when she told him they were through.

Thoughts scattered from the topsy-turvy week, she entered Brenna's kitchen and was drawn immediately to the fragrant smell of coffee. She poured some into a mug she found upside down next to the maker.

The break with Cameron had been coming for a while. Will's public lambasting of the writer had only made the propitious moment appear. Cassidy liked spending time with Ryan; Cameron had never wanted children. She preferred socializing with a small group; he preferred public venues such as conventions, premieres, and awards ceremonies. Then there had been the little things, things Cass now realized she had glossed over. He also had not bothered to attend Ryan's party or bring him a present.

She sipped the coffee thoughtfully. *Now that's just petty. But then,* she castigated herself, *you were far from perfect, too.* She thought about all the times she had declined his dinner invitations because of a late work schedule or an early set call the next morning. Resentment had been inevitable, she realized, as they both continually were not there for one another.

There was something else, too, she realized. Over the last several weeks, she had begun to regain a sense of purpose and self-determination that had apparently been subverted, first by Mitch and then by a well-meaning Cameron. She took another sip, nodding to herself.

Cassidy leaned on her elbows on the counter, eyes surveying the interior of her colleague's home. The furnishings were elegant but practical, and they energized the room with vibrant color and texture, much as Brenna herself effortlessly did in any space she occupied.

She moved to the back, looking out on the yard, noting the gardens and a deck that looked new. The dominant furniture was an A-frame wooden swing that made Cassidy think of lazy Missouri summer nights. She leaned against the wall, sipping her coffee and studying the dew-draped trees.

"Like it?"

Brenna's voice drew Cassidy around to see the other woman unconsciously mimicking her pose ~ hip perched against the entry to the kitchen as she gazed toward the taller woman. She straightened but was caught and held by a pair of smiling blue eyes. "The coffee's delicious. Thank you. You have a fabulous view from here, too."

Brenna let out a breath she had apparently been holding and

straightened as well.

This isn't Hanssen and Jakes, Cassidy thought, even as she found conflicting signals rushing through her body and her skin tingled. She finished the coffee, more to have something to do than out of any need for the fortification of the caffeine. Brenna walked up alongside her and gazed out on the horizon as well. The woman's presence offered warmth that Cassidy found hard not to move toward. *Why do I feel like Hanssen when she's about to do something reckless?*

"The boys have finished moving everything." Brenna's voice was quiet, as though she were distracted.

"Is it a long drive?"

Brenna's shoulders moved in a shrug. "Couple of hours."

Cassidy felt the tightness in her chest slowly unfurl, spreading warm tendrils through her arms and legs. "I'm looking forward to putting L.A. behind us."

Pouring the rest of the coffee into an insulated bottle, Brenna nodded with a smile that intrigued Cassidy. "Me, too. Let's go."

Brenna pressed the remote to open her garage door and watched in her rear view as the blonde drove into the shadowed recesses. They were storing Cassidy's car in the Lanigan garage for the weekend. Brenna closed the garage and waited for Cassidy to get into the front passenger seat and secure her belt. "Everyone set?" Finding Cassidy's gaze on her, Brenna covered the tightness in her throat by turning around and looking at the three boys in the back seat. Ryan still slept, his head resting in Thomas' lap and his feet on James' knees. Brenna's eldest shifted carefully to avoid disturbing Ryan as he made sure the boy's seat belt was secure.

"All set," Thomas responded.

She caught Cassidy's nod and put the Mountaineer into gear. "Then we're off."

The pre-dawn lighting was peaceful, and for a while silence settled among the group as Brenna concentrated. Once they were on the highway headed north out of the valley and into the foothills, Brenna reached for a CD from her glove box. The motion was a little blind as she focused her gaze on the road at the same time.

"What are you looking for?" Cassidy asked.

Straightening up, Brenna offered sheepishly, "I thought a little music?"

"Tell me what you want, and I'll get it for you. I don't mind."

"The CDs are in the glove box." Brenna shot a quick look at her passenger. She wondered what Cassidy would think of her music collection. "I...Well, see if there's something you like."

She felt their age difference acutely at that moment. Cassidy thumbed through the titles, but she was keeping her opinions of the selection to herself. Brenna worried nervously at her bottom lip as she returned both hands to the wheel. Certainly the thirty-year-old wouldn't have the same tastes. Brenna was more than ten years her senior. She glanced into the rear-view mirror to recheck her position amid the light morning highway traffic.

She held her breath as Cassidy slid a CD from its case, into the player, and adjusted the forward speaker volume. Curiosity changed to surprise when Brenna heard the opening promenade of an original cast recording of *Allura*. She had caught the obscure musical during a trip last year to New York City.

Cassidy adjusted the volume again, raising it to catch the voices of the singers. "I've never heard this," she ventured.

"It's a something I caught on stage last year. I had a chance to speak with the producer afterward, and I asked for a recording."

"What's the play about?" Cassidy leaned back with her elbow in the window, head resting in her palm, gaze fixed on Brenna.

"It's a love story between a dancer and his partner."

"Period or modern?"

"Period. 1920s," Brenna said.

"Like our last story. So, was it accurate?"

"More or less."

"What drew you to see it?"

"The lead actor was a classmate of mine in high school."

"Really?"

Brenna nodded. "We were...an item, I guess, and worked in all the drama productions together, went to Homecoming and Prom together. That sort of thing."

"So you went to see him in his first Broadway play?"

"Oh no, not his first, but the first I'd seen, yes. He and I were both stage struck. He has been in New York since we were eighteen. He got steady work; I didn't. After leaving a soap, I drifted away from New York, bitten by the big-screen bug. I came to L.A."

"Do you want to go back?"

Brenna nodded solemnly. "Someday. Maybe after *Time Trails* is finished, I'll find an apartment in New York and try my luck again."

"I have no doubt you'll make it." Cassidy smiled, her hand covering Brenna's on the gearshift for a moment.

"You think so?"

"I've seen you act, remember?" Cassidy chuckled.

Brenna's smile returned. She pulled her hand from beneath Cassidy's and brushed her hair from her face as she chuckled, too. "What are you going to do?"

"When *Time Trails* is over?" Cassidy dropped her head and studied her hands in her lap. "I haven't had any offers yet. But," she added quietly, "I really haven't been looking."

"Because of Cameron?"

"Yes."

"I'm really sorry about how things turned out."

"Don't be. He's just...We didn't have the same priorities."

"That makes it hard to make a relationship work," Brenna acknowledged, feeling guilty about not speaking with Kevin in over a week.

"The hours. The pace." Cassidy sighed. "Why do we do it?"

"Because we love those hours, that hectic pace," Brenna responded with a wry twist to her lips. "Thomas knows." She glanced over her shoulder and asked with a smile, "Don't you?"

"Mom's a nut case less than a month into hiatus," Thomas provided, which made Cassidy laugh. "Short vacations are okay, a weekend here or there, but longer than a couple of weeks and she's climbing the walls. She built the deck last summer."

Cassidy laughed again. "Handywoman, huh?"

"My set-building days left me with a few skills," Brenna supplied with a blush.

"I'd say so. I saw the deck and that swing. Nice work."

Brenna was warmed by the compliment. She dwelled on it for a few moments, almost missing their turn off. At the last possible opportunity, she changed highways, heading more east than north.

When they arrived at the park entrance, Brenna displayed their pass and was waved inside. The ranger gestured them forward. "Follow the road ahead. Parking for the hiking trail to the campground is the second one on your left."

"Thanks," Brenna told him, then pulled away from the station.

"You really do come here a lot," Cassidy commented as they drove into the park.

"Yes, we do." Brenna rolled up her window and looked in the rear view, noticing Ryan had finally stirred. "Just in time," she said with a smile, reaching back between the seats to tickle a sock-covered foot.

Cassidy leaned between the seats and brushed his hair smooth. "Sleep well, buddy?"

He nodded. "Could I have juice?"

"You're thirsty?" James asked. The youngster's blue eyes lifted quickly to the dark-haired teen, and he nodded. "Mom, is it all right if I pull one of the juice pouches for him?"

Brenna deferred to Cassidy. "It's all-natural."

"That's fine, thanks," Cassidy said. "It'll help him wake up."

"That's what I thought," Brenna replied as she pulled into the lot. Parking, she looked around and spotted Mike Connell, the charity director. "Looks like we aren't the first."

Brenna tossed her keys to Thomas while she went to catch Mike's attention. "Good morning."

Connell was a tall, spare man with brown eyes, curly brown hair, and a face worn from years in the sun. He wore a wide-brimmed hat and a leather jacket over what was really a skydiver's jumpsuit. "Hey, Brenna."

"Thomas is here," she said before he could ask. The two of them were conducting the central attraction of the weekend ~ a rock climb up a fifty-foot rock face. "I wanted to introduce you to a friend first." She waved Cassidy over. The blonde had the hiking pack half on when Thomas spotted his mother beckoning and quickly helped her finish.

"I remember her from the Halloween party," Mike noted, holding out his hand and shaking Cassidy's. "Good to see you again, Miss Hyland."

"Cassidy, please." She shifted awkwardly under the weight, and Mike reached back and held the pack's support beam above her head while she adjusted the balance. "Thanks."

Brenna watched the woman push her hands through tousled blond hair and swallowed against her suddenly dry mouth when the blue eyes met hers briefly. *She looks relaxed. That's good, right?* Brenna had worked hard the last week to keep news of the blowup from leaking out and was pleased to see that her efforts had paid off. Seeing the way Cassidy had been torn up by being thrust into Will and Cameron's pissing match, she had needed to do something. She dragged her attention away from Cassidy, where it was straying far too often. "How far to the campsite?"

"Second change in the tree line," Mike supplied. "About an hour up the side. It's not too steep and a pretty basic hike. It will put us next to the feeder spring and just below the rock face we're climbing tomorrow."

"Sounds good." Brenna shook his hand again and returned to the car and efficiently secured her own backpack. Primal energy flowed through her as she adjusted the belly strap. "Thomas, how are you doing?" She glanced toward her sons and found both Thomas and James already wearing their packs, kneeling next to Ryan.

"I want one!" the little boy pouted.

Cassidy started forward, but Brenna grasped her hand, stopping her.

"They'll find something small for him to carry," she assured. "I promise they won't give in to his request for a pack."

As the two women watched, Brenna's sons performed a negotiation worthy of Commander Jakes. Soon Ryan had his *Wild Things* monster tied to his back with about six feet of tent rope. He was grinning ear to ear as he reached for his mother's hand.

The five joined the gathering crowd, children and adults of various ages and sizes, a host of them wearing long-sleeved LAKE logo shirts and carrying packs with personal utensils and sleeping bags. Adults carried tent bundles. Brenna and Cassidy had split the materials for their own tent between them.

Thomas and James had done the same for the tent they would share with Ryan.

Mike moved to the front of the group and welcomed everyone. "All right. Everyone ready for the best weekend of your lives?"

Cheers rose throughout the group, and Brenna looked at Cassidy, who was scanning the surroundings with a quiet, expectant smile. *I am so ready for this*, Brenna thought as the group started out. She fell into step next to the taller woman. She heard Thomas and James behind them, already chatting with other teens. Between her and Cassidy, Ryan darted every which way, trying to take in the whole atmosphere at one time. Brenna pointed out birds and squirrels, and a frog jumped away from their path as they continued through the woods and the trail began to angle upward.

The sun found Cassidy's face and lit the pale skin with a soft golden fire as her eyes met Brenna's. Thudding in her chest, Brenna's heart sped up in response. She dusted her hand through Ryan's hair as she looked ahead on the trail, wondering what waited around the next bend.

It was nearing nine o'clock when the group reached the campsite. While the youngest children played tag, the older ones assisted in setting up camp. Despite the cool November temperature, the exertion had them all sweating very quickly. Wielding a hammer, Brenna had just finished sinking the first stake in her last tent when she stood, stretched, and pulled off her outer shirt. Tying its arms around her waist, she returned to her work in her tan cotton tank top, arms bare and glistening.

Steadying a pole for a tent across the way, Cassidy studied the loose fall of auburn hair concealing Brenna's face from her view. She considered the smoothly muscled arms and could easily picture the other woman laboring on her deck. Familiar energy swept her through her loins. She recalled watching Susan kiss Virgil and sighed.

Diverting herself from the budding feelings, Cassidy took a deeper breath of the pine-scented fresh air. Out here it felt like anything was possible. She worried fretfully at her bottom lip as she moved to hold the next pole. She was assailed by a strong vision of brushing Brenna's sweat-dampened hair away from those high-colored cheeks and—

"Ouch!" Cassidy blinked and looked down to where the man she was helping had just rapped her booted foot with the stake hammer.

"Sorry," he offered.

"It's all right, Gerry." She patted his dark shoulder absently and wriggled her toes. The sudden impact had hurt, but thanks to her footwear's thick leather and sturdy construction, she could already feel the ache subsiding. She judiciously moved her feet back as he resumed his hammering, fighting down a blush as she felt Brenna's eyes on her from across the clearing.

Brenna's color was high, and her smooth skin was highlighted by wet sunlight. Cassidy stole another glance toward the working woman and sighed again. Brenna had made a lot of adjustments over the year they'd worked together. When the actress eventually told Cassidy how much she respected her work, her reaction to the revelation had surprised her. The more she thought about it, though, the more she realized that Brenna's respect was something she had desperately wanted.

Gerry proclaimed the assembly finished, and Cassidy let go of the last pole. Brushing her palms together, she dropped onto a log. Sitting by one of two unlit fire pits, she pulled off her own outer shirt, using it to wipe the sweat from her face and neck, thankful that she had already pulled her hair into a ponytail.

A thin towel suddenly draped across her shoulders, sliding down into her hands. She looked up to see Brenna sitting on the log beside her. Cassidy returned her friend's quick smile. She lifted the towel to her face to mop at the sweat, pausing abruptly at another scent already on the towel. *Brenna.*

"Want to go for a swim before lunch?" Brenna asked.

Despite the evaporation of sweat from her back and shoulders, Cassidy still felt hot. "I could use the chance to cool off." She dropped her gaze quickly from the warm glow of Brenna's sun-touched, smiling face. She squeezed the towel reflexively, not sure why she was suppressing the sudden urge to grasp Brenna's hands, which were fidgeting in her lap.

We're friends, right? Friends could touch, and no one would think anything of it. The two of them had even touched in comfort before. However, she knew her earlier daydream had not had mere comfort in mind.

The opportunity fled, as Brenna stood in the next moment. "I'll round up the kids."

Her hand brushed across Cassidy's damp shoulder, sending conflicting waves of chill and heat along the nerves. Mopping at her face, Cassidy watched Brenna walk away and wondered what the hell she should do. Clearly the gesture was an invitation. But to what?

Cassidy thought about Hanssen being gay, about the idea of her wanting Jakes. Jakes and Hanssen were fantasy. This was reality. *Does that make a difference?* Cassidy was not sure.

Walking away from Cassidy and the curious pale blue eyes that had followed her all morning, Brenna reached a cluster of trees where the younger children were racing about. Catching one girl under the arms and swinging her around, she announced loudly, "Swim time!"

Shrieking, the children raced to their tents in a mad scramble, eager to be the first dressed and into the water. Mike stepped from his tent, already clad in plaid green swim trunks. The teens, Thomas and James among them, loped over more sedately, also ready to change.

Brenna caught a wave from James and waved back, fretting when she realized her arm and chest were still tingling from her light contact with Cassidy's shoulder. As she walked toward their tent, Cassidy approached from the other side. She found herself studying the other woman's figure.

So, she's physically attractive, Brenna. You knew that a year ago.

In the beginning, Cassidy's physical beauty had scared Brenna, professionally and personally. She agonized for months over what she had done, or not done, to lose the confidence of the production staff. Why had they brought in someone younger, taller, and a former model, to boot? Looking at Cassidy now, she felt no jealousy. It also was not protectiveness filling her chest, since she wanted to wrap much more than her arms around the younger woman.

Brenna was feeling very energized, she realized. While working on the tents, she had found her progress constantly disrupted by side glances toward Cassidy. Checking on the first-timer's progress, or so she told herself. However, it was clear that Cassidy was fine. *Very fine*, she noted, tracing the backs of her legs, the way her hair had worked free from her ponytail. It was insane the way she had tracked drops of sweat from Cassidy's hairline down her cheek, throat, and onto her collarbone before tossing a towel across the lean shoulders. She wanted suddenly to be very active, very sexual, but couldn't understand why a woman she was just barely beginning to know ~ and had until recently largely ignored ~ would be at the center of the whirlpool of emotions.

She and Cassidy reached for the tent flap simultaneously. When their hands touched, the vibration ricocheted through her body. It came to a stop deep in Brenna's groin, where it crouched like a wild cat coiling to pounce. She quickly pulled back. She motioned Cassidy inside, pacing outside as she tried to bring her reactions under control.

Aware of the necessity for propriety, but reveling in the chaotic feelings sweeping her body, Brenna was surprised when Cassidy suddenly reemerged and straightened up before her. Her gaze swept the trim body, noting the sleek black one-piece suit.

"Your turn." Cassidy stepped out of the way.

Just as the tent flap started to fall, Brenna felt a fleeting touch on her back. Startled, she looked back, but Cassidy was looking off into the distance. Then the canvas obscured everything.

Brenna bit off a gasp as she hit the surface of the cold spring. Diving shallowly, she came up and tilted her head back, letting the water wash the hair back from her face. She stroked evenly to the shallow side, where the youngest children were being supervised by adult partners.

Screeches and nervous laughter arose as little toes hit the cold water. She stood and stretched against the sandy bottom, watching Cassidy coaxing Ryan into the water. Abruptly, he jumped. When he came up spluttering, his mother tucked a hand under his stomach. He laid out, arms and legs splashing in a sloppy crawl stroke.

Thomas swam past Brenna, briefly diverting her attention. He had partnered with a young black boy, probably ten years old. Thomas paused frequently to check his buddy's progress. She smiled, and her chest filled with pride. *He's growing up so fast,* she thought, watching her eldest child stand and shake the water from his hair. Thomas was beginning to look a great deal more like his father. Thinking about Tom made her think about Kevin and their fight. Resolutely, she pushed the issue aside.

She moved through the water toward a sputtering boy whose head had dropped beneath the surface. Grasping him under the arms, she helped him clear his face and directed him back to his partner. The boy's uncle waved to her as she moved off again.

A splash behind her drew her around to see that someone had brought a volleyball, and a group of adults and children were siding up, batting it back and forth among themselves. Mike leaped up, intending to intercept the ball but missing, landing heavily in the water. The resulting wave smashed into Brenna. Staggered, she snatched at the ball he had missed and smacked it back with the heel of her hand. Mike laughed, as did others.

As the game continued, Brenna heard splashing coming closer and turned again, expecting to find another child in need of a hand. Instead she found Cassidy ~ walking along, keeping a firm palm under Ryan's stomach as he propelled himself forward, his puffed cheeks regularly dropping into the water. Finally, he tried taking a deep breath and swallowed some water. Catching him around the stomach and pulling him up, Cassidy waited for him to stop coughing, unalarmed. Her gaze lifted from him and found Brenna. "Hi."

"Hi." *Hi?* Brenna castigated herself for the singular response. *Come on, for crying out loud, talk to her.* "He swims pretty well," she noted. "Lessons?"

"No. Just the waterproof baby class at the Y when he was two."

"Oh." Brenna fell silent, feeling like a teenager at a prom. The rush of sensation she experienced in Cassidy's presence was both exciting and terrifying, and she exhaled slowly.

Howls and loud splashing drew the women's attention to the rocks. Brenna spotted James leading off a series of wild cannonball jumps, each splash bigger than the last as the group's teens hit the water.

"James!" Brenna shouted. Her worry subsided when her son surfaced. The joyful expression on his face demonstrated he was fine and eager for another run. He looked at her, shrugged, and slowed his steps for about three paces before he ran to the end of the line of kids. Brenna shook her head, decided against starting a battle of wills, and splashed the water surface lightly in her distraction.

"Lessons?" Cassidy asked, her voice sounding in Brenna's right ear at the same moment Ryan's small hand grasped Brenna's forearm.

Brenna inhaled and exhaled to release the shiver of reaction the double assault had on her senses ~ one innocent and the other unintentionally seductive. Cassidy had a warm, throaty voice when she talked softly. Shaking her head, Brenna fought to just answer the question, trying to avoid letting her own voice go equally soft in response. "No, just pure gumption."

"I wonder where he gets that from," Cassidy mused, her eyes dancing with laughter, though not so much as a chuckle passed her lips.

Despite the flutters in her stomach, Brenna bantered back, "Oh really?"

Cassidy nodded. "You've got more guts than ten people put together. I really believe that, especially after this week."

Brenna flushed under the praise. "Just trying to help," she said quietly.

Cassidy did not respond. In her curiosity, Brenna looked back. She found a softening light staring at her. She felt as though the gaze were swallowing her whole. *Are you feeling what I'm feeling?* She almost opened her mouth to voice the question and then suddenly clamped her jaw shut as a voice in her head warned, *Don't go there.*

It was barely audible over the pounding of her heart.

Two hours later, the springs were abandoned to cries of "I'm starving!" and the crowd descended on the campsite. The portable grills were lit and hamburgers and hot dogs set to cook. Brenna monitored one, and Mike monitored the other. Both had helpers to pass the paper plates of buns back and forth to the campers. Next to her, filling the plates, Cassidy was silent. Taking her cue from that, Brenna focused on the meat.

After a while, Cassidy asked, "Want to trade? You could go eat."

"No, I'm all right." Brenna flipped over another patty and then looked up. "Why don't you make yourself up a plate and go sit. I've got this."

Cassidy scanned the groupings, apparently considering who to join. Brenna watched Cassidy's face slip into a bemused, indulgent smile that lit up her fair features. Brenna followed the gaze and saw what had her attention.

Thomas had coaxed Ryan into his lap, and the two were alternating bites of hot dog and chips. The boy, with a young version of his mother's intense look, painstakingly pulled off bites and fed them to Thomas, who playfully snapped his teeth over each morsel.

"I've never seen him do that," Cassidy marveled.

Brenna laughed. "Thomas did it to get him to eat. He was probably too excited to settle down."

The two women watched a while as the interplay between their sons continued, then Cassidy turned to make up a plate for herself.

Brenna watched the bent head, aware of the smile still playing on the full lips and the corresponding tightness in her own chest. Flexing her grip on the spatula handle, she suddenly realized her hand was hot. "Ow!" Brenna jerked back from the flames that had licked her palm. The spatula dropped with a clang. A cold wet paper towel was suddenly pressed around her injured hand as she gripped the wrist with her left hand.

"Are you all right?" Cassidy asked, carefully supporting Brenna's hand while she removed the paper towel to look underneath at the angry red skin.

"I...Yeah." Brenna grimaced as Cassidy turned the injured palm up, stretching the skin near her wrist painfully. "Ow." Cassidy immediately stopped pulling.

"There's no blistering yet," Cassidy reported, the relief plain in her voice. "We can put a salve on it and wrap it up." She wet the paper towel again and pressed it against the tender redness. "Does it hurt much?"

"It's numb," Brenna admitted worriedly. "I'll go find some first aid cream."

"Go sit. I'll bring your lunch over. Hot dog or hamburger?"

"Burger with ketchup." Brenna grimaced again as the light pressure keeping the towel in place aggravated the abused skin. "Damn," she cursed under her breath.

Cassidy went to work on the two plates, pulling the rest of the burgers and dogs off the fire and following quickly as Brenna looked for a place to sit. She settled on a grassy spot just outside those circled around one of the unlit fire pits. Cassidy was at her side quickly.

Caroline, another chaperone, noticed Brenna's predicament. "Burn?"

Brenna nodded, and Caroline jumped to her feet to grab a first aid kit. The hand was salved and gently wrapped. Throughout the treatment, Brenna felt Cassidy's hand on her shoulder. Though she felt absurd for having done something so careless, Brenna appreciated the quiet presence.

The emergency handled, Brenna accepted her plate from Cassidy, balancing it in her lap and eating awkwardly with her left hand. When she looked up from her hamburger, she found Thomas studying her, Ryan still in his lap, secured with a big hand. Thomas' head tilted in question. Shrugging, Brenna offered a twitch of her injured hand conveying that the pain was minimal. Her son nodded and returned to entertaining Ryan and a young girl next to him with the "disappearing potato chip" trick.

A scavenger hunt took up the afternoon. Still nursing her hand, Brenna declined to lead a team. Her son, James, and his team, the Blue Bombers, found all thirty items first, earning a grab bag assortment of movie tickets and coupons, as well as baseball and other trading cards.

When her hand began to throb and itch, Brenna gave up on trying to keep a public face and retreated to her tent to rest and read. The noise of the zipper opening drew her attention as Cassidy stepped inside and hunched over, crowding Brenna for a moment before folding up on her own sleeping bag.

The taller woman stretched out, offering up a sybaritic sigh. Rolling over and propping her head on her hand, she took a deep breath and exhaled. "I haven't had this much fun in months." She nudged the book in Brenna's hands. "What are you reading?"

Turning it over, Brenna presented the front. "*The Red Tent.*"

"Enjoying it?"

"It's pretty good." Brenna started to turn the book back. Its spine bumped her injured hand, and she winced.

"How's your hand?" Cassidy wrapped her fingers around Brenna's hand.

Brenna felt as though she had swallowed her tongue. "It's sore," she managed in soft protest, withdrawing from Cassidy's touch.

The other woman nodded. "I'll rewrap it while you tell me what the book's about."

"It's biblical fiction, about Jacob's four wives and his only daughter, Dinah. She's the narrator." As she talked, Cassidy retrieved the first aid kit from her own supplies and applied more burn salve. Brenna's eyes watered at the renewed pain.

"I'm sorry," Cassidy offered, brushing Brenna's lower arm soothingly with her thumb.

Putting down the book, Brenna wiped her eyes with her uninjured hand. "It's not your fault."

"I know. I feel bad all the same." She held Brenna's hand gingerly in her lap as she took pains to wrap the gauze without further aggravating the skin. "Tell me more about the book."

Watching Cassidy's hands move around her own, Brenna had lost her train of thought. "Oh...Um..."

"How do they handle jealousy?" Cassidy prompted.

"Culturally, it's very different. There seems to be a lot of negotiating going on."

"Humans just can't help being jealous," Cassidy said thoughtfully. "Monogamy just...is, I think."

"Many ancient cultures practiced polygamy, but like you, I have a hard time seeing how it would all work. That's why the story's fascinating, I guess. It seems to work for them."

"Is that a recommendation?"

"I could loan it to you when I'm finished." As Cassidy let go, Brenna flexed her rewrapped hand, making only a mild face. "Thank you."

Cassidy leaned back, tucked the kit back inside her bag, and crossed her hands under her head, staring up at the tent peak. "Best I can do."

Rolling onto her side, Brenna could see Cassidy struggling to explain herself. "It'll get better."

"I know," she said finally. "Do you think you'll be all right to climb tomorrow?"

"Not without my gloves, which I was planning to wear anyway."

"I should probably go take your place in the dinner prep," Cassidy said suddenly.

Brenna's bandaged hand on her arm forestalled her. "It's only four o'clock. Relax."

Cassidy relaxed back against her sleeping bag. "You don't mind the company?"

"Go on. Sleep." Brenna watched Cassidy's eyes close as the blond head turned into the cushioning of the bag.

"I am a little worn out. Must be all this fresh air," Cassidy mumbled.

Brenna's right hand lay between them. It was covered gently. Book forgotten, Brenna leaned back and watched the gentle rise and fall of Cassidy's chest, soon drifting off herself in the quiet.

CHAPTER TWENTY-ONE

"MOM? MS. HYLAND?"

Cassidy stirred as the call came again from outside the tent. She flexed her wrist and arm and found an unfamiliar texture pressing against her palm. Focusing, she realized she held Brenna's injured hand in her own. Gently she released her grip and tracked up to the other woman's profile, finding the distinctively featured face turned toward her. A sharp pang of desire made her breath catch.

Is it possible to fall in love in a day? She shook her head. *This has been building for a lot longer than a day.* What she had always felt as admiration was finally blossoming, having been buried under work and their intense and adversarial relationship for weeks, probably months.

Cassidy grasped Brenna's other arm and shook gently until Brenna stirred. Blue eyes blinked open, capturing her, and she gasped.

"Cassidy?"

The husky voice flowed over her senses with a shocking tenderness. "It's dinner call," she guessed, drawing away quickly as Brenna sat up.

"Boy, I really sacked out." Brenna sighed, rubbing her cheeks with her palms and wincing as she aggravated her burn.

"Mom?"

Brenna glanced to the tent opening. With a sigh she shifted to it, unzipping it. "Dinner, I guess. Hmm?" she invited over her shoulder to Cassidy, who had not moved.

Looking away as Brenna exited the tent, Cassidy tried to pin her emotions down and contain them. She knew what lust was about. She had even experienced it in the context of a woman once. This was different. The urge to touch, yes, but more...the desire to hold and cherish was also present. At last she released a long breath and followed Brenna into the evening air.

Brenna's son, James, stood a few feet away, looking at the women as they emerged, straightening their sleep-wrinkled clothes. He held Ryan by the hand.

Stepping forward, Brenna brushed her son's hair from a cheek and kissed his temple. "Thanks," she said.

"You were sleeping?"

"Yes. That's not so strange." Brenna ruffled her son's hair. "I've had a long day." She looked at Cassidy with a wry expression. "And I'm not as young as I used to be."

Mike hailed them from the grill. "Corn on the cob? Fish?"

Giving James a parting pat on the back, Brenna led the way to Mike, took two plates, and passed one to Cassidy. "Thanks. Did we miss anything?" Carefully, Brenna picked up the cob in her left hand and bit into the kernels, enjoying the sweet savor on her tongue.

"Not really. Thomas and I double-checked the equipment for tomorrow. Most people relaxed in their tents for a little while." He turned a pair of fillets. Spearing one, he held it up. "Fresh fish? Can't beat it."

Biting into the one delivered to her plate, Cassidy agreed. "Delicious."

Seated on a log by a now-lit campfire, Brenna and Cassidy listened to the hum of conversation around them, content for the moment to be quiet. An orange glow lit the western sky as the sun set.

Caroline slid over. "How's the hand?"

Brenna flexed her bandaged hand, able to stifle the wince. "Not so bad anymore." When she dropped her hand and looked up, Cassidy's deeply concerned gaze intersected hers. "Really," she insisted.

Unnerved by the fire that began flickering behind the concern in pale blue eyes, Brenna felt the need to escape. "I think I'll take a walk."

She handed her plate to Caroline and set out of camp. Passing the main table, she plucked an apricot from the basket of fruit. Aimlessly, she turned onto a path that would take her higher up the mountain. Determined to sort out her feelings, she followed the narrowing path, trying all the while to dispel the image of kissing away that doubting look from Cassidy's face.

She's a woman, her inner voice pointed out. Brenna was surprised to find that the inferno inside her did not dim for a second.

You're married. All right, that caused a brief flicker. However, her heart softened again at another visit from her memory: Cassidy's face as they hugged in the Pinnacle lot the week after Ryan's mishap in Sports Warehouse. The fires roared back to life.

Brenna was forced to acknowledge that it was desire she felt ~ not protectiveness, not simple friendship. Her belly was thick with it; her chest ached with it. Her breaths shortened. *I can't be feeling this.*

She felt like turning tail and running. Her heart pounded, her head throbbed, and her knees shook. She couldn't move. Sinking to the ground against a tree, Brenna closed her eyes against the images that would not stop now that they had come forward to be recognized.

The crack of dry wood breaking brought her head up sharply. Twilight shadows concealed the face, but it wasn't necessary to see; she knew who had followed her.

She dug her hands into the tree behind her and rose slowly, steadying herself in the maelstrom of emotions assaulting her, challenging her conscience. *Should I flee again? Or is it time to stop running?* She studied Cassidy's silhouette. The other woman's head was tilted, her shoulders rounded. She hesitated, but then stepped forward.

All contrary arguments were crushed under the weighty evidence of a reality far more powerful as Brenna realized, *I do feel.* "How did this happen?"

"So you *do*...I wondered if it was just me." Cassidy stepped hesitantly forward into a beam of moonlight that pierced the canopy of trees.

Brenna held her breath. *What will she ask of me?*

Neither knew who reached out first, but they fell into a hug which became an embrace, their heads turned into one another's shoulder. They inhaled in surprise and sensation, and their lips touched lightly. The tiny flames in their souls licked up through their chests and joined where their lips melded in a nascent, delicate kiss, the faintest brushing of their lips one against the other. The sensations ~ warm, cool, and dewy soft, like rose petals brushing against their sensitized skin ~ rocked them both.

Brenna gasped for breath, and Cassidy reluctantly let her go.

"We can't do this," Brenna said huskily, though this was exactly what she had wanted since that morning in the car.

"You want this," Cassidy countered softly, knowingly. Her palm warmed Brenna's cheek as the other woman fought against the desire to lean into the caress. "All day...I saw you. I watched you."

"I know. But this isn't some fantasy, some role." Brenna's words sounded unconvincing, even to her own ears.

Cassidy shook her head. "No, you're right. It's real."

Brenna's eyes widened, her expression worried, hopeful, and alarmed in quick succession. Palms tenderly held her cheeks, and Brenna's stomach flip-flopped as warm, full lips brushed hers again.

"It's very real," Cassidy assured her quietly again. Leaving a layer of cool air behind filled with the scent of passion making Brenna shiver, Cassidy disappeared into the darkness alone.

What the hell do I do now? Brenna leaned weakly against the tree still holding her somewhat upright. Traitorously, her body shook with the desire to run after Cassidy.

A woman of forty plus years shouldn't be reduced to a puddle of mush from a single kiss.

Ah, hell, who was she kidding? This wasn't about what should be. As she had told Cassidy, there certainly seemed to be something here.

So what do I do now?

Go after her.

Brenna stumbled away from the tree and through the darkness tried to find a path out.

The chaperones and children had gathered around the fires, each carrying sticks stripped of their bark. Several adults were armed with bags of marshmallows, graham crackers, and chocolate bars. The shadows were deep; it was hard to see people until you were right on top of them. Rubbing her face to hide her emotional turmoil, she stepped into the milling group. Where she promptly bumped into Mike.

"Oh, hey. Saw you go off earlier. Everything all right?"

"Yes," she said. "I just went to stretch."

"Sure. Here's your stuff." He supplied her with the s'more makings and pointed out an unoccupied log by the furthest fire.

As she passed each group, she looked at the fire-lit faces. She worried when she did not see one in particular. *Did Cassidy even come back?* She looked back at the woods, worried that the blonde might be still out there somewhere. *And you hurt her.*

With children crowding around her, Brenna settled to a log. Someone prompted from the darkness, "Sing-a-long!"

Suggestions were passed around and Brenna listened. Finally *Little Rabbit Fufu* was selected. She started to sing and do the hand gestures for the story-song, the children mimicking her and the other adults.

> *Little rabbit Fufu*
> *Hopping through the forest*
> *Sneaking up on field mice and*
> *Batting them over the head*

> *(spoken) Along came the Good Fairy, who said:*

By the second verse, Brenna's eyes had adjusted to the firelight, and faces took shape across the campfire. Her heart skipped a beat. Head down, helping her son with the song motions, Cassidy was singing softly. Brenna's awareness shrank down to the other woman's voice. It was very different with the folk song than it had been during her role as a lounge singer in their last episode. She thought she heard a rawness that suggested Cassidy had been crying. She rubbed her own throat as it tightened. Scared about what that meant, Brenna returned to the song:

> *Little rabbit Fufu,*
> *I don't want to see you ...*

There were middle verses, but Brenna had not heard them in years. Falling silent, she listened as, amazingly, about a dozen others did keep singing. Cassidy was among them. Brenna shook her head and joined in the ending of the song:

> *...I'll give you one more chance.*
> *But if you don't stop, I'll turn you into a goon.*

> *Little rabbit Fufu*
> *Hopping through the forest*
> *Sneaking up on field mice and*
> *Batting them over the head*
> *Along came the Good Fairy ~*
> *Who turned him into a goon.*
> *Which just goes to show you:*
> *'Hare today and goon tomorrow'*

Groans echoed all around. Brenna watched Cassidy move off the log, lean back against it with Ryan in her lap, and gaze up at the sky. She wondered what the younger woman was thinking. She was torn from her thoughts when a collection of sticks appeared before her. With a smile, she pushed a marshmallow onto each one. "When you finish toasting those, I'll show you what to do with them."

Cassidy assembled a pair of graham crackers, the melted marshmallow from Ryan's stick, and a square of chocolate. Ryan gleefully ate her demonstration model as she passed out ingredients and watched several children near her make the s'more treat.

Kissing Ryan's head, she leaned back and studied the canopy full of stars. "How about *Twinkle, Twinkle?*" she suggested aloud. She heard a murmur of agreement and joined in the opening lines.

Across the fire she saw Brenna sitting alone, her mouth moving over the song extremely softly. *She's unsure of her voice,* Cassidy realized. Listening carefully, she filtered out the other voices until only Brenna's remained. Not sounding particularly trained, Brenna's voice was nevertheless entrancing, suggesting the romance of a bygone era, smooth whiskey, and hazy smoke. *Where's there's smoke,* Cassidy thought, *Brenna could certainly be the fire.*

Dropping her chin, she admired the way the firelight caught the lighter browns in Brenna's hair, making them appear more red. When she had held Brenna's cheeks as they had kissed, her fingers had drifted through the soft strands for the very first time. Even now her fingertips tingled at the memory.

She remembered the first time she had touched Brenna's skin, too, though she was just brushing away tears with the back of her knuckles. Brenna had been crying while talking with someone on the phone.

Her husband, her memory supplied helpfully.

For God's sake, she scolded herself. *The woman is married.* She put a hand over her eyes. *How in the hell could I lose sight of that?* Uncovering her eyes, she looked at Brenna again. The refrain trailed off: "Twinkle, twinkle, little star, How I wonder what you are."

Cassidy had been certain that Brenna had invited their kiss. The escalation in their relationship had been Brenna's idea, too, hadn't it? She had given Cassidy the slippers. There was the physical comfort when Ryan was lost. The invitation to camping had come even before that. She paused.

Is it possible that Brenna didn't mean those things the way I took them? Her face heated at the possibility. *I need to explain.*

Just how do you plan to do that?

I have to let her know I didn't mean it.

But you did mean it.

The sounds of giggling children faded as Brenna's gaze met hers across the fire. Cassidy's heart hammered in her ears.

The gathering broke up as happy, stuffed youngsters started to fall asleep in soft laps. Brenna saw Ryan curling into his mother's body and suddenly imagined herself doing the same. *You're nuts.* She blushed.

"Mom?"

Brenna turned to find James behind her. "Going to bed?" she asked, cocking her head to the side.

"Yeah, you?"

She nodded. "After a bit." She put her arm around his shoulder and squeezed, briefly tucking her head against his. "Did you have fun today?"

He nodded, catching her right hand lightly. "I saw you getting this wrapped up. What happened?"

"Burn from the lunch fire," she said. "Doesn't hurt anymore, though."

"You should be more careful."

That's pretty good advice for more than just fires, she thought ruefully. She kissed his cheek and watched him walk away. She stood alone, an island in the sea of people moving toward their tents.

Another island emerged nearby. Thomas and Cassidy talked quietly, Ryan between them. The five-year-old did not seem happy to be spending the night in the boys' tent. Brenna listened but resisted stepping in.

"I've got cookies," Thomas offered, finally hitting on Ryan's weakness. The boy's eyes lit up; he looked less upset and more intrigued. "Cookies? For Fred, too?"

Brenna could see that Cassidy, also quiet, was grinning, too.

"Who?" Thomas looked at Cassidy, then back at Ryan.

"My monster, Fred," the boy explained with an air of "you should know that."

Brenna chuckled softly as Thomas recovered admirably. He stood, held out a hand, and assured Ryan seriously, "I have cookies for Fred, too. Come on."

Ryan trailed after Thomas. Soon Brenna and Cassidy were the only ones not inside their tent. Brenna fidgeted with her bandaged hand. The taller woman strode toward her, blue eyes soft and full lips beckoning. Brenna lifted her hand. Whether the gesture was to ward off Cassidy or pull her close, she could not decide.

Cassidy decided for her, grasping the bandaged hand carefully. With a quiet, even voice, she said, "I'll rewrap it for you, if you want."

Want? Brenna inhaled. Heat from their connection seared her. *What do I want?* She nodded, unable to break free of the other woman's gaze. "All right."

At the tent, Brenna entered first and lit the lantern. They circled on their sleeping bags, and Cassidy reached for the first aid kit as Brenna unwrapped her hand.

The silence became oppressive. They both felt the need to fill it.

"I wanted to-"

"Could I ask you-" Cassidy shook her head. "You go first." Examining the red splotches on Brenna's hand, she applied the cooling cream. She wrapped it loosely to let the skin breathe.

Brenna swallowed, alternately watching her hand in Cassidy's and the other woman's bent head. "I wanted to say that I'm sorry."

"It was my fault. I shouldn't have...I misread-"

"No, you didn't." Brenna's voice was soft, afraid of the admission she was making but unwilling to have a lie between them.

Cassidy's motion stopped. Their eyes met, and Brenna read the astonishment clearly. A cool collectedness emerged which Brenna recognized as Hanssen. "Don't. I need Cassidy here right now," she begged. "No confusion."

Cassidy shook herself, and the composure washed away. "I...I'm sorry. I...just...I don't know what to say to you."

"I don't know what to say either," Brenna admitted. "I didn't plan this."

"I'll go."

Brenna shook her head. "No, we just need to slow down."

"Are you sure?"

"I don't want to lose our friendship."

Cassidy exhaled sharply. "Thank God. I don't think I could stand it if you made me leave."

Brenna acknowledged that admission with a nod, though it was far more impassioned than she wanted to deal with at the moment. "I've never done anything like...that," she said, her voice barely audible.

Brenna was looking down at her hands, fidgeting with them in her lap again. Cassidy recognized the habit from earlier in the day. This time she did not resist reaching out. She wanted to touch this woman. And Brenna wanted it, too. "Would you do it again?" Cassidy asked.

The faint smile on Cassidy's lips drew Brenna's gaze like a magnet. Before she could demur, Cassidy had covered her hands with one of her own, pinning them to the sleeping bag between them, and was leaning forward, closing the gap between their bodies. At the same moment gentle fingers caressed Brenna's left cheek and into her hair, and Cassidy's full lips touched hers.

The earlier kiss had shocked Brenna, reducing her to a gasping puddle of mixed sensations, but this one rocketed her past shock into a place of hypersensitivity. She noted the texture, the scent, and the adoration passing from those lips to hers. She freed her hands from beneath Cassidy's and gave in to the need to touch in return. She caressed the other woman's pale cheek, brushing her thumb over the satin skin, holding her still, even as they both trembled.

When the kiss broke, Brenna's head dropped forward. Cassidy's lips trailed across her forehead. "I didn't even use to like you," Brenna admitted on a deep breath, inhaling the delicate lavender again.

Cassidy's laugh, soft and lilting, washed over Brenna in absolution. The long fingers in Brenna's hair caressed the nape of her neck, spreading a delicious tingling. Brenna lifted her head. Mesmerized by her own hand lifting to Cassidy's cheek, she stroked the smooth planes. *A woman's face. This woman.*

"You are..." She couldn't find words. Cassidy turned her face into the touch and closed her eyes. A lump welled up in Brenna's throat. "It scares me that I don't understand where this is all coming from," she managed.

"You snuck inside me, too." Cassidy's hand dragged slowly from the back of Brenna's neck onto her cheek, over the arch of her nose and down over her lips, where the other woman's breath warmed them.

Brenna leaned forward to seek another kiss from the soft mouth. Cassidy's arms went around her shoulders, hugging her close. Gradually their bodies bore them down to the sleeping bags together, breasts pillowing against one another. When Cassidy's knee unexpectedly slipped between Brenna's thighs and made her groin clench, Brenna broke their kiss. "I...I can't..."

One arm instantly moved away, though Cassidy's other hand remained gentle on Brenna's lower back. Soft fingertips covered Brenna's lips. "Then I won't."

Brenna started to ease away, aware of her body's reluctance to part. Cassidy did not force her, but the gentle strokes on her back convinced her to remain partially on the leaner, longer body. She rested her head in the curve of Cassidy's shoulder, watching the pulse tick in her throat, lulled by the gradually slowing tempo of Cassidy's heart under her ear. She felt the body under her shift. Cassidy reached above their heads and lowered the lantern's flame until they were enveloped in the night's shadows. Gingerly Brenna moved her hand against Cassidy's stomach, nearly jumping away when the muscles clenched in response.

Cassidy's arms held her in place, tightening briefly around her back. "I promise I won't."The whispered words sifted through the hair on top of Brenna's head. The tension took some time to melt away, and Brenna was unsure what the morning would bring, but her eyes could stay open no longer. She slept.

Arms wrapped around Brenna, Cassidy stirred between wakefulness and sleep in a hazy, half-dream state. She heard a commotion outside. A glance at Brenna's face made her pause. She brushed her fingers against the woman's tousled hair, noticing up close the light freckles across Brenna's cheeks. *God, she is beautiful.*

Reaching over her head, Cassidy turned up the lantern flame, their conversation echoing in her mind. She sat up and wrapped her arms around her bent knees, considering everything.

Okay. So the kiss was consensual. She sighed, rubbing her face briskly. *What do we do now?*

The noises outside came closer, and, as only a mother could, she recognized the plaintive voice of her own son whispering anxiously to someone else. With a sigh she set aside her own problems for the time being, opened the tent flap, and looked outside.

The filtered lantern light provided just enough illumination to identify her son being led along by James. "What's up?" Looking up at the teen, she found herself suddenly transfixed by how much he looked like his mother ~ from the shape of his chin to the slope of his nose.

"He won't go to sleep." James' voice clearly displayed his agitation and his exhaustion.

"All right." Cassidy held out a hand to her son. "Come on, buddy. You can sleep in here."

"Thanks," James said in relief.

She held her son still with one hand and stood, exiting the tent. She could see James was uncomfortable. "I'm really sorry he bothered you."

"Well...I...It..." He stumbled to a halt. "When I couldn't wake Thomas to deal with it, I figured I better get you."

"Come to me anytime, all right?" she said. She accepted then that her feelings for Brenna were more than lust. Apparently they included insuring that her boys were all right, too.

James frowned and shrugged. "Yeah. Whatever."

Cassidy watched him walk back the way he had come. Turning to Ryan, she was startled to see Brenna leaning out of the tent. "I'm sorry I woke you," she whispered.

"I...wasn't really sleeping," Brenna admitted. She didn't elaborate, instead looking in the general direction where her son had disappeared. "Trouble?" she asked, pulling the flap aside and gesturing both Cassidy and Ryan inside.

"Not unless you count sleeplessness."

"Mine or yours?"

"Mine causing yours."

"Ah." Brenna turned to Ryan, who was curling up quickly against his mother's right leg. "Too excited to sleep, hmm?"

"Mmm hmm." He hugged his monster tighter.

"Well, why don't you lie down right here?" Brenna smoothed open her sleeping bag and patted the interior. "Come on."

He looked from Brenna up to his mother, who nodded. "Go ahead. I'll be right here." He lay down on his back as Brenna pulled the top layer up, covering his face. He laughed and pushed it away.

Brenna chuckled. Cassidy realized it was intentional, the sleeping bag becoming the mechanism for an impromptu game of peek-a-boo. Ryan was too old for it, but it clearly it amused him that this woman would play with him. Cassidy realized that's what Brenna had intended. Brenna was feeling the need to connect with her son ~ just as she had tried to connect with Brenna's.

"You're fun," Ryan finally declared, rolling onto his side, clearly ready to try sleeping again.

"Thank you," Brenna acknowledged seriously, smoothing her hand over his pajama-covered shoulder. When his eyes had closed, she looked to Cassidy, who displayed an adoring smile. "It's instinct," she protested quietly.

"I know. I did the same with yours a minute ago." Cassidy inhaled slowly. "This just got really complicated, didn't it?"

Brenna sighed. "Cassidy, I don't know what I'm going to do." Uncertain whether or not she should touch Cassidy, she moved away from Ryan, who was already breathing evenly, and closer to Cassidy, who remained stiff. Not wanting to be overheard but unwilling to wait until morning to address what was between them, she whispered, "I can't stop what I'm feeling. Despite everything against it, there's a part of me that doesn't want to stop," she added ruefully.

Her tone set off an alarm in Cassidy's head. Bluntly she said, "You told me about those fans talking about getting Hanssen and Jakes together, and I could tell it bothered you."

Brenna sighed. "I'm not against gays or even playing a gay. I never expected to be attracted to you, but I can't get involved with you." She swallowed hard as she looked away from the woman beside her. "Will and I...It didn't work," she admitted bluntly with a sigh. "That's probably part of why he's such a mess."

That Brenna had had an affair with Will Chapman surprised Cassidy so much that she almost missed Brenna's other admission.

"Even then I was at least single, divorced. I'm married now."

"You said it yourself, these feelings are not going away." She put her hands over Brenna's, which were resting on the other woman's stomach. The muscles quivered at her touch, and Cassidy smiled, knowing she felt the same. "We may not know where exactly they came from, but shouldn't we see where they go?"

"I'm married." Brenna bit the inside of her cheek. "I don't have another answer I can give you."

"Don't you?" Cassidy brushed her lips over Brenna's and felt the brief response from trembling lips before Brenna stopped herself and pulled back. Tears pooled in the corners of blue eyes turning them a sad gray, and Cassidy brushed at them.

"What a mess," Brenna murmured. Unconsciously she dropped her head to Cassidy's shoulder nestling closer for comfort, and then suddenly she realized what she was doing and jerked away.

Cassidy lifted Brenna's chin, guiding the mulberry-shaded lips to hers, offering the solace Brenna had been unwilling to seek.

"I can't have an affair," Brenna said in a small voice when they parted.

Exhaling across her lips, Cassidy whispered, "I don't want an affair either."

Tears streaming down her cheeks, Brenna accepted the kisses. Cassidy moaned against her mouth, and Brenna gasped as her nipples tightened, her groin pulsed, and her heart pounded hard and fast. She laid her hands against Cassidy's shoulders, drawing them up along the skin of the other woman's throat and into the fall of straight blond hair, never once breaking the contact of their lips. Finally they parted, panting softly.

Cassidy pulled Brenna into her body, hugging the other woman securely. "I remember telling myself when I first walked on set that I was going to make you like me." She nuzzled Brenna's hair and inhaled.

"Honestly, this wasn't what I had in mind."

Brenna buried her face in Cassidy's neck to stifle the laughter bubbling in her chest and the embarrassing heat burning her face. "God, what am I going to do with you?"

Cassidy showed a full toothsome smile and offered cheekily, "Anything you want."

Despite her misgivings, the thought of giving up their newfound closeness actually made Brenna feel sick. She let Cassidy pull her down until they were sharing the same sleeping bag, nestled close for the rest of the night.

Lying awake in Cassidy's loose embrace, Brenna stirred as soon as she heard the faint sounds of camp activity. The soft, warm body next to her made the decision to leave the sleeping bag a difficult one. After barely a night, she was addicted. Rolling over carefully, she studied Cassidy's face only inches from her own, tranquil in sleep. Filled with awe, she traced a fingertip over the slender jaw. Her Catholic conscience took a swat at her.

Brenna Renee Lanigan, you are not thinking what you're thinking.

Glancing down between their bodies into the darkness of the bag, Brenna could not deny she was curious. *This is not the time or place,* she concluded, again hearing noises outside the tent.

She looked around the interior and sat up. Adjusting to the dim lighting, she saw Ryan obliviously and soundly asleep, tucked in her sleeping bag.

Cassidy's arm moved across Brenna's thigh as the long-limbed woman stretched, waking slowly. Brenna's body shifted into the unintentional caress.

"Oh. Mmm. Morning." Blue eyes blinked open and searched Brenna's face as muscular shoulders flexed. Cassidy's head lifted, their lips meeting for a brief kiss.

Brenna inhaled, literally tasting the natural scent of Cassidy's body. Her stomach coiled in sexual anticipation, and she broke off the kiss with a gasp. Closing her eyes to the searing sensuality in Cassidy's gaze, Brenna pulled away, despite the desire clawing at her. "Not here."

Cassidy nodded and sat up alongside her. "I know." She rose from the sleeping bag, tantalizing Brenna with the nearness of her cotton-clad hips. "I'll take Ryan and get him changed," Cassidy said, turning around in time to catch the blush staining Brenna's cheeks. Aware of the desire she and Brenna both were stifling, she kept her voice business-like. "You can change while I'm gone."

"Right."

Cassidy collected her son gently, rousing him with a kiss to his temple. "Time to dress for morning swim, buddy."

Once Cassidy was gone, Brenna pulled on a pair of thick denim jeans and a peach tank top. She was unwrapping her hand to look over the damage when Cassidy returned to the tent.

"I'll do that," Cassidy offered.

"No, actually I should be able to go without a bandage. It's almost completely pain free."

Cassidy scanned Brenna, causing her to duck her head a little at the appreciation reflected there. "Let me take care of you, Brenna, please." Cassidy's voice drew her gaze back up. "Where are your gloves?"

Brenna licked her lips. "I...uh, the gloves are in my bag." She removed the last of the white gauze from her palm. The worn leather gloves Cassidy handed her were lined with soft cotton twill. Easing her right hand inside, she flexed her fingers.

"How's it feel?"

"Not too bad," Brenna answered with surprise. "Are you ready for your first climbing lesson?"

The women joined the gathering outside that was separating into two groups. The youngest and those adults not interested in climbing were returning to the spring to swim.

In his role as co-leader of the climbing group, Thomas strode down the line, checking everyone's attire. He directed a pair of girls to go back and change into full shoes. They'd have to stay behind otherwise, he decreed in a tone that invited no argument. Standing at the end of the line, Brenna chuckled as they tried to change his mind by offering rather blunt enticements.

"He doesn't get his head turned easily, does he?" Cassidy whispered in her ear.

Brenna shook her head, then glanced to see he was only a couple of people away from them. "Straighten up," she said with amusement. "Time to see if we pass muster."

Cassidy laughed, and Brenna caught a glance of surprise from Thomas. Since the laugh had a similar effect on her, she instantly recognized the entranced delight in her son's face.

Thomas came over to stand in front of them, glanced once at his mother, and declared, "I know you're ready." He turned his attention to Cassidy, his expression very attentive. "Have you ever climbed before?"

"No."

The two were not quite eye to eye, but Cassidy only had to lift her chin a fraction to meet Thomas' gaze. His gaze swept down her attire. "Sturdy boots," Thomas said. "Thick jeans." He noted her bare hands. "Gloves?"

"I didn't think about it," Cassidy admitted.

"All right." He picked up her hand. Brenna's face tightened as she fought to keep her expression neutral. He sized Cassidy's fingers against his own. "We're about the same size. You can borrow my spare pair." He pulled them from his back pocket and presented them.

"Thanks."

Cassidy's smile made his throat turn red, and he ducked his head away, turning back to the group at large. "All right, everyone, collect your rope and pitons from the pile. Mike, we're ready to move out."

Thomas stayed at the back of the group with his mother and Cassidy, explaining as they walked how the best climbers moved up a mountainside. Keeping quiet herself, Brenna listened to both her son's voice, very animated, and Cassidy's interested questions.

They talk so easily, Brenna lamented. With a deep breath, she looked around at the scenery, trying to remember how nice it was to be in the mountains again.

Someone nudged her arm. "What?" Brenna found Cassidy had fallen back into step with her. Thomas had gone ahead as they neared the rock face.

"Are you all right?" Cassidy's smile was bright, sinking Brenna's spirits lower.

"Yes, I'm fine," Brenna lied, absurdly jealous of her own son.

CHAPTER TWENTY-TWO

"WATCH HIS rope!" Mike Connell shouted.

Thomas immediately rappelled alongside Vince, a beefy football-lineman type in a gray tank top and knee-length shorts.

"Vince! Stop!" Thomas ducked his head under the muscle-bound arm that Vince flailed as he tried unsuccessfully to regain his footing against the rock. "Hold still!" Finally Thomas grabbed the man's hand and wrapped it around his rope.

"Pull your right foot up. There's a spot for it about knee high." The big man's anxious huffing couldn't drown out Thomas' firm voice. Vince nodded automatically. "All right." Thomas checked Vince's harness again, then patted the dark shoulder. "You're fine now. Go on up to Mike."

Holding position, Thomas watched Vince's first few cautious movements, shot a thumbs up to his partner, and let out his line again, checking on the others trailing further down the cliff face. The climbers were grouped about one-third to one-half the distance up the mountainside. It wasn't a sheer drop, but roughly a seventy-degree angle to the plateau. He shouted to his mother, who looked over with a smile, flashing him a thumbs up.

Half a body length above and to Brenna's left, Cassidy looked down to adjust her footing. She wrapped her gloved hand around a higher section of rope and hauled herself another full body length before pushing her right boot into a crevice.

Cassidy tapped in a piton and clipped her belt harness to the metal loop. Looking up, then down, she absorbed the heightened sensation of freedom as she dangled between earth and sky.

A familiar auburn head crested against the rocky surface. Sure gloved hands and tanned arms snaked over the surface. A moment later Brenna stopped alongside and tapped in a piton to take a break. Her face was flushed, and sweat ran freely down her face and throat. Brenna offered Cassidy a grin, close to the expression she affected for the all-knowing Commander Jakes. "Great climb, isn't it?"

"Incredible view."

Brenna turned and looked down to the top of the canopy of trees and beyond, occasionally able to pick out the trail they had hiked from the bottom as the trees parted. Out further, the western horizon blended into blues and greens as the foothills surrounding the mountains pointed the way to the ocean.

She inhaled deeply, the fresh look at the spread-out earth making her marvel at the possibilities of life. Turning back, she studied Cassidy, who had turned her face to the sun's light, eyes closed in surrender to the sensations. Her lips curled into a cat-like smile of contentment. Brenna reached across the brief space separating them and ran her gloved fingers over the muscled wrist wrapped around the rope.

Cassidy's face turned from the sun, and eyelids opened slowly as even white teeth appeared in a sensuous smile. Then her eyes widened, and the smile dimmed slightly as she focused on something behind Brenna.

"Tired already, Mom? Come on, you're holding up the climb."

Flexing her shoulders, Brenna turned into the rock face, looking over at Thomas with a shrug. "We're coming, we're coming."

"How're you doing?" Thomas tossed his inquiry to Cassidy with a quick lift of his chin.

"This is incredible. How long have you been climbing?"

"Since I was twelve," Thomas answered, taking a moment to slip over to her side and adjust one of her ties before it twisted on her. "I learned on a scouting trip." He gestured to the north. "The ridge is north of here, called Domino Peak."

Brenna, who had moved ahead of both of them, paused and called down, "Now who's the slowpoke?"

Thomas looked away from Cassidy and grinned up at her. "Be right there." He smiled winningly at Cassidy. "That's her competitive spirit. Excuse me."

Cassidy laughed and watched mother and son for a moment before resuming her own climb. She heard Thomas laugh at something his mother said and looked up to see the woman moving swiftly away on the rocks. She particularly appreciated the firm rear and rippling shoulders as Brenna moved.

Damn this is fun, she thought, grinning as she pulled herself ever closer to the top.

When she reached the level plateau, Brenna spread out on her back, arms splayed. Breathing heavily, she could not muster energy to care about the dirt mixing with her sweat.

This is freedom, she thought triumphantly. She had beaten Thomas to the top, if only by a few seconds. He shook her hand and hugged her before he rappelled down to help others. She wondered if her competitive spirit had been in part due to Thomas' obvious attraction to Cassidy. She rolled onto her side and propped her head on her hand, watching the edge for the blonde's appearance.

Though Thomas was on the side, probably with Cassidy, Brenna hoped he would let her offer congratulations first when Cassidy completed her climb. Shaking her head at herself, she pushed to her knees and moved to the edge, peering over to find her...

Castmate? Friend?

Brenna sat up slowly as she contemplated their relationship. She could no longer consider Cassidy "just another member" of the *Time Trails* company. She had moved past the feelings of animosity, straight into...*What?* They had certainly passed "'friend" with the kisses the previous evening.

Lover?

She swallowed. Despite coming very, very close the previous evening, they had not crossed that line. *Not yet.*

A hand appeared over the top of the rocks, finding purchase on the granite. Then Cassidy's face appeared, upturned and smiling as Brenna grasped her hand.

"Hey, partner!"

The eager voice filled Brenna with joy.

Partner?

"Hi," Brenna returned with a grin, pulling Cassidy the last feet onto the plateau. Stopping herself from assisting, she watched as Cassidy detached her own safety harness. Relief flooded her as they hugged firmly. Brenna could not find words to speak. She only squeezed tighter, delighted when Cassidy returned the grasp.

"Congratulations on completing your first climb, Cassidy." Mike broke free from another group that had also just reached the top.

Keeping an arm around Brenna as she steadied her legs, Cassidy flashed a huge grin. "I can't wait to do that again." She laughed, dizzying Brenna's senses.

"Well, we'll be going down in about twenty minutes." He passed her a water bottle. "Have some water. Walk around. Check out the view on the other side while we get the rest up here."

Cassidy tilted her head back and swallowed lustily from the bottle, splashing herself and Brenna in the process. She passed the bottle. Brenna drank a little, splashed her throat, and returned it.

"Want to see the other view?" Brenna asked as Cassidy's arm fell from her back.

Cassidy's eyes revealed rising passion as they lifted to meet Brenna's. "Yes."

Together they walked around some boulders and sparse vegetation and perched on a smaller boulder on the eastern rim. The panoramic view was spectacular. The Sierra Mountains sheared into the sky to the southeast, and through a valley Cassidy could see what was probably the edge of the desert.

For a while they just sat there, shoulder to shoulder. Brenna felt warmed by the sun and cooled by the breeze. She could feel the bond between them tempering, as though in a forge. Brenna pulled off her gloves and set them in her lap, studying her hands as they tingled. Cassidy did the same. Brenna's throat caught on thoughts she couldn't put into words. Brenna recalled Cassidy's earlier words. *Shouldn't we see where they take us?*

Glancing over, she saw Cassidy smile faintly at some private thought as she looked over the view. The body posture conveyed a powerful confidence, and her sweaty shoulders rippled when she rubbed her hands together.

She rose abruptly, offering her hand to Brenna. "Ready to go?"

As Brenna reached out and their fingers touched, she felt the heat of fear rising in her. A promise shone from Cassidy's eyes in reply. "Yes," Brenna finally answered, standing. *I want to see where this goes, too.* "Yes," she said again. Her heart pounded faster, and her face flushed.

Cassidy's answering smile brightened the morning sky as if it had previously been the middle of the night.

James splashed with his brother in the springs. Lunch had been spent with the two of them sitting with their mom and the Hylands. The women had talked about the climb, wondering aloud if they could find time to get together to do it again. Personally, he found that weird. They all knew Mom's contract finished up in the spring. She was corresponding with her agent to find her next project. She had even talked about going to New York, even though Mr. Shea was in Michigan.

James wasn't happy about moving anywhere. High school had proven to be fun, and he didn't relish the idea of moving somewhere else to start over again. Friends never seemed to happen quite the same way.

May would likely find the two women on opposite coasts. It seemed pointless to form a friendship that was going to end so soon. He looked over at the two women splashing one another in the shallows. They had never been chummy. He vividly remembered the things his mother had said when Ms. Hyland had been cast in the series.

Her first months on the set had made his mother, by turns, angry and anguished. She had even considered leaving the show. That had been just before she married Kevin Shea. James and Thomas had both thought the marriage sudden, but they didn't say anything. After all, it was their mother's life, not theirs. In the beginning, she had spent at least a weekend each month with him in Michigan. The visits had trailed off since spring, though. During the summer, she had built the deck out back and spent a lot of time lying out in the sun reading.

Mr. Shea had come out twice, but it was clear he didn't enjoy Los Angeles. Mom had only taken them for a visit the once this fall.

Thomas nudged him. "They get along pretty nice, huh?"

"Who?"

"Mom and Cassidy."

James blinked at his brother's use of the woman's first name, then he looked at Thomas' face and groaned. He had seen that infatuated look before. *Sheesh...*

James watched his mother pick up the Hyland boy from the water and swing him around, splashing him down to squeals of delight. He realized she looked happier right then, soaking wet and laughing with Ryan's mother, than she had on the entire trip to Michigan.

"Hey, James!" Thomas climbed up onto the rocks. "Move, will you?"

James stroked out of the way and pulled himself out of the water as his brother performed a smooth, shallow dive. Thomas stroked underwater to the other side of the spring. James rolled his eyes when Thomas "accidentally" bumped into Ms. Hyland before springing up out of the water.

Holding his nose, James shook his head and cannon-balled into the water.

Thomas burst to the surface beside Cassidy, startling her into jumping backward.

"Thomas!"

He looked to his mother, who was frowning deeply. Ignoring her for the moment, he returned his gaze to Cassidy. "So, have you and Mom decided when we're going camping again?"

"No, we haven't," Cassidy answered with a laugh.

"Then how about coming over to go to the gym? They've got a climbing wall." She smiled, and he felt his chest swell. *She might consider it. Yes!* He tried to contain his excitement, unaware of how his eyes glowed with expectation.

Cassidy's gaze left him and flitted briefly to his mother. After a moment, Brenna shrugged. Cassidy nodded, then shifted her eyes back to

Thomas. He straightened up quickly. "Well, I suppose I could, when my schedule gives me some time."

"Our schedules," Brenna interjected with a smile.

"Right." Cassidy patted his shoulder, and Thomas beamed.

His mother interrupted the moment. "Looks like everyone's headed back," she observed.

"We're breaking camp, aren't we?" Cassidy asked.

"Yeah," Thomas said without inflection. He was bummed, but he walked with them, pulling his body out of the water and snatching up his towel to pull around his neck. Holding the ends, he watched pensively as his mother took Ryan from Cassidy so that the blonde could pull herself out of the spring.

The three walked back to camp while Ryan ran around their legs, laughing and chasing frogs. Thomas laughed when the boy caught one and proudly showed it to Cassidy. She screamed, then laughed nervously as she stepped out from behind his mother.

"What is it?" Brenna asked. Ryan obligingly shoved it at her. She backed up abruptly, tripped, and fell over.

Cassidy's laughter was musical as she watched Brenna, on her hands and knees, wrap Ryan in a rolling bear hug. Her body protected Ryan's as they rolled over and over on the ground. Brenna looked so natural, laughing, open, and playful, it must have been a game she played with her own sons when they were small. Coming to rest, she tickled the five-year-old as he rested on her stomach. When she got back on her feet, letting Ryan scamper ahead, she had wood chips and leaves in her hair, and her damp arms were spattered with dirt.

"I think I'd better take another quick dive," Brenna said ruefully. "You two go on ahead. I'll be there in a few minutes to help you dismantle the tent, Cass."

"All right."

Thomas stepped forward. "No problem, Mom. Take your time. I've got the tent."

Hands on her hips, she scrutinized him. Finally she nodded. "All right."

Thomas looked to Cassidy and said, "Come on. I bet we can have most of the packing done before she gets there." He jogged the rest of the way to the camp, Cassidy easily keeping up with him.

Everything was tucked into their packs, and the campsite returned to its unoccupied state. The fire pits were raked over and doused again with spring water. Firewood they had cut but not used was stacked neatly at the edge of the large clearing for the next campers. Brenna surveyed the empty campsite as she adjusted the balance of her backpack.

"Ready to go?"

She looked over her shoulder at Mike. "It was a successful weekend, wasn't it?"

"Everyone had a lot of fun," he confirmed. "Thanks again for arranging this."

"My pleasure," she assured him, patting his shoulder.

He nodded, then raised his voice to address the whole group. "All right, everyone, move out!"

It was after five in the afternoon when they reached the parking lot at the bottom of the trail and loaded everything into the waiting vehicles. Brenna waved as the last vehicle drove off, then walked to the Mountaineer.

Through the rear window she saw Thomas and Cassidy talking. James and Ryan were already dozing, each head resting against an opposite side window. She opened her door and pulled out her keys. "Well, another weekend's come and gone," she said with a melancholy smile.

"Been the most amazing time." Cassidy smiled at Brenna, then apparently decided that might be too much and looked back to Thomas. "Right?"

"Definitely," Thomas replied, sitting back and securing his belt.

Definitely, Brenna echoed silently as she put the car in gear and started home.

CHAPTER TWENTY-THREE

"CAMERON, SIT down!" Victor pulled the man back into his seat and looked toward the sole female in the room, who had spoken very little. They had called this meeting to address the specific story arc for the current episode. Will had pushed until he got the meeting, but they had decided only the key players needed to be there. He still wondered how Rich Paulson had entered the side area. Victor wished again he had taken this meeting up in the executive building where he could close doors. "Cassidy, do you have something to say?"

She looked from Will Chapman to Cameron Palassis and then to Victor Branch. "You seemed to have decided everything," she said.

"What do you want?" Will demanded. "C'mon."

She bit her lip, then sighed. "No, this is about what you want, Will. I'm just a convenience."

"You can soften Hanssen with this," he countered.

"This guts her character," she snapped. "She is not a mushball romantic. She certainly wouldn't sleep with Raycreek just because they're stuck together ~ temporarily ~ in a screwed-up timeline."

"Would you rather have Jakes?"

In her anger, Cassidy didn't check her words. "She kisses better than you do I bet!"

Will Chapman sat down, never taking his eyes from Cassidy's face. His gaze narrowed searchingly. Cassidy stood to leave.

Branch put out a conciliatory hand. "Please sit. We've got to have something to shoot. Here." He passed her a script. "Read it over. If you see any merit in it, we'll rewrite it with any slant you like. Otherwise, we'll toss it and go with our back-up when shooting starts again in January."

She pursed her lips, knowing as well as anyone what rearranging shooting could do in collateral damage to production values. "There has to be something we can do."

Will shrugged, his expression smug. "For the record, I like it as-is."

Cassidy's anger sparked again. Did he want the series to crash and burn? She turned and yelled at him, surprising everyone. "I won't crawl into that gutter with you!"

"It's not a gutter, it's an alley," Chapman retorted.

Can I even act like that with him? Cassidy wondered. She recalled lying with Brenna in their tent, leaning against a tree caressing her body, kissing her...She had done kissing scenes before, even on-screen lovemaking, but she had at least genuinely liked those men as friends. Chapman was making that impossible.

She realized she had to do something if she did not want to be at the center of another fight. She returned to her seat. "Can we take it more slowly, at least? Could I meet with another writer? Talk about it some more?"

Victor nodded. "I'll tell Paul to come over."

"Today?"

He nodded. "All right. Today."

She stood. "Are we finished?"

Victor stopped her as she reached the door. "Could you send in Bren? We've got the drafts of January's scripts. If we need to make changes and move things up, we'll want to be sure to get them done now."

Cassidy nodded. "Sure. I'll see if I can find her."

Rich Paulson followed Cassidy as she walked away. Though present at the meeting, he had remained silent. He spoke when they were out of earshot. "Cass?"

"Yes?"

"I'd just like to say I agree with the changes you want."

"The writing is best when it's about all of us...working as a team." She paused. "Why would only two team members go into such a situation anyway? Jakes would never allow that."

"She *is* usually much more proactive than this script suggests," Rich agreed.

"I want to put some ideas together for fixing this episode, Rich. Would you help me?"

"Anything I can do," he assured her. "Where to?"

"Not just yet. I have to find Brenna first." She rolled the script in her hands and looked back over her shoulder at him. "Would you meet me in my trailer after lunch?"

"Sure."

He looked pleased. She smiled at him warmly, then patted his shoulder. "Thanks again." He nodded, and she walked away through the rest of the soundstage.

"Rich?"

"Brenna?" He turned around and found Brenna Lanigan walking up behind him. "Victor wants you in the script meeting."

"Thanks." She looked past him. "Was that Cassidy?"

"Yeah, her meeting went badly." Brenna nodded as if she had surmised as much. He wondered if she had seen the script. "Hanssen having sex didn't go over so well."

"Sex? With who?"

Okay, so she hasn't read the script. "Apparently, Cameron wrote Hanssen into a sex scene with Raycreek in order to satisfy something Will asked for."

"That's absurd! What are we saying if we do that? This is supposed to be a family show!"

"That's what Cassidy said," Rich replied, clearly surprised. "If she can't get a rewrite done quickly, the January script gets moved up into that production slot." He gestured back to the conference room set. "That's why Victor wants to see you."

"Right. Thanks." Brenna spun on her heel and strode over to the conference room, leaving him standing alone and still a little befuddled.

Cassidy walked through the sets toward the back of the lot and the haven of her trailer. She passed the speakeasy set, still up from the previous episode and now... Stepping carefully around the equipment, she acknowledged nods from some of the engineers as they filmed a short business scene. She stopped, her attention caught by the closeness of Rachelle and Sean.

You wouldn't know they were just friends. Rachelle and Sean were married, not to each other, and yet their scenes exuded love and support, even now, during some simple "business."

She relaxed, enjoying the opportunity to watch others work, letting her own thoughts quiet, absorbed by Rachelle and Sean's easy friendship which was becoming so much more under the hot camera lights.

When Jeremy pulled Luria from her chair and they danced around the empty set, Cassidy felt her heart moving with them. This was what she had felt burgeoning between Brenna and herself this weekend. Too much not to move with it. Too much coursing energy not to try to grasp it, hold it, caress it. *Caress her...*

"Cut!"

Startled by the director's loud voice as the Victrola's music cut to silence, Cassidy straightened quickly, embarrassed to be caught daydreaming.

Spotting her light coloring against the dark backdrop, Sean waved at her. "Hey, Cass."

"Cassidy?" Rachelle, who had started to walk off in the other direction, turned around. "How was your weekend?"

"Nice," she supplied. "I've found a new hobby."

"Yeah? What is it?" Sean asked.

"Rock climbing."

Rachelle grinned and patted her shoulder. "That's great. I've never done it, but I like skydiving. Same thrill, I bet."

"Probably. I might have to ask Thomas."

"Thomas?"

"Brenna's oldest son Thomas was the co-leader on the climb."

"That's cool. So what'd Brenna do while you were climbing?"

"She was right there."

Sean shook his head in disbelief. "No kidding?"

Cassidy smiled. "Nope. She actually beat Thomas to the top in a challenge climb."

"That doesn't sound like Bren."

"Well, it was," a husky, amused voice intervened.

Rachelle spun. "Bren."

Brenna walked up to the group with a smile on her face. "Yes. Hi. On a break?"

"Yup," Rachelle said. "Did I hear right? You were rock climbing this weekend?"

"I've enjoyed rock climbing for about five years. When my son wanted to learn, he needed a partner. I nominated myself. A mother's work is never done."

Sean chuckled. "Man, oh man. That just boggles."

"Why?" He had the good grace to look sheepish. "Sean!" she waved her hand dismissively, "don't answer that. I don't want you to say what you're thinking."

"What was I thinking? You're fit as a fiddle."

"I'm flattered," she said with obvious irony. She looked at Cassidy. "Can I talk to you for a minute? I just got out of my meeting with Branch."

Cassidy nodded. Rich had undoubtedly told Brenna about the earlier meeting. "Let's go find someplace quiet." She looked at Rachelle and Sean. "Catch you later, all right?"

"Yeah," Rachelle said. "See ya."

Cassidy led the way outside. "My trailer okay?"

"Sure." Brenna followed her up the steps. "Are you all right?" she asked when they were inside. "They want to move up the January shoot." She sat down on the couch and Cassidy moved next to her. "I agree, by the way, about the sex."

"They insisted Raycreek be the love interest."

"I guessed."

"What should I do?"

"They gave you permission for a rewrite. So...You make some changes ~ soften the blow to Hanssen's character, make it more logical."

"I want to toss the whole damn thing," Cassidy said derisively. "It's all about clashing egos, not about the show."

Brenna shook her head. "I know." She reached for Cassidy's hand and found the script rolled up in her fist. Gently she eased it out. "This it?" Cassidy nodded. "Why don't we see what's salvageable?"

Hands freed, Cassidy put them on Brenna's shoulders. "How was your night?" she asked, changing the subject.

"I was very happy for a mattress," Brenna mused, closing her eyes as Cassidy's fingers began a soothing massage over her neck. "I'm so sore." She reached up and grasped the distracting digits. "You'd better stop." When Cassidy nuzzled her hair, Brenna pulled away.

"What's wrong?"

"I'm just not sure yet."

"You seemed sure yesterday."

"I know," Brenna acknowledged. "It was like another world out there."

Cassidy nodded. "I felt it, too." She let her hands fall away from Brenna's shoulders. She could not keep her hands completely off her, however, and found her fingers lingering against the slight hips. "So...was it just time and place?"

Brenna lifted her chin and looked at Cassidy seriously. "My son is infatuated with you."

"Thomas?" Cassidy nodded. "Yes, I noticed."

"I don't think I can stomach competing with my own son."

Cassidy chuckled softly. "There's no competition. He's sixteen."

"Seventeen," Brenna corrected. "To his way of thinking, that's completely grown up."

"I promise I'll handle him carefully." Brenna remained silent, and Cassidy prodded her with concern. "What's wrong?" She rubbed her thumbs across the tight muscles in Brenna's lower back.

Brenna groaned appreciatively. "I feel so old right now," she admitted in a faint voice.

"I don't care how old you are," Cassidy assured her. Tucking her leg up on the couch, she drew Brenna back into the cradle of her body as she brought both hands up again to work on the muscles in the stiff shoulders. "I find you incredibly sexy," she confessed. "I think I've thought so for quite a while ~ even if I couldn't exactly say what it was, but the possibility of getting a negative reaction if I even spoke to you scared the hell out of me."

"And now?" Brenna couldn't deny how good Cassidy's touch felt, comforting her in a way she hadn't experienced in years.

"Knowing you don't hate me, just my character...I needed to take the chance."

"I don't hate Hanssen," Brenna said uneasily, "and I didn't hate you. I didn't want to get to know you, though. I was scared about what Hanssen's presence implied about Jakes, what you implied about me." Brenna eased out of Cassidy's embrace and turned around, holding the long-fingered hands gently away from her body as she spoke with unvarnished honestly. "I am over forty. When *Time Trails* came along, I'd had just one project in the previous five years that was worth the time I spent on it creatively. Do you know what that meant to me?"

"You are *not* old," Cassidy refuted emphatically. "The industry is a bunch of fools."

Brenna laughed abruptly. "Yeah, but this industry is still where I want to work and where you want to work. Right in the middle of a series run I was just settling into, they snatched the red carpet out from under my feet and put it under yours."

"I..." Cassidy thought about that time and what Cameron had done for her. "Brenna, I have something – "

Brenna had only paused for breath. "You're what, thirty, right?"

"Thirty-two."

"When they told me you were joining the cast..." She laughed mirthlessly. "It was two days after my birthday, actually." Her gaze grew melancholy. "I'd spent the day alone. I'd broken things off with Will, so I wasn't even dating at the time. Then they tell me you've accepted the job permanently. It was like getting slammed by a torpedo."

Cassidy's eyes shimmered with sympathetic tears. "I never meant for anything Cameron did to hurt you. I joined the cast to work with you, you know." She wiped at her face as Brenna wiped at her own tears. "Right from the beginning, I've wanted, needed, to reach out to you. Until you accepted the invitation to Ryan's party, I thought I had exhausted every means possible. I was so...grateful you came."

"Shh." Warm fingertips brushed over her cheeks. "That's in the past now." Brenna turned to the script. "Let's see if we can untangle Hanssen from her little mess, all right?"

"I had a few ideas earlier. Want to hear them?"

Brenna nodded. They rearranged themselves on the couch, Cassidy wrapping herself around Brenna, the script in Brenna's lap as she rested her hands on Cassidy's thighs. Flipping to the scene that concerned her most, Cassidy tested dialogue changes while Brenna read along.

CHAPTER TWENTY-FOUR

CASSIDY TURNED her face into the setting sun while she waited for someone to answer the doorbell at the Talbot home. *God,* she thought idly, *life is wonderful.* She felt warm, exultant, open, and very positive. She and Brenna had worked on script changes for a few hours. Then, when Brenna left, Cassidy reluctantly left for her meeting with Paul.

What stuck in her mind, what flowed through her body, though, was the shimmering glowing happiness of talking with Brenna. Talking that had become cuddling, cuddling that had turned to kissing. The fit of their bodies, Brenna's hips pressed into her pelvis, had felt so natural and right.

The door finally opened. "Oh, hey. Come on in. We're just about to eat." Gwen smiled and pulled Cassidy inside. "You're incredibly early," she remarked in a low voice.

"I didn't have any reshooting today. I have one song to rerecord in the sound studio tomorrow. I don't even have to go in to work on Wednesday at the moment." Gwen waved her to the seat next to her son at the dinner table and placed a plate in front of her.

"Plans for the holidays?"

"I haven't stayed in town for the holidays yet," Cassidy admitted. "I thought Ryan and I could find out what it's like."

Chance piped up, "We could go to Disneyland!"

Gwen shook her head ruefully, but said nothing. Her husband, Lou, changed the subject. "Time for grace."

Cassidy linked a hand with Ryan and one with Gwen at the end of the table. The young Talbots on the other side also joined hands with their parents. Chance and Deter tried to escape notice as they thumb-wrestled. She bit her lip against a chuckle as Lou prayed, "Thank you, Lord, for the bounty your love has shown us." He paused. Cassidy looked up, catching his fleeting frown before his face smoothed over again. "Amen."

"Amen" echoed around the table, and she released Gwen's hand as she felt the woman tug slightly.

"So tell me," she asked sociably. "How's the semester finishing up?"

"My students have their first research papers due just before the break," Gwen answered.

Cassidy wrapped her mind around the idea of fourth grade research papers. It couldn't possibly be anything like her college philosophy papers. "What sort of topics are they doing?"

"Sharks, surfing, dogs, cats, that sort of thing." Gwen gave a half-shrug.

Cassidy nodded. "Good luck with that." She turned to Lou. "How are things with you?"

"Fine."

She nodded politely. He was seldom as talkative as his wife, but his tone told her that was all she would get as a response. With an internal grimace, she decided she'd have to make some inquiries with a particularly gossipy neighbor and figure out the source of the odd feeling she was getting from Gwen and Lou. *Besides, I ought to get home so I can finish working on Paul's ideas.* She returned to her dinner, a casserole dish that was among Gwen's best recipes, as Lou informed her in the small talk that filled in the silence.

When Ryan had finished, Cassidy excused them, collecting his schoolbag and waiting while he put it across both shoulders, backpack style, as he had done since they had been camping. She quickly tendered their goodbyes, then paused at the door. She automatically reached for the check she had written, a regular agreement to defray some of the costs of the Talbots keeping Ryan so frequently late into the night. "I forgot it," she said. "Tomorrow, all right?" When Gwen hesitated before nodding, Cassidy thought she had her answer to their atypical behavior. Cassidy being a day late with the check usually did not bother her.

Cassidy leaned over and kissed Gwen's cheek. "Thanks for everything," she said sincerely. "I didn't expect dinner. It was lovely."

"Sure," Gwen said, a little more quickly. "See you tomorrow."

Following Ryan into the kitchen, Cassidy put her bag down and set the draft script on the kitchen table. "You just had dinner. Snack is after your bath," she said as he opened his mouth to ask.

The order of events given, Ryan ran into the bathroom. She heard the taps twist and water start to fill the tub. Grabbing a fresh towel and washcloth from the linen closet, she entered the bathroom. "Are you going to wash yourself, too?"

"Yes, Mommy."

She returned to the kitchen. Flipping on the radio to a soft volume, she sat down at the end of the table and opened the script and the notes she had gathered in her conversations with Brenna, Paul, and Rich.

Cassidy kept one ear out for alarming sounds from the bathroom but threw the rest of herself into the work. The writing staff had been more open to the actors' suggested paths for their characters since Rich's script, *Aleutian Blues,* had been accepted last season. Cassidy had remained quiet about her character's development, though ~ until now.

She sighed, releasing her residual anger. Most of it. The general outline of this script had to have been in the works for months. Cameron had not mentioned it to her once, even in passing, and he loved to talk about work when they were together. The original interaction appeared to have been intended to be between Chris and the other mission member, Rich's character Dr. Pryor. Cameron had substituted Chapman's Lieutenant Raycreek. He'd also expanded the interaction, taking the camaraderie, which would have been fatherly from Pryor, too far. Cassidy was working at reining it in ~ for Chris Hanssen's sake, as well as her own. After experiencing Brenna's touch, she could not imagine having any physical contact with Will Chapman, even if it was acting.

A spark of jealousy flared. According to Brenna, she and Will had had a brief affair. Cassidy admitted that stung, but she also knew that it was irrevocably over now, if it hadn't been before. Brenna calling him out in front of reporters certainly sealed that.

Inhaling, she put her pen down, her mind flying back to the momentous occasion: The Kiss. She was unable to forget a single nuanced movement of having Brenna in her arms, their lips pressing against each other, her own lips moving from Brenna's to taste soft skin along her jaw. She had not planned it, hadn't even really fully identified the emotion that was gripping her, until they were microseconds away from that first contact. She just knew that she'd been growing warmer and warmer all day, as she watched Brenna work on the tent or splash with Mike Connell in the mountain spring. She certainly had not expected the rush of connection she felt while innocently treating Brenna's burned hand.

Kissing Brenna had been precipitous and revealing. By then, she had needed to know. She had seen a question, and what she thought was invitation, in the gray-blue eyes. She had needed to *feel* the other woman's reaction, needed to know if Brenna experienced the same sparks when they touched or talked. During their dinner, she had decided to take a chance and had followed when Brenna left the camp. Her guess had been right, but that had only served to make things more complicated.

Cassidy burned whenever she looked at the woman. Knowing Brenna would never have an affair, Cassidy forced herself to hold her desires check.

On set today she had been partly successful, mostly by staying away. *But when we were in my trailer...*

Cassidy closed her eyes. Her mind drifted back over lean muscles and conjured up the unforgettable scent of Brenna's soft skin.

"Mommy?"

Shaking her head, Cassidy straightened up to see Ryan with damp pajamas clinging to his body, anxiously looking up at her. "Yes?"

"I finished my bath."

"I see that."

"Can I have my cookies now?"

She suppressed her chuckle at her son's one-track mind, nodded, and stood. Ryan immediately sat on her vacated seat and propped himself on the table.

"What're you working on?" He reached for the papers.

"Something I have to do for tomorrow," she explained, moving the pile out of the way as she set a glass of milk and a plate of chocolate wafers in front of him. Cassidy sat down and picked up the script as Ryan munched away, dunking the wafers into the milk before eating them.

He finished with a slurp before she had finished reading a lengthy section of dialogue between Hanssen and Raycreek. She resisted striking the entire exchange and cut only one of his lines strongly suggesting that intimate relations were possible, along with her reply. *God, that one made Chris sound like a teenager.*

Finally she put down the pen, inhaled and exhaled to clear her mind, and announced bedtime. "What should we read tonight?" Together they went through his shelf of books and selected *Goldilocks and the Three Bears.*

Since he had been learning sounds and letters in his pre-K class, Ryan sounded out far more words in the tale than Cassidy expected. She ended up listening more than reading. Pride filled her, growing stronger until, when the story was finished, she praised him profusely. He giggled; she tickled him, making him laugh harder. When they quieted, she brushed his bangs back and kissed his forehead. "Good night."

"Good night, Mommy." She tucked his covers to his chin and walked out, turning off the light as she went.

Once again in the kitchen, facing an evening of quiet, Cassidy listened as a news brief concluded on the radio, then a voice announced the start of an hour of jazz. Cassidy returned to the kitchen table and picked up the pen. After another hour, she felt a more acceptable version of events was unfolding in the pages. It wasn't perfect, but she hoped it would result in less damage to Hanssen overall.

Near the end of the script, there was a rescue scene, where Hanssen and Raycreek were recovered by a second team led by Jakes. In the original version, the search party, which had not included Jakes, actually came upon the two in very compromising state of undress. Cassidy's version had already put the clothes back on. Now she changed the dialogue to a considerably more business-like, "Time to get out of here."

Trying out the new lines, Cassidy almost could hear Brenna's inflections change as Jakes' concern about Hanssen's physical injuries grew. She closed her eyes and just listened as the woman's voice played in her head. *Yeah,* she thought. *It works.*

Cassidy laid her pen aside and reread the entire act she had just finished. She bit her lip. In the action text, Hanssen gravitated toward Jakes, almost scornful of Raycreek. She realized that she had better soften that. Chapman might take exception at being shoved into the background again. She inserted a short exchange between Raycreek and Jakes, hoping it would be enough to satisfy Will Chapman's ego.

"Welcome to Dr. Swanson's Waiting Room," the radio announced, interrupting her train of thought.

Dr. Swanson's voice was soothing, his advice to callers reasonable, and Cassidy found herself sitting quietly, just listening. Twenty minutes later, her head was resting on the table, and she slept.

She knew she was dreaming, but the woods were familiar. They had to be the ones surrounding the campgrounds from the weekend. She moved deeper into the foliage, and the terrain changed, leading down to a riverbank. The water sparkled in the sunlight, and she walked to the edge for a drink.

Reaching for the water, she froze when a splash drew her attention out into the water's flow. A small reddish brown bear crossed the stream, coming directly toward her. It ambled through the water, not bothered by the current. Cassidy settled carefully to one side and watched it as it emerged onto her bank.

It looked at her, considering her for a moment, then rooted around a prickly bush full of berries. The bear's paws grew raw against the thorns and soon it stopped rummaging, soothing its paws with its tongue.

Cautiously Cassidy approached, earning a wary look from the bear. She passed by it, going directly to the bush and carefully pulled off a handful of the berries, compelled to offer them to the brown bear.

It watched her for a while, and they sat together in silence, each munching on berries. When she made no further moves toward it, the bear started watching her more often than eating from its dwindling supply.

Cassidy plucked more berries and held them out carefully, palm open. The bear sniffed, its breath washing warmly across her hand. Its cool nose eased into her palm and gentle nibbles with the vaguest edge of teeth rubbed against her fingers. She felt her heart begin to pound, nerves and excitement combining as she shared a moment with the gentle animal.

When it finished, the bear angled its head toward her and ambled forward, crowding Cassidy against the bush as she tried to back up.

It was then that she saw something else, another animal inside the berry bush. A rabbit, spotty brown fur from nose to tail, nibbled on the berries from the safety within. The brown bear watched Cassidy as she removed the rabbit, cuddled it against her chest and fed it several berries. The bear settled to the ground and watched them.

The scene was idyllic. The sun sparkled on the water, the cool breeze ruffled through Cassidy's hair. She reached out toward the bear. Head lifting and eyes wide, it held very still, as if poised to run, but it permitted her to touch its fur. She rubbed its scruff and watched it nose her thigh as it squirmed under her hand. The rabbit in her lap stopped quivering, and the soothing sounds from the bear made Cassidy sleepy.

Abruptly the brown bear lurched to its feet. It bared its teeth toward something Cassidy couldn't see. It backed up and moved around her, facing out, standing between her and some approaching threat.

She put the rabbit carefully aside just in time. The ground vibrated slightly under her as she rose to her feet.

A massive bear with brown-black fur lunged out of the bushes. It scraped the ground and air with huge claws. Its lips were drawn back in a snarl, and it bared its teeth ferociously. Rising to its hindquarters, it challenged Cassidy at her own height and scraped at the air again. It released a terrifying bellow that made her cover her ears and stumble backward. She couldn't find her voice to scream, so she looked around for a place to run.

A growl suddenly sounded beside her, and she fell to her knees. As she scrambled away, she saw the brown bear, only half the Kodiak's size, raise its hackles and growl at the monstrosity. She tried to reach for it, to hold it back, but missed as the small bear leaped into the air.

She screamed then, drawing the bigger bear's attention. It snarled at her and advanced. She looked beyond it to see the brown bear circling again. With an open-mouthed snarl, it leaped again, landing atop the Kodiak's back, snapping its jaw at the back of the thick neck.

The massive bear shrugged and easily threw off the brown bear before advancing on Cassidy again. Thorns from the berry bush behind her cut into her legs and her hands. She scrambled around it, briefly glimpsing the rabbit which had retreated inside.

Eyes gleaming, the Kodiak tore at the bush.

Cassidy realized it wasn't after the berries or herself, but the rabbit. She struggled through the bush and grabbed the rabbit, fighting to release them both from the tangle of brambles. The Kodiak's massive paws clawed down her back, drawing blood, just as she broke through to the far side.

The brown bear was there, snarling and snapping over and past her to deter the Kodiak from continuing its advance. The massive bear claws landed again on Cassidy's legs.

She curled up around the rabbit and kicked out, screaming. The sound of the water rushing nearby filled her ears and the snarling bears continued their fight.

Cassidy woke herself with her scream, her heart pounding its way out of her chest. *Oh my God,* she panted.

Shaking, she got to her feet and turned on her kitchen tap, splashing her flushed face and throat. Still shivering, she shut her eyes tightly and concentrated on bringing her breathing under control. Finally she turned around and faced her kitchen, letting her surroundings come into focus. She heard the radio playing something obscure, classical, and soft. With a gasp, she shut it off.

Taking another deep breath, she listened to the house and heard snarling coming from outside.

Grabbing a flashlight, she ran to the porch and quickly shined it into the yard. His spotted coat easy to identify, Ranger crouched in the middle of the yard. She aimed her light the direction he was facing and found a cat. She called the dog off and watched the cat leap away the instant the dog turned his back. Weak-kneed, Cassidy leaned against her house and snapped off the flashlight.

Returning inside, she glanced at the clock. It was after two in the morning. Closing up the bound pages of script and smoothing them out, Cassidy sighed and turned off the kitchen light, deciding she had better finish the night in her bed.

Despite knowing how much it would complicate things, as the last of the nightmare slowly faded away Cassidy wished she could curl up with Brenna. Hugging a pillow as a poor substitute, she closed her eyes.

CHAPTER TWENTY-FIVE

BRENNA WATCHED the sunrise through her front window, seated at the dining room table while Thomas and James ate their breakfasts. Dressed casually, she mentally went over her Tuesday off and made plans for what would be a quiet, at-home Thanksgiving.

"Mom?"

"Mmm hmm?" Brenna finished chewing her bite of eggs and then patted her lips with a napkin, turning her attention to James. "Yes?"

"Are you going to take us to school today?"

"I don't have a set call. I have some pages to read on another script, but I had planned to do that here. Why?"

"I was wondering...could we pick up Marcie?"

Brenna thought about her younger son's girlfriend, remembering a brunette girl who was quite shy. "What happened to her usual ride?"

"Her mom's got problems with her dad, and well, could you, please?"

Brenna reached for a half slice of buttered toast. James did not often make requests of her. He barely tolerated the times she dropped them in front of their high school. She mentioned none of that now, however, having learned it was better to just go with the flow. "You'll have to navigate to her house."

"Thanks, Mom." He seemed distracted and had since getting off the phone with his girlfriend the night before. Without another word, he finished his eggs and returned to his room.

I wonder what that was all about. She turned to Thomas. "What's your schedule today?"

"Just classes. If you're going to be home, do you want us to come here directly after school?"

"Please. We have to work on Thanksgiving dinner."

"I'm surprised we didn't plan to go to Mount Clemens," he said.

She shook her head. "It looks like I'm going to have to work with a reorganized shooting schedule. There were problems with another script being ready in time."

"Problems?"

"I don't know. Cassidy said that the changes were going over well. She had more work to do last night, but the turnaround on these things is never fast enough for the production team." She watched Thomas shift in his chair, signaling a change in topic.

"Mom, I know you had a lot of problems with Ms. Hyland when she first joined the cast. Does this mean you two get along now?"

"We're working out our differences," she answered neutrally.

"Is that why you invited her camping?"

"We had talked about camping, so yes, I invited her along." She opted not to mention that the discussion of camping had taken place after the invitation.

"I liked her."

Brenna tread carefully. "Did you?"

Thomas finished his orange juice in one lengthy swig. "She doesn't seem like a pin-up."

Brenna quirked a smile; her eyes unknowingly turned dark blue. "No, she's not."

"Do you think she was humoring me about the rock climbing?"

Ah. Brenna suppressed a smile. "No, why?"

"I've never met anyone like her. I don't know what to make of all the stuff she said."

"Are you getting at something?"

"If I can really get her to come over for climbing at the gym, would you mind?"

"I did invite her on the camping trip, didn't I?" Brenna said with an understanding smile.

"That's a relief." The clock on the wall chimed, and he stood. "Oops, time to go."

Brenna rose, and the two of them swept the dishes into the sink. She snatched her keys and purse from the small shelf by the front door. "James!"

Her other son appeared and tossed a backpack at Thomas, who caught it handily. "Ready to go."

Twenty-five minutes later, Brenna returned home, finding the phone ringing. Catching it up, she tucked it against her ear. "Hello?"

"Hello?"

"Kevin?" She blinked, then recovered. "I wasn't expecting–"

"I wasn't expecting to find you at home."

"Oh? Um, well, what's up?"

"Shouldn't you already be at work? I was just going to leave a message."

"I didn't have a call to the set. I'm reading a script that is probably going to move up in production." She reached for it, flipping through the script idly and highlighting her dialogue.

"Oh, would that make it inconvenient if I was going to come out to L.A.?"

The highlighter went down. "Coming here? You hate L.A."

"But...I love you." There was a long pause as he formulated something else. "We haven't had much of a chance to talk. I decided you were right."

About what? she thought but did not say.

"I haven't been thinking about you very much."

"Kevin?"

"I knew when I called last time that you probably couldn't come here. So, I thought I'd come see you instead."

"When?"

"Is Thanksgiving too soon?"

"You're coming here for Thanksgiving?"

"My plane lands at LAX Thursday morning at seven. I could take a cab if you can't pick me up."

Brenna could feel her palms sweating. She wiped them before resettling the phone on her shoulder. "Of course I...Of course I'll pick you up. How long will, do you plan to stay?" She winced.

"The girls have school again Monday," he said.

"Oh, so they're coming too?"

"No, my mother's going to have them over. You'll have me all to yourself."

Brenna was silent, upset at her uncontrollable surprise.

"Brenna?"

"Sorry, I was just thinking. I'll have to add a few things to my To Do list." She walked around the living room, spotting a shirt tossed across the back of the couch. She sighed as she realized the house needed work.

"Don't go into a tizzy. Please. I don't care if the pillows aren't fluffed and the carpets aren't steamed. I just want time with you. I don't care about anything else."

She closed her eyes and pinched the bridge of her nose. *Would you care if I kissed someone else?* "All right," she said finally. "I'll see you Thursday."

Kevin's voice rolled over her. "I love you, Bren."

Brenna sat down hard on the couch cushion and put the phone aside. *What am I going to do?*

She closed her eyes. Instead of Kevin's pleasant face and soft brown eyes, she was immediately immersed in a physical memory of bodies sliding against one another in a sleeping bag. She saw the heat in adoring blue eyes and felt her own pulse race in response.

Dear God.

She rubbed her face sharply and forced her mind back to Kevin, searching for the memory of his face on their wedding day just fifteen months ago. She submerged her senses in the recall of the emotions and the event.

Brenna arranged her mother on the rocker in the small bedroom at the back of the Shea home before she pulled the summer dress from the closet.

"Brenna Renee?"

She winced as her mother used her full name. She always felt about six when she did that. "Yes, Momma?" Brenna settled on the bed, carefully tugging on white stockings.

"Shouldn't you already be in your dress?"

"Just another few minutes."

"Have you asked your sister about the bouquet?"

Brenna winced. Carefully she recited, yet again, "Evelyn can't be here."

"Still jetting with that boyfriend of hers in Paris?"

Brenna shook her head. Her younger sister was dead, having succumbed to breast cancer four years earlier. "No, Momma. Evie...couldn't break away." She shrugged. "I hadn't expected her to."

Her mother questioned, "Who's doing your hair, then?"

Evie had stood up with Brenna in her first marriage and calmed a retching and nervous bride-to-be by soothing her with a long hairdressing session. Brenna had seen her hair tugged in fifteen different styles, and she was laughing, no longer scared or nervous. Her throat caught at the memory. She missed her sister fiercely. She fluffed her shortened style. "I'm just going to twist it up."

The door opened then, surprising both Brenna and her mother. The latter looked blankly at the face peering around the edge. It was Kevin. "How are you doing in here?"

"Hi." Brenna grinned at her groom. "We're not ready yet, as you can see." She winked, raising her arms to display her slip-clad figure. She watched his face curve into a smile and felt very appreciated.

"I've got some very anxious gentlemen out here to see you," Kevin said. "Can you make yourself decent to see them?"

Something in his voice made her smile giddily. "My brothers?"

Kevin grinned back. "Tommy, Mike, Scanlon, and Gary are all cooling their heels in the living room. But they're finally here."

"Oh, Kevin. Yes." He closed the door, and she pulled a robe from the closet.

"I thought you were dressing, sweetheart."

She patted her mother's hands. "Momma, the boys are here!" Her brothers were so infrequently together in one place. No sooner had she finished tying the belt of the robe than there was a knock at the door. "Come in," she called, turning around and flipping her hair out from under the collar.

In a matter of seconds she was enveloped in the happiness of four big men, two with lighter brown hair just barely touched with the red of their Irish heritage and two with shocks of red mops and faces full of freckles. Her own coloring was the link between the extremes, as was her personality.

Scanlon, freckles on his thirty-three-year-old face still able to remind her of the gangly teen he had been, swept her up first, kissing her cheek. "Bren! Damn, you look good!"

She hugged and kissed him back, then found herself handed off to Mike, the eldest. "Mike!" Her financier brother, now forty-four, looked as he did every time she saw him: reserved blue suit, red Republican tie, and a far-too-serious look in his eyes. He hugged her back and kissed her temple.

He asked, "Happy?"

"Ecstatic," she answered. She pressed her hands to either side of his face, able to read his equal joy on her behalf despite his restrained expression. "You really need to smile more." To which he blinded her with a brief, unforgettable smile that consumed his whole face. Then it was gone, though the glow remained in his eyes.

Gary and Tommy hugged her next. "So, giving up the single life again, eh, Bren?" Gary ribbed.

"I know you never will," she prodded her playboy sibling. "Do you have a date today?"

"Just with a beautiful redhead and her new husband," he laughed, kissing her cheek. She lightly slapped his arm.

Then Kevin was in the doorway again. "Now, I'd rather she not be late to her wedding," he chided the group. "Out!"

Mike escorted their mother, leading the group back out to the living room, leaving Brenna and Kevin together.

She hugged him. "I'm so glad they're all here."

"For that smile every morning, I'll chain them to the couch." He chuckled, nuzzling her ear. "Ellie has already declared your brother 'dreamy'," he revealed.

"Which one?" she asked throatily.

"Gary."

She laughed. "Don't tell him."

"It's just a crush," he said. His hands slipped around her back, and they indulged in a leisurely kiss.

"Not from her point of view, I'm sure." Brenna leaned back in the circle of his arms. "It's got nothing on the crush I've got on you," she murmured. His mouth pressed over hers, and she felt a quiver in her stomach. "Oh, why do we have to wait?" She felt cherished in his embrace.

"Then get dressed ~ so we can get married, already."

Returning her focus to the present, Brenna inhaled and nodded ruefully. They had played tourist in the Bahamas for a week after the wedding, walking every morning and night in the blue-green surf, holding hands. Talking endlessly, they had dined by moonlight, and he held her tenderly, making love every moment between.

Kevin's devotion and attention had been a balm in those days. He cherished her at a time when she had been very low. Cassidy's abrupt arrival had caused major disruption and stress on the set and in Brenna's world order.

Cassidy.

Brenna's world order fell askew again at the mere thought of the slender blonde. Heat filled her, and she swallowed it down with difficulty, remembering the laughter they had shared playing in the spring with Ryan. To counter it, Brenna consciously thought of Kevin's laugh. Cassidy's returned quickly, and with it came guilt.

Didn't I promise to make my second marriage better than my first? She had started by choosing someone who supported her. Now here he was demonstrating that support again. Here he was making the gesture to come to her, when she couldn't find the time to get away and see him. Angry about a misunderstanding, she had let their relationship become distant.

Brenna castigated herself. Allowing herself to succumb to a physical attraction to someone else when Kevin was not around was not worthy of that devotion. "He deserves better." Standing, she made a decision.

Pulling out a dust rag and the vacuum, she set about cleaning up her home and pushed thoughts of Cassidy from her mind. The longer she cleaned, the more her throat tightened. Like the house, she would work on her marriage, and thoughts of Cassidy would go away.

Cassidy scanned the call board and sighed. The sets were being used for crowd shots on the previous episode. None of the central cast was required for any of them. An early Thanksgiving wish "Happy Turkey Day ~ See you Monday" was scrawled across their names.

Brenna was probably at home, Cassidy realized, stepping away from the wall.

"Hey, Cass. I didn't expect to see anyone else."

Cassidy turned to find Rich Paulson sauntering up, his hands stuffed in the pockets of a pair of tan Dockers. "Rich, what are you doing here?"

"Probably the same thing you are ~ delivering a script for approval." He grinned. "How'd the work go last night?"

"I've got most of it, I think. I think I saved Hanssen from being turned into a sexpot, but I don't know if Chapman will buy into it. He seemed really determined."

"No one blames you."

"Brenna said–"

"She'd be the first to reassure you. I remember her running through the press that day of the fight..." He thought better of continuing that line of thought. "By the way, Brenna won't be in. I was talking with Victor when she called. Her husband is coming into town."

"Oh." Cassidy lost focus for a moment, feeling a sharp reaction that took her a moment to completely submerge. "I, um, was going to ask for her advice. I changed a lot of her dialogue. Would you mind looking it over?"

"Not at all. Let's go to the conference room and have a look, shall we?"

Cassidy nodded and followed. "I hate being forced into this situation," she lamented.

"I figured that. You were more vocal than I've ever seen you in the story meeting. But," he added, "when you feel that strongly, it does nobody any good to remain silent about it."

Cassidy nodded sadly. "I guess you're right. I think I was maddest that no one thought to ask me about it before it got that far. I feel like a game show prize."

"Why did that happen?"

"I wish I knew. I thought Cameron and I were okay until that day. We'd hit a comfortable patch. Maybe Will's demands just pushed him beyond reason."

Rich sat in a chair, and Cassidy sat next to him. He opened the script. "Where do you want me to look first?"

"The ending. I want to find a way to make the story isolated. I don't want Chapman feeling there can be a continuation of this plot thread."

"That would mean finding a way to either put a halt to Raycreek's interest or..." he shrugged, "show Chris is interested in someone else." He offered Cassidy a wiggle of his eyebrows and feigned a salacious grin.

She laughed. "Sorry, I could never date a doctor. Terrible hours."

Rich chuckled. "Yeah, me neither." He dropped his gaze to the page, read through several scenes, then paused to read one more slowly. Cassidy peered over his shoulder. He looked at her curiously. "You want to leave this part like this?" In the throes of a fever, Hanssen was interacting rather openly with Jakes.

"Don't you think it works?"

"Oh, it certainly will cut Raycreek off at the knees." *And threaten other parts of his anatomy, too.* "Will Brenna do this?"

"I don't understand."

"Maybe you should have Hanssen weaker, less feverish? She's revealing a lot, perhaps too much."

Cassidy pursed her lips, studying the dialogue more critically. "You're right." Her gaze dropped, and a blush touched her cheeks. "I can't be that obvious."

Cassidy's cheeks were suddenly very pink, and Rich was stymied. He burned with questions, but he realized that this was not the time to pose them. "Maybe you'd better get that to Paul."

He waited until she was out of sight before letting his jaw drop. *Is it possible? Cass has feelings for Bren? And Bren for–?* Rich was only surprised that he had not recognized the situation before. He flashed on an image of Brenna on the big day of interviews. He had come to talk to Cassidy about a scene they were working together and found her hovering over Brenna's shoulder while the shorter woman conducted an interview. Brenna's hand had rested over Cassidy's the entire time.

Then there had been the later incident. Brenna had rapidly defused the confrontation between Chapman and Palassis when Cassidy was caught in the middle so publicly. It should have become a press relations firestorm, a real nightmare. Instead it had died, never making it to print or air anywhere that he had seen.

They certainly came a long way in a year, he thought. *From cold shoulder to warm thoughts, apparently. If not more.* He wondered if anyone else had noticed.

Cassidy stood in the doorway of the small office, watching pensively as the writer inside took the pencil from behind his ear and scratched a note in the margin of the script, mumbling, "Mmm hmm."

"Paul?"

"Hold on." Not looking at her, he held up a hand and kept reading. He scratched out a line and then made more notations.

She crossed and uncrossed her arms and leaned more heavily against the door jamb. Opening her mouth to speak, she shut it quickly. Having turned the page, he was now reading the scene that most concerned her. Cassidy watched his face, nervous about his reaction. He offered a half-smile, then a curt nod, and circled something before closing the bound script. He finally looked up at her. "Not bad."

She heard the cautiousness of the praise and swallowed. "Will it work?"

"This is how you feel? No chance of going back to the original script?"

"No." She was firm. "Chapman wanted the scenes, he's got them, but I am not sacrificing Hanssen to his ego."

"I'm probably going to lengthen the infection scene, just to draw the audience's attention, make it more obvious that's what's causing the delirious behavior. That will mean trimming somewhere else."

"Where?" Worried about where he might cut, she considered explaining her reasoning to convince him to keep the script basically as it now was. However, if the key scene was shortened, or cut entirely, at least the audience would know Chris was not in her right mind.

"Seconds here and there, no entire scenes. It's really quite cogent. I'm surprised you haven't said anything much before now," Paul mused. "We writers are going to be out of work if you guys keep doing rewrites this well."

"I heard about the union problems," Cassidy said. "I don't want to be a writer. I just want to act."

"That's a relief," he said with a chuckle.

Cassidy walked away from the office, collecting her breath a bit at a time, resenting that she had needed to "save" Hanssen. She looked up to find she was at Cameron's door. She ought to be sure he knew how she felt. She lifted her hand and knocked. The door, not completely latched, slowly opened inward.

"Cameron?" She stepped forward, pushing in, and froze.

Cameron sat on his power-napping couch. A petite short-haired blonde had her head in his lap. Cassidy's face heated when she realized the woman's head was bobbing enthusiastically. Cameron's head lolled back on the cushions as his fingers moved through the woman's short hair.

"Cameron!"

The woman abruptly fell back onto the floor as he sat up, closed his zipper, and came to his feet. "What the hell do you want?"

Cassidy straightened. "God, Cameron, here?"

"What's it to you? You dropped me, remember?"

"You are really fucked up. You decide Chapman's words are some sort of dare and change a script into a horrifying character assassination, which I have fixed by the way. Now...you're into underage girls?" Out of the corner of her eye she saw the girl pulling her top together. "How the hell old are you?"

Cameron retorted, "Well, you won't have to worry about me after this. Thanks to that shit Chapman pulled last week, Victor has moved me over to another series."

Cassidy jabbed a finger at the girl. "Is she your new assistant?" Feeling absurd and angry, Cassidy swiped a hand over her face to calm herself and turned on her heel. She took some pleasure in shoving the door into the wall with a loud thud as she left.

Collapsing against the wall outside the studio offices, Cassidy waited for her heart to stop racing. She was not jealous, she realized. She was appalled, realizing that at some point that could have been her.

She crossed the open lot and re-entered the soundstage, finding a chair where she could sit quietly. If someone needed to see her they could, but the single chair didn't invite others to come and chat. She swallowed hard, accepting some of the responsibility for the situation. She had allowed herself to become wrapped up in Cameron to such an extent that she had culpability in this mess.

Her mind tumbled over the other news she had gleaned from the confrontation. *Cameron is off the series.* She exhaled. Maybe now things would calm down on the set. Chapman would not be able to get in Cam's face every day, demanding things. She wondered who would take over the writing and what the change would mean to Chapman ~ or any of them. It would not break the show, but some people were bound to see his departure as her fault.

With a sense of the inevitable, she covered her face with her hands. After a moment to settle her nerves, she left the set behind, along with all its troubles, looking forward to seeing her first Thanksgiving Day Parade in L.A. She had promised Ryan they finally would attend one.

CHAPTER TWENTY-SIX

MOVING WITH the traffic flowing away from the Los Angeles International Airport, Brenna watched Kevin adjust more comfortably into the passenger seat. Thomas and James sat quietly in the back, elbows on the windows, gazing out at the passing traffic. The radio played so softly she could not identify the song. She was quiet, still absorbing that Kevin was here, in L.A., with her. Her gaze kept sliding sideways to watch him.

He wore a forest green polo shirt instead of the familiar suit and tie, and she wondered why. Previously whenever she had asked him to change into something more casual, he had insisted that a candidate should always look professional. Nervously she rubbed her hand on the gear shift.

Kevin's hand covered hers. She glanced away from the road long enough to catch his smile and offer a faint one back. She turned her hand over, palm up, and briefly squeezed his fingers before looking once in each rear-view mirror. She put both hands on the wheel to change lanes. Her hand never returned to the central console.

"How are Ellie and Marie?" she asked.

"Eleanor, if you please, and Marie Curie," Kevin supplied wryly. "Eleanor's been trying to find the 'most grown-up gown' to wear to the Christmas dance at the church, while Marie can't be bothered. She's taken an interest in physics and joined a rocketry club last month. Her entire room is papered with trajectories and math equations that are years beyond me."

Brenna suppressed a chuckle. "I bet there's a boy involved," she surmised.

"That's what I thought too. She and a classmate, Kirsten, both joined up. Heard it might get them an angle on a scholarship, I think."

Shaking her head, Brenna shrugged. "If she likes it..." She changed the subject. "How's Ellie's dress hunt coming?"

"My sister took her shopping last weekend. Five hours and not a single thing she found suitable. They're going out again this weekend."

Brenna let the silence grow, but it did not feel the same. Usually silence between them was light, a time of communion. She felt anything but communal at the moment, so she concentrated on the road.

After catching the temperature on a bank sign as they passed, Kevin filled the void. "It's warm here. Barely in the mid-thirties back home."

"Oh?"

"Yeah. We had snow two nights ago. Just a couple inches, but it'll probably stick. Nice white blanket for Christmas, I figure."

"It was almost seventy when we were camping," Thomas interjected.

Kevin turned around in his seat. "When did you go camping?"

"Last weekend," Brenna supplied. "Thomas had taught the LAKE kids to climb, and this was their first chance on something other than the gym wall."

"Yeah, everyone did great, even Cassidy."

"Cassidy?"

"Yeah, that blond actress from Mom's show."

Kevin studied Brenna. "Sounds like you had fun."

She shrugged and considered what to say to that. Knowing he was not inclined to go camping, she had not even thought to invite him. *Is he bothered that I had a free weekend and didn't come to see him?* He didn't sound upset, but she could not see his face. *Damn.* Brenna wished she were not driving so she could study his face and come up with the right thing to say. Instead she shrugged again. "Yes. I think everyone had a good time." Her brow furrowed a little even as she tried to stifle it.

There was silence again; she almost reached for the radio dial to break it.

Kevin looked out the window, then mused, "I passed up riding in the parade at home today. Do you want to go see yours?"

"Hmm?"

"I was just noticing the signs blocking off the route and indicating parking. Would you like to go see the parade?"

"But, the crowds..." Brenna felt she would much rather spend the morning at home. The turkey was already in the oven, but she liked puttering around the kitchen. It always reminded her of Thanksgivings as a child.

Kevin shrugged with unconcern. "We'll just be a few more nameless faces in the madness." He put his hand on her knee as he turned around and addressed the boys. "What do you think, guys?"

"If we get somewhere near Del Ray Drive, maybe I can find Marcie. She said she and her family were going to view things from there."

"I'm sure there'll be too many people to find just one."

"We haven't seen a parade that you weren't in, in years, Mom," Thomas coaxed. "Come on."

Paused at a stoplight, Brenna looked from one face to another, then into Kevin's hopeful smile, and she conceded to the majority. "All right."

To guard against too much sun, they purchased hats from a street vendor hawking "LA 2000" downtown revitalization project logo gear. Thomas and James turned theirs backward, sauntering along with big grins until Brenna turned and gestured once with a finger. Sheepishly they both turned the caps around properly and straightened their shoulders.

Brenna pulled a golf-style visor low over her sunglasses and looked up as Kevin pulled the baseball cap brim low over his eyes. He wrapped his left arm around her bare shoulders and tilted his head to capture her lips.

She stiffened in surprise, then forced herself to rest her hand against his cheek, and willed the kiss to tantalize her. When Kevin pulled away, she blinked.

That certainly didn't work, she thought, thankful the glasses hid her eyes. She was very aware of how different his kiss was from Cassidy's ~ less absorbing, less able to take her to a realm of forgetting where and who she was. With a sense of loss, she turned away to watch where they were walking.

Thomas flanked her left and James took Kevin's right, slipping behind the adults when the path narrowed. Brenna worried that the boys would be bored. Adults liked parades for the nostalgia, and little kids liked them for the colors, noise, and candy at the end. She remembered herself as a teenager finding parades painfully dull unless she was surrounded by friends.

"I've missed you," Kevin whispered against her ear, brushing the lobe with his lips. His left arm moved down her back, then abruptly he grasped her hand.

She offered a tremulous smile. "So, where should we sit?"

Thomas and James forged ahead through the crowd. Brenna and Kevin followed, ducking the elbows of in-line skaters and holding their hats against the jostle of the rest of the crowd.

"Are you sure this was a good idea?" she asked.

"Sure. See?" They broke through the line, and Brenna lowered herself to the curb behind the parade rope next to a pair of preschool-age children licking fruity-smelling Italian ices. She inhaled appreciatively, identified grape and cherry, and wrapped her arms around her upraised knees as Kevin reached down, brushed a spot clean and sat next to her. Thomas and James crouched behind them.

James leaned forward, putting a hand on his mother's and Kevin's shoulder. "Mom, can I go look for Marcie?"

"There's no way you'll find us again if you leave," she protested.

He looked up and pointed across the street. "That's the Piccadilly's. Only one for miles. I'll meet you back here in one hour, I promise."

Brenna looked to Kevin, who pursed his lips, then nodded reluctantly. "I guess it'd be all right." She grasped her youngest son's hand. "Be careful."

"I will." James disappeared into the throng before she could change her mind.

Thomas' gaze was fixed on something, Brenna realized, as she turned and caught his face. "You aren't going to leave, too?"

"Well, I don't know. So far I haven't seen a prettier lady to spend my time with." He laughed. She grasped his chin and caught his kiss on her cheek as he patted her shoulder. "So, what's your favorite entry in a parade?"

Brenna opened her mouth to answer, when Kevin began offering his response. "The bands. Not that I'd be biased, having played in one all through high school myself, of course."

Thomas laughed. It hurt Brenna to see Kevin smile at her, pleased by her son's reaction to him.

"What about you, Mom? What's your favorite part of a parade?"

She fell back to a time decades earlier ~ a parade with her brothers. She couldn't have been more than seven. She saw painted faces, smiling, dancing eyes that made everyone laugh. Telling stories from behind masks that hid the truth. "I like the clowns," she said wistfully. "I always have."

Kevin put his arm around her shoulder, and they leaned forward to look down the stretch of road for any signs that the parade was nearing. Calliope music, accompanying the opening float, reached them over the din of the crowd laughing and hollering good-naturedly around them. Kevin's arm nudged her backward, and she felt her shoulders conform to the curve of his chest. Gradually she relaxed her posture until he was almost completely supporting her. She felt his cheek nuzzle her hair and closed her eyes, waiting for the magic.

Tears gathered instead. She did not feel a wash of protectiveness or the sudden rush of blushing affection. His hand was caressing her lower back, but it raised no tingles. Cassidy had raised so much more from across a campfire. She opened her eyes, startled that the blonde was once again foremost in her thoughts, and leaned back harder against her husband's chest. As if on cue, Kevin wrapped his arms around her, catching her hands in her lap as his body hugged hers. "Bonny Brenna's got a blush on," he said in her ear.

She was not blushing because she had shared her childhood fondness for clowns. As her mind filled with the memory of a woman who was forbidden, the first marchers turned into teary blurs before her eyes. She turned her head away, lifted her sunglasses and brushed at her cheeks.

Filled with renewed misgivings, Cassidy viewed the crowded street. She grasped Ryan's hand more firmly as the flow of bodies around them threatened to tug him away from her. She thought about just sitting right there, but the view of the parade would be less than optimal, and she wanted Ryan's first memory of the pageantry to be the best possible. She looked around and located the entrance to Piccadilly's. The route mapped in the paper had shown this as the location of the parade's second turn. She scouted the area, looking to avoid the crowd-scanning cameras. Ryan tugged her leg. "This way, Mommy."

He was gesturing toward the curb nearby, and she decided it was suitable. Tucking herself on the edge, she positioned him between her thighs. Cassidy circled her arms around him and pointed out the blue and red uniformed band marching past. "Would you like to play music someday?"

"Yes!" He jumped excitedly. "Drums!"

Cassidy ruffled his hair as the drumline marched past, feeling its rumbles clearly beneath her sneakers through the surface of the road. She resisted putting her hands over her ears and instead sat back, listening as Ryan named off the other instruments they were seeing. He paused when he could not identify one.

"What are those gold things? Tubas too?" He pointed to a golden line.

"Those are called French horns," she explained. "Don't ask me why."

"Why?"

She sighed and hugged him. "Probably because they were first made in France or something. I'll ask the score director at work."

That seemed to satisfy him. "Okay." Then he paused. "Mommy?"

"Yes?"

"Will you see that lady at work again?"

"Which lady?"

"Ms. Lan...gan?"

"Lanigan. Yes, of course." Cassidy thought of the compact woman and smiled wistfully, wondering what she was doing this holiday morning. She frowned. *Probably waking up with her husband,* she thought wryly.

"Will you tell her I like her hat?"

"What hat?" Cassidy was confused. Brenna had not worn any headgear on the camping trip, which had surprised Cassidy, actually. She still remembered the sunshine on the titian locks as they paused on the mountainside during Sunday's climb.

"The one she's wearing." He pointed.

Cassidy followed the line of his finger through the break in the parade.

She recognized Brenna, but certainly not because the woman was trying to be recognized. A sun visor was pulled low over her face and her sunglasses hid her eyes. However, there was no mistaking that jaw or the soft lines of shoulders bared to the sun.

Cassidy swallowed. *Or bared to her husband's touch.* She had never met Kevin Shea, but that had to be him, curled around Brenna's body, his hands stroking her shoulders. Her throat tightened.

"Mommy?"

"Yes?" she managed.

"Will you tell her?"

"I...I'll try to remember. I'll certainly try." Cassidy sat up as the street became busy again, filling with the GE "Bright Ideas" float moving past, surrounded by dancing light bulbs, one of whom dropped candies which Ryan scrambled to get.

She caught his jacket tail, preventing him from going too far, and soon he was back in her arms, watching the rest of the parade as Cassidy contemplated how Brenna looked enclosed in Kevin's arms. She looked away from the street to brush her eyes and saw couples walking hand in hand, occasionally looking at the passing parade but more often wrapped up in each other. The whole tableau made her sigh. Her gaze slipped back toward the street, and she saw a couple on the near curb from the back, one's hand tucked into the other's rear jean pocket. One brunette head turned and two sets of soft, feminine lips connected.

Normally one to glance away from public displays of affection, Cassidy dropped her chin lightly on top of Ryan's head and let herself covertly study the lesbian couple with great interest. She felt a swirl of arousal in her groin. When their kiss ended, the smaller woman tucked her head against the other's shoulder. Cassidy felt a twinge in her own arm around Ryan, which she now recognized as the need to hold, to cherish. She watched as the women caught pieces of candy thrown from the float and unwrapped them, offering the pieces to each other.

She swallowed and finally turned away, glimpsing Brenna on the other side of the street. Her arms were tucked around her knees and her mouth was open, laughing. Cassidy felt a pain in her chest. She sat back, releasing Ryan for a moment as she tried to catch her breath.

Ryan took the opportunity to bolt out for another piece of candy. Cassidy righted herself and grabbed for him, but missed. She looked at the oncoming parade and did not hesitate. She leaped for her son, now in the middle of the street as the mounted division of the Los Angeles Police Department clip-clopped past. The horses that might have stepped on them stopped instantly. The disruption of their rhythm made a few officers look down.

"Back to the side, ma'am."

Cassidy stood, walking around the two horses to reach the curb.

It was not her curb. Disoriented, Cassidy had sought a section of empty curb, thinking it was where she and Ryan had been sitting.

"Hey, Ms. Hyland!"

Recognizing Thomas Lanigan's cheery voice, Cassidy looked up as she sat, realizing she was about to sit on Brenna's feet. The other woman moved, drawing Cassidy's bewildered attention to the shadowed face. Heart hammering, Cassidy lifted her chin and met the curious expression on Kevin Shea's face.

Cassidy shook herself and looked at Thomas. "Hi. I'm sorry, I didn't see you here."

"Looks like Ryan was getting himself in trouble again," Thomas said. "Saw him dart out ahead of the horses."

Brenna could not breathe. She had stiffened against Kevin the instant she recognized Cassidy settling on their curb. She practically identified the woman by the curve of her rear in her jeans as she bent at the waist. No need to go higher and actually see her face. Mortification renewed, she tried for nonchalance, forcing herself to relax against Kevin, whose hand stroked over the muscles in her upper arm.

You ought to make introductions, her mannered conscience prodded.

Her terror issued a curt *No.*

No one's paying attention to the parade, her conscience prodded again.

Both Thomas and Kevin had fixated on Cassidy. For a measure of calm, and since no one could see her eyes clearly, Brenna focused on Ryan in Cassidy's lap. "I'm sorry, you've never met. Um. Kevin, this is Cassidy Hyland, from *Time Trails*. Cassidy, my...husband Kevin Shea, and you already know Thomas."

Brenna offered up thanks as Cassidy's gaze left her and Cassidy grasped Kevin's hand. "Nice to meet you," Kevin said politely.

"The same." Cassidy returned her hands to her son's shoulders, where Brenna watched them move slowly up and down the boy's small arms. "This is Ryan, my son."

Kevin nodded. "How old is he?"

"Five." Both women's voices mingled in the answer.

Brenna sat up and turned so she was crouched over the curb without being supported by Kevin. "His birthday was back in October. Cassidy threw a party and invited the cast."

"Oh." He rubbed her back. "So, how do you like working on *Time Trails*, Cassidy?"

"I'm sure Brenna's told you all sorts of stories."

"A few," Kevin acknowledged.

Brenna's stomach began to twist. *I'm imagining the rising tension, right?*

"I should probably try to cross back to our seats," Cassidy said.

Thomas' hand shot past Brenna's shoulder and landed on Cassidy's. "Stick around. You'll never find your spot now. At least there's room here."

Brenna turned her gaze from the slender throat swallowing nervously and the dimpled chin angling up to meet Thomas' gaze. His hand rested on Cassidy's jacketed shoulder. Cassidy's throat moved as she prepared her words. Brenna wished, just for a moment, that she had not raised such a well-mannered child, as Thomas squeezed the shoulder, silently convincing Cassidy to accept the invitation.

"All right," Cassidy finally answered. Glancing once more to both Brenna and Kevin, she settled back on the curb and wrapped herself around Ryan.

The matter decided, everyone turned back just in time to be showered by the water sprayed by the thirty-foot watering spout on the Bromeliad Society's garden float.

Wiping her face required her glasses to come off, Brenna realized. She did not want to, but the light refracting through the water droplets bothered her eyes. Reluctantly she tugged off the glasses and wiped them on the bottom of her cotton top. Lifting her head to put them back on, she caught Cassidy's sidelong glance. The other woman also held sunglasses in her hands.

The intersection of their gazes hit Brenna in the stomach, hard. Her lips trembled and her breath caught. Shaken, she looked away to the parade.

The remains of the turkey will barely be enough to cook down for soup stock, Brenna lamented, surveying the scattered dishes.

James reached for the bowl of creamed onions, then paused. "Anyone else want these?" He looked at her expectantly.

As if I have room for another bite. She shook her head. James grinned and scooped the remains of the creamy vegetable onto his plate, setting aside the empty serving dish.

"More sweet potatoes?" Brenna asked, reaching for the pan by her elbow. She cast a significant look at Kevin opposite her.

He raised his hands. "None for me, thanks." Picking up his wine glass, he sipped.

Thomas spoke up from her right. "I'll take them."

Brenna passed the pan, and soon the yams were gone as well. "We used to have leftovers," she complained good naturedly.

It had all been devoured by the boys. She herself had only a single plate, with small portions. She'd eaten reluctantly, trying to cover her lack of appetite and anxieties which lingered from the day.

"They're growing boys." Kevin chuckled.

"It's great stuff," James chimed in, reaching for the bowl of stuffing and serving himself a heap.

"I'm glad." She dropped her eyes from her son and collected her napkin from her lap. When she looked up to put it on the table, she found Kevin studying her. "Yes?"

"I was just thinking that we could leave the bottomless pits here to clear the table and do the dishes." He lifted the remains of the bottle of red wine they had drunk with the meal. "Want to sit on the deck and watch the sunset?"

The tenor of his voice bothered her, but Brenna nodded. "All right." She looked at Thomas. "When you finish in here, you can come out and join us."

"Dishes?" James pouted, still eating.

Thomas shrugged. "Sure."

She leaned forward, grasping Thomas' hand and kissing James on the cheek. "Thanks."

Kevin had risen meanwhile and stood at her shoulder when she straightened. "Ready?" he asked.

She let him pull her chair back, and retrieved her wine glass before following him out to the back deck. The light breeze picked up her hair, and Kevin slipped his arm around her, pulling her into his warmer frame. "It's a nice night," he said as she settled beside him on the A-frame swing.

Brenna didn't answer, her pulse nervously thrumming in her ears.

"So this was your summer project?" Kevin stroked his fingers over the scrollwork on one of the swing's arms. She nodded into his shoulder. "Nice workmanship," he complimented.

"Thank you." She had hunted for weeks for the right wood, and the ash had taken the stain beautifully.

"Something like this would look nice in our yard back home."

"I, well, I'm sorry I didn't come to Michigan then, but, the boys, Thomas, he had Little League coaching. James had joined the summer league through the high school." She frowned. "I was here. And I..." She trailed off wondering how to put into words the unsettled anxieties she recalled suffering. "I needed a place back here to read," she said softly. "It was stifling being inside all the time." She looked into his face for a moment and then uncomfortably looked away, noticing that her rosemary patch seemed a little wilted, in need of attention.

"Is that why you went camping?"

"The camping trip was for charity. But I like it, yes."

"I'm not much of a camper."

"I know."

"But I would have come if you'd asked."

She swallowed. "I know."

The motion of the swing gradually pushed their bodies together, hip-to-hip. She steadied herself with a hand on his thigh and felt his arm drop lightly across her shoulders. His fingers swirled against the bare skin of her arm. She tried not to feel jumpy, but the fact remained, she was. When she angled her head to study his profile, she found his eyes closed. "Kevin?"

He turned to meet her gaze. "Yes?"

"How are the girls?"

"All right."

Brenna tried to calm her mind and think only of the moment, but the sounds around them distracted her too easily. She could hear the scuffling as James and Thomas quarreled over who would wash or dry. Thinking she should help, she started to stand.

"Where are you going?"

She turned, finding their gazes level, and sheepishly shook her head. "I was thinking of helping the boys inside."

"Don't. They'll be fine. I..." He straightened slowly, and she leaned back a bit, watching him. "Here." He reached down and retrieved the wine bottle. "Help me finish this?"

Brenna held the glasses while he poured the last of the alcohol into them. She handed him his and they sat again in the swing. "This was a nice vintage with dinner," she said, letting it remain on her tongue for a moment before swallowing.

"Thanks." The only sounds were crickets. She was taking a sip when he spoke again. "Do you intend to stay out here?"

"With you, of course. I just said~"

"No, I meant here in California. After the show is over."

"You want me to come to Mount Clemens."

"Yes."

She accepted the brush of his lips against hers, tasting the light wine flavor, but ended the kiss as he touched his tongue to her lips, tasting her.

"Nice sunsets out here," he said, caressing her shoulder as she concentrated on the red-orange western sky. "Guess it won't be so tough for me to stay out here 'til the end of the show."

"You shouldn't. There's things to do back in Michigan."

"I'd be willing."

"No. That's not...Don't do that."

"Bren, I feel I need to do something."

"Why?"

"We should be together."

"It's just another five months." Brenna tried to shrug. He put light pressure on her shoulders to stop the motion.

"What about after that? I know you don't want to come to Mount Clemens, so, where do you want to go?"

"I like Mount Clemens just fine. It's just...it's not..."

"It's not L.A.," he supplied.

His expression made her hold her tongue when she was inclined to denial. "I had an offer to join a theater company here," she explained.

"I guessed. I came out here so we could at least talk about it." He sighed and sat back. "I feel like we're drifting apart. I don't want that to happen."

"Kevin, I..." Brenna bit her lower lip, unknowingly presenting a very endearing image. She was startled when Kevin groaned and grasped her hands.

"There's always regional theater, good stuff."

"I worked a long time to get where I am," Brenna said. "It's what I've wanted my whole life."

"A year ago you were ready to give it all up."

Brenna nodded. "Things change."

"Apparently. You haven't written or called much in the last several months."

"I've been busy."

"I know. So have I."

They were silent. Brenna felt crowded, as though Kevin was too close or she was too small. She wanted to get up, to get some space. She braced her hands on the wood, careful not to touch him. She tensed the muscles in her arms to push.

His voice broke the silence. "I still dream about you, Bren."

Her arms went slack. She blushed. "When the series is over..."

"That's a long time to wait." He brushed his forefinger and thumb over her chin and lifted it, bringing their mouths together. "We could make up for it." His breath caressed her lips. "I've missed you."

He pulled her back across his thighs, and wrapped his arms around her waist, nuzzling her hair as they watched the sun finish its descent. For a long time they just sat, and Kevin sipped his wine.

Brenna could not bring herself to do anything. She was frozen between rising and running and just sitting there crying. She knew that Kevin deserved a wife. She had wanted that once, too, wanting nothing more than to leave L.A. and all its competitiveness ~ where she was never good enough, never pretty enough, never young enough ~ behind her. But now, when she closed her eyes and tried to envision a future with Kevin, she felt pain grip her heart and she fought against the tears. *No, I can't.* She blinked, releasing two tears down her cheek.

In her mind's eye rose a memory of Cassidy's smile, soft fingers lifting to her cheek, the whisper of breath against her face just before they kissed...

"We haven't done this since we first were dating."

Brenna jumped at the sound of his voice. "What?"

"Just sit together, contemplating life, the universe and everything," he mused. She stiffened as she felt his lips press against her temple. "About the show. You know, I am glad to know that you're getting along at work again."

"Hmm?"

"Well, her appearance startled you, but it was good to see you smiling with Ms. Hyland. You had such trouble with her at first. Her son certainly likes you."

Brenna's breath caught at the image of Cassidy from that morning ~ her hair loose and blowing around her face in the breeze. She could only nod as her throat constricted with the memory of Ryan crawling into her lap and complimenting her hat. She had fallen easily into playing games with him.

"It was time to make amends. She didn't have any control over events," she explained, unable to prevent the halting as she composed her reply.

"How are things with the show itself?"

"Fine, though it feels more like the end every day. The production team is already being split between us and a new show. The questions from reporters are all about 'the end'." She lifted her hands in the air and formed the quotation marks with a grimace. "It's depressing." She realized her melancholy showed when Kevin brushed his fingertips across her cheeks.

"I'm sorry I brought it up."

Brenna remained silent, and he let her. The sounds around them seeped in slowly, and she realized the house behind them was quiet. "Did they kill each other?" she asked in a worried voice.

"I doubt it," he whispered back.

The door to the house suddenly opened. At the sound Brenna turned with Kevin, spying one of the boys backlit in the doorway.

"Mom! Are you coming inside?" Thomas' voice reached them easily.

Brenna looked up at Kevin and raised a questioning brow. He shrugged at her silent query. "If you'd rather..." he answered, leaving the option open-ended.

"It'll get cold fast now that the sun's gone," she reasoned.

"I wouldn't want a Popsicle in bed later." He chuckled. "We'll be there in a minute," he called to Thomas. "Let's go inside," he said softly, turning back to her and pulling her against him with subtle desire.

Brenna's heart tripped against her ribcage as his hands caressed her throat, brushing over her breast and onto her hip where he tugged, lifting her briefly onto his lap for a hard kiss.

On the pretext of becoming uncomfortably lightheaded, Brenna broke the kiss. "It's not late enough to send the boys to bed." Her voice was tremulous as she laid her palms against his chest. His eyes were searching hers, and she knew what he wanted. She was unsure she could give it to him.

Arguing against the old proscription, he coaxed, "They're old enough now. We can just go into your room..." His voice trailed off when he began nibbling her throat, humming against the skin the way he knew she liked.

It didn't bring a magic rush of desire, and she began to despair. However, his hands seemed to compel her. *He's my husband,* Brenna fretted, but she couldn't think very clearly. She felt like she was betraying someone, but could not decide if it was Kevin...or Cassidy. What she did know was that her heart was not in this.

She closed her eyes, and Cassidy's face floated easily into her mind: cool blue eyes filled with a warming fire, the dimple in her chin that begged to be touched. As Kevin continued kissing her, Brenna seized on the warm desire her imagination was causing and the heat it was sending to her loins. She drew in a long breath. "All right." Shaky, Brenna found herself set on her feet. Kevin led the way back inside.

"All done?" Cassidy sighed as Ryan spread his mashed potatoes and gravy around his plate rather than eating it. "Yeah, you're done."

He looked up at her with half-closed eyes. The meal had been late; both of them had fallen asleep when they returned from the parade.

She patted his back and urged him from the table. "We should pack some of this for the Talbots, don't you think?" Cassidy looked at the leftovers and nodded.

The gossipy neighbor, Mrs. Sandsmarsh, had been less than helpful, but agreed that Cassidy's guess about the Talbots' finances might be right. "Especially seeing as it is Thanksgiving and all," suggested the older woman, a lifelong housewife who frequently hung her laundry while dressed in a bathrobe.

While Ryan settled on the floor, marching his Transformers around, Cassidy gathered a collection of Tupperware and began scooping up the leftovers. Ten minutes later she closed the last container and found a plastic bag to carry them. "Come on." She interrupted Ryan's play and opened the front door. "Let's go visit Gwen and Lou."

"And Chance!"

"And Chance." She coaxed him out the front door while he was still pushing his arms into his coat.

The streetlights were already on as they crossed to the third home on the opposite side of the street. "Now promise you'll be good. We won't stay long." Cassidy watched Ryan circling on the stoop as she waited for her rap on the door knocker to be answered. The door opened and Gwen looked out.

"Cass?"

"Hi, Gwen." She lifted the bag. "I brought some stuff over for you."

"What is this?"

"Leftovers. I made too much for our meal tonight. I thought you might like to have it. We'll never manage to eat it all before it spoils."

Gwen shifted the door wider. "Well, I...We don't really need it ourselves." She motioned Cassidy inside the entry. "Just a minute."

While waiting, Cassidy noticed the Talbot family was still at the table. Lou sat at the head of the table in view. Gwen went up to him and spoke quietly into his ear. The man shook his head. Gwen said something else. Lou's gaze found Cassidy's across the distance. She saw his jaw tighten and firm as his eyes narrowed, but he nodded at Gwen.

Gwen returned, glancing at the bags. "There's tons here. How is it you made so much? Didn't you have guests?"

"It was just Ryan and me tonight. I'm so used to Missouri spreads..." Cassidy shrugged.

"You had no one over? What about...Cameron?"

"No, we broke up."

"I didn't know that." She nudged Cassidy onto the front stoop, closing the door between them and the rest of the house. "Lou wanted me to talk to you. I don't think it's anything, but we wanted you to be aware that Ryan was telling us about your camping trip." She smiled uneasily. "He mentioned your co-star, Lanigan, is it?"

"Brenna invited us to go along on her charity's trip."

"Ryan really enjoyed himself. He kept going on and on with stories." She inhaled, then shook her head. "He told us you 'slept with Miss Lanigan.' We assume that he meant that you two shared a tent and he was just confused."

Cassidy felt her face flush and tried to joke, "Well...yes...of course. What else?"

Gwen studied her for a moment. She checked the door behind her and found it securely closed. Turning back, she grasped Cassidy's hands, feeling them shake. "My God, you did!"

Blood drained from Cassidy's face. "No, no. We didn't." She drew a breath to get her reaction under control. "I kissed her." She frowned. "It's complicated."

"I bet. I knew you felt like she didn't resent you anymore; I had no idea it had gone so far. Guess the hatchet's really buried." She frowned as apparently other implications occurred to her. "For God's sake, don't say anything to Lou."

Cassidy sighed. "You won't say anything?"

"No, I won't."

There was a long pause, and Cassidy thought that would be the end of it, then Gwen asked, "How did it happen?" Clearly "not saying anything" did not mean she would not satisfy her own curiosity.

"It was completely innocent," Cassidy explained. "We had to share a sleeping bag because Ryan couldn't sleep and came into the tent for the night. There were only two bags. He had one; we took the other one."

"Surely you could've shared with him ~ or just slept. So...what else happened?"

"I...I had kissed her...in the woods."

"Cass, are you serious? You're...straight. And she's married, right?"

"Yes." Her hands shoved in her pockets, Cassidy looked around, at the sky, the ground, then back at Gwen. "We haven't done anything."

"Are you still pursuing it?"

"I don't know. I don't even know if she wants to."

They looked up as Lou's voice reached them through the closed door. "Gwen!"

Cassidy shook her head and frowned. "You'd better get back inside. I can't talk about this now."

"I'll have to figure out something to tell Lou. He was disturbed by the story." Her expression told Cassidy he had been more than disturbed. "Maybe we can get together Sunday."

Cassidy nodded reluctantly. She really did need someone to talk to. "Maybe."

Kevin rolled onto his back, taking Brenna with him. Their bodies were covered in a fine sheen of sweat, and the sheet stuck. He laughed, clearly pleased, and kissed her repeatedly. Brenna turned her head aside, pretending to want to curl down and fall asleep. Kevin whispered how wonderful she was.

All the while, Brenna was emotionally distraught at what she had done. *Oh my God! I just gave my husband a sympathy fuck.* Her face hot, but not from exertion, Brenna shut her eyes tightly and fisted her hand against Kevin's chest. As soon as she felt him fall asleep, she would leave the bed.

She swallowed back a sob, knowing, even as she thought such things, that she could not invite questions from him by betraying her emotions with tears. The truth would have to come later, when she was collected and calm.

Tonight, when she could not put another out of her mind, she had learned the truth: Her heart had gone elsewhere. Kevin was still a wonderful man ~ socially conscious and caring for his daughters, her, and even her sons. Brenna knew, though, that she could never do this charade again. Her chest hurt from withholding the tears ~ wanting to cry out in passion, but finding that nothing he did moved her. The usually pleasant soreness between her legs felt instead like a violation of her soul. She needed to slip away and wash herself.

CHAPTER TWENTY-SEVEN

ON SUNDAY, Cassidy, waiting at the window, spotted Gwen coming across the street. She tucked the grocery list in her purse and called for Ryan. "We're going, Ryan! Come on."

Bolting in from the back of the house, Ryan drew to a sudden halt at her feet. "Ready!"

She swept an assessing glance over him. His baggy jeans and tee shirt were acceptable. "Do you have your sneakers?" He pulled up the pant legs and showed off the hidden footwear. She shook her head. "All right. Let's go."

Opening the door, Cassidy found Gwen just reaching for the knocker. "We're all set."

Gwen nodded, then looked down at Ryan. "Chance is waiting for you at my house." They watched him run down the walk and cross the street, without looking both ways. He ran up to the Talbots' front door and knocked enthusiastically.

"How've you been since Thursday?" Gwen asked as they walked to Cassidy's car.

"Right into it, hmm? I've been trying to enjoy an all-too-brief vacation."

"I'm just curious. Ryan is so fixated on you two at the camp, I figure it must've been pretty intense. I told Lou that Ryan had simply noticed Brenna because she's pretty but different from his mother. That seemed to appease him." Gwen paused outside the passenger door. "Have you heard from her?"

Cassidy slid behind the wheel. "No. I don't expect to, either."

"So...have you figured out what you're going to do?"

Shaking her head, Cassidy said, "You don't understand."

"Then help me understand. Were you experimenting, acting out something? I don't get it, Cass. You've never done anything like this before."

"Once." A sudden warmth suffused her cheeks. She had told no one else about this. Gwen was looking at her expectantly. "It was...college. We...Her name was Misty. We'd both been dumped during finals week, and we decided to take a ski trip to Colorado. It was late; we'd been drinking, snuggling by a fireplace. We...I...She..." Cassidy's blush deepened, and she lowered her voice. "The next morning, she made me promise to forget anything happened."

"Sounds like this is the same thing."

Cassidy thought about what she felt when she looked at Brenna or even just happened to think about her ~ the rush of adrenaline she experienced or the equally powerful flood of calm. "No comparison, Gwen. I constantly want to touch her. Talking with her is both the most difficult and the easiest thing I've ever done. She's so physical. Alive. She's intelligent, sharp-witted, private, personal, focused. When we talk acting, I can feel her passion for it. She really gets into it. She doesn't share that with just anyone."

"Passionate, huh?"

Cassidy blushed and changed the subject slightly. "She loves her family, as much as I've seen anyone could. Her boys adore her in return. That's part of the problem. I don't want her to change. If I can't find a way to live with this, it'll hurt her...not to mention her marriage."

"Is her marriage good?"

"I don't know." Cassidy had read nothing but anxiety from Brenna at the parade, anxiety that she knew her presence caused. Certainly Kevin had behaved lovingly while the group was together. *Though*, Cassidy thought ruefully, *I'm certainly not a good judge*. Mitch, and recently Cameron, had showed her that.

"If the marriage isn't good, it's not likely because of you."

"I can't know that, not for certain. That's why I have to stay away until she makes her decision. She asked me to."

"What about the parade?"

Cassidy pulled up at the store and parked. As she set the auto-lock from her key chain, she said, "That was entirely an accident. Most of this seems to happen by accident."

"How'd it go?"

"She introduced me to her husband."

They each grabbed a cart from the corral outside the store. "That had to be awkward."

"I could feel her tension."

"Nothing confrontational happened?"

"No. We all sat together. Her oldest son talked to me while we watched the rest of the parade."

"Her son?"

"We'd gotten to know each other a bit when he taught me how to climb."

"When?"

"The camping trip."

"So, the mother *and* the son?" Gwen pressed her hands over her eyes dramatically. "Sheesh, you don't do things simple."

"I'm not in love with Thomas."

"You're in love with her? You're positive?"

Cassidy delayed her answer as a man walked around them and grabbed a box of spaghetti off the top shelf. When he was gone, she whispered, "I don't just want to go to bed with her, Gwen. That's Cameron's M.O., not mine."

"Speaking of...Why aren't you still dating Cameron?" Gwen picked up two different bottles of pre-made sauce and compared labels while awaiting Cassidy's answer.

"It's over. He handled a colleague badly and really made a scene, put me right in the middle, demeaning me."

They pushed on to another aisle. "You had to have had a clue before that."

"There were times when Cam...It was more about sex and..." Cassidy finally admitted to herself what had been lingering since the night at the club with Griff Torend, "and showing me off than any emotional connection."

"Maybe what you feel for her is because you had a breakup. She's become a friend, someone to talk to. So maybe it's some sort of rebound."

"It's not all me, Gwen. I feel something back from her."

"Last year she hated you."

"She apologized."

Gwen was skeptical. "When you were kissing?"

"No," Cassidy said defensively.

Gwen nodded. "All right. Can you stay away from her and still get your work done?"

"That's a problem," Cassidy admitted wryly. "Since I touched her, I find I need that. We...fit in a way I've never felt before. When she's stressed or upset, I can feel it. When she's happy, she glows." She thought about the time in her trailer when she and Brenna had curled up on the couch together to work over the script rewrite. Despite the sudden changes in their relationship that had prompted Brenna to request that they slow things down, they had fallen into the position so naturally and remained comfortable for hours.

Gwen sensed the awe. "Wow. You never talked like this about

Cameron."

Cassidy scanned the dairy case, checking the stamped dates, and selected a gallon of milk. She nodded. "I told you."

"Does she know how you feel?" Gwen retrieved a package of sliced cheese. "I mean, *really* know?"

"I can't tell her. Not right now. She's trying to sort herself out. It wouldn't be fair of me to complicate that."

"All right. Well, may I suggest that you try not to be alone with her off-camera?"

"That's helpful," Cassidy said with sarcasm.

"Only advice I can give you. If it's meant to happen, it will." Gwen clasped her shoulder briefly, then moved away, picking up a six-pack of Lou's favorite beer. "Just don't expect it to be easy. If this breaks publicly, regardless of what you've actually done or not done, it's going to be uncomfortable ~ at the very least. And it won't just be tabloid reporters who will cause you problems."

"I know," Cassidy admitted. "Are you finished?" she said as they both selected apples and dropped them into bags.

"Yes, I'm finished. You?"

"Just one more thing," Cassidy said. "Wait here."

"Sure." Gwen leaned on the handle of her cart. Going to the card aisle, Cassidy searched for her holiday season cards. One of the boxed sets had caught her eye when they passed earlier. She read the interior message of one with reindeer on the cover and decided they would do. Perusing the wide variety of individual cards, she chose more personal cards for her parents and other family members. One with a mistletoe sprig on the front and a soft gold trim caught her attention. She read the message inside and smiled, then tucked the card in with the others. *Perfect.*

Back in the produce aisle, Cassidy caught up with Gwen, who noted the box and selection of cards. "You're certainly getting an early start this year."

"I have work right up until the holiday. It's better to get them done and mailed."

"You're right." The two headed for the checkout lanes.

Stepping out of her bedroom, Brenna quietly shut the door. Out in the living room, she curled up on the couch and checked the time. It was only just after seven.

"Did Kevin already go to bed?"

She uncurled a little and looked up at James walking through from the kitchen, his hands filled with a plate of leftovers and a glass of milk. "He's going to lose a lot of sleep going back to Michigan tonight, so I suggested the nap."

He leaned on the couch back and met her gaze. "Been a pretty cool weekend."

She could not agree but nodded her head anyway.

"You just gonna sit out here and read?"

"I need to keep an eye on the time. His plane's at midnight."

"You should've come with us yesterday to Groveland Park."

She shook her head. "It was a guys' day out. But I'm glad you all got to go. It gave me a chance to do some things around here."

"Got a phone call from work, didn't you?"

She was a little surprised at his intuition. "Yes, they've rearranged production again. I have to be on the set at six tomorrow."

"Well, it won't be for much longer," he said. "Guess you're ready for it to be over. Have you decided what you're doing next?"

"No, I haven't." She paused, then asked, "What would you like to do?"

James blinked. "You really want to know?" She nodded. "I'd really like to stay here. At least until I finish school."

"Mount Clemens is much smaller, more personal," she said, playing devil's advocate.

"Yeah, I know, but five years in one place has been a long time."

Brenna considered that and realized he was right. "I hadn't thought about that."

"I don't mean to make anything difficult for you, but I really want to stay here."

"Kevin would want what's best for you," she assured him.

"Is he going to move here, or are we moving there?"

She was taken aback. Thinking it had been only a preliminary discussion they'd had on Thursday night, she hadn't expected Kevin to bring the boys into things so soon. "He told you?"

"I told you, you should have come to the park. That's all we talked about." James straightened. "He wants us to help convince you to go to Michigan as soon as *Time Trails* is over."

Brenna frowned, feeling a rush of anger that Kevin would put either of her children in such a position. "We honestly haven't even discussed it fully ourselves. I'm sorry he put you boys in the middle of this." She laid her hand on James' forearm where it rested on the back of the couch.

James pressed his lips tightly together. "You guys gotta do what you gotta do."

"I'm still glad you told me what you want. That matters to me," Brenna promised.

"Is it going to mess things up?"

She shook her head emphatically. "It will not." *Certainly no more than they're messed up now.* "No matter what happens, you must never believe that." He tilted his head, and she wondered if she had said too much.

"All right," he offered cautiously.

She accepted his kiss on her cheek and then watched him as he left the room. With a sigh of misery, she went back to the bedroom and spied Kevin rolling over on the bed. "Kevin?"

"Yes?'" His voice was filled with sleep.

"Did you mention to the boys that we were discussing where to live after *Time Trails?*"

"Yeah."

He sat up and flipped on the bedside lamp. She averted her eyes from his naked chest, trying to give the impression that the light had startled her. She turned back. "We didn't decide."

"Will you come home for Christmas? Bring the boys, and we can hash it all out as a family."

Resignation weighed heavily on her as she gave in. "All right."

"You look like you could use a hug," he said, patting the mattress beside him.

Brenna knew she did, too, but she looked at the bed and shook her head. "Get some sleep. You've got a plane in just a few hours."

She remained as still as possible while he studied her, not moving until he reached up and turned off the light. She closed the door and returned to the living room. In the corner of the couch, she pulled a pillow across her lap, feeling the rest of the cushions hugging her back. She closed her eyes, just for a moment, sipping in a startled breath as the memory of Cassidy's scent suddenly seemed to surround her.

You should have just told him you wouldn't come for Christmas. Burying her face in the pillow, Brenna stifled her groan of self-disgust.

CHAPTER TWENTY-EIGHT

HEAD DOWN, Brenna walked into the soundstage, trying to compose herself despite the early hour. Rachelle's smooth voice interrupted her progress.

"How was your holiday?"

Looking up into the friendly face, she offered a tight smile. "Hmm?"

Rachelle blinked and lifted a hand to Brenna's arm. "Are you all right? What time did your plane come in?"

"I didn't...Kevin...His plane left at twelve-thirty this morning." She rubbed her face briskly with both hands.

"Kevin came for a visit?" Rachelle's grin held a hint of a leer, and she elbowed Brenna, patting her on the arm. "Well, now I know why you look like you hardly slept."

I did hardly sleep, Brenna thought, so she nodded. In truth, the complex tensions she had struggled with for four days had more to do with her current exhaustion. Since Thursday night she had tried several times to broach any of the many subjects she and Kevin needed to discuss. She had found herself agonizing over word choice before she even opened her mouth. It had been painful, exhausting, and in the tend, she had not said anything. He was on his way to Michigan, and she had even found a way to avoid giving him a goodbye kiss. She had never before depended so much on her ability to act and yet at the same time despised it so much.

"Let's get some drinks," Rachelle suggested.

"Please," Brenna breathed. They walked along, following the faint smell of coffee. "What did you and Jacques do?"

"We took Rose home for my family's traditional blow-out ~ all the trimmings. Even my brother and sister-in-law flew in from Seattle."

Rachelle had clearly enjoyed herself so Brenna consciously brightened. "That's wonderful. Are you going back for Christmas?"

"Probably."

They both grabbed Styrofoam cups and filled them from the big coffeemaker. Brenna added Half and Half to hers, while Rachelle slugged it back black.

"So, where's everyone meeting?"

"Your office set."

"Why there?"

"Personally, I like the cushions," Rachelle commented, then shrugged. "Beats me. That's just where Victor said he wanted to run the meeting."

"Branch is leading the meeting?" Brenna wondered why the producer would be leading a pre-dawn meeting usually only called by the director.

"That's what he said," Rachelle confirmed, dispensing more coffee for herself and sipping at it.

Brenna followed the brunette to the office set. Many of the rest of the cast were already assembled. She exchanged grins with Terry, who sat on the desk, legs crossed at the ankles and dangling above the floor. "Morning, Terry."

Brown smiled broadly. "You look good."

Brenna's eyes dipped in acknowledgment. *Apparently a smile and coffee go a long way toward repairing my appearance.*

A semi-regular actor who filled a junior officer role darted in past her and sat on the floor along one of the couches, his muscle shirt showing off where he had spent the holiday weekend ~ on the beach getting sunburned. He grinned at her. She nodded back, her lips curling. "Hurt much?"

"Nah."

Scanning the rest of the room, Brenna considered where to sit. Legs spread as he sat casually, Sean Durham caught her eye and changed his position, freeing up a section of cushion beside him. Brenna shook her head.

Rachelle left her side at that moment and pounced on the space, falling into Durham's lap with a come-hither growl. He wrapped his arms around her and gave her a staged kiss as nearly everyone laughed.

Brenna however could not, assailed by the reminder of her own acting over the weekend. Instead she took advantage of attention being elsewhere and moved to the upper level, sitting on the stretch of couch under the window.

With a silent nod, she acknowledged Chapman on the other couch, sipping from his own coffee. He offered her a smile which she couldn't find in herself to return. Cheron and Durham finally sat side by side.

Shoes clicked on the bare concrete just outside the set. Branch and co-producer, sometimes writer, Lonny Nickel stepped up onto the set flooring. "Good morning."Nickel was younger than Victor, but not much, maybe only forty, with curly black hair and a scarecrow-like build instead of a paunch. His tweed suit jacket sported large patches on each elbow. Brenna wondered why he would cultivate such a professorial look.

Just behind them, excusing herself, Cassidy slipped past, her arrival snaring Brenna's attention. She drank in the sight with a hunger she struggled to suppress. She wore a soft blue cotton pullover sweater, slightly off her right shoulder, over form-fitting cotton workout pants and athletic shoes. Brenna took in the whole and then, over the rim of the coffee cup, directed her gaze up to the other woman's face.

Cassidy looked tired, and Brenna suspected she had slept just as little she had over the last four days.

"Well, looks like we're all— Wait, where's Rich?" Branch took the chair behind the desk, while Nickel set another one for himself next to the producer.

Meanwhile, Brenna fixated on the sight of Cassidy crossing through the set, both pleased and anxious about the woman's direction – toward her. Her breath caught in her throat as their gazes met for the first time since the parade. She put her coffee to her lips to hide their trembling.

At that moment, Rich Paulson bounded in. His lean frame filled the doorway, then sagged dramatically, allowing the man to fold up on the floor in a staged fall.

The low murmuring conversations became stunned silence. Paulson rolled over onto his back and panted as if he had been running miles. "Freeway backed up. I just got out of the car and ran."

Sean grabbed the cushion next to Rachelle and pitched it at him. "Ham!"

"Salad!" responded Paulson, rolling to his feet. "Good morning, everyone!"

"We need to get started. There's a lot to cover."

At Branch's words, Cassidy spun and sat down where she stood, curling her body on the carpeting to the left of Sean and Rachelle's couch. When Brenna looked away from the blonde she discovered Chapman looking at her. She pointedly looked away, focusing on the executives.

"First off, I've appointed Lonny to be the on-set producer for the remainder of the season. Cameron has moved over to work start-up for a new fall series." Brenna grimaced. Even when she was diverting the press from printing anything about the incident between Will and Cameron, she had not expected that would resolve the problem.

There was a murmur of reaction among the others. She glanced down to see Cassidy's back stiffen, as the woman tried to cover a tension that made

Brenna's fingers itch to rub it away. She did not blame Cassidy for the move, though others might. Brenna had a fleeting awareness that as recently as a year ago, she would have been one of them. All she wanted now was to hold Cassidy, protect her. She sighed.

"Brenna?"

She realized she apparently hadn't been quiet enough, as Victor looked in her direction. "Hot coffee," she explained. "Sorry."

Sean boldly asked what was on everyone's mind. "Is this because of the fight?"

Victor frowned as he shook his head. "We decided the new series needed Cameron's special touch." There was a "company line" quality to his voice. No one would say differently.

Brenna nodded. While on the surface the cover story protected Chapman and Palassis, she knew it also protected Cassidy, who had been at the center of their argument in a very demeaning way.

Two runners came in. Victor waved them over and instructed them to distribute the scripts they carried.

"These are the scenes being shot tomorrow," he explained, as everyone received one set. "We're able to go with 264 as planned. Its working title is *Crash*."

Brenna caught Victor's nod to Cassidy, who dropped her gaze to her folded hands on her knee. The Raycreek/Hanssen script. Brenna inhaled and exhaled, trying to figure out why she felt so uneasy about it. After all, she had helped Cassidy with some of the rewrite.

"You'll get the rest of the pages after we've cleared them through set production, as we finalize the filming schedule. It's a little last minute..." *Certainly not uncommon*, Brenna thought ruefully, recalling other scripts that had been extensively rewritten even as they were filming. "...so check the call board every morning. We've also got more newspaper, magazine, and wire folks coming out. As their credentials clear, they'll be sent to you."

"So, no hanging out in our undies?" Sean pouted. "Damn, I was thinking of rehearsing *The Full Monty* with the guys in the back lot."

Branch let the laughter die naturally. "*Crash* is a character piece, limited action for most of you, but there are some key moments early in the script. Let's read." Since most of the cast had not yet seen the script, several flipped pages to finding the teaser. "The director is coming in after lunch. He's checking out the sets right now."

Everyone flipped back to the start, and the scene began to unfold as they tried out the dialogue for the first time.

\#

"Interesting opening," Will said neutrally, drawing everyone's attention to him for the first time since the reading began. He had not had a single line in the teaser.

Victor nodded. "Practice. Read. Walk the sets. We'll reconvene here after lunch, around one."

The meeting broke up quickly after he exited with Nickel. As Cassidy was standing, with help from Rich, Brenna and Will intersected as their way down from upstage.

Brenna eyed Will warily. "How was your Thanksgiving?"

"Just fine. I'm really looking forward to this, though."

Moving alongside Cassidy, Brenna vented her ire on Chapman. "We had to work pretty hard to recover from the mess you caused."

"It's all right," Cassidy said softly, touching Brenna's arm.

She looked at it a long moment before looking back up at Will. "She's more forgiving than I can be."

"I guess that's why I'm getting involved with her and you're not." His expression was significant and cutting.

As Brenna opened her mouth to respond, Rich stepped forward, landing on her foot. "Hey!" Brenna glared up at him.

"Sorry," he offered blithely. "It's crowded here." He looked at Cassidy. "Why don't we all sit down somewhere quiet?"

Catching sight of the other actors watching the four of them with curiosity, Brenna stepped out of the group. "I've got some things to do," she said. "Good luck." She looked from Cassidy to Will; he nodded.

"I'd like to talk to you later," he requested civilly.

"Fine." She strode away, the script rolled in her fist.

Cassidy watched her go, then turned on Chapman. "Why do you have to hurt her like that?"

"She's not hurt, she's confused."

"You baited her."

"She doesn't know what she wants," Will answered.

He met her gaze squarely, and realization hit her. Coolly, she responded, "It's her life, her decision to make, not yours."

Rich looked confused. "Cassidy, I thought–"

"He knows. Don't you, Will? How long?"

"Give me some credit. I have a little experience knowing Brenna's moods."

"And you use that to go around manipulating people?" Cassidy spat. "Have you been enjoying your game?"

"It created a united front, didn't it? I saw you two go off after my fight with Palassis. So, when did it happen? This past weekend?"

Cassidy ignored that. "She thinks you hate her for dumping you. You've been kicking around here like an angry mule."

Chapman sighed and looked away for a moment. "She has been seeking something for a long time. I wasn't it. Shortly after you arrived, when she went home during the hiatus, she was scared. I didn't expect her to come back married. She was so hungry for affection, for approval," he said with a quiet pain that caught Cassidy off guard. "That was when I realized how strongly she was reacting to you. I also realized I'd seen it before with..." He trailed off, took a deep breath. "With someone else. She just didn't understand what her body was telling her. She needed a push so I provided it, to let her feel you needing her. "

"*You* pushed?"

"Bren needs to feel needed."

"She *is*."

"I'm glad you two finally connected. Her tension was going to kill her."

"It's not that simple. She's married."

"Yes, she is. She's cleared some sort of hurdle, though. She readily and openly defended you just now."

"She did look pretty upset when she walked out of here," Rich mused. "Maybe you should go talk to her," he suggested to Cassidy.

"I promised her I wouldn't pursue things. I won't hurt her." She frowned at Will, pondering his proclamation that he had purposely done things to get Brenna and her together. *Was he always acting?* She didn't know anymore. He seemed sincere. Still, it wouldn't hurt to issue a clear warning. "Don't push her again."

Abruptly, Will grinned. "Deal."

"Thank you." Cassidy leaned up and impulsively kissed his cheek.

#=

In the shadows off set, Brenna watched the trio, unable to hear, but fully able to see Cassidy's expression transforming from anger to relief. Brenna caught her breath at the kiss. *What prompted that?* When Will hugged Cassidy and led her off the set in the opposite direction, she leaned hard on the wall and sagged down.

"Brenna?"

She quickly straightened. "Rich. I'm sorry, didn't see you."

"It's all right. Where are you headed?"

"My trailer, I guess."

"All right. See you later."

CHAPTER TWENTY-NINE

BRENNA WAS exhausted. The last reporter finally left her alone, and she signed out, already imagining the bath waiting at home. She had tried to avoid the set itself most of the day. Unfortunately, each time she got a few minutes away, she got another call to report back ~ for a lighting check or a technical sound check or an interview where she had to force herself to smile and be cheerful. Each time she passed the set where Cassidy had practiced with Chapman, her heart ached a little more.

"Brenna?"

Her head jerked up, and she stopped abruptly at the sight of Cassidy leaning against the wall ahead of her. "I was just going home."

"I'm sorry. I didn't mean to startle you."

Brenna noted Cassidy looked worn. "Um...how did your rehearsals go?" she asked, drawing in a breath to steady her nerves.

"It seems to be working." Brenna nodded, too tired to do anything other than register the words. Cassidy started to reach for her, Brenna even swayed toward her, then they both pulled back. "Did Will talk to you?"

Brenna shook her head. She had sidestepped him a dozen times until, she hoped, he had given up trying to talk to her. "The reporters kept me too busy."

"I'm sorry." Cassidy watched Brenna for a moment. "I should go."

Brenna looked up at her, her feelings a jumble of loss and hurt and frustration and want. Cassidy looked around at the empty area before taking a step forward. Brenna started to take a step back, then stopped. "Cass?"

"Yes?"

"I wish..."

Cassidy enfolded Brenna in a hug. She closed her eyes at the wish-fulfilling contact of their bodies. "Shh." Cassidy rubbed her hands over Brenna's tense shoulders and back. "I'm sorry about the parade. I didn't plan that. You wanted space...I didn't give it to you."

Cassidy's voice stumbled to a halt as Brenna wrapped both arms suddenly around Cassidy's back, accepting what she could no longer deny. After a long moment, Brenna's voice filled the silence. "No. Not...I couldn't...do..." Exhaustion was shattering her thoughts. She breathed in but hiccupped on an aborted sob. "I'm going to file for divorce." Brenna blinked back tears, searching the taller woman's gaze for comfort for her soul.

Cassidy leaned back and lifted Brenna's trembling chin. "What happened?"

The years of moral precepts ingrained in Brenna's upbringing were hard to overcome, but she forced out a whisper through the lump of propriety lodged in her throat. "I realized that I love you." Cassidy's arms were raising tingles where they rested on her hips. "I don't know what to do..." It was terrifying and she wanted to hide, but the heat of their touching skin and the feel of Cassidy's heart thudding under her ear fueled her courage. "Help..."

Brenna's words were a soothing balm. Cassidy bowed her head, and tears trickled down her cheeks. Will had told her during practice that Brenna would likely come around when she saw Cassidy with him in the love scenes ~ in the same way he had noted Cassidy's reactions when Brenna had been romantically involved as in her role as Susan Jakes.

He had not yet spoken with Brenna, not explained his actions. Nor had they begun filming. Cassidy was elated. Brenna had not been prodded into making this move.

She pulled Brenna into her body, rejoicing in the comforting touch of their curves melding once again. There was a half-gasp, half-sob from either or both of them. It didn't matter. Their mingled body heat intoxicated Cassidy as she moved her lips away from Brenna's and down the soft column of her throat. She felt the woman tremble and weaken in her arms and murmured, "I've got you."

Brenna lifted her eyes, and Cassidy saw pain and fear slide away, replaced by wonder which mirrored her own. She caressed Brenna's cheek with shaking fingers before returning to the soft mouth for more absorbing kisses.

In their groping, Brenna slid her hands under Cassidy's sweater, warm skin meeting her fingertips. She leaned back and closed her eyes, luxuriating in the sensations as Cassidy's head fell to her shoulder, and she stroked silk skin and taut muscles.

Cassidy groaned with pleasure but shook her head, lifting it to pierce Brenna with darkening eyes. "Don't..." she gasped again as Brenna's innocent touch sent a bolt of desire directly to her groin, "don't do anything you'll regret."

Brenna swallowed and stepped back. The separation was painful, more painful than she could have imagined. "How?"

"We'll do something...impulsive, and you'll wake up afterward, hating yourself...and me."

Brenna nibbled her lip. "That's what happened actually."

"When?"

"Kevin. I...He...We went to bed. I...couldn't think of anything...I...was dead afterward. Cass, I can't do that again."

"Then we wait." She grasped a trembling hand, letting Brenna lead the way as they left the set.

Out in the late fall air in the parking lot, the brisk wind helped settle Brenna's nerves. "Time to go, hmm?" Her car was closest.

Cassidy leaned against the SUV with Brenna, studying her face in the lights of the parking lot. "It is after midnight."

"Do you need to get home to Ryan?" Brenna asked.

"I should," Cassidy admitted, but she reached out for Brenna's hand in the darkness. "But I'm kind of in a daze right now."

"Me too," Brenna admitted. "I can't believe I'm doing this."

"Why did you change your mind? What exactly happened this weekend?" Cassidy asked earnestly, reaching out as the auburn-haired woman's chin dipped. "Brenna?"

"After we got back from camping, I told myself it was...the moment, the change of pace, simply getting to see you in another role. I don't know. Kevin called, and I resolved to work on things with him."

"So you have been having problems?"

"Yes...no...or at least I didn't acknowledge them. We've been finding more and more reasons to have separate lives. I haven't been to Mount Clemens in a while and he hasn't been out here in almost a year."

"What brought him to L.A. over Thanksgiving?"

"He thinks we're drifting apart." Brenna sighed. "I lied. I said we were fine."

Cassidy forced herself to be Brenna's friend first, though the ache in her arms was fierce to hold the woman, protect her from anything that upset her so. "Why lie?"

"It's supposed to be what I aspire to ~ a husband, two kids..."

"That's June Cleaver, not Brenna Lanigan."

"It's what I was raised to believe."

"What about your work?" Cassidy prompted.

Brenna shook her head. "I'd have to stop acting." She moved away from Cassidy and stepped carefully into the breeze that pushed her hair from her face as she hugged her arms around her chest. "I can't do that. Acting is all I've wanted to do since I was a teenager. And I'm good at it."

"You are. So is that why you want the divorce, so you don't have to give up acting? You thought you loved him once. Wasn't that why you married?"

Brenna frowned. "Kevin...made me feel...desirable when I didn't feel it from anyone else."

Damn, maybe Will actually had it right. Somehow he had managed a clear view the rest of them never got ~ of Brenna, the series, even her. She watched Brenna formulate her answer. The look of serious concentration created as she furrowed her brow and covered her mouth was hopelessly endearing.

"He's the perfect husband."

"Obviously not."

Finally her arms dropped, and Cassidy could see Brenna's narrow shoulders square resolutely. "I'd been alone for almost six years. Kevin cares for the boys. My mother likes him." She corrected herself. "No. Mother loves him. He and I apparently grew up across town from one another. She knew his mother through some civic organization back in the Sixties. When I was home on hiatus, she encouraged me to meet him."

Brenna fell silent.

"In the beginning he was right there, every time I turned around. Now..." She sighed, pausing as she assessed her feelings honestly. "I feel more like it's not him I fell in love with, but...the idea of his stability, the support." She groaned and covered her face with her palms. "Does that make any sense?"

"It does." Cassidy stepped away from the Mountaineer and put her hands on Brenna's shoulders, drawing the woman's hands from her face. "Still, it amazes me that Will was right."

"Chapman? What does he have to do with anything?"

Cassidy's lips curled in a grin as she leaned her forehead against Brenna's temple. "He's been trying to put us together for months."

Brenna opened her mouth to fume, but Cassidy's smile took away her sense of having been caught in a sting. "So it was all an act."

"No. He still hates what's happening in the show," Cassidy revealed. "He just didn't see why it had to ruin us, too."

"Incredible. So, he thinks Nickel will be an improvement?"

"I didn't ask him that. But, from what I discovered about Cameron, he certainly has to be." Cassidy frowned as she recalled the tableau she had walked in on in Cameron's office the previous week.

Brenna observed the frown and prodded, "What happened?"

"I'd been at Paul's office, getting the changes approved to *Crash*,"

Cassidy started. "I went to Cameron – to let him know how we'd changed his script and to give him a piece of my mind." Brenna smiled at that. "I found him on his couch getting a blowjob from some teeny-bopper."

"Oh my God." Brenna covered her mouth in surprise.

"I think I was in love with some facade...or dream, too," Cassidy considered. "I'd known he was...somewhat on the edge. I used to find it...exciting. And God, he did help me get away from Mitch..."

Brenna put a steadying hand on Cassidy's arm as the woman drifted back to an obviously painful time. "What exactly caused your divorce?" she asked.

As if quoting from a brief, Cassidy looked off blankly and recited, "Extreme psychological distress from physical and emotional domination."

The tone and words ~ so neutral, so clinical ~ scared Brenna. Muscles tensed, she remembered Cassidy's conversation with Mitch on the phone. *And she agreed to meet him in a park? Dear God.* "You were abused?" Brenna grasped Cassidy around the waist. "And this all happened while you were struggling to adjust to *Time Trails?*"

Cassidy nodded. "It...intensified after Chris became a recurring character. My counselor said Mitch was threatened by my success. My previous roles had been guest appearances. He thought if I really hooked up with a series as a regular that I would get away from him. Lucky for me, that's exactly what happened.

"I hadn't even seen it as abuse. He's a lot like my father ~ likes things 'just so,' very definite about what he wants from life, and a wife and family. Mitch kept saying Ryan needed more of me, which is completely true." She took a deep breath. "When I was supposed to return home on the weekends, Cameron started finding reasons to keep me in L.A. ~ extra filming, a publicity event, anything. I slept on his couch for about three weeks. Then, well, he asked me once and I..."

"That's how your affair began, when you were at your most vulnerable." Brenna shook her head. "You don't have to explain." The story was disconcertingly familiar. The details were different, but both of them had felt trapped by their situations and someone had miraculously appeared to resolve everything. "So, we're both here now, I guess...losing our minds again."

Cassidy felt immense relief flood her body as she lifted Brenna's cheek in her palm. She shook her head. "Maybe it's finding our hearts for real this time. I know that I haven't been able to talk as honestly about all of these things with anyone else."

"The fact that we're both women doesn't bother you?"

Cassidy shook her head. "It surprised me, Bren, but...I'm...not unfamiliar with it." She hesitated at Brenna's surprise, then quickly went on. "When we were apart, I missed you in the space of just a few hours. Seeing you at the parade, knowing you were close but untouchable...I was hoping you'd find me today on our way out." She smiled and took a step closer, reaching out to catch Brenna's hand. "You did." When Brenna's gaze met hers, she said gently, "This might be unfamiliar territory for you, but you're here too."

Brenna's throat moved in an uneasy swallow. "I...I've never had feelings like this." Cassidy felt Brenna's fingers shifting in her hand, turning around and intertwining with her own fingers. "I've never been distracted day and night by thoughts of someone other than the one I was with."

Nodding ~ the words conveyed her own feelings, too ~ Cassidy tugged until Brenna was snug against her chest, the softness of her body warm against her own. Their hearts pounded together. She lowered her head slightly and poured her feelings out over Brenna's skin, her lips and cheeks, meeting her eyes, inhaling the sweat-sweetened scent of her hair. She returned to the soft satin of bow-like lips, delving into the sweet recesses of Brenna's mouth.

Tentative fists at first, Brenna's hands soon opened, caressing Cassidy's body, conceding to the unexpected passion between them. As Cassidy held her face with a tender finger, nuzzling and kissing the rapidly fluttering pulse point under Brenna's chin, Brenna gasped with spiraling need matching Cassidy's own. "Oh God, Cass, I want you." Brenna's fingertips worked beneath Cassidy's top, reaching the bare skin of her stomach, and she unleashed a soft predatory growl in Cassidy's ear. "Now."

Cassidy's stomach muscles clenched in sexual anticipation. The effect threw off her balance, and she shifted to find a way to make contact with Brenna's bare skin. The passion continued lapping at their awareness. They exchanged nipping kisses, chased one another's tongues, and swallowed one another's groans.

Stumbling against Brenna's car, they were abruptly reminded that they were standing in plain sight in the Pinnacle parking lot. "Oh God," Cassidy stuttered, trying to regain control. "We have to stop."

"What?"

Brenna's passionate outrage would have made Cassidy laugh if she, too, had not also been suffering the destabilizing effects of interruption. Blowing out a deep, regretful breath, Cassidy calmed herself and stroked Brenna's arms to soothe her as well. "It's just the place. I do want to make love with you, but here and now is probably not the brightest idea."

Brenna nuzzled into her. Cassidy felt her heart expand at the clear signals that she was receiving from the other woman. Stroking Brenna's hair and back, she reveled in the sudden feeling of protection. She had always been the submissive one in her relationships, used only for someone else's benefit. The men she had dated called it gallantry, but she had suffered it as domination. No way would she not go slowly with this more precious person. "Bren," she leaned back. "It's late."

"I don't want to go."

"I know."

"Cass, I want to see where this goes." Brenna's gaze followed the stroking of her hands on Cassidy's arms, upward and inward along her shoulders, then down her torso. "I don't know how, but I...I'll learn."

"It will be perfect because it will be with you...but not tonight. We have work again in just a few hours."

Brenna's hands stilled on Cassidy's chest. Slowly she nodded in agreement with some inner thought. When she met Cassidy's gaze, she asked, "Would you like to come over to the house this weekend? On Saturday?"

Brenna's passion was amazing; Cassidy felt it washing over her in waves ~ from her darkening blue eyes and from the sensuality of her body's caress. "That's a tempting offer." Brenna's hands moved under Cassidy's top again, the touch making her groan in renewing passion. "Too tempting." She hesitated, gently tugging Brenna's hands free. "I don't want regrets. If we rush this, that could happen."

"The whole day together." Brenna pressed her case. "What about another climb?"

"Camping again?"

"No. There's walls at the gym."

"So we would just get together, work out?"

"You could bring Ryan over. I could make dinner."

Cassidy loved how easily Brenna included Ryan in making plans. "What would he do?"

"I have a spare room at the house where the boys have all their play space, video games, television. I...don't have coloring books, or ...well, there's my sons' old primary reader books."

Her grin widening as Brenna considered turning her teen sons' space into a children's playroom for an afternoon of family-like togetherness, Cassidy realized that the depths between them were growing. Since she didn't want to rush their physical joining, a day surrounded by their children sounded like a proper start. "All right." Brenna smiled, and Cassidy kissed the curvaceous lips. "Our first date." She stepped back and opened Brenna's car door, holding Brenna's hand as she got into the Mountaineer.

Their hands met at the belt catch. Cassidy's and Brenna's happiness bubbled up into a shared laugh and another kiss.

"Drive safely," Cassidy wished as she pulled back.

"You, too."

With reluctance, Cassidy stepped back and closed the car door. The SUV engine roared to life. Holding herself perfectly still to preserve the moment, Cassidy reveled in the heated ball of joy ricocheting around inside her as she followed the vehicle's progress until Brenna was out of sight.

The house was dark when Brenna entered. Turning off the front porch light, she flipped on the foyer light and dropped her coat and purse on the small table by the door. The wall clock over the kitchen entry showed it was after two. She listened for activity in the house and heard nothing.

Keeping as quiet as possible, Brenna stepped out of her shoes and picked them up. Combing her fingers through her hair, she retreated to the master bedroom. There she turned on the light and shut the door to the hallway. She reached for the button on her pants and tugged them off her hips, leaning back to rest on the side of the bed as she pulled them over her feet.

Brenna rubbed her feet for a minute, mind wandering over the time she had done the same for Cassidy. She had been on her feet all day and then stayed in costume for the charity party afterward. Back in her trailer after things broke up, an exhausted Cassidy had fallen backward onto her small couch. Brenna had tugged her shoes off and provided a mini massage. With the clarity of hindsight, she realized the tingling she'd felt in her fingers during that incident had been lust, not nerves. Just like tonight. When it became clear they would be embarking on an intimate relationship, the same searing tingling had returned, and Brenna had become giddy with desire.

Brenna was not a sexual novice; she knew they had been engaging in foreplay. She wanted to make love with Cassidy, but from a practical standpoint, she had no idea what sex with a woman would actually be like.

Pulling off her clothes, she hung her blouse over the back of a chair to air and then lay back on her bed, tangling in her sheets, aware of their coolness against her bare skin. Overhead the fan's slow rotation lulled her, and she laced her fingers over her stomach. The light touch on her abdomen and the faint sensation of moving air over her bare nipples made her stomach quiver, much as it had when Cassidy had kissed her in the tent. Tasting the passion that awaited her fantasy, Brenna lifted a hand to her right breast and circled the nipple, closing her eyes to focus on the images in her head.

Come on, Brenna. You have a fabulous imagination. Just imagine it. Those words of advice from her acting coach two decades earlier rippled through her mind, inviting her to find her soul.

First, she found Cassidy's eyes. As Hanssen or off the set, her gaze always compelled Brenna to meet it. The eyes were not a pure blue, but swirls of blue and white, like a cloud-filled sky. Sometimes they were colorless, giving Brenna the impression that she could fall into them and drown in a soul as wide and as deep as any ocean.

Brenna imagined those eyes heating with passion as they drifted down to watch her caressing herself. She brought her other hand up, lifting her left breast, pinching the nipple between forefinger and thumb.

When Cassidy's head dropped, Brenna would see her hair falling forward around her face. Without the stage lights, the strands were more the color of honey than flax. She knew the texture was soft and fine, imagined the strands brushing against her chest and tangled in her fingers, as Cassidy lowered her head further still.

In vivid panorama, her imagination weighted her down with Cassidy's body, their breasts pressed together as they had been in the tent, the smooth legs tangled with her own. This time when the strong thigh nudged between her legs, she did not protest. The kisses she remembered so well caused her to arch into the phantasm above her, the sheets tangled tightly around her thighs and groin as she pulled at her nipples ~ which were swelling and rising in response to the attentions being paid to them by Cassidy's mouth.

Groin throbbing, Brenna arched spasmodically. She moved one hand away from her breasts, searching out the ache, knowing what she needed.

She started quivering even before her fingers reached the patch of hair covering her mound. Her fingertips slid through the evidence of arousal on her inner thighs, and when she finally parted her folds, she bit her lip to keep from taking herself over the edge immediately. She ran the tip of her tongue over her lips, tasting the perspiration already gathering from her effort to go slowly and fully explore the sensations.

She curled onto her side, drawing her knees up as she moved both hands to her silken heat. She imagined Cassidy against her back, arms securely wrapped around her. She imagined both their hands finding her center, and finally, stifling her gasp of reaction, she orgasmed. Lightly stroking herself as the sensations ebbed, Brenna sighed. "Cassidy."

The whisper passed her lips as she burrowed under the sheet, a satisfied smile curling her lips, then drifted off to sleep for the two hours that remained before she would have to get up again.

Cassidy knocked at the front door to the Talbot home. Lou answered it, still tying a robe around himself. "I'll take Ryan," she said.

Lou waved her off. "Leave him sleeping. We've got a change of clothes for him for school."

"I shouldn't."

"Shoulda thought of that three hours ago when you called and said you were on your way."

"Something held me up," Cassidy said quietly.

"I bet."

"I just started a pretty heavy script. Do you want me to arrange to bring him to the set after school, so you don't have to keep him overnight?"

"That set is no place for a five-year-old," Lou remarked. "I saw last week's broadcast. That farce...what was it? *Brains and Brawn?* Sick. You really want your son to see you acting like that?"

Cassidy blinked. "Excuse me?" The body-swapping script had been a fun one to do. As well as enlightening her to Brenna's physical touch, experienced as Commander Jakes had consoled the body-switched officers ~ her and Durham's characters. She always enjoyed working with Sean, and helping him expand on his character had been a creative challenge. She wondered exactly what Lou's problem with the story had been. Maybe it was her kiss with Rachelle's Luria...*Hmm*...Cassidy shook her head. "I don't write the scripts."

"Ah, so that makes it okay?"

"It's just acting, Lou."

"Kids don't see it that way. My kids don't." He added, "Yours didn't."

Cassidy lifted a brow. "Excuse me?"

"Don't think I believe that line Gwen told me about Ryan misinterpreting things. You aren't just acting."

"Whatever it is you're talking about, it's not your business," she pointed out.

"No, but it is Mitch's."

Cassidy inhaled. She wasn't sure why he was doing this now. "You don't like me. I get it. Give me Ryan and I'll go away."

He remained an obstacle, meeting her eyes for a long assessing moment. She felt the beginnings of real panic. "Please."

Lou Talbot finally stepped back. "Get him, then go, so I can go back to sleep."

She moved quickly to the back bedroom where Gwen typically put Ryan down on the trundle bed in Chance's room. She collected him and his school bag, cradling his sleeping form against her chest and hurrying out the door. She stood on the stoop with Ryan in her arms and watched as Lou shut the door. The front porch light was turned off, leaving her in the darkness in more ways than one. Obviously talking openly to Gwen had not been a very good idea. Resigned, she tucked Ryan in the car and quickly drove the short distance home.

As she collected him again, he stirred. "Shh, go back to sleep," she whispered. With the ease of practice, she wrangled her key into the deadbolt and let them into the house. She walked through the dim hallway and placed him on his bed. He was already in pajamas, the pair she left with Gwen each week in case he had to sleep over.

She sat on the floor of her son's bedroom for a long time after she tucked the covers up to his chin and smoothed the hair off his forehead, just watching him sleep. She hoped that, at least tomorrow, she could manage to get Ryan to and from school and then keep him at the set with a minimum of fuss.

Standing, Cassidy glanced up at the small clock on his dresser. It was almost three in the morning. With a stretch that was only slightly successful in loosening her muscles, Cassidy crossed the hall to her bedroom and pulled off her shoes. Stripping down to her underwear, she crawled into bed. Cassidy spread herself across the sheets, and her body, well-trained by hundreds of nights of knowing she would only get a couple hours of sleep, was unconscious before she had finished curling around a pillow, imagining Brenna's warm body instead of the cool linen.

CHAPTER THIRTY

THE NEXT day, during a quick break from shooting, Cassidy ran to fetch Ryan from pre-school. Traffic conspired to make her return to the studio much later than she had hoped. A small backpack on over his tan coveralls and blue shirt, Ryan jogged alongside her long strides as she crossed the lot toward the tutor's trailer.

A young girl scampered down the path. Cassidy knew Sandy Tillman was fourteen, though with blond hair styled in pigtails, she looked much younger. She had a recurring role as Lilibeth, the daughter of one of *Time Trails'* base administrators. While her father frequently challenged the existence of the program, she was a proponent of the program and planned to grow up to be a Time Squad member.

"Mrs. G said you have–" The girl charged directly for Ryan. "This is your son? Cool!" She skidded to a halt as they all met on the walking path. "Hi, my name's Sandy."

Ryan looked up at his mother. "It's all right, Ryan. This is Sandy Tillman. She works with me sometimes."

Satisfied, her son looked back at Sandy. "I'm Ryan."

She looked at the paper bag in his hands. "What's that?"

"His dinner," Cassidy supplied. "We were running a little late."

"My shooting managed to speed up a little bit for the afternoon session, so I got a long dinner break. Ryan here is going to help me get out of homework, aren'cha?"

"Where's Mrs. Grinaldi?"

"Mrs. G's in Trailer Fourteen. Come on, I'll lead the way." Sandy offered her hand to Ryan, who looked at his mother uncomfortably.

"It's all right."

"Yeah. There's cool stuff. I've got my school books, but there's games and toys, too."

Ryan took Sandy's hand, and with Cassidy following behind, the trio crossed to Trailer Fourteen.

A nearby trailer door swung open, and Rachelle Cheron appeared on her steps. "Hey, Cass, glad to see you made it back. Coming to dinner?"

"In a minute. I've got to get Ryan settled first."

"Ryan?" Then the woman spotted Cassidy's son. "Oh, hey there!" She waved. "Meet you in the commissary later." Still in costume, she crossed the lot at a fast walk.

Cassidy turned to see her meeting an extra who was out of costume. Once inside the tutor's trailer, Cassidy shook hands with Karen Grinaldi. "Thank you for doing this."

"No problem. Kindergarten?"

"Pre-K."

"So, no homework."

"He usually stays with a neighbor after school, but some changes occurred recently and she can't do it any more."

"I've worked as a set tutor for a dozen years. Ten right here at Pinnacle." They turned to see Ryan had settled with Sandy on a rug near a set of shelves. The girl had pulled down a copy of Candyland™ which Ryan had excitedly pointed out.

"I know this one," he was saying.

"Looks like they'll get on fine." Mrs. Grinaldi set Ryan's dinner on a nearby table. "I'll get him to sit and eat when he's hungry. The rest of the staff's kids are already gone. I watch the writers' and execs' kids too from time to time. Sandy just has to stick around for an hour now until her mother can pick her up, but she's finished her shooting for the day. I'll keep Ryan here until you're done."

"It won't be too late. I just have a re-recording session and a handful of C.U.s. I'm really sorry about this. Might be ten o'clock?"

"Like I said, no trouble at all."

"Thank you, Mrs. Grinaldi."

"Call me Karen."

"Thanks, Karen." They shook hands, then Cassidy crouched and hugged Ryan. "Take care, buddy. I'll see you later."

Outside, Cassidy found Brenna standing at the foot of the steps, leaning on the railing. The way the other woman's gaze sought hers made Cassidy's breath catch. She saw so much warmth in those eyes.

Brenna's hand covered Cassidy's on the railing as she reached the bottom of the steps. "Is everything all right?"

"Yeah. I didn't even know this was here. I mean I did, but I figured it was just for the underage actors."

They walked across the lot together, and Brenna shook her head. "I used Karen's services myself. James was only ten when I started here. Thomas was twelve. A year later, I felt they were old enough to go home as long as I had my housekeeper, so I stopped needing to bring them here."

"Rachelle must use her from time to time when Rose is sick. I should've thought to ask her."

Brenna shook her head. "Rachelle has Jacques, and they have daycare in the city. Nope, it's just us single moms who need these."

"Single moms?" Rachelle was at the condiment stand when Brenna and Cassidy entered, and she'd caught the end of Brenna's statement. "What about single moms?"

"Cassidy just left Ryan with Karen Grinaldi. I was telling her that I used her services, too."

"Oh, yeah." Rachelle nodded. "Certainly didn't think you were single now."

"With Kevin in Michigan, it's still much the same thing."

"Oh. Well, come on over when you've got your plates." She finished gathering up her ketchup packets and napkins and walked across the busy commissary. Looking out across the crowded tables, she spotted no familiar faces until she got to the cluster of tables pulled together for the *Time Trails* cast on their break. While Pinnacle was the shooting home of *Time Trails* and a handful of other first-run series, it also shot dozens of movies ~ both for television and theater release.

Brenna and Cassidy stepped into the buffet line and selected salads. Brenna picked up a diet cola and watched as Cassidy collected a coffee. "Are you going to make it?" she asked in a low voice.

"Yeah. I should be out of here by ten."

"I'd love to listen in. If I finish up my C.U.s before it's too late, would you mind?"

"All right."

"I'll pick Ryan up and bring him with me."

"I'll call over and tell Karen it's okay."

Brenna smiled as they stopped at the condiment counter before walking over to join the rest of the cast. They settled into the remaining empty seats, between Rachelle and one of the *Time Trails* regular extras, who played an officer in Luria's department.

"Good to see you again, Alex," Brenna offered. "How's life on the outside?"

The Amer-asian male shrugged, chewing a bite of his Salisbury steak. " I've been lucky, picking up commercials, but a lot haven't been so lucky. Projects are dying quickly and quietly. The writers' strike looks like it might happen."

"Just as pilot season is prepping?" Brenna asked in disbelief. "I doubt anything will happen. Someone's going to blink."

Cassidy shook her head. "Actually, I'm not sure. Even Paul was anxious about it last week."

"I've read the party lines. What's really at stake?"

"The way work is credited," Sean put in. He was the most experienced among them on the other side of the camera. "I haven't figured out how I'll vote yet."

Brenna nodded. "Won't get me straddling the line. If you wrote it, you should get the credit for it. End of story."

The actor-director groaned. "And a director's vision doesn't count? Many of them rewrite whole sections of scripts."

"You don't."

"I don't have to; I work with the original writer. In some cases, they're not on set."

Brenna shook her head. "I still don't see the argument as valid. Put the director's name in as co-writer then. Or as teleplay writer."

"Then the original writer gets less of the take." Sean changed focus. "And what about all the reality shows? Writers do have a decent gripe about that."

Cassidy saw that Brenna and Sean were going to really get into it and decided to intervene. "We won't solve the issue here. We'll just have to wait to see how the vote turns out." Brenna shook her head, hair falling across her face as she bent to eat. "Right?" Cassidy prompted, trying to draw up the blue eyes to look into, just once.

The woman's head came up and she smiled. "Right."

Conversation switched to catching up. While Brenna had heard about Rachelle's Thanksgiving, it was a chance to find out what everyone else had done. Across the table, Will elaborated on his time off, spent in Arizona with his sister.

"She's ready to pop," he said with a sigh. "So's her temper. Man, I don't think I've put my foot in my mouth that often since I was in junior high trying to ask a girl out. She jumped on everything."

Brenna remembered him telling her some time ago that his sister was expecting. "Pop? Your sister hasn't had her baby yet?"

"No, and she and Terry are just dying of anxiety."

"Do they know whether it's a girl or a boy?"

"Nope. They want it to be a surprise."

"Do they still need anything?" Rachelle asked. "We could get together a care package and send it to them."

"That'd be a nice gesture," Sean agreed. "They're extended family after all."

Will shrugged. "I guess they could always use things. All right. I'll give the office the address."

"We'll pack the stuff up ourselves," Terry Brown suggested. "I'll bring some wrapping paper."

Brenna looked around at the others and smiled. "Looks like your sister's going to have reason to forgive you for foot-in-mouth disease."

"Here's hoping." He lifted his cola in mock toast. Everyone laughed. The meal finished quickly after that.

Brenna found herself alongside Will in the back of the group as they returned to the set.

Finally he broke the silence between them. "I haven't had a chance to talk to you."

"I know."

"Is everything okay?"

"Cassidy told me what you did. Why, Will?"

"I'm sorry if it hurt."

"What you did was pretty strange."

"But things are working out?"

"I haven't exactly figured out what to do yet."

"You will."

"Since you're playing matchmaker, maybe you can break it to Kevin for me," she said sarcastically.

He shook his head. "You'll have to do that yourself, but I think you'll find a way."

She sighed. "I'd love to know where you get off being so intelligent about this."

"Let's just call it deja vu." He did not sound pleased, but rather resigned at his knowledge.

"All right." Brenna shook her head and walked ahead, stepping up onto the set and taking her place. She watched him set up across the way and waited for the director's instructions as everyone else, stagehands aligning them, also took up their positions.

"We're going to do the C.U.s in short order, but everyone is to hold their marks to keep the background consistent."

When Brenna stepped off the set an hour later, Cassidy had already gone to her re-recordings, the close ups on her side of the set finished. Brenna changed in her trailer, removing her tunic gratefully. It was already after nine, so she hurried to Trailer Fourteen and stepped inside, drawing Karen's attention when the door latched. "Hey."

"Hello there. It's been a while, Brenna."

"Yeah. My boys are pretty much on their own now."

"How old are they?"

"James turned fifteen back in February. Thomas just turned seventeen."

"High schoolers. Geez, time flies."

"Who've you got today?"

"It's just me and Ryan. I had Sandy when Cassidy brought him, but she wasn't here long."

"Cassidy's still over in recording, I think. She said she'd call and okay me bringing Ryan."

"She did. Well, I'm on my way then. I'll walk over with you." She collected Ryan and his backpack, and they joined Brenna near the door.

"Hi!" Ryan said with a smile. "Are you going to take us camping again?"

"No. I did come to take you to your mom, though," Brenna said. "Is that okay?"

"Sure!" He freed his hand from Karen's grasp. The tutor looked on in surprise as he immediately attached to Brenna's hand.

"Let's go, buddy." Brenna caught a strange look from Karen and wondered what she had said.

When the sound booth "do not disturb" light went out, Brenna pushed open the door. Ryan left Brenna's side and charged his mother. "Mommy!"

She swung him away from the overhead microphone and onto her lap, accepting his hug as she looked up at Karen. "Thanks."

"No problem. He's pretty self-entertaining. Tomorrow?"

"At the moment, let's say yes, if that's all right?"

"Sure. Good night." Karen waved at Ryan and Brenna as she exited.

"So, how'd it go?" Brenna asked.

"Thankfully we did most of the work on the interior sets. I only needed to redo about half my lines," Cassidy declared.

Brenna laughed as she took Ryan. "Only half? When I was in here yesterday, I had over a hundred lines to redo."

"Slipping?"

"I've got a lot on my mind lately."

Cassidy nodded. "I know the feeling."

Meeting Cassidy's gaze, Brenna felt her hormones sit up and beg. It was embarrassing. She ducked her head away.

Lightening the mood, Cassidy asked, "Anybody wanna do a sing-a-long?"

Brenna held out both hands in protest. "*Happy Birthday*'s the only thing you'll get out of me."

"Whose birthday?" Ryan interrupted curiously.

Brenna kissed his head and brushed her fingers through his hair. "No one's, sweetheart. I'm just explaining my shortcomings to your mom."

Cassidy chuckled. "Not very convincingly, either," she pointed out. To Brenna she said, "I heard you at the campground. You're good."

"My first husband thought I sounded like Grable on a bad day."

Puzzled, Cassidy remarked, "Grable was never a singer."

"See, I told you." Brenna offered a toothy smile and stood. "Time to go home, anyway."

"I suppose you're right."

"Of course I'm right. That's why they put me in command." Cassidy laughed, and Brenna chuckled. "Let's go home." Ryan bounded out of the room ahead of them, and Brenna flipped off the light.

"See you in the morning." Cassidy reach out and captured Brenna's hand. Their fingers meshed for a moment, and gazes caught before they parted.

CHAPTER THIRTY-ONE

STANDING AT her kitchen sink, Brenna rubbed a towel over the waffle iron she had just washed. Thomas and James sat finishing their breakfasts before having to run for the bus. "How's breakfast?" she asked.

"Great, Mom. Thanks," Thomas answered first.

"Sure thing," James added.

After placing the iron back in the cabinet, she leaned over the counter. "Thomas, honey, could you reserve the climbing wall at the gym this weekend?"

"I guess so. Why?"

"Cassidy– Ms. Hyland," she corrected quickly, "mentioned that she was free this weekend. She often comments on how much fun she had on the mountain. I thought that maybe you'd like to refresh her climbing lessons." Brenna tried to sound nonchalant. She need not have worried. Suddenly Thomas wasn't paying any attention to her.

He leaped for the telephone. "I'll reserve the coolest wall. There's this one at World Gym that I think she'll find really challenging."

"You can wait and call after school."

"By then it'll already be reserved. What time does she want to go?"

Brenna snatched a time out of the air. "Two o'clock Saturday?"

"Very cool. All right." He turned and plugged his left ear while listening to the call ringing through.

"Mom?"

Brenna turned and met James' gaze across the dining room table. "Yes?"

"Is Ms. Hyland coming over just to climb?"

"No." Brenna shrugged a shoulder. "I thought we could have her and Ryan to dinner afterward."

"Saturday night?"

"Yes."

James frowned and put down his fork. "Well then, I guess I'm going to miss the fun."

"What?"

"Yeah. Marcie and I have a skate date Saturday night."

Brenna studied him, getting the distinct sensation that he was lying to her. "James, what's up?"

"Well, I'm bummed I'm gonna miss seeing that cute kid," he said, returning to his food.

"When did you set up this date? I don't remember you asking for permission."

"Well, I only asked her yesterday. Didn't get a chance to mention it to you."

Brenna circled the table and put a hand on his shoulder; he tensed under her touch. "Didn't you enjoy meeting Ms. Hyland and her son on the camping trip?"

"Like I said, cute kid."

"James," Brenna prodded anxiously.

Her youngest sighed. "Mom, I don't want to spend an evening watching Thomas make gooey-eyes at her like he did at the parade."

Having been unable to find his girlfriend in the crowd, James had returned to the group after Cassidy and Ryan had joined them. She had been too caught up in Cassidy's presence herself to notice his discomfort or Thomas' behavior. "I didn't realize you felt that way about her."

"Mom, I..." James frowned again, screwing up his face as he tried to find a way to put his thoughts into words. "I can't help but look at her and remember they brought her in to replace you."

"That's not true," she corrected sharply.

"So maybe not *replace*. But they didn't think you had 'it,' and she does, and I remember how hurt you were about that." He shook his head. "You didn't used to like her, now she's everywhere." He turned his head away angrily. "What happened to keeping work and us separate?"

"James," Brenna began, not exactly sure what to say. Then she began carefully, "I was wrong to be upset with Ca...Ms. Hyland. When I realized that, I took some time and got to know her. She's...just an actress, like me, trying to do her job."

"You think 'cause you helped find her kid that makes her your friend?"

"No, I did that because she needed help. And I...*we* were in the right place to do something."

"You should've never let your guard down. She's just going to stab you in the back."

"No, she won't." She reached for him, but he pulled away. "You've never told me any of this. We should talk about it."

Frustration stiffened his body, and Brenna watched his expression fluster and sour by turns. His fists opened and closed. She hadn't seen him like this since he tried out for soccer and didn't make the third round cut to join the team.

"Damn, Mom, Thomas is so ga-ga over her. She's just some pretty face. You said so."

"I was wrong. There's no reason to get so upset."

"What happened that you've got this thing about making amends? The series is over in five months."

"I hadn't taken time to know her. Now that I have, I find she's intelligent and thoughtful. Fun. I want to spend time with her outside of work. She and Ryan are pretty special people."

James shook his head and sighed. "I just don't get it." He pushed to his feet. "I gotta get my stuff."

"James, stop. Could you please just...take some time? Give her a chance? Be here Saturday, I think you'll be surprised." Brenna leaned on the table and tilted her head back, looking up at James. She could see the tension in his shoulders as he struggled with what she was asking of him. *What is so hard? What has he been thinking about?*

He never answered. The hall clock chimed the hour, making it too late to continue their conversation. "Gotta go. See you tonight." He turned around and jogged for the door.

"James, wait!" Brenna called as he opened the door. He was gone in the next breath. "Damn," she muttered under her breath. "He's never lied to me."

Thomas rested a hand on her shoulder. "Go ahead and tell Ms. Hyland the wall's been reserved. I'll talk to him."

She patted his hand absently, then watched in silence as he grabbed up his own bag and left the house.

Picking up a fork and cutting into the cooling remains of James' half-eaten breakfast, Brenna released some frustration in silence. She bit into the waffle. *Damn, damn, damn!* The sweetness of the syrup went down bitterly.

Brenna straightened the collar of her costume's undershirt and tugged the jumpsuit smooth across her stomach. Double-checking her makeup in the mirror, she headed for the soundstage where she was expected to meet with the *Variety* people and do an interview. As she entered, she could hear the sounds of voices, and she slowed her steps. She told herself it was because she didn't want to risk making a sound that would be picked up by the on-stage microphones. Stopping at the edge of the nearest set, she listened to the dialogue between Hanssen and Raycreek.

```
"I prepared a fire for our meal," Hanssen said.
"Good thing I brought the wine, then," Raycreek
responded.
"When do you think they'll get the vortex reset and
find us?" Hanssen asked.
"If I know Susan, she's working on it right now."
```

Brenna swallowed. She knew from watching practice that this was the moment the two of them were huddled in a "homeless camp," an alley lit by the garbage burning in a city trash can. Curiosity pushed her slowly around the barrier. Between her and the raised area of the set, the entire film crew was scrambling around doing their jobs ~ adjusting sound and angle and microphone levels to catch the drop in both voices as they became more intimate.

Brenna's eyes saw past all that to the two people alone in the middle. She covered her mouth, abruptly stifling the jealousy that flared at seeing them so close. Will was practically leaning on Cassidy's left shoulder. Her *bare* shoulder, Brenna realized, seeing Cassidy's costume for the first time. *God, what a mess!* The vortex effect had taken its toll on both their costumes. Chapman wore torn uniform pants and no shirt. Cassidy's uniform was strategically torn to reveal a lot of skin.

Cassidy looked over her shoulder at Chapman's face, her hair falling across her cheeks and over her eye in a look of devastating sensuality. Brenna's stomach twisted as Chapman's face twitched into an amused smile. She tried to focus on some place other than their faces, inches apart, and found Cassidy's hands, curved together, elbows resting on her knees. Cassidy straightened as Chapman lifted his left palm to her cheek. Brenna couldn't stop staring as he kissed her.

Face hot, Brenna backed up. She shut her eyes to blot out the image. And abruptly opened them again~ having found herself, during the brief moment behind the darkness of her eyelids, taking Will's place in the scene.

"Ms. Lanigan?"

"Hmm?" Brenna turned to the whispered voice that sounded just next to her right ear.

"Sanderson, *Variety*. We have an interview?"

She put her hand over his mouth and shook her head. Relief filled her as she led them out of sound range but not too far to prevent her from keeping an eye on the filming. "Now, how is it you didn't know not to step onto a live set?"

"I'm sorry, ma'am." Brenna raised an eyebrow at him. "Excuse me, I mean, I..."

She smiled at him then, completely upsetting his already precarious control. "Well, now that we've established you're new at this, how about I ask you a question?"

"I..."

He was completely flustered. Brenna almost giggled. He was a small young man, barely five-six, she guessed, and his inexperience suggested he was an intern at the industry magazine.

"Sure?"

"What's your first name?"

"Barry?"

She grinned. "Good. Now, how familiar are you with the series?"

"I've been watching since the first episode," he admitted bashfully. "I thought it was great that they put a woman in charge."

She grinned. "I don't think they knew what they were in for."

"What's it been like so many years on the same series?" he asked, warming a little to his intended topic. "Longest role you've ever had, isn't it?"

"Yes, it is. Jakes is such a full-bodied character. I've enjoyed living in her skin. It'll be hard to see her go."

"No movies?"

"They haven't made any plans."

He glanced over his shoulder as commotion from a break in filming drew his attention. "What's that all about?"

"Ah, that'd be a spoiler," she warned. "Can't print anything."

"I know, I know, but off the record?"

"What's it look like?" She was curious as to whether he saw any falseness in the acting.

"Hanssen's getting together with Raycreek? I didn't think those characters spent any time together."

"The vortex transit was rough."

"Pretty sudden, still. And," the young man went on, "doesn't Jakes have the hots for Raycreek herself?"

Brenna answered honestly, "Not anymore. He's more like the brother she never had." She scrunched up her nose. Sanderson chuckled. "Now, I bet you have other questions."

"Yeah. I, hey, would you like to do this over a cup of coffee?"

Brenna shook her head. "As you can see, I'm in costume. I can't leave the set."

"What are you shooting today?"

"Just a couple of scenes in my office."

"Could I see it?"

"All right."

During a half-interview, half tour, Brenna led the young man around the soundstage, steering clear of the shooting, and finally sitting with him on one side of her office desk and her on the other side.

He picked up a prop from the desktop. "These things really are just cobbled parts," he realized aloud. "Just...look at this, a disposable razor, a toothpaste cap? All painted gray. Funky."

Brenna laughed. "None of the science is real. We make it up. Well, the writers make it up."

"So, were you ever interested in science or space exploration?"

"No, I've always been an actor. That's what I love."

He frowned. "I got into the science. I like engineering."

"I'm glad there's an inspiration out there from the things we do."

"Anybody else in the cast like science?"

"You'd have to ask them." Brenna began to piece together the clues. "Can I ask you a question now?"

"I, well...yeah, go ahead."

"How did you get on this set?"

"Excuse me?"

"You're not from *Variety*, are you?"

"I...um, well..." He stood up quickly. She grabbed his wrist. "I'm sorry." He looked up to see someone coming toward them. "Listen, I really just wanted to meet you. I think you're great. I'll leave now. Don't report me, please?"

Brenna shook her head. "Pretty elaborate scheme to get in to see one actor."

"I'm secretary of your fan club. Really. I'm a student at UCLA. I've been following you since before *Time Trails*."

"Following me?"

"Not stalking or anything like that, honest, just always trying to find out more about you."

"I see."

"Who's this?"

Brenna looked up at Cassidy standing over her left shoulder. "Hi, Cass." She redirected her attention to the young man. "My interviewer, or so I thought. It just struck me that I was giving a tour as much as I was giving an interview."

"Really?"

"You're not going to report me, are you?" He looked at Cassidy with big eyes. "Please?"

"Bren?"

"I think he's harmless."

Barry sagged with relief. "You're not going to report me."

"No." Brenna shook her head. "If I were you, I'd get out of here, though, before someone else comes along." She stood up and pointed toward the exit. "And I'd better not hear word one of any spoiler getting out about the upcoming episode." He shook his head vigorously and scrambled toward the door she had indicated.

When he was out of sight, Cassidy said, "How could you spend an hour with him?"

"How'd you know it was an hour?"

"I noticed when he first came up to you."

"I thought you were filming."

"I was." Cassidy leaned close. "I always notice when you enter a room. I get this jumpy feeling in my stomach."

Brenna found herself face to face with a very sincere, very sensual expression. Cassidy's hand had risen from her side. Brenna intercepted it and placed it against her chest, letting them both absorb the feeling of her pounding heart.

"I looked for you before filming started," Cassidy said quietly. "You got in late."

The recollection of the morning brought several things to mind. "Thomas reserved a climbing wall ~ he says it's the best in the area ~ for two o'clock Saturday afternoon."

"That sounds good."

"Could I ask you a favor?"

"Anything."

"Would you consider talking some to James? He's...I don't know what's wrong, but he's bothered by all the visits between us. He views you as some evil, backstabbing witch."

"Sounds like an inherited viewpoint," Cassidy said drolly.

Brenna protested, "I haven't thought about you like that in months."

"That's certainly good to know," the blonde chuckled ~ she fingered the open collar of Brenna's vest ~ "because I'd like to think I've shown you another side of me."

"Rest assured, I've seen all sides."

"Not all," Cassidy teased softly. "Not yet."

Brenna couldn't help it; she leaned forward. As though pulled by gravity, Cassidy's hands moved down her sides and around her back. She inhaled the healthy aroma of perspiration caused by Cassidy's exertion under the lights.

"I needed this," Cassidy said as they hugged. "Will's definitely not my type."

"Anytime I can help," Brenna said, stepping back. "We'd better get back to work."

"Are you going to watch more filming?"

"Do you need me there?"

"I'd like it."

They stood together, bodies lightly touching, each drinking in the planes of the other's face. They heard footsteps and separated.

Will Chapman appeared around a corner, instantly taking in the scene. "Glad I came for you instead of a stagehand." He looked pointedly at Cassidy. "Come on, we're needed back on the other set."

Cassidy left with him. Brenna remained behind, resting her palms on the desk, steadying herself from the heady rush of hormones still cascading through her body like a flash flood. She closed her eyes and absorbed the true precariousness of the indulgence she'd shared with Cassidy, breathing deeply to calm her heart. She really was going to have to find a way to stay away from Cassidy during filming. "Be one hell of a story if we got caught together," she muttered. *Damn.*

Cautiously she slipped around to watch the rest of Will and Cassidy's scenes, listening as lines were flubbed, spoken too softly, or stumbled over. Cassidy kept making eye contact with her, causing reshoots time and again.

At least there weren't any more kisses. Both Brenna and Cassidy were grateful for that mercy.

CHAPTER THIRTY-TWO

"THANKS, SWEETHEART."

James Lanigan had known he was in for it when his mother gripped his chin, kissed his cheek, and uttered those words. She had not even asked, just assumed that he would be okay watching Ms. Hyland's kid for an hour. His mother, Thomas, and Ms. Hyland were climbing walls at World Gym.

James sighed. He was probably being unfair. His mom had not asked because of two simple facts. One, he was not climbing. Nothing could get him even four feet off the ground onto that wall. Two, Ryan was also not climbing. *Well,* James amended silently as he pulled the five-year-old off the Road Rally Virtual Racer, *he's not climbing the walls.* "Do you want to play something?"

"I want to race the cars!" Ryan responded firmly.

Feeling like his mother when he spoke, James shook his head. "You're not big enough."

"You could push the pedals," the boy answered. "Please?"

Crap. James looked with misgiving at the bucket seat, then sighed and dug into his pocket for the tokens obtained with his mother's ten dollar bill. "All right. Let me sit first, then you can sit on my lap."

Leaning forward, James dropped in the necessary tokens. As soon as he sat back, putting his hands up on the steering wheel, the boy was pushing his way onto his lap and determinedly squeezing in across his already cramped knees. *Sheesh, couldn't they make these things closer to real size?* "Ready?"

Ryan beamed. "Yep."

Obediently James only worked the brake and gas pedals as the boy steered like the five-year-old he was. Given four lives a game, Ryan quickly expended them ~ dumping the race car into a gorge and driving it into a spin-out with a giant sand scorpion, a river, and finally a cliff wall. They did not even make it a quarter of the way through the course.

The competitor in James took a big beating, especially when Ryan glanced up at him over a shoulder. "Can we go again?"

James sighed. "We've only got an hour. Wouldn't you prefer something else, simpler, maybe?"

Ryan's reply was uncomplicated and uncompromising. "No."

Stymied, James counted out more tokens. This time he gave them to Ryan to insert. Five minutes later, Ryan had again lost all four lives, but they made it halfway through the Desert Rally course. *Only because there are fewer things to hit*, the teen thought morosely.

Inevitably Ryan asked, "Again?"

So they did it again. This time James convinced Ryan to let him "help" steer.

Twenty minutes later, they made it through the course, dead last.

James looked at his watch. *At least we made it*, he allowed with a half smile. "Time's up. Let's go find our moms," he said, a little too cheerfully. Pushing the boy from his lap, James stood and stretched. Bending over to rub the cramp in his left calf, James was startled to feel arms around his throat.

"Thanks, I had fun," Ryan squealed directly into James' left ear.

"Hey!" He rubbed his ear to ease the ringing in his eardrum. "Yeah, yeah. You're welcome." He stuck out his hand, and Ryan put his small one into it. "Let's go."

Standing at the edge of the gym's main room, James scanned the room for his mother. Constructed in faux rock, three climbing walls stood against the far wall. He spotted his mother and Ms. Hyland on the right two, apparently in a race to the top. His mother climbed steadily up the middle. Thomas stood at the bottom and to her right, under the blond woman, cupping his hands around his mouth and shouting encouragement. James could not tell who was ahead. He sent a bit of a wish toward his mother.

The women neared the top, both finding their handholds efficiently. In the end, due to James' wishes perhaps, his mother topped the edge first. She smacked the sensor, triggering the light and buzzer a full second ahead of the taller, younger woman. James applauded madly, then grabbed Ryan's hand and dragged the boy over to the walls. He continued cheering as his mother switched to the slide lead and quickly returned to the floor, bouncing once on her feet before turning around.

She pulled off the green bit of fabric she had used to tie her hair back, and the tresses promptly fell to surround her face, which was lit with high color. Sweating profusely, she was laughing as she caught her breath. Thomas slapped her on the back once, then turned to spot for Ms. Hyland as she began her slide down the wall face.

Ms. Hyland landed beside their mother and offered her a high-five before turning to Thomas. James' brother clasped her hand and whooped, making both women laugh. "You'll need a few more lessons to beat Mom," Thomas said. "However, I'm game if you are."

"Colluding against me?" their mother said. "My own son? Shame on you." She wrapped an arm around his neck. "Now where's my towel. God, I need water."

Laughing, Ms. Hyland walked over to a bench and fetched both their towels and gym bags. She scooped out a bottle of water. Her own skin shiny with sweat, she took a healthy chug herself before passing it over. "I'll get the right pace eventually," she warned.

"You can't beat me at handball. I'll stay ahead of you here, too." Brenna laughed.

James was surprised when she popped her towel at the other woman, making her jump backward.

"I have to point out, kindly," the younger woman teased back, "that that is scripted. *This* is not. Your days are numbered," she countered, accepting the return of the water bottle and tossing back another swallow.

The women fell silent, sharing big smiles, then realized the boys were staring at them.

"Shower?"

"Yeah." Ms. Hyland flipped her hair free of the ponytail tie and looked at Thomas. "We'll be out soon. Watch Ryan for a few minutes?"

"Sure thing," Thomas replied. He offered his hand; she shook it. "You really did great today."

"I had a great teacher." She flashed him a toothsome smile and brushed his shoulder lightly before following their mother into the locker room.

"Well, let's go sit and wait," James sighed.

"You're right. It'll probably be ten, fifteen minutes. Want to go to the Game Room?"

"Yes!" Ryan pumped his fist in the air.

"No!" James objected. Thomas shot his brother a questioning look. "I just spent the whole hour in there with him," James said defensively.

Thomas held out his hand. "Well then, give me the tokens. I'll take him."

"You just want to keep on his mother's good side," James said crossly, handing over the tokens.

"What is it with you? That night at the campsite did Cass and Ryan poke you in the ass or something?"

"No." James subsided with a pout, stuffing his hands in his jean pockets. "Fine. Let's just go."

"Come on, I'm your brother. Tell me what's up."

"Have you ever seen Mom act like this?"

"Far too rarely."

"What is it with that woman that's got you so nuts and Mom acting like last year never happened?"

"They've obviously worked things out. Shoot, you should be happy. Mom's got few enough close friends as it is. Most of them are back in Michigan. At least now she's got someone she can joke around with, do fun stuff."

"But things don't just go away like...that." James snapped his fingers.

"Maybe it's something on the set. They decided to bury the hatchet in order to get through it. Hell, I don't know. I don't care." Thomas sat Ryan in front of a space shoot 'em up and popped in the coins. "You being upset isn't going to change anything."

James frowned. "I know." He put his hand on the game console and exhaled loudly. "I can't get over the feeling something is really messed up. We're just missing it."

"You're just not giving Cassidy a chance."

"And you're giving her too much of one," James retorted. "Damn it, Thomas, she's over thirty. She isn't going to like you no matter how much you fawn over her or her kid."

"I happen to think she makes a pretty cool friend."

"So is that why you watched her butt sashay out of here just a minute ago?"

"Listen, she was telling Mom and me today just how cool all this is. How she had never gone for the Outdoors Club in college but now wished she had." He laughed. "She scared Mom nearly to death when she did her first plummet, but she had great form. She suggested skydiving might be next."

"So she's got a death wish. I'm supposed to like her now?"

"She just loves excitement. I think Mom's finding that refreshing. She's got an adventurous streak in her, too, that I think she's just beginning to let out."

"Our mother is not going to skydive."

"Maybe she isn't. But if she does, you can bet it'll be because she wants to do it."

"She's our mom!"

"But," Thomas lifted Ryan down from the game as the telltale sound of the last life lost played out, "she's a person, too."

James crossed his arms over his chest. "You are such a dweeb, Thomas."

"And you've got some growing up to do. Mom's finally breaking out of her shell, and I think it's great."

In the locker room, Brenna grabbed a full-sized towel from the courtesy rack and headed for the showers. She noted all the stalls were occupied and paused.

"Come on, let's go," Cassidy suggested, coming up behind her.

"Where?"

"The communal shower."

"I don't–"

"It's just to rinse off. That's all we need." Cassidy was already moving; Brenna automatically followed.

At the end of the row of stalls, the floor opened up to a lowered space. Spigots lined the far wall at chest height. Brenna shook her head. "I need a shower."

"Then feel free to wait." Cassidy stepped out of her shoes. Putting them up on a bench, she dropped her gym bag next to them, then pulled off her socks. Bending over, she stepped out of her shorts and dropped them on top. She remained in her white tank top and underwear as she pulled the chain under a spigot and stepped into the water flow. Turning around, she dropped her head under the spray and combed her fingers through it before tossing her head back. She looked at Brenna as she brushed the hair back from her cheeks and forehead.

Brenna drank in the sight of lean curves hidden inside the clinging wet tank. "You're soaked."

"Yes, but I'm cool now," Cassidy answered with a mischievous smile, stepping away from the water. "You ought to try it," she suggested, running a finger through the sweat dotting Brenna's near shoulder. Wrapped up in her towel, she sat down on the bench, picked up her bag, and fished out a cotton sweater, fresh underwear, and a pair of slacks.

Looking from the spigot to Cassidy, Brenna saw the blonde's smile widen slowly and her eyebrows dance. She was being challenged to drop some of her inhibitions.

Bending over, Brenna plucked off her shoes and socks. The shorts followed. There was a tingle down her back ~ she felt she was being watched ~ but when she glanced over her shoulder, Cassidy was bent over, putting on her sneakers. The blond head started to rise, and Brenna turned her face away, averting it before Cassidy could catch her looking. *So she wants a game? All right.*

Keeping her back to Cassidy, Brenna pulled off her tank top and stepped forward into the spray, flexing her shoulders as she scrubbed her fingers through her wet hair. The ice cold water teased her nipples hard before running down in rivulets to her center and continuing down her thighs.

The shower was not cooling her off. Knowing those eyes were on her, appreciating the view, made Brenna feel like a ball of fire, the white hot core of which was centered just below her pelvic bone.

She rubbed her hands down her chest and abdomen, sluicing off the excess water. Only then did she turn around. A towel was held up at face level, blocking her view of Cassidy, who was holding it out.

"Dry off," Cassidy said tightly. "Or I'll get us both very wet."

Brenna gave her a daring leer, then wiped the expression from her face as she took the towel and wrapped it around herself. Studying Cassidy, who was determinedly looking at the floor, she felt energized and said evenly, "Don't challenge me. I always play to win."

"I'm beginning to believe that." Darkened eyes, hungry with desire, flickered over Brenna's face. "Sometime you'll have to tell me where you developed that competitive streak."

"In a household with four brothers we call it a survival mechanism."

Cassidy was silent for a long moment, then quirked her brow. "You like nude sunbathing too, I bet."

"What makes you say that?"

Cassidy's smile broadened, showing her teeth before she turned away. "No tan lines."

A flush caught Brenna from head to toe as she settled quickly on the bench to cover her weakened knees. "I'm a mother," she protested innocently. "How could I dare do that?"

Cassidy watched Brenna as she covered herself in a billowy green blouse and black slacks, then stepped into low-heeled sandals. "A year ago I'd have guessed tanning salon," she mused. "But I didn't see this adventurous competitor in you then."

"True," Brenna acknowledged.

"Though I wouldn't be surprised to discover that's why you built the deck in your backyard."

Brenna's cheeks flooded with heat, and she dropped her eyes.

"I swear you've bewitched me. I can completely see you in that yard...More beautiful than any fairy princess." As Brenna's head came up, Cassidy swept in and planted a quick kiss at the corner of her lips. Aroused but wary, Brenna looked around, noting they were well hidden from others in the locker room.

Exhaling sharply, she grasped the nearby tiled wall separator and watched Cassidy leave. *God help me, I've never felt anything this totally consuming in my life.* Collecting her wet things and rolling them into her towel, Brenna stuffed them into her bag, tossed the bag on her shoulder, and strode out.

When she stepped out into the gym again, Brenna spotted Cassidy standing among their children. Ryan was in her arms as she spoke with Thomas on her left and James looked at them from her right. A sensation of family slammed into her with the force of a physical blow. At that moment, she resolved to make that snapshot a permanent picture in her life.

Wrapping her arm around James' shoulder, she addressed the group. "Everyone ready for dinner? I'm starved."

CHAPTER THIRTY-THREE

BRENNA STOOD at the stove, tending a skillet of chicken strips sautéing in a white wine and mustard sauce. She glanced at the timer, noting the wild grain rice still had ten minutes. *Just enough time to finish the chicken thoroughly.*

She looked over her shoulder at the kitchen's other occupant. Cassidy's face was in profile as she skillfully chopped vegetables on the cutting board. *Odd enough for a first date,* she thought with a smile. *Dinner with my kids and me.* Cassidy looked far from daunted. When all three boys disappeared into the game room, she had offered to assist. Right now she was cutting mushrooms to add to the salad in a bowl by her left elbow. The fall of her hair obscured her face somewhat, so Brenna shifted to catch the profiled chin and nose, admiring the smooth features.

"Salad's almost finished." Cassidy spoke without turning, alerting Brenna to the fact that she knew she was being watched. "You'll burn your hand again if you don't pay attention to what you're doing." She turned her head slightly until their gazes met. Brenna blushed under her amused smile.

You're distracting me, she thought. She tried to hide her blush and covered it with, "The chicken and rice are almost done."

Cassidy nodded, pushing the mound of cut mushrooms from the board into the bowl, then tossing the salad briefly. "Well, why don't I tell them dinner's up?" She flashed a quick grin, dropped the knife into the sink, brushed off the cutting board, and put it back on a hook over the sideboard.

"All right." Brenna returned to minding the chicken, pleased with the ease with which they'd divided the responsibilities.

Cassidy had learned how to walk silently in order to get herself in and out of the house while tiptoeing around her ex-husband's rages. She employed the talent now, to get a peek into the game room before the boys knew she was there.

Peering around the edge of the doorway, she surveyed the room. Thomas coached Ryan through a flight simulator video game. Both were seated cross-legged on the floor, control pads in hand. Ryan bounced frequently, giving Thomas a running commentary. The older boy cocked his head and listened. He maneuvered his own ship through the same obstacles on the split screen with the other half of his attention. As he had with her at the gym, Thomas was encouraging, prodding Ryan into making better choices. *He would probably enjoy being a camp counselor*, she thought, wondering exactly what he thought he might do with his life, knowing he would be graduating from school in May.

Brenna's younger son, James, was a different story. In the corner of a small futon couch, lowered so that she could barely make out the top of his brown hair, he read a book propped on his bent knees. He seemed pretty absorbed by the contents of the small paperback. Noticing his exhaustion when she collected Ryan before the group left the gym, she had tried to talk to him. He had rebuffed her, politely, but it had been a rejection all the same. She wondered if it was personal or if he was just mad at the world, as some teenagers were wont to be. He did not seem the "mad at the world" type. His mother was just too involved in his life to let it get that far. *No*, she thought sadly, *it must be me*. She thought about how Brenna had said the same thing when Cassidy had been shivering on set one day. *Well, not everything has to be about us*. It was interesting to think that Brenna had been seeing the relationship that interconnected them even then. She smiled and stepped into the room.

"Dinner," she announced. Three sets of eyes turned to her, expressions ranging from interested to excited to wary. She smiled as Thomas and Ryan stood. The seventeen-year-old flipped off the game console, and James rolled to a sitting position, still warily watching her.

"I'll set the table." Thomas stepped past her and left.

Ryan looked up at his mom. "Can I help?" When she nodded, he ran after Thomas.

Amused, Cassidy turned back to James. "Coming?"

"In a minute."

He returned to the page he held open, and it was clear to her that he'd become interested in the reading again. "Good book?"

He shrugged, trying to tuck the book out of sight. "Just something I picked up."

"Something for school?"

"No." He stood up, pushing the book aside. "Come on, before Mom comes looking for you."

She remained in the doorway, studying him. She wondered at his choice of words: looking for her, not for him or for both of them. Meeting his gaze, she waited until he broke the connection and said, "I may not have said it, but I sure did appreciate you watching Ryan this afternoon."

"Yeah."

The silence spread like a fog, making it difficult for her to gauge what he was feeling. She was put in mind of Commander Jakes' stoic mask. It was a phrase that director after director had used while coaching Brenna. *"Nothing's supposed to get through the mask. When it does, that's the drama."*

On the other hand, Hanssen was supposed to be a contained but forthright individual. Getting at the unflappable Jakes was her form of rebellion. Cassidy was frequently instructed, especially during her first months on the series, to deliver lines with the intent of breaking the mask.

Brenna's "mask" was a tight jaw, and eyes that wouldn't look quite at you. She always looked as if she were holding her breath. Cassidy saw that now in James' face.

She tried to break through. "James, tell me something." He looked at her, but the mask stayed in place. "Do you watch the show?"

"No."

She judged the response to be too quick. "Your mom doesn't like you to?" Silence again as he, again, wouldn't look directly at her. "So," she poked carefully, "what do you think of her portrayal of Susan Jakes?"

His gaze snapped to hers. Defensively he said, "I told you, I don't watch."

"Maybe you should," Cassidy prodded. "She's very good, you know. I've always thought so."

"What do you know? You're just a..." He cut himself off and turned away from her. "Dinner's getting cold."

Careful to avoid any expression that she was startled by the unfinished comment, she stepped back. "I may be anything. That's what acting is all about. I happen to be your mother's friend. That," she assured him, "is not an act." Stepping out of the doorway, she returned down the hall. She found Brenna at the end of it, gaze upturned to meet hers.

"I was beginning to wonder what happened to you."

"Just turning off the stuff." James edged his way around them.

"Oh." Brenna watched him stride out of sight. She turned back to find Cassidy studying the spot at the end of the corridor where her son had last stood. "Are you all right?"

"Yeah. I'm fine. Let's go eat before the food's cold." Cassidy rested her hand companionably on Brenna's shoulder, then gradually dropped it away as they entered the dining room.

Until she started a conversation with "Ryan loves baseball," Brenna was sure the group would have been content to remain silent. Even the normally sociable Thomas had alternated between watching Cassidy and watching his plate. Brenna knew Cassidy was uncomfortable; she had stopped meeting Brenna's gaze across the table.

Responding to the cue, Thomas began regaling Cassidy's son with the stats from his latest season of baseball. Ryan *ooohed* and *aaahhhed* and asked many knowledgeable questions.

Thomas asked, "How'd he learn all those stats?"

"TV," Cassidy explained. "I've started letting him get the cards, but mostly he just listens to the commentators."

"That's very cool," Thomas praised. "Have you ever seen a live game?"

"Mom took me to one this year."

"Who was playing?"

"Oakland A's and Baltimore Orioles," Ryan reported proudly. "A's lost."

"That was a great game," Thomas said. "What position would you play?"

Ryan grinned. "First base."

"There's an active Little League in L.A. Besides playing for the high school team, Thomas helps coach one of them. Perhaps you could let Ryan join up." Brenna prompted an expansion of the conversation with a look at Cassidy. "The new season starts up just after our filming finishes," she added.

"Please, Mommy?"

Cassidy nodded. "I guess you could."

"It's T-ball until age eight, but I think he'd have a lot of fun," Thomas said.

Cassidy chuckled. "Between climbing together and Ryan's games, you may see too much of me."

"Don't forget, we'll all have to go watch Thomas play," Brenna responded with a smile. Her smile faded as James stood. "James?" He looked toward her. "Done already?"

"Yeah. I've got stuff to do."

"We've got cobbler for dessert," she said.

"Call me." Then he was gone.

"All right," Brenna said to his back. Disconcerted, she slowly picked up her fork.

\#

Disheartened and confused, James listened as his mother, Ms. Hyland and Thomas started up the conversation again as he left. He bristled at the woman's inquisitiveness. He really wished she would just go away. Now his mom was talking about seeing the Hylands more often, inviting them to Thomas' baseball games, even getting her son involved in the Little League.

Flopping down on the couch in the game room, James sighed. She had seldom brought any of the *Time Trails* cast to the house, except for hosting the occasional holiday party when she had briefly dated one of the other actors. That had all stopped when she married Mr. Shea.

Cassidy Hyland was the last person James had ever expected to see sitting at their dining room table. In the beginning, when she was alone in her room when she thought no one could hear, his mother had cursed the blonde. Socializing with her should be the last thing on her mind. Now, that seemed to have all changed. He just did not get it.

Thomas was right; it was his mother's life. However, she was changing rapidly, right before his eyes. She barely spoke to her husband any more; weekly calls had dwindled to less than once a month. James hadn't seen her writing a letter in weeks. It made no sense. Thomas said he had seen them kissing out on the deck before they disappeared into her room at Thanksgiving.

He immediately terminated that line of thought. Thinking about his mother having sex was just *icky*. He had only just gotten into petting with his girlfriend, Marcie. He knew what he wanted to do with her, but thinking about his mother and Mr. Shea doing the same thing was just...He groaned and closed his eyes, shoving the heels of his hands against them to rub out the images. *Ew.*

She was more enthused about physical stuff lately, too. She worked out and swam a lot when she first got the job on the series. That had tapered off as the series itself provided her with more than enough exercise. Now she was actually racing Thomas when they climbed. Thomas seemed unsurprised, saying her competitive spirit was reawakening.

Why was it happening now, just when he thought she was ready to leave this role behind? Why hadn't this happened when she married Mr. Shea?

Damn it, he cussed. *Why the hell do I think Cassidy Hyland has everything to do with it?*

Pulling the remote control from the table, he lost himself in television.

"Thomas, would you please take him out of here?" Brenna held Ryan's hands to prevent him from sticking them in the sink where his mother was washing dishes. Brenna had turned around to say something to Cassidy and nearly tripped over him for the fourth time.

She herself was finding containers to store the leftovers. Since James had left the table early, more food than usual remained. He had always been her most robust consumer.

Thomas, who was bringing the dishes in from the table, put down the glasses he carried and held out a hand to Ryan. "I could show you my baseball cards. Come on. Let's leave the moms to do the tough stuff." He grinned cheekily at his mother as Ryan trotted over and took his hand. "Right, Mom?"

She blew him a kiss. "Thank you." He laughed, and in a moment the two boys were gone.

Cassidy stepped back from the soapy water. "I have never seen Ryan worship anyone so fast."

Brenna reached over and flipped on the radio, grabbing a towel to dry the pans filling the dish rack. The quiet music was a pleasant backdrop as they continued to work. "Thomas has always been great with kids."

"Has he thought about being a camp counselor?"

"He has. Until he has a car of his own, it's just not feasible."

Finished, Cassidy dried her hands and leaned against the counter, crossing her feet at the ankles and easing herself back on both hands. "You could get him a car."

"I don't work that way," Brenna said. "He'll get a job in the summer and earn his own."

"I guess you're right."

"I'd rather Thomas earn something himself, than for me to get him something he won't appreciate."

"You didn't raise him to be shallow."

"No, I didn't."

They fell silent. Brenna reached into the refrigerator and drew out two wine coolers. "Drink?"

"All right." Cassidy took one, glancing at the label. "Raspberry. Nice." She opened it and sipped, then paused as she listened to the tune on the radio. "Wow, that brings back memories."

"What?"

"This song."

Brenna listened to the tune. "I don't recognize it."

"It's an oldie, but that was all the Armed Forces heard overseas."

"Armed Forces?"

"My dad was...*is* retired military. Marines. I was born in France."

Thomas had come back in with Ryan and asked, "We were wondering. Wasn't there supposed to be dessert?"

"Oh, right," Brenna answered distractedly, caught up in the image of Cassidy as a small girl, probably in pigtails, running around a military base. "Go on," she encouraged. "Sit down and I'll get things together."

Thomas, Ryan and Cassidy settled at the table. Brenna grabbed the vanilla ice cream and set it on the counter. "We should probably tell James," she said, recognizing that her younger son was still absent. She looked to Thomas, who got up quickly and went on a search. Then she turned back to

Cassidy. "You said you moved around a lot."

"I did, but from birth to six, I lived just outside Paris. Since I started school there, it's still the best foreign accent I do." She chuckled. Easily changing her accent to reflect a French influence, she said to her son, "Don't you think so?" He giggled.

"So you traveled a lot as a child." Brenna emerged with the tray of plates. The smell of warm peach cobbler filled the air, and steam rose from beneath the cool splashes of vanilla ice cream that she added on top.

"There were two bases in France. We lived in Texas, Tennessee, then Missouri ~ where he retired. There were also stops in San Francisco, London, and Bremen. Though I didn't go, since he was posted there only two months, he was stationed in Thailand for a training assignment when I was fifteen."

Thomas returned at that moment with James, and they both sat down. Brenna passed James a plate. "Cassidy was just telling us about growing up on Army bases."

"Uh huh."

Cassidy decided it probably would be best to go while things with James were just strained instead of completely out of hand. He clearly had issues specifically with her, but she was getting nowhere with resolving them. "I learned a cool language out of it, I guess." She sat up. "Maybe it's time I took Ryan home."

"It's only eight o'clock," Brenna protested.

"Can't we stay?" Ryan looked at her pleadingly, cobbler dribbling from his spoon as he lifted it to his mouth. "I'm not finished."

"Let him finish his dessert, Cass. You, too." She tapped the edge of Cassidy's untouched plate with her spoon.

Relenting, Cassidy fell silent, trying to enjoy the cobbler. James finished quickly and left the table even as he was putting the last bite into his mouth.

Watching Ryan take his last bite, Cassidy wanted to end the evening on an up note, to try and make Brenna feel less like she was being driven off by James' indifference. She stood, grinned at Thomas, and nodded at Brenna. "*Merci. Vous semblez délicieux. J'ai eu l'amusement dans la douche.*"

"What'd you say?" Thomas asked curiously. "That sounded really nice."

She chuckled. "I said, 'Thank you. The food was delicious. I had fun...at the gym.' Impress your friends, confound your enemies ~ learn a second language."

"Of course, you're right." Brenna stood. "I guess I'll see you Monday, then. Would you like some of the leftovers?"

"No thank you. Why are you going in Monday? There's no shooting."

"It's just for a little while. I have interviews and a meeting with my agent."

To spend a moment alone with Cassidy, Brenna waited until she had said her goodbyes to both boys. Thomas flushed a bit at Cassidy's hug, taking a quick step back after she let him go. Brenna bit the inside of her cheek to prevent a chuckle from escaping.

She walked Cassidy and Ryan out to their car and leaned on the open driver's door. Ryan secured his own belt over the booster seat in the back. Cassidy started into the driver seat. A soft hand over hers on the top of the door made her pause. Brenna's eyes were slightly obscured by windblown hair. Cassidy's hand reached up and brushed her face free. "Yes?" She appreciated the heat that rose in Brenna's cheeks and the way her lips parted, her breath caught, and the tip of her tongue came out to wet her lips.

"What did you say? Really."

Cassidy glanced at the front door, then leaned closer to Brenna and whispered, "I said, 'Thank you. You look delicious. I had fun in the shower.'" She leaned back, meeting Brenna's gaze again. The smile widened, and the intention was overtly lascivious.

"That can't possibly be something you learned when you were six," Brenna said breathlessly.

Cassidy could see that her words had piqued Brenna's desires. "I took a refresher course in college."

"What else did you learn that I should know about?" Brenna asked coyly.

She leaned close again, surprised by how much she wanted to kiss Brenna, right there in the open, in front of God, Creation, and the kids. Instead she issued her words across Brenna's lips in faint puffs of breath. "One weekend in particular comes to mind. I'll reenact that with you some other time. Privately." Clearly her words had an effect. Brenna's pupils widened with desire.

"Would you like to get together again sometime? Soon?" Brenna's invitation was hopeful.

"There's the 'office' Christmas party on the seventeenth," Cassidy reminded her.

Pursing her lips, Brenna nodded. "I forgot."

"Aren't you going?"

"I have to, but I haven't...Kevin escorted me last year."

Gambling, Cassidy suggested, "You could go with me."

"A date, you mean?"

"I'm willing," Cassidy said. "But we could just tell the reporters we're friends. I'm going stag. No Cameron this year."

Brenna's brow knitted in sudden anxiety. "I...I need some time."

"Are you unsure of the press, us, Kevin, or the kids?"

Nibbling her bottom lip, Brenna was the very definition of adorable. "It's...I have to talk to Kevin first." She lifted her gaze to Cassidy's. "Can there be another time during the hiatus?"

"I'm not sure yet whether Ryan and I will be headed out to St. Louis to visit my parents for Christmas."

Brenna nodded. Cassidy's hand brushed hers lightly in parting before Brenna had to step back and watch the other woman get into her seat, fire up the engine, and back out of the driveway. She watched until the taillights disappeared into the evening.

CHAPTER THIRTY-FOUR

When Brenna returned inside, James and Thomas were in the kitchen polishing off the remains of the cobbler. "That was pretty cool," Thomas remarked when she walked in to check things. "You think we'll be able to do it again?"

James shook his head. "It seems to me from what Mr. Shea said that we should be cutting ties, not making more of them."

Brenna put a hand on his shoulder. "We're not leaving L.A. tomorrow; there's all spring. A lot could change."

"Are you planning to stay here after *Time Trails*, Mom?" James asked.

"There are a lot of options," Brenna replied noncommittally. "I'm just saying that you shouldn't get anxious about it. I thought you said that you wanted to finish school here," she said.

"Yeah, I do. Come on, Thomas, get with me here. I don't want to start over totally someplace else."

Thomas shook his head. "Mom, I...is Kevin going to escort you to the Pinnacle Christmas party? Maybe we could all talk then."

Brenna frowned. "I haven't talked to him about it."

"I'll escort you if you want."

"Sorry, that's not possible." She hesitated. She would rather go alone, making it possible to meet up with Cassidy, but she knew that the press could have a field day with that. If Kevin came out to L.A. for the party, they could talk, and she could end it then. She was afraid. If she went to Mount Clemens to give him her decision, surrounded by their families, she wasn't entirely certain she could hang on to her nascent resolve. Looking at her sons awaiting her decision, Brenna knew guilt. She was looking for them to supply arguments for her to avoid telling Kevin the real reason she wanted a divorce.

Well, that is going to stop. She wanted and needed Cassidy, needed to make her own way. Out on the driveway, she had been a breath away from Cassidy's lips, wanting to kiss her, only stopped by the sight of the lights in a neighbor's house across the way. She decided convention would no longer hold her back.

"I'll call him right now and see if he can come," she said sharply, reaching for the phone. Her eye caught the clock, and she unconsciously converted the time ahead. "It's almost midnight there." She put her hand down, only to be startled when the phone rang. She snapped it up and hit the button. "Hello?"

"Hi, Bren."

"Kevin?" She blinked, looking from Thomas to James. "It's late."

"I hoped I'd find you in," he said. "I know it's late for me, but this time differential..." He seemed to shake himself. "Anyway, I called to...We didn't get a chance to finish talking about everything."

She felt her stomach get queasy. "I know. We've got a weekend coming up."

"You want to come here? I can make up the boys' room."

"No, Pinnacle's got a party, like last year's, our final one ~ press and everything. The execs are throwing it for the cast and crew."

"Oh."

"It's the seventeenth." Thomas and James sat on the couch, watching her. She turned slightly aside, expecting anger at the lateness of the notice.

Instead Kevin was unnaturally calm. "That's this Saturday."

She winced. "Yes. I know."

After a long pause, he answered, "I'll fly in Saturday morning."

"I could go alone."

"I will fly in."

She felt a frisson of anxiety as she heard the deliberation in his tone. "All right."

"We can talk more when I get there."

"I know." Brenna pulled back the receiver and swallowed back her nerves. *Come on, Brenna, seize the brass ring.* Returning to Kevin, she said simply, "Bye."

"Good night."

"Mmm hmm." She dropped the portable back onto its cradle and sat down on the couch.

Thomas spoke first. "Mom, what's wrong between you two?"

She shook her head. "I'm sorry, Thomas, but our problems...I have to talk to Kevin about them." She started to her feet, but her son's hand grasped her arm and she settled back down, meeting his light eyes.

"Mom, can I let you know one thing?"

"What?"

"It seems like all fall has been a real roller coaster for you. Whatever is going on, all I want is to see you happy."

James nodded. "Me, too."

"I'll be all right," she responded. "Kevin and I will talk, and things will be resolved." That was as much as she was willing to say. She went to the calendar. "Your school dance is the sixteenth," she realized.

Thomas leaned over the couch and looked at her. "Yeah."

"Looks like we go tux shopping tomorrow after church."

James and Thomas groaned. "Can't we just wear suits and ties?"

"What's the attire requirement?"

"Formal," James supplied with a grimace.

"Then it's tuxedos. Have your dates picked their dresses yet?"

"Yes."

Brenna nodded. "Tomorrow's a busy day. You'd better get to bed." She crossed the room again and accepted a kiss on the cheek from each son as they passed her. She kept a lingering hold on James. His reticence around Cassidy bothered her. "Are you all right?" She rubbed lightly between his shoulder blades, feeling the layer of tension there.

"Just anxious about all the changes," he stated. "I'll get over it."

"Promise me you'll tell me if anything gets to be too much." She brushed her fingers through his hair. "Yes?" He nodded but said nothing. She pulled him into her body and rejoiced at the way he clung to her for a brief moment. *My son.* "I love you. Good night, James."

Letting him go, she stood quietly, watching them both walk to their rooms. With a small smile, she had a moment of faith that everything might actually work out. She went into her room and closed her door, picked up the phone and dialed a now-familiar number.

Cassidy stepped into the house, putting her keys and purse aside. Ryan charged to the bathroom. "A quick bath," she reminded him. "Then it's story time."

"Will you read me a story?"

"Sure," she answered, leaning in the doorway. She grinned as he splashed into the filling tub. "Keep the water off the floor."

"Okay."

"Did you have fun today?"

"Yes." Cassidy started out the door to get his pajamas. "Mommy?"

"Yes?"

"Are we going to see Ms. Lanigan again?"

"Probably." She smiled warmly at the memory of Brenna's face in the twilight.

"Are we going to be able to see Daddy anymore?"

"What?"

"Now that you're dating Ms. Lanigan, will I get to see Daddy?"

"What makes you think Brenna and I are dating?" Cassidy knelt at the side of the tub and soaped a washcloth, helping him by washing behind his ears and over his back. "We're just friends."

"You don't kiss 'just friends,' Mom," he said, rolling his eyes.

Cassidy carefully stifled her inclination to deny it. *He must have seen us kissing in the tent during the camping trip.* Obviously he had continued to think about it. At least he was finally talking to her about it. "Does that bother you?"

Ryan shook his head. "She's really nice, and Thomas is a lot of fun. James doesn't like me."

"So, what's bothering you?"

"When you were dating Mister P'lassis, I didn't get to see Daddy. I want to be able to see Daddy."

"Who I'm dating doesn't affect you seeing your father."

"Does that mean I can see him again?"

"Why do you want to see him?" Cassidy had kept Mitch's image as pristine as possible for Ryan. During the divorce, the youngster had not been old enough to understand anything other than that he no longer saw his father every day.

"I asked Thomas if he ever saw his dad, and he said no. He hadn't seen him since his mom married Mister Shea."

Cassidy wondered if that was Brenna's doing or her first husband's. "I don't know the reasons," she admitted, "but we shouldn't guess. It's not nice."

"Okay. So, are you dating her?"

Were they dating? Tonight could be considered a first date, even though they had been surrounded by their children. Or had the camping trip been the first one? She wanted to take Brenna out on a date sometime, just the two of them. That would be their first date, she decided. She finally shook her head. "No, we're not dating."

"Would you like to be?"

Smiling at her son's "cut to the chase" manner, she said, "Yes. But it's our secret, all right ~ yours, mine, and Bren's. Okay?"

"Okay." Ryan nodded and turned away from her, standing up in the tub. "I'm ready for my story."

At her son's typically abrupt change of subject, Cassidy stood and wrapped him up in a towel as he stepped out of the water. "I'm glad you approve." She laughed, rubbing his hair briskly under the terrycloth. He giggled when she tickled him and helped him into his pajamas.

Together they went into his room and pulled out *Jack and the Beanstalk*. They shared the reading and oohed and aahed together over the various mishaps and marvels in the giant's home and the final triumph as Jack cut down the beanstalk.

When they finished, she tucked him under the covers. "Good night, Ryan."

"Good night, Mommy."

The phone rang. Hurrying out to the living room, Cassidy settled into the corner of her couch and answered it. "Hello?"

"Cassidy?"

Brenna's voice slid through the phone and wrapped around her. It was soft, Cassidy realized, likely in order to keep their conversation private. She pictured the woman in her bedroom, lying across her bed. She shook herself to damp down the desire aroused by that simple image. "What's up? I don't think I left anything at the house."

"You didn't. I just wanted to tell you, I got off the phone with Kevin a few minutes ago."

"You didn't tell him over the phone!" She brought her voice down to a more normal pitch and volume and said again, "Brenna, don't tell me you did that."

"I didn't. I...chickened out. He's coming here, though. He'll escort me to the Christmas party."

"Oh." She stifled her disappointment. "Everyone will expect that, I guess."

"I know. We'll talk after the party, though. I...wanted your permission...to tell him about us."

Cassidy was torn. "Do you really want to do that? I thought you had other reasons that were precipitating the divorce."

"I do, but I realized they're all excuses, reasons to avoid coming right out and saying I don't love him. He recognized at Thanksgiving that we've been drifting apart. So, that's what I should tell him."

"Brenna, I don't know. My divorce was very messy because I'd had an affair. That's part of the reason I agreed we shouldn't do anything until you were...able to." She gripped the phone. "Besides, have you thought what that would be admitting? Are you really ready for the publicity? He's a public official, if a small-town one. The firestorm would be~"

"Oh God, unbearable." Brenna sighed. "I don't want to hurt him like that. I just want to be able to tell someone how much I love you," she ended with a whispered pledge.

Cassidy blushed at the lowered, enticing tone. "Brenna, I~"

"I had an incredible time today. All day," Brenna admitted with soft amazement. "I felt like we were a real family."

"James might have a problem with that," Cassidy pointed out.

"I think he'll come around. I had a talk with them."

"About us?"

"Not exactly, but I told them I was unhappy, that Kevin and I have problems."

"But you didn't actually mention divorce."

"No."

"What did they say?"

"That they want me to be happy." Brenna sounded a little stunned.

"I love your sons," Cassidy said. "We have a lot in common."

She heard the bedsprings as Brenna shifted on her bed. Imagining activities she could share with Brenna on that bed made her weak in the knees. She could almost imagine Brenna breathless and writhing under her touch.

"I, uh, should get some sleep," Brenna said reluctantly. "I have to take the boys to a men's shop tomorrow and rent tuxedos for their dance next Friday."

"Tuxes? That must've gone over well. I bet they'll look smashing, though. They've got their mom's genes, and you looked incredible in that men's suit in *Wild Horses*."

During a time jump, they had all been swept through a vortex to the American Old West. A fun romp, the episode had been a breather from their usual characterizations. Jakes had portrayed a Calamity Jane type and Hanssen, one of the "upstairs girls." One of Hanssen's johns was supposed to be stopped from killing the town sheriff. Creighton had insinuated himself as the bartender and provided the modern, untraceable compound slipped into the drink. Jakes delivered the poisoned drink to their suspect during a high stakes card game.

"How long did you say you've been attracted to me again?"

Cassidy could just picture the sensual smile curling those kissable lips. The same look had innocently met the gaze of the sheriff, the man they had saved, though without his knowledge. Cassidy countered with a question of her own. "And what's the favorite outfit you've seen me in?"

"As Chris?"

"As Chris."

"I rather liked the flight jockey look on you in *Brains and Brawn*," Brenna replied huskily. "Before that, the gown from *Wild Horses*."

Cassidy grinned and chuckled softly. "See you Monday?"

"I'll be there."

"Good night, Bren."

"Good night, Cass."

CHAPTER THIRTY-FIVE

CROSSING HER feet at the ankles, Brenna leaned forward to get a better look at the script just laid in front of her on the small table in her trailer. "You really think I should consider it, Ray?"

Raymond Aruth, a slim man with brown hair and eyes, adjusted the lapel of his gray suit jacket. "Yes, I do. It's got an energized group already assembled. The script is original, bold."

"It's shooting in England."

"Tops you'd be there only...four weeks." He put a hand on her shoulder to close the sale. "They loved the clips I sent. They want you."

"When?"

"May. However, you have to go out before that specifically to read for the part, otherwise the government won't issue the work visa."

Brenna groaned. "Good thing my passport's up to date. When do they want to do that?"

"As soon as possible."

She looked at the opening pages. Ray had highlighted the role he had considered for her. The plot was elemental fantasy. She wondered what the pages would reveal.

"Read it. Think it over." Ray patted her hand. "Now, tell me how it's going here."

She set aside the script. "Good."

"Really?"

"Yes."

"Anything you need? I heard there was a top-down shake up."

Brenna nodded. Cameron and Will's fight still unnerved her. "Positive results from that so far."

"All right. How are Thomas and James?"

She smiled. "We had a good break together camping. I've gotten the time I wanted with them."

Ray stood. "That's great. So, it's still working. Happy?"

Brenna had an image of Cassidy the last time she had seen her. "Yes." She grinned. "It's proving to be a good season."

"I like that smile, Brenna. I do. It's been a while since I've seen it." He reached for his briefcase. "I've represented you for ten years, and that smile is a promise that I'll do it for a lot longer. Right?"

She stood and hugged him. "I promise I'll look at the project. England's daunting, though." She winced. "We'll see."

Opening the trailer door, Brenna let Ray hug her as he passed onto the steps. She leaned on the railing as he moved down to the sidewalk. Suddenly she joined him. "I'll walk you out."

They passed several crew members headed out to other soundstages. On another walkway, she glimpsed Cassidy and caught a small wave.

"I was looking at some of your recent tape," Ray said. "I'd like to add a couple of scenes from *Brains and Brawn* to your audition reel."

Brenna smiled, remembering the shoot and how hard she had worked on it. "Go ahead." They stopped on the path. "I'll call you after Christmas with my verdict on the movie proposal."

"Excellent. Give my love to your family."

"I will."

With quick strides, Brenna returned to her trailer to pick up her scripts. She was looking forward to the holiday break.

An unexpected visitor rose from her couch. "Cassidy?"

"Forgot what I looked like already?"

"I mean, what are you doing here?"

"I had to be here for a few meetings myself. I saw you with..."

"That was my agent, Ray Aruth."

"I thought I'd see how you were."

Brenna pulled her door shut. "I'm good."

Cassidy sat back on the couch, and Brenna watched her getting comfortable. In deference to the cool temperatures, she wore a light blue sweater Land wool slacks. A jacket lay over the couch arm next to her. "I thought about what you said," Cassidy interjected into the silence.

"What?"

"About telling Kevin about us. I'm still not sure you should, but I don't want to tell you how-"

Brenna knelt on the couch cushion, one knee on either side of Cassidy's thighs, and put a light hand over full lips. "You didn't. You expressed an opinion that I asked for. And you're right," she added, "about the press it would generate. I won't let you or Ryan be hurt." She leaned forward, removed her fingers, and kissed Cassidy soundly.

"So now, tell me about what Ray brought you?"

Brenna chuckled as Cassidy tugged her down until she was sitting on her lap. "It's a script to be filmed in England," she said.

"Sounds interesting."

"It sounds far away," Brenna countered.

"Well, read the script before you decide. If it's worth a look, you'll find a way."

Brenna blinked. She had thought with them feeling their way into a relationship, her leaving the States right now would have been at the bottom of Cassidy's suggestion list. "You're serious."

"Don't I sound serious?"

Cassidy's fingers combed through her hair, and Brenna couldn't deny how wonderful it made her feel. "What about us?"

"There isn't any us...yet," Cassidy pointed out. "But even if there was...Brenna, you're a brilliant actress. We'll find projects together or close to one another, or I'll wait while you work, and...I hope...you'll wait while I work. I won't ever tell you that you can't do a project that you want."

Cassidy was in earnest; Brenna saw the proof of it in her face. A lump of emotion lodged in her throat. She rubbed her eyes to avoid the tears burning in them. Hands slid up her arms to her shoulders and pulled her against a warm, soft chest. "Thank you," she murmured against the soft skin of Cassidy's throat.

Fingers brushed against her chin, lifting it. "So...tell me, was the tux hunt fun?"

Brenna laughed at the change of subject. Obviously her getting emotional over the statement of support made Cassidy uncomfortable. *Well, damn it, no one had ever just said, "Do it" before.* "They suffered, but now Thomas and James are properly outfitted for Friday."

"Have any pictures?"

"In my bag."

"Let's see." Brenna withdrew the Polaroids, and Cassidy encouraged her to recline into her chest to share the viewing. Her fingers moved gently over Brenna's shoulders, raising tingles, then down her sides under her arms before tucking around her stomach.

The first picture was of James. Cassidy traced the outline of his frown as he fidgeted with the cummerbund. "He doesn't look pleased."

"James would rather curl up with a book than dance, but he's going because he's totally in love with Marcie."

"Do you like to dance?"

"I love it," Brenna replied, as Cassidy's hand slid across her abdomen. "I took a little time on Sunday night to show them both how to lead." She grinned, remembering the awkward moments as they stepped on her feet or just stumbled on the idea that their mom was teaching them to dance. However, she had seen the pride in their eyes when she declared them "fit to serve." She switched to another picture ~ James adjusting Thomas' bowtie. "They managed passable ties, too."

Cassidy looked more closely at Thomas' figure. "He really takes after you," she murmured. "I love that smile."

"Thomas has always been...more balanced. Maybe it was the fact that he was already in school when I divorced Tom. James...cried for months, upset at the least little change in plans or routine." Brenna fell silent, pensive as she recalled those difficult days.

"What happened with your first marriage?" Cassidy nudged her into the curve of her shoulder. Brenna lifted a knee and adjusted her position to be more comfortable. Cassidy's chin dropped gently onto her right shoulder; her faint breathing sounding reassuringly in her ear.

"I was becoming miserable. I love my boys, but I wasn't working. I hadn't worked in almost three years. I felt a part of myself dying." She sipped in a breath. "Tom said it was for the best. I should just quit entirely, he said. Stay home and raise the boys." She swallowed the bitterness that still rose at his total lack of support. "He did not understand at all. There he was with his work; I had nothing." She pursed her lips and frowned, then inhaled and exhaled slowly. *God, it still hurts ~ feeling that alone.*

"So, I got out. Custody was tougher. He was working; I wasn't. I knew that without Thomas and James, something in me would die."

Cassidy brushed her cheek against Brenna's. "Mitch did the same to me. I'm so sorry."

Soft lips traced over her brow, and Brenna turned into the touch. Finally she felt surrounded by someone who honestly could understand. Their lips met; Cassidy's mouth soothed over hers. Waves of desire washed over her, through her. There was no shooting to interrupt them, no script demanding rehearsal. No time constraints at all.

Putting aside the pictures, she curled into Cassidy's body and murmured, "I've thought about you, about this. If you have time," she went on, tilting her chin to bring her lips into contact with the smooth curve of Cassidy's jaw, "I'd love one of those lessons you promised."

Cassidy nuzzled her ear. "If you like."

Beneath her hands, Brenna felt Cassidy's heart rate pick up, confirming her interest. She turned around and straddled Cassidy's knees, resting her hands on the slender shoulders, looking down into an upturned face. "I'd like." She ducked her head to capture full lips. Cassidy's hands remained on her hips as Brenna balanced her weight onto her knees to either side.

"You said you've done this before," Brenna pointed out. She trailed her fingers under Cassidy's top, watching Cassidy's eyes drift shut as Brenna warmed her hands against tight muscles and delicate skin. "You'll have to tell me if I'm doing it right." Cassidy's eyes opened as Brenna found a spot along Cassidy's ribs that made the other woman jump. She moved her hand away from the ticklish spot, and her fingertips grazed the soft weight of another woman's breasts for the first time. She inhaled, entranced by Cassidy's direct and intensifying gaze.

Cassidy's hands moved from resting on her hips to resting just below Brenna's bra. Brenna felt the difference in touch like an epiphany. The fingers were slender, soft, and smooth and made her arch into the contact. Cassidy moved her hands around Brenna's back and undid her bra, moving it aside. The edge of the fabric abraded a nipple, hardening it. Silk soft fingers moved over the outline of her breasts, while Brenna maintained eye contact. Slim fingertips trapped her nipples as she did the same to Cassidy's. The intense connection she always felt around Cassidy, and had never quite understood, strengthened as they both tweaked sharply.

Brenna was startled by the intensity of the shock that shot to her groin. Her fingers flexed unconsciously, and Cassidy arched into the contact, encouraging exploration. She felt the nipples harden against her palms and huskily asked, "Will you take it off?"

Cassidy smiled. Her marvelous hands left Brenna's skin for a brief moment as she tugged off the top. When her arms came down, she found Brenna studying her torso. "The costume changes the look," she explained bashfully.

"You're beautiful." Brenna was surprised her sharp desire to taste the nipples hardening under her fingertips. She met Cassidy's eyes. "Please tell me they're as sensitive as mine."

Cassidy laughed, and there was a sign of patience and restraint in the catch of her voice. "As sensitive as yours, I can't say, but you're welcome to find out." Covering Brenna's hands with her own, Cassidy moved their hands together over her breasts.

Brenna considered what turned her on and tentatively followed imagination with action. To her delight, Cassidy writhed, offering up moans of pleasure that Brenna stole away with kisses. The textures were familiar, yet not. She was surprised how much she felt deep in her own groin as Cassidy continued to voice her appreciation. The gentle scent of arousal, both hers and Cassidy's, rose between them. Slowly she pulled one hand away, and down, feeling Cassidy's stomach muscles constrict as she passed over them. She captured an abandoned nipple in her mouth as her fingers pulled at the waistband of Cassidy's pants.

Massaging Brenna's scalp and hair with languid pleasure, Cassidy's hands left tingles in their wake. Despite the definite wetness between her thighs, Brenna felt no need to rush, only to indulge. Cassidy's body was responsive, but again there was no push from her to move faster, nothing like she had experienced from men who wanted to get down to business.

Brenna moved her attention up Cassidy's body once again, capturing her lips briefly before returning attention to Cassidy's breasts. The woman's reactions thrilled her as she indulged both their desires.

Cassidy's pulse thrummed hard in her throat, but she only continued to stroke Brenna's hands, cheeks, and hair as Brenna explored her breasts. Brenna found she liked the weight in her palm, lifting it and licking the hardened nub before returning it to between her teeth and sucking on it. Moans and cries of her name wrapped Brenna in more love than she thought she could hold.

Brenna pulled back and met Cassidy's gaze, finding the same hot blue gaze she had inadvertently caused in the gym shower. Slender fingers cupped her chin.

"You..." Cassidy began unsteadily, pausing to moisten her lips with her tongue, "don't need lessons."

Brenna rested her palms across Cassidy's stomach and felt the quivering muscles. The sensation slowly dissipated, and Cassidy's eyes stopped looking quite so glazed.

"Is that good?" Cocky pride edged her voice as she realized that, even in her inexperience, she could move Cassidy to such an intense reaction.

"Brenna, cockiness is very attractive on you." Cassidy sat fully upright and stripped Brenna's shirt off, along with the bra.

"Must be why they made me Commander," Brenna teased back, trying to mask her anxiety as Cassidy looked at her, studying her body intensely. "Like what you see?"

Cassidy loved what she saw. Brenna's breasts were just a handful. Much to the other woman's enjoyment, she tested their fit in her palms. Brenna closed her eyes and bit her lower lip endearingly. Freckles liberally dotted her upper chest. The nipples were taut, and a golden tan blended into wide areolas. "I was right," Cassidy said, dragging her eyes up to Brenna's face.

Brenna's eyes opened with surprise. "About what?"

"You do sunbathe in the buff." Drawing her fingertips down evenly tanned skin from sternum to stomach, she felt the muscles jump as she nudged her fingers under the waistband. "Don't you?"

"Yes." Brenna's blush spread down not only her throat, but her upper chest as well, making the freckles, which Cassidy now kissed, stand out.

"How could you chain this free spirit for so long?" Cassidy asked, honestly curious. "It's incredible. I only glimpse it when you're beyond exhausted at the end of a day of shooting." She lifted her chin to nibble Brenna's lips as their bared breasts brushed together. Brenna's open-mouthed moan slipped hotly between her teeth.

Gasps of delight blew softly through the hair on Cassidy's temple as she lowered her mouth to taste Brenna's sun-kissed skin. She watched the muscles flex in Brenna's shoulder as the woman's arm encircled her neck. Cassidy nudged her nose into the tendons in Brenna's throat. The jumping pulse under her palm on Brenna's left breast told her she had found a ticklish spot. She kissed the skin more firmly and licked the mild salts.

Moving Brenna off her thighs, she arranged the woman against the couch pillows. She trailed a fingertip over Brenna's throat, cheek, lips, and nose, drawing their gazes together. A low quiver started in her own stomach again, and she realized she wanted to go all the way ~ right now, right here. Aware of other limitations, though, she inhaled and exhaled, catching sight of a clock on the nearby table. "I'd better stop," she murmured. "I have to meet with my agent in twenty minutes."

Rising onto her elbows, Brenna nodded. "Okay, but that gives us, what? Fifteen?" She offered a searing, passionate expression.

Cassidy would have willingly burned to a crisp had Brenna been actual fire. However, she did not want to explain to her agent that she was late for their meeting because she was having sex with her co-star. It would cause far too many questions too soon. Cassidy acknowledged she was willing to face those questions eventually. She would have even escorted Brenna to the Pinnacle party and weathered the questions then, but Brenna was right to hold off. They did not want press, not right now when this was so new for the two of them.

She indulged them both in the distraction of another absorbing kiss. Brenna's mouth was flavored by her morning coffee and her teeth were pearl smooth. *Her tongue...*Cassidy sucked the little muscle into her mouth and felt her head spin when Brenna initiated a sensual duel. She broke the kiss, panting softly. "God, Brenna." She found herself captured by a grin, seduction narrowing Brenna's eyes and curving her wine-shade lips.

"Later?"

Regretting now that she really did have to go, Cassidy nodded. "Not too much later." She sat up and reached for her top. Pulling it on, she watched Brenna do the same. "I'd like to take you on a date," she said abruptly.

"What? Where?"

"Somewhere away from work, away from kids. Just you, me, and an open evening."

Brenna thought for a moment, "I don't know when we could work that out." They stood, with Cassidy at her shoulder bestowing a kiss behind her right ear. She leaned against the taller woman, feeling her breasts pillow against her back. Together they drifted into a zone of sensation as their body heat rekindled. "But I'll come up with something."

"Your husband will be here Saturday."

Brenna's hand slipped from the doorknob, and the door opened slowly. Without thought, she turned hotly into the mouth and hands that drew sensation out of her every pore. She wrapped her arms around Cassidy's neck and pressed wantonly against her. While tasting the full lips, she offered a hungry promise: "I'll call you."

Cameron Palassis grumbled. He had to cross the whole lot these days to reach the sets being built for Pinnacle's newest series. He was supposed to oversee the PR shooting they would use to entice the rest of the actors they wanted, now that their principal was in place.

Looking up, he realized he had reached "trailer row" behind the *Time Trails* soundstages. He frowned, still angry about being pulled off the dramatic series. *All because of that asshole Chapman,* he bitched. The sound of a door opening, coming from the end where Chapman had his trailer, drew his attention. Cameron's hands flexed. What he wouldn't give to rearrange the man's face. He walked closer.

The open door was not Chapman's trailer, but Lanigan's, and she was not alone. It took less than a breath for him to identify the blonde standing with her. *Cassidy?* Stepping back in surprise, he saw Brenna's arms slide around Cassidy's neck and pull her head down.

Cautious but curious, he edged around the trailer and looked on as Cassidy's hands slid down Brenna's butt. He had never thought of Brenna as attractive, really, but watching the long-fingered familiar hands stroking over the small ass, he grew hard.

Son of a bitch! his mind screamed. *Brenna and Cassidy, his Cassidy, were kissing!* He could not deny the total turn-on as he reassessed his thinking that Cassidy was prudish. Obviously, he had been mistaken. *What a fucking turn-on. Hmm.* He wondered if Cassidy might be persuaded to invite him to their playtime.

Not now, he thought with some sense. *There will be a better time to make a deal.* So he held his knowledge close and retreated quickly before either woman saw him.

CHAPTER THIRTY-SIX

"FRONT AND center," Brenna called, standing by the front door. Still adjusting his bowtie, Thomas appeared first. James appeared at the end of the corridor, his shoes in his hands.

"I'm not ready yet," he protested.

"Well, you're going to have to be, young man," Brenna teased. "Never keep a lady waiting."

He leaned against the couch arm and tugged the shoes on. Standing, he held his arms wide. "Better?"

She grinned and held his cheeks between her palms, kissing him soundly. "Perfect." Brenna turned to Thomas and looked him over with a loving, critical eye. She reached out and adjusted the lapel of his jacket. "There."

"Thanks, Mom." Thomas stuffed his hands in the pockets of the jacket. Almost immediately, his mother tugged his hands out. "This cummerbund is awful." He grimaced but resisted adjusting it. "Mom, do men really wear this stuff?"

"All the time. It's not the throwback you think it is." She patted his cheek. "I promise."

James straightened up and grinned at Thomas. Stockier than his brother, who had the lean build of a runner, James was considerably slimmed by the formal tailored suit. "I like it. Thanks, Mom."

"Kiss up," Thomas snorted.

"Hey," Brenna warned.

"Sorry."

"You both look wonderful." She lifted the camera pulled out for the occasion. "All right, line up."

Thomas and James rolled their eyes, but they stood in the entryway, in front of the door. Arms around one another's shoulders, with the occasionally bunny ears over one another's heads, they posed for their mother. Brenna snapped the shutter a dozen times and then finally set the camera aside.

"Now," she picked up the Mountaineer's keys, "one a.m.?" Thomas nodded as his hand closed around the fob. "I'll be waiting up," she promised.

"Yes, Mom."

She feathered her fingertips through his hair, setting it to rights. She turned her gaze to James, combed her fingers through his hair as well, then trailed them down his cheek and chucked his chin. "You look really handsome," she said, pride and love filling her chest. She swallowed it down and patted his cheek. "You'd better go. You don't want to be late."

She hung at the door, watching Thomas back them out of the drive and head off to pick up the girls. Dinner would be first. The boys had reservations at Michael's. The dance would be at the Radisson ballroom starting at eight p.m.

Offering up a prayer for their safety, she sat down on her couch and reached for the script from England. With a soft exhalation, she pushed her slip-ons off her feet and sank deeper in the cushions seeking a comfortable position. She tried to concentrate on the pages of dialogue, but they blurred. Rubbing her neck, she let her head drop back to rest against the couch arm.

Brenna's body told her loudly exactly what was missing. Or, rather, *who* was missing. Not going to the set for four days had felt terribly strange. Before, set breaks had simply induced boredom. The additional duress of not seeing Cassidy each day had brought her close to stir crazy. The boys were going to be gone almost seven hours. Looking longingly at the phone, she asked herself if it would really hurt anything to spend those hours with Cassidy. *Conversation, a movie maybe?* She nodded, agreeing with herself, and picked up the phone.

As it rang, she wondered what to say. *What if Cassidy can't find a sitter?* She would enjoy having Ryan, but she recalled Cassidy's request for a date, just the two of them.

"Hello?"

"Hi." Pleasure filled her voice at the sound of Cassidy on the other end of the line.

"I just finished reading to Ryan. What's up?"

"I just sent Thomas and James off to their dance. You, um, don't have to, but...I've got movies, or popcorn?" She shrugged at the phone as her nervous tongue stuttered to a stop. "I would love to see you." Brenna bit her lip, waiting.

"I'd love to see you, too." There was relief in Cassidy's voice. "How's seven sound?"

"Think you could arrange it?"

"I'll be there," Cassidy promised.

Cassidy hung up the phone, dazedly considering her good fortune. The series was on hiatus until after New Year's and she had heard nothing from Brenna since their tryst in her trailer. Nearly a week had passed, and Cassidy had begun to wonder if she'd dreamed their mutual explorations or if perhaps Brenna had simply decided it was all too much.

Looking down at the coveralls she had worn while refreshing the all-weather white paint on her back porch, she decided she'd better change. She had come inside on a break from the project, and Ryan had asked for a book, leaving her only the chance to pull off the paint-spattered smock. She reached for the phone again and took it with her when she went into the bedroom to search her closet. It had been two weeks since Gwen had last looked after Ryan. She hoped the time away had settled the Talbots' situation. "Gwen," she greeted as the line opened.

"Hello, Cassidy. What's up?"

"I need a sitter."

"Going out?"

"Yes, can you? I don't know how late I'll be out. I know it's last minute, but I'd rather he be with you for the night rather than ask one of the Treacle girls down the street." Cassidy waited, counting her heartbeats in the silence.

Finally Gwen responded, "We'll keep him all night. I'll return him in the morning."

"I'll call tonight around ten." Feeling butterflies in her stomach, Cassidy realized she was nervous about seeing Brenna. She, unlike Cameron, would have no problem at all if Ryan had to come along, but honestly, what would he do at Brenna's with her boys gone? She wanted time with Brenna, and the woman had made a point of reminding her that her own sons were at a dance for the night.

"No problem," Gwen assured her. "I'll deliver him in the morning. You have a good time."

"Thank you."

"Leave an emergency number?"

"My cell is always on."

"All right."

"See you in a few minutes." Cassidy hung up the receiver and looked through her open doorway into Ryan's room. "Ryan?"

"Yes, Mommy?" He appeared at the doorway, Legos in hand.

"I'm going out for a while. Pack up so I can take you to Chance's house."

"Okay."

He handled the change in plans with such calm it made Cassidy wonder. *Have I spent that much time out?* "Ryan?"

"Mmm hmm?"

"We'll be going to Grandma's for Christmas, okay?" She had not wanted to leave town for the holidays, but maybe a little concentrated time with Ryan would be good for both of them. Certainly she could not sit here in L.A. wondering how Brenna was faring with Kevin's visit. She had no idea how long he intended to stay. Besides, she did not want to get in the way if Brenna decided to use the time to talk to Kevin about a divorce.

Cassidy sighed. *Why'd I have to fall for her after she married?* she asked, knowing that she had barely known Brenna prior to her marriage, not only because of her abrupt arrival to the series, but because of her own problems, affair and divorce.

Melancholy words of a romantic song tripped across her brain. *"It's sad to belong to someone else when the right one comes along."* Desperate to get away from Mitch, Cassidy had decided Cameron was "the right one" and jumped from one ship to another, completely overlooking the woman who was the reason she had agreed to join the series in the first place. She paused, realizing the implications of her thoughts.

She recalled the tapes her agent and the Pinnacle executives had shown her to convince her to accept the role of Lieutenant Hanssen. She even remembered the scene that had clinched it. Commander Susan Jakes had been injured, and Brenna played opposite a very talented actor, Brett Heslip, who portrayed a man who believed the injured commander was his daughter.

The range of emotions on Brenna's delicate, determined face had immediately captured Cassidy's attention. Brenna had played the lines written, but Cassidy recognized that what made the words work was Brenna's special gift ~ portraying the riveting emotional turmoil of a woman torn with real love for her rescuer. The Pinnacle people had not needed another session; Cassidy agreed to the part. She wanted the chance to play opposite that kind of depth.

But instead of working closely as allies, their characters were set against one another, and life seemed to imitate art. Despite that, though, Cassidy had intensified her attempts to break through Brenna's icy reserve toward her off-camera.

Standing in front of her closet considering her choices, Cassidy recognized the nervous indecision that accompanied going on a first date. Brushing her hair back from her face, she shook her head. *Come on. This is Brenna.* The agenda was a movie and popcorn, which strongly suggesting a casual evening, so Cassidy reached for a pair of capri pants in a neutral taupe. She stepped into the comfortable cotton Lycra mix, then looked through the sleeveless tops she favored and finally decided on a v-neck in pale blue cashmere that was not form fitting. She dusted her hair off her face and examined her appearance in the mirror. Shaking her head, she went to replace the capris with dark blue jeans.

Splashing water on her face, Cassidy studied her features in the small bathroom mirror, hoping Brenna would approve. She chuckled as she rubbed her damp palms on a towel. *God, I am so nervous about this. What's up with that?* She thought about the compact woman and the glimpses of skin she had seen in the gym and in the trailer. *Because I want something to happen tonight.*

Thinking back to her one college experience, Cassidy was suddenly plagued by self-doubt. Would she be able to make Brenna's first same-sex experience pleasurable? Just thinking about it made her stomach swirl with desire.

Her time with Misty had been an experiment, a solace for both of them for losing boyfriends. She had enjoyed herself, but the feelings had been ultimately casual, not emotionally entangling, no matter that she had been in a daze for an entire week. Her feelings had not even been hurt when Misty abruptly announced she was going to bed a fraternity brother who had caught her eye.

With Brenna, it was not going to be a game, and it was so far from casual as to feel in another universe entirely. Cassidy wanted to make Brenna cry out with pleasure. She wanted to have Brenna lie in her arms afterward and for the two of them to whisper together of future dreams and wishes. She wanted to share a life with Brenna for years to come.

Walking out to the front door, she called for Ryan. "Come on, buddy." With his small hand in hers, Cassidy felt steadier. She glanced in her front hall mirror and frowned. Grabbing a brush from the table, she stroked several times through her already perfect locks before ushering Ryan into the evening air.

No car sat in the Talbots' driveway. Cassidy knocked; Gwen answered.

"Lou's out," she said when asked.

Cassidy handed over Ryan's bag. "Are you sure you want him all night?"

"It'll be easier on him. If you get home early, just get some sleep. We'll see you after breakfast." Gwen patted Ryan on the back and sent him to find Chance.

"When will Lou be home?"

"Sunday. He's checking a job lead upstate."

"So he did lose his job."

"Yeah."

"I'm sorry."

Gwen shook her head. "Somebody will pick him up." She leaned over. "So, is this a date with Brenna?"

"Snacks and a movie."

Gwen pursed her lips. "Friends? She's still married."

"Yes."

"Be careful."

"Thank you, Gwen. That means a lot." Cassidy grasped her friend's hands briefly, then hurried out to her car.

Eagerness to see Brenna drove her across town quickly. She stopped at a florist shop on the outskirts of Pacific Palisades and chose two perfect roses surrounded by baby's breath before proceeding to Brenna's.

Gripping the roses in one hand, she raised her empty one and rapped with the engraved knocker. *This must be why men bring something on a date,* she thought, hiding her shaking hands under the tissue paper. She had a sudden carnal image of grabbing Brenna as soon as she opened the door, pushing her against the wall, and kissing her hard. Excitement warred with anxiety as she waited.

Brenna had stepped out of the shower twenty minutes earlier. Aside from brushing her hair, she had managed to decide on her underwear and not much else. Seated at her vanity, she looked to the closet open to her left and at the array of clothes scattered on the bed ~ and wished the butterflies in her stomach would go away. She stood and shook her head at her image in the mirrored door.

Her little voice prodded with uncertainty, *You really want her to see you?* Her gaze swept her figure. Forty-plus years glared back at her ~ from the uneven sag of her breasts to the extra swell at her stomach. Tiny crow's feet shaped the corners of her eyes.

Cassidy, on the other hand, was young, fit, and trim. Brenna sighed with pleasure, reliving the feel of soft breasts nestled in her palms. She fisted her hands in her lap. Cassidy was not just a body, though Brenna had thought that when Cassidy first arrived. Since that original erroneous assessment, Cassidy had more than proven she was smart, forthright, and not at all arrogant, as Brenna had also wrongly assumed. Cassidy had gifted instincts as an actress and a giving nature.

That she could have fallen in love with a woman shocked the Midwestern Catholic part of Brenna. Trying to set that aside, she was clinging to the possibility that she had finally found someone who accepted her completely.

She scooped up her black sweater and stepped into her favorite steel gray slacks. *Informal,* she staunchly told herself. She stepped into sandals and crossed through the living room and from there to the refrigerator, where she checked on the bottle of wine she had chilling.

There was a knocker rap at the front door. Drying her perspiring hands on her hips, Brenna went to welcome her guest. "Hi. Come on in." She looked at the short, deep brown leather coat Cassidy wore. "Can I take your coat?"

"Thanks." Cassidy pulled it off, and Brenna opened the front closet, pulling down a hanger for the coat and then placing it back inside. Wondering at her brief thought of it never leaving, she left the coat with a lingering stroke down the arm.

As she turned around, Cassidy stood close over her shoulder. "How was the drive?" Brenna asked, feeling like her heart was doing a marathon.

"Fine."

Cassidy's arms moved, and Brenna jumped as something appeared between them. She looked down in wonder. "Roses?" She studied the entwined pair, a red rose and a golden rose. "Where did you find these?" She looked up into Cassidy's face. "They're incredible."

"I thought of us when I saw them." Cassidy blushed. "God, I've never said that to anyone before." She leaned in for a fast kiss.

When they could part, Cassidy still nuzzling Brenna's hair, Brenna took Cassidy's hand and led her into the living room, her stomach aflutter with nervous butterflies. She couldn't tell who was shaking more as they gripped hands and settled on the couch.

"When I invited you, I had every intention of just sharing a movie and popcorn with you."

Cassidy curled on the couch and looked back at her steadily. "A first date," she replied, "never goes too far. I grew up with the same mores."

Their grasps on one another's hands tightened, and they leaned closer. "So, do we start the movie?" Brenna's voice quavered.

"What's the movie?" Cassidy's voice was even less steady, and she did not break contact with Brenna's eyes.

"*The English Patient.*"

"I hear it was good." Cassidy's mouth was only a breath away.

Brenna's breath was short. "Very good," she barely voiced. "One of my favorite movies." Their mouths fell together as she finished. Hands and arms tugged bodies close.

"Four days." Cassidy hid her head against Brenna's shoulder as she murmured her fear. "I thought...Four days and you didn't say anything. I thought that you had decided you couldn't –"

"I never stopped thinking about Monday," Brenna replied, still keyed up and slightly raspy. "I couldn't find any time alone to talk to you."

Cassidy leaned back, and Brenna turned so their bodies settled together, her arm across Cassidy's stomach. "So, um..." Cassidy's fingertips circled over Brenna's forearm in a slow manner as they both caught their breath. "How about that movie?"

"All right." Brenna slipped from her cozy spot and put in the tape. "The movie." She handed Cassidy the remote. "Popcorn?"

Nodding, Cassidy turned on the television and then the tape player, amused by the absence of up-to-date equipment. It was a VHS player, not even a combination DVD/VHS machine like she had in her own home. Brenna had a turntable, too, obviously a classic, for records that were on another shelf. As the previews played, she adjusted the sound level then turned to watch Brenna in the kitchen. "Need help?"

"No." Brenna paused and turned around. "Well, yes. I...there's something in the refrigerator I thought we might enjoy."

Cassidy was immediately on her feet with an eager smile. "Chocolate?"

"Ah, the perfect aphrodisiac," Brenna remarked. "I've never had to think like a seductress, so no, chocolate never occurred to me. It's a bottle of wine."

Cassidy opened the refrigerator, found the wine bottle, and read the label. "Wine and popcorn ~ a first for me."

"Well, it *is* a first date," Brenna quipped. "Lots of firsts," she set the pan of kernels over the gas burner, "in lots of things." Concentrating on the popcorn, she felt Cassidy come up behind her.

The younger woman's hands caressed her shoulders. "You're shaking as much as the pan."

"I guess I am."

"How late are Thomas and James going to be out?" Cassidy asked. "Just for reference."

"Their curfew is one a.m." As Cassidy did not move, Brenna began to relax. Their bodies were close but not touching. The heat was incredible ~ addictive, seductive. She moderated her breathing to concentrate on not burning the popcorn. When the silence was broken by the first kernels exploding, Brenna stepped back directly into Cassidy's chest.

"Careful." Cassidy's hand closed around Brenna's and steadied the pan. "You have this nasty habit of acquiring burns when you're around me."

Brenna chuckled and more of the expectant tension broke, leaving her closer to the lightheartedness that characterized their easiest conversations together. "I'm glad you came over."

"Are you all set for tomorrow?"

"Yes." Brenna nodded soberly. "Kevin arrives in the morning." She pulled the pan away from the fire and poured the popcorn into a large earthenware bowl. "I don't want to think about tomorrow. Let's just think about tonight."

"If I do that, we won't be doing much talking." Cassidy said, popping a puffed kernel into her mouth. "But if you're worried about Kevin...Are you going to be okay while he's here?"

"I haven't figured out what to say to him. He's...I mistook need for love," she said sadly. "He was stability when I needed it."

"Do you think you ever loved him?"

"Once, maybe. I'm not sure anymore."

"What's different with us?"

Brenna shook her head. "I'm not any better at putting that into words, but I feel...like you might understand me...all the little parts that don't make sense sometimes...even to me."

"I can't wait to discover all those little parts," Cassidy said with a smile. "Ready for the movie?" They returned to the living room, wine and popcorn in hand. Brenna and Cassidy sat together on the couch, and Brenna found the remote and pushed play, keeping the volume low.

Easing her arm around Brenna's shoulder, Cassidy asked, "Have you looked over the English script?"

"A little. I like it."

"I read somewhere you'd done another movie overseas before," Cassidy said.

"A mythic romance." Brenna sipped her wine. "I was twenty-five. It was in Scotland. Tom hated that I was gone for a month. After that, he wouldn't let me do anything unless it was shot in L.A. Understandably, the project offers tapered off."

"But you liked that movie."

"I loved it," she enthused. "It was epic. How I carried the role really mattered. He just didn't care." She took a long swig.

Taking the bottle from her, Cassidy nodded. "Tom was a director, right?"

"Still is, though he does fewer projects."

"So, Kevin is totally opposite. I can see it."

"So could I. It was the only clear image I had during those days."

"I really am sorry we didn't get a chance to talk like this when I first joined the cast," Cassidy said. "I gather I was the devil incarnate for much of the first year?"

Brenna winced. "That wasn't fair of me."

"I could have told Cameron to stop setting up all those PR appearances. All that extra publicity work kept me away from Mitch, but that build-up wasn't fair to you."

Brenna waved that off. "Even if he had ulterior motives, he actually did help you. It doesn't sound as if your marriage was ever good. How did you meet Mitch?"

"At a cabana bar when I first got to L.A. after graduation," Cassidy said. "I did a little modeling. He was working the beach bar, and going to school. After he finished his masters in finance, we moved back to his hometown, Highland, Illinois, which was across the river from St. Louis. My parents liked having us closer too, and for a while it was all right. Like you though, I wanted to get back to L.A., to maybe do a little acting. At first it was all right with Mitch. I'd stay with Gwen and Lou when I came out for short parts.

Then I became pregnant with Ryan, though, and Mitch really began working at holding on to me. Forbidding me from leaving, and, well, hitting me when I didn't listen."

Brenna and Cassidy eased together as they talked more about their early marriages, about what they had done to their lives as they discovered what they really wanted. About how marriage and motherhood had changed them and their expectations of what was important. About all the missteps they had made anyway.

Shaking her head, Brenna lamented, "I ran away from the anxiety your arrival generated in me and walked right back into a marriage ~ and all out of fear. Kevin should have a woman who loves him. I can't be her."

"Do you think he'll understand?"

"I don't know. He may feel like I've been lying to him. Trouble is, I'm not certain I wasn't. I certainly was lying to myself. Doesn't that mean I lied to him?"

Cassidy hugged her and kissed her temple. Caught by the scent of Brenna's hair, she continued nuzzling the fine strands. "I don't know the answer."

"It's enough that you listen," Brenna replied, her hand stroking Cassidy's leg as they sat in a half-dark room illuminated only by the television's flickering. "Really." She moved closer and melded their torsos together, pressing a tender kiss to the full lips.

Cassidy didn't let her pull away, instead wrapping her arms around Brenna's back while she explored Brenna's mouth. Both their heartbeats ticked up a notch. "First date?" Cassidy asked breathlessly when they parted briefly.

Brenna found it so easy to slide her hands under Cassidy's sweater. "Um. Maybe...There was..." She brushed Cassidy's lips, remembering their first kiss in the woods. "Camping...we shared a sleeping bag. Then there was...um, the gym and dinner? So...third?"

"Certainly kissing is permitted on a third date," Cassidy murmured, pressing her lips to Brenna's and then sliding her tongue into wet warmth.

"Absolutely," Brenna concurred breathlessly as she pulled back. Slowly her fingers edged the cashmere up Cassidy's ribcage. "We've showered together already," she pointed out. Hands shaking slightly, she eased the top higher, "And seen each other nude."

"Partially nude," Cassidy corrected.

"Maybe, we could just...satisfy our curiosity?" Brenna murmured the question against Cassidy's breastbone, inhaling the scent of skin and light perspiration.

"Are you sure?" Cassidy pulled back and watched the need clear a little from Brenna's face. "I don't want you to regret anything. I don't want to regret it either."

Brenna exhaled. "I know that I want to connect with you completely." She bit her lip. "You excite me," she pointed to her heart, "in here. It's lust, and love...I think. For the first time I'm not really able to articulate everything I'm feeling, and it's a bit frustrating. I'm no novice, you know, but it feels...wonderful and scary. But right. Does that make sense?"

Cassidy pulled Brenna to her to place a tender kiss on her nose, cheeks, and then finally her lips. "It does. It's not something I understood either, until I looked at you and wanted the same thing."

"So, um..." Brenna licked her lips, aware there was a precipice looming, "does this mean we should move to the bedroom?"

"We could sit here," Cassidy mused, "if you want your sons to find a wet spot on the couch."

Brenna shivered and her groin convulsed at the thought of how they might cause that wet spot. "Let's clear this stuff into the kitchen."

"We should wash our hands." To illustrate her point, Cassidy traced a popcorn-greased finger down Brenna's cheek.

They made quick work of putting away the bowl and bottle and turned off the television, taking turns at the kitchen sink with soap and water. Warm, damp hands brushed together, and Brenna, still trembling, led the way to the bedroom.

Closing the door carefully, Brenna and Cassidy looked at the array of clothing covering the bed. "It took me three outfits to figure out what to wear, too," Cassidy confessed with a hint of laughter.

Scooping the clothing to the vanity chair, Brenna turned to find Cassidy sitting on the bed. Her hands splayed across the sheets, tracing their whimsical blue and white flower pattern before she looked up. Brenna reached up and tucked her hair behind her ear as Cassidy's gaze lingered. *She's here. She's really here. In my bed.* She started to tug her sweater over her head. Suddenly hands wrapped around her waist, and she was falling to the bed. Cassidy completed the removal of her top, tossed it aside, and rolled half over her body, warm fingers stroking over her stomach.

"I was taking too long making up my mind, wasn't I?"

"Oh no, not at all. My body heat was just about to set your bed on fire. You could've stood there as long as you wanted; I'd have just burned up the bedroom around you." Cassidy chuckled and pulled off her sweater, tossing it to the floor with Brenna's.

Brenna's hands slid up Cassidy's arms and shoulders, then down, slowly circling the breasts. "Partial nudity achieved," she reminded with a grin.

Cassidy's hand caressed Brenna's thigh and calf to tug off her sandals. Their gazes locked. Reversing direction, she moved her hand up the inside of Brenna's thigh until the heat from her center guided her the rest of the way. Softly she covered the area for a moment, reveling in the heat and her own rising passion, then reached for the top of Brenna's pants.

Lifting her hips as the slacks were removed, Brenna felt Cassidy's touch along the bare skin of her inner thighs for the first time. She hooked her fingers into Cassidy's waistband and tugged in return. Warm skin, smooth and familiar in an unfamiliar way, met her palms as she spread her fingers across the taut abdomen. Braced over her, Cassidy copied the touch against Brenna's stomach.

They looked their fill for several minutes. "Touch me." Cassidy lowered herself onto her side on the mattress and combed her fingers through Brenna's hair as the other woman's fingers explored over peaks and valleys. With whispered encouragement, she told Brenna how each touch made her feel.

Brenna moved against her, and Cassidy's tremors quaked through her as Brenna first brushed her fingers through the hairs covering Cassidy's mound.

Cassidy's hand slid over the roundness of Brenna's butt, nudging her fingers toward her intimate flesh from behind. Brenna arched into the contact and they kissed as they each found wetness for the first time. Nervous laughter served as a vent to their passions.

Brenna felt the penetration in detail. An intimacy far keener than simple sex, Cassidy's fingertips circled in her wetness. "Cass." She moved her hips into the contact, encouraging it deeper. She felt her muscles ripple around the digits as her own fingertips explored between Cassidy's folds. She kept her eyes open, watching intently as Cassidy's chin dropped and the muscles around her fingers convulsed. She moved her fingers slightly and slipped deeper without conscious intent. The blond head fell back, and Brenna tasted the perspiration shining on the exposed throat. Appreciative moans spurred her arousal.

Cassidy arched abruptly and pulled away from Brenna's fingers. With her mouth she sought out Brenna's taut nipples. Crying out and curling in reaction to the hard suckling, Brenna lodged her knee between Cassidy's thighs, bumping her groin. As her own orgasm spiraled closer, Brenna felt Cassidy rub herself against the intruding leg.

Cassidy's orgasm was a beautiful thing ~ primal, wild. Golden hair fell in disarray around her face. Eyes shut tight against the acute sensations, her body became rigid, then collapsed bonelessly against Brenna.

Gently, rhythmically, Cassidy rubbed her knee between Brenna's thighs. Fingers in her hair drew their gazes together. "Mmm," Cassidy murmured unintelligibly against Brenna's lips, then the fingers and knee moved again. Brenna gasped as her idling passion surged. She groaned, her voice rising into a keening as her orgasm crashed through her.

CHAPTER THIRTY-SEVEN

THEY WERE both covered in a thin layer of perspiration. *At least that's not new*, Brenna thought. The sensations flooding her body held her suspended in a pleasurable daze. She rubbed her fingertips together, and viscous fluid coated the pads of her thumb and forefinger. She remembered the delightful feel of moving inside of Cassidy and wondered what the other woman tasted like. Lifting her fingertips to her lips, she flicked out her tongue and experimentally tasted. When she lowered her hand, she found Cassidy studying her.

Cassidy's lips wrapped around the fingers, tasting Brenna's skin, saliva mingled with her own essence. The gesture was incredibly intimate and arousing, Brenna thought, feeling a fresh rush to her groin. "How'd you know what I was thinking?" she asked when Cassidy let her fingers go.

"It's the first thing I thought about, too," Cassidy confessed.

"You, um, never told me about your first time." Brenna eased into Cassidy's shoulder, resting her chin against the back of her hand over the other woman's breast. "Who was she?"

"A classmate in college."

"How did you...did she seduce you?"

"We were drunk. There wasn't much seduction involved."

"Did you enjoy it?"

"It was experimentation," Cassidy admitted. "As long as something didn't hurt or wouldn't get me kicked out of school, I was game to try it. This was a case of 'broken hearts,' though. She and I had both been dumped, and it was a way to still feel wanted."

Brenna nodded. She could easily picture it. She had sometimes gone to bed with some director, or another actor, just to feel connected. Easing her thigh over Cassidy's, she brushed her knee against her center. The other woman's eyelids drifted closed. She felt the smooth arms tighten around her back. "Let me assure you, you are very much wanted," she said. She nibbled down from the known quantity of kissing and conducted teasing forays on her breasts, which had Cassidy writhing beneath her.

"I keep finding more and more things to like about you," Brenna said with a smile. She pressed a hand between their bodies, and while it was awkward with their slight difference in height, she found Cassidy's center again as the other woman's fingers curved up inside her.

They withdrew with gentle touches, caressing whatever skin lay within their reach. She traced her own fingertip across Cassidy's lips and inhaled sharply when Cassidy sucked the finger into her mouth. Sharing the experience, they rubbed one another's essence on their lips and kissed. Cassidy replenished her wet fingertips frequently, and Brenna was surging toward another orgasm from the intermittently interrupted and resumed sensations.

She tasted both of them strongly in their next kiss, as Cassidy filled her with three fingers. Gasping, she moved her hips in rhythm. "Oh, God," she groaned appreciatively.

Cassidy's palm splayed across her stomach, holding her down, and the full lips trailed kisses from her mouth to her breast and back up again. Brenna tried to pay attention, but the woman clearly had her number, as every touch drove her higher and higher. She rapidly lost focus and just gave over to the sensations.

When Brenna, panting and covered in perspiration, opened her eyes, Cassidy was intently studying her. Her groin clenched as she watched Cassidy inhale and leisurely lick and suck at her wet fingers.

Cassidy rolled onto her back, bringing Brenna with her. "Did you enjoy yourself?"

Cassidy's curves were softer and the skin smoother than any other body Brenna had cuddled. "Yes, I did." The loving connecting them expanded in Brenna's chest as she watched Cassidy lift her arm across her eyes, panting lightly.Brenna remained keyed up in a way she found exciting, yet comfortable. She decided she could either do it all over again or simply fall asleep with a contentment she was uncertain she had ever truly felt before. She almost thought she had drifted off when Cassidy spoke.

"I have a confession to make."

Brenna cupped her palm against the underside of Cassidy's breast and murmured, "What?"

"I'm very happy right now." Cassidy's lips smoothed over Brenna's forehead. "I think I've been wanting this a lot longer than just the last couple of months."

Perching her chin on Cassidy's chest, Brenna wondered what that meant. So she asked. "I'm not sure what you mean."

Cassidy sat up and skimmed her palms over Brenna's skin. She could not get enough of how smooth and warm it was. Brenna's hands covered hers on her breasts. "I wanted to work with you, but now I'm thinking I really wanted to *be* with you." Moving back into the circle of Brenna's arms, Cassidy heard regret in Brenna's response.

"I'm sorry I didn't let that happen."

Looking back over her shoulder, Cassidy captured Brenna's palm and kissed it. Brenna curled toward her, her breasts lightly pillowing against Cassidy's back as she intertwined their legs. "When you finally did...I really enjoy the person I've met. I loved watching you with the kids at Halloween, the way you dealt with the police for me when Ryan was lost." She sighed as Brenna kissed away the fear that passed over her features. "I enjoy just sitting with you, munching on a lunch bar and arguing out a piece of script, climbing in the state park, watching you swim, and," she concluded softly, "Ryan loves you, and that means you're perfect."

"I'm far from perfect." Brenna brushed her fingertips across Cassidy's nose, amused by the crinkle that formed in the bridge as Cassidy smiled. "Ryan is a handsome little boy, and I think you're doing a wonderful job raising him. It's not easy doing it alone. I know."

"Cameron could never be bothered with Ryan. Mitch uses him against me." Cassidy sighed. "I just want..." She faltered.

Brenna brushed her hands over Cassidy's hair. "I know," she said with a soft chuckle. "Why can't life just be normal?" She lifted Cassidy's chin. "If it had been, though, would we have met?"

"Probably not."

Brenna heard the distraction caused by her nuzzling Cassidy's ear. "Are we done being serious?" she asked. "We've gotten so much out in the open," she said. "I was thinking we could get back to some *fun*." Brenna lifted her chin and offered a sensuous smile.

"Fun, hmm?" Cassidy asked, smile returning.

Cassidy grasped her wrist and guided her fingers. Torn between watching Cassidy's face as she touched her and watching her fingers moving over the intimate flesh, Brenna darted her eyes back and forth. She began inserting two fingers, but Cassidy shook her head. "No, just..." Voice strained, Cassidy repositioned the touch until Brenna was just on the edge, massaging her center.

Cassidy's back arched, and Brenna licked dry lips as nipples pebbled before her eyes. Cassidy reached for one of her own nipples, pulling and twisting it tightly. Brenna dropped her chin and sucked on the other, trying to keep her fingertips in contact as Cassidy arched with growing need, her moans the sweetest music.

Moving down further, Brenna's lips drew circles on the quivering stomach. She offered kisses across the skin to soothe the tension she felt gathering in the body beneath her. Fingers threaded through her hair ~ Cassidy appreciated the increased tempo ~ and she rubbed more determinedly. Brenna slipped her middle finger inside and continued with her thumb across the bundle of nerves.

Then inspiration struck as Cassidy's breast bumped into her cheek. Brenna twisted the nipple in her teeth, recalling Cassidy's reaction to this same action in her trailer. *Brilliant!* She congratulated herself as Cassidy's chest expanded suddenly. The woman gasped for breath, whimpered, and then scared Brenna by growling and bucking.

Gradually, the flutters slowed under Brenna's palm and finally Cassidy's heart rate slowed. Brenna's groin throbbed with empathy. Cassidy's palm slipped down and found the wetness. They lifted their fingers to one another's lips and both comforted and aroused each other with their juices mingling.

Brenna traced the tear streak on Cassidy's cheek. "I'm sorry. Did I hurt you?"

"No, it's okay." Cassidy swallowed hard and captured Brenna's hand in her own, kissing the knuckles.

Brenna wrapped around her, feeling the light aftershocks. Squeezing a little, Brenna felt the gentle touch of an arm stealing across her waist. "What was that?"

"Beginner's luck," Cassidy replied whimsically. Then she kissed Brenna until she was dizzy.

"Do you always come like that?" Cassidy shook her head, hiding her face in Brenna's shoulder. "Good, because that would make it really hard to hide that we're...together." She kissed Cassidy's tear-stained cheek. "Thank goodness the house is empty."

Adjusting their positions to snuggle, they had to move when Cassidy's thigh landed in a wet spot. They laughed, dozed a little, and talked a bit more. The sound of gravel crunching under tires abruptly shattered the tranquility. Headlights illuminated the cul-de-sac outside. Brenna sat up. Beside her, Cassidy moved off the bed. "The boys are back," she said.

Brenna stood quickly, finding Cassidy's clothes mingled with hers on the floor. She passed them over and pulled on her own top and pants. "I'll go see. You can use the bathroom."

"But..."

Putting a finger to Cassidy's lips, Brenna iterated clearly, "Popcorn and movies." Cassidy started to speak, but Brenna quickly left, dusting her hands through her hair to set it in a semblance of order and pulling the door shut behind her.

In the living room, despite her nerves, Brenna moved methodically to the couch and turned on the TV and VCR. *The English Patient* was about thirty minutes from the end. She looked at the time; it was just after midnight.

Seconds passed, but the front door did not open. Brenna stood and walked into the foyer. Finally she opened the front door and stepped out onto the stoop. Only Cassidy's hatchback sat in the driveway; her Mountaineer was nowhere in sight.

When she came back in, Cassidy was half standing and half sitting on the couch as she turned toward the door.

"Nobody," Brenna said. Cassidy collapsed on the cushion and laughed, making Brenna chuckle as well as she sat down on the couch beside her. "Look at us." She reached out and grasped Cassidy's hand.

"Well, if you'd rather explain things..." Cassidy left the thought unfinished as the front door opened and light from the porch poured onto the foyer wall. Their hands dropped apart, and both turned to face the door.

James stepped into view first, bowtie hanging loose around his neck and cummerbund askew. "Your car?" he asked Cassidy.

"Yes."

"Thomas parked on the street so you could get your car out." James turned to his mother. "He thought it was Ms. Hyland's. I wasn't sure."

"I decided on a night of popcorn and movies," Brenna said. "I called Cass to see if she was interested."

Thomas appeared at the entryway. "Hey, Cassidy."

"Hello, Thomas." Cassidy stood at Brenna's shoulder and watched the boys with a faint smile. She could feel Brenna's nervousness, so she tried a diversion. "Was the party fun?"

Grinning, Thomas nodded. "Yeah, it wasn't bad."

"So, do you forgive me for the tuxedo?" Brenna asked.

"Okay, I forgive you," Thomas said. "Cheryl said I was the hottest thing on the dance floor."

Brenna laughed. Cassidy questioned in astonishment, "Should you be telling your mother that?"

He looked at Cassidy and blushed. "Sorry."

Brenna patted his shoulder, "That's okay. I'm glad you had a good time."

"Is Ryan in the spare room?" Thomas asked.

"No, he had a sleepover, so I took your mother up on her invitation."

Brenna moved into her younger son's path. "You're awfully quiet; didn't you have fun?"

"It was okay. Thanks for the dance lessons earlier."

She rubbed her thumb over his cheek as he met her eyes. Behind James, Brenna saw Cassidy smile at her. Hoping her blush was invisible, she turned back to James. "Well, get yourself comfortable and get some sleep." She leaned in and kissed his cheek. When he sniffed, she stepped back. "Okay?"

"Yeah. Whatever." He looked at her and frowned, then shook his head dismissively. "Good night."

"Good night." Brenna watched both boys disappear down the hallway and then felt a tentative hand on her lower back. "Wait," she murmured.

The light in the hallway went out, and Brenna turned around, facing Cassidy. "They looked all right. I guess the dance broke up early."

"Guess so."

Brenna sat down but Cassidy remained standing. "It's all right to stay a bit," she said. "It would look odd if you left right now," she added quietly, pulling Cassidy to the couch. "Something to drink?"

Realizing her mouth was quite dry, Cassidy nodded. "I don't think the wine."

"Iced tea?"

"All right."

Brenna stood, and Cassidy followed her into the kitchen, where they took a few moments to pour the drinks. As they stood together in the kitchen, sipping in silence, they realized the mood had fled.

"Any ideas?" Cassidy studied the dark hallway where the boys had disappeared.

"None," Brenna admitted.

"Still shaken?"

"A little."

"We ought to say something eventually."

"I know." Brenna put down her glass and idly traced her thumb through the condensation. She glanced at Cassidy. "Thomas' statement about Cheryl gives me hope that he's getting over his crush on you."

"It does seem that way."

They walked to the front door. Brenna retrieved Cassidy's coat from the closet and helped her into it. The natural motion of Cassidy adjusting the leather on her shoulders pulled Brenna in close, and she was assailed again by the scent of their lovemaking. Cassidy turned into her, and Brenna barely restrained herself from a kiss. Cassidy grasped her hand and turned her lips into the palm. She inhaled and whispered, "Step outside with me?"

"All right." Brenna followed her onto the stoop, rubbing her arms against the cold air. "I'll see you tomorrow...tonight, I mean, at the party."

"What time does Kevin fly in?"

Brenna shook her head. "I don't know. He's going to call from the airport."

Cassidy kissed her fingers one by one. "You might want to shower."

"You, too."

"I mean before Kevin gets here." Cassidy slipped Brenna's fingertips into her mouth for a brief moment, conveying her message without words.

Mortified, Brenna closed her eyes. "That must've been what James sniffed." Her cheeks turned pink with embarrassment.

"I do think you smell wonderful, it's just..."

"I know." Brenna watched Cassidy get in her car, start it up, and back out of the drive. Pensively, she returned inside, closing the door and setting the bolt.

Thomas was at the refrigerator in shorts and a tee shirt. She stopped at the counter. "I thought you were in bed."

"Just getting some milk." He pulled out the carton and poured it into a plastic mug he'd already set on the counter. "So, Cassidy came over for movies?"

Brenna nodded. She considered how to explain it. "Who wants to sit around the house all alone on a Friday night, right?"

"Yeah." He studied her a moment as he drank his milk. She watched him set his glass in the sink, then, as he neared her, he stopped. "Good night, Mom."

"Good night, Thomas."

After giving him a few moments to clear the hallway, Brenna entered her room and began tidying up her space. She opened the window to let the air circulate. Hanging the clothes strewn on the vanity back in the closet, she found a pair of lace underwear under the untidiness and blushed, tucking them into her own underwear drawer. *How on earth did Cassidy forget these? Too easily,* she concluded, remembering the speed with which they had dressed.

She stepped into her shower and washed her hair and face. Running the washcloth over her shoulders, neck, and breasts, she sighed wistfully as she recalled Cassidy's touch. Nude, she stepped into her room and pulled on her satin nightgown. The clock told her it was nearly one-thirty in the morning. Tired, she crawled between the sheets and closed her eyes.

She was next aware of voices in the hallway.

"Thanks, Thomas."

It was Kevin just outside her bedroom door. Brenna stole a glance at the clock, alarmed to find it was after seven. As the door opened, she rolled over and sat up. As Kevin approached the bed, she shivered in the cool air blowing in the open window.

Leaning in as his weight shifted the mattress, he kissed her cheek as she turned her head. "Good morning. Thomas says you all had a late night last night."

"Yes." She rubbed her eyes and watched as he crossed the room and pulled the window shut. "Thanks. I wanted a little fresh air last night."

Kevin sat on the mattress almost on her feet. She bent her knees and wrapped her arms around them, then looked up at him. "How was the flight?" she asked, her voice burring groggily.

"Wow. You are tired. Why don't you get yourself together? I'll fix you breakfast and bring it in here." He put his arm around her waist, balancing his weight with his opposite hand. "With all the frequent flyer miles, we'll probably be able to take a free round trip to Singapore by summer." Usually the comment would have elicited a chuckle. She simply nodded. He kissed her quickly. "I'll see to that breakfast." He paused, then leaned in close for a kiss. After a moment, he smiled. "Smells like you missed me last night," he said softly. "I could send the boys out."

Brenna quickly rose. "No. We've got little enough time to be together today as it is," she said, moving toward the bathroom. "Just give me a minute to tidy up, and I'll join everyone at the table."

"All right."

He stood, and Brenna watched from the open door of the bathroom as he let himself out. With a quiet exhalation, she girded herself for the day ahead.

Chapter Thirty-Eight

Brenna had long ago realized that she could no longer attend any party resembling a simple cast party like those she cherished from her younger acting days. The Millennium Holiday Gala was part formal ball and part public relations for Pinnacle Productions. Attendance was mandatory for all actors and even most of the creative staff. As Commander Susan Jakes from *Time Trails* Brenna was expected to literally give a command performance. Stepping out of the limousine, she stood for a moment at the end of a crowded walk carpeted in blue-gray that led to the Hyde Hotel's Grand Marnier ballroom. It was sunset, and the photographers' flashes popped randomly as she discreetly checked the smoothness of her full length gown. Tucking her black purse under her arm, she placed her hand inside of Kevin's elbow.

She heard the buzz of national entertainment reporters recording their segments and local personalities from radio and television news reporting one of the city's most famous studio-sponsored events. The entire block was cordoned off. She nodded to the dress uniformed L.A. police officers as one of them requested her purse and checked its contents.

Accepting her bag back, Brenna allowed Kevin to lead her inside. The high-ceiling ballroom was festively decorated for the holiday in greens and reds, mistletoe, and Christmas wreaths. The company's theme colors of blue and purple were also prominently displayed throughout, decorating the mounted placards proclaiming the various series and movie projects sponsored by Pinnacle and its parent company.

At her shoulder where they stood outside the entry doors, Kevin asked,

"Ready?" Passing through the velvet brocade rope barrier would mean officially joining the party and submitting to the interview-hungry press.

Spying Victor Branch dancing with his wife, Brenna steeled herself for duty. "Let's do it," she said. Kevin led her down the two steps into the pandemonium.

Cassidy had escaped the stir that ensued when she arrived at the event alone and had sought out Rich Paulson and his wife, Linda, in the throng. They were presently discussing Linda's work as a Department of Children and Families foster placement specialist. The conversation had turned to the topic of what exactly constituted a nurturing environment.

"It seems to me that all varieties of family models will work," Cassidy observed, "if a child's needs are put ahead of those of the parents."

"It's more of a balance, I think," disputed a woman with short brown hair and a happy air about her. Her date leaned easily against her shoulder, a younger woman with feathered short blond hair. "If you're not happy, your kids won't be either, no matter what environment you try to provide for them. There are an awful lot of miserable rich kids. And a hell of a lot of happy poor ones."

"It seems we put a lot of pressure on people to conform to some ideal," Rich said. "When in fact, there is none. A lot of ancient civilizations provided communal childcare, a small percentage of the females doing the caretaking while everyone else worked to provide for the other needs of the community."

Cassidy reached for a wine glass from a passing tray. "Only the women should be responsible for the caretaking?"

Linda shook her head. "No, many men are very capable. I've argued for custody being given to several fathers following messy divorces. They were simply in a better position to provide the appropriate care."

The brown-haired woman nodded. "Equal opportunity."

"Just so," Linda agreed.

Conversation around them ceased for a moment, causing nearly everyone to look toward the entrance to identify the new arrival. Cassidy's chest squeezed in surprise. On Kevin's arm, Brenna stood scanning the room. Alarmed that the heat rising in her face might be noticed, she took a step back from Rich and Linda to assure that she remained inconspicuous and could observe Brenna without the press observing her.

She sighed with pleasure. Brenna looked wonderful in a floor-length, tank-style, red silk gown. The daringly low décolletage was covered by a red, gauze-thin wrap that hugged her upper arms while leaving her shoulders bare. She had swept her hair up into a softly gathered twist of curls that brought out the red highlights. *God, I want her.* Her fingers itched at the tactile memory of the softness of Brenna's hair and how satin her skin felt.

With a dry swallow, she diverted her attention to observe the man at Brenna's side.

Kevin Shea was built along the lines of a defensive lineman and towered every inch of six feet. His broad face was weathered and framed by wavy gray hair, only hinting at the dark brown it must once have been. Not unkindly, Cassidy compared him to her father and found him a handsome man.

She watched him lead Brenna through the photographers and executives. He lightly put a hand on her lower back, as if afraid she would break. The doting glances he gave her when the smaller woman was not looking were embarrassing to observe. The tenderness brought a lump to Cassidy's throat. It was clear to her that Kevin loved his wife.

As Brenna and Kevin started down the steps, Rich moved forward to greet their titular leader. Cassidy hung back, wishing she dared to approach but not trusting her body, much less her voice. Brenna's smile, she noticed, was tense. The photographers were the usual bunch, but still she ducked away from two photographers whose flashes went off less than a foot from her face. Her mind was apparently on something other than publicity.

Cassidy felt a presence come up on her left side. Taking a sip from her wineglass, she offered quietly, "Evening, Cameron."

He sipped from a small tumbler, and she recognized the sharp smell of a Triple Sec Speeder, a drink for which Cam had a penchant when his sole professed purpose was to get rip-roaring drunk. It was likely his first, since the evening was still young, but she knew it wouldn't be his last. When he spoke, his words were the unmeasured tone of someone not interested in watching his language.

"Bitchin' cool party, I guess."

"Mmm hmmm," she replied noncommittally.

"Hey," he said, pointing as he slithered an arm around her waist. She stepped away from the embrace. "I've only been off the set what, two weeks? Chapman's looking buffer than usual."

She nodded. "He switched gyms."

He looked to another cluster of celebrities. "Isn't that Spellman? Look, Brenna and her husband are headed over to say hello to him. Why don't we join them?"

Cassidy was stunned. He was acting as if they had never broken up. "What's going on, Cameron?"

"Oh, I'm just thinking we could spend some time together ~ you and me. Can't I be sociable?"

"This isn't sociable. You're drunk, and you're fawning."

"Ah, but I've seen the woman I love in the arms of another. Shouldn't I fight for her?"

Cassidy froze. "What?"

"That was a very hot kiss on her trailer steps. Which of you did the seducing? I've always wondered how dominance works in a relationship like that," he went on, deliberately ignoring her discomfort.

"I think you've had too many drinks, Cameron. You're imagining things."

"Not tonight. I just wanted to get my facts straight ~ pardon the pun ~ before I go over and share them with her husband. Now, it was...just last week. Right? On her trailer steps..."

Cassidy's eyes widened with alarm. "You're fishing. There's nothing," she tried bravely.

Cameron didn't buy it. "What is it worth to you for me to keep your secret?"

"Secret about what?"

"I can blurt it out right here and now if you like."

Cassidy grasped the hand he raised to gesture to Kevin and Brenna. Through clenched teeth, she drew him to a quiet corner. "What do you want?" she asked cautiously.

"Just what Chapman said. You can act, right? So, I want you to act like we never parted ways. I came to this damn thing alone, and that got me dozens of stares. I'm not going through that again."

"You want me to be your date tonight?"

"Not just tonight," he corrected. "However, it'll be a start. I rather like everyone in the room envying me."

A reporter drew a bead on them at that moment, directing his cameraman to follow. "Mr. Palassis, Ms. Hyland, having a good time tonight?"

"Pinnacle knows how to throw a party," Cameron replied. "Right, sweetheart?" He pressed his mouth over Cassidy's and boldly licked her lips.

Cassidy exhaled carefully through her nose to keep herself from doing something publicly she would later regret. She put a hand on his arm so he could not wrap it around her shoulders. She collected herself when the reporter addressed Cameron.

"There was a rumor that you'd been moved from *Time Trails* because of some differences between you and the cast."

Cameron shrugged. "Rumors. My expertise was needed on the new sets. *Time Trails* gets along fine now that I've set her on the straight and narrow. But the move has meant less time together for me and Cass, and you know how rumors are."

The reporter nodded. "I guess so. Well, you two enjoy your evening."

The reporter moved off. Cassidy exhaled sharply when Cameron's elbow happened to "bump" her ribs. "Do a better job," he warned. "You don't get multiple takes, so I suggest you get into character."

"I can't do this, Cameron."

"Well then, let's see, where's...Oh yes. Looks like the cozy couple is dancing. Shall I cut in for you?"

Cassidy grimaced. Cameron took her silence as agreement and immediately pulled her into a dance embrace. She looked toward Kevin and Brenna and relaxed when Cameron started them off in the opposite direction. "Why do you want to hurt her?" she whispered.

"She seduced you; my manhood must be avenged," he declaimed dramatically.

He was playing with her. Whatever his true motivations, he would not be sharing them. "What if I told you it wasn't like that? Maybe I seduced her. Maybe I'm the one with a broken heart because she turned me down flat."

"You are anything but flat," he said pointedly, rubbing against her as they danced, drawing her attention to her chest with the salacious maneuver. "Absolutely anything but."

Cassidy gambled, "Well, I did. She's lovely. It's true. I hungered for her. Approached her. The kiss you saw? She left me begging afterward."

"Poor darling." He nuzzled her cheek with his nose and whispered harshly in her ear, "If I believed you for one second, I'd be furious on your behalf. You are completely irresistible. I don't believe it. She's defended you too ardently lately. That was really spectacular how she helped you rewrite my script so quickly," he added. "Everyone was buzzing about it."

"She's married."

"Didn't stop you from taking up with me. Come on, you women are all alike ~ take your thrills where you can get them and play coy when it suits you." He changed their direction. She followed his lead and tried not to stiffen as they moved alongside Brenna and Kevin.

"Hey, there," Cameron opened.

"Cameron?" Brenna looked over her shoulder at them. "Hello, Cassidy." Brenna's smile managed to be both welcoming and cautious. She glanced up at Kevin. "You remember Cassidy Hyland and Cameron Palassis?"

"Ms. Hyland, a pleasure to see you again. Has your son gotten in any more trouble since Thanksgiving?"

"No, thankfully." Cassidy felt Cameron tense beside her, and she smiled genuinely at Kevin. This affable exchange was exactly what he had not expected to see. "Has winter hit Michigan yet?"

"Yes. We had a light first snowfall just after I returned home. It'll be a white Christmas, for certain." Kevin glanced down at Brenna. "I'm trying to convince her to come home with me for the holiday itself. Maybe you can add your persuasions?"

Cameron smiled at Brenna's unease, so obvious to Cassidy. "Got plans in town?" He leaned forward and kissed Cassidy's neck as Brenna studied them.

Brenna's eyes flashed dangerously, but her voice was calm when she responded. "There's too much chance I'd get snowed in and stuck out there when filming is supposed to resume. Like I did our first year, Cameron, remember? I've always just found it safer to stay put. Summer's better for trips anyway." She stopped dancing. "I think I should go freshen up."

Kevin nodded. "All right." Cassidy stood beside him watching Brenna move quickly off the floor to the alcove containing the powder rooms. "Mr. Palassis, would you mind if I took your lovely lady for a spin around the floor?"

Cameron inhaled sharply, and Cassidy almost laughed at the triumph she felt. "I'd love to," she answered, taking her hand from Cameron and putting it in Kevin's. She followed the older man easily, feeling a burst of joy. Cameron could not possibly continue clinging to the idea that she and Brenna were involved if Kevin were this congenial. Certainly a man would know when his wife was unfaithful. *Right?* She looked at Kevin, suddenly uneasy.

He smiled at her. "I have to admit I didn't ask you to dance just to pass the time," Kevin said in the lengthening silence. "I have a question to ask."

Cassidy steeled her jaw to keep her mouth from gaping. Carefully she nodded, then cleared her throat. "What is it?"

"I need to know what's bothering Bren. She won't tell me. Maybe I'm just not able to understand, or so she thinks. Do you think you could ~ if you know what it is ~ tell me?"

"Are you bothered that she's not going to Michigan?" He nodded. "She is right about the shooting demands. She's heavily featured in the next episode. There are a lot of lines and a lot of scenes. It would mess up shooting if she got stuck because of a storm. I used to have to avoid going home this time of year, too."

The forthright answer seemed to pacify Kevin. "I guess you're right. It's just..." His voice trailed off as he kept the changing thoughts to himself. "Never mind."

Cassidy found herself in the unenviable position of dancing with the spouse of her lover, expected to sympathize with the estrangement that he could feel but for which he could not see an apparent cause. "She's uncertain about a lot more than just being here when shooting resumes," she allowed.

"You're her friend. Has she told you what?"

Cassidy hesitated, uncertain whether she would be breaking a confidence. "She's been offered a job in England. She has to make a decision soon, I think."

"England?" Kevin sighed. "We'll have to talk."

"Apparently they want her badly enough to wait until she's finished with the series in May."

"Oh." Kevin's frown deepened. The song to which they were dancing came to an end. "Well, I'd better return you to your date."

"All right." Cassidy squeezed his shoulder. "Have a good holiday."

"You, too."

They returned to the side of the ballroom. Cassidy did not dare leave Cameron and Kevin alone. Though derailed abruptly and thoroughly, Cameron was no doubt planning another way to use his knowledge to his benefit. She immediately pushed him out to dance, leaving Kevin on the side of the floor waiting for Brenna's return.

Brenna found the restroom a quiet haven. The loud music was muted there, and the strain of conversing with Kevin was also gone. Seeing Cassidy in Cameron's arms had startled her, but it was when Kevin took Cassidy off to dance that she understood exactly what she was feeling. She was not jealous that Cassidy was dancing with Kevin because Kevin was her husband; she was jealous that she could not be dancing with Cassidy herself.

You're going to tell him tonight. Brenna knew what she had said to Cassidy the night before, and yet, she had continued to wrestle with how to tell Kevin it was over. She was in love with someone else. Remaining married to Kevin would be wrong. She would just have to come out and say it.

She emerged back into the ballroom and scanned the crowd. Cassidy and Cameron were dancing. Kevin was coming toward her, as were Will and Terry. *It would be better in private,* she reasoned. She turned and greeted her co-stars first. "Hi. Having a good evening?" She looked up over her shoulder as Kevin stopped behind her. "Kevin, you remember Terry Brown and Will Chapman."

"Terry. Will." He shook their hands in turn and then rested his hands lightly on her shoulders. She shivered. "Why don't we get something at the buffet?"

"All right." She eased away from Kevin's hand on her lower back guiding her lightly through the milling crowd. Cameron and Cassidy were also at the buffet. "Hello again."

Brenna caught Cassidy's startled look and noted that Cameron had his hand wrapped tightly around her wrist and the knuckles were white. It made her look at Cameron more closely. He did not release Cassidy's wrist. Instead he pulled her against him.

"Nice spread," he said, looking directly at her as his hands roamed Cassidy's butt. Cassidy's face was growing steadily redder.

Whatever was going on, Brenna knew she had to stop it. Obviously Cassidy was not with him by choice. The realization that there was manipulation going on also clued Brenna into something else. Cameron knew, or thought he knew, there was something to tweak in her relationship with Cassidy. A year ago she would have said he was doing it to see her get mad because Cassidy was stepping into her limelight. Now though, she wondered if he actually did know something.

"Excuse me," she said, easing forward to collect a plate. "Looks delicious. What do you think we should try, Cassidy?"

"The capers?"

"All right." Brenna smiled and edged along the table, guiding Cassidy along in front of her, Cameron preceding them, unwilling to relinquish Cassidy. She felt her husband step into line behind her. Brenna took in the layout of the table, taking particular notice of the punchbowl at the end, its red juice and floating balls of ice cream beckoning. She speared the capers and nudged a few onto Cassidy's plate. "Here you go."

"Thank you."

Caught between Cameron and Kevin, Brenna and Cassidy exchanged grimaces. *I will get you out of this,* Brenna vowed, moving along the table. Walking backwards as he kept his eyes on them, Cameron did not notice he was next to the punchbowl until his hip bumped the table and he stumbled. The punchbowl rocked unsteadily and splashed. Brenna grabbed Cassidy's hand out of his and stepped back, unerringly kicking her own shoe forward and under Cam's foot.

Chapman and Brown were behind Kevin when Cameron toppled. They stepped out and around, offering Cameron a hand up.

The reporters and nearby guests all caught the commotion and turned. Several flashes went off as Cameron stood, his suit dripping with punch. "Cameron, let's get you cleaned up," Will offered.

Cameron hesitated and looked around. Straightening, he walked out. Terry and Will moved to flank him as he left.

Terry discreetly kicked Brenna's shoe back to her and she slipped her foot inside, exchanging a quick nod with the dark man, who then followed Will and Cameron out to the restrooms.

The distraction was over almost before it had completely built up. Brenna mentally patted herself on the back.

Cassidy nodded and squeezed her hand, excusing herself. "I'll say good night, now. Kevin, good to see you again." With a brief smile at Brenna, she turned and made a graceful solo exit.

Brenna ached as Cassidy left, wanting to follow the other woman out, to assure herself that she was all right, that Cameron had done nothing more untoward than coercion. She started forward. She saw Terry come out of the corridor with the restrooms and cross to follow Cassidy out. *Should I follow?* Then she felt Kevin's hand on her elbow and the flashes of light receding and knew she had to stay to deflect everyone's attention from Cassidy's early departure. The notion was reinforced by Victor Branch leading his wife to their side a moment later.

"Get out there," he hissed.

Kevin looked to her. She knew he would do whatever she asked, even if he did not know immediately why. She was grateful for it even as she recognized she was using it to advantage. "Just a dance or two."

She smiled disingenuously and followed Kevin's dance steps out to the center of the floor, circling several times before other couples joined them and they could slip to the fringe once again. They stopped for the cameras, and she answered the pertinent questions from reporters about the series, sounding excited for all that she was far from it.

Kevin's expression grew more confused as the evening's performance wore on. He said little. He drew them to a stop as Will Chapman approached. "You had probably better perform a little more," Kevin said, handing her off to Chapman. "I'm going to get a drink."

Brenna realized Kevin sensed she was off kilter, though he seemed to think it was caused by her responsibility to 'perform' for the press tonight. "Just one dance," she assured Kevin before she took Will's hand, wanting to talk with him about Cameron and aware that the wagging tongues might be quieted even more if she spread her attentions around.

Stepping out with her, Will smiled, and Brenna saw in his eyes a brotherly affection. "Thank you," she said earnestly. "And Terry, too, for the save."

Will nodded. They circled in the dance, pausing near a flower-bedecked column for photographers. In a low voice, he acknowledged her words. "Terry saw she got to a limo fine and told the reporters who followed them out that she had been caught in the punch spill also."

Brenna exhaled, most of her questions answered by Will's quick explanation. "How did she seem?" she asked anxiously.

Will's reply took a few moments, as they were stalled by Victor and his wife. Though they exchanged greetings, Brenna declined Victor's request to swap partners, asking him to catch her for the next dance, pouring on the charm as he frowned. "I'd rather have an entire dance with you."

Will offered his assessment of Cassidy's departure low, for Brenna's ear alone, as they danced away. "She seemed anxious to be away; otherwise Terry would have pulled her back onto the dance floor, too."

"I know." *Always with the appearances*, she thought with a frown, though she quickly replaced it with a winsome smile up at Will. The deliberate posing was caught forever on film as a camera flashed.

She danced next, as promised, with Victor, Will taking Victor's wife Melanie out for a spin to the quick, jazzy number. Brenna was grateful that the tempo limited the conversation.

"Word about is that your husband is running for office, and you've got a job offer from England."

"He actually has already been elected. And yes, I've been shown a movie project."

His brow furrowed. "Have you been happy with *Time Trails* overall,

Bren?"

Genuinely surprised by his question, she nevertheless answered honestly, "It's been a learning experience."

"I read your interview with SciFi Magazine. You didn't sound like everything was peachy."

"Working was tough, Victor."

"Was? You do seem to be enjoying rehearsal a little more. Well, except for that fiasco with Palassis."

"He's got quite a hot temper," she concurred, and added, "I'm glad he was moved off."

"Is that what tonight was about?" Victor asked, clearly having talked her around to the topic he most wanted to discuss.

"Tonight?"

"That mess at the buffet."

Brenna shook her head. "An accident."

"Nothing you do is accidental, Bren." She could say nothing to that, realizing she had just been told that he viewed her as calculating.

In the strained moments that followed, Victor's dance steps led them back to where Kevin stood sipping from a small glass with ice. He put it down on the tray of a passing waiter as they approached. "Mr. Shea, thank you for the privilege."

Bren found her hand placed into Kevin's. She looked up between the two men and wondered what her producer would say further.

"You may go," Victor said coolly. He turned away without changing expression and took his wife back out onto the dance floor for the song just starting.

Kevin studied her quizzically. She lifted a shoulder in a shrug though she was far from feeling at ease. But, she had been granted her reprieve. For now. "Ready to go?"

It was nearly midnight when they returned to the house. Brenna remained quiet as the limo driver wound through the neighborhood streets and pulled into their driveway. Relaxing at her side, Kevin loosened his bowtie. "Bit of an odd evening."

"Mmm hmm."

He took the keys from her hand and opened the front door. "Are you going to tell me what that was all about?"

"Pinnacle's annual meet 'n' greet," she said.

"No, that bit of sabotage you did."

"That was an accident."

"You aren't that clumsy."

She pulled the wrap off her shoulders and put a hand on his left arm. "Me?"

"Yes, you. Whenever you saw him tonight, you bristled. Has something happened on the set that I should know about?"

"No. He's been reassigned, actually," she said, perhaps with too much of a smile. "He's working exclusively on a new series." She led the way to the deck in the backyard, and Kevin sat on the swing.

"So you don't see him a lot?"

"Nope. One thing about this set I will not miss is the politics that play off-camera."

"Are you finally thinking about afterward? Ms. Hyland said you have an offer from England."

"I do." She smiled. "And I'm thinking of taking it."

"I thought we were going to settle down, take a break from things."

Brenna shook her head. "You've got your life to live, and I've got mine."

"That's rather harsh," he said. "Just come home for the holiday, see Ellie and Marie. We'll visit with your brothers."

"I'm not going to Michigan with you. Not now...or in the future."

"What are you saying?"

Brenna exhaled, girding herself for a fight. "Kevin, you said you felt we are drifting apart." She nodded. "I agree. It's not fair to you to be distracted like this."

"You mean how you're distracted by set politics?"

She shook her head. "You deserve someone who can focus on you, who *will* focus on you. I...I tried to, I wanted to, but...there's..." *No, not good to tell him about Cassidy.* She started again. "I can't go back to Michigan with you."

"You're still working, I know." He lifted a hand and laid it gently over hers on her lap. "There'll be other jobs. I...I'd like you to take a little time off for a while, just be...a mom." He paused. "My wife." He nodded. "Get the anxiety about all this out of your system. We can just *be* for a while."

Brenna shook her head. "Kevin, I shouldn't be with you at all." She looked at her hands ~ small, nearly hidden by his one big one. Gingerly she pulled free of his light touch. The wedding band on her left hand, put there for tonight's publicity event, glinted in the deck lighting. She pulled it off.

She lifted his hand and pressed the ring into his palm. "I was wrong to take this from you," she said, afraid as her voice cracked. She wanted to do this; it was the right thing to do. *So why am I about to cry?* She looked up from his hand into the stunned expression her words had put on his face. "I want a divorce."

"Bren...I...We...we're married. You're my wife. I love you–"

"But I don't love you," she interrupted, forcing her voice to remain even.

"This is just a rough patch we're going through. You're lonely." He cast about for words. "I'll move out here. We'll work it out." He tried to press the ring back into her hand. She pushed back. "I'll support~"

"No, Kevin." She stood abruptly, causing the bench to rock erratically. "You are...a wonderful man, but...I can't. I can't lie any more...to myself or to you."

"Lies?" His shock was palpable.

Brenna nodded. "I married you because I was too afraid to face things on my own. That was wrong. I...You're a strong, steady rock. You...were everything I thought I should need." She blinked away tears. "But I was lying to myself about some very important things I needed to face."

"I'll help you face them. What's brought this on tonight ~ the weird encounter with that writer?"

She shook her head. "No. I just realized tonight what I want and what you are for me...I was using you to be able to avoid...someone."

Kevin shook his head. "I don't understand, Bren. You're avoiding someone? Who?" He started to his feet. "If it's someone at Pinnacle, I'll make it right. That's what I'm here for ~ for you, for whatever you need me to do."

Brenna exhaled. She was going to have to say it. "Kevin, I have been trying to avoid this, but...please, listen to me. I don't deserve you; I have been unfaithful to you."

"We've barely been married a year!"

"Yes, I know. I spent our first anniversary waiting for you to come home from a political rally."

"Were you with him that night? Were you upset I was gone?"

She shook her head. "You know I wasn't. And I wasn't angry with you," she hastened to add. "I used to wonder why. I should have been, if I loved you as much as I professed." She sat down on the swing. "I've been unhappy so long, I didn't even know I was faking my happiness."

She looked into his face. "The bottom line, Kevin, is I don't love you. I admire you a great deal. You're a great family man, the kind of person my mother was right to point out to me, and I should love you. I think you're smart, and I've been treating you very, very stupidly." She shook her head at herself.

"You're at least admitting the affair. It's over. We can recover from this."

"It's not over, Kevin. It's only just beginning."

"You swore you needed fidelity, not the least because Tom never gave you his."

"That's why I have to let go, Kevin. You're right ~ I want fidelity. I asked it of you, and I can't let you believe you have it from me, when you don't."

"Can I at least know the name of the man? Is it that writer? Is that why you were so abrupt with him ~ because you wanted to cover up in front of me how you lust for each other?"

The notion of her being interested in Cameron Palassis was so absurd, Brenna laughed out loud. "No, no, Kevin. He is nothing to me, not even a colleague I have to suffer for the sake of the job. No, Kevin. Cameron was, however, acting an ass for an entirely different reason, and she is why I tripped him, risked complete public humiliation, and now must confess and end the charade with you."

Kevin's brow furrowed as he processed what she'd said. Finally he seemed to deflate. "You're having some sort of intimacy with Ms. Hyland?" He looked utterly confused.

"Yes."

"But you're not gay. We've made love and I'd...know."

"I've had sex with you. I thought it was...all I was supposed to feel." She struggled to explain. "But...until I...she...it's different," she finished lamely, aware that explaining further would just hurt him unnecessarily.

"Am I that a bad lover that you would go to a woman?"

"Kevin..." She shook her head. "No."

"Then why the hell are you leaving me for some lesbian?"

"I didn't *know* Cassidy felt the same."

"Did she seduce you?"

Brenna shook her head. "It was mutual."

Kevin stood up looking sad, angry, confused. His posture went rigid, hard. Brenna leaned forward, clasping her hands together, arms braced on her thighs, looking at her now bare finger, not even a mark to indicate a ring had been there. She really had never worn it honestly. *God, how could you make me so blind?*

"I'm truly sorry," Brenna said. "Whatever you want in the divorce, I'll...pay it."

Kevin's brows lowered angrily. "I want *you*," he snapped. "I married you for love, Bren. That's what I want."

She nodded. "I know."

"I'll have a lawyer draw up the papers." He threw the ring into the darkness; they both heard it hit the pool surface with a plop. *Down the drain,* she thought as he walked away, leaving her in the yard alone.

When she went inside later, reluctant to face him but driven in by the chill, she found he had left. His overnight bags were gone. She heard a car drive up and looked out her window in time to see him bend down and get in the back seat of a cab. Gone.

CHAPTER THIRTY-NINE

CASSIDY REMOVED the pins from her hair with relief and dropped them on her bathroom counter. Finger-combing her locks, she caught her gaze in the mirror.

I wish we'd had a chance to talk privately, she lamented. She had fully felt overwhelming love and protection in those few seconds surrounding Cameron's "accident." It made her want to curl up in Brenna's embrace.

Just twenty-four hours ago she had indulged that want. She had touched Brenna in the ways she had imagined, even tasted her. Rubbing her cheeks as they heated with the memory, she inhaled slowly.

So why did I feel Brenna's love just as palpably across the separation tonight as when surrounded by the scents of our passion?

Indulging in the quiet since Ryan would not be returned by Gwen until morning, Cassidy relaxed back on the couch and relived the evening with the perspective of time. The conversation had been pleasant and stimulating. Rich and his wife, of course, Cassidy had known. The brown-haired woman had been a new acquaintance. A singer by trade, as soon as she'd learned Linda's profession, she had turned the topic to childcare by bringing up one of the segments from a women's issues program that she hosted.

At the time, Cassidy had not thought about her conversation companions. In reflective retrospect, she saw the sandy brown hair, the warm brown eyes, and remembered her from a recent news story. *Something about her children. The woman and her previous partner...Lesbians.*

She thought about that word. She'd been referred to so often as a blond bombshell, treated like a dumb blonde. What would being labeled again would do to her career?

She loved Brenna. De facto, the press would label her a lesbian. *Well,* Cassidy thought with a slight quirk of her lips, *at last something they say about me will be true.*

Immediately Brenna's features coalesced in her mind ~ the rounded chin, softly slanted eyes nestling above smooth high cheekbones, and her dainty, kissable lips. Her heart expanded with acute joy. When Brenna had entered the ballroom, Cassidy knew she had stopped breathing. The older woman was compact, luminous, gracious, and scintillatingly sexy. And later, in her eyes, Cassidy recognized what love really looked like.

Cameron's face interposed itself over Brenna's, with the half sneer he had worn when talking to her about witnessing the kiss. "*I know. I saw,*" he taunted. Cassidy sighed. She may have prevented the publicity from breaking tonight, but that grace period would not last forever. She had overheard the light buzz concerning Brenna's husband's political aspirations. His wife wanting a divorce would be popular news. That same wife having an affair with a woman would give the tabloids fodder for page one stories for months to come.

Cassidy knew that the timing of advancing her relationship with Brenna to a physical union could have been better chosen. She could foresee the coming difficulties. She wondered if the storm clouds on the horizon, formless and swirling, might blow everything away. She suspected that if the publicity caused any problems with the roles she was offered, the effect would not last long.

She briefly considered that Mitch might cause a problem if he knew about her relationship; his continual badgering that she was a poor parent might gain new traction. However, Ryan would probably be all right with Brenna being around a lot more. He was too young to understand everything, but he had seemed genuinely unconcerned by the concept of his mother "dating" Brenna, however his five-year-old mind might define "dating".

Brenna's sons, on the other hand, were old enough to have definite opinions about it, and those were not likely to be favorable. But they loved their mother, and they wanted her to be happy. If they accepted Cassidy, it would be because Brenna asked it of them.

Shaking her head and not understanding why her stomach twisted, Cassidy flashed back to the previous evening. During their lovemaking, Brenna had been indulgent, offering Cassidy her passion freely, finding numerous ways to give pleasure. While Cassidy had been shaky, Brenna had responded to the possibility of discovery with utter calm. She had regained herself with quicker aplomb.

Has Brenna not fallen as far, or as deeply? Will our one night together be enough to convince her to not turn her back on what we have when the press breathes fire down our necks?

Another thought sprang to mind, and the crushing weight of it made it difficult for Cassidy to breathe. *She's already expressed fears about her ability to continue her career because of her age. How much more fear will it create if she is branded a lesbian and alienated from her family?*

Enveloped in sudden depression, Cassidy finished with the cloth on her face and splashed in the water. Going to her bed, she burrowed under the covers, reluctant to face the dawn.

Morning coffee percolating and still wrapped in her full-length thermal robe, Cassidy stepped onto her stoop to fetch her newspaper.

"Mommy!"

She looked up from her crouch in time to catch Ryan, dressed in a pair of jean coveralls and a plaid long-sleeved shirt. His arms slipped around her neck, blocking her view of Gwen walking up behind him.

"Lazy morning?" Gwen asked.

"Not too bad." Cassidy stood. "I've got coffee on. Want some?"

Ryan raced past her into the house, and Gwen entered ahead of Cassidy. "Do I get to hear all the details before they show up in the paper?"

Cassidy shrugged. "It was a press party," she said wryly. "I went. I talked ~ mostly to reporters mind you ~ and that was that."

Gwen helped herself to a cup from the coffeemaker. "What I wouldn't give for a night out among all those hot names." She leaned on the counter while Cassidy poured a bowl of cereal for Ryan at the kitchen table. "So, who was there?"

"You met some of them at Ryan's party. Rachelle and Jacques Cheron, Rich Paulson and his wife Linda..."

Gwen shook her head. "Who *else* was there?"

Cassidy lifted an eyebrow and nodded, knowing Gwen's tastes among the other actors who worked at Pinnacle Studios. "Kyle Gramercy was there. Daniel Pettigrew, too. Oh yeah, and Spellman. Brenna talked briefly with him and his wife..."

"So, she was there?"

"Of course."

"Did you..."

"We had a brief conversation with her husband Kevin, then he took me out on the floor dancing. After that we went to the~"

Gwen grabbed her arm. "You danced with her husband?" The brown head shook in disbelief. "My God, that is just plain weird."

Cassidy smiled broadly, recalling a similar reaction. "It was strange, but I'd do it again, just to see that stymied look on Cameron's face."

"Why would Cameron care? I thought you broke it off with him."

"He decided to play a little game of blackmail," Cassidy explained with a grimace. "I was supposed to pretend we were still together, or he'd tell Kevin that he saw Brenna and me kissing." Gwen looked alarmed. "Don't ask me how. I was positive we were alone, but~"

"Oh, Cassidy, please tell me she's already gotten separation papers, something. She hasn't?" Gwen shook her head again. "Shit, Lou is gonna flip."

"No, Gwen. You can't tell him. I know, I just know this is going to break soon, but please ~ you know how he gets about gay subjects." Cassidy shivered. "I need time to figure out what to do about Mitch myself."

"He'll find out."

"I just need a little time to prepare." Cassidy was determined. She brushed her hair back from her face in exasperation. "Somehow."

She watched Ryan climb down from the chair, his empty bowl left on the table. "Ryan, clean up."

He had gotten halfway to the sliding door. "Yes, Mommy." Ryan moved his bowl to the sink with a clatter. Cassidy grimaced at the sharp noise. "Can I play with Ranger now?"

"All right. Then we'll figure out what to pack for Grandma's."

"Going to Missouri, then?" Gwen asked as Ryan ran outside to the excited barks of the four-year-old Dalmatian.

"Might be the last chance I get for a while."

Oh my God. Brenna rolled slowly over onto her back, blinking into the morning sunlight cascading into her bedroom. She swallowed against a painfully dry throat and rubbed the heels of her palms gently against her eyes, which felt puffy from crying.

She stretched her shoulders and back, achy from sleeping across bunched covers all night. *I'd better clean up.* Standing and stretching with several groans, Brenna stripped off the wrinkled remains of her gown and stockings. Then, with a gasp of shock, she stepped under the stinging spray of gradually warming water.

Her heart thrummed fast, making her breathless as she opened her mouth and gargled.

Well, here we go again. Divorce. She recalled her mother's reaction to the news six years ago that she and Tom were divorcing.

"You're breaking a contract God made, Brenna Renee Lanigan. Who are you to question God's will?"

Brenna's throat tightened at the sharp note of disgust in her mother's voice. However, she tried to defend herself. "I didn't break it, Mama," *she said.* "Tom did."

"You've obligations. He's your husband, father of your children."

"You want me to forgive him? Mama, he took another woman into the bed he shared with me!"

"Don't you talk to me like that! You have a duty."

Her mother had raved about damnation and excommunication. Brenna had stopped regularly attending church several years earlier, but the sense of disappointing her mother had stuck. She had disappointed her before. Divorcing Tom had been strike one. Divorcing Kevin might be strike two. As for partnering with Cassidy... She shook her head.

Stepping out of the shower, Brenna dried slowly. Standing at the sink, she checked her face. The puffiness was almost indiscernible. She conjured up Cassidy's face, and her lips curled up at the corners. The sensation of a reassuring hug across her shoulders made her stomach twist, her nipples tighten, and her groin heat.

She thought about the party and wanting to escape with Cassidy to the bathroom, even for just a moment to talk. The touch of winsome blue eyes had steadied her. She had done what was necessary.

Thinking about Cassidy led to thoughts of Cameron, whose behavior at the ball had been beyond the pale, even for him. His direct gazes while pawing Cassidy had been designed to taunt her specifically.

Brenna did not regret backing him into the punchbowl. She wondered what happened after he was escorted away. She sighed. No doubt she would learn all in great detail when she returned to the set.

Holding her robe closed at her throat, Brenna stepped into the mid-morning sun and went down the front walk to collect the Sunday paper. On their small cul-de-sac, she could see two girls playing on the front drive of a nearby home. She smiled and turned back inside.

She worked through much of the newspaper and was about to get herself a second cup of coffee when James appeared in the kitchen. He poured himself a glass of pineapple juice and settled next to her at the dining room table. He was barely conscious. She brushed his hair out of his face and commiserated. "Rough night?"

Busy draining the glass, for a moment James did not speak. Mouth wet and eyes blinking, finally he nodded.

"Anything you want to talk about?"

"No." He looked at one of the discarded sections of paper and picked it up, flipping through the sports news. "How was the party last night?"

"Nice."

He seemed to straighten, then. "Is he still asleep?"

Brenna shook her head. Abruptly there was another presence behind her. She jumped when Thomas' hands caught her shoulders and he kissed her cheek. "Good morning," her elder son greeted then crossed through to the kitchen.

Sighing, Brenna knew there was no sense in putting off the announcement. "Kevin's not here."

"Did he go out?"

"He went home. About three o'clock this morning."

James frowned and shook his head. "Mom?"

Thomas stepped in from the kitchen, his orange juice clutched in his hand. "What's up?"

"We had a fight last night. I asked for a divorce." James got up and walked into the kitchen. She could see him leaning on the counter while he poured his cereal. Brenna winced as she saw him slam the box on the counter with a sharp thump.

From the kitchen, James asked, "Does this have something to do with Ms. Hyland coming over Friday night?" The question made Brenna look up at him in surprise. "It does, doesn't it? You become friends with her, and suddenly everything you have isn't enough for you, is it?"

"Kevin and I have had problems for a while now. I talked sometimes with Cassidy about them, but she did not make me do this."

"You're such a doofus, James."

"Shh." Brenna laid a quieting hand over Thomas' on the table. She studied James' face, trying to gauge how much he should understand. Obviously the divorce was angering him. *Is it this one, or recalling the first one?* Telling him at this point that she was involved with Cassidy would be inappropriate additional information.

"Some things just can't be gotten past. Kevin wanted things I couldn't give to him and still have the things I want. We'd thought it would resolve itself when *Time Trails* finished. I learned that's not going to happen. Our goals are too different. I really want to keep working. He doesn't see that as important."

"Why didn't you know this before you got married?" James let his frustration and confusion show, stalking away from the counter and out of sight.

"Because nobody's perfect." Brenna entered the kitchen and found James standing away from her as if staking it out as a defensive location. He cringed when she reached for him but when she pulled him into a hug, he collapsed against her. "Kevin's not. I'm not." She kissed his hair. "I've always told you that things have a way of working out the way they should."

James' arms slowly moved between their bodies, and he pushed away. She let him go. "I saw this coming. Damn." He turned away. Brenna looked to Thomas, who had gotten up and walked to the outside of the counter.

"So what happens now?" he asked.

"Our lawyers will be getting together. Kevin and I actually didn't have a lot of joint property, so it won't take long." *Or at least it shouldn't.*

James suddenly looked up at her with concern. "Will Dad have to be involved?"

"Your father? No. Why?" Brenna suddenly wondered what her first husband's reaction would be. "You two are staying with me. That's not up for negotiation."

"So you'll have to go to court," James asked.

"At least once. In Michigan."

Thomas grimaced. "Will we?"

"I doubt it. Unless you want to come for support. It's your choice." She wasn't certain they did support her, but she wanted them to have the option.

Thomas rested a hand on hers on the counter between them. "Mom, are you going to be okay?"

Old habits died so hard. She was tired of causing so many people so much pain. "I'm just sorry to be putting you through this again."

"It's a shock," Thomas replied honestly. "But, we're older. It's not like divorce isn't common, y'know?"

Sighing, Brenna agreed, but she didn't want either of her sons to feel that divorce was the predictable end to all marriages. "Don't think it has to be this way for everyone." She picked up her coffee mug and looked into its emptiness. "You can do better." She exhaled and filled the cup. "The most important thing is that you don't lie to yourself about who you are or what you want."

Pretty smart words, she castigated herself. *Too bad I have to drag my sons through my lessons. Twice.*

"Mom?"

"Yes, James?"

He pinned her with a questioning look. "What do you really want?"

"Cassidy" immediately came to mind, but she held the name back. *In a while*, she thought, *after they've adjusted a little more.* But James needed an answer. "To be loved for who I am and not what someone wants me to be."

He bit his lip. She reached out and pulled him against her, feeling him squeeze lightly around her waist. She looked over to Thomas, who nodded. "Thank you," she said quietly.

CHAPTER FORTY

CASSIDY PUT her and Ryan's suitcases on the end of the full-size bed that took up much of the space in the cozy corner bedroom. Two windows draped in gingham that matched the bedspread opened on the view of the modest backyard of her parents' suburban St. Louis home.

The squat dresser was dominated by a large mounted oval mirror. Looking into it, seeing the room's reflection, was like dropping back in time. Cassidy plucked a picture from its carved wood frame. She smiled at her self at sixteen on horseback. After living several years in one place and finally feeling settled, she had learned to ride. By high school graduation she had become an adept horsewoman and spent some of her happiest hours in the saddle. It had been a true break from her heavy academic load and the extracurricular activities of Key Club, Student Government, and drama.

Maybe when the snow cleared she could come back out and take Ryan across these hills for his own equestrian experience. He was old enough now. *Actually, Brenna might enjoy it, too.*

Cassidy smiled at the thought of introducing Brenna to her family. She would probably get along well with Cassidy's mother. With a sigh, she set the picture back in the frame and wished anew that she had been able to see Brenna one last time before the holidays. She'd had to settle for a brief phone call as she rushed for the airport. As she shuffled clothing from the suitcase to the dresser drawers, she pulled off the long-sleeved blouse she had worn out of L.A. Reaching into the left-hand dresser drawer, she pulled out the North St. Louis High School River Rats sweatshirt and donned it, completing her homecoming ritual.

"Cass?" Her mother appeared in the doorway. "Oh, good. I see you found everything."

"Of course I found everything. You and Dad haven't changed a thing in this room since I left for college."

"Always good to have a place to come home to." Her mother, Sylvia, sat on the bed. "Are you sure you don't want to put Ryan in with Jimmy?"

Cassidy shook her head. "This way I'll be able to read his bedtime stories." She turned back to the clothes in Ryan's luggage, pulling them out. Setting the pajamas to the side for the night, the rest she tucked in the top drawer of the empty dresser.

"But it isn't right you should sleep with your son. He's old enough to sleep on his own."

Leaning back against the dressing table, Cassidy waved off the concern. "We're comfortable with it. He likes knowing where I am."

Sylvia frowned. "Well, if you change your mind, we'll pull out the trundle." She stood. "I have to get back to the kitchen. There's cocoa and coffee available."

"I'll be out in a minute to help with dinner."

"We'll be going to the service tonight," Sylvia said. "What's Ryan wearing?" Cassidy pulled out a red turtleneck and long pants from Ryan's things. Sylvia asked, "Didn't you bring a suit for him?"

After a moment of confusion, Cassidy shook her head. "No."

Her mother's frown deepened. "I'll see if I have one of Jimmy's old suits in the basement trunks." Shaking her head, Sylvia left the room. Cassidy looked at the turtleneck, finding it perfectly suitable.

She moved from her son's things to her own, pulling out an off-white pantsuit and forest green cotton scoop-neck blouse. She hung each in the closet after a quick shake to loosen the travel wrinkles. After hanging the rest of her things, she moved to tucking away her undergarments in another drawer.

She frowned at a small shallow box wrapped in shiny maroon paper trimmed with dark green velvet ribbon. "I thought I left this at home." It was Brenna's gift, but with the change in her flight time, Cassidy had not had a chance to take it by her home. "I'll just have to give it to her when I get back to town." With a fond smile, she tucked it back into the suitcase, hoping Brenna would like the silk scarf and small rose clasp. Brenna favored scarves as final touches on her outfits, and Cassidy hoped her selection would be an acceptable way to express her private feelings for Brenna without being obvious to the public.

She was looking forward to presenting Brenna with the gift. She'd been smiling ever since purchasing the gauzy red scarf, and her fingers tingled at the prospect of pinning it on her.

"Something for under the tree?"

"Oh, no." Cassidy turned to find her mother standing in the doorway, now holding a small stack of folded clothes.

"For Ryan. Hopefully everything will fit." Sylvia passed the clothing.

Cassidy looked at the gift box, considering again whether Brenna and her mother might like one another. "Mom, the next time I come for a visit, would it be all right if I brought someone?"

Sylvia's gaze lit up. "Are you considering marrying that fellow from L.A.?"

"Cameron?" Cassidy shook her head. "No. I–"

"Mommy! I ran all the way to the fence and back and didn't fall once!" Ryan pushed enthusiastically past his grandmother and plowed into his mother's legs, wrapping his arms around them and looking up her body as he gave a rambling recounting of his adventures outside in the snow-covered yard.

"Stephy got a snowball, but Jimmy hit her first."

Sylvia asked, "Jimmy hit Steph?"

"She was all wet. Jimmy ran away from her and fell down, but I didn't. I didn't, Mommy!"

"That's very good." Cassidy ruffled his hair, pleased by his high color and excitement. "It's time to clean up for dinner now. Change to dry clothes."

Sylvia nodded and left before Cassidy could re-address the topic of her bringing a guest.

Despite the request to change, Ryan kept pausing in the task and telling his mother how to pack the "best snowballs," demonstrating with his hands while his pants remained around his ankles. Cassidy finally grasped his hands, kissed his nose, and helped him finish changing ~ helping him step out of his pants, pull on new ones, and change to a long-sleeved green shirt.

"Do you want a cup of cocoa?"

"Yes!"

With a smile, Cassidy led the way out of the bedroom, into the main area of the house, joining her gathering family. As an only child, and traveling as much as she had with her father's military postings, extended family was the one constant.

Her Uncle Travis, her father's brother, looked up as she entered and then sprang to his feet. "Hey, Cassie girl! How's it going?"

Across from him, leaning back in a big stuffed brown leather recliner, Uncle Floyd, her mother's brother, chimed in. "When'd you get in?"

"A couple of hours ago."

"Cutting it a little close, ain'cha?" Travis wrapped one of his linebacker arms around her shoulders and ruffled Ryan's hair as her son wrapped his slender arms around the man's tree-trunk thigh. "Howdy, squirt."

She kissed Travis' clean-shaven cheek and accepted a kiss on her own cheek before stepping back. Travis sat down and pulled Ryan into his lap. "I'll be right back with cocoa."

"We've got it all together, don't we, Ryan?" Travis chucked him under the chin and tickled his stomach.

Cassidy heard the creak as Floyd lowered his chair. "Stay," she encouraged. "What can I bring you?"

"Nothing, thanks." He followed her into the kitchen. "Just hoping to catch up with you." Floyd, her mother's younger brother by two years, watched her move around her mother in the kitchen, finding the hot kettle on the stove top and pouring cocoa mix into two mugs, one for herself and one for Ryan. "Wasn't sure we'd see you this year."

"I did have some trouble getting a flight, but at the last minute a space came through."

"You still happy out there among all them stars?"

Cassidy stirred the cocoa and put down the spoon. "Just working hard like anyone else."

"Are you going to be finishing up soon?"

"They tell us it'll be done in April. We aren't being renewed."

Moving the turkey from the oven to a platter on the counter, Sylvia interjected, "That's good, then. You can move back here so Ryan can start school."

"I wasn't planning to move home."

"You can't raise Ryan out there all alone."

"I'm not alone, I've got friends, and I will get another job." By rote, Cassidy took the turkey platter from her mother's hands, walked out to the dining table, and set it in front of her father's seat at the head of the table. "Is that the last item?" At Sylvia's nod, she said, "Excuse me, I'll take Ryan to wash up." Feeling unsettled by the discussion, Cassidy left her mother and uncle and took Ryan to the bathroom, where they washed their hands for dinner.

While she was doing that, Sylvia called the rest of the family to the table. Cassidy found Steph and Jimmy ~ her Uncle Floyd's children ~ washing up at the kitchen sink, directed by their mother, Lydia. Floyd, her father, Gerry, and her mother were already moving to their seats. Travis entered from another room. "I've got Brenda down," he reported, taking his seat.

Cassidy pushed Ryan's seat in and took the one next to him. "How is she doing?" she asked.

"Bren? Oh, fine. She's too little yet to know much about what's going on."

Cassidy reached over and gave his hand a light squeeze in silent support. She felt him squeeze her hand back. Virginia "Ginny" Hockman, Travis' wife of only two years, had died of a staph infection, leaving Travis with their newborn daughter, now just seven months old.

"Travis is moving into the old Arbor place down the street so we can help him out," Sylvia said.

"Time for grace," Gerry said, as he held his hands out to either side. Ryan took his right hand, Steph took his left. Everyone at the table grasped hands, and Gerry dropped his eyes, closing them briefly before speaking.

"Dear Father in Heaven, You have gathered us together to witness the birth of the Living Word as the Wise Men foretold. We bless You for all that we receive in this world and in the Kingdom to come."

Cassidy echoed "amen" with the rest, surprised at how awkward she felt inside at the sentiments her father expressed. She didn't recall grace at the table being so religiously formal. There had always been thanking God, but it had not seemed so much like an invocation.

Her father carved the turkey, and plates began to circulate. As the dinner items moved from person to person, from cranberry sauce to cornbread stuffing to the creamed string beans, Cassidy served herself and Ryan, remaining quiet as she listened to the conversation that started up around her.

Steph had entered junior high in September; Cassidy marveled at her poise. She sat quietly, unhurriedly eating, back straight, hair pinned up tidily. By contrast, at that age a pigtailed Cassidy had been always been in a hurry to get back outside, whether it was to run around the Army base playing tag or act out the skits she and the other military children had scribbled out. When she had gotten to high school and found the drama department, it had been an epiphany. She had been ecstatic when her father retired and she was told they would finally be staying put.

Jimmy, at ten, seemed unusually quiet. He did not look up as the adults talked. He ate quickly, clearing his plate. Instead of asking for seconds, he asked to be excused. Lydia nodded her permission, and he was quickly gone from the table.

Ryan ate with energy, commenting on everything ~ from the decorative lamb-shaped holiday salt-and-pepper shakers to the "stringy beans" catching in his teeth. And of course he had to show everyone the one missing incisor he had that made it "hard to chew right."

Several times as Cassidy reminded him to eat, she caught her mother studying them. She felt a surprising amount of disapproval coming from her, despite the fact that she never said anything directly.

Her father was less restrained. "Ryan, sit down." Ryan sat with a frown. "So, Cassie, tell us when you'll be done with this television thing."

"*Time Trails* taping ends in April."

"So will we see you in the summer? Do you want us to come help you move home?"

"I wasn't planning to move back to St. Louis," she said again.

"Your divorce is final. Without Mitch supporting you, you obviously can't raise Ryan by yourself. Your mother tells me that you're no longer dating that writer," her father said.

"It's time to give up this silly thing and come home," her mother added. "Your room is still as you like it, and the other room will be Ryan's."

"That won't be necessary." Cassidy shook her head. "Ryan will be starting school next fall. Our life is in L.A. now. We're doing fine." The sensation that she had already had this conversation with Mitch was unnerving. "Have you talked to Mitch recently?"

"He did call here to wish us a happy holiday."

"He did?" Cassidy chewed quietly as she considered why her ex-husband would be contacting her parents.

"He seemed rather concerned about your arrangements for Ryan."

"I've got that all worked out. After school, he's on the set with me." From the expressions on their faces, that seemed to be the wrong thing to say. "He spends the time with a professional caregiver, and I get to see him on my breaks."

"And you plan to continue doing things like you've done on this show?" Her mother sounded the word distastefully.

"Until April, certainly."

"And you'll find another job from the friends you've made on this one?"

Cassidy nodded. "There's a theater run by one of them. I might try that for a while. I haven't decided yet."

"Ryan can't live in that kind of environment."

"Is your problem with me, with L.A., or with something on the show?" Cassidy asked.

"We object to the content, yes."

"What content?"

Her mother looked pointedly at Steph and then Ryan across the table. "We'll discuss it later."

That brought the topic abruptly to a close. Too abruptly. Cassidy looked from her mother to her father, then to Travis and Floyd to inquire silently if they felt the same. No one said anything. She returned her gaze to her mother. "It seems to be something everyone agrees on."

"In this house," her mother said.

"I see." Not sure what to say and aware that whatever it was they did not want it discussed in front of the children, Cassidy pushed herself away from the table. "Excuse me, I'm finished. Ryan, come on; time to change our clothes."

She led Ryan from the dining table. In the room, she looked at the size of the pants her mother had provided. Realizing they would be too long for him to wear, she put him in the clothes she had brought. Pulling the turtleneck over Ryan's head, she sent him to the bathroom with instructions to potty, wash his hands, and brush his teeth. While alone, she quickly changed and joined him in the bathroom, brushing his hair and then her own and cleaning her own teeth.

They were finished and emerging as Steph and Jimmy walked up, changed as well ~ Steph in a short jumper dress in green plaid, a crisp white turtleneck underneath. Jimmy wore a pair of green slacks, with deeply pressed creases down each leg, and a white oxford-style button shirt, a hunter green tie finishing off the semi-formal appearance.

Lydia stood in doorway of the other bedroom holding a dress jacket in her hand.

"Lydia," Cassidy sent Ryan off with a nudge to his back, "can you tell me what's going on?"

"It's not my place."

"What isn't?"

"Floyd told me it's none of our business what you do, but we don't have to watch it."

"What did I do?"

"I didn't see it," Lydia said sharply. "I was at choir practice with Steph."

"Something on *Time Trails?*" Cassidy asked, beginning to understand somewhat. "They're upset about one of the episodes? For that they think I can't run my own life and need to come home?"

"As I said, it's not my place." Lydia stepped back as Steph and Jimmy returned to the room. She shut the door to tend the final preparations of her children, leaving Cassidy staring at the wood.

During the church service, Cassidy put the issue from her mind and tried to enjoy the pageantry of the holiday service. She lifted Ryan to see as they sang *Good King Wenceslas*, *On a Midnight Clear*, and *Silent Night*.

The assembly filed out past the live manger scene, several members portraying roles in the hay-covered, rustic barnyard-style scene. She knew something about the landscape of Judea at the time and knew that it was more likely to have been a cave than a barn, but she thought the distinctly Midwest interpretation would have appealed to Brenna. She left the church smiling after shaking hands with the minister and his wife.

Out in the parking lot, she looked around to find the rest of the family. She noticed none of them had Ryan in tow. Hearing chuckles and sounds of a disturbance, she realized he had climbed inside the manger area. She found him petting the lamb that was curled up on the floor. "Come on, my little farm boy." She picked him up, laughing easily.

Thomas watched his mother curled up on the couch. Her gaze, though supposedly on the book in her lap, was a little vacant and lost as she reclined, propping her chin in her palm. Wanting to help but not sure how, he waited another moment before crossing through the living room to the kitchen. As he'd expected, she jumped at the noise of his passing. "Mom?"

"I'm sorry. What is it? Has James come home yet?"

"Not yet." He set his cup on the counter. "Are you sure you're all right?" He reached into the upper cupboard for the cocoa mix. "I'm having some cocoa. You want a cup?"

She started to shake her head, but he tilted his head in question. "All right," she conceded. She started to rise.

"No, I've got it. You sit." He put a teapot on and set out another cup of mix. "You've been awfully quiet," he began. "Everything okay?"

"What makes you think something's wrong?"

"Well, let's see." He stepped out from behind the counter and tapped off his observations on his fingers. "You've been sitting there reading the same page in that book for the last twenty minutes. Before that, you sat in the chair and read the comics page for half an hour. Before that, you sat at the desk and worked on a letter for almost an hour."

His mother waved off any further commentary. "I get the point. If you've been watching me, what have you accomplished in the last two hours?"

"Finished wrapping presents," he said proudly.

"I see." The teakettle whistled, and he turned away to pour and stir. When he carried the cups into the living room, offering her one as he sat down, she blew on it and took a sip, then asked, "When did you have time for shopping?"

He shook his head. "Who says I shopped?" Thomas grinned at her. "Don't ask me what I got you, and I won't ask what Santa's bringing me."

She laughed heartily. "You and James haven't believed in Santa in almost five years."

"So why is there a package marked 'From Santa' under the tree?"

His mother pursed her lips. "I got a little something for Cassidy's son."

"Pretty big box."

She swatted his arm. "Now who's being nosy?" She lifted the mug in her palms and sipped, then exhaled. "It's a kid-sized hiking pack, if you must know. He liked yours so much, I thought I'd get him his own."

"Was that phone call you took from Ms. Hyland?"

"Yes. She took Ryan to Missouri for the holidays."

"Well, I guess I'll hold her present until she gets back then."

"You bought her a present?"

"Well, yeah, I did. I got her a pair of climbing gloves," he answered sheepishly. She frowned at him. "What's wrong?"

"Thomas, she's...I'm sure she'll love the gloves, but, sweetheart, you shouldn't continue this infatuation with her."

Thomas felt his face get hot. "I like her."

"She's twice your age. It's not healthy." She hesitated as she decided how to continue. "I thought you were doing well with Cheryl."

"Cheryl's nice, but she's more interested in dances and going shopping than things that matter."

"Thomas," she patted his arm, making his frown deepen. "Yes, you are more mature than the average teen. I admire that. But there is such a thing as growing up too fast."

He pulled away from her and stood, pacing away from the couch. "I don't want to spend time with empty-headed girls, worrying about my clothes or my hair." He wanted to convince his mother of his earnestness. "I've been thinking about Ryan, too. I'd be good for him. We get along so well. I can show him things he should know."

"Thomas, you can't possibly be thinking that you could be a father to that boy. You aren't even responsible for yourself yet." Brenna stood, squeezing a couch pillow between her hands. "I know you find her fascinating and she's very engaging, but Thomas, she'll never feel the same way about you."

"I thought we really hit it off," he said, sitting down, deflating a little in the face of his mother's objections.

"You did...as friends." She drew a short breath, sat beside him, and put an arm around his shoulders. "You taught her to climb in a single afternoon. That takes incredible talent. You impressed her, but that's very different from love."

He leaned forward over his knees and braced his elbows on them as he covered his face. "You're telling me I've been obvious?" When he turned his head toward her, she nodded. "God, she must think I'm such a-"

"I just told you ~ she thinks you're talented."

"But I'm only seventeen to her."

"You *are* seventeen. That's not a bad thing. You've got a lot of choices ahead of you." She leaned back and rubbed between his shoulder blades; he shrugged off the touch. "Come on. What's wrong with being her friend? I enjoy that role myself."

"Mom, it's not the same thing."

"No, it's not." She straightened. "It's not going to be. She and I are peers. But you two can be friends. I'd like you to be. If you're comfortable around her, she'll be comfortable around here. That's important to me." She grew wistful.

Thomas hated when his mother got uncertain. He quickly assured her, "Don't worry, Mom. I'll figure it out. I promise."

"Thank you, sweetheart." She hugged him. "Someday you will find someone suited just for you."

He pursed his lips and nodded tightly. It felt unlikely at the moment. Cassidy Hyland was, as his mother had said, both captivating and engaging. She also stirred him in ways Cheryl or his other girlfriends never had. When he was around her, he felt smart, thoughtful, respected. She made him feel mature, though he knew there were many things he still needed to understand. He took a deep breath. Maybe there would be only friendship for them, but he suspected he would always harbor a love for Cassidy for sharing that with him.

Brenna stood as he did and touched his shoulder. "It's Christmas Eve. Would you like to attend midnight Mass?"

"What about James?"

"Curfew's in another few minutes," his mother said. A vehicle pulled up outside even as she spoke. "Probably him now. Let's get changed, and we'll all go."

"All right."

The door opened, closed, and James swept into the living room. Thomas noticed immediately something was wrong. When his mother called to him, James only dropped his head and waved before quickly passing through to his room.

"James?" Brenna tried again. She brushed past Thomas, turning back as she reached the hall. "Go on and get changed. I'll talk to James."

She hurried to James' bedroom door only to find it shut tight. "James, sweetheart?" She tried the knob and found it locked. "Can I come in, find out about your evening?"

"Go away."

His voice was muffled enough that she could not discern any particular emotion in it. "If you're hurt about something I'd like to help."

"You can't help. I just need to be alone."

Brenna swallowed hard, fighting the emotions stirred by her conversation with Thomas. She had come so close to telling him more, much more, than he should know about her relationship with Cassidy.

"James, unlock the door." There was a long silence while she waited, then came the telltale noise of the lock disengaging. She reached for the knob and turned it, pushing inward. James straddled his desk chair, his head down on crossed hands on the back of the chair.

"Mom..."

She heard the pain lancing through his voice now that it was no longer muffled by the door. "What happened?"

"Marcie dumped me." He pulled something from his pocket and tossed it on the desk. "I've been walking around downtown for the last hour trying to figure out what I did wrong."

Her heart clenched with sympathy ~ and with fear. "That's so dangerous, honey." She stood close but didn't touch him.

"I know; I'm sorry. What did I do wrong, Mom?"

James turned, and Brenna saw the tear stains on his face. "You didn't do anything wrong; sometimes it just happens." She crouched next to him and put a hand on the desk, looking into his face. "I know it hurts. It won't make this any less painful, but, there will be other girls."

James' jaw hardened, just like his father's did when he was trying to suppress emotions he thought inappropriate to display. She rubbed her thumb over his chin, feeling it tremble slightly. His gaze cleared just a little at the familiar, comforting touch. Knowing him as she did, she changed the subject. "It's Christmas Eve. Thomas and I were going to attend mass."

"I don't want to go out. People will laugh at me."

"No, they won't. You've always enjoyed the music. It might ease the pain, just a little." He nodded briefly. Quickly, as he preferred, she caught up his head and shoulders in a hug, no more than a squeeze, and stood away. "Get changed and I'll see you in a few minutes, all right?"

Brenna left him and went to her own room. She wanted to tuck the last presents under the tree before the boys came out. Quickly she changed for the service, pulling on a jade green pant suit and draping a diaphanous emerald scarf around her shoulders. Then she pulled two objects from her closet shelf ~ one wrapped in navy blue with a mistletoe print and the other, a round cylinder, papered in metallic red. Putting on soft leather green pumps, she carried the presents out and set them beneath the tree that glowed in the far corner of the living room.

She was just standing when her sons appeared, ready to go. Each had chosen a simple green dress shirt to wear under a blue suit jacket. Thomas' was a vertical striped forest green and black. James wore a solid aquamarine. She grinned at both of them and stood.

"Presents?" James asked.

"You'll see them in the morning." Brenna saw that James had washed his face and looked better than he had a few minutes earlier. She put a light hand on each shoulder. "Let's go."

Putting the children to bed after hanging up their stockings, the adults gathered in the living room. Some had coffee, Travis with a shot of whiskey in his, and Cassidy had chosen cocoa. The stocking stuffers, little baubles and toy knick-knacks, were pulled out. As they parceled out the treats, filling the children's stockings, Cassidy was surprised at the unusual solemnity. Normally this task, the adults' last one on Christmas Eve, was joyful, and even though they couldn't talk loudly, they would usually whisper back and forth. No one tonight was saying a word, and Cassidy was disturbed to feel that she was the reason why.

"Can we talk about what the problem is?" she asked. "I can't address it if I don't know what I'm supposed to have done wrong."

Her father scowled at her. "As if you didn't know."

"Well, I don't know. Obviously it's something I did on the show, or something someone else did. But I thought I didn't have to remind you that it's all a fantasy. I act for a living. I'm not a secretary or a teacher; I'm an actor."

"So what you do is a game?"

"I take it very seriously. You know that."

"Then how could you participate in something like that? You kissed a woman, and all our friends think you're a *lesbian*." Her mother hissed the last word.

Oh boy. Cassidy exhaled. "An accident had switched our bodies. It was supposed to be seen as Luria - that's the other character - kissing her husband."

"That doesn't excuse it."

"Did you even see it? Do you understand what it was actually about, or are the neighbors your judges now?"

"How dare you!" Her father's voice rose angrily. Her mother put a hand on him quickly to quiet him. "You blindly think we'd accept such a display? Homosexuality is a sin against God."

Cassidy hung the stocking she had been working on, a sinking feeling making her chest feel heavy. She strove for a calm response. "I'm sorry that you've been embarrassed by your narrow-minded neighbors."

"They're our friends."

"I'm sorry."

"You're sorry; that's all? You're sorry?"

Her father stared at her with an angry expression and Cassidy felt her adrenaline start to flow. The longer he stared at her, the more hurt and surprised she was, feeling just as she often had just before Mitch hit her. Her father hadn't struck her since disciplining her as a very young child. Abruptly, he backed up, pushed away Sylvia's hand, turned, and walked away. Travis reached up from the couch and tried to grasp his arm. Gerry brushed that away as well.

"I'm going to bed."

"Dad," Cassidy called after him.

"Everyone," Sylvia said, "I think we're all tired. Time for bed."

One by one the family left the living room. Cassidy looked after them. Travis was the last to stand to leave. "Uncle Travis?"

"Hopefully there won't be any more shows like that one," he said. "Gerry was not happy."

"But it's just a show. You know that, don't you?"

"Yes, I do," he said gently. He rested his hand on her shoulder and kissed her forehead. "Good night, Cassie."

Restlessly rolling around beneath the covers, Ryan woke. His mother lay beside him, and from the quiet sounds he knew she was sleeping. Uncle Travis had read the story about Santa Claus, and Ryan still had the pictures in his head. He had to see. Getting to the floor, he stumbled over something. When he looked, he found another present his mother must have forgotten to put under the tree. He thought he could do it for her and carried it with him out to the den. The fire glowed orange and the stocking Grandpa had helped him hang bulged in the dim light. *Santa's already been here!* he thought excitedly, putting the box under the tree with the other presents.

"Mommy! Mommy!" He ran back into the bedroom and launched himself onto the bed with a squeal. "Santa's been here!"

His mother rolled over and sat up, brushing her hair from her face. "What? Ryan, it's..." she squinted toward the bedside clock, "it's only three a.m. At least wait until six. Jimmy will be up then, all right?" She pulled him down with her under the covers and murmured, "Now try to go back to sleep."

Obediently, he closed his eyes, but sleep did not come. He squirmed. "Mommy?"

"Yes?" She sounded tired.

"How much longer?"

"About three hours. Please go to sleep." She brushed his hair with her fingers and kissed his forehead.

"I can't. Can I wake Jimmy up now?"

Cassidy moved away from him, and then suddenly the room was filled with light. He blinked as she looked down at him from the edge of the bed. "I know it's Christmas and I know you're excited, but you really need to sleep."

"Read me a story?"

Sitting up in the bed, she pulled a big book out of the nearby bookshelf. "Just one story, all right?"

"Okay." He settled between her legs and helped her open the book to a story. "Little Red Riding Hood," he read carefully. The squeeze on his shoulder told him he had gotten it right.

A tale unfolded of a little girl hunted down by a wolf who pretended to be her grandmother. Ryan was excited by the end of the story where the woodcutter killed the wolf with his axe. "He saved her from the mean old wolf," he cheered at the end. "He saved her."

"Yes, he did." She kissed his cheek and pulled the book away. "Now, that's your one story. Let's try to go back to sleep." He yawned, and after she turned off the light and pulled him down across her chest, he closed his eyes as she patted his back, with her heartbeat strong in his ear.

"I love you, Mommy."

"I love you too, Ryan."

Her voice was soft, sleepy. Ryan found it easy to succumb to sleep himself.

CHAPTER FORTY-ONE

COMFORTABLY ENSCONCED on the couch, Brenna sipped her coffee as she watched Thomas and James opening their presents. Gift cards from their father were already tucked in their wallets for the holiday trip to the mall tomorrow. Shaking her head about the absurdity of a father who neither called nor wrote except to send money, Brenna watched James opening his last gift from her. It was the package she had tucked under the tree at the last minute, but the one she'd worked longest on in preparation for the holidays. She hoped he would still like it. Music tastes changed so fast.

He unfolded the white tee shirt, looking blankly at the back for a moment before turning it around. His eyes widened, and he yipped, "Lifehouse! This is so cool! How'd you get all the autographs?"

She grinned as two oblong pieces of paper fluttered from the folds of the fabric. "There's more," she said.

He set aside the tee shirt and snatched up the strips of cardboard. "Tickets to their concert! Cool!" He tucked the tickets into his shirt pocket and turned back to the tee. "How *did* you get the autographs?"

"They *are* an L.A. band, you know," she said with a smile. "I...ran into someone who knows them."

"No way."

Laughing, she responded in teen parlance, "Way." Obviously boggled at the autographs, James immediately pulled the shirt on over his other one, which made her grin broaden.

Thomas, who had watched quietly through the exchange, finished opening the small present from his Uncle Gary, her brother. "Thomas, what have you got there?"

"Uncle Gary sent tickets to spring training exhibitions for the Dodgers. Says he got me some batting and pitching practice with them, too."

Brenna looked at the tickets. "There's two here for each game."

"Yep." Thomas read more of the note his uncle had included. "Says he's going to take me. Looks like he's coming for a visit."

"There's a half-dozen games here. That's...what ~ three weeks worth?"

"Yeah, probably. It's usually two games a week." He tucked the tickets safely in the small box and then turned to open the present from her.

Brenna suddenly realized there might be some conflicting dates. Biting her lower lip anxiously, she awaited Thomas' reaction.

His brow furrowed as he read, "U.S. Department of Forestry."

Brenna's heart sped up at the slow-building smile, finally laughing when he burst out, "I'm going to co-op with the Forestry Service!"

"What?" James asked.

"Yeah. Mom? How did you do this?"

"I had a talk with your counselor about how interested you were in hiking and climbing and how much fun you have with the LAKE kids. He looked up the contact information and the requirements."

"I've got enough credits to do this?"

"You'll get two credits, as well as get paid. Mr. Thierry can tell you more, but I've already set up an account for you on the bus line." She gestured to the tube. Thomas looked inside and when he shook it, the credit card bus pass dropped out into his palm. The magnetic strip would debit the account, allowing him to not always have to travel with change for the bus. "After lunch you take the bus to the forestry office and get home around eight o'clock." She hesitated. "I was just thinking it might make getting to some of your Dodgers games a little tough."

"Don't worry about that! This is fantastic!"

He skimmed the letter again, and she registered with pleasure the wonderment on his face. "I'm glad then that I thought to talk to your counselor."

"I can't believe Thierry didn't tell me about this opportunity himself."

"Apparently it's not a widely publicized program," Brenna explained. "I guess that my asking if there was something along those lines caused him to go looking in the right places."

Thank you, Cassidy. Cassidy had mentioned the idea of Thomas being a camp counselor in the first place. The Forestry Service co-op would give him a chance to see all the related outdoors careers and let him find his own place, if he chose. She would have to tell Cassidy how well the gift had been received. *Actually, I would like to tell Cassidy a lot of things.* She suddenly missed her very much.

"More coffee, Mom?"

At Thomas' question she looked up, only then realizing that she had been staring into her empty mug. "Thank you." She passed it to him for a refill.

James stood up and retrieved a present from under the tree. It was square ~ about a foot long on a side and an inch deep. He passed it to her. "For you."

"James?"

"Just a little something." He shrugged and sat down, looking nervous as she took it carefully onto her lap.

It was quite heavy. She tore through the plain navy blue paper. Inside was a framed piece of art, a portrait, she realized, identifying a shoulder before she removed the last of the paper and revealed the face. Her face.

Awestruck, she looked at a portrait of herself rendered in pastels. The figure was in three-quarter profile, from the shoulders up, and the skin tone was flawless, shadowed well enough to suggest the muscles in her throat and face as she smiled. *He really sees me this way?* "It's...beautiful," she whispered.

"I had a good subject," James said, smiling. "I did it in art class."

Still studying the portrait, Brenna realized the shadows above the figure's left shoulder were not just random swirls. "There's another face in here."

"It's you...as Jakes," he said.

She picked out the shadowy face and shoulders of an almost ethereal rendering of her on-screen alter ego. It was..."Truly amazing," she breathed. "Thank you." Looking at the picture, she said, "I didn't know you could do anything like this." She traced the swirled 'JL' signed in the lower left corner.

"We had a portrait unit in class. Mrs. Vetter thought this was good enough to enter in the district art fair."

"Did you?" When he nodded but remained silent, she patted his arm. "Well? Are you going to tell me, or make me drag it out of you syllable by syllable?"

"I won second place in the pastel category."

He grinned at her, and she squeezed his hand. "That's wonderful!"

"Thanks."

"Thank you." She pulled him down for a kiss. "Let me know when you do another show." James looked surprised. "I'd really like to go."

"Uh. Sure." He blushed and stepped back.

Thomas appeared over her shoulder with her coffee. "Here you go, Mom." He caught a glimpse of the portrait. "Man, James, that's nice." James accepted the praise with a nod. Thomas looked at his mother. "You might not want mine now."

"Of course I will." She reached up and patted Thomas' cheek. "Go on." As Thomas retrieved a package from under the tree, she noted the similar dimensions; it looked suspiciously like another picture.

He introduced it as he passed it over. "I know you've seen some of the pictures I took on the camping trip. I thought you'd like this one to remember it best, though."

Brenna tore aside the paper and found another framed image, this one a photograph, blown up to 8 x 10. It was a picture of the mountain they had climbed, shot from above. Framed centrally between golden brown rocks and the green forest, Brenna and Cassidy had their arms wrapped around their ropes, resting in the grandeur. The sunlight seemed to beam on them both, illuminating them against the tan of the craggy surface. Looking up at Thomas, she said, "But you were on the mountain with us."

"That was taken on my second stop at the top. I pulled out the camera and captured it, then rappelled down to meet you." He dropped his chin, swallowed hard, then returned his gaze to her. "I'm giving Cassidy a duplicate of the shot."

"She'll love it." Knowing he was concerned she would be upset with him, Brenna reached out a hand. When he leaned past his brother and took it, she assured him, "It's an appropriate gift." He smiled with pleasure, and she let him go.

"Thanks, Mom."

She looked to James, then at the pictures. "I'm going to have to build on a gallery room," she said with a chuckle. "Both of these deserve more of a display than the living room wall." She squeezed their hands. "Thank you. And, you know, I love you."

Predictably, her younger son sidestepped the mush. "If we're finished, how about some lunch?"

"A snack," she suggested. "Dinner is early today." She stood. "You two get something together, and I'll hang these."

It was two in the afternoon when the Hockman family began to wind down the opening of presents. The last ones around the tree were being distributed by Steph and Jimmy. Ryan was playing with a new race car. Cassidy looked up from unwrapping a sweater from her parents to see Jimmy carrying a familiar-looking box. "Jimmy, what have you got there?"

"It looks like it's for Brenda." He crossed to Travis, who was giving his daughter a toy he had just unwrapped.

Cassidy reached for it, but Travis got his hands on it first. Brenda, having heard her name, pulled it from him.

Travis looked at the card, "To Bren, love Cass."

She cleared her throat. "That's not for Brenda. I'm sorry, Travis. It got mixed in by mistake."

"That's the present I brought out Mommy," Ryan said proudly.

"Thank you, Ryan, but it's for Brenna back home."

"Oh." He brightened. "Is it pretty?"

At that moment Brenda tore into the paper, and the box was opened. Gerry reached over the back of the couch and pulled the box with the scarf and pin from Brenda's hands. "It certainly is pretty." He fingered the silk. "Who is this for?"

Cassidy was unnerved by his tone. After last night's very one-sided exchange, she could not them know she was involved with Bren. "Brenna Lanigan, a woman I work with." She stood up to take it from him. As he plucked out the note, she remembered what she had written. Everyone else found out, too.

Obviously surprised by what he read, her father read it aloud, as if asking her to confirm it. " 'A silken embrace to remember me.' " His eyes darkened in plain anger and disgust as he continued reading silently. He looked at her with suspicion. "Rather intimate for an office gift."

Her heart beginning to hammer, Cassidy saw the terrifying glint of steel in her father's blue eyes. She reclaimed her property. "I'll just go put this back in my bag."

"You'll explain who this woman is to you." His voice was deep and dark.

"Cassidy, what kind of trouble have you gotten into?" Her mother's tone was anxious.

"What trouble?" Cassidy exhaled. "Yes, it's a present for my friend on *Time Trails*. We work together sixteen hours a day!"

Her father's voice exploded through the room. "It looks like a note to a lover!"

Little Brenda wailed at Gerry's shout. Travis bent to soothe her even as he was rising to stand between Cassidy and her parents. Cassidy had also taken a quick step backward at her father's loud exclamation, almost tripping over Ryan. She righted herself as her mother exclaimed, "Gerry!"

"I told you she'd get perverted ideas out there!" Gerry accused. He threw the scarf box down on the couch.

Cassidy quickly retrieved it, tucking the contents gently back inside, holding it tightly. "Get ideas?" Cassidy was jolted by his patronizing tone. "I've been in L.A. eighteen months working on my job. I've been on my own working since I was twenty. I'm thirty-two, not ten or twelve."

Her father shot back, "We sent you to college to get an education."

"And I earned my way all by myself." Her scholarships for academics had paid the bulk of her tuition, and the money from a few small beauty pageants ~ and commercials as she was cutting her teeth in acting ~ paid for the rest of the fees at the state university. She hadn't asked her parents for anything. Apparently they remembered things differently.

"I told your mother that place would corrupt you. First you take up with that playboy and get a divorce!"

"Playboy? Cameron? He's just a writer."

"We've heard all about casting couches," her father retorted.

"Well, I've never auditioned on one," Cassidy replied evenly. "I got the job on *Time Trails* through hard work, and I've kept it the same–"

Her father's hand landed hard against her cheek. "You don't talk to me like that."

Cassidy's eyes watered as she gingerly touched the stinging hot skin of her face. Biting the inside of her cheek, she kept the tears at bay. Silence blanketed the room. She took a step back. "I didn't think you were the same as Mitch."

"It's your own fault. He wouldn't have done anything to you if you hadn't made him jealous," her father retorted.

"My fault?" Cassidy shook her head. "Not my fault."

"You get it in your head that you want to act ~ instead of being a mother to your son ~ and you claim that your husband getting tired and jealous isn't your fault?"

"And so it's okay that he hit me? Something you've never done before, I might add," Cassidy retorted. "Why are we discussing this?"

"If I'd been less lenient with you as a child, maybe you would've paid more attention to how things are supposed to be."

"You're talking nonsense."

"I should've beat all those fool ideas of acting out of you in high school, but your mother thought it was 'harmless'." He turned to Sylvia again. "Harmless, hmm?" He jabbed at the note. "I'm not a little girl."

"No. But damn well you're my daughter and I won't have it." Gerry turned his back abruptly.Cassidy had never heard her father spew such vitriol. "I'm no different than I was just yesterday when I came home to spend some time with my family for Christmas."

"*Christmas?*" He tried to grab Cassidy, but she backed away and he stumbled forward, knocking around the furniture noisily. "You are no Christian, behaving like this! No respect for your parents, all we've done for you! Sleeping with a man while you were married!"

Travis stood. "Gerry, please. Shh. you're scaring the baby." Gerry shook off his brother's hand on his arm.

"I'm sorry, Uncle Travis." Cassidy apologized though she had not been the one yelling. Her father said nothing. She looked from her father to her mother and back again at her father's sternly set jaw. She set her own jaw and then exhaled. "It would be better, I think, if we went home. This obviously isn't the best time to talk about this."

"I don't want to hear you say anything but that you're giving up all these damn fool notions," her father retorted.

"You've made that perfectly clear." Shaking inside, Cassidy drew on her acting skills to maintain an outward appearance of calm. "Which is why we have to leave."

"You can't leave now, we haven't had dinner," her mother protested.

Cassidy studied her father, who gave every appearance of not relenting. He stood with his back to her, his arms over his chest. He seemed proud of himself as he walked away and settled ~ in what Cassidy could only characterize it as a "king-like" manner ~ on his recliner, his arms splayed outward over the padded arms, hands wrapped around the ends. He looked like he was waiting.

Abruptly Cassidy recalled how he would do the same thing to her when she was younger, his silence conveying disapproval of something she had done. She would buckle under that look and apologize, promising profusely not to do whatever it was again. Though today was the first time he had struck her, the rest of the situation made her feel like she was twelve again, being grounded for some unspoken infraction.

Only now she wasn't twelve. She was not going to be cowed into apologizing for doing something wrong when she felt she hadn't. She had learned a great deal in the last year about herself, particularly when it came to making her own choices and directing her own life. Mostly from Brenna. She smiled at that, and her spine straightened with resolve.

"Maybe I'll see you in the spring after *Time Trails* finishes up." She saw her father's eyes narrow and felt vindicated that she had surprised him by not capitulating. She tried to lean in and kiss her mother's cheek, but the bewildered woman pulled away, eyes wide. Stepping away, Cassidy took Ryan and went to pack.

"Cassie?" Her Uncle Travis stepped out of the doorway of the second bedroom.

She stopped, gauging his expression but finding nothing but the question. "I'm going home," she said quietly, continuing past him.

Travis followed her into her bedroom. "Do you need a ride?"

"I can call a cab." She pulled out the luggage and set it on the bed, haphazardly repacking what she had unpacked only the night before.

"Most likely double the price today."

Cassidy automatically went through the process of changing Ryan's clothes while she responded. "I can handle it."

"I could see you safely on the plane."

"I've got to change my flight. It'll probably be a few hours before we can find space to L.A."

"I wouldn't mind waiting with you and Ryan."

"Dad wouldn't take it kindly."

"Doesn't seem right ~ you leaving on Christmas Day."

"I won't let them continue to treat me as if I'm a child. Besides I've got someone who will be happy to see me back in L.A. just as I am."

Cassidy finished securing the lock, and Travis grabbed the luggage. "You can tell me about her on the way."

The tension thickened as Cassidy, leading Ryan by the hand, followed Travis out through the living room. Her father stood, and they regarded one another warily, Cassidy not moving a muscle and keeping her face expressionless and her father frowning deeply. Her mother stood beside him, a hand on his arm, not restraining him, but the gesture suggested that she was holding him in place nonetheless.

"Cassie, please don't go. Let us help you."

She shook her head. "I don't want, or need, the help you want to give."

"We're your parents. We know what's best for you."

"When I was ten, maybe. You seem to have forgotten I grew up."

Her father took exception to her tone. "Don't talk to your mother like that," he growled.

Cassidy nodded. "Goodbye."

Uncle Floyd and Aunt Lydia, each with a hand on a shoulder of their two children, remained seated on the couch. Cassidy directed a "Goodbye," to them. Travis said nothing, but the suitcases in his hands spoke volumes. She followed him to the hallway, put Ryan in his warm coat, and pulled on her own long winter coat. Sylvia followed them but didn't say anything more.

Travis addressed himself to her. "I'll be back when I've seen her safely off. Maybe after dinner. See to Brenda, will you?"

Sylvia nodded, and Cassidy watched her close the door, leaving them outside standing on the porch. The silence was oppressive, and Cassidy felt suddenly as heavy as the door barring her from her parents' home. She exhaled. "Let's go."

"Where are we going, Mommy?"

"Home."

"Christmas is over?"

Cassidy nodded. Ryan took her hand as they walked down the snowy wet front steps. She belted Ryan into the back seat of Travis' large four-door gray sedan. The car rocked a little as he closed the trunk lid.

"Got everything?" he asked as he entered the front seat.

Cassidy checked her purse for the tickets she would have to exchange. She considered the keepsakes she had left in her old bedroom ~ the pictures in the mirror, the yearbooks in the closet. St. Louis was only the last stop in her family's many moves, but it was the home she remembered most. Now it all felt like her things belonged to someone else. She now understood that her parents had believed she was supposed to stay that same amenable girl. She wasn't, and she would have to wait them out until they realized that as well.

She shook herself, rubbing her cheek where it still hurt from her father's hand. "Yes, I've got everything." She got in on the passenger side of the front bench seat and secured her belt. "All right. Let's go."

The doorbell sounded as Brenna, Thomas, and James were finishing their holiday cleanup and sampling a fruitcake sent by Rachelle Cheron. James went to the door.

Looking through the peep hole, his face took on a puzzled expression, and he opened the door. "Ms. Hyland?"

Brenna paused in folding together her wrapping paper collection. *Cassidy?* She pushed to her feet and dusted off her hands. "Cass? I thought you were in St. Louis." She pushed the door open wide and watched as Cassidy nudged Ryan forward first. Cass looked tired, and her face seemed a little drawn. Her left cheek was bruised.

"We were in St. Louis until this morning. I decided to come home early."

"Well, we're just finishing cleaning up. Come on inside; I'll make some coffee."

"I'd like that."

Brenna watched as Cassidy crouched and helped Ryan off with his coat. Sensing something unsettled about her, Brenna gave in to the impulse to put her hand on Cassidy's shoulder. Cassidy rose with Ryan's coat in her hands and turned to meet Brenna's gaze.

"We need to talk," Cassidy said quietly.

CHAPTER FORTY-TWO

THOMAS AND James stood as Cassidy and Ryan entered the living room, Brenna walking in behind them. "It's good to see you," Cassidy said to them.

"Mom told me you were in St. Louis visiting your family," Thomas said with concern.

"I was. We had...a problem." Cassidy looked to Brenna. "They don't like what I'm doing," she elaborated vaguely.

Brenna wondered exactly what Cassidy meant, but clearly the woman didn't want to speak in specifics without a private word first. "Thomas, would you take Ryan into the game room? I'll make some cocoa with our coffees and bring them in a minute."

Thomas looked as if he were about to balk at the request, and Brenna noticed how he fidgeted toward Cassidy. "Just a few minutes," she added.

Finally he nodded. "All right. Ryan, c'mon. Let's see how you do on my latest Playstation game."

James actually led the way, clearly eager to leave the whole group.

Brenna nodded toward the kitchen once she and Cassidy were alone. "It's not perfectly private, but obviously something's on your mind."

Cassidy followed her to the kitchen and helped pull out the makings for coffee and cocoa. "I'm sorry. I didn't really think about this; I just knew I needed to see you."

Shaking her head, Brenna flipped on the coffeemaker and then reached over to grasp Cassidy's hand. "You should feel you can come to me about anything. So, what happened at home?"

"My parents didn't like the same sex kiss I did with Rachelle. I mean, *really* didn't like it. I found that out Christmas Eve."

Brenna pulled down mugs with a light clatter to the counter. "Controversial stuff. We knew that."

"Unfortunately, that was not all. They've decided that somehow L.A. has corrupted me. They basically demanded I come back to St. Louis to live with them."

"That's nonsense. You're thirty-two and have a great job."

"They don't care about that; they think they need to 'fix' me."

"What?"

"They...We had already argued about what I was doing out here in L.A. I had a present for you. It accidentally got mixed in with the others under the tree. When my father intercepted it, well, he..." Cassidy's explanation trailed off as she recoiled from the memory of her father's contorted angry features. "He hit me."

Brenna closed her eyes and inhaled, caressing the bruise. "So that's where you got this. Damn."

"This is not about you and me, I swear I didn't tell them. Too much could go wrong. You and I together only can decide who learns what and when. But my father... I've lived meekly...I didn't realize it. My few visits home were relatively quiet. I didn't suspect they harbored these kinds of feelings. They apparently felt ...or at least my father felt, that my acting is a game. My mother called it a phase I was supposed to grow out of."

"I'm sorry."

Cassidy nodded. "Their narrow-mindedness and lack of understanding hurts. I actually thought for a while that you might like to come to St. Louis the next time I visited. There are a lot of things that I'd like to share with you from my growing up." Cassidy shook her head. "But I won't be going back to see them for a while. At least until they understand that I won't change to suit them."

"That bad?"

"My father was...unrelenting. I decided to leave, but more to prevent being thrown out and making more of a scene in front of Ryan or the other children." The teapot whistled, and Cassidy poured water into three mugs of cocoa mix, stirring each.

"I remember saying something about our families when we started this." Brenna sounded regretful.

Cassidy shook her head. "It matters, yes, but we're adults, Bren. It's our life. My parents don't get to tell me what to do with it."

"But your family is all you have."

Taking Brenna's hands, Cassidy pulled her against her body and kissed her. "No, please. Ryan and I have you." Trying to convey her conviction, Cassidy lifted Brenna's chin and kissed her solidly.

Thomas stood in the kitchen doorway staring at the two women as they parted. A shocked moment of silence was shattered by his "What's going on?"

Brenna exhaled and swallowed, then felt Cassidy's arm around her back and the long fingers wrapping around hers. "I think it's a good time for a family meeting."

Thomas turned sharply, striding quickly down the bedroom hallway. Before they could catch up to him, he pounded on his brother's bedroom door. Brenna shushed him. "Stop!"

James, half-undressed, appeared at his doorway. "Mom has something to discuss," Thomas said quickly.

"Can't it wait until morning?" James asked, leaning against the doorframe.

"I'm not listening to this alone."

Thomas pushed open the door, and James' exhaustion fled instantly, replaced by anger. "What the fuck's up with you?"

Brenna cleared her throat, reminding them she, and Cassidy, were right behind Thomas. "Family meeting. Now."

James grabbed a robe and arrived in the living room as Brenna was directing Thomas to sit on the couch. "Being angry won't change what I have to say," she started.

"About what?" James sat in nearby chair, looking up expectantly. With her hand on Brenna's arm, Cassidy was moving both Brenna and herself onto another seat, the divan, and foot stool. Cassidy sat up behind Brenna, who leaned forward on the stool.

"This is nuts!" Thomas' outburst was emphasized by him jumping to his feet.

"Sit down!" Brenna ordered. "Sit down, please," she added more softly.

Thomas did as she asked. James continued to wait and watch, with growing curiosity.

"Ryan?" Cassidy asked.

"Busy with Mario Brothers," Thomas answered curtly.

Brenna looked over her shoulder, meeting Cassidy's gaze, squared her shoulders, and turned back to face her sons. "Cassidy and I have grown very close over the last few months. We didn't realize at first what was happening." She reached for Cassidy's hand. "*I* didn't realize what was happening," Brenna amended. "But I couldn't...didn't want to stop it."

Thomas ground out, "When?"

"When what?" James asked.

Cassidy answered, "It started getting really serious on the camping trip."

"When you were flirting with me?" Thomas snapped. He turned on his mother. "Why you?"

"What's wrong with me?" Brenna retorted sharply.

"I was not flirting with you, Thomas." Cassidy sighed. "I genuinely think you're a great guy, but it's not...I'm in love with your mother."

"You're in love with Mom?" James blurted. "How the hell did that happen?"

Brenna's gaze darkened in dismay at his language, but he was uncowed. So was Thomas. "She...You..." He shook his head and stormed to his feet. "So all that stuff you told me, about being her friend?"

"It's all true, Thomas. I am Cassidy's friend. When I opened myself to that much, I realized I felt more than just friendship."

"So you...This is why you're getting the divorce?" James asked.

"Kevin and I were a mistake I made."

"The fight you had, you said he left."

"I had to tell him the truth."

James nodded. Thomas countered, "And the gym climb, dinner ~ that was a...a...date?"

Cassidy answered. "Dating is part of being together."

"Together? So...you...you have been...physical?" Thomas closed his eyes, rubbing them quickly. "Forget it, I don't want to-" He cut himself off again. "I'm going out." With quick jerky motions, he stalked to the front door, grabbed a coat, and slammed out of the house. Brenna was on her feet after him, watching in dismay as he took off on foot.

"Thomas!"

"Bren, wait."

"But it's..."

Cassidy turned her back inside. As they reached the living room, James was just entering the hallway. "James?" Brenna asked.

"You've said what you need to," he said with a shrug. "I'm going to bed." The door to his bedroom closed loudly in the sudden silence.

Brenna sat down heavily on the couch where Thomas had been just a few moments earlier. "Well, I can see that wasn't the best way to do this." Cassidy sat next to her, wrapping her arms around Brenna as she turned into her chest.

"You should get some sleep while I go after Thomas," Brenna said after a few minutes struggling for calm.

"Any idea where he would go?"

Brenna thought. "It's late. It's Christmas. I don't know."

"He knows that, too."

"He was still in love with you," Brenna said ruefully.

"I gathered."

"I'm sorry. First you have the scenes with your family, then here."

"I've been gifted with a lot in the last few months. I'm not giving it up easily." Cassidy stood, pulling Brenna up with her. "Let's go look for Thomas."

They helped each other into light coats, then got into Brenna's car. "There's a park down the street," Brenna suggested.

"All right."

They were just out of the cul-de-sac, reaching the first corner to turn when Brenna's headlights picked out a figure walking on the south sidewalk toward them. The light caught his face and Brenna quickly stopped. She was out of the car on her side as Cassidy strode across the grass.

"Thomas?" Cassidy called.

"Yeah." He sounded winded.

"Your mother was worried."

He looked toward Brenna, then up at Cassidy. "I just needed some space."

"Are you all right?" Brenna asked.

"With this?" He gestured between the two women. "No."

"I'd like to think you are smarter, and kinder, than that," Cassidy said gently. "Can you at least give us a chance?"

Thomas' ears reddened. He looked away from Cassidy but nodded.

"That's all we're asking."

"Will you come home?" Brenna asked.

He nodded again and moved to the back door of the SUV. Reaching for the handle, his hand met Cassidy's. They said nothing, but Thomas let her open the door for him and close it after he was inside.

Cassidy put herself in the front passenger seat as Brenna went back to the driver seat. They were silent for the short turn around to the house. Thomas said nothing to them as he entered. He disappeared into the bedroom hallway before they could ask him for his coat.

Cassidy hung both her and Brenna's coats. "I should probably take Ryan and go home."

They walked into the empty living room. Brenna nudged Cassidy into the couch cushions. Then she also sat down, pushing herself further back, coaxing Cassidy to turn her back into her chest. As they nestled together, Brenna stroked her fingers through Cassidy's hair, untangling it with her fingers but also relishing the feeling of its softness against her skin.

They settled into an embrace, arms around one another, each breathing in the other's scent and sinking slowly into the sense of warmth and peace being together generated for them. Out of the corner of her eye, Brenna caught the twinkling of the Christmas tree lights and remembered her present for Cassidy. "I have something for you." She brushed her lips over Cassidy's and sat up.

"No, it's – "

Brenna's fingertips silenced her. "Shh. Humor me?" She retrieved the small cube-shaped package and watched anxiously as Cassidy studied it. "Do you remember one of the first real conversations we had? In my trailer?"

Cassidy's brow furrowed. Now curious, she tore the wrapping and withdrew the unmarked cardboard box. The top lifted easily after a fingernail was judiciously applied to the bit of tape sealing it.

Brenna smiled, love shining from her eyes as Cassidy tipped the box to the light and looked inside. Slender fingers withdrew two ceramic figurines, and Cassidy smiled. "Rocky and Bullwinkle?" Her voice filled with amazement and amusement.

"Friends through thick and thin," Brenna explained, kneeling on the couch cushion. "A promise." She bent toward the uplifted face and kissed the full mouth with infinite love pouring through their connection. "I do love you," she murmured as their lips barely separated for a breath.

Cassidy put the figurines aside and grasped Brenna's shoulders, and then, unromantically, she yawned. "I'm sorry," she said, dropping her face away.

"You don't have to collect Ryan now." Brenna shook her head. "Please stay?"

"Thomas isn't going to handle that very well."

"I missed you." Brenna reached for Cassidy's hand. "When I saw you on the doorstep, it was...I thought about you so often today."

"Me, too." They wrapped their arms around one another. In the relative privacy, they reveled in the contact and kissed lightly.

"Then please, stay. We'll have breakfast tomorrow. I'm taking Thomas and James to the mall with their gift certificates. Maybe we can...I...it might feel 'normal' for them."

As Cassidy considered the offer, her brows knitted then relaxed slowly. "All right." Brenna smiled and quietly led Cassidy to the bedroom. As she was being guided inside, Cassidy stopped. "I should go sleep with Ryan."

"We can put him to bed." Brenna led Cassidy to the game room, and showed her how the sofa folded out to a single bed. She watched Cassidy change her son's clothes to pajamas, and waited at the door as mother and son said good night. When Cassidy got to her feet and came to the door, she grasped her hand. Cassidy looked to protest.

Brenna kissed her. "We'll be up long before anyone else," she whispered persuasively. Cassidy let herself be led into Brenna's bedroom.

Passion was there, riding a hot crest in Brenna's stomach as Cassidy undressed. However, she only reached for Cassidy to position them both in the middle of the bed, arranging the covers around them. She brushed her lips across Cassidy's nose and closed her eyes. "Go to sleep."

Gradually their bodies curved and settled into one another. Their breathing quieted, evened out, and finally slowed into sleep.

CHAPTER FORTY-THREE

EDGING AWAY from the dark anxiety of her dreams, Cassidy moved closer to Brenna as early morning sent rays of light through the gaps in the curtains. With a deep breath, she inhaled the soft sweet scent of the woman next to her. Her uneasiness faded away, safely closed off to be dealt with another time, and she opened her eyes. A smile curved her lips when another gaze met hers.

She blinked sleepily into blue eyes that were almost indigo in the indistinct light. Lips met hers again, filled with love and comfort. Brenna's fingers splayed over her back, the tips circling along her spine and raising tingles. *All in all, a pleasant way to wake up.* It was then she realized that her borrowed tee shirt had been eased up and Brenna's hands were moving over her skin, not through the shirt.

"Good morning."

Brenna's words were breathed against her ear. Pleasure coursed over Cassidy in sauna-like waves of wet heat. "Good morning," she offered back, concluding on a groan as Brenna's knee grazed against her center with just the right pressure. Brenna rose and loomed over her for a moment, just studying her, and Cassidy rolled onto her back to meet her gaze. She found desire and a soul-deep connection looking back. Fingertips trailed through the long locks of hair at her temple, eyes following with a reverent intensity. The contact filled Cassidy with the contentment of being cherished.

Even when the light touch skimmed over her bruised jaw, there was no pain, only healing. Listening to Brenna's murmurs of disbelief and comfort regarding her parents' treatment, Cassidy felt the rawness of her spirit being mended as if it were being rewoven in a loom. Torn apart by her parents' revulsion and rejection, Cassidy felt Brenna's love and support making her whole again.

Satiny lips soothed over hers, and an invitation was issued by the gentle nipping on her lips. Cassidy met Brenna's eyes and found the dedication, protectiveness, and all those qualities she so loved in their out-of-bed moments that moved her so much. The realization that she was a whole person to this woman who had so completely captured her heart ignited Cassidy. She answered the invitation as it was given ~ with a kiss. She poured her feelings into the connection and was gathered up and held safe in her arms.

Tenderly she held Brenna's face above hers, bringing their mouths together from the faintest to the deepest of kisses. When Brenna's arms shook, unable to hold her weight steady any longer, Cassidy welcomed the soft curves against her own and moved her attention to Brenna's face and throat, bringing their bodies into fuller contact.

They both gasped as hardened, sensitive nipples brushed against the inside of fabric. "Take it off now," Cassidy growled, pulling at Brenna's shirt. When the blue eyes widened at the rough huskiness of her demand, she swallowed down the keenest edge of her passion and added softly, "Please?"

With a grin, Brenna sat up, straddling Cassidy's abdomen as she pulled her shirt off over her head. Before she could lower her arms, Cassidy was on her, kissing hard against her throat and shoulders and across the swell of her breasts where she covered a nipple with her hot, wet mouth.

"Ah," Brenna gasped.

Cassidy felt soothing arms come around her shoulders and massage over them and down her spine. She pressed Brenna down, trapping her between the cool sheets and her own heated body, then tugging Brenna's shorts from her hips. She slid them off her legs and tossed them to the floor. "I'm glad I came home early." Her voice thrummed with a low growl, as she undressed herself. She pulled Brenna sharply against her body, surging skin on skin. She sighed at the feel of the down between Brenna's thighs brushing against her stomach.

Her mouth moved from Brenna's breasts down the firm plane of her abdomen. The muscles quivered. Brenna's hips surged beneath Cassidy, and she spread her hands wide across the peaks and planes of Brenna's chest.

"My parents are nuts if they think I'm ever going to give this up." Cassidy's voice was harsh, firm in its defiance of the parental disapproval that had hit her so hard.

Brenna's heart ached. She understood Cassidy's instinct to distance herself from the hurt, but family was so important. *How could they treat you like a child?* Only wanting to soothe, she drew Cassidy up and swirled her tongue in the woman's mouth as they kissed.

"Don't...don't think about it," Brenna murmured against her lips, then treated Cassidy's face to tender kisses from chin to temple to nose and back again. Her voice hummed against Cassidy's throat at the juncture of her shoulder. "I'm glad you came home early, too. It wasn't right without you and Ryan here."

"I feel the same."

Cassidy's head fell back, and her hands encouraged Brenna down with her. Skimming her touch down Cassidy's sides, Brenna felt the stomach muscles contract pleasurably with each kiss she placed down the woman's chest. When she swirled her tongue in the slight depression of belly button, Cassidy arched her hips. Brenna did not linger there, instead returning to the full-lipped mouth, letting her hands smooth over throbbing muscles. They sat up again, kissing devotedly with patience not present in their first joining.

"I love you." Breathing the words across Brenna's shoulders, Cassidy turned her in her arms until the lean back was pillowed on her chest and rounded hips rested between her thighs. Brenna's heart thrummed a rapid tattoo under her palms. *We are one body,* Cassidy thought wildly, as their heartbeats matched and sped up together. Strong fingers pressed into her thighs as her hand skimmed down Brenna's stomach and soft wiry hairs met her fingertips. "Let me show you how much." As they experienced the first feel of silky wetness, their sighs mingled and combined into one voice.

"Cass."

"Bren."

To still her own voice and listen to her lover, Cassidy closed her mouth over Brenna's shoulder, sucking lightly on the velvet soft skin. With a reverent devotion that she mirrored in her strokes below, she swirled her tongue over salt-sweet skin.

Brenna turned her head and lifted Cassidy's face, inhaling as she climaxed on warm fingers. When Cassidy subsided and rested her hand on the inside of the damp thigh, Brenna turned around and held Cassidy close for a lingering kiss. Embraced in a tight hug, Cassidy felt Brenna's hands splayed on her lower back. Cassidy's quivering rocked through both of them.

Brenna rolled them over until she lay on her back on the sheets. Cassidy gazed down as the fine-boned hands guided her hips until their mounds were pressed tightly together. The sensation of hairs tangling made Brenna's back arch in an aching sensuality. She kept her eyes locked on Cassidy's to witness every emotion playing across her features.

All Brenna's love seemed poured into their connection; tears pooled in her eyes. "So beautiful," Brenna said.

Her voice filled Cassidy with so much emotion, much as Brenna's fingers filled and satisfied her ache and longing inside. At the feather-light touches, like capturing a live wire, an almost electrical feeling passed between them. Cassidy arched as Brenna's fingertips pressed between their bodies. Her climax engulfed them both in its flashpoint heat. Tearfully biting her lip to keep little more than a whimper from escaping, Cassidy bonelessly collapsed. Brenna welcomed her into a sheltering embrace. Soft fingertips brushed over Cassidy's cheeks, drying her tears.

As Cassidy's heartbeat slowed, her lips moved reverently over the breast pillowed under her cheek. She heard Brenna's heartbeat slow, too. *That was...so different*, she thought dazedly.

Arms tightened around her shoulders when she would have moved off. "No. Don't go," Brenna murmured, a noticeable hesitance in her voice. "Stay."

Cassidy's whispered reply came against Brenna's lips. "I'm not going anywhere." She moved only enough to settle her weight mostly on the bed and intertwine their legs, then her head fell back to the curve of Brenna's shoulder.

The auburn-haired woman looked down into Cassidy's face as she looked up. They both spoke softly at the same moment, the same words. Their hands intertwined, and they kissed their joined fists at the same instant. "Thank you."

Bemused, they moved their hands aside and drank wonderingly of the sight of one another, combing fingers through locks of soft hair ~ dark and light. With light touches they explored damp bodies, not out of arousal, but for contact.

"I need you so much," Cassidy whispered. "You make me whole." She soothed her palm over Brenna's breast, cherishing the heart beating so strongly within. "You were wonderful," Cassidy commented softly. "So different." She nuzzled Brenna's throat and reveled in the strong arms moving over her back in a secure hug. Sure hands moved to her nape and coaxed her head back up for a leisurely kiss which went on for several minutes.

When Brenna bent her knees, Cassidy rested naturally in the cradle formed by her hips. They floated in the daydreaming world of mutual heat and, for the moment, completion. Her eyes were almost closed, her body lulled, when Brenna's voice wrapped around her, strong and soft.

"With everything I am, I love you," she said.

To Cassidy, the inflection was clear in a way she had not heard before...from anyone. *You.* The totality of who she was. *Friend. Lover. Daughter. Mother.* Here, in this woman's arms, she felt, for the first time wholly Woman as well. *Nothing ever will or could be wrong with that.*

"Hey, are you awake?"

James vaguely registered the whispered question before rough hands were shaking his shoulder. "Go away," he grumbled.

"Come on. I need to talk." More insistent shaking followed.

"Is the house on fire?" James pushed the hands off his arm, then pulled the covers around his head. "No? Then leave me alone."

"You can't leave me to face them alone" came back a pleading whisper.

He furrowed his brow. "What the hell are you talking about?"

"Mom and Cassidy."

Rolling onto his back, tucking the covers under his arms, James stared up into the shadows. His brother loomed over his bed, hands on his hips, fully expecting him to get up and participate in this conversation. "What about them?"

"Do you think they're out there?"

James glanced at his bedside table and the LCD clock. "At five o'clock in the morning? Not unless there's some emergency...like this is *not*," he grumbled, turning away and pulling his pillow over his head. His muffled voice issued up from beneath the pillow. "Besides, it's a holiday. You know how much Mom likes to sleep in when she gets the chance."

"Yeah, but what about Cassidy?"

"She doesn't strike me as a morning person. She's probably still asleep, too."

There was a long moment of silence and James hoped that Thomas had left, though he hadn't heard the door closing. His brother's voice broke the silence.

"Do you suppose they're sleeping together?"

Damn. From beneath the pillow, James bit out, "I. Don't. Care."

Thomas' voice became agitated. "Why are you taking this so calmly?"

James rolled toward his brother again and answered sarcastically, "Maybe because it's five o'clock in the morning?" He sighed. "Just go back to bed."

"I can't. I had to go to the bathroom, and then I..."

Groaning, James pulled the covers over his head, blocking out the rest of whatever his brother was saying. *What is it lately with people sharing much more than I really need to know about their personal lives? First Mom, now this.* Firmly, to be heard over his brother's rambling, he bit out, "Shut. The Fuck. Up."

His brother did fall silent, but instead of leaving, he dropped to the end of James' bed. The mattress jostled. James groaned. Thomas moaned, "I don't know if I can go out there."

"I'm not sharing the bed," he said dryly.

"You saw how they were last night."

True, James acknowledged silently, then muttered, "Mom is more sensible than that." When Thomas asked him to repeat it, he did, adding a few choice words for effect. "They are not *fucking* on the *damn* couch."

"But..." Thomas paused; James could imagine him shaking his head.

"What if I-"

"Go and look?" James threw off the pillow and rolled to his feet enthusiastically. "*Great* idea. You go look and report back. Later. *Much* later. Like after noon, okay?" He pushed his brother toward the door. Thomas pushed back.

"This only gets more complicated if you make it that way. Frankly, I'd rather you not upset the balance by getting into a pissing match with our mother." He opened the door and pushed Thomas out. "Go. Do whatever. Just leave me alone." He firmly closed the door in Thomas' face

Turning around, Thomas realized he was stranded in the hallway, in nothing but shorts. *What do I do now?*

Too keyed up to go back to sleep and uncomfortable about possibly encountering their houseguest, who would undoubtedly be tousled and painfully beautiful fresh from sleep, Thomas retreated to the only safe haven he could think of ~ the game room. Too late he recalled that was where Ryan had been put to sleep. The five-year-old stirred even as Thomas was closing the door as quietly as possible.

James returned to his bed and flopped down, pillowing his head on his hands as he tried to empty his mind and return to sleep. Thomas' visit bothered him. Even though James had ribbed Thomas about it, apparently his brother really had fallen for the blond actress who, it now appeared, had been gradually becoming involved with their mother.

While James did wonder how his mom had come to the conclusion that she returned those feelings, the explanation made sense of many things he had been observing over the last several months. That was really the only thing he required, since emotionally he had no attachment one way or the other to anyone other than his mother in this little drama. Considering his mother in a lesbian relationship was only slightly more unsettling than considering her as any kind of sexual being at all. Definitely it all fell into the category of "too much information," and he preferred to ignore it, so long as the situation was ignorable.

Thomas however was reacting out of his emotions concerning Ms. Hyland, which meant he was jealous of their mother. When the relationship had been revealed, Thomas had even asked, "Why you?" making their mother defensive with her "What's wrong with me?" James recalled the camping trip and what he'd heard about the challenge climb between Thomas and their mother. Now he realized it had been a competition for love, like Romeo and Tybalt in *Romeo and Juliet*, which they'd been reading in English class.

James sighed. As a matter of fact, Marcie had dropped him because he wouldn't become jealous over her. She had told him that another guy had asked her out. James had shrugged and said if she wanted to go, she should.

He had thought that giving her the space to do as she needed was most important. That's what his mother had said she had most wanted from Mr. Shea.

Marcie had wanted him to react more possessively. He didn't see the intelligence in fighting a football player who could easily pound him into the turf. So, Marcie told him they didn't need to see each other at all. *Why wasn't she pleased that I left the choice up to her? Isn't that what they all want ~ no man making all their choices for them?* He frowned and closed his eyes, admitting it was all too confusing to be unraveled at five-thirty in the morning.

"I should go."

The whisper in the dark lured Brenna from her half-dream state. She was feeling content with her choices, wrapped up pleasantly in the circle of Cassidy's arms as they languidly stroked each other's skin. "You don't have to," she murmured back, lifting her chin. Unerringly, Cassidy found her lips with the kiss she had sensed coming. She purred into the contact and turned until their breasts touched when the kiss became deeply arousing.

Cassidy's chuckle tickled her lips, voiceless as it was. "I think I had better not be coming out of their mother's bedroom when I first see your sons today. I didn't really think how it would complicate things for you when I came straight here from the airport instead of going home." She indulged them both by stroking down Brenna's hip and then over her buttocks, tugging until they were perfectly fitted together, breasts to breasts, stomach to stomach, and hips to hips. A knee nudged between Brenna's thighs and the slight pressure against her center made her want their interlude to continue.

"It had to happen eventually," Brenna pointed out. "I needed to tell them." She reminded Cassidy of her words the night before. "We told them. Together. That was right to do."

"Ryan had already guessed." Cassidy sounded pleased.

"I'm not surprised. He's seen us together a little more often than Thomas or James." Brenna sighed. "And clearly Thomas still thinks he's in love with you."

"There is at least one thing we can do," Cassidy said solemnly, withdrawing from Brenna slowly. "Give him time. I really should go to the guest room." She sat up and slipped her legs off the bed.

Brenna studied the long lean line of the other woman's back and moved a hand over the muscled surface. She nodded. Cassidy was right. Their children's acceptance was important. Brenna's sons would need time to adjust, and, because they both cared deeply about those affected by their decisions as well as each other, they would have to take things slowly in making a family together.

"It wouldn't hurt to shower first," she said, moving across the mattress to press herself indulgently against Cassidy's back and place a kiss behind her ear. At the touch the woman's back arched in a sensual shudder. Brenna reached around and filled her palms with the soft fullness of warm breasts. She squeezed lightly. "What would you say to that?" she whispered hotly.

"I...could do that." Cassidy's voice was halting, the woman clearly and quickly affected by the sexual play. She turned her head slightly and inhaled Brenna's breath before sealing their lips together in a hard kiss. "You so don't play fair," she said breathlessly when she tore herself away. "Come on, before we lose any more time."

Brenna's small smile turned into a confident grin as Cassidy pulled her to her feet. Already nude, they stepped into the master bathroom together. After letting the water warm, Brenna switched the flow over to the shower head, then drew the sprayer off its mount, and they soaped and washed one another.

Cassidy knelt in the tub and soaped down Brenna's thighs, then rinsed them by directing the sprayer. Brenna shuddered when the spray hit her center. She reached out to steady herself on Cassidy's shoulder. The blonde set down the shower head, leaving its water spraying up slightly around their ankles, then she leaned forward.

Brenna thought Cassidy was going to wrap herself around her waist, but then full lips trailed quickly over her stomach and– She gasped when the grip firmed on her butt, and Cassidy nuzzled through the hair covering her mound. "You shouldn't...Oh...God..." she groaned. She threw her head back as Cassidy used her mouth to pleasure her. *Kevin never did this at all,* she thought wildly, *and Tom was never this good at it.*

She felt every little movement of Cassidy's tongue and lips, as if the area were sensitized tenfold; the sensations consumed her. Her fingers moved through Cassidy's wet hair, which grounded her and steadied her nerves. She was panting and groaning with the pleasure rapidly spiraling out of control. She shifted her feet to remain upright. Her hands found the towel rack over her head. Cassidy's hands moved to steady her as well, spreading wide to support her back. As the waves overtook her, her essence pulsed into Cassidy's avid mouth and her entire chest vibrated with a cry of ecstasy.

Almost instantly, Cassidy's mouth retreated. She rose to muffle Brenna's cry of frustration with a kiss, but her fingers deliciously drove Brenna through the orgasm until she was panting and spent. "Shh," Cassidy murmured quickly. "You don't want to wake the boys."

The hell with that, Brenna thought rebelliously when Cassidy's touch continued to ignite small fires throughout her body. When the sensations ebbed and she was wrapped up in Cassidy's strong grasp, Brenna sighed. Cassidy was right, though. Had she done as she wanted, the screams would have awakened their sons. The kisses that followed, where she tasted herself on Cassidy's lips, made the aftermath so much sweeter than she could have imagined.

Cassidy watched Brenna dress. From her own bags, she had retrieved a long-sleeve cashmere sweater top, and jeans. Brenna was pulling a sweatshirt on over her bare breasts. The logo swept Cassidy back through wonderful memories. She reached out to caress the lettering. Brenna looked up at her curiously.

"I remember the first time I saw you in this," Cassidy said with touch of melancholy. "I knew I was seeing the real you."

"I don't understand." Brenna hugged her quickly. "Is something wrong?"

"Remember Ryan's birthday party?" Cassidy began. Brenna nodded against her shoulder. "You came in this sweatshirt, a pair of blue jeans, and with your hair in a ponytail. You took my breath away."

"I don't understand why that should upset you."

"I love sweatshirts," Cassidy answered. "I even have a ritual at home where I slip into one of my old high school jerseys the minute I get into my bedroom. It's my way of saying 'I'm home'." She gasped in sudden distress and tried to pull away, but Brenna held her firmly. "I guess that won't be happening anymore."

In Brenna's embrace, Cassidy safely cried until the tears stopped. Brenna pulled the sweatshirt off and held it out, her meaning clear. Cassidy leaned back, stripped off her sweater top, and pulled on the sweatshirt. Brenna helped her smooth it over her chest. As their gazes held, Brenna said, "Welcome home."

It was aftΩr six-thirty when the women finally peeked out of the bedroom doorway, looking up and down the hall before stepping out together and walking to the kitchen. Cassidy leaned on the counter and watch Brenna grind the coffee and prep the coffeemaker. "Anything I can do?"

"If you want some juice, the glasses are in the cabinet to the left of the sink," Brenna said.

"Would you like some?"

The "yes" that replied wasn't Brenna's voice.

Together they turned and saw Ryan standing in the entry to the kitchen, looking up expectantly at them. A welcoming smile curled Brenna's lips as she took in the sight ~ still in his pajamas, looking only mildly sleepy. "Good morning, Ryan."

"Hi," he said to her, then turned to his mother. "Good morning, Mommy."

"Good morning." Cassidy scooped him up in a tight hug before releasing him. "You're thirsty, hmm?"

"Yes."

"One orange juice coming up." Brenna collected the small glass, poured the juice, then passed it to him. "Got it?" She watched him carefully put his hands around the base of the glass before she released it.

He nodded. "Thank you."

"You're welcome." She brushed her fingers lightly over his hair. "Why don't you go sit at the dining room table?"

Brenna leaned next to Cassidy, who gazed across the counter into the dining area, following Ryan's progress. She put a light hand on Cassidy's back and held the blonde briefly against her shoulder before stepping away and pouring them each a glass of juice.

Thomas stood just out of sight in the bedroom hallway, listening to the exchange between Ryan and his mother. He ached at the affection in her voice. *God, she's really happy.* Nudging around the end of the wall, he remained silent, the position allowing him a chance to watch them without them seeing him.

It wasn't anything overt, but he saw Cassidy's face as she handed his mother a glass of juice. Clearly, Cassidy was in love with his mother. He thought back to the times the three of them had shared together. He winced, realizing that the laughter and the looks they'd exchanged had been more than camaraderie. He had not seen it before because he had not wanted to see it. Feeling foolish and hurting, he wondered if he could fall out of love as quickly as he seemed to have fallen into it.

He stepped forward, and the noise of his entrance drew their eyes to him. Thomas squared his shoulders and affixed a careful smile. "Good morning."

"Good morning." Cassidy answered first; she was sitting at the table next to her son.

His mother's greeting preceded a pat on his arm. "Have a seat. Here." She set her glass of juice in front of him and returned to the kitchen to pour herself another.

"So, what's on the agenda today?" he called to her.

"I'm going to drop you and James at the mall to spend your Christmas money. I'll be taking Cassidy and Ryan home."

CHAPTER FORTY-FOUR

THE MALL was already busy when Brenna pulled to a stop in front of an entrance. She had decided against parking at all. News vans were everywhere, covering the post-Christmas shopping crowds.

"Can I come?"

Cassidy turned around and put a restraining hand on Ryan's thigh to discourage him from following the older boys, who were getting out of the backseat. "Don't you want to go home?"

"I want to play video games with Thomas."

Cassidy looked wryly at Thomas, then Brenna, who shrugged and left the decision to her. It was Thomas' expression that decided her. Standing on the curb, he had his jaw set carefully, and though he looked at her son, he wouldn't look at her. "You two go on and have a good time. Ryan and I really need to get home."

"Mom?" Thomas drew his mother's attention.

She fished in her purse and handed a twenty dollar bill to each of them. "Don't spend it all at the arcade. Eat some lunch, too. I'll be back at five to pick you up right here."

"Okay, Mom." James looked at his mother, then briefly to Cassidy. "See you."

"Bye," Cassidy responded with a faint nod. From her place in the front passenger seat, she kept her hand on Ryan until both rear doors were closed. He squirmed and pouted but remained quiet. Brenna did not drive off immediately. Her gaze followed her sons until they were inside. Cassidy watched her face. When the blue eyes darkened, indicating she was getting upset, Cassidy asked, "Are you all right?"

The upset vanished quickly, and a smile turned to her. "Yeah." Patting her knee lightly, Brenna went on, "Yes, I'm fine. Ready to go?"

As Brenna drove north to Cassidy's side of town, Cassidy said, "You can park at my house. The Talbots are only on the corner." Directing Brenna to make a left, she added, "Gwen's been feeding and walking Ranger while we were gone. Right, Ryan?"

"Can I walk him when we get home?"

Cassidy shook her head. Disconcerted, Brenna said, "I didn't see a dog at the party."

"We left him at the Talbots' that day so he wouldn't misbehave with all of the excitement. Ranger's a Dalmatian. I got him when Ryan was three."

"Dalmatian's a big dog, right?"

Cassidy chuckled. "Brenna, are you afraid of dogs?" The other woman did not answer. "Ranger's a softie," she assured. "That's why I chose the breed ~ because they are obedient but active enough to keep up with children."

"I didn't know that." Brenna pulled into Cassidy's driveway. "Well, we're here."

"Home!" Ryan unbelted himself and was in the yard in a couple of bounces.

"Keeps up with kids, huh?" Brenna laughed. Cassidy chuckled, coming around. "You know, I think I remember meeting Gwen at the birthday party. I remember thinking you were...rather intimate," she added the last under her breath as Cassidy led her across the street.

"She's just a friend," Cassidy said, sealing the assurance with a kiss just before she rang the doorbell.

Brenna felt the appraisal begin as soon as introductions were made. Since Cassidy did not make mention of their changed relationship, she suspected that somehow Gwen had already learned about it. It was the oddest sensation to be aware that another person was skirting a subject that she wanted, just as desperately, to broach.

She looked around the modest home as Cassidy shared the first part of her trip to Missouri. Those events ~ getting to spend time with her uncles, aunts, cousins, and their children ~ brought a fond smile to her face, Brenna noticed, particularly when she mentioned Travis and Brenda. Each time a story veered close to referring to her parents, though, Cassidy shifted the subject to another relative or one of Ryan's snowy adventures.

Brenna hurt for her. She also acknowledged to herself that rejection by her family was a very real fear of her own. If Cassidy's family had responded so violently, what could she expect, with her family being almost another full generation older?

She suspected how her mother might react, but she and her siblings had never had cause to discuss such an issue, so she had no basis on which to figure out what their response might be. Despite his political stances, when it came down to her personally, even Kevin's biases had come out, with him believing she was "not like that" and "not one of those people."

Preoccupied by her jumbled thoughts, Brenna started nibbling her bottom lip. She did feel different. She was sure it wasn't because her lover was a woman, though, but rather because she was finally, really, truly in love. The discovery made her feel calmer about everything.

"Bren?"

Cassidy's voice drew her from her thoughts. "I'm sorry. What were you saying?"

Cassidy turned to Gwen. "I think I'll get the house key now, then Bren can go home."

"No, I...It's all right. I've just been thinking."

"About your work? I catch the show frequently," Gwen offered. "You're quite good."

"That wasn't actually what I was thinking about, but thank you." Brenna stood as the other two did. Gwen excused herself.

"Brenna, are you all right?"

"Just learning to live with secrets," she whispered. She fell silent as Gwen returned and passed the key to Cassidy.

"Well, it was nice to meet you," Gwen said.

"You, too. Thank you."

"Ryan!" Cassidy called.

He came running out with a boy Brenna now remembered from the birthday party as well.

"Say goodbye to Chance," Cassidy said. "Time to go."

"Mommy!"

"Sorry, but it's time."

Ryan turned his blue eyes on Brenna. "Ms. Lanigan, tell her I want to stay."

Brenna knew her eyes sparkled with amusement, but she kept her voice serious. "Honey, if your mother says it's time to go, then I suggest we listen to her."

"Yes, ma'am." He hung his head, dropped the toys in his hands on the floor, and, shoulders slumped, exited the Talbots' home.

"Good budding actor you've got there, Cass," she said with a chuckle. "I don't think I've ever seen a pout quite that perfect."

Cassidy sighed. "Come on. Let's go." She turned to Gwen. "Thanks for looking after things."

"Anytime." Gwen looked Brenna over once more as she showed the women to the door.

Brenna paused on the stoop after the door was closed. Cassidy had already started down the walk. She turned back, her expression curious. Nervously Brenna asked, "She's your friend. So, what's the verdict?" Cassidy smiled, and it untied the knot in Brenna's stomach.

"She likes you."

They walked across the street and up to Cassidy's home. "She knows, though ~ about us, I mean ~ doesn't she?" Cassidy nodded. "She's burning with questions. It was unnerving."

Cassidy keyed the knob, then the bolt, and stepped back, letting Brenna enter first. "When I was pretty confused, she was good to talk to."

"You were confused?" Brenna tugged off her light jacket, and Cassidy hung it in her closet.

"Very."

Ryan ran past them. She watched him enter what she presumed was his bedroom. The toys he poured onto the bedspread with a clatter confirmed it. She turned back to find Cassidy in her bedroom across the hall opening the luggage and sorting clothes into drawers, her closet, and a wicker basket by the bathroom door.

"Are you going right back to the mall?" Cassidy asked.

"No. James and Thomas would really hate if I joined them so soon. I should give them some normal space and not go back until the time I said I'd pick them up."

"How about some Irish coffee?"

"I'll make it," Brenna volunteered.

"Supplies are in the kitchen. Help yourself. I'll be out in just another minute."

Ryan joined Brenna in the kitchen when he heard her clattering around. "What'cha doin'?"

"Making something for your mom to drink."

"You're being very nice to Mommy. No wonder she likes you."

"She said that?"

"Yes. I knew already, though."

Cassidy had mentioned Ryan had already guessed about them. Brenna crouched down to talk to him. "What do you think you know?"

"I know you kissed. I saw that."

"When?"

"When you took us camping. In the tent."

"I thought you were asleep."

"I wasn't."

"Are you okay with your mom and me kissing?"

"I like when Mommy's happy."

"That's all?"

"Yes."

"I like when your mommy's happy, too." Brenna could not stifle her amusement. She looked Ryan squarely in the eye. "Your mother raised a very smart boy."

"Me?"

"Yes." She hugged him. "I love you."

"As much as you love Mommy?"

"Just as much." He smiled broadly at that. She stood and ruffled his hair. "Would you like a snack?" He grinned, and she saw his mother's features so clearly, she felt her heart beat faster. "Let's see what we can find, hmm?"

"Okay."

Together they raided the refrigerator, locating a pair of apples. While she ate hers whole, she cut the second into wedges for him. They sat together at the kitchen table. When she'd finished and was rising, Cassidy appeared from her room. "All unpacked?"

"I ran across this," Cassidy said, holding out the unwrapped box. "Sorry, it's a little worse for travel."

Brenna took the box, lifting off the top and withdrawing the scarf.

"There was a note with it, but I think it got lost in the..."

"Confusion?" Brenna supplied an innocuous descriptor.

"Yes."

"It's a beautiful gift."

"I was hoping you'd like it enough to wear it...around."

Brenna looped it around her throat, tucking it into the neckline of her blouse. The blouse's color was not really suited to the silky red, but the effect caused an immediate and broad, lust-filled smile from Cassidy. "Done."

Cassidy reached out to caress the silk, lightly brushing the skin beneath. "You're beautiful."

"Want an apple, Mommy?" Ryan held up his last apple wedge.

Smiling at Brenna, Cassidy dropped her hand from the silk and took the apple piece from her son. "Thank you."

"Ryan says he's happy we're together."

"One down, two to go?"

Brenna nodded. Despite the anxiety clouding her eyes, she bestowed a loving smile on Ryan and brushed her fingers through his hair. She turned to Cassidy abruptly. "I was just about to finish the coffee. Still want a cup?"

"I'll get the whiskey." She moved toward the cabinet over the stove. "The whipped cream is in the refrigerator."

With Ryan in his mother's lap, Cassidy and Brenna sat on the couch, sipping their coffees. Brenna had cut more apples, which the trio nibbled as the women talked.

"Have you heard anything more from the British production?"

"I have to contact them after the first." Brenna sounded pensive. "What with everything, I haven't finished reading the script." She thought for a moment. "What are you planning to do after *Time Trails?*"

As much as she wanted to talk about all of them making plans together, Cassidy carefully kept her news neutral. "A few series pilots have been dropped off, but I'm not interested in a starring role. I'd like another ensemble. The hours can be much better for Ryan and me."

Brenna nodded, then finished her coffee with one final swallow, and patted Cassidy's thigh. "Well, I should probably be going."

Cassidy heard the strain. "Brenna, do you want to talk about doing something together?" From the averted eyes, she had her answer. "Ryan, look over there, okay?" She pointed to the porch. Preceded by such an absurd request ~ what five-year-old would look away when told? ~ Cassidy leaned forward and kissed Brenna quickly on the lips, stunning her. She felt the other woman's tension gradually melt away under her nibbling kisses and finally leaned back.

Brenna blinked, clearly gathering her so-pleasantly-scattered wits back together. "What was that for?"

"To relax you. You don't have to be nervous. I would love to do something with you."

"That probably won't happen."

"Neither of us thought this would happen, either. Obviously anything is possible," Cassidy said earnestly. A buoyant energy streamed through her as Brenna accepted her optimism with a careful nod. To be able to provide someone else support made her feel good. It was not something she was used to. Setting Ryan on the floor, Cassidy stood up. "We've never just hung out. How about we go back to the mall together?"

"Do we dare?"

"I'm not going to ravish you over the perfume counter," Cassidy assured her. "I don't want to hide away, either. Besides, we'll have Ryan with us."

Brenna took her hand. After spending a moment clearing their few dishes into the dishwasher, Brenna drove the three of them back to the mall.

\#

Brenna felt as if she hadn't smiled and laughed so much in years. She, Cassidy, and Ryan started at the end of the mall furthest from the food court, looking through the racks in a designer store. She purchased a blouse that would go perfectly with Cassidy's scarf. When she stepped out of the small dressing room wearing the combination, having kept the scarf in her handbag, Cassidy's expression, so full of fiery passion, almost buckled her knees. The touch of their hands was electric.

Standing at the counter waiting for the purchase to ring up, they chatted about nothing in particular and everything ~ clothing, fabrics, decorating, early apartments, Cassidy's college dormitory, getting too drunk on a date, not getting drunk enough ~ all the time wishing that half the people they had known over the years had been half as easy to talk to.

At the perfume counter, Brenna discovered her favorite scent on Cassidy was Emporio White Elle by Armani. The floral woodsy scent transported her immediately back to November. When she leaned close, inhaled deeply, and whispered the direction of her thoughts, Cassidy's laughter sent sensual shivers through her. Cassidy acquired the scent in a body lotion, promising under her breath to let Brenna apply it any time she desired.

To reward Ryan for his patience while the two women tried on clothes, they next stopped in a toy store. The five-year-old headed immediately for the baseball equipment. Though Cassidy protested weakly, they eventually split the cost of a regulation-size baseball, junior wood bat, and glove, not forgetting the oil, as Brenna told him that Thomas always worked his gloves for weeks before ever using them.

They talked about the Little League team Thomas helped coach. Brenna found her phone book, and Cassidy programmed the head coach's number into her cell phone.

They talked a bit at that point about the spring and working out the situation with their sons.

"I found Thomas an internship with U.S. Forestry," Brenna revealed. "It was your suggestion actually that led me to go and talk to his counselor."

"Camp counseling?" Cassidy asked.

"No. The group, as I understand it, will survey many of the jobs available through the National and State Park systems."

Cassidy smiled. "He'll love it."

"He did seem pretty excited. The news even trumped his uncle's tickets. My brother Gary always sends him spring training tickets and comes to town to accompany him," she explained.

Ryan pulled at his mother's hand excitedly. "Thomas!"

The women looked up to see they had reached the arcade. Inside, Thomas stood at one of the games, wrestling with a joystick, several shopping bags piled at his feet.

Thomas turned at hearing his name called. As she let Ryan run to Thomas, Cassidy asked Brenna quietly, "Ready?"

Ryan "helped" Thomas with his purchases, opening each bag as he asked, "What'd'you get?"

Without answering, Thomas picked up the bags. He didn't seem angry at Ryan or at either of them as they walked up.

"We're early," Brenna said. "Sorry."

"I was done."

"Is James in here?" Brenna looked around.

"No. I did run into him coming out of Blick's with an armful of sponges and grease pencils."

Cassidy was surprised. "James dabbles in art?"

"Draws mostly, but there's a new art teacher who has been encouraging him to work in other mediums," Thomas answered. "For Christmas he gave Mom this fantastic portrait he did of her."

Brenna blushed, and Cassidy decided she would have to see this portrait. "Where are you going to hang it?"

"I have to completely rethink the living room wall," Brenna answered. "Thomas gave me a photograph he took on the mountain."

The foursome turned out of the arcade and started for the food court tables when Cassidy spotted James coming out of an odds'n'ends shop, just putting away a receipt in the bag in his hand and readjusting the bags under his arms. He looked up just as they reached the tables. "Oh, hey."

"Fruitful day," Brenna remarked.

"Yep."

They all put their bags down. Brenna conferred with Cassidy while Thomas and James went off to choose their food. Cassidy stayed at the tables, pulling two together to give them enough space, and watched Ryan while Brenna picked up two salads at Salad Express and a burger meal at Hokey Joe's for Ryan. Thomas and James returned with barbecued beef stacks, fries, and super-sized sodas.

Ryan informed everyone about his acquisitions, explaining that he would be the "best player on Thomas' team." He tried to pull out his bat to show it around. When his mother intercepted it, he showed the vial of oil and the new glove instead. Thomas took it from him and showed him how to work the oil into the leather. Before long, he was finally smiling easily and laughing as Ryan irrepressibly rattled off the statistics he believed he could rack up when he began to play.

Brenna quickly took a forkful of salad, but Cassidy did not miss the gleam of tears gathering in her eyes, or the way the tension finally left her shoulders. Under the table, Cassidy nudged Brenna's knee as they sat side by side, giving her a smile when she looked up. The corners of Brenna's lips turned up, and her eyes dipped in acknowledgment.

EPILOGUE

NUDGING OPEN the door with her hip, Brenna balanced the champagne flutes and wine bottle in her hands. Stepping into her back yard, she turned at the first crack of fireworks and spied Cassidy with her head tilted back, eyes skyward. The bright sparks of blue and red faded from their blossoming formation. Cassidy turned at the sound of the screen door slamming into its frame.

"Thought we might celebrate the start of the year properly," Brenna said with a shrug, nodding at the glasses and wine.

Cassidy met her halfway along the garden walk and took the glasses. "All that will take is the traditional New Year's kiss. First one of the year always brings good luck to the relationship." Cassidy chuckled, kissing Brenna's ear, making the other woman shiver in reaction and fumble as she started to work on opening the bottle.

Finally wresting the foil and wire mesh from the bottle's neck, Brenna paused at another explosive crack. The two of them watched a pair of green fireworks blossom overhead. The light display altered the shadows over Cassidy's face. Brenna was entranced by the delicate bone structure and the look of peaceful repose.

"Thank you for inviting me," Cassidy said, her gaze on the fireworks.

"I'm glad Thomas thought to take Ryan to the park to see the display from there so we could have some time together."

"He's...adjusting well," Cassidy remarked, turning to look at Brenna. "He bolted with Ryan after twenty minutes instead of five." She turned back to the fireworks. "Where's James?"

"He went to the park earlier. I think he's trying to get back together with his girlfriend."

"Did he know Ryan and I were coming?"

"I didn't hide it from them."

"You would tell me if there were problems, right?"

Brenna sighed. "The shock has worn off. I was working with my lawyer on the divorce papers. James didn't like it. He said I was being selfish. I told him it would be more selfish to stay with Kevin just for appearances." Brenna sighed. "Until I said it, I didn't realize that's what I'd been doing all along, letting appearances govern my actions. My reaction to you, in the beginning, was like that. You appeared to be everything I should fear, and yet, even in the beginning I couldn't stop focusing on you. I hated it, and that made me lash out."

"I've lived for appearances, too," Cassidy replied. "I had to be the perfect actor, fit in here without raising any questions." She took the bottle from Brenna's hands, trading her the champagne flutes. Pressing the sides of the plastic cork with her thumbs, she turned away and worked it out of the neck. A little bubbly spilled as the cork popped free. Tucking it in the pocket of her pants, she filled both glasses as Brenna held them up.

Cassidy lifted her glass. "To two thousand one, a new century."

"That was last year," Brenna pointed out.

"Last year was the end of the twentieth. Nothing against it, but it was a tough one. I'd rather the century start with a good year."

"To a good year." Brenna tapped her glass against Cassidy's.

Cassidy watched Brenna sip from her flute, the muscles in her throat moving gently, tantalizingly. As Brenna's glass lowered from her lips, Cassidy could no longer resist. She leaned in, caressed Brenna's cheek, and claimed her lips, tasting the light flavor of the champagne lacing over Brenna's own unique taste. The moan that met her kisses thrilled Cassidy endlessly. "I love you," she murmured, trailing away from Brenna's lips to nip and suck at the skin where her jaw met her throat.

Brenna's husky voice made Cassidy's heart skip. "Oh, God. I love you too." There was a soft thump as the champagne glass slid from Brenna's fingers and hit the grass. *No shattering*, Cassidy thought, pleased, as she let her own glass slip free so that she could wrap both her arms around Brenna. Brenna's arms encircled her neck, and she lifted the small woman up. Their eyes met, both reflecting their rising passion.

Cassidy's fingers skimmed a warm and now familiar path to arousal over Brenna's shoulders and down her stomach. Moving her fingers beneath the hem of the low-cut black cocktail dress, she recalled her first sight of it ~ as she was let in the front door. Brenna's figure was shown off to full effect, even more than it had been the night of the Pinnacle party.

She had wanted to say it then but had been too tongue-tied. "I want you." She said it now, pulling the smaller woman closer still, supporting her fully as she felt Brenna's knees give way. She slowly sank to the ground with Brenna, the grass soft and cool against their flushed skin. Her fingers found the clasp of Brenna's garter. She gasped at the bolt of lust that shot through her own groin.

Brenna dislodged pins from Cassidy's hair. "Now, let's see about starting the New Year off right with a really big bang."

The fireworks in the sky faded into the background as they melded in their own explosions together under the stars.

TURN FOR HOME

With grateful support from family and the community, she presents this story to her longtime readers and invites new readers to slip into the world of Brenna and Cassidy.

Prologue

Brenna Lanigan pulled up to the curb just outside the entrance to Pacific Heights High School. It being just after seven in the morning, she was not the only parent delivering her sons to the new semester.

"What time tonight?" she asked as she stretched her right arm over the space between the front two seats and looked squarely at Thomas, next to her in the front passenger seat. At age seventeen, he was beginning to chisel and thicken in the chest. James, a little rounder and softer at fifteen, was pulling his book bag together in the back seat. Both were turning away from her already, their doors open.

She grabbed Thomas' shoulder before he could get out of range. He didn't look back as he answered, "No need. I've got orientation with FIRE. I'll catch the city bus when it's over."

She released his shoulder. "James?" she directed to where he stood outside the vehicle.

"I've got stuff planned with friends," he answered.

"Will I see either of you for dinner?" she asked. Thomas paused, but without turning back to look at her, he shook his head. She glanced at James and saw that he was looking at her, though she couldn't interpret his dour expression.

"I'm making Chicago deep dish," she offered. "All the toppings you like."

James shrugged. "Sorry, Mom. I won't be in 'til curfew."

"Thomas?"

"That's a big meal. We having company?" Thomas hazarded a glance toward her. His eyebrows drew together briefly, betraying his anxiety, before he assumed a bland expression.

Brenna had been thinking of inviting her new lover, Cassidy Hyland, and her son Ryan. She missed the blond woman terribly. The last time they had all been together, Cassidy had come over for New Year's Eve. Thomas and James had gone off to the Palisades neighborhood park, reluctantly taking Ryan with them. At the time, it had been wonderful, giving Cassidy and Brenna time alone together. But any ground she thought had been gained in her sons' adjustment to her new relationship was short lived. Up before dawn most days, both boys then stayed gone all day for the remainder of their holiday.

Any time Cassidy's name came up, Thomas and James acted as if they didn't hear a word Brenna said, and the last time she'd tried to talk to them about it, she'd ending up getting upset. The school driveway was no place for a scene, so Brenna reluctantly said, "It'll be just the three of us."

After a moment Thomas said, "I should be home by six."

"Thank you. James?"

Something near the building caught his eye, and his response was hurried. "I'll reheat. Catch you later."

He slammed the back door and she watched as he ran to catch up with someone. She decided his objective was a girl, despite the black leather jacket that hid most of her upper body. The jeans were just a little too snug on shapely legs to belong to a young adult male.

She turned to see Thomas walking away more sedately, but no less intent on some point in the flow of students entering the front entrance of the school building.

A horn honked behind her and Brenna reluctantly turned her attention to guiding the SUV away from the curb and into the flow of traffic exiting the school grounds. Safely in the flow of vehicles on her way back to her Pacific Palisades neighborhood, she turned her thoughts to the continuing problem of what to do with her sons' clearly expressed discontent with her new relationship.

Stopping at the grocer's for a short list of items, she wandered aimlessly, the dawdling giving her time to think. It had been a week since New Year's. It would be another week before she returned to work on the Pinnacle Pictures lot where she portrayed Commander Susan Jakes on the science fiction series Time Trails. She had already cleaned her home top to bottom—refreshing drawer liners and shelf paper, cleaning out the refrigerator, and running the self-cleaning cycle on the oven which had been used heavily during the holiday season just past.

Unless she went against their not so subtly expressed wishes, this cold shoulder from Thomas and James would mean another week without seeing Cassidy.

Brenna hadn't given a second thought to going weeks without seeing either her first husband, Tom, or her second, Kevin. She had attributed that to their mutual understanding of conflicting schedules, or knowing their responsibilities had been as busy and demanding as hers.

She knew now that didn't actually account for her diffidence to being apart from her spouses. Her new relationship made her feel so different, and not just because of the obvious difference that her lover was a woman. She called Cassidy nearly every night, just to hear the sound of her voice, to share a thought or two, or find out about her day.

Brenna was forty-one, with an anything but sheltered history of lovemaking—from a series of affairs to two marriages—but for the first time she understood the physical craving that went with truly being in love, a craving that went beyond physical pleasure to emotional completion. She didn't understand how she could have ever settled for anything less, except perhaps because she had never known there was supposed to be anything more.

In the aisle that held magazines in addition to groceries, she studied the industry periodicals and her attention was snared by a cover with two semi-nude women kissing in a lovers' clinch. Curiosity piqued, she studied others nearby and made a selection. Picking up a travel magazine showcasing the Oregon portion of the Rocky Mountains for weekend getaways, she wondered how Cassidy might react to another invitation to go camping. Or, Brenna thought, maybe we can do something a little more indulgent, a little more romantic, just the two of us. Her face flushed at the thought.

In the checkout line, Brenna found herself looking at the other patrons. Did she ever respond to another woman with the same quickened heartbeat, the same catch in her breath, the same visceral, mind-stuttering desire that she did whenever she looked at, or even thought about Cassidy Hyland?

Watching the brunette ahead of her in line interacting with the cashier, how her hands moved from her wallet to her purse, Brenna listened to her voice—a quick patter...no easiness to it. The woman was close to her own age, laugh lines not quite defined at the corners of her eyes. Brenna assessed her emotions and found nothing beyond polite awareness, similar to when she had first met Rachelle Cheron when they were both reading for the Time Trails roles. Abruptly the woman turned to look at her and Brenna ducked her gaze to the tabloid rack.

The man monitoring self-checkout came to bag her groceries as she stepped up to pay the cashier. Brenna let him help, taking some time to consider her reaction to him as well.

He appeared older, probably having taken the job to supplement a retirement income. He chatted about the local news, his voice pleasant but unremarkable. When he offered to push her cart outside, she met his eyes and noted they were a vague brown. She smiled politely and declined. "Thank you, I can manage."

The interaction apparently dazzled him, because he smiled wider. He reached for the cart again, but she shook her head. "I've got it."

"Come see us again," he said after a moment, and she detected the hopefulness in his voice.

After placing her groceries in her trunk, Brenna climbed into the driver's seat and started the engine. She brushed the central console, surprised at the strength of her memory of Cassidy's hand caressing hers as it had rested there.

Once home, she unpacked the few groceries and put them away. Standing at her desk, she glanced through the mail and saw a reminder that the Satellite Awards were in two weeks, and she sighed at the reminder that she still had not acquired a gown for the occasion. That made her wonder whether Cassidy would like to go shopping with her. Just the chance to see her lover again propelled Brenna back to her car and she sped north toward Cassidy's home in Altadena.

CHAPTER ONE

THERE WAS a click of her bedroom door and the rustle of feet crossing the floor, and the blonde under the covers rolled onto her back. She opened her eyes to the sight of Ryan, her five year old son, leaping onto her bed. His "Good morning, Mommy!" made her ears ring a little as his body fell into her open arms. Inhaling, she detected more than the scent of his hair. Startled, she looked toward the door. It smelled like...

"Breakfast." Her lover of only a few weeks used her elbow to push open the door on her way into the bedroom bearing a tray laden with filled glasses, mugs, and plates. "Well, brunch, maybe," Brenna corrected, as she set the tray down on the bedside table. "It's almost ten, Cass."

Cassidy could see toast with a pale jam, coffee, and glasses of a red fruit punch. She looked at Brenna again and smiled as the other woman stepped out of her shoes—face partially obscured by a loose fall of auburn—and sat on the queen-sized bed next to her. The bedsprings creaked under the additional weight.

"Thank you," Cassidy said as darkening blue eyes caressed her face, coming closer. She reached out with both hands and tugged on the open collar of Brenna's light blue cambric shirt, encouraging her lover closer. "When did you get here?" Though they had spoken almost every night, discussing the impasse Brenna had come to with her sons, Cassidy hadn't seen Brenna since New Year's Day. Cassidy eagerly searched the beautiful features to see what, if anything, was changed, as well as to gain some insight into her present mood and the reason for the unannounced, but welcome visit. "Is everything all right?"

Brenna's eyes shone as she quirked a smile and leaned in. "It is now." The edge to Brenna's voice was husky, brushing warmth against Cassidy's ear. "I arrived just a little while ago."

When Cassidy tasted Brenna's lips, she discovered the jam on the toast was orange marmalade, and devoured her first morning kiss in over a week.

Brenna's lips were soft, supple, and little moans issued from the duo as their connection deepened. Ryan squirmed against Cassidy and dampened her rising arousal. She pulled back. "I missed you."

Brenna's gaze never shifted as she caressed Cassidy's cheek. "God, I missed you too."

Ryan interrupted impatiently, "Are you hungry, Mommy? Miss Lanigan made you breakfast for bed."

Watching Ryan's expectant smile grow, Cassidy blinked. She was ravenous, but not for food. Gazing at her lover, Cassidy knew Brenna was feeling the same swirl of emotion.

"I already fed Ryan," Brenna explained.

"She made me scrambled eggs in a sandwich," Ryan supplied.

"So you let her in this morning?" Cassidy asked. "You know you're not supposed to let people in when I'm not awake."

"But Miss Lanigan's not a stranger."

Brenna's smile faltered. "It's my fault. I should have called first. I'm sorry."

Cassidy reached out and caressed Brenna's cheek. Her son's opinion of Brenna was important to their continuing relationship. Ryan was right; Brenna was not a stranger. Finally, she said, "It's all right." Ryan flung his arms around her neck, hugging tightly. Over her son's head, Cassidy said to Brenna, "I'll give you my spare key."

Brenna grasped her hand and leaned forward, pressing her lips to Cassidy's temple. "Thanks."

Disengaging Ryan, Cassidy then watched as he got down from the bed and in the way only her son could, crept to the door, leaning over his legs and thumping away like an elephant. He shut the door with a loud thud behind him. Brenna, who had watched the whole thing, laughed out loud, rolling back onto the pillows with Cassidy. "What a charmer he's going to be, Cass."

"I bet he planned that whole entry with you," Cassidy replied, having learned a little about what could happen when the two people she loved most put their heads together.

Brenna snagged a piece of toast and passed it to Cassidy with a glass of juice. "He really wanted to go along with the surprise. I'm sorry that his letting me in was against the rules."

Cassidy sipped the cranberry-apple juice and took a small bite of the toast, truly moved by the gesture. "This is wonderful, Bren," she said with real appreciation.

"I hope it's not too inconvenient. After I... Well, I got Thomas and James off to school then I decided to come see you."

Cassidy held out the toast and Brenna took a bite. Watching Brenna chew, that delicious mouth twitching slightly, the muscles moving in her throat as she swallowed, Cassidy had to tamp down a flash of lust. Quickly she took another bite of the marmalade and toast, her taste buds tingling with the sensory satisfaction. Clearing her mouth with a sip of juice, she arranged the pillows so she and Brenna could lean back, legs stretched out side by side. "I can't recall the last time I had breakfast in bed."

"I'd like to do it more often," Brenna said, taking up a mug of coffee from the tray.

Cassidy lifted her own mug while she considered how to answer. She inhaled the scent of the deep rich roast, laced with cream the way she liked. She could do this more often as well, but there were considerations. "We'll be back to work next week," she said.

"I know," Brenna leaned against Cassidy's shoulder and picked up another piece of toast from the tray, "but our situation won't have changed. You'll still have your place, and I'll still have mine, and we'll still go our separate ways most nights."

Cassidy's nose nuzzled against the fine hair that smelled of fresh peaches. "You switched shampoos," she murmured.

"I did. Do you like it?"

"Marvelous." Cassidy kissed the crown and the fine silky strands tickled her lips. "We're together now," she said by way of answer to the last question hanging in the air.

"But Ryan's outside."

"So snuggle with me while we finish your wonderful breakfast in bed."

Brenna settled against Cassidy's shoulder as she lifted her coffee mug to her lips again. "I can definitely do that."

Deciding they couldn't leave Ryan to his own devices for too long, as soon as Cassidy finished eating, Brenna led the way from the bedroom carrying the breakfast tray. Cassidy, pulling the belt of her robe secure, was a step behind her. "Ryan!" Cassidy called out.

The sliding glass door to the back porch was open. While Brenna went to the sink to deposit the tray, Cassidy went to the open door and called, "Ryan! Time to come inside!"

The blond boy suddenly raced into view, a barking Ranger leaping and running at his side. The taxidermy animal they had acquired several months earlier was once again their toy. Cassidy sighed. "Come inside, please."

"Why don't we take Ryan and Ranger for a walk?" Brenna asked.

"Where?"

"You've got a neighborhood park."

"Yeah, but—"

"I don't want to go home yet," Brenna admitted.

Cassidy looked back over her shoulder, her nervousness manifested by the teeth worrying at her bottom lip. "All right."

"Are you tired?"

"No. I... It's... We don't really want to be caught by cameras."

Brenna shook her head. "Neighborhood park, not the local mall. Furthermore, it's your neighborhood, not mine."

"There's always a chance."

"Is it your parents? Cass, your parents are in Missouri. What can they do?"

Brenna was right, the chances were slim, but Cassidy had a distinctly unsettled feeling. And, while her parents might disapprove, they were more than a thousand miles away. She made her decision looking down into Ryan's expectant face as he slammed into her legs coming through the doorway. "All right. Let's go to the park." Wrapping his arms around her legs, he kissed her left thigh.

Brenna gently peeled Ryan off Cassidy and sent her lover to her room with a kiss. "Dress casual. We'll be waiting."

Cassidy returned wearing jeans and a long-sleeved aquamarine flannel pullover, her hair brushed and pulled back in a ponytail at the nape of her neck. Brenna grasped her right hand and Ryan's left, and led the way to the street.

Halfway to the corner, Cassidy spotted Lou Talbot in his driveway, poking under the open hood of the family car. She gave a friendly wave as his gaze rose to them. "Good morning."

"Hmph."

"Friendly sort," Brenna commented as they walked on.

"That's Gwen's husband, Lou Talbot. You met Gwen."

"She's married to him?" Brenna shook her head.

After walking two blocks of sidewalk, Brenna and Cassidy entered the park through a high arched gateway. A path encircled the park's central feature—a duck and fish pond, large enough that there was a small dock out over the water on the far side. A walking path, a biking path, and an exercise path all separately circled the pond.

"It's about two and a half miles, three including the walk back to my house," Cassidy revealed. "So here you have my morning gym." She pointed at the equipment along the exercise path. "You remember; I told you about it during Ryan's birthday party back in October."

Joggers flashed by them, and a man in tight shorts but with a bare chest was hoisting his meaty frame on the chin-up bar. Brenna smiled. "Clearly it's a popular place."

"When Gwen showed me through the neighborhood, I knew I wanted to be right here."

"You said that you stayed with her and Lou when you came out from St. Louis to do small parts."

"It was a strain. At first I thought it was all me, traveling so much, not sitting still, always just getting on or just getting off a plane. But Lou... Well, I made a good bit of money from the vampire role, so I thought about renting something. Gwen liked having me around, so she showed me a few rentals in the neighborhood. When I was finalizing my divorce and knew I would stay, I talked the rental agent into letting me buy the house I'm in now."

Ryan ran for a children's jungle gym and they watched for a while as he threw himself over and under the various posts and poles.

People milled about, but it wasn't crowded. On the weekends, Brenna imagined this was a popular place for the neighborhood families. She could see the vendors Cassidy had mentioned, and picnic tables, in the grass by the dock. A grandfather and grandson—their apparent age difference making her assume the relationship—were seated, feet dangling over the water, straight poles with lines dropped in search of a fish's nibble. "This is wonderful," she concluded.

"Probably the best feature of the neighborhood," Cassidy agreed. "And not a reporter in sight."

"You don't like large crushes, formal events, do you?"

"I like my privacy. I don't hate the events, but I guess I'm still more the girl from the St. Louis suburbs." They walked along the path while Ryan ran around them.

"Is that guiding your choices after Time Trails?"

"Maybe. I haven't fielded a lot of offers."

"If you're staying here, I probably shouldn't go to England." Brenna paused. "Unless you'd like to come along." She found herself eagerly considering the idea. A little seclusion, just their families, time alone.

"Terry mentioned his theater," Cassidy replied.

"Or we could do that."

"But you should take the British part if you want it."

Unwilling to leave Cassidy for the length of time it would take to film that movie, Brenna grudgingly allowed, "I'll think about it."

"With Thomas graduating, you've only got James at home."

"If I can get him to adjust to us." Brenna was melancholy. She was dreaming dreams with someone who really mattered to her, and her sons, who mattered as well, were less than happy about it, despite their forced words to the contrary when she confronted them.

Cassidy caught Brenna's mood shift. "Have they said anything more about it?"

"No, that's just it. They aren't saying anything." Brenna sighed. "Thomas told me once he liked being someone I could confide in. But now, he's more scarce even than James, who just seems to disappear and reappear, without explanation."

She inhaled and exhaled the fresh air, finding the pine, palm, and pond scents calming.

"It probably feels to them as if you've been keeping secrets from them. You're different, and they don't know how to react to that."

"Am I different?" Brenna considered that. Inside she felt happier than she could recall in any other time in her life. She guessed maybe it showed outwardly in ways she wasn't aware of. "I guess I am a little different, but I'm still their mother."

"I've seen them with you. I think they'll come around."

Cassidy and Brenna leaned together on the bench, gazes intent on Ryan, minds mulling over Thomas and James, ears attuned to each other's quiet heartbeats.

"It's really quite nice."

"Weekday mornings the vendor has sausage and egg rolls, and coffee. He brings out hot dogs by noon."

"So we're just in time."

As if on cue, the vendor, with his supply of hot dogs, rolled his wheeled cart past them, and Ryan's attention was immediately drawn by the aroma of food.

The trio walked over to a picnic table near the dock, and Brenna sat with Ryan while Cassidy collected three hot dogs. When she returned to the table, she found Brenna and Ryan with their heads bent close, her son whispering to her lover. "Am I interrupting?"

Brenna lifted her head and smiled widely. "Not at all. I was just listening to Ryan showing how high he can count."

"What was he counting?"

"Ducks."

"How high did you get?" Cassidy asked, sitting down and distributing the hot dogs in their white crenellated carriers.

"I got to fifteen."

"Very good."

All of them were silent for a few minutes, consuming the foot long hot dogs. Ryan saved the heel of the bun. "May I go feed the ducks?" he asked when he'd finished the rest of his hot dog.

"Yes. Wait, though. Someone should go down to the water with you."

Brenna swallowed her final bite. "I say we both go."

"All right." Cassidy stood and Brenna took her hand. Ryan took his mother's other hand, holding the piece of bun in his right.

About three feet from the water's edge, Cassidy tugged Ryan to a stop. "Close enough. Try reaching the ducks paddling this way."

Ryan tore the bun into pieces and threw a handful of crumbs, most of which landed on the ground in front of him as they caught the air and fluttered down.

The ducks were undeterred. Long used to being unafraid of humans, they waddled out of the water, long necks stretching this way and that, black beaks snapping up the bits. Ryan had to back up and quickly throw away the remainder as a larger duck realized Ryan was the source of the bounty, and lifted his beak in search of more.

Brenna snatched Ryan out of harm's way. Startled by the larger person, the ducks squawked in alarm and quickly waddled away.

Cassidy wrapped her arms around Brenna and Ryan, and laughed away her anxiety. Brenna had been closer and had taken care of the situation without a moment's thought or outward alarm, but Cassidy's heart had been in her throat when she realized what was happening.

"Thank you."

"You're welcome. I think it's time to go home, though." Brenna nodded at Ryan snuggling against her chest. "I think someone's tired."

"It's nap time." Cassidy took Ryan from Brenna and the women walked back with more speed and purpose in their stride than during the slow amble to the park. In ten minutes they were back inside Cassidy's home and pulling Ryan's shoes off as he drooped sleepily on the edge of his bed.

As she and Cassidy retired to the couch and snuggled together, Brenna realized it was almost one-thirty. "All things considered," she observed aloud, "it's been a wonderful day."

"Anytime you want to come over, just come," Cassidy said.

The breath whispering through her hair sent tingles of pleasure down Brenna's spine which then lodged warmly in her abdomen. She squirmed in response and lifted her head, knowing she needed to go instead of dallying here. For now.

"I've got to get my sons adjusted. I'd like to have you and Ryan over to my place again, especially when the weather warms up and I open the pool."

"Now that school's back in session, the sense that your boys have their own things to do may help."

"I hope so." Brenna's breath sighed against Cassidy's collarbone. "I want everything with you. It's been a long time since I felt as if I had a friend and a lover in the same person. I want to wake up with you every morning. I can't do that until Thomas and James understand that their silent treatment, or even outright anger, is not going to change my mind."

"Thomas' and James' opinions matter, Bren. I wouldn't want them not to." Cassidy wrapped her arms around her lover, letting their curves fit together.

"I won't let Thomas or James push us apart."

"All right. So, what now?"

"What would you say to going in to work together on Monday?"

"Are you serious?"

"Thomas and James can get themselves to school. I'm sure they'd prefer it. I'll come here, and take you and Ryan in my car."

"I've got Ryan's car seat."

"I'll move it to my car," Brenna suggested. "It's not a major display, but it's a half hour drive back and forth, time that we could be together."

Cassidy grasped Brenna's hands earnestly. "Not yet. It's too soon. Let's try smaller things first."

Brenna was reluctant to agree. "Why?"

"Do you really want your sons inundated by the press before they are comfortable? And what about the détente you reached with Kevin?"

Brenna sat up. "It isn't fair that we have to hide."

"No, it's not," Cassidy agreed. When Brenna got up from the couch, Cassidy followed. "Are you all right?"

"I haven't even left yet, and I miss you already." Brenna snuggled into Cassidy's embrace.

As she wrapped her arms around her lover, Cassidy couldn't help thinking the same thing. Putting other people's feelings first, when she'd been used to ignoring her own for so long, was frustrating.

"I'll be waiting when you get to the set Monday."

"Maybe I can find more time to get away this week."

"Take some time with Thomas and James. Maybe they just need a little attention from Mom."

"Maybe." Brenna's lips turned down at the corners. "I offered to make Chicago deep dish tonight, their favorite. I finally got Thomas to promise to be home. James, who knows where he'll be."

"It will work out, Bren."

"Promise?"

"I promise." They shared one last lingering kiss before they reached the front door.

CHAPTER TWO

CASSIDY SMILED as she and Ryan entered the surroundings of the Time Trails soundstage on the Pinnacle Studios lot. The whole of it—with crew people scrambling thither and yon, unrolling cables, testing boom mikes, everyone smiling—provided a wonderful sense of familiarity.

Sean Durham, Time Trail's Jeremy Dewitt, gave her a wave, his sandy blond hair pinned under a blue baseball cap flipped backward on his head.

"Good morning," she offered.

"Sure is." He tapped the end of a ball point pen against the neon orange clipboard in his left hand. "Hey, brought the little man today. Did you have a good break?" He dropped his foot from a director's sling chair and approached her.

Cassidy nodded. "Did you?"

"Went to see some family out of state," he said. In the next moment they were both distracted by the door opening behind him.

Rachelle Cheron, Time Trail's Luria Dewitt, entered the soundstage through a door held by her companion. Rachelle was walking backward and elaborating on a story, hands flowing rapidly through the air. Brenna, Time Trail's Commander Susan Jakes, brushed her fingers through her short-styled auburn hair. Her blue eyes twinkled as they caught Cassidy's gaze past Rachelle's head.

"...and he didn't believe me!" Rachelle finished.

"I can't imagine why your brother didn't believe you," Brenna commiserated, though her tone was amused. She shifted her eyes away from Chelle and the melancholy gray became suffused with passionate blue.

Rachelle spun around. The cocoa-skinned woman was clearly agitated, her dark skin unable to hide the high color in her cheeks. "Oh, hey, Sean, Cass." Without preamble, the small woman threw her arms around Sean's neck and kissed him soundly.

He returned the affection. "Your brother didn't believe you about what?" he asked.

"That Rose's school had already taught her the basic colors, numbers, and was beginning on letters."

"I thought your brother had kids," Sean said.

"He apparently pays no attention at all to their education," Rachelle huffed.

"So, tell me everything." Sean slipped an arm around the diminutive woman and led her away, Chelle launching anew into her story.

For Cassidy, the conversation quickly faded into the general din as she feasted on Brenna's appearance. A warm smile and gleaming blue eyes hinted at the fiery and passionate nature Cassidy knew was hidden within. Today Brenna wore a maroon wool pullover, the white cambric shirt underneath visible at her wrists and collar. Drawn to Brenna's hands, Cassidy watched them move forward, reaching toward her, and then awkwardly try to hide away in the tight pockets of the name brand denim jeans. Following the arm back up to Brenna's face, she broke the silence as their gazes entwined. "I... Hi." Brenna's smile made Cassidy's stomach flip.

"Good morning."

Cassidy's heart raced at the warm tone, its smoky resonances blocking out all other sound.

"Good morning," she returned with more assurance. Brenna's hand slid over Cassidy's forearm, just below the three-quarter sleeve of Cassidy's pale blue, stretch cotton blouse. The contact caused a tingling deep in Cassidy's chest.

"How are you?"

Cassidy let Brenna take Ryan from her arms, amused briefly by the startled grunt the woman made as Ryan's full weight settled against her.

"Why don't we take Ryan to Karen's together?" Brenna suggested.

"I'd like that," she replied.

As they crossed through the soundstage area, Cassidy stuck close to Brenna's side. She wanted to reach out, put her hand on Brenna's back, but each time she came close, a rigger, or other tech, appeared from somewhere.

Once they stepped outside, Cassidy holding the door for Brenna, she rested one hand on Brenna's back and the other on Ryan's, and leaned in very close. "I've been waiting for you."

Brenna's scent, warm and spicy, assailed her. Helpless to resist, she nuzzled Brenna's hair, feeling the woman lean into her. Looking around and finding themselves in shadows and alone, she nudged Brenna's back, causing the woman to lift her chin to see what Cassidy wanted. Perfectly positioned, she thought. She smiled and brought her lips to Brenna's, intending a chaste and quick kiss.

Brenna's moan made her throb, and Cassidy reached for Brenna's shoulder to turn the woman more fully into her body. With Ryan nestled against both their shoulders, she wrapped her arms around the two people she loved most.

When they parted, Cassidy stroked Brenna's hair lightly.

"I missed you so much," Brenna murmured. "I should have found more time away. One day since New Year's wasn't nearly enough time together."

"We will work all this out," Cassidy promised.

Ryan lifted his head and looked at Brenna. "Did you miss me?"

"I missed you too," Brenna answered him seriously, sincerity clear in her voice.

With Ryan awake, Brenna stood him on his feet. He put himself squarely between the two woman, taking hold of a hand from each. "Where are we going?"

"To see Miss Karen," Cassidy replied.

He grinned and bounced their arms with his excited arm swinging. They let go of his hands, linking their own, as he ran around them, up and down the sidewalk, as the trio picked up the pace to the child care trailer.

Cassidy wanted Brenna next to her but the other woman hung back as Ryan ran ahead inside the trailer, leaving her standing on the stoop talking with Karen Grinaldi, the studio's tutor and caregiver.

"Anything special I should know?"

"No." Cassidy shook her head, but then a glance at Brenna gave her an idea. "Wait, yes. I'd like to make sure that Brenna can come pick him up, if need be."

"So you want to list her as an alternate?"

Out of the corner of her eye, Cassidy saw Brenna start up the steps, looking upset. "Yes, I would. We work odd hours. It might come in useful."

"Well, step inside here and we'll sign the paperwork."

"Thank you." Cassidy held the door for Brenna and put a light hand on her back to encourage her ahead, following Karen inside the trailer.

Brenna said, "I... shouldn't."

Cassidy shook her head. "Most nights we'll leave about the same time, but there could be late calls. For either of us."

Karen fished in her desk for the proper form, coming up with it quickly. "Are you rooming together?"

Brenna looked at Cassidy. "I... no. But..." She hesitated. "You're sure?"

"Yes." Cassidy watched as Brenna mulled over the situation, pleased to see how seriously she was taking it.

"It won't happen a lot, I'm sure," Brenna said aloud, clearly convincing herself that this was a small thing.

"It would make me feel a lot easier, knowing he's with you." Cassidy waited for her answer.

"I guess it's all right," Brenna finally said slowly, her words sounding more confident with each syllable.

Karen smiled. "Then sign and print your name and contact information right here." She pointed to a place on the form.

Brenna said nothing more until they were outside the trailer headed back to the set. "Cass, was that a wise idea?"

Cassidy leaned close and held Brenna captive with her gaze. "It makes me feel pretty wonderful."

"Me too," Brenna answered in a low whisper, their hands overlapping on the door panel as Cassidy reached for it.

Cassidy held the door as they reentered the soundstage. "It's a very early day today. Would you like to do something after work tonight?" she whispered.

Brenna's shiver of pleasure did not go unnoticed and Cassidy smiled.

"Your place, or mine?"

"Mine," Cassidy said, and it sounded more like she was claiming Brenna rather than simply stating her preference of location for their third official date.

Will Chapman, Time Trail's Mark Raycreek, drew the attention of both women as they stepped out from the shadowed corner where they had been speaking. "Are you ready to get to work?"

"Ready," Brenna answered with a smile. Trailing behind Will, each woman grabbed a bottle of filtered water as they passed the small catering table.

"Bren. Cass." Already seated, Rich Paulson grinned at Cassidy and Brenna as they appeared around the edge of the set wall. "Looks like vacation was good to you."

Cassidy blushed. A quick glance to her right saw Brenna was doing the same. Smiling brightly back at Rich, Cassidy nodded. "Ryan and I stayed in town for most of it."

Rich puzzled, "No family?"

Cassidy felt Brenna's reassuring touch on her back as the woman passed behind her to get to her seat. Cassidy wrapped her hands around the back of her own chair. Catching Brenna's nod out of the corner of her eye, Cassidy turned back to Rich with a steadier gaze. "A little."

"Something the matter?" Rich asked.

"No. We hadn't spent a holiday here in the city before, is all. What did you and Linda do?"

"We spent a week in the Pocono mountains," he said. "Perfect snuggling weather."

Recalling the breakfast in bed Brenna had brought her as a surprise, Cassidy smiled. "Yes, it was."

"Cass?"

Cassidy blinked, embarrassed she had "checked out" on her colleague. As she was debating what to say next, she felt a large presence move behind her. Cassidy stepped aside as Will Chapman brushed past. He seemed quite distracted.

"Is there news on your sister, Will?" she asked politely.

Uncharacteristically, he grinned widely and expansively spread his arms. "I'm an uncle! Christmas Day. Seven pounds eight ounces."

"Congratulations! Boy or girl?" Rachelle asked.

"Oh? Um..." Will was clearly flustered as several others in the cast pounded his back congenially. "It's a girl. My sister's doing great, too."

"That is good news." Brenna took her seat.

Cassidy watched as something intangible passed between Brenna and Will, then Brenna dipped her chin in acknowledgment of something and Will took his seat next to her with only a light brush of his hand over hers. Cassidy flashed back to Brenna's revelation that the two had a brief affair little more than eighteen months ago.

Forcing her mind from the disturbing thought, Cassidy was sitting down when she heard Brenna's voice again, this time filled with great warmth and surprise.

"Max! Brady?"

Cassidy glanced at Brenna and saw her face light up. Unable to resist, Cassidy turned around to study the two men, new faces to her, now standing in the doorway.

"Good to see you again, Bren." The older man, dark-haired and redwood-tall, quickly circled the table and enfolded Brenna in a bear hug as she came to her feet.

"No one told me you were in this one, Max."

"When I won the casting call, I asked them to keep it quiet so I could surprise you."

Cassidy noticed how Brenna patted him affectionately before she turned to the younger man, also dark-haired but leaner in build. His facial features were similar to Max's. He stepped up to Brenna, who had to look up about six inches to meet his gaze. Brenna's next words caught Cassidy off guard again.

"My God, you're your father twenty years ago. James and Thomas would love to see you." Brenna wrapped both arms around Brady's neck, hugging him while kissing his cheek. "You both have to come to the house." Turning to Max, she asked, "Did Mary come with you?"

Max shook his head. "I'm afraid I'm at the mercy of the commissary or take-out this time. Mary's with her mother on a cruise in the South Pacific."

Brenna could not seem to take her eyes from Max very long, nor from Brady next to him. She asked after Brady's studies, surprised to hear this wasn't a lark, but that he had chosen to go into acting. "My old man has so much fun at it," he finished, "I thought I'd check it out."

"Do you like it?" Cassidy asked.

Brenna beamed at her as Brady turned to answer Cassidy's question. "I've only done a few roles. Dad's helped pick them out, and advised me a couple of times, but overall, yes, I do."

Max and Brady circled the table shaking hands, trading greetings and introductions. The social conversation ended as the director and the episode's writer appeared. It was Cassidy's turn to be startled, though not in a good way. "Cameron?"

Cameron Palassis, one of the studio's writers, had been moved off the series early in December. She had ended her intimate relationship with him at the same time.

The last time she had seen him, he had pawed her in public and made them both a spectacle at the studio holiday party. Now he did not look at her. Instead he kept a guarded expression trained on Will Chapman and Terry Brown, who both stood as he had entered the room.

Either ignoring the standoff, or oblivious to it, director Jackson Tierson pulled out the chair at the head of the table. "Let's start."

The cast settled around the table to begin reading through the newest script. Across the table, Cassidy found Brenna's gaze, watched her smile fade into an uncertain frown as she looked at Max before following the page as Terry's voice started on the opening line.

```
    Chris:   Lieutenant,   I  thought  I  was  taking  the
point position.
    Susan: Heatherly was spotted this time. I'm going.
    Chris:   Creighton?
    Creighton: The commander is joining us.
    Chris:   Right.
    There  is  a  Vortex  effect  and  briefly  everyone
vanishes from sight. Raycreek is standing aside with a
smile. Luria at the console reacts to a bad reading.
    Luria:   Interference  at  the  reception  site.  I'm
going to reverse the stream, bring them back.
    Raycreek: You will not, Lieutenant. Wait for the
recall signal.
    A console light begins flashing.
    Luria:   Damn it!
    Luria  performs  the  recall  protocol.  The  Vortex
effect is radically different and when it clears, there
are  four  people  on  the  platform:  Chris,  Creighton,
```

Susan Jakes (prime) and Susan Jakes (Alt), who is considerably older.

Max let out a low whistle. "Two of you," he said to Brenna. "Yum."

"And you won't get either one," she teased.

"Damn," he said with a laugh.

Cassidy's stomach flip-flopped as Brenna laughed along with him. It was good to see her lover happy, but she was surprised at her own spurt of jealousy. She wondered who, exactly, Max was.

"So, wanna do some blocking?" Max asked.

"Cass?" Brenna looked at her.

"I'm just going to my trailer to work on my lines." She wondered whether Brenna would come with her. After all, it had been a week since they'd been together.

However, Brenna didn't pick up on her unspoken invitation, or was declining, since she looked up at Max and then answered, "All right. I'll see you when we're done."

Cassidy watched in surprise as Brenna put her hand on Max's offered elbow and walked away. All the while, she tried to tell herself that Max was obviously an old friend, and Brenna probably wanted to spend time catching up. It didn't cure the ache, but it did galvanize Cassidy into moving off in the other direction.

CHAPTER THREE

A REPORTER stopped Cassidy outside, requesting "a few minutes". Taking him at his word, she led him to her trailer steps, sat down, and gave a simple interview.

Finally she entered her trailer to get some memorization done. Just nearing the end, she heard her stomach rumble, suggesting she find some lunch, Cassidy heard a knock at the door. She hoped it would be Brenna.

Cassidy definitely wanted them to do something together off set, like get something to eat, just not too far away. Maybe with some clothes shopping afterwards. And then they could come back to the lot and pick up Ryan from Miss Karen.

However, the visitor at her door proved to be a Peter Murray, who said he was with the Virginia Dispatch newspaper.

"Ms. Hyland?" he asked.

"Yes?"

"I'd like to ask you some questions about the series and the final wrap. Do you have a few minutes?"

Hoping it would be only a few minutes, she didn't invite him inside. Leaning against the railing alongside her trailer steps, she said, "All right."

He started off by asking whether she had been enjoying the work. She answered by rote until a question came out of the blue.

"Do you have a favorite designer shop in the mall?"

Since she had just been thinking about clothes, she wondered whether she had said something out loud. Cassidy gave him her full attention. "Excuse me?"

"I was picking up gifts for my kids at the mall, and I spotted you at the food court."

"Me?"

"You are quite recognizable." He gestured toward the set. "So is she."

"Lanigan?"

"Yes. This is her, right?" He held out a small photograph. It had been taken at the food court at the mall when they all were there the day after Christmas. Centered in the frame, she and Brenna were leaning over a table, passing out food. "Who are the kids, yours or hers?"

"The two teens are hers," she supplied evenly, knowing lying would be stupid. She began thinking of ways to convince him to give her the picture—and the negatives. "The youngest is mine." She hadn't even seen a flash go off. Well, she reasoned, I was distracted. At least it wasn't when they had their heads bent together, quietly discussing Thomas and James.

"Ms. Hyland, the general belief is that the two of you hardly speak. I'd like the scoop if that's changed."

"Working hard together creates friendships in the toughest situations, Mr. Murray." She vaguely recalled Brenna saying something similar months ago.

"So you were just Christmas shopping together?"

"Yes," she answered. "Mind if I show her the photo?"

He stepped back from her outstretched hand. "That's all I needed," he said hastily. "Thank you for your time."

Cassidy watched him leave then, feeling a presence, spoke to the shadow behind her left shoulder. "I was waiting for the right moment to get the picture," she said. She did not have to turn to see the hard look Brenna had shot the reporter go slack.

"Picture? All I saw was your face go pale—"

"How can you tell under the makeup?"

"You're not wearing any, and neither am I." Brenna's expression turned tender as her voice became softer, private. "I learned to pay attention. I care."

"I'm sorry. I didn't mean to snap." There was silence as their eyes met. Cassidy swallowed. "I was thinking about doing something with you, now I'm not so sure."

"Why?"

"I didn't get the pictures from him."

Brenna raised an eyebrow in query. "Pictures of...?"

"Us at the mall with the kids."

"We can explain that easily, right?"

"But how many more are out there?" Cassidy fretted.

"Would it really harm anything to be seen out shopping together? Or having dinner?"

"Bren..."

"Why don't we go out after work? It might be fun. Nothing intimate, just shopping, a little dinner. Someplace nearby." Brenna shook her head, her hair in such disarray around her features that when she looked up, she had to brush the locks behind an ear to see Cassidy.

"Why don't we go back to the set, work on some walk throughs, and then call it a day?"

"I'd like that."

"You need to meet Max," Brenna said.

"Do I?" Cassidy asked, hoping her jealousy wasn't evident in her voice.

"He's got a wicked sense of humor."

Cassidy smiled at Brenna's gaze, all for her. "All right. Let's go."

Hours later, Cassidy understood a little of what Max was to Brenna. They'd been walking through several different scenes, and though Brenna hadn't memorized her lines, her interactions based on Max's cues were spot on, and he had the uncanny ability to pull spontaneity from Brenna. Out of the corner of her eye, Cassidy saw someone walk through carrying a coat. It made her think of the time. Looking at her watch, she said, "It's after four."

Immediately Brenna stopped talking to Max. Cassidy resisted the desire to smile broadly as Brenna turned to her. "You ready?"

"Been ready," Cassidy answered.

Brenna said to Max, "I'll catch you for dinner another night. I've got a date."

"Really?"

Brenna couldn't contain her pleasure. "Yes."

Cassidy saw the surprise on his face, but if Brenna was unconcerned about his reaction, she decided she could be as well. She casually followed Brenna out of the soundstage.

Once they were outside, Cassidy pulled out her cell phone and dialed Karen Grinaldi, letting the caregiver watching Ryan know they would be off the studio lot for a few hours. Karen assured her everything would be fine, and Ryan would be waiting for them whenever they were finished.

CHAPTER FOUR

"I DO. I think it's a good script." Cassidy lifted her glass of chardonnay to her lips. A light smile touched the bow-shaped lips and the candlelight from the small tea light between them on the table flickered in the darkening blue. Cassidy blushed. In a low voice, she commented, "You're staring."

Brenna shrugged. "You're beautiful."

Brenna's voice was pitched just as soft, but its huskiness rolled over Cassidy with palpable effect as her groin convulsed.

They had found this little jazz place only a few blocks from the studio and after their afternoon spent perusing shops without anyone interrupting their time together, Cassidy had begun to relax. No one seemed to be following them. She was still concerned about Mr. Peter Murray and those like him, but it was hard to worry when Brenna seemed so happy.

The musical interlude from the band made their words private, even if their looks and touches couldn't be. "When you talk like that," Cassidy said, "this is the perfect setting."

"What do you mean?"

"Your voice, it makes me... actually made me from the very beginning, think of smoky jazz clubs."

"You'd be the torch singer," Brenna corrected. "God, when I recall 'Hold Tight'..."

"You liked that?"

"Loved it. I think I half fell in love with you. The looks you gave me didn't help."

"I liked the song too."

"It felt like you were singing to me. I checked to be sure you hadn't rewritten the lyrics."

"I hadn't, but I felt something then too," Cassidy admitted.

Brenna shook her head and Cassidy found herself watching the firelight dance among the brown and red strands of her hair. Apparently she was quiet and thoughtful too long, as Brenna broke the silence.

"Cass?"

"Yes?"

"Something wrong?" Brenna asked with concern.

"No, everything is right." She started to reach across the table to clasp Brenna's hand resting just to the outside of her wine glass, but stopped. Looking up again, she added, "I'm glad we decided to do this."

Brenna nodded. "Me too."

The music stopped and there was a commotion as the vocalist headlining the evening at the tiny jazz club took the stage after her break. Cassidy shifted her chair around the table so she could watch the performer; it was no coincidence that it also gave her an excuse to sit closer to Brenna. She caught Brenna's smile and returned it as their hands joined under the table.

The floor before the stage slowly filled with couples as the sultry voice began with a danceable jazz standard. "I wish we dared dance." Brenna's breath brushed over Cassidy's throat as she spoke close and very low to be unheard by others.

"Should we finish our drinks and go?"

"Not just yet. It's still early. Maybe after this set."

Leaning back a little, Cassidy saw Brenna move closer, then freeze. Slowly Brenna moved again. She lifted her left hand awkwardly between them and shifted a lock of her own hair as if she was putting it back in place, though it hadn't moved. Cassidy realized that Brenna had just barely stopped herself from resting her head against Cassidy's shoulder.

"More wine?" Brenna asked, reaching forward to fill her glass from the bottle in an ice bucket at the table.

"If I have any more, I won't be responsible for my actions."

Brenna groaned as Cassidy accompanied her words by easing her right arm onto Brenna's lower back. She looked around quickly then let out a breath, hopeful the low lighting was keeping their intimacy unnoticed.

Cassidy leaned back and sipped on her wine, letting the music and the ambiance wash over her. Brenna's weight gradually eased against her body.

A small frenzy erupted at the entrance, drawing their attention as well as everyone else's as a couple popular with the paparazzi entered. The club's security quickly stymied the press, but the flashes continued from outside for several minutes.

Brenna moved away, and with a sidelong glance, Cassidy could see that Brenna had drawn in on herself. She herself was also concerned about the possibility of them being caught in the attention. "Do you want to go?" she asked.

Biting her lip so long that Cassidy wanted to kiss it and make it better, Brenna finally nodded.

"I'll go get the car," Brenna said.

"I'll pay the tab and meet you across the street at the garage in about five minutes."

Brenna stood quickly and ducked past a waiter walking by their table. The next sighting Cassidy had, Brenna was beside the short corridor leading to the rest rooms. She was able to track her to the front door, approaching it from the opposite site of the club. Cassidy shook her head and discreetly waved down the next waitperson. "I'd like my check, please." The young brunette nodded and disappeared briefly. When she reappeared, she wore a small frown. "There are two dinners here."

"Yes. Thank you." Cassidy did not explain, simply handing over her credit card.

A slight frown still marring her features, the waitperson stepped away, returning in a few minutes with the credit slip. Cassidy signed the slip and withdrew a few bills as she put the credit card in her wallet. She handed the money to the young woman. "Thank you for a pleasant evening."

"You're welcome."

Cassidy made her way outside with only a brief stop at the front door by a reporter who noticed her despite his tracking of the other couple inside. "Have a nice evening, Miss Hyland?"

"Very nice. Always excellent service," she added, though this was the first time she had been to this club, which was why she and Brenna had chosen it.

As she gained her bearings, looking up and down the street, another question came.

"Out on your own this evening?"

Past the flash of his camera, for which she automatically froze, Cassidy spotted Brenna's Mountaineer about a block away. "Yes, of course. Good night."

The hasty retreat unfortunately drew more attention as the single reporter started after her and his flurry of motion drew other eyes. She quickly crossed to the other side of the street, hoping to lose herself in the shadows between the streetlights before crossing back to meet up with Brenna.

The Mountaineer was stopped at a light and Cassidy wondered if Brenna could see that she was being followed. When the light changed, the SUV went on through instead of turning down the street toward her.

Cassidy exhaled as her heart rate increased. It would be up to her to catch up to her ride.

She ducked into the parking garage, searching through the darkness for the way to the other street exit. Crowd noises and shouted questions behind her drew her gaze backward. The security guard for the garage, meaty and fit for the job, looked small against the wall of surging reporters. Cassidy ducked around a support post and found her solitary way to the other exit.

The SUV door was already open, Brenna leaning toward the passenger seat.

"Everything all right?" Brenna asked with a frown.

Her question turned Cassidy around from looking over her shoulder.

"Yes." Cassidy pulled herself quickly into the vehicle and shut the door. "Let's go."

Brenna's hand on hers gradually slowed her heart rate as the SUV moved them further and further away from the scene.

Brenna had also nearly relaxed by the time she pulled the SUV into the Pinnacle Studios lot. The gate guard nodded them through, and she parked outside of the pool of illumination provided by a light pole.

While in the dimly lit restaurant, she had relaxed, with Cassidy's encouragement. Now Brenna was stiff, withdrawn, as she had been when she caught sight of the one reporter looking past the other couple he had come to track. The look on his face was as if he was mentally poring through an album of celebrity images, and she had looked quickly to be sure that Cassidy was mostly in shadow.

Cassidy's touch had relaxed her, but the enjoyment had gone from their time together.

Though they were alone now, Cassidy did not take her hand as they walked through the dark lot. "Do you think we've got a problem?" Brenna asked.

Cassidy did take her hand then, which made Brenna smile.

"I don't want our relationship splashed through the papers as something tawdry. Maybe we should work with our agencies to generate some positive press before it becomes a negative issue."

Brenna sighed and briefly rested her head against Cassidy's shoulder, jostling with its movement as they walked. "If I could get the divorce decree done tomorrow, I would."

"In an ideal world," Cassidy lamented.

"I'll bug my lawyer to see what she can do to hurry things up."

Their conversation stopped as they entered the child care trailer and found Karen sitting reading a magazine while Ryan slept soundly on a cot. Cassidy gingerly picked him up, and Brenna took his backpack from Karen.

Once outside, Cassidy spoke more quietly, as she asked, "Have you spoken with Kevin recently?"

Brenna swallowed. She had, and the conversation had not gone comfortably. "He's hurting, but... he's got his daughters to consider, as well as his campaign hopes. I don't want to hurt Ellie or Marie, either, so I've spoken with them."

"How are they taking it?"

"Marie—she's older—says that she knows a girl in her classes who likes girls, and in class, they've talked about homosexual relationships."

Cassidy winced. "It sounds like a 'but' is coming."

"But she says it's weird because I 'don't wear fatigues or dress like a boy'." Brenna sounded as aghast as her expression suggested.

Cassidy chuckled. "Clearly high school is not filled with 'lipstick lesbians'." Brenna looked disturbed. "What's wrong?"

"I never thought there would be a 'type' I was expected to be."

"So, what Marie said bothered you? Don't worry, Bren." Cassidy adjusted Ryan in her arms and leaned in to kiss her. "It's not like I have expectations of it all, either. I fell in love with you exactly as you are."

"And when the press asks, which you know they will?"

"How much did you say to them about your relationship with Kevin?"

"They never really asked me. Kevin talked about it. I did the usual pre-wedding spreads in Celebrity Monthly and People."

"Publicity." Cassidy nodded. "I guess we have to think about it, but..." She frowned. "I'm not really interested in 'coming out' and playing some political angle. What we have means a lot to me, and it's private."

"We don't want it tainted, or misconstrued."

"Exactly." When they reached her car in the parking lot, Cassidy put Ryan in his seat in the back.

Cassidy started to lower herself into her driver's seat, then stopped. "Bren?"

"Yes?" She leaned on the frame of the open door.

"I'll see you tomorrow?"

Brenna was disappointed that their conversation was at an end. "Yeah."

Cassidy's leaned across the car door and nuzzled Brenna's cheek. "I'm just not ready yet to share you with the rest of the world."

"Oh." As she stepped back, Brenna's blush was evident, even in the low parking lot lighting. "I'll see you tomorrow."

Brenna fought against the melancholy which welled up as she watched Cassidy drive away. She quickly went to her own vehicle and followed Cassidy's car out of the lot, turning right when Cassidy turned left. She didn't see the vehicle which turned and followed her to the outskirts of her Pacific Palisades neighborhood, turning off its lights in the parking lot of a darkened corner store.

CHAPTER FIVE

THE NEXT morning Cassidy woke to the insistent ringing of the telephone. Glancing at the clock, she saw that there were still ten minutes before her alarm was supposed to sound. Rubbing her eyes, she glanced at the caller ID and quickly picked up. "Bren? Something wrong?"

"We're in the papers."

Brenna sounded flustered.

Cassidy sat up, brushing her hair from her face with one hand while adjusting the phone against her ear with the other. "What?"

"Entertainment wrap up. That reporter with the photos must've been with EW."

"He said he was with the Virginia Dispatch."

"That lying sack of—"

"Whoa!" Cassidy cut into Brenna's vehement outburst. "We don't know that. What exactly does the caption say?" She wished she could read over Brenna's shoulder; her own copy of the LA Times was still on her front stoop.

"'Not known for their close association, Brenna Lanigan and Cassidy Hyland were both seen at the opening night of Suede's tour stop at Jazzy Jay's. According to the wait staff, the couple shared a check, ducking out separately during the uproar surrounding the arrival of current hot-n-heavy couple, Jeff Masters and Gail Oberlain.'"

"That doesn't sound too bad. We might get a few questions on press day about it, but truthfully, we can say we're friends and we went out for a break after work."

She could not see Brenna's face, but envisioned the half smile at her response:

"Nothing more than friends?"

Cassidy chuckled. "We don't have to say any more."

"All right. I'll practice my straight face."

That made Cassidy laugh outright. "See you in an hour on set?"

"Are you bringing Ryan again today?"

"Yes."

"I'll see you in an hour then. Love you."

Cass heard the sound of a blown kiss through the phone and offered one in return.

"Love you, too."

"What's up with you and her?" Max asked Brenna as she responded yet again to a wave from the blonde passing through the soundstage.

She erased her expressive smile and turned back to Max. "What's up?"

"I know we haven't worked together in a while, but I seem to remember you being a little more focused at work."

Brenna considered for a moment and then decided it would be a good opportunity to share a little of how much better she felt about her life in general with a long-time, close friend. "Max, I'm a lot happier now than I have been on a set in a long while. The work's not any easier, but it's more fun."

"Like at the beginning?"

"Something like that, I guess. But now I know what I'm doing, so the shine's off of the business and more on the... relationships I am building."

Max's brow furrowed. "Isn't Time Trails about to finish up?"

"Yes. These are good people. Did you know..." She trailed off, thinking that she didn't want to mention Cassidy first. "Terry Brown has a playhouse in La Jolla. He's invited me to join up."

"Plays? So you're thinking of leaving the small screen behind?"

"I don't know about full time. I've also got a movie in England in April."

"A movie? You haven't been this busy since Thomas and James were very young."

Brenna noticed Cassidy standing at the edge of a temporary wall. "Why don't we go to lunch and we'll catch up?"

"Am I going to get a home-cooked meal?"

"Nope. Commissary." She smiled, stood, and waved Cassidy over. "Do you mind if Cass joins us?"

"I... well..." Max hesitated and then shrugged. "I guess not."

Brenna was already moving to catch Cassidy's attention. "Cass, will you join us for lunch?" she called.

Cassidy turned, and for a moment her features registered surprise. "All right."

Brenna watched Cassidy's appraisal of Max as he stood to his full height. He was an imposing man, dark hair and thick, and he was assessing Cassidy right back.

Brenna stepped between them, reasoning that she wasn't jealous, but unable to articulate why the mutual study bothered her. "Let's go."

Cassidy's gaze dropped to meet hers and the quick sure smile eased the knot which had started to form in her stomach. "How long have you known Bren?" Cassidy asked Max.

"More than twenty years," he replied. Brenna caught Cassidy's surprised glance at her. Brenna's unease started up again until Max gleefully added, "So, how many dirty secrets do you want to know?" She turned in time to catch his wink.

Cassidy laughed out loud, and Max offered them each an arm. While Cassidy took the left with alacrity, Brenna was slower to take his right. She caught Max's eye and lowered her brow. His smile did nothing to assure he understood her unspoken plea.

Max is a lovely man, Cassidy thought, as she laughed at another story of a prank he had played on Brenna when he took her out for her first legal drink.

"She wanted a Long Island Iced Tea, having heard they contained several varieties of alcohol. I had the waiter bring plain tea, sweetened. I kept telling her if the drink was properly made, a person shouldn't taste the alcohol, which is true. She drank three rounds before she realized she wasn't anywhere near tipsy."

He rubbed his shoulder. "Still hurts when it rains," he said with mild accusation, but a broad smile.

"When I finally had a real Long Island, I actually couldn't tell the difference, but I had watched the bartender make it."

Stifling a chortle, Max bit into the deli turkey sandwich. "In another life, Bren, you were definitely a teetotaler."

"I snuck alcohol at home a few times before I was legal," Cassidy admitted. Brenna's gaze held hers for a moment with a gentle smile. "My father would have killed me if he knew."

"So what's your choice these days?" Max asked.

"Wine, or Irish coffee," Cassidy answered.

"Did you introduce her?" Max asked Brenna.

"No," Brenna replied with a smile. "Just something we found we have in common."

Cassidy nodded. Catching sight of a clock, she realized abruptly she had better go. "Wow. I didn't realize how long we've been at this. This has been very interesting, but I think I'd better go see how Ryan's doing, and get back to Terry for rehearsals."

"I'm going to send Max to his hotel in another hour, and then I'll come and watch," Brenna said as Cassidy stood up.

"All right."

"Come on, Bren, not even a single home-cooked meal?" Max sighed.

"You should take Max home, Bren, and catch up. I'll see you tomorrow."

Brenna nodded, but Cassidy could tell that Brenna was bothered by their separation. Frustrated by her inability to communicate openly with Bren, Cassidy left quickly.

"Max, let's go." Brenna stood as soon as Cassidy was out of sight. "The sooner we get the blocking done, the sooner we can get going."

He hadn't risen. "Bren, are you upset that I'm here?"

"Of course not. It was a surprise, but it's good to see you."

"You forget how well I know you. What's wrong?"

Retrenching, Brenna realized she had to take Max home. "Max, it's all right. I'm sorry. It is good to see you, and I'll take you and Brady home to see James and Thomas tonight."

"You'd rather she came along, though."

Brenna glanced toward the door through which Cassidy had gone. "She's the newest member of the ensemble."

"Bren, I read entertainment news too. She was your 'date' the other day, right?"

He didn't make the motion, but she heard the quotation marks in his pause over the word.

She sighed. She couldn't lie to him. "Max, will you accept that I can't discuss this here?"

He stood. "Will we eventually?"

Brenna looked away again, thinking about how to talk to Max, her oldest friend, about her newest lover. He had been with her through some of the toughest times of her life, but she still had no idea what he would think. Eventually, she just didn't answer his question. "Let's go finish our blocking." She led the way back to the soundstage, where they spent the rest of the afternoon.

Will and Sean were working with Brady, Max's son, when Cassidy arrived back at the set. "How's it going?" she asked, as Sean stepped back from a position pretending to hold a weapon.

"The bad guys have been apprehended," he said with a broad smile.

"Need any help from me?" she asked, picking up her script from a nearby navy blue canvas chair.

Will thumped Brady on the back. "Well, 'Heatherly Junior' here seems to like the ladies."

She circled around, smiling as Brady's gaze followed her. "Divide and conquer?" she said pointedly to Sean.

Sean laughed. "All right. Let's stage this thing again."

The four separated to their marks for the beginning of the scene, and the walk-through began, allowing her to put real life from her mind for a little while as she inhabited Chris Hanssen's life and times.

CHAPTER SIX

BRENNA CLEARED the table while the four males sat around it talking. Thomas and James had both come home in time for the late dinner she'd put together for Max, Brady, and herself. She had sheepishly told Max that she wasn't sure what her sons were planning for the evening, but she had made enough for everyone in case they did show.

Thomas was in the process of explaining the FIRE program to Max, who listened and asked about a variety of conservation topics. Brady had fallen into conversation with James, who seemed more open with him than Brenna had seen her son with any of his peers in a while. They talked of art shows and something called a CAP project, which apparently had to do with public school art programs partnering with galleries.

Each time Brenna had injected a comment, her sons would nod, but seldom responded, so she had decided to vacate the room.

She looked at the phone several times as she passed between the dining table and the sink, and after washing the last dish, she retreated to her bedroom and called Cassidy.

The phone rang twice before Cassidy picked up.

"Hello?"

"It's Bren. How did the rest of your day go?"

"Quietly. Ryan and I got home about twenty-five minutes ago. I just put him in the tub. How's dinner with Max and Brady?"

"They're enjoying conversation with Thomas and James." Brenna settled on her bed and stretched out her legs. She reached for the neighboring pillow and hugged it against her lap. It was a poor substitute for Cassidy's head there, but a firm comfort as they talked.

Cassidy must have heard the resignation in her voice. "Is it going well?"

"Now that I'm out of the way, I think it is."

"Bren, I'm sorry."

Brenna exhaled. "I'm sorry, too. I don't know that Max senses anything wrong. He hasn't seen the boys since they were in grade school."

"Before Time Trails then. Max seems like a fun guy. Did you ever date?"

Brenna detected the undercurrent. "It... No, he's just known me a long time."

"Would he be surprised, do you think?"

"Surprised? About us? At least."

"So that's why you were off at lunch," Cassidy probed.

"No, I was off at lunch because he was giving you a very deliberate once-over. Didn't you notice?"

Cassidy's laugh was light through the phone, and it made Brenna smile. "I was too busy tamping down butterflies every time you looked at me."

"So, I'll see you at work tomorrow?"

"See you."

"Love you, Cass."

"Love you, too, Bren. Good night."

"Sleep well."

Brenna rejoined Max after Thomas and James turned in for the night, taking Brady with them to set up the game room space for sleeping. "Anything for you?" she asked Max, going into the refrigerator for fruit juice.

"A little straight talk," he replied.

He joined her in the kitchen, standing in the middle of the entry arch, leaning against the wall, arms crossed over his chest as he considered her.

"All right. What do you want to know?"

"Will you tell me about you and Cassidy?"

She leaned against the counter, crossing her arms over her chest in imitation. "It's a long story."

"Then why don't we go out to the pool deck? It's a nice night, and we can sit as long as we need to without any interruptions."

Brenna exhaled. He had never let her get away with anything for very long. "All right."

Out on the deck, she sat in the bench swing and he settled in next to her, leaned back and put his arm across the back of the bench. Brenna leaned forward, starting the swing rocking. She remembered sitting there with Kevin, just like that, when her own recognition of her irrevocably changed feelings had finally dawned on her.

"You haven't asked about Kevin," she said.

Something on the side table had drawn his attention but now he turned back. "The politician you married?"

"Yes. He... I... We're not going to be married much longer."

"So you're getting a divorce." He nodded at some silent thought. "Doesn't surprise me."

"It doesn't?"

"Brenna, I... When you are excited about something, you always share it with me and Mary." He looked down at his feet then back up at her. "I knew something was up when I read about your marriage in the paper instead of hearing about it from you."

"I'm sorry. I apologize."

"I'm not upset about that. I am upset that it took you a year to realize he was wrong for you."

"Just a little longer than that," she admitted. "It's not his fault, though."

"So he was a good guy?"

"Yes. I just wasn't suited to him."

"You're more suited..." He seemed hesitant to make the leap of logic.

"To Cassidy. She and I began an intimate relationship a little more than a month ago." She braced herself for any number of possible negative reactions.

"I don't think I've ever known you to have feelings for a woman before."

His observation wasn't particularly negative, just unexpected. She relaxed marginally. "I haven't."

"She's quite a bit younger, isn't she?"

"She's thirty-two. Her son Ryan is five."

"Does she have a history?"

Brenna knew what he meant. "A youthful episode. She says she never gave it much meaning."

"She seduced you?"

Brenna smiled. "No."

"So you..."

Brenna took some time to put her thoughts into a semblance of order, brushing her hands together and recalling the nuances of her emotions in Cassidy's presence, in her arms, when they made love. She slowly sat up.

"Max, I love who I am when I'm with her. She... I am totally me, and whatever I think, feel, do... She's... I don't know how, and I sometimes wonder why, after I treated her so badly, she can even stand to look at me. But when I do... her eyes never let me go. There's a connection I can't deny; I don't want to deny."

"I have known you through some of the highest ups and lowest downs of your life, Bren." He put a big gentle hand on her shoulder. "It didn't occur to me that a woman would ever capture your heart. You seemed to find pleasure rather freely with men."

Brenna considered her relationships and an even deeper recognition occurred. "Max, I never felt this level of completion with any of them. It's that ... my soul is happy, I think."

Max's lips curled into a smile. "You've never said that about any relationship." He squeezed her shoulder. "I guess I'm happy for you. Do you think it will last?"

Sighing, Brenna lifted one hand and ticked off potential barriers with the fingers of the other. "If we can get Thomas and James to relax, complete my divorce from Kevin, survive the press storm when our relationship inevitably becomes known. I also want to reconcile Cassidy and her parents..."

Max's chuckle filled the air as her voice trailed away. "Brenna, you are as bull-headed as they come. I have no doubt you will make it all happen."

"God, I hope you're right."

Impishly he said, "And when it's all over, I have no doubt you will be grand marshal at a Pride Parade somewhere."

Brenna's eyes widened, then she closed them and covered her face with her hands. "You think I'm going to grandstand."

"You never do anything halfway."

"Cassidy wants to keep us as quiet as possible for as long as possible. I don't want to unintentionally do something until she's comfortable."

"Then I'd say you should do your research discreetly." He looked at the small table again and picked up the dog eared copy of Curve magazine. "The store where you bought this, anyone could talk."

Brenna groaned and took the magazine from him. "I picked it up on my last trip to the grocer's."

Cassidy was just readying herself for bed when the phone rang. She didn't recognize the Caller ID, but it was a local call. With a sigh, she picked it up. "Hello?" The line was silent, then a click indicated the caller had hung up. Puzzled, she replaced the receiver and shook her head, lying back and closing her eyes.

CHAPTER SEVEN

CASSIDY WALKED onto the set in full costume and makeup and saw Bren and Max, with Brady between them, chuckling as they came in through the doors she knew led from the parking lot. "Hi," she called.

Max dipped his head in her direction and smiled. Brady blushed, clearly caught up by his hormones as he looked at her. Cassidy, however, was most pleased with Brenna's expression. A flush crept up her throat, and she swallowed several times. *Hormonal rushes aren't just for teenage boys,* Cassidy thought with a smile.

Finally Brenna summoned a "Hi." Max swatted Brenna playfully on the back of the head and she yelped, "Hey!"

Brady ducked past Cassidy and she saw him stop to chat with Sean and Chelle.

Cassidy approached Brenna and Max, and just caught the tail end of what Max was whispering.

"...a hormonal teen."

"Who? Brady? Don't worry; I'm used to it," Cassidy said with a chuckle.

"No," Max replied. "Bren here had her tongue practically on the floor. If the two of you want to keep it under the gossips' radar, you'd better be more circumspect."

Cassidy's humor instantly changed into concern. "Bren?"

"We had a long talk last night."

"Brady seems okay with it," Cassidy said with a puzzled frown.

"He wasn't there. Max waited to browbeat me until after the boys were in their rooms for the night."

"Oh." Cassidy lifted her gaze back to Max. "She seemed to think you might be surprised."

"In this business? When every fifth person I've worked with is gay? Please." He turned away from her and abruptly stopped speaking. Cassidy turned around to find Jackie Gabby, the episode's second unit assistant director.

The young woman tapped her clipboard with the side of her pen. "Mr. Brightman, we need you over at Set C for the battle baton choreography."

"Right." Max excused himself.

Jackie paused before turning away. "Ms. Lanigan?"

"I'll be right there, Jackie."

"Yes, ma'am."

Cassidy felt Brenna brush against her as she moved, presumably to watch Jackie walk away. "Another day apart," Cassidy replied.

"Let's try a slightly different outing tonight."

"What?"

"Let's take everyone to Terry's playhouse."

"So that's why he's not here today."

"No, it's what he's doing when he's not here." Brenna smiled and Cassidy shivered, from that, and the sensation of Brenna's fingertips across the back of her own hand. "I'm done here at four. The play starts at eight."

"You want to take Max, Brady, Ryan, Thomas, and James to a play out of town?"

"James and Thomas won't come. Ryan will enjoy it, and Max will be a less annoying cover than a publicist, so I can spend some time with you. And," she nodded, "yes, it's a bonus that it's out of town."

Cassidy laughed. How could she refuse? "All right. And maybe if we can get everyone used to seeing us together, you can accompany me to the opening of Vampyra."

Brenna shrugged. "How long have we got?"

"Opening is in three weeks."

"A vampire movie on Valentine's Day?" Brenna's quick distasteful twist of her lips made Cassidy laugh again. "I don't know about that."

"Would you rather we go to a chick flick romance?"

Brenna's expression turned to one of consideration and Cassidy ended the conversation before Brenna could say something which might be overheard. "Better get to your set."

"All right. I'll see you later."

Cassidy walked toward her own set call as Brenna walked in the opposite direction.

As soon as she had shut the door to her trailer, Cassidy flopped onto her couch. With a groan, she pulled off her shoes and lifted her feet in the air over her head, grasping one in each hand to massage them. When her cell phone rang, she considered ignoring it, but then thought maybe it was Karen Grinaldi with something about Ryan. She quickly rolled to her side and grabbed the phone from the desk. "Hello?"

She heard a click as the line closed. Shutting her phone, she waited a few seconds to see if the voice mail chime sounded. When it didn't, she looked at the caller ID. *Mitch? What is he doing calling?*

She wondered if she should call him right back. Part of her quickly said no; another part was curious about what he might feel the need to say to her; and another part was wary. In the end, she decided she didn't need the aggravation and did not return his call.

After work, the group of playgoers piled into Brenna's Mountaineer. With Brenna following directions as Cassidy read them, Los Angeles was soon left behind. The winding route put them on a two-lane road which turned around a mountain and entered foothills just off the Pacific Coast Highway. Vineyards, some old and clearly no longer cultivated, and others with rangy young vines, closely bordered the roadway on either side.

The road was relatively free of other cars. However, as they rounded a turn, a sports car behind them gunned its engine and passed, despite the double yellow lane lines.

Brenna jerked the wheel as the sports car cut back into the lane far too closely, only to speed away before she could get a good look at the vehicle in the headlights of the Mountaineer. She flashed her brights angrily at him, and pulled off onto the very narrow shoulder.

Taking a deep breath, she looked at each of the other occupants. "Everyone all right?"

There was a chorus of "fine" and "yes", while "what the hell was that?" came from Max. Brenna shot him a dirty look for using that language in front of Ryan.

Cautiously, Brenna pulled back onto the road and continued. Finally the sign for the playhouse diverted them onto a dirt road which they bumped over, much to Ryan's laughing delight but to the sorrow of everyone else's tailbones.

The art crowd seemed to be the only type of patron present. *At least no one looks to be a reporter,* Cassidy thought as she ruefully rubbed a sore shoulder from the jostling she had taken in the SUV.

Brenna approached, leading Ryan. "Sorry about the ride."

"No. It wasn't your driving. What was wrong with that idiot?"

"I have no idea. He seemed in a rather pointless hurry." Brenna looked around and grasped Cassidy's hand. "I'm glad we're here, though. I like the place."

"Does Terry know we're coming?"

"No. I purposely didn't tell him. I didn't want to draw attention to us."

"He'll see us, though."

"Yeah, and he'll figure out we want to be quiet about this."

Cassidy nodded. "Shall we go find our seats?"

Brenna took hold of Ryan's hand and turned around. "Max, get lost, will ya?"

"What? Who me? Such a big, lovable guy?" He smiled, lifted his arms and shoulders in a shrug and ambled off, throwing one arm around his son's shoulder.

Cassidy put her arm around Brenna's waist and laughed. "I think I really, really like Max," she said.

"We've been friends a long time."

"What would you have done if he hadn't been accepting of our relationship?" Cassidy asked.

Brenna looked momentarily upset at the prospect. "I was worried about it." She smiled. "But it didn't happen."

Cassidy remembered her own thoughts after the holiday gala. "I keep waiting for the other shoe to drop."

Brenna, who was leading the way through to the audience area, paused. "What?"

"I mean, we've had small, easily explainable mentions in the paper; your sons have a problem with it, but mostly because they just don't want to 'see' it. My parents have expressed their disapproval. You've had a long time friend not really blink. All pretty benign reactions. I can't help feeling that we're living on borrowed time."

Brenna slipped her free arm around Cassidy's back. "Let's just enjoy the show."

Cassidy admittedly felt better because of the cozy squeeze.

"All right."

After the play, Terry Brown walked up to them through the mingling theatergoers. "I thought I saw you two. Glad you could make it." He looked at Ryan clinging tiredly to Brenna's legs. "Did you bring the whole crowd?"

"Mine don't want to be seen in public with me right now," Brenna admitted. She was casually brushing her fingers through Ryan's hair as she sipped on a bottled water which Cassidy had purchased from the snack table.

"So it's just the three of you?"

When Terry's eyes fell on Cassidy, she shrugged. "We came out with Brenna's friends."

"Max is being a good friend?"

"Yes," Brenna acknowledged.

"Good." He grasped Cassidy's hand. "I'd really like you to think about coming here after Time Trails finishes."

"It's become a lot more complicated than when you asked me five months ago, Terry."

He laughed. "So, maybe I can get two for the price of one?"

Brenna nodded slowly. "It would be a good way to keep roots here when I have to go to England."

"As long as we haven't been driven underground by the press before then," Cassidy said.

Terry was confused. "What?"

"Cass thinks the other shoe's going to drop soon."

Surprisingly, Terry was on Cassidy's side. "You don't think so?" he asked Brenna.

"The only people whose opinions matter to me have already expressed their feelings. We'll work it out. That will be it."

Terry looked at Cassidy. "You don't see it that way?"

Cassidy thought there was more than a little wishful thinking in Brenna's assertion. "Terry, I..." She didn't want to argue with Brenna in front of Terry, and she couldn't really put her finger on why it all felt just too tenuous to believe. She gave a half-hearted shrug but fell silent. Brenna continued rubbing Ryan's hair.

"So, you want to hang out here for a while?" Terry asked. "I can promise there's no media. We're practically invisible to them."

Cassidy commiserated. "I'm sorry to hear that. It was an excellent play." Terry shrugged. "We probably shouldn't stay any longer tonight, either." She looked down as Ryan shifted to her legs from Brenna's, rubbing his face against her pant leg. "I think we should get Ryan home to bed." Brenna started to crouch to collect Ryan, but Cassidy scooped him up first. "It's all right, I've got him."

"Cass?"

"Good night, Terry."

"Good night, Cass, Bren."

Brenna followed Cassidy to the entry doors. "Hold on. We've got to get Max and Brady."

Shaking her head, Cassidy stopped walking. "I'm sorry."

"Are you mad at me?"

What Cassidy felt wasn't anger. "No. I'm... I thought we'd be more of the same mind about keeping things quiet, I guess."

"So you're disappointed in me?"

Whether they saw eye to eye or not, Brenna clearly didn't want to upset Cassidy. "I'm as tired as Ryan," Cassidy admitted. "Maybe I'm being just overly emotional."

"Good thing I'm driving, then. I remember worrying over you in the parking lot after you had that argument with Cameron."

"You did?" Cassidy watched as Brenna turned aside, waving at the air. She looked to see that Brenna had spotted Max. The man tapped his son on the shoulder and they joined the two women at the door.

"Going home?"

"Ryan's tired," Brenna said dispiritedly.

Max gave her an understanding smile. "All right. Let's go."

Brenna took Max and Brady by their hotel first. Once they were alone in the car with Ryan asleep in the back, Brenna asked, "So..." She hesitated. "My place is closer."

Cassidy looked over the seat to Ryan asleep in the back. "Bren, I..."

"No, I'm sorry I upset you. Please let me make it up to you?"

Cassidy asked, "What about Thomas and James?"

"It's nearly midnight. They're home, and asleep."

"Are you sure?"

"Cass, they aren't going to get used to us spending time together if we let them keep us apart." She reached across the center console and squeezed Cassidy's thigh.

"But I don't have a change of clothes for tomorrow."

"I seem to remember a sweatshirt in your size."

Out of objections, Cassidy reluctantly acquiesced. "All right. But I'll have to change as soon as we get to the set."

Brenna made the turn onto the highway headed south. "Done."

The house lights were off when they arrived. Brenna unlocked the door, flipping the switch for the foyer as she stepped back and let Cassidy enter ahead of her, carrying Ryan. "Come on, we'll tuck him into the guest bed and then get some sleep ourselves," she whispered.

Leaving the foyer light on to illuminate their way down the corridor, Brenna leaned in to flip on the light in game room. "No, leave it off," Cassidy whispered. "It'll be easier to keep Ryan asleep."

Navigating by the light of a nightlight in the wall, Brenna flipped open the futon and put on sheets from the storage drawer beneath. She fetched a blanket from a closet. Turning back, she saw Cassidy efficiently stripping her son to his underwear. His eyes were closed and he moved like a rag doll, obviously asleep on his feet. Soon Cassidy had tucked him between the sheets and stepped back. Brenna arranged the blanket over him. Standing in the doorway, she held Cassidy as they watched Ryan breathing easily.

Cassidy's head drifted against Brenna's. "Come on, time for you," Brenna said, guiding the woman out of the room and the few feet to her bedroom.

After closing the door, they turned on a bedside lamp. Cassidy automatically started to strip, and Brenna just watched her for a moment, marveling at her beauty. She was far too tired, and they had to get up far too early for Brenna to do anything about her arousal, but she loved watching the shadows and light flowing across Cassidy's curves as she moved.

She went to her closet to look for something for Cassidy to wear, inhaling sharply as a naked Cassidy pressed up against her back. "We don't need anything," Cassidy said.

"I was just thinking we don't have time for me to ravish you," Brenna said, turning around. She let Cassidy unbutton and remove her blouse.

"So, how about I ravish you?" Cassidy's whisper trailed off and her hot breath brushed Brenna's skin as it was uncovered by Cassidy removing the rest of her clothing.

Brenna stepped out of her shoes and pants as Cassidy instructed.

"I'd like that."

"I know."

Their body heat alone was enough to keep them warm as they slid between the sheets together, naked. Brenna stroked every bit of skin she could reach as they entangled themselves, feet over ankles, knees between thighs, bellies and breasts pressed together.

Cassidy's hands stroked up and down Brenna's back until she cupped Brenna's buttocks, pulling her up slightly.

"Mmm, good." Cassidy's murmur brushed Brenna's temple with warm breath. Her movements slowed, then stopped.

Brenna drew her head back and chuckled softly, brushing Cassidy's hair from her cheeks. "Sweet dreams." She kissed Cassidy's breastbone and snuggled back into her lover's arms, joining her in sleep.

CHAPTER EIGHT

THE NEXT morning, leaving Cassidy warmly wrapped in her sheets, Brenna pulled on a robe and stepped out of her bedroom. She checked on Ryan, who was still sleeping soundly.

Coming out of the game room, she met Thomas walking out of his room, a radio still playing inside. "Good morning," she said.

"Morning," he replied. "When did you get in last night?"

"Around midnight."

He looked at the door to the game room. "Ryan's here," he guessed.

"Yes."

"So she's sleeping in your room?"

"Of course." She put her hand out. "Come on, Thomas, please. Cassidy is important to me."

"I don't want to deal with this right now."

"When?" she demanded.

"Mom, why don't you understand that I can't?"

"Because you aren't talking to me," she replied with exasperation. "You and James—"

"What have I done now?" James appeared at his door, rubbing his hand over his head and face sleepily.

Her second son's appearance forestalled Brenna's response to his question. "What are you doing sleeping in your clothes?"

He looked down at himself. "I, uh, fell asleep as soon as I got home."

"What time was that?" She saw him cast a look at Thomas. "What's going on?"

"Come on." Thomas shoved James down the hall in front of him. "We'll make our own breakfast, Mom. You'd better get ready for the set. See you around."

Brenna grasped his shoulder. "Stop. What's going on? What time did you get home last night?"

"About eleven-thirty," Thomas answered. James said nothing.

"James?"

"Eleven-thirty."

She had the distinct impression he was lying. "I told you we were going out to the playhouse. Knowing I wouldn't be home, did you go somewhere, as well?"

It was Thomas who answered. "We made it in before curfew."

"That wasn't what I asked." She pointedly directed her gaze. "James?"

"I hung out with some friends."

Cassidy appeared in her bedroom doorway, and Brenna watched both Thomas and James eye the blond woman then quickly push past.

"Gotta go."

Brenna leaned against the door jamb. "Well, I guess I wasn't going to get any more anyway."

"Problem?"

"I think Thomas and, or James broke curfew last night," Brenna said, "but I don't have any proof."

"And my appearance ended the interrogation. I'm sorry."

"Don't be. Come on. We'll get dressed. Maybe I can try again over breakfast."

"When do you have to report to the set?" Cassidy asked, stroking Brenna's arm as she embraced her on her trailer sofa. They had dropped Ryan at the childcare trailer and retreated here for some private time.

Looking at the small digital clock on Cassidy's desk, Brenna settled a hand atop Cassidy's, which was lying across her stomach. "Not until eight."

"We have a whole hour together?" Cassidy asked. "No demands, no kids, no colleagues, no reporters?" She sighed happily and bent to inhale the scent of Brenna's hair. "Alone at last."

Brenna kissed their laced fingers. "I love spending quiet time with you," she said. "It's amazing."

Cassidy's hand slipped away from Brenna's arm and down her side to her hip, stroking suggestively close to Brenna's crotch. "And here I was thinking we were in the same bed this morning and I completely missed out on some serious groping because someone had to get up and see why her sons missed curfew."

Laughing, Brenna turned slightly and Cassidy eagerly kissed the offered lips. "Mmmmm....oh," Brenna murmured. "So you really want to make love now?"

"I never thought I'd be randy enough to do something like this, but I can't imagine anyone else I'd rather be the first I do it with. I have been wanting to get into your pants for hours," Cassidy's words sounded dramatic but they were a true expression of her desire, nearly constant, for her lover.

"Ah, I get to be your first." Brenna chuckled, lifting herself up over Cassidy and straddling her thighs. Cassidy rested her hands against Brenna's hips, holding her easily as they fanned each other's arousal with deep, long kisses, tasting lips and tongues. Between kisses, they bared each other's skin and indulged in heated exploration.

Cassidy lay nude but warm under a blanket, and dazedly happy on the couch in her trailer. Brenna had just left to go to the set for her call. Cassidy's call wasn't until later, and they decided she should stay and relax until she was officially due on the set.

Initially there to change from the borrowed clothes to the spare things she kept in her trailer, Cassidy had finished what she had barely started the night before. She curled her knuckles against her lips, still able to smell Brenna's scent on them.

The next time she saw Brenna, they would both have to be in character, but the interlude had been sustaining, and thoroughly fulfilling.

She was surprised at their creativity. The trailer couch was narrow. It should have been impossible to pleasure each other, but they had found a way. Shared oral sex had been the most intoxicating experience. They were both so new to their intimacy, it was as much an exploration of the tastes as it was of touches that would please. Even as Brenna requested a particular touch, she ushered Cassidy toward climax as well. Brenna's way of making love had Cassidy feeling, for the first time, the difference between being someone's prize and being a treasure.

She could still feel Brenna's breath, hands, and tongue moving over her skin. As she had shuddered in release, crying out that she was falling apart, Brenna's strong, soft embrace held Cassidy together, and the rich husky voice whispered over and over again how much she was cherished, showing her a mutual lovemaking unlike the possessive, forceful way every man had ever touched her.

Rubbing her thigh where Brenna had nipped her when she orgasmed, Cassidy recalled experiencing the moment when Brenna let herself go, and her orgasm washed over Cassidy's fingers while her nails pricked into Cassidy's legs and her mouth closed over Cassidy's thigh to muffle the sounds of her ecstasy. In the aftermath ensconced on the sofa, wine-red lips soothed over the faint marks, but Cassidy relished their presence. The tenderness of her breasts and the wetness renewing itself between her thighs just at the thought of Brenna's touch felt wonderful.

Finally sitting up and going to the bathroom to clean up, Cassidy delighted in the flavors on her lips as she licked them. Combing her fingers through her hair to smooth it, she studied herself in the mirror with bemusement. A satisfaction that had been too long missing curled her lips; color accentuated her cheeks; and barely submerged passion still had her pupils wide. She lifted her fingers to her nose, again inhaling the scent of Brenna's sweat and sex.

She sighed. She wouldn't see Brenna again until after she had lunch with Ryan and reported to the set for a short filming session.

The phone rang. She checked the Caller ID and recognized it as an on-set number. It had to be Brenna calling from a set phone. They'd had such a hard time parting. Invitingly, she answered, "Hello."

"Love that whisper of want there, Cass."

Her blood instantly turned to ice. "Mitch?" Why is he calling now? "What do you want?"

"Seems you're a mighty popular person. Made the news lately."

"What do you want?"

"Been interesting reading. Seems you're done with that writer fellow. Moved on to someone else."

"I've made some friends in the cast," she replied.

"Your friend," he said snidely, "what's her name? Brenna Lanigan, right?"

"The papers are wrong, Mitch. She's just a friend."

"You've been staying at her house. You weren't home the other night. She's a lesbian. I won't have my son raised by lesbians."

She wasn't going to get into a discussion with Mitch. He didn't need to know Brenna's re-orientation was a new thing. "The custody has already been decided, Mitch. That won't change. This is California."

"I came here to talk to you about that."

"You're here at the studio?" she said. "Come by the house later."

"I don't want to wait. I went by Gwen and Lou's place and they said you started bringing Ryan here with you, so I thought I'd come for a visit."

"It's not your visitation time. You don't have that choice." Cassidy's knees quivered, but she was proud of herself.

"Damn you've gotten pushy. Certainly not the good girl I trained you up to be. Why don't you come to where I am with Ryan, and I'll tell you all about it before I take him away from all the fancy Hollywood queers."

Flabbergasted at his words and his cool threats, her breath rasped harshly through the phone. "You are not taking Ryan anywhere."

"Oh, but I've already got Ryan. How about we pick you up and have a nice family lunch?"

"You can't have Ryan," she insisted, panic chasing the calm from her voice. "I'll call the cops, Mitch. That's kidnapping."

"Why don't you come and say goodbye? We'll be leaving in a few minutes."

"Don't move!" Cassidy shouted into the phone and slammed it down on its cradle, shaking and angry. *God, he's got Ryan. No! No.* She tried to think. *He has to be bluffing. Ryan is safe with Mrs. Grinaldi.* She picked up the phone and dialed the extension in the tutor's trailer. It rang three times then a fourth without an answer. Her heart raced when the number of rings reached ten. *Oh God!* She burst out of her trailer and hurried toward trailer 14.

CHAPTER NINE

MITCH HYLAND grinned as he hung up at the pay phone just outside of the Time Trails soundstage. *You are a genius, my man*, he congratulated himself as he turned around and saw his ex-wife exit one of the trailers. Run scared, sweetheart. It'll all be over soon. With care for the distance between them and remaining out of sight, he followed Cassidy, knowing full well that she would go directly to wherever she had Ryan, to assure herself of his safety. Then, and only then would she draw others into a search for him.

He had planned on that.

He had been surprised to hear the news about Cassidy's new choice in lovers, but then again, she had always been too adventurous for her own good. It had attracted him at first, and after years of molding her, he had thought her completely his, bound to him by their son.

She stupidly clung to her acting, though, first taking up a guest role on some limited series. He should have put a stop to that. However, she had sweetly made love to him, just as he liked, and addled his brain. From there, these Time Trails people had seen her and enticed her away from him. If I had only followed her here in the beginning. When she told him about the open-ended offer they'd made, he had punished her for even considering leaving their son.

Mitch had underestimated the writer. He frowned, trying to recall the name. Palassis. He wondered briefly if the man was around somewhere. They certainly had a score to settle for taking his family from him.

Mitch considered the woman he had seen on the set. Brenna Lanigan. That lowly, tiny woman now stood in his way too. With her lesbian seduction of his wife, she had disrupted his plans to pull Cassidy back when the series was over and she was out of work and desperately in need of protection again.

Getting on the lot had been surprisingly easy. He had thought the restraining order Palassis had taken out might still be in effect; he had even planned for that contingency. However, the guards had let him pass without even noting his name. Not surprising, considering the hundreds of people they must check through every day.

The tour forming up had readily taken him in, and the group passed through many areas of the lot. When he saw the first sign for the Time Trails soundstages, he waited, then broke from the group, wending his way through unfamiliar equipment and corridors. What a mess, he had thought derisively. His wife deserved to not work in such squalor.

Ahead, on the path, Cassidy reappeared from a small trailer. Since no one had come outside with her, he suspected where she had led him. Now that she had brought him to Ryan, it was time for him to make his move, and he stepped out from the bushes, whistling Dixie.

"Mitch!"

"Hi, sweetheart," he drawled, hands tucked in his pockets, presenting the non-threatening posture that so often made her drop her guard. He kept his eyes on her hands, watching the cell phone attached to her hip.

"Stay back!" She circled just out of reach of an easy lunge.

Come on, baby. Trust me like I know you can. Her body moved fluidly, despite the fear he could see widening her eyes.

"Where's Ryan?" Cassidy growled.

Ryan wasn't in the trailer? Interesting. He could use that information to his advantage. "In the car. I came back to get you. Let's 'do lunch'. Isn't that how these Hollywood types say it?"

She shook her head. "No!"

Her rejection of his invitation infuriated him.

"Really?" He lunged, catching her off-guard with a feint and able to get around behind her, grabbing both shoulders and pulling them tightly toward her back. "You want to see Ryan again, you'll cooperate."

He started dragging her toward the trailer nearby, but she screamed and surprised him by tripping him up. As she wrenched herself from his grasp, he stumbled as he tried to regain his footing.

"Bitch!"

"I'm not going!" she screamed, and she surprised him with a fist into his throat.

He grabbed her arm, but it slipped until he only had her wrist. He heard it crack as he twisted and wrenched hard. Her face turned white and she screamed in pain.

Pulling the wrist again he twisted harder. The agonized sound she made filled him with pleasure. "Now are you going to come quietly? I have to save you from the queers. You know I do," he cajoled.

With a scream, she yanked herself free. As he reached for her again, she ducked away but he tackled her and they fell against the paved walk with a thud. She grunted and rolled under him. Terror filled her eyes as he settled his weight on top of her.

"Let's go," he ordered brusquely, standing up and grabbing her injured wrist. He didn't care if it was separated or broken; he dragged her up the steps and into the trailer.

During a break in the filming with Max, Brenna looked over and saw Mrs. Grinaldi leading Ryan through the soundstages. Filled with an uneasy flash of concern, she asked, "What is it?"

"When Ms. Hyland didn't come to pick up Ryan for lunch, I thought she must be here with you."

"She isn't," Brenna offered, carefully keeping the alarm from her voice. Cassidy wouldn't leave the set without Ryan, her little voice told her emphatically. And she would feel terribly guilty if their tryst had made Cassidy miss lunch with her son. Brenna crouched at the edge of the soundstage and spoke to Ryan. "Why don't we go and see if your mom fell asleep in her trailer?"

"Okay."

Coming up behind Max, Will noted the looks of concern. "Something up?"

"Cassidy didn't pick up Ryan for lunch."

Will pursed his lips. "I saw Cameron earlier. Do you think they got into an argument?"

"Maybe." Brenna stood up. "I'm going to go looking for her."

"I'll be right behind you," Will said. "Just let me tell the director where we're going."

"Right." Brenna grasped Ryan's hand and strode ahead of Max and Karen toward the row of trailers.

Stumbling as her ex-husband pushed her, Cassidy tried to think past the pain radiating through her fingers and up into her left elbow. In an odd sort of disassociation, she tried to flex her wrist, able to ignore Mitch as the agony became her focus.

"Fucking bitch! Ignore me? Damn you!"

The epithet-filled outburst was accompanied by a backhand knocking Cassidy's head up and aside. The blow made her jaw ache and her ear ring so badly she forgot about her wrist as she stumbled again, this time into a low desk and child-sized chair.

Grabbing the chair as she fell, Cassidy thrust it into Mitch's body when he came after her. With a quick inhalation, she used her undamaged arm to haul herself a few feet away before trying to get her legs under her and stand.

"Where did all this fight come from?" he asked, tossing the chair against the wall. "Do you have any idea how mad this makes me?"

Cassidy lurched against a bookcase, unable to silence the agonized scream which bubbled up when her wrist struck the wood. "Mitch, leave me alone. You don't want to do this!"

"What the hell do you know about what I want?" He smashed his body into hers. The force of his forearm against her chest knocked the wind from her lungs and she gagged and sagged, his weight the only thing holding her up as she fought for breath.

"You are mine! Ryan is mine!" He punctuated each pronouncement with his fists.

Gasping as she pushed, trying to force some space between them, she yelled at him, "Ryan will hate you!" As he pressed forward, she threw herself to the side and slammed her head into his face.

"My boy loves me."

"I'll tell him everything!"

Heedless of the chairs, Mitch lunged through the debris, eyes wild. "The hell you will!"

Oops, wrong thing to say. She got behind the tutor's large desk, circling it as he stalked around the other side.

"Always hiding behind something, or someone, aren't you?" he sneered at her. "Do you hide behind your lesbian friend?"

"No!" Cassidy did not want to let him get on the subject of Brenna. She could take him belittling her, even his physical attacks, but if he turned his venom on Brenna, Cassidy was not certain she wouldn't end up dead trying to make him regret the words. "She has nothing to do with this! Ryan's custody is between you and me!"

"I told you I will not have a lesbian raising my son."

He turned his back, as if to make for the door.

His feint drew her out. Cassidy threw herself after him and caught his lower torso, and they went down in a tangle. His hands wrapped around her head and she struggled to remain conscious as he slammed it against the floor.

Brenna! She conjured the woman in her mind's eye. Soft auburn hair curling around smooth tan features flushed with love, mouth whispering 'I love you', blue eyes sparkling with desire. It kept the mental cobwebs at bay as she fought to get free.

"Wait here, Ryan." Brenna let go of his hand and hurried up the steps to Cassidy's trailer door. Rapping twice, she called inside, "Cassidy, it's Brenna." She pressed her ear to the surface, listening for sound inside though she realized her heart was racing almost too hard to hear anything. She stepped back and knocked harder. "Cass!"

Sweeping the assembled group below with her gaze, she caught Will's eye. He frowned and nodded, and Brenna yanked open the door.

The lights inside were off. She reached for the switch and illuminated the space. It was tidy. She looked into the open door of the bathroom at the back. "Cass?"

She laid a worried hand against the sofa cushion. It was cool to the touch. Cassidy had not been there for some time. Where are you?

She hurriedly exited the trailer, reporting, "She's not here."

Terry turned to Mrs. Grinaldi. "Maybe she went to pick up Ryan and just missed you?"

"That's possible," the tutor considered, but no one felt reassured.

"Let's go," Brenna ordered briskly.

Terry pulled out his cell phone as they walked hurriedly along the path. "What's Cassidy's cell number?" he asked.

Brenna quickly gave it without slowing her pace. "What's up?"

"Just thought I'd try the line. Pinnacle's a big place."

"What if she's not wearing her phone?" Brenna asked worriedly.

"You didn't see it in her trailer, did you?" Brenna shook her head. "Then let's just try it." Terry pressed the 'send' button and put the device to his ear. "It's ringing."

Chapter Ten

CASSIDY'S HEAD felt like lead balls were rolling around inside. When she swallowed, she tasted blood in her mouth and smelled the coppery stuff filling her nose. Pinned under two fallen toy shelves, she could not recall anything about the last few minutes. Frantically she looked around the devastated classroom.

Agony ripped through her and she retched, trying to turn over. One toy shelf moved, freeing her left leg. Automatically she said, "Thank you."

"Much better." Mitch scowled and yanked her to her feet.

His face was bruised around the nose. She guessed she had managed to break his nose with one of her attempts at head-butting him.

"Now let's talk custody."

The pain in her chest was excruciating. Breathing shallowly, she shook her head. "You will never get Ryan!" She shook her head again, groaning at the sensation of her brain sloshing around in her skull. "Ever!"

A dull ringing sounded in her ears. *The cell phone!* She had forgotten she was wearing it.

She fumbled the tiny phone from her hip, lost it, and watched it slide across the floor, making a scraping sound against the linoleum. Diving after it, she took her eyes from Mitch.

Something struck her leg and she turned to see Mitch wielding a short, dark blue baseball bat.

"He's mine!" he snarled.

The solid wooden bat aimed for her chest.

Raising her arms defensively, she felt the bat land against her forearms instead. Winding up again, Mitch swung for her head. She ducked but felt the swoosh of air as the weapon passed over her. Inhaling sharply, she dove after the electronic lifeline.

Mitch grabbed her leg and her body slammed into the floor, breaths wheezing agonizingly from her lungs. The phone continued to ring. One chance. *God, help me.* Her knee twisted and gave a sickening pop as she lunged from Mitch's unrelenting grasp. With her other foot, she kicked him in the head. Her hand wrapped around the cell phone.

Just as she pressed the 'talk' button, Mitch brought the bat down against her hand, crushing it and the phone. Bits of metal and plastic drove into her tightened fingers and she screamed.

He hauled her up and threw her against the wall. "Who was that?"

Clawing at his face, she screamed, "I don't know!" Her fingers left a red trail across his cheek.

"You better hope they don't look for you." He raised his fist. "Especially your lesbian lover. All she'll find is a dead body!"

A fever ripped through Cassidy. The cell phone had been her last chance at summoning help. She was on her own, alone, the only thing standing between her manic ex-husband and Ryan. *It's him or me,* she realized. Watching as he edged toward her, Cassidy propelled herself off of the wall and had a momentary glimpse of Mitch's wide eyes before she landed against him. The surprise took him down more than her weight. She clawed at his face as his flailing arms tried to block her way.

He pushed at her. She pushed back. Her fingers dug into his cheeks and she heard his howl with feral satisfaction. The only way she was going to get out of this was if he died first. It was up to her to save Ryan. She forced her hands into fists and smashed them into his face. His head snapped up and back, and his skull made a loud crack against the floor. She howled in animalistic delight as her prey struggled. She drove her fists again and again into his face, his arms, his upper body, landing punches solidly. The bones under her fingers crackled like paper. She snarled as Mitch reared up.

"What the—"

Clutching his face with her fingers clawlike, she felt the skin shred. She plowed her knee into his groin. As he hunched over, she bashed her fists to the back of his head and brought her knee up against his face.

I will kill you! You will die! Her vision became red; her breathing suddenly seemed easier. Mitch fell to his knees before her. When she kicked him in the head, he dropped to the floor face first.

She followed him to the ground, all fists and claws. *Die!*

"Bitch!"

His fist closed over her jaw. As she wrenched herself away, she distantly she heard the bones separate.

Terry frowned. "I had a connection, then the line went dead," he puzzled.

Brenna was still trying to figure out what he meant when there was a thud against a wall somewhere close by, then another, followed by a scream of such raging volume and pitch that it sounded like an animal. Brenna leaped into action.

"The childcare trailer!" Releasing Ryan's hand, she ordered, "Stay!" and was up the stairs to the trailer before anyone else could take another breath.

Behind her she heard Terry yell, "Call 911!" She looked back to see him and Chapman bounding up the steps behind her. There was no guessing exactly what they would find, but Brenna feared Cassidy was in real trouble.

Will reached the door Brenna had flung wide. "Bren!"

Brenna ran headlong toward a hulking man wielding a baseball bat while Cassidy cowered on the floor, her blond hair streaked with dark patches and matted with fresh blood. Her face was a mass of black and blue, and blood. *So much blood!* With surprising strength, Cassidy shoved a desk at her attacker.

The man wasn't Cameron. Blond and muscular, there was something in the shape of his face that made Brenna think of Ryan. It had to be Cassidy's ex-husband.

She yelled, "Mitch Hyland!" and green eyes swung toward her, gashes bleeding sluggishly in his cheeks and forehead.

The bat in his hands continued its downward path toward Cassidy's head, and Brenna lunged to intercept his attack. She hit Mitch's legs with the full force of her lunging body, striking sideways at his knees. Mitch, the bat, and Brenna all hit the floor inches from Cassidy's head.

"Run!" Brenna encouraged as she wrestled for possession of the bat. Her hands met Cassidy's, and she saw a wild, sightless glaze in her lover's eyes, one of which was nearly swollen shut. Cassidy's lips drew back, her jaw opened, and Brenna only just got out of the way as the woman's teeth closed on Mitch's forearm.

Startled, Mitch reared up, and Brenna had her chance. Her hands closed around the bat and she looked down wild-eyed, seeing Mitch as if in the distance beneath her. She tried to swing the bat but caught a table's edge instead, jarring the muscles and bones in her shoulders, neck, and back.

Mitch lurched up and threw her off.

"The Security team is here."

The sound behind Brenna was almost unintelligible. Immediately on her feet, she advanced on Mitch, still carrying the bat, ignoring the pain shooting down her back. Mitch's attention was on her. Hopefully Cassidy could catch her breath and somehow move away.

Mitch moved to her left; Brenna followed, guarding Cassidy. People swarmed around her to the right and left. Mitch looked away from her, eyeing the newcomers with panic. Her lips drew back in a snarl as she spied the bleeding bite mark Cassidy had inflicted on his arm.

Mitch lunged for Brenna, but the security guards, wielding nightsticks, wrestled him into submission between them.

She heard the door open again and spun around to assess a new attack. Instantly she identified the tutor Grinaldi. "No! Stay with Ryan!"

Mitch took advantage of the men's slackened holds and burst free. His momentum took him at top speed toward Cassidy, who was just beginning to rise shakily to her feet.

"Cass!" Brenna yelled, rushing forward.

Mitch's head and shoulders collided with Cassidy's chest. Everyone in the room heard the sickening crunch of ribs breaking. Cassidy's screams went silent. She coughed up an alarming amount of blood as she sank to the floor, head lolling.

Brenna tried to go over Mitch to reach Cassidy, but his forearm slammed against her head, bringing her down and blinding her for a terrifying instant. She scrambled on the floor, blinking to clear her vision. Her fingers miraculously closed around the bat, her nails biting into the wood.

Through narrowing vision, Brenna saw Mitch struggling between the two security guards who were pulling him away. Mitch's head snapped back as one of the men landed an upper cut. Brenna growled and launched herself at Mitch, bat raised over her head. She unleashed a scream with her swing. "Aiiiiieee!" Again the bat jarred in her arms as it failed to reach her quarry. She screamed in frustration, struggling to free her arms from a muscled grip.

"Bren! Brenna! Stop!"

She struggled wildly as the bat was stripped from her hands, and her thrashing hands curled into claws.

"Bren!"

Her head hit something. "Shit!" The arms around her adjusted and she broke their hold, only to find herself in other arms.

"Bren." This voice was calm. "It's over. He's down. You're safe. Cassidy is safe."

She screamed and the haze slowly cleared as the arms gradually loosened.

"Oh...God..." Brenna's knees buckled and she fell to the floor beside Cassidy. "Oh... God... Cass..."

Tenderly she brushed aside the blood-matted hair to examine the blue, black, and purple face. With shaking fingers she checked the pale throat for a pulse.

There was a faint flutter under her fingertips. She tried to carefully rearrange the still body, feeling the heat and softness in Cassidy's ribs.

Moving the torn blouse aside, she found mottled bruises covering most of Cassidy's chest and stomach.

"Ambulance! We need an ambulance!" Turning around, she kept a hand supporting Cassidy's wrist and hand with its puffy fingers and blue knuckles; it looked broken.

"Already called." A security guard fastened handcuffs on Mitch and shoved his prisoner toward the other officers, then approached Brenna. "What the hell happened here?"

"He," Brenna spat, "is her ex-husband." She stroked Cassidy's face and hair. "Howinthehell did he get on site?" Fury warred with worry that deepened the longer Cassidy remained unconscious. There was a disturbingly soft, spongy area on the right side of Cassidy's head. She bent close to the blond hair and nuzzled close, hiding her tears.

Will appeared at the officer's shoulder. "Bren, the EMTs are here."

"I don't think she can be moved," Brenna worried.

"We'll take it from here." A medical technician carrying a kit came around the other side of the overturned table. He moved it aside and surveyed Cassidy, then reached for her limp hand in Brenna's. Brenna did not move and did not release the hand.

"Ma'am, I really need her hand."

"Her, her wrist, I think it's broken."

"Hand, too, I'm guessing," he considered, pressing gingerly around the knuckles. Brenna felt the blood drain from her face. "Ma'am, listen, we'll get her fixed up. It's what we do." He patted her shoulder and she eyed his hand, disconnected from the sensation.

"Bren?" Will's voice sounded behind her then his hands were on her shoulders.

She jerked her gaze to Cassidy. Pulling away from Will, she leaned over and pressed her lips to Cassidy's forehead, then whispered fiercely, "You'll be all right. I love you."

A flash of light drew her eyes to the side. Terry Brown wrestled a camera from a reporter who had somehow gained entrance to the small trailer in the confusion.

He protested, "I've got a valid pass!"

"Then have some respect," Chapman barked.

"Who is it?"

"Cassidy Hyland," Brenna informed him sharply. Shaking as she stood, she looked down at Cassidy, hugging herself in an attempt to hold herself together.

"Who's he?"

Brenna spun to Mitch Hyland, seated in a chair, handcuffed and being treated for his broken nose and the cuts on his face. "Don't you treat him!" She rushed over and batted the medic's hand away. "He tried to kill her!"

Strong hands grabbed her shoulders and she couldn't shake them off.

"Let me go!" She covered her face, crying her pent up anguish. "Let me go!" She fought harder.

Arms wrapped around her chest and she struggled to breathe. She spun away, gaining her freedom and falling to the floor. The position put her next to Cassidy.

Cassidy had been moved onto her back and an apparatus supported her head and neck. The medic held her right arm in his lap, swabbing something over her inner forearm. Then he pulled out a syringe, removed the plastic covering and tapped the needle clear.

"What is that?" Brenna demanded. He didn't answer and Brenna watched the injection. The plunger tube was removed and another tube inserted, this one connected to a bag of fluid. Saline solution, she realized.

"You need to move now, ma'am. We need to get her onto a backboard."

Brenna stood up, still shaking. As the haze left her, she saw Will staring at her.

A loud thunk behind her made her spin. The second EMT had set down the backboard. Her heart pounded in her throat as she considered the paralysis Cassidy could suffer if anything went wrong. Brenna covered her mouth to stop the helpless sounds from escaping as she watched them secure Cassidy and the board to the gurney with straps.

"Time to go," one said to the other.

"We'll clear the way." Brenna's rough voice was unfamiliar to her own ears. "Will and Terry, help me." She grabbed the reporter and shoved him out ahead of her. Stepping outside, she was blinded by flashbulbs and bludgeoned by questions.

"Who was hurt?"

"What do the medics say?"

The medics bearing Cassidy behind her, Brenna tried to descend and clear a path. Someone jostled her; she shoved back. "Get the hell out of the way!"

"You're covered in blood. Were you hurt as well?"

"It's not me I'm worried about," she barked. "Now leave us alone." She hovered as the medical personnel lifted the gurney into the back of the waiting ambulance.

At the doors, Brenna grabbed an arm and demanded, "Why is she still unconscious?"

"She suffered several major traumas. Actually, being unconscious is the best thing for her."

"She's... It's not a coma, is it?"

"Her pupils are reactive."

Brenna had no idea what that meant, but the ambulance engine roared once and the EMT pulled away from her before she could ask.

"Gotta roll," he said with an apologetic shrug.

"What hospital?" She grabbed the outer bar to haul herself into the back.

"Get down," he ordered. "Pasadena General."

Brenna shouted the information back to Will Chapman and then tried to follow the paramedic into the rear of the ambulance with Cassidy. Someone behind her grabbed her shoulder.

"No, ma'am," a male voice said firmly.

She turned furiously. "I'm going."

"She's critical, ma'am. They can't take you in this one." The policeman looked her up and down. "Are you hurt?" His gaze paused at her face and a frown furrowed his brow. He reached up and touched her cheek.

Ducking away from his touch, Brenna tried again to mount the truck. He held her back and she began to panic; she could hear the ambulance had just changed gears. "I'm fine."

"Nasty shiner. You sure you don't need treatment?"

She looked at him. Something in the way he said "sure" suggested there might be a way around the regulations, and she waited.

"If I get an ice pack," he said with a smile, "maybe they'll take you up front."

A monitor going off accompanied a rough command from inside. "I need help here."

"Help her," she begged, while the police officer looked at the medic for his call.

The man growled under his breath, but rummaged in his bag and handed her a chemical ice pack. "You take that up front with you. The hospital can check you when we get there."

He was already half inside a second after handing her the cold bag. Just before he slammed the door, she caught a glimpse of Cassidy's face as it was obscured by a hand-pump and mask. Brenna hurried to the front of the truck and banged on the door.

"Let me in!"

The third man up front behind the wheel leaned over and pushed the door open. "What the hell?"

"They said I'm to ride up front with you," she said, as business-like, I-do-this-all-the-time as she could manage.

"Well, get in. We gotta get outta here."

Brenna exhaled quickly and pulled herself into the high seat.

"Seatbelt," he ordered. She complied just as

the ambulance followed a police cruiser out through the back gate.

"How long?"

"Depends. Five to eight minutes." He grabbed the radio microphone and barked into it, "Pasadena General, this is Rescue 1-8. We're transporting a beating victim. ETA in five."

A disembodied voice confirmed. "Roger, 1-8. ETA in five. Already in communication."

"Great." Putting down the microphone, he concentrated on driving.

Brenna turned to look into the back, straining against the thick distortion, finding it nearly impossible to see through the window separating the cab from the back compartment.

"Friend of yours?"

"I... uh, yeah. She's a friend."

"What's your name?"

"Brenna."

He concentrated on a turn for a second, the ambulance siren on as he moved against the traffic signals through an intersection. "What's your friend's name?"

Brenna continued trying to look into the back. "What are they doing?" she asked.

"Stabilizing her." He asked again, "What's her name?"

"Cassidy."

"How's your head?" he asked. "Need the ice pack anymore?"

Brenna looked at the bag resting on her lap. Her face did throb. Sheepishly she put the ice bag against her face. "I'll be fine. What's going to happen?"

There was a faint sound from the back. Brenna looked quickly to make out Cassidy struggling with the paramedics before being restrained. Her own panic resurged. "What's going on back there?"

The driving paramedic tapped the window with his fist, then the radio next to him crackled and he picked up the mouthpiece. "Can you give us a status on our patient? Lady up here wants to know."

"Briefly conscious. She wanted to know where someone named Ryan is."

The driver looked at Brenna. "That's her son," she answered. "Tell her he's safe with Karen."

"Will do," answered the paramedic from the back. "What's our ETA, Chaz?"

"Less than one."

"I've got Trauma on the other line. PG's scrambled the heart surgery team."

"Got it." The driver switched the radio. "PG this is Rescue 1-8. ETA update, pulling through the drive now."

To Brenna's relief, the last turn they screeched around was just beyond a sign declaring "Pasadena City General".

"You'll need to pull around to the dock. You've apparently got hot cargo there, Chaz. Reporters have already hit the place."

"Got it." He circled around past the drive leading to the large overhang labeled "Emergency" and took a service drive to the west wall where a loading dock was hidden by a line of bushes.

Brenna's mouth was too dry to speak as he put the vehicle into park and leaped out. She unbelted and reached for the door.

"No!" The driver's sharp voice froze Brenna in her tracks. "Let the doctors get her going inside. You take yourself around to the ER and check in." Leaving Brenna to stare after him, he turned to help his partner unload the gurney from the back of the ambulance.

CHAPTER ELEVEN

WHEN JAMES came out of the game room, he found his brother stalking around the living room and punching numbers into the phone. Every few seconds he would stop and stare at the television. "Yes? Pasadena General? ... I need word on a patient, Cassidy Hyland." Thomas slammed a hand into the wall, rattling the pictures. "What the hell do you mean you don't have her? I just saw the damn news report!"

"What news report?" James asked.

"Shut up!" Thomas barked at him, then returned his attention to the phone.

James turned back to the TV. "Special Report?" He sat down. "What's going on?"

A reporter on site had a microphone and was recapping the breaking story. "At approximately one p.m. today, domestic violence claimed a very public victim."

Tape rolled. A melee scene filled the screen and the camera zoomed in.

"Shit, that's Mom!" James recognized their mother, and grabbed the air fruitlessly for his brother, still stalking, still on the phone, and apparently still on hold, cursing steadily. "Who's that she's leaning over?"

"On the busy Pinnacle Studio lot, an ex-husband took his former wife on a journey of terror."

As James watched the tape continue, his mother moved aside, revealing the victim.

"Popular star, Cassidy Hyland, Time Trails' sexy rebel officer, Chris Hanssen, was severely beaten in a trailer on the Pinnacle lot, allegedly by ex-husband Mitch Hyland."

James inhaled. "Man, she's really messed up."

"As her costars hovered helplessly, Ms. Hyland was transported to Pasadena City General Hospital, apparently unconscious, possibly comatose, as a result of her injuries."

The tape followed the woman being carried on a backboard then loaded on a gurney. Next to her, James also saw his mother, spattered with blood. Over his shoulder, James heard Thomas gasp.

James watched his mother climb aboard the ambulance, using forceful language he had never heard from her. He called over his shoulder, "Mom'll be there at the hospital too."

"Mom? Shit, what the fuck happened over there?"

"Ms. Hyland's ex, apparently." As Thomas headed toward the door, James called, "Where are you going?"

"To the hospital."

"In what? Mom's got the car."

Thomas kicked the wall. "Shit!"

"You couldn't do anything if you did go." James grabbed his arm. "Mom will call."

"They said Cassidy is comatose!"

"They said she might be."

Thomas sank to the sofa, dropping his head in his hands. James grabbed his shoulder, feeling it shake as his brother gave in to his emotions. Watching the TV, James wondered how their mother was doing.

He had just known there would be trouble eventually, but he hadn't figured it would be this bad.

The gurney legs snapped down noisily and Brenna followed as they wheeled through a supply corridor. A nurse approached and grasped Brenna's arm as she tried to follow the gurney into the exam room.

"Do you know the patient?" When Brenna nodded, the nurse said, "Follow me."

"But—"

"We need some information from you."

Brenna sighed. "This won't delay her treatment, will it?"

"The trauma team will stabilize her. After that, we'll see."

Brenna was ushered through a doorway and emerged at the end of a large waiting room.

She was settled on a chair in a small room just off that, looking at a woman perched before a computer and holding out a clipboard. Brenna automatically took it, and the nurse left before she could ask another question.

"Patient's name, date of birth, home address, insurance, and any known allergies. Please."

The request was issued in a monotone, as if she said these words dozens of times an hour. Which no doubt she did. Brenna blinked, putting aside the ice pack and studying the clipboard. "I'll do my best."

"Insurance card?"

"No. Everything's back at the set," Brenna explained, indicating her attire. She was still in her own costume from filming.

The secretary's eyes widened then narrowed with realization. "God, you're the two they've been looking for." She nodded out into the waiting room that could be seen through the small window in the door. "They have been pounding my door every twenty seconds to find out when you were coming in."

Brenna briefly recalled throwing one reporter to the ground back at the trailer. How long could her energy hold out against a room full? From the growing commotion just outside the door, it sounded as if she was about to find out. Groaning, she looked pleadingly at the secretary. "Couldn't we just ignore them?"

"If you can do it, I can do it," the woman said with a conspiratorial grin, turning back to the computer.

They worked through the necessary information, as much as Brenna could provide, while the reporters hovered just outside, snapping pictures through the security-threaded glass.

Brenna hoped all they got was glare from the glass. "Please tell me there's another way out of here. A tunnel under your desk would be fine."

"Nothing so devious, but there is a back door to the exam room bathroom. We can get you out that way." She nodded toward a slender door on the opposite wall, mostly invisible because of an angled bookcase.

"I'd really appreciate it. I need to get back to see her as soon as possible."

"What happened?"

"I won't know everything until she wakes up, but we found her ex-husband attacking her in an empty trailer on the studio lot. We tried to break it up."

"You got caught in the middle, I see." Brenna nodded, starting to return the ice pack to her cheek when she realized it was no longer cold and set it on the desk. "Well. So... how did you get nominated to come along? Usually a studio grip brings the workman comp paperwork."

"There was no way I was not coming," Brenna stated emphatically. "Please, can we go back? I need to see her." For all her politeness, she was nearing the end of her rope.

The secretary nodded. "Give me the studio number so we can get her file from them. We'll also need a next of kin..."

"She will make it," Brenna insisted firmly.

"But only next of kin can make her medical treatment decisions... unless we find a health care proxy in her documents, or a living will?"

Brenna frowned. She didn't know whether Cassidy had either of those documents, but she knew that in any event, her name was not on them. She swallowed and nodded. "I... I'll see what I can do."

Finally, the secretary led Brenna into the antiseptic white and green hallway behind the office. Behind her there was a burst of clatter against the secretary's door. She sighed. God, I want to get out of here! She closed her eyes and amended, but only if Cassidy's coming with me.

"Here's the nurses station. Let's find out what room your friend is in." The secretary leaned over the desk and spoke to the nurse sitting there going through the clipboards. "I've got to get back to the office. What do you want me to tell the reporters?" she asked Brenna.

"To go away. Barring that, give them the number for the studio's PR office." Brenna sighed. She grabbed the back of a prescription pad and wrote two numbers. "The first is for HR. They've probably got Cassidy's medical file. She was in last year, I think, for a sprained ankle during a publicity event." The secretary nodded. "The second is the studio's PR." The secretary nodded more enthusiastically. "Thank you for everything."

"She's in exam room 8." The station nurse pointed then handed her a pad. "If you'll just sign in, you can meet with the doctor."

Brenna breathed a sigh of relief and signed the form. At last. "Thank you."

Taking back the sheet, the nurse asked, "What's your relationship to the patient?"

After a thoughtful pause, Brenna answered, "I'm her lover." Ignoring the gaping reaction, she turned on her heel and strode down the hall.

Pushing the door open to room 8, Brenna stepped inside, her eyes quickly locating the bed. The room was crowded with equipment, but she only had eyes for the woman looking small and hooked up to most of it.

An oxygen machine rasped to one side, the accordion pump hissing as it compressed and expanded, feeding Cassidy oxygen through a tube wrapped around her cheeks and under her nose. The heart monitor beeped slowly but steadily.

Stepping closer, Brenna laid her hand gently across the sheet-covered chest, feeling the reassuring rise and fall. A tube fed out from under the sheet, flowing with a murky liquid. She was not sure whether it was good stuff going in, or bad stuff coming out.

She lifted Cassidy's bandaged right hand and kissed the fingertips just peeking out beyond the edge. "Can you open your eyes for me? Please?" There was no response to her touch, not even a flutter of eyelids. She bent close. "Please get well."

"She's not going to be well for some time."

Exhaling, Brenna turned. "Doctor?" She was face to face with a man of Asian descent, in a green smock wearing a stethoscope around his neck. He was about her height, giving her a clear view of the fact that he was not smiling.

"What do you know?" She had not meant for the question to sound like a challenge. She amended, more softly, "So far."

He examined a few readouts and made some notations, all the while leaving Brenna hanging for the answer to her question. "Your friend here—"

"Her name's Cassidy. Cassidy Hyland."

"Well, Ms. Hyland suffered several separated ribs. When the x-rays come back, we'll know how many are broken. There's at least one. It punctured and collapsed her left lung." Brenna looked at Cassidy in alarm. "We've already reinflated the lung," the doctor assured her.

He checked the tape sliding out of the heart monitor and frowned. Brenna noticed the expression. "What's wrong?"

"There's some pressure buildup around her heart. She may have pericardial bleeding. Or it could just be fluid build up. The lab has several samples, so we'll know shortly what we're dealing with."

"What can you do?" Brenna forced herself to remain more composed than she felt, but she had to work hard to focus on the doctor instead of the limp hand she cradled in her own.

"We'll have to relieve the pressure. That will involve surgery. I'm scheduling an O.R. with our cardiac surgeon as soon as she's stabilized." He flipped through a printout he had brought with him. "You signed her in?"

"Yes."

"Is there any family we can contact for the admissions paperwork and the permission to do surgery?"

"No one is local. Her family's in Missouri." Brenna added, "She has a five year old son. Her ex-husband did this to her, so I guess that leaves me."

"Do you have a medical power of attorney to act as her health guardian?" She shook her head. "Are you a relative?" She shook her head again. "Then who are you?"

"I'm... We're involved, though it's only recently, you see, but—"

"I'm sorry, you're going to have to leave."

"What?"

"I need to discuss Ms. Hyland's medical condition with someone who can authorize the treatments. Her injuries are extensive and severe. We need to determine—"

"You need to heal her!" Brenna interrupted emphatically.

"Within the guidelines of her wishes and those of her family, yes." He left the rest unsaid, but Brenna heard it in her head, and wanted to scream. You're not family.

"How long before surgery will be absolutely necessary?"

"Her blood pressure is still too low. Probably by morning, unless she goes into respiratory failure before then. We're moving her up to CCU as soon as I can get someone to authorize her admittance."

"Who can do that?"

"Her insurance company. Or her employer."

Brenna felt the tendrils of hope. "Where's a phone I can use? Local call."

"You can use one at the nurses station but then you'll have to return to the waiting room. You can't stay back here." She started to protest and he reiterated firmly, "You can't stay here."

Turning to look at Cassidy's face, she kissed tenderly alongside a bandage covering most of her injured jaw. "I'll be back; I promise." Maybe the studio could authorize her to act in their stead. *There has to be something that can be done so that I can stay with you,* she thought. *Because I am not leaving you alone.*

Back at the nurses station, Brenna made her call as the duty nurse hovered. "Human Resources. ... Yes. This is Brenna Lanigan. Tell them I'm— ... Yes, that's right. Pasadena General. ... They need to admit Cassidy." She grabbed a pen and a piece of paper. "Right." She wrote quickly. "No, they don't know everything that's wrong yet, but she's in trouble. ... I guess you should. Ask Victor Branch to handle it. I'll... do this." She frowned then hung up.

The doctor reappeared. "Well?"

"I've got your authorization here." She waved the paper at him. "Personnel already faxed her file. There's no living will."

He nodded. "We're not there. Yet." He went on, "Family?"

"The studio said they'd contact her parents." Brenna could not stop the dejection from entering her voice. "Another colleague is on his way over with her son, though."

"But you said he's five. He can't authorize anything."

Brenna was firm. "He needs to see his mother. He was there when she was put in the ambulance and whisked away from him."

The doctor frowned and strode away, and Brenna handed the authorization note to the nurse. "Please notify me when they move her. He probably won't think to do so."

The nurse nodded slowly. "Can I ask you a question?" Brenna nodded. "Are you and she really dating?" When Brenna nodded again, the nurse shook her head, wearing an expression of confusion. "You sure don't act like the others that come through."

"What others? Actors?"

"Nah, the gays. They wave those health proxies around like red flags."

Brenna inhaled and exhaled slowly. She needed a friend back here. "We haven't been seeing each other very long."

The nurse shrugged. "Haven't had your second date yet, huh?"

There was a hint of amusement in the voice and Brenna fumed.

"Thanks for nothing." She stalked away, leaving the exam area and emerging into a cacophony of light and sound. The press still crowded the waiting room. She couldn't even see the other patients waiting for emergency services.

"What's Ms. Hyland's condition?"

"Serious," she supplied with a growl.

"Is she being admitted, or released soon?"

"I just said serious!" she snapped. "What the hell does that suggest to you? Now get out of my way." She pushed through the throng, heading for an empty chair, but they followed.

"What was your role in the events that occurred?"

"I helped break up the fight."

"Who was her attacker? Her husband?"

"Her ex-husband. Can't you ask the police these questions?" She pushed past the empty chair and more of the reporters in exasperation.

"They say it was a domestic dispute. Jealousy?"

Brenna was still upset she had not known Mitch was in town. She had not fully understood the level of danger he posed to Cassidy. The question hit on that. "I found him standing over her with a baseball bat! She was barely conscious!"

Pushing her way through them again, she stumbled against a door, and noticed the universal sign for the ladies room. Thank God! She pushed inside and shoved the door closed, locking it before sliding down to the floor and huddling while reporters posed their questions loudly through the door.

Tears streaming down her cheeks as the tension finally overwhelmed her, Brenna prayed. She prayed for the reporters to go away. She prayed Cassidy would recover. She must have dozed because suddenly there was a sharp rap on the door and a thick male, authoritative voice demanded, "You have to leave the restroom, ma'am."

"Are the reporters gone?" she asked weakly.

"We've ordered them off the premises."

"Thank you," she breathed, rising to her feet. Unlocking the door, she stepped out and looked into the quiet waiting room. No one carried a writing pad, or a camera. She exhaled in relief.

"Are you Brenna Lanigan?" one officer asked her.

"Yes."

"Man here says he's a friend of yours and a patient inside. He has a little blond kid with him."

Brenna pushed through the throng of officers and spotted Terry Brown—God bless his familiar and friendly face—seated beside Ryan Hyland. Both looked up as she rushed forward. She got a strong one-armed hug from Terry as she lifted Ryan and hugged him, pressing her face into his jean jacket. She kissed his hair and caressed his cheek.

"I thought you might need these as well." Terry held up two handbags.

"Her insurance card should go to the nurse in there. Also, we need to know if anyone in town is authorized to sign treatment forms."

"Just Pinnacle, I think."

Brenna frowned. "That's what I thought, too. The office is looking up her parents' number but that may not get her help."

"Why not?"

"Over Christmas, she had to leave their house of her own volition or be thrown out."

"What for?"

"They learned that she and I had become involved."

"Yes." He shrugged. "But what does that have to do with this?"

"I don't know. Maybe it doesn't have anything to do with it. But they're apparently the only ones who can authorize treatment, and they're not exactly on speaking terms."

"What was Mitch doing on the set? She used to have a restraining order against him."

"How did you know that?"

"Brenna, just because you didn't want to know anything about Cassidy when she first arrived, doesn't mean some of us didn't know something about her."

"So you knew she'd been abused in her marriage."

"It wasn't hard to decipher."

"Except for someone who was ignoring her with every fiber of my being."

"Now you're being hard on yourself for no reason."

"Damn it, I'm an idiot. Cassidy was afraid of our relationship getting out. Even when she couldn't put it into words why. Damn, I should have listened to her. She must have known that sonofabitch Mitch would pull something."

"Mr. Hyland has been transported to the police station," Terry reported evenly. "He struck two of the officers as well."

Brenna closed her eyes and offered up a silent 'thank you'. "He tried to kill her with a baseball bat," Brenna hissed softly, looking toward Ryan. "How can I tell that to Ryan?"

"You can't, until Cassidy advises you."

"She hasn't awakened since the ride over."

"It's that serious?"

She nodded. "They need to operate to relieve some pressure around her heart."

"What can I do?"

Fishing in her purse, Brenna came up with her car and house keys. "I'm going to call Thomas and then...Could you take Ryan to my house?"

"Your car is still at the studio." He looked her over. "And you're still in costume."

"I know. You can take the vest with you, but the rest will have to stay. I don't want my sons here; I want Ryan to stay with them. I'll catch a cab and retrieve my car later." She rubbed her cheeks in fatigue, wincing as she aggravated her bruised eyes. "But not until Ryan and I have seen Cassidy." She reached out and coaxed the boy off the chair to take her hand. "Ready?"

"Where is she?" Terry asked.

"Hopefully by now they've gotten her settled into CCU. I have no idea, though. I got thrown out of the exam room and then mobbed by the press out here."

"Productive afternoon," Terry offered dryly.

"What time is it?" She caught sight of a wall clock. "It's after five already. God, the boys will be frantic." She withdrew her change purse and headed for a pay phone booth along the front wall of the waiting room.

"I'm hungry," Ryan complained, snuggling into her lap as she dialed. "And I want to see Mommy."

"I know, sweetheart. I'll find you something to eat in a minute and we will see your Mom." She dialed.

"Who are you calling?" Ryan asked curiously.

"Thomas and James."

Ryan smiled, looking tired. She kissed his head and held him against her chest more firmly.

"Hello, Thomas. ... Yes, it's me. ... I'm okay."

Her elder son's voice was worried as he asked, "And Cassidy?"

"She's hurt very badly, but I don't know much more than that."

"It's been more than four hours," he commented anxiously.

"It's complicated," she said firmly. "Thomas, listen." He fell silent on the other end of the line. "I've got Terry Brown and Ryan here. After I take them in to see Cassidy, I want to send Ryan to you. I need to stay here."

"Do you want us to come there?"

"No, it's better if you don't... not yet."

Thomas fretted, "Is Cassidy going to be all right?"

"They're doing everything they can," she countered, knowing how little comfort those same words had brought her.

"I'm sorry. I'll watch Ryan. It's fine."

"I'll call you again in an hour. We'll have a better idea what's happening then."

"All right."

"Thomas?" She offered him as much reassurance as she could. "I don't know what the news stories said, but I don't want Ryan seeing any of the reports, all right? I'll try to explain something to him while I have him here. You're only responsible for making sure he gets some sleep. And keeping your chin up, all right?"

"Mmm hmm."

"Sweetheart, I love you. Thank you."

"I know, Mom. I... Yeah."

"Bye."

"Bye." Brenna hung up the phone, her son's farewell still echoing in her ear. *God, he sounded almost as bad as I feel.* She stood, hefting Ryan in her arms. "Let's go see your Mom."

Chapter Twelve

"...HER LOVER!" Brenna bit her lip. The nurse finally nodded and pointed.

Terry looked at Brenna as they walked away from the desk. "That... approach was effective."

"I can't seem to get anywhere without saying so," She cupped Ryan's hand and found a small joy in how easily the boy accepted her touch.

At the elevator she pressed the button to summon a car. T

Terry nodded. "A reality of the situation. How will Cass feel about that information getting out? It's certain the press will play it up."

Brenna sighed. "What will she think about me 'outing' us publicly? Yes, I know that's the term, Terry. Don't look at me like that. I never pictured myself in this situation, but I'm not naïve." She shook her head, stepping into the summoned car. "Cassidy didn't want it to come out abruptly. She sort of figured we'd get people used to us being friends first. I'd hoped to have my divorce final..."

"Will told me you finally broke it off with Shea."

"Will's definitely known for a while. Did he tell you?"

"We've discussed the situation."

"I don't know that I like that."

They stepped off on the fourth floor. A sign pointed the way to CCU.

"You didn't want to see what you were doing to yourself or Cassidy, remember? You avoided her off camera. I'm surprised all it took was a birthday party to get you to open up."

"It was more than that, but I get your point." They had reached the nurses station. Brenna leaned over the counter and stated, "We'd like to see Cassidy Hyland."

One of the nurses sitting before the monitoring stations looked up. Must be the one assigned to Cassidy, Brenna thought.

Predictably, the woman asked, "Family?"

"This is her son, Ryan." She skirted actually having to lie.

"Right this way. I have to tell you she didn't take the transfer very well. Her fever spiked and the bleeding resumed. She had a mild heart attack." Brenna looked alarmed. "From the stress her body's going through. Her condition's been stabilized for now."

They stopped at the doorway to the heavily monitored room.

"She's the second bed. Now that you're here, we can get all the approvals done for surgery in the morning. The doctor didn't seem to think you'd get here this quickly."

"That's okay. How long can we stay?"

"A few minutes inside, but there's a lounge nearby." She offered one last piece of advice. "Be careful of the tubes, we had to intubate her. Can he keep his hands to himself?"

"I promise Ryan will be good." Brenna waited until the nurse left and Terry took up a sentry position.

When Brenna turned around, she found Ryan walking toward the curtain around the far bed. The first bed was empty.

"Mommy?" He pulled aside the curtain and Brenna stepped quickly to his side. Ryan looked up at the bed. "Wake up." He reached out and touched the bandaged hand that lay on the edge of the blankets. "Mommy." He nudged the hand. "Miss Lanigan, what's wrong with her?"

"She was hurt at work today. You saw us take her in the ambulance, right?"

He nodded. "I saw Daddy, too. He didn't come here. Policemen took him away."

"Yes, they did." Brenna exhaled to keep her voice even, trying not to reveal the anger she felt.

"Will Mommy wake up now that we're here so that we can go home?"

"Your mommy needs her sleep. You're going to come home with me for a little while."

"Can't I stay here with her?"

"No, sweetheart, you can't. But we'll come back tomorrow, and every day until she's better. Is that okay?" Brenna moved alongside Cassidy's head and brushed her fingers over the lank blond hair. It still had much of the blood Brenna had first seen and she paused a moment to study the rust color on her own fingers. God, I'm sorry, Cass. The blood on Cassidy's face had been washed away; what remained visible was the bruises, though bad ones. Brenna touched one gingerly and felt the heat under the skin.

Ryan climbed up on a chair beside the bed and leaned over the railing to look down at his mother's face. "Her face is dirty," he said, reaching out to clean it.

Brenna gently but firmly kept his hand away.

"She's not dirty; those are bruises. Like when you fall down?"

He touched the oxygen tube tucked under his mother's nose. "What's this?"

"It helps her breathe." Brenna recalled the nurse's information about a heart attack and had to calm herself before she could speak again. "Don't touch."

Ryan cocked his head. "What's that noise?"

"Which one?" she asked.

"The beeping."

"The machine listening to her heart." Brenna pointed to the far side of the bed.

"Can I listen too?"

"I'm sorry but we have to be very gentle with your mom. She's delicate right now."

Ryan climbed down and found his mother's hand again, taking it more surely in his own. "Is this okay? I can hold her hand?" He looked at Brenna for permission. She granted it with a nod. "Mommy," he said, addressing her hand, "Miss Lanigan is going to take me home with her."

Brenna tucked her hand around Ryan and Cassidy's joined ones. "You just think about getting well. We'll be here."

At first Brenna thought she or Ryan had moved, then she felt the motion again. Cassidy's fingers flexed around her son's; her knuckles moved inside Brenna's palm.

"I love you, Mommy." Ryan leaned forward and kissed his mother's hand, his lips touching Brenna's fingers too. She closed her eyes and let the tears of relief come.

In the hospital cafeteria, Terry coaxed Brenna to nibble on an apple turnover along with her coffee. Beside her, Ryan devoured a hamburger and French fries.

"You should go home. You've already been here longer than six hours," he reasoned.

"I can't leave her alone."

"Actually, I wasn't thinking that. You need to settle Ryan. I can stay. I'll call you if something changes."

"I can't ask you to do that."

"You didn't. It shocked us all." He put a hand on her shoulder. "You're going to have enough people not offering help." He added with a quirk of his lips in a half-grin, "As a group, we might be able to frustrate the reporters before they can frustrate you."

Brenna sipped her coffee as she thought. It would help Ryan if she settled him rather than just sending him everywhere. "It was quite a run-around just for me to get to see her. If I leave, I might have to start the process all over again."

"We can be sure that doesn't happen."

"We?"

Terry picked up his cell phone and pressed the button along the side, initiating a long tone. The cafeteria doors behind Brenna swung wide, and she turned at the sound. Terry's wife, holding up her own cell phone, walked in at the head of a sizable crowd.

"What have you done?" Brenna recognized half the cast and crew from the set. Spouses seemed to make up the rest of the entourage. A cacophony of support flowed from the group as they surrounded her. Hands patted her shoulders, touched her back, gazes offered a mix of smiles and supportive determination.

Rachelle stepped forward bearing a bundle. "We suspended shooting." She put the bundle in Brenna's hands. "I went through your trailer. Thought you might like to change."

Brenna looked surprised as Rachelle enveloped her in a hug. Against her ear, Brenna heard Rachelle's soft, private words. "You've been in those all day, and frankly, I think Wardrobe would like a chance to get the blood out." As Rachelle stepped back, Brenna looked down at herself. *Cassidy's blood. Probably even some of Mitch's*, she thought with revulsion.

The reaction must have shown because Rachelle wrapped her up in a tight hug again. "God, I'm sorry this happened." She pulled back and brushed Brenna's tears from her cheeks. "But really, I don't know how else to handle this. It's kind of shocking."

"Which? That Mitch beat her up or that I'm involved with her?"

"Both, but... How could you let me find out like this?" Rachelle put her hands on her hips and feigned an injured look. "I knew you were finally relaxing around her, but this... I'm surprised."

A small smile tugged at Brenna's lips. "Cass took me by surprise too."

"Oh, I like that smile," Rachelle complimented. "Can we all go up and see her?"

Terry intervened. "I was just trying to convince Brenna to go home for a while."

"So Cass is doing better?"

Brenna shook her head. "She's in CCU. Only family can see her. She's going into surgery soon."

"Depending on what?"

"Whether the pressure around her heart gets better or worse."

"Her heart?"

"Yes." Brenna swallowed again, collecting herself. "The attack seems to have caused heart damage."

"God." Rachelle's hand covered her mouth and several others registered similar shock on their faces.

Brenna shook her head, turning to Terry. "I can't leave. I just can't."

"Then we'll stay in shifts with you," Rachelle suggested. "I'll take the first shift."

"I'm not going to be able to argue that point, am I?" Brenna sat down. Ryan scooted into her lap and she put her hand on his back. "We've got some pretty wonderful friends, hmm, Ryan?" He nodded against her chest. "All right. The doctor is probably on rounds somewhere. I'll find out what's happening and then decide what to do." She looked at her bundle of street clothes and added, "First, I think I'm going to change."

Terry and Sean Durham entertained Ryan while Rachelle accompanied Brenna to the restroom.

"So, I heard the reporters had you cornered in one of these earlier?"

"Yeah," Brenna answered from within a stall. She appeared a minute later, her costume over her arm, pulling her blouse's collar straight. Rachelle stepped forward from where she had been leaning on the sinks and helped. "Better?" Brenna asked with a weak smile.

"Much. It'll be a little easier for you to go incognito now." Rachelle took the uniform pieces. "Jacques'll drive me back to the studio and I'll deliver these. Do you want me to return with your car?"

Brenna nodded. "I need to get Ryan to my place."

"Terry will be happy to do that." Blinking at her reflection, Brenna acknowledged the help. Rachelle met her gaze in the mirror. "So, are you going to tell me everything?"

"I've told you all I know."

"Not about this. Well, I'm sure it will get back to this, but I meant about you and Cassidy, and Mitch... And don't you still have a husband?"

"You seem to be one of the few who didn't see it. I didn't see it," Brenna admitted. She leaned over the sink and splashed water on her face before answering. "But she's just... I've never met anyone like her." In her mind's eye, she could see the beautiful face studying her across a campfire in the middle of the mountains. "I've never met anyone with the intensity she has..." *All directed at me.* "The freedom she gives herself to just feel..." Brenna shook her head and tossed the paper towel in the trash. "She's mischievous and playful, unassuming and even shy."

"Shy? Cass?"

"It's all a front, Chelle. Since the beginning. Only Cameron knew, and he made sure no one else did. Remember how she didn't sit in any scenes?"

"That was blocking."

"That was planned that way because she was recovering from broken ribs Mitch gave her when she told him she'd gotten the contract to work with us."

"So she really was abused? God, that's awful."

"I didn't know for the longest time. We started... talking. Do you remember when she said she'd been camping with my charity group?"

"Yeah. What about it?"

"We... talked... and... well, that weekend it... it became something more than just friendship."

"Really? She was pretty happy the week after that."

"We just kept growing closer. After the gala, I asked Kevin for a divorce."

Rachelle blew out a deep breath and then asked hesitantly, "Is this something more than friendship? Sexual?" Brenna nodded. "That's a surprise."

"For me, too." Brenna blushed.

"The media isn't going to let this go."

"Maybe they will. It's not like we're the first they've ever seen."

"But you are the first where a man has tried to take his ex-wife apart bodily for being involved with another woman."

"Sensational," Brenna sighed sarcastically.

"Exactly."

CHAPTER THIRTEEN

BRENNA CALLED home again, as promised, to tell her sons Ryan was on his way with Terry Brown. Brown agreed to stay the night with the boys and return in the morning to the hospital with Ryan. While Rachelle and Jacques Cheron went to fetch Brenna's car, Sean Durham accompanied Brenna back to the fourth floor to find out what they could about the doctor's latest visit.

"She responded to Ryan, squeezed his hand," Brenna was explaining with pleasure as they entered the room where Cassidy had been assigned.

The dividing curtain was thrown back, revealing the second bed was empty, made up with fresh sheets. They quickly returned to the nurses station, where Brenna accosted the nurse at the desk, a different one from her earlier visit. "Where's Cassidy Hyland, 408?"

Looking at her charts, the nurse pulled the appropriate board. "Ms. Hyland went to surgery twenty minutes ago."

"Twenty minutes? Why didn't someone tell me?"

"Ma'am?" Scanning a list, she asked, "What's your name?"

"Lanigan. Brenna Lanigan. I came in with Cassidy this afternoon by ambulance."

The nurse shook her head. "The family issued a list of visitors. I don't see your name."

"The family issued a list? When?" Sean asked because Brenna was struck silent by the double blow. She stepped away from the desk white as a sheet.

"About an hour ago. Admissions dropped it off."

Brenna exhaled her question in a rush. "Does it say why Cassidy went into surgery?" Back to the matter at hand: news about Cassidy. She required it. Now.

The nurse returned to the chart. "Pericardial pressure. She had another Code Blue."

"But she was responsive when I was up here with her earlier with her son. She squeezed his hand."

"These cases can turn very quickly. I promise you she's under excellent care." The nurse picked up another clipboard. "Can I tell the family you stopped by?"

Brenna's eyes widened. Face Cassidy's family? "No. I... No." Brenna walked away from the desk.

Sean asked, "Is there any way she can see Cassidy? Just look at her?"

"Certainly not before she's out of surgery, but even then... CCU's policy is family only. She isn't a relative, is she?"

"As close as you can get. They've worked together sixteen hours a day for the last year and recently started a relationship."

"Perhaps she can speak with the family. Maybe they just overlooked her."

Brenna overheard and stormed over. "They didn't overlook me. They excluded me." Anger vibrated in her chest like a living thing as she lashed out. She shook her hand toward the empty room. "Her family wouldn't care if she dies!"

Anguished and astonished at her outburst in the face of the nurse's startled expression, Brenna moved away quickly and sat in a lone chair. Covering her face with her hands she cried.

Sean tried again. "There has to be something."

The nurse returned her attention to him, clearly consternated by Brenna's reaction. "Yes, um... I... Well, there's Patient Advocacy. They've been known to get domestic partners visitation rights when no other avenue was available."

"Are they open now?"

"There's always one rep on duty. The office is down next to the hospital chapel."

"Would you call down there when Cassidy returns from surgery?" He waved his hand to forestall her objection. "I know, there's regulations, but... one phone call can't hurt."

The nurse nodded, watching him walk to Brenna's side. He grasped her shoulders and pulled her to her feet. "I think I know where we can wait." Brenna looked toward the nurses station and he assured her, "She'll call."

"Where?"

"Patient Advocacy."

"They can get me in to see her?"

"It's the only possible option to being on the family list. And..." He frowned. "Was that, um, true about her parents?"

Entering the elevator, Brenna sagged against the wall. "I don't know. I'm just scared I won't see her again. It's wrong to think they would let her die, but Cass says that her father was not at all understanding over Christmas. He hit her. She left their house and told me she won't go back."

Brenna stepped out on the first floor and they followed the signs to the advocacy office. Noticing the chapel signs, she thought about how she had prayed, sitting on the bathroom floor. "Sean, wait."

She looked into the small room softly lit with candlelight and a few halogens recessed in the ceiling. The far wall was dominated by a stained glass window, backlit by the night lighting outside.

She entered, feeling the softness of the place seep into her. It was very different from the rest of the hospital. Light refracted through the glass and she found herself watching it dance through the air. She stopped at a table of candles near the front, some already lit, watching the tiny flames.

Using memory as her guide, Brenna selected a votive candle and lit it, setting it among the others in the box. Memories flowed over her, a soothing balm to the stresses of the day, of doing this with her mother at her side when she was a little girl and a relative was ill. Now she knelt against the altar railing with more purpose than she had in those young, naïve years.

Through the litany of her memorized prayers, Brenna poured out her soul. In silent uncertainty, she questioned whether she even had a right to ask for intervention. She cried when Cassidy's face appeared in her mind's eye. She prayed earnestly Cassidy would be whole and healthy soon, alive with the love they had found together. *I didn't look for it, but it found me. She found me.*

Brenna had to believe she and Cassidy had been brought together for a reason. She thought of how Cassidy had fled her husband and joined Time Trails. Cameron, yes, had done that, but then he had thrown it away. Everyone, it seemed, had taken Cassidy, used her, and thrown her away. Her husband, Cameron...

She examined her own life and its choices. Driven by acting, she had left her home and struggled through a young adulthood in New York City. She had found what she thought was love, only to have it thrown back in her face when it produced a child. Unable to do anything less, she had carried the baby and then given it up for adoption.

It seemed she had been searching ever since for another heart to hold, to promise to take care of, to love her as much as she loved them. Tom, she thought first. He had proved inconstant, unable to offer her support or accept hers. Her relationship with Kevin had merely been grasping at something she thought she was supposed to have.

Then came a birthday invitation tucked shyly in a mirror, and Brenna had awakened to the realization that her impression of another person had always been colored by circumstance, not by who they really were. When she finally got to know Cassidy, she found the woman behind the cool exterior, replacing fear with something deep and cherished.

Her mind filled with images of their times together. She remembered being enveloped in intensity staring back at her from behind the veil of character. Remembering their earliest talk off-camera made her smile. She blushed at remembering when she had flirted. *God, did I really do that?* The memory filled her mind:

Brenna presented two pairs of slippers.

"Go on. Blue cotton or Bullwinkle J. Moose?" Cassidy laughed and reached for the brown character slippers. "I figured you for a Bullwinkle fan," Brenna commented when Cassidy settled to the sofa to slip them on her feet.

"Really?" Cassidy sighed in relief as the thickly padded, one-size-fits-all interior hugged her achy feet.

"Really. Don't ask me how I knew. I just took one look at you and said, 'Bullwinkle.' But you can see I took the blue plain ones, just in case I was wrong."

"I find it odder that you would like Bullwinkle," Cassidy admitted.

Brenna shrugged. "I grew up with this earnest moose who seemed to mess everything up."

"But it usually came out right in the end."

"Serendipity." She smiled.

"Or his buddy Rocky," Cassidy chuckled.

She remembered now being struck silent by the laughter, something heavy in her chest dislodging as genuine like shoved out wariness and replaced it.

Her mind skipped ahead to how much she had wanted to tear the store apart, helping Cassidy look for Ryan. She had also wanted to strangle the store manager for shattering Cassidy with his talk of kidnapping:

The manager asked one more thing before turning around to catch up the intercom microphone. "How long do you want to wait before we call the police and report a kidnapping?"

Cassidy's face went even paler at the blunt question. Supportively, Brenna wrapped her arm around Cassidy's waist. "Just make the announcement," she ordered sharply. The manager shrugged and turned around.

She remembered how good it had felt when Cassidy turned into her body, the feel of her hands on her hips, how that had broken every barrier she had ever established, shattering her need for distance from this woman like a stone wall being breached.

She remembered being absorbed in Cassidy's pain following Cameron and Will's fight:

Cassidy drew a ragged breath and Brenna could see some of the blond woman's composure slowly returning. Brenna helped her tug the inner top off her shoulders. "Thank you." With the intensity Cassidy had offered her, Brenna knew it was about more than the costume.

"You're welcome." She hoped Cassidy knew she meant more than just the costume too. She leaned away, picking up a loose t-shirt. "Here." With a quick pull, Cassidy's chest was covered again, falling to her sofa and tugging off the lower half of her costume. Brenna settled next to her and slumped forward, a defeated posture.

"Brenna, I'm really sorry."

"You don't have anything to apologize for. Cameron should. Hell, Will needs to make a trip to a confessional. I've come to realize something," she said quietly. "All you've ever done is your best. And I admire that."

Cassidy was silent; Brenna easily read her surprise.

"You do?"

"Yeah. I do." Brenna smiled gently and patted Cassidy's leg, only realizing as she felt the warm skin beneath her palm, that Cassidy hadn't yet finished dressing.

She remembered the entire camping trip, every minute—from watching Cassidy as they drove down the highway, to setting up the tents, to swimming in the spring together, and that mountain climb. She recalled the days afterward—being in a daze from feeling so much. Every look they shared conveyed so much emotion, much more than she thought she could handle. But damn, she'd come alive then. Like being reborn. Cassidy had felt it too. She remembered being so alive when they tried a simple 'popcorn and movie' evening and instead romped with passion on her bed. A laugh bubbled up, warming her insides and filling her with sunshine in the darkness.

Resolve and peace filled Brenna. She looked up at the stained glass images. Several of the panes together looked like hands reaching toward one another. She nodded in affirmation.

"Miss Lanigan?"

Brenna turned to see a spare man with brown hair and glasses wearing a dark suit and tie. She nodded. "Yes, I'm Brenna Lanigan."

"I'm Paul Heath with Patient Advocacy." He offered his hand. She took it, then withdrew. "Your friend said you might want to ask me some questions?"

She looked past Paul. "Where is Sean?"

"He said he had to go, but a Rachelle is waiting outside."

She nodded. "They're staying with me here in shifts. I don't know why. I can't get in to see her and her parents will be here in the morning and—"

He held up a hand. "Who is 'she' we're talking about?"

Brenna swallowed. "Cassidy Hyland. She's a patient in CCU."

She followed him out into the corridor. Rachelle put a hand on her shoulder as they all walked down the hall to Paul's office.

"You're involved with her?"

"I love her."

"Her parents don't approve and they left you off the list."

"Sean told you all that?"

He shook his head. "I've heard the story before." He sobered. "I've told the story before." Brenna's eyes widened, but he shook his head and returned to her. "Why don't you tell me your specifics?"

"Can you get her visitation?" Rachelle interjected. "Cass is in emergency surgery right now."

"I would like to be there for her," Brenna acknowledged.

"Now?" Paul questioned.

"Her ex-husband beat her with a baseball bat today." Brenna shuddered at the remembered horror.

Paul gave a low whistle. "She came out of the closet to him?"

Brenna shook her head. "I don't know. I don't think so, but he learned about it. About us."

"What makes you say that? Did you witness the fight?"

"No."

"How long have you and... Cass, you said? How long have you been involved?"

"You mean...?" Brenna looked at Rachelle whose eyes sparkled with interest waiting for the answer. "Sexually?"

Paul nodded. "Yes."

"I... About a month." Brenna studied her hands in her lap.

"This is your first relationship?"

"I've been married twice." Paul looked at her startled. "Oh, you mean of a ..." She blushed scarlet and sighed, "Yes. I...I didn't expect it."

"You're obviously struggling with identity issues at the same time. I can hook you up with a local support group, but we need to address your immediate problem." He smiled and took her hand. "Can't have such a promising start end prematurely."

Brenna sighed. "Is there anything you can do?"

"Have you at least seen her since she was admitted?"

"Once. I accompanied her in the ambulance. I haven't left the hospital since. I sent her son—he's five—to my home to stay with my sons. Another co-worker took him over."

"You've certainly tried to tend to her business for her." He nodded and jotted something down.

"Will that help?" Rachelle asked.

Paul answered, "It could be shown as concern beyond some mere physical relationship or desire for personal gain." He turned back to Brenna. "How did you find out you weren't on the approved list?"

"I went up to check on her and talk to the doctor. When she wasn't in the room, I went to the nurses station and found out she was in emergency surgery and that I wasn't privy to any further information."

"Until then your questions were reasonably accommodated?"

"I think so. I know there are rules for the patients' privacy, but..."

"But you think Cassidy needs you."

"I brought her son up to visit and I know—I know—she responded to him, to us."

"Her son has seen her already?"

"Yes. He needed it. He'd seen her taken to the hospital. I learned with my own sons that you don't keep them in the dark. Give them an explanation, or show them something, and they'll deal with it."

Paul nodded again, making more notes. "Are her parents here in the hospital?"

"Not yet. They're due in the morning."

"Did you call them?"

"No. The studio did. I should be okay with that. They're her parents. But Cass said her father hit her when they argued at Christmas. I saw the bruises."

"I'll talk with them in the morning, but you have a pretty solid argument here for visitation. You have her son. What's his name?"

"Ryan," she answered with obvious warmth in her voice.

Paul smiled indulgently. "You've also tried to take care of other things. You filled out her paperwork when you arrived here, right?" Brenna nodded. "I think we can get you in to see her."

"Tonight?" Rachelle asked firmly. Brenna put a hand on her arm to quiet her. "No. Listen, you need to see her. She needs to see you. It will help."

Paul raised a hand. "I've heard enough for me to sign you in and let you spend the night up on the CCU floor."

"You're serious?" Brenna asked in astonishment. She really had not expected anything.

"You can take your friend here up with you." He patted her hands as her eyes went wide. "Give my best to Cassidy when she wakes up and sees you."

"I... I'll do that. Is it going to be all right to bring Ryan back in the morning?"

"He's her son. Even though you're acting only temporarily, you are watching out for him. Definitely make sure he continues to see his mother. It's important to his health as well as hers." He stood. "Come on."

Brenna stood, supported by Rachelle for a brief moment as she let the shock fade and the hope return. Paul held the door and led them out.

CHAPTER FOURTEEN

BRUSHING BACK her dark hair, Rachelle watched as Brenna paced around the empty bed in CCU room 408 yet again. The agitated woman ran her hands over the silent monitoring equipment then paused to look out the window and hug herself.

"There's still a news van out there. I'll bet that reporter knows more about her condition than I do," Brenna commented mirthlessly, forlornly grasping the edge of the curtain.

"Paul said you would be updated. The doctor will visit after the surgery."

"It's been almost three hours." Brenna circled back to the near side and flopped onto a chair tucked up by the headboard. Her arms splayed along the chair's arms and her head dropped dejectedly.

Paul had left them over an hour ago. Now, with the hour passing midnight, Brenna was agitated beyond anything Rachelle had seen on the set as they worked together. She had long since fallen silent on the story of the attack.

"Do you want to talk?" Rachelle invited.

Brenna rolled to a more normal sitting position but then leaned forward over her knees and covered her face. "I'm becoming unhinged, aren't I?"

"I have never seen you like this," Rachelle assessed frankly.

"I don't think I've ever felt this helpless before."

"So let's not talk about this. Let's look forward. What are your plans after Time Trails?"

"Cass and I haven't worked that out yet, but I have an offer to do a film in England. Terry's also got his playhouse. Somehow we'd like to work it out as a family."

Rachelle smiled. "You really see yourself as a 'family'?"

"More than I did with either of my husbands, Chelle."

"Have you ever been attracted to women?"

Brenna shook her head. "Not that I'm aware of."

"Did you get this idea from Luria kissing her in 'Brains and Brawn'?"

Brenna groaned. "That did shock the hell out of me. I barely remembered my next line."

"Cass was surprised too. Will had the idea; Sean liked it. I was game, so we blocked the scene that way. So, seeing her and me..."

"No jealousy. I didn't know what was what yet." Brenna looked at Rachelle with open curiosity. "How about you?"

"Nope. Like kissing a sibling. Stage kisses always are."

"Not for me."

"Not for Cass either, I think. I don't think she'd ever thought of kissing another woman."

"She has."

"Oh?"

"Just once, though, in college." Brenna paused.

"A little jealous?"

"Well, it did make our first time a little easier."

Rachelle laughed. "A little easier. Right."

"Can we change the topic?" Brenna was finding herself drifting into melancholy. Lovemaking was a nice topic, but not if her partner wasn't there to share it with her. "Catch me up on Rose? How is she doing?"

"Good. She wants to know what everything is, so she holds them out until we tell her then she repeats it. We have a little myna bird."

"Thomas was like that, always parroting. James, though... He seemed to wait forever. When he finally did talk, it was like he had a tape recorder. Everything was exact."

"How are they?" Rachelle asked.

"I hope they're at least trying to sleep. Thomas was very upset."

"Did they know about you and Cass before the news coverage today?"

Brenna exhaled. "Yes. Only since the holiday break, though. Thomas had developed a crush on Cass."

"So your son had a crush on your girlfriend."

"She wasn't... We weren't together yet." Brenna sat back and focused on some distant point in time.

"So, you opened up and became friends. That's easy enough to understand." Rachelle continued with open curiosity, "I just don't... What turned you on to her physically?"

Brenna responded sheepishly, "Her feet."

"Excuse me?" Rachelle choked on a startled laugh. "Her feet?"

Trying to find a way to explain, Brenna stood up and stepped away from the chair. "What part of your body hurts the most at the end of a shooting day; what's the absolute worst?"

Without hesitation, Rachelle responded, "My back. Playing Luria just kills my back." Looking up in bemusement, she asked, "What about you?"

"My feet. My calves. Jakes is a strider. When I turn her 'off', my first order of business is a foot massage, then I can actually drive home." Brenna sat down on the edge of the bed. "I caught Cassidy once, just collapsed in her trailer. I don't remember why I thought to follow her. She had her arm over her face. I remember I just grabbed her shoes off," Rachelle nodded, "and I massaged her feet."

Leaning back across the foot of the bed, Brenna sighed.

Staring at the ceiling, she added, "Cass looked at me and it wasn't 'have you lost your mind?' It was more like, 'Thank God, I could just kiss you.' I felt fire in my stomach, Chelle." Brenna's hands folded over her abdomen and she traced idly, obviously remembering. "My fingers tingled and my chest ached. And I wanted her."

Rachelle felt a rush of heat from Brenna's retelling, as if her friend had just told her how she and Cassidy made love. "God," she managed with a steadying breath, "was that the first kiss?"

"No. That came on our camping trip."

"The one Cassidy came back from all excited about mountain climbing?" Brenna smiled fondly as Rachelle asked, "Did she climb more than just the Sierra peaks?" Brenna blushed, but shook her head. "You didn't make love then?"

"No, but we both knew we would."

"Brenna, how did you, you know, know what to do?"

She shook her head. "Cass did. I didn't. When it first happened, instinct failed. I think we over thought the whole thing," she considered honestly.

"But you're together now?"

"The night she came back from her parents, neither of us thought very much at all. It was all feelings." She exhaled. "It was the most incredible experience. Never have I had this happen. Not with Tom and not with Kevin. Not even Will, though we had a lot of fun briefly. Lying there together..."

Rachelle's blush indicated she was envisioning the two women wrapped around one another. Brenna's voice was soft and awed as she continued.

"I didn't need to say anything, not a word, and she didn't either." Brenna inhaled raggedly and hugged herself. "I saw it in her face. Like I was reading her mind."

Brenna fell silent, rubbing her shoulders and thinking of that night, shaking from the mere memory of the emotions. There was a sound from down the hall—worn, badly oiled wheels rolling against linoleum. Bolting to her feet, Brenna ran to the doorway, Rachelle quickly at her side.

An intern in hospital greens pushed an occupied gurney toward them. A gauze cap covered his head, and a mask still hung around his throat. Pausing at the nurses station, he lifted the clipboard from the dangling IV stand, signed it and handed it across the counter. He spotted the women outside 408. "Hi," he said with a friendly smile. "Friends of the patient?"

The patient was covered chest to toes by a green sheet and a cotton blanket. The head was covered in white gauze. Brenna stepped close, reaching out hesitantly, but anxious to see for herself.

"Something like that," Rachelle answered. Brenna had finally given in to her need and was gingerly running a fingertip over Cassidy's bandaged cheek, so Rachelle asked, "How is she?"

The intern pushed along again, and Brenna followed. "The doctor'll be up here after he's cleaned up. She was in real trouble. We did a lot of work on her chest and her stomach. Whoever did this managed to bang her around pretty good. We had to reset her jaw, too, and put a steel pin in to stabilize it."

"What about her heart?" Brenna finally asked. Rachelle reached out a hand, cupping her shoulder.

"We drained off the fluid and that should stabilize on its own now. She's going to have to be very quiet for several days. Then there's all the healing she'll need for the broken ribs."

"How many were broken?" Rachelle asked.

"Three. A total of five were floating, though. She'll need intensive care for now. A regular room might be possible in a few days. She'll be recovering from this for a long time, though it doesn't look like there was any permanent spinal injury."

"Thank God," Brenna breathed. She pulled down the sheet and watched, holding her breath, as the intern moved Cassidy to the bed.

"She'll be under for a while longer, so don't worry. The doctor can tell you more about her post-op care when he gets here."

Brenna grasped his hands. "Thank you," she said earnestly, looking up into his face.

"Pretty special lady?"

"More than I can express."

He nodded and left.

Brenna immediately returned to Cassidy's bedside, leaning over the railing and staring down at the still face.

Rachelle came up along the other side of the bed. "Mitch broke her jaw?" she asked, noting the heavy bandaging and recalling the mention of a pin.

"I guess. God." Brenna's eyes trailed down Cassidy's chest. Rachelle watched as Brenna found the puffy blue and black left hand and cupped it in her own, tracing over the scrapes with her fingertips.

"Looks like she got in a few good hits on him herself," Rachelle said.

"She did. I saw his face. She's got one mean right hook."

Rachelle saw Brenna's frown. "What?"

"I'm going to find out when Mitch is scheduled to be arraigned," she said, a definite chill in her voice. "I want to testify. Mitch Hyland needs to stay behind bars. He could've killed Cass. He would have if we hadn't found them when we did."

Brenna's eyes watered as she brushed hair from Cassidy's temple. Much of it was trapped under bandages and Rachelle suspected some of it had been shaved away. Brenna leaned forward and pressed her lips to Cassidy's. The look on Brenna's face made Rachelle feel like she was intruding on a very private moment. She waited until the other woman straightened. "Well?"

"She looks better."

Rachelle took in what was visible of Cassidy's bruised face, though it was almost completely hidden behind the bandages covering her jaw. Next her gaze drifted to the cast-bound right wrist, and the heavy strapping around Cassidy's waist immobilizing her damaged ribs. And there was all the internal damage the intern had mentioned which she couldn't even see. "This is better? Jesus." She couldn't imagine much worse.

The skewed images began to fade from her mind and pain invaded. Cassidy groaned and opened her eyes. Curling on her side, or at least making the attempt, sparked agony, and her eyes widened. The dimly lit room took shape. She was lying on a bed. Overhead she made out the runner for a curtain and turned her head to find the source of a low hum. The monitor beeped periodically. She couldn't make out what was on the blurry green screen.

She swallowed; her mouth was dry and uncomfortable. The muscles in her face and throat also were not responding as she expected. Putting a hand to her face dumbfounded her as the dulled sensation of bandaged flesh met other bandages.

"Where am I?" she thought, but the sensation in her throat suggested she had spoken aloud.

"You're in Pasadena City General Hospital."

She turned toward the voice and found a woman wearing a white smock covered in flowers standing at the foot of her bed. She had a clipboard in her hand. "You're a nurse."

"Yes. I'm sorry my checking on you woke you up."

"What time is it?"

"Four-thirty in the morning. Your friend there finally fell asleep about half an hour ago, after the brunette left."

Cassidy's gaze followed the nod down to her left side. There was an arm across her abdomen, creating a dull pressure. The woman's right arm was bent under her face, the sight of which created a warm stir of familiarity. "She can't be comfortable," Cassidy remarked, moving her hand until it brushed the slack upturned cheek.

"She settled there and hasn't moved. I offered her the empty bed, but she wanted to be close by in case you woke up."

Carefully moving her bandaged hand, Cassidy let her fingertips absorb the sensation of fine hair as she stroked the sleeping woman's warm cheek. She is clearly someone I am very close to, she thought, recognizing the fullness in her chest as deep affection.

Fine lashes flickered against skin and eyelids fluttered open, revealing clear blue eyes that gradually focused on her. Cassidy's chest hurt with anxiety as she waited. "Hi," she offered uncertainly.

Almost as tangible as a warm blanket, the woman's husky reply soothingly wrapped around her. "Hi," the woman said as her lips curled into a tired but adoring smile. Then she sat up, reaching out a hand toward her.

Cassidy pressed back uneasily into the pillows. "Um." Warm fingers brushed over her forehead. A smile that made her insides melt held her attention.

"Cass? It's Bren. How are you feeling?"

A sense of trust replaced her hesitation, and of all the questions plaguing her, she asked only, "What happened to me?"

Brenna stood up and Cassidy let her gaze follow her up until the pain in her neck and back stopped the motion. She listened carefully as Brenna spoke.

"Would you mind if I turn on a light?"

"No. I mean, go ahead."

The light bar above her head flickered on and Cassidy studied Bren's back before she turned around again. The woman's face—such a beautiful, demurely featured face, Cassidy thought appreciatively—was suddenly alarmingly serious. "What do you remember?"

"From when?"

"Anything at all in the last twenty-four hours?"

Cassidy closed her eyes, willing something to float to the surface of her mind. She furrowed her brow, momentarily making her headache worse. A brown cartoon moose and a squirrel in an aviator's cap appeared, completely befuddling her. What are their names? She opened her eyes. "Why would I be seeing a pair of cartoon characters?"

Brenna met her expression with a confused one of her own. "Who?"

Searching her reluctant-to-respond brain, Cassidy puzzled, "A moose and a squirrel? The moose is... Bull... winkle? The squirrel is... Rocket?"

"Rocky," Brenna corrected softly. Cassidy could see tears glistening in the pale eyes. "Oh boy," Brenna worried.

"You haven't answered my question."

"What question?"

"What happened to me?"

Brenna sat down again. "You're in the hospital. Your ex-husband, Mitch... we found him beating you in the childcare trailer. I don't know what set him off."

"He..." Cassidy tried to think. "We were arguing... custody. He wanted to take Ryan away because I was dating a lesbian." She screwed up her features. "That doesn't sound right."

"We're dating, Cass."

"We are?" Cassidy shook her head. "You're a lesbian?"

Brenna cupped her cheek and kissed her lips. Cassidy suddenly had a flash of holding this woman down and kissing her in a darkened tent, the material of a sleeping bag against her legs. She smiled. "Seems you are."

Brenna laughed. "Actually, before you, I had no experience at all with women. You're the one who had a girl in college."

"I don't think so. My parents would have killed me."

"Maybe that's why it didn't last." Brenna fidgeted. "I need to tell you something."

"What is it?"

"Your parents are on their way here."

Cassidy frowned. *My parents are coming?* She felt a wave of nausea and closed her eyes, hoping it would pass, but the sensation only grew stronger. A face, fleshy and mottled red in rage, appeared in her mind, accompanied by physical pain, which suddenly constricted her chest, choking off her breath. She gasped.

With a firm touch, Brenna cupped her cheeks. "Shh! Shh, it's okay. Shhh."

The whispered reassurances gradually calmed Cassidy and the disruption in her breathing subsided, but the alarm had sounded when Cassidy's heart rate sped up and tripped the threshold on the monitor, so the nurse appeared.

Brenna looked back over her shoulder and said clearly, "She shows... signs... shhhh..." She interrupted herself to soothe Cassidy again. "She's disoriented, not sure of some things."

The nurse nodded. "I'll get the doctor."

"My... parents," Cassidy gasped, aware of tears painfully clogging her throat as she clung to Brenna. "I had an image of a very angry man."

Her lips against Cassidy's hair, Brenna asked, "Describe him?" Still shivering, Cassidy did. "Must be your father, as you last saw him. Your ex-husband, Mitch, doesn't look anything like that."

Cassidy felt another kiss against her temple.

The sensation of the hug and the kiss awakened another memory. "Ryan?" She looked around. "Where's Ryan?" She had a sudden memory of being in a small office, wondering where Ryan was. Brenna had been with her.

Brenna exhaled and pulled back, meeting Cassidy's gaze. "This is probably going to sound like a stupid question, but... humor me?"

Instinct driving her, Cassidy agreed. "Yes."

"What's Ryan's connection to you?"

Cassidy blinked then answered with some assurance, "He's my son."

Brenna's smile was brilliant and Cassidy's heart lurched with pleasure.

"How old is he?"

"He's... five. He... His birthday was... several months ago, October 8th. I gave a party."

"Yes, you did." Brenna's smile softened and she cupped Cassidy's chin again. "Ryan is at my house for now. Terry Brown will be bringing him by later today."

"Why is Ryan staying with you?"

"You, um, didn't have anyone else to watch him. He gets along well with my sons and I thought it would be okay."

"We work together." Brenna nodded. Cassidy went on, grasping at facts as they occurred to her. "Terry Brown. He... works with us too." Cassidy had a scary flash of a dark-skinned man grasping her and yelling in her face. It left her vaguely unsettled, but not as much as the image of her father. "He's not usually scary."

"Not usually. You must be remembering filming a scene with us. I vividly remember one about six weeks ago that scared you."

"Filming?"

"You're an actor. So am I. We work together on a series called Time Trails."

Cassidy studied Brenna. A sensation of intimacy flowed through her as their eyes met. "And we're dating?"

"Yes. It hasn't been very long to wrap our heads around it."

"That was a nice kiss. I don't think I'd have forgotten for long."

Brenna blushed, but tried to explain. "Mitch's attack gave you a concussion. That's how it works sometimes."

"So that's why some things are hard to remember?"

Another voice answered, "You took some pretty hard blows to the head."

Cassidy and Brenna looked toward the end of the bed. Brenna straightened up and turned toward the doctor. "She does seem to be piecing things together."

"Does she remember anything about the incident that caused her injuries?" he asked. Brenna shook her head. "It will probably come back to her." He turned back to Cassidy, addressing her directly. "You'll have trouble for a little while. Your brain was severely bruised." He studied her chart. "What's your name?"

"Cassidy Hyland," Cassidy answered automatically. Seeing Brenna's surprise, she added, "That's good, right?"

The doctor nodded. "Good. Birthday?"

She hesitated, clearly searching her foggy memory. "February 18th, 1968."

"Excellent. Just the short term memory centers are affected, apparently." He put down the clipboard and pulled a scope out of his coat pocket. "I'm going to take a look inside your head."

For reassurance, Cassidy held Brenna's hand while the doctor examined her eyes and ears. "Do you have any ringing in your ears?"

"No."

"Any dark spots in your vision?"

"No."

Removing the pillow from behind her head, he helped Cassidy lie back flat. Again holding Brenna's hand, Cassidy grimaced at the prodding and gasped at one particular poke to her left ribcage. "It's going to be a good six weeks on those ribs," he said, "but your chest sounds are finally clear."

He checked the IV bag. "I'll have a different antibiotic switched into your drip. How's your stomach feel? Your chest?"

As he palpated those areas, she bit her lip to keep from making a sound, but she had to squeeze her eyes shut, and still tears dripped down her cheeks. At last he stopped probing her.

"You had a hemopneumothorax and lost a lot of blood. There was heavy damage to your liver and spleen. Surgery took care of some of it, but there's going to be a lot of drainage. You'll have another day or two on IV fluids, then start on a liquid diet. Maybe Saturday you'll be ready for something more substantial. If you're very good," he added with a smile. "We'll get you into a general room as soon as I'm sure there is no danger of blood clots."

"But she is getting better?" Brenna asked.

He addressed Cassidy. "You're conscious. Fairly self-aware. Your eyes are clear and alert. There are no indications the swelling around the base of your skull cut off anything vital and the swelling has gone down. A day or two more and I'll be able to make a better prognosis, but I'd cautiously project that full recovery is quite possible."

Cassidy squeezed Brenna's hand, exchanging a shy smile with the other woman when she turned. "Thank you, Doctor."

"I'll be back for my regular rounds at eight." When Cassidy nodded her understanding, he left.

Brenna exhaled in relief. "Thank God."

"You were worried about me."

"Yes, I was. I saw what Mitch did to you and it scared the hell out of me. I thought I might lose you."

Contentment filled Cassidy. Adrenaline reserves began to fade, leaving her exhausted. She blinked sleepily. Soft lips moved against hers then Brenna pulled back.

"Now maybe we can both get some sleep."

"Will you stay?"

"I won't go anywhere. And when you wake up, Ryan should be here."

CHAPTER FIFTEEN

"MAX!" ABOUT to step back into Cass's CCU room, Brenna had her hands on the shoulders of a small boy. She smiled at Max then restrained the boy. "Just a minute, Ryan."

Max Brightman met her halfway. Though there was a weary grayness to her blue eyes, she smiled warmly and hugged him with energy. "Quite a stir," he commented.

"Everything's going to be fine soon," she replied.

Terry Brown walked over. "How are things on the set?" he asked Max.

"Shooting has restarted. Front office is all over, keeping the press mostly at bay. They wanted a status report on Cass."

"It's been a long night," Brenna answered. "I should have sent a report with Rachelle when she left." She smiled then. "But Cass has shown improvement even since then. She woke up around four-thirty and the doctor thinks she'll make a full recovery over time."

"Encouraging," Max concluded.

Brenna shook her head.

"Very encouraging," she corrected with another smile. "I'm taking Ryan in to see her now." Brenna grasped Ryan's hand and stepped inside. Max started after her, only to feel a hand on his shoulder.

Terry shook his head. "They need time alone."

Max moved into the room but remained back, observing as Brenna watched over the reunion between mother and son. His friend of nearly twenty years had one hand lightly on Ryan's back and the other on Cassidy's shoulder.

"Someone's here to see you," she said quietly.

Taking his cue from Brenna, Ryan also spoke softly. "Mommy?"

"Ryan, hi." The voice was very tired, but even so, Cassidy was very happy to see her son.

Max watched Brenna bend over the railing to lightly kiss her forehead. Over the years of friendship, Max had seen Brenna at many hospital bedsides, and in many relationships.

It was clear to him that this was different; Brenna was different. It was in the way she met Cassidy's gaze; there was a directness in her expression that he hadn't seen for anyone else. The younger woman's expression also was filled with pure devotion. There was no way he could see to interpret their connection other than that they were in love. While he had been flip with Brenna, he still hadn't been sure. He had even seen them at the play and been wary of believing it. But seeing Brenna with Ryan on her lap in the chair at the head of the bed, he finally believed. She was telling the boy about his mother's many bandages. Occasionally she kissed his cheek as she and Cassidy spoke.

"I'll take Ryan downstairs for breakfast while you sleep."

"You should... go to the studio," Cassidy replied, her voice washed out so Max had to read her lips to understand what she had said.

"When you're out of here, I'll go back to work. Not before," Brenna insisted. "Consider that incentive to get well, all right?"

"I really messed things up," Cassidy said sadly.

"No you didn't; Mitch did. I will make sure he pays for this as fully as possible."

The determination in Brenna's voice was to be expected, but not the underlying pain. Max had heard that specific mixture of determination and pain only once, back at the very beginning of their friendship.

"You will do no such thing."

A male voice accented from somewhere in the South or Midwest interrupted the quiet conversation. It came from almost on top of Max, and he stepped back to see a man and a woman standing in the doorway, both staring at the tableau around the bed.

Max watched Brenna stand up, set Ryan down by her legs, and turn to face the new visitors. She appeared to struggle a bit for composure before speaking. Still, her voice shook.

"Mr. and Mrs. Hockman." She nodded at each but her eyes darkened with anger and lingered on Cassidy's father. "I'm Brenna Lanigan. I've been with your daughter since the attack."

Max was taken aback by the amount of tension suddenly filling the room, and the very dark and dangerous look on the face of the older man. Before Max could speak, though, Cassidy's father barked, "You've been with her longer than that! It ends now. Get out of my daughter's room."

Brenna kept her eyes on Cassidy's father, even as she held her place at Cassidy's bedside. "Mr. Hockman," she began. She paused, reconsidering her deference. They were all adults, and the stakes were high. "I have permission to be here," she concluded firmly.

"Not from me! Get out!"

Behind her, a small hand clutched at her pants. Brenna glanced down at Ryan, who was wrapping himself around her leg and staring up at his grandfather with wide-eyed uncertainty. Soothing the boy with a gentle touch along the side of his face, she found it easier to steady her own nerves. "No."

"You are not in charge here. I left orders who was allowed in, and you are not on that list. I will not have you influencing Cassidy."

"She has the right, and the ability, to make her own choices," Brenna replied evenly.

"Not in this. Not when she's my daughter."

"Is that why you struck her and drove her from your home? Because you're afraid of what her choices say about you? No one should live through their children that way." Brenna stepped back. "No one should control their family through fear."

"Holiness is only attainable through fear of God."

"You are not God, Mr. Hockman, and neither is your former son-in-law. God does not beat people to death." She gestured toward the bed, drawing the Hockmans' attention to their daughter. She was sure that when they saw what Mitch had done, they would not remain steadfast in their condemnation of Cassidy.

"What happened?" Sylvia tentatively stepped closer. "Oh, dear sweet Lord..." She looked to Brenna questioningly. "Can I?"

"Sylvia!" Mr. Hockman—Gerry, Brenna mentally corrected—sent a warning glare toward his wife.

Brenna took another step back from the bedside and gestured encouragement to Cassidy's mother. "Go ahead, Sylvia." She gambled by using the woman's first name. It got her a worried, uncertain look, but the woman did step forward, her gaze returning to Cassidy's face as she reached out and hesitantly touched the bandaged hand.

"Now you get out!" Gerry shouted, taking a step toward Brenna.

Brenna stood her ground and made herself very clear. "Lay a hand on me and you will not enjoy the consequences."

"Who did this to her?" Sylvia asked softly.

"I would have thought someone would have given you some of the details. Mitch did this to her. I arrived in time to stop him from doing worse." Sylvia frowned. "He's in jail awaiting a bond hearing. Didn't the studio explain when they called?"

"Gerry?"

Sylvia looked toward her husband and Brenna realized he had been the one to take the call.

She directed her remarks to Cassidy's father.

"Being selective with your facts, Gerry?"

He looked away. "She deserved it. No decent wife would want this acting more than she wanted her husband."

"No one deserves this." Brenna exhaled as she tried to keep her voice calm. "Damn it, no one!"

Cassidy awakened at the sound, and Brenna twisted quickly to stop her as she struggled to move.

"Cass, no." When Cass met her gaze with understanding and determination, it set Brenna's heart singing, despite the gravity of the situation. She adjusted the bed so Cassidy could face her father.

Cassidy exhaled carefully then begin to speak. "Would you prefer Mitch had killed me?" Sylvia's face went pale, but Gerry's hardened at his daughter's breathy, pain-filled voice. She caught her breath and went on. "Sorry to disappoint you..." She had to stop and collect herself, tears wetting her cheeks at the amount of effort it took just to speak. "...again." Cassidy dropped her head back against the pillows.

Brenna's tears threatened to fall as she squeezed Cassidy's shoulder, offering what support she could.

"Go... away," Cassidy wheezed as her energy failed.

Ryan reached up and prodded his mother's arm, plaintively calling out, "Mommy?" Cassidy did not respond.

Brenna felt Cassidy's tremors fade away as her eyes closed in exhaustion, and quickly checked the heart monitor for reassurance before turning back to Gerry.

Sylvia fell heavily into the bedside chair, covering her face with her hands. Gerry walked toward the bed and every muscle in Brenna's tensed as her body flooded with adrenaline. She took a step forward, placing herself between Cassidy and her father. Slowly, she straightened, tucking in the covers as Gerry stopped at the foot of the bed. He looked as unmoved as before, but Brenna thought perhaps there was a flicker of doubt in his lowered gaze. Perhaps if she left, gave them some time to think about what had happened between them, they would see what they had done was terribly wrong, regardless of their reasons for doing it.

"I'm taking Ryan down to the cafeteria for breakfast. Maybe by the time I return, you'll be ready to be reasonable."

She withstood the withering glare from Gerry with a neutral expression. Taking Ryan's hand, she noticed how he clung to her, watching his grandfather warily. She reassured him with a squeeze of his hand and led him out of the room.

In the corridor she went to the nurses station, greeting Cassidy's nurse with a terse smile. "She's sleeping, so we're going down to breakfast. Her parents are with her." Terry Brown reached her then. "Terry, would you stay please? I think Cassidy got through to them, but... Just watch out for her?" He nodded and she turned to go to the elevator. Max appeared alongside as they waited.

Wracked with tension, Brenna had forgotten he had briefly been in the CCU room with her, Cassidy, and Cassidy's parents. Now, she appreciated his quiet, steady presence. The elevator emptied into the lobby. One by one, milling reporters identified them and began circling.

Brenna held tight to Ryan, but probably need not have worried. Scared by the closing crowd shoving microphones in their faces and calling out questions, he clung to her.

She answered an update question with, "Her parents have arrived." She answered a status question with, "She's sleeping now." A few of the questions made her realize that her statement about their relationship had made it into entertainment press rooms around the country.

"When you return to shooting, will the characters be re-written to reflect your changed relationship with Ms. Hyland?"

She stared at the questioner. "Excuse me?"

"Will the writers put Jakes in a romance with Hanssen?"

"I have no idea what the writers plan. Now, if you'll excuse us." She pushed past the reporter, only to be faced by another.

"Ms. Lanigan, does this mean your character will be coming out of the closet and admitting she's gay?"

Brenna groaned. "What Jakes does is her business, and Pinnacle's, not mine! Excuse me."

She shoved past the rest and entered the cafeteria. With everyone jostling for the perfect angle to take pictures, the media crowd could not immediately follow them through the narrow doorway.

Max stood with them in line, his jaw flexing with anger. "You're not going to get a moment's peace."

"It'll blow over. The media will figure out what's real and what isn't, and eventually leave us all alone. This is just sensationalism," she rationalized. "A star is beaten up by her ex-husband and they immediately assume jealous rage. So they have to figure out who he was jealous of."

"You are the one he was jealous of."

"No. Mitch is a chronic abuser. If it wasn't about me, it probably was about custody, but it could have been about anything else. He created excuses to do what he wanted." Looking at her buttered toast and coffee, Brenna closed her eyes.

"All right. Do you need me to stick around?"

"You probably should get back to the set. I'm sorry your time here during the shoot couldn't have been more pleasant."

"It has been good to see you, Bren."

"I'm glad you were here."

He put his hand behind her head and kissed her temple. "Me, too." He got to his feet and she watched him walk away, pushing easily through the crowd of reporters because he simply did not interest them.

Turning back, she watched Ryan eating his scrambled eggs.

"Miss Lanigan?"

"Yes?"

"Will we go back to see Mommy?"

"After you've eaten," she assured him. He redoubled his efforts to eat quickly. "Slow down. You don't want to make yourself sick," she coaxed, pulling the fork away from his mouth and encouraging him to put it down for a moment. To give his body a chance to catch up with the food he'd already stuffed in it, she asked, "What would you like to get as a present for your Mom from the gift shop?"

"A toy motorcycle," he said with a smile.

"That sounds like it'd be more for you than for your Mom," she commented with a smile and a light ruffling of his hair. "How about some flowers, or a picture frame?"

"Who would be in the picture?"

"I still have your mother's purse. Why don't we find a picture of you to leave with her after you go?"

"I can't stay?"

"We should get someone to take you away from this mess. You don't like the reporters, and unfortunately they aren't going away."

"Why do reporters ask so many questions?"

"That's their job. But we can avoid them sometimes."

"Okay." Calmed by the quiet talk, Ryan returned to finishing his meal.

When the pair returned to CCU, Brenna carried a vase of carnations and Ryan carried a small box. When they emerged on the floor, Ryan immediately spotted his grandfather talking with the doctor and stepped behind Brenna's leg. "It's all right," she assured him. "Let's just go see your mom."

Sylvia stood at Cassidy's bedside, looking more concerned than when Brenna had left. An oxygen mask had been pulled over Cassidy's bruised features and a fresh bandage covered her throat. "What happened?" Brenna asked, putting the flowers down on the rolling table.

Her voice barely audible, Sylvia answered, "They argued. She complained... her chest hurt."

Afraid that Cassidy had had another heart attack, Brenna asked heatedly, "What did the doctor say?" Sylvia frowned, but Brenna urged, "She almost died while I watched, Sylvia. Please tell me!"

Cassidy's mother studied her, obviously conflicted. "Please?"

Perhaps it was a recognition that Brenna cared for Cassidy as much as she did, or just a way for Sylvia to reach out for support she needed. In any case, Sylvia finally nodded. "Her left lung had collapsed again. They revived her."

Brenna quickly went from alarm to relief. "Thank you," she breathed. Ryan climbed up onto the chair next to the table and opened the box, putting up the picture so his mother could see it when she woke. Brenna stepped back to let him work diligently on his own, arranging things as he wished.

Out of the corner of her eye, she saw Sylvia watching her with puzzlement.

Reaching out, Brenna offered, "Don't go. I don't want to be in conflict with you."

"But it's a sin," Sylvia whispered, clearly shocked.

"We're not that different," Brenna insisted.

"You're a—"

"I'm a mother, too," Brenna interrupted firmly.

"You're shameless!"

"No, I'm not. I'm very ashamed of how I treated Cassidy when she first joined our cast."

"Your series caused her divorce!" Sylvia charged.

Brenna shook her head. "It probably saved her life. She had been keeping it all inside. Only one person even listened to her, and it wasn't me. I ignored her, too. You wouldn't believe her when she said Mitch was awful. You and I, we both left her to twist alone, until she had nowhere to turn."

Sylvia looked stunned. "She always sounded so sure of her choices."

"If she had admitted her mistake in marrying Mitch, what would you have said?"

Sylvia's face froze then she frowned.

"How could you know?"

"Because I thought my mother would say terrible things when I made a horrible mistake as a young woman. Unlike Cassidy, I took the risk and told my mother. And she said the terrible, hurtful things that I thought she would. So I know it happens."

Brenna swallowed. The pain was still sharp. Years later, Brenna was sure her mother had ultimately showered her with love only because illness had taken away her memories of those earlier disappointments.

Feeling too vulnerable, Brenna walked away from Sylvia but could not leave the room. Cassidy needed her. Settling into another chair, she turned so Sylvia could not see her face.

"What the hell is going on in here?" Looking up, her muscles tensed,

Brenna saw Gerry Hockman filling the doorway. "I told you to get out."

"Gerry," Sylvia called to him from Cassidy's bedside.

"What is it?" He sounded exasperated, but he crossed the room. Brenna suppressed an instinctive cringe as he passed her.

"What does the doctor say?" his wife asked.

"She can't be transported anywhere right now."

Brenna surged to her feet. "You can't be thinking—"

"She needs the best care."

"She'll get that here."

"She needs family around her."

"What about Ryan? He's her family, and he needs his mother."

"We're taking him with us."

"No, you're not!"

Gerry raised his fist at her. "You don't have any input here."

Damn, Brenna thought, taking a step backward. There has to be some other option.

Terry appeared, drawing all eyes to him at the doorway where he stood with a man at his side. Brenna recognized Paul Heath, who inclined his head toward her in silent greeting.

"Who the hell are you?" Gerry demanded.

"I'm Paul Heath, Patient Advocacy. I represent Ms. Hyland's and Ms. Lanigan's interests."

"You called in a lawyer?" Hockman asked her in shock.

"Not formally," she replied. "But I will."

"Since when do my rights as her father get questioned?"

"Ms. Hyland is an independent adult with her own rights. From what Mr. Brown told me, she had already conveyed her wishes that she not be removed from this hospital," Heath answered calmly.

Gerry frowned but did not say anything else inflammatory. Brenna hated thinking the only things he would respond to were legal threats. She also lamented the interruption, feeling she had almost connected with Sylvia, was almost able to appeal to a shared outrage at the violence, getting the woman to see her as something other than a rival for her daughter's affections.

Sylvia Hockman was weak, though, when faced with her husband. Brenna wondered if there was abuse there too, if only mental.

"What now?" Gerry asked, sounding more reasonable.

"We wait until Ms. Hyland wakes up, then we all hear what she has to say," Paul explained. "Or I call Security and no one sees her except her doctor and her nurse." He indicated the doorway. "There is a lounge on this floor where you can wait."

Brenna made the first move to follow the directive, taking Ryan into the corridor and looking for the lounge sign. Finding it to the right, across from the elevators, she led Cassidy's son to the leather-padded chairs in a small room with two round tables and a drink machine. Terry followed close behind, sitting beside her as Ryan curled up in her lap.

"Do you need me to stay?" he asked.

The question drew Brenna's eyes away from the doorway as Paul entered, followed by the Hockmans. Cassidy's parents took the opposite corner from Brenna and Ryan. Paul settled at one of the tables, flipping open his portfolio notebook and beginning to work in the silence.

Brenna considered Terry's question. With Paul there she felt less vulnerable to the wishes of the Hockmans. "You should go to the lot," she said. "Ryan and I will be fine. Cassidy'll wake up and this will all be settled. As soon as that happens, I can probably go in myself for a few hours."

"Are you sure? I can call someone else to stay with you."

"It will work itself out," Brenna insisted. "Go on."

Terry stood. He returned a nod from Paul Heath then left the lounge. A few moments later, the beep of the elevator's arrival signaled his departure. Wearily Brenna met the wary gazes of the Hockmans and then closed her eyes, feeling Ryan tuck himself up under her chin as she dozed.

Chapter Sixteen

THE DOOR to the lounge opened with a click. Brenna looked up from the table where she sat looking over Ryan's drawing efforts. She recognized Cassidy's nurse. The woman's smile made Brenna's heart lift in anticipation. She put her hand on Ryan's shoulder and kissed his head.

"She's awake. The doctor says she can see you now."

Brenna pushed her chair back and rose, sweeping her gaze to the other side of the visitor lounge. The Hockmans also rose from the corner they had staked out over two hours ago. Neither looked particularly relieved that Cassidy was awake. Sylvia had been crying quietly for a good portion of the wait. Brenna had heard her in the tense silence, but breaching the separation had been out of the question while Gerry was present.

Gerry, on the other hand, cast yet another angry glare her way, as he had most of the time in the lounge. When he returned his attention to his wife, it was to make her walk out ahead of him. Brenna turned away, helped Ryan to put the borrowed crayons back in the sturdy plastic box provided by the floor nurse, stalling for a moment before guiding him out to see his mother again.

The first thing she noticed was Cassidy lying flat on her back; even the pillow had been moved away.

Since Cassidy's parents stood alongside the head of the bed, Brenna moved Ryan and herself to the end. Paul Heath, whether he realized it or not, was the buffer between the two groups, standing at the lower corner.

Cassidy looked up at her parents. Anxiety shaped her features, drawing her eyes down before furrowing her brow when she met her father's stare.

Brenna held her breath as Cassidy lifted her bandaged hand up, past the rail, toward her mother. "Mom."

Sylvia's reaction was a combination of fear and indecision. She started to reach for Cassidy's hand.

Gerry snatched Sylvia's hand away. The move so sudden, that Sylvia gasped. Cassidy cringed.

"If you want forgiveness, girl, you know how to get it." As Cassidy pulled her hand back and met his eyes, he added, "We're waiting."

Cassidy's lips trembled and her eyes went glassy. Twisting her gaze away, Cassidy next noticed Paul. "Who are you?"

"I'm Paul Heath. My job is to speak for patients' rights in situations like yours."

"Like mine?"

He nodded. "Yes. Your parents want to transfer you to another hospital."

"I told them I didn't want that," Cassidy reiterated. "I need to stay here."

"You need your family around you," Gerry said sharply.

Paul was not fazed. "As long as your wishes remain unwritten, Ms. Hyland, your parents are the authorities that the legal system will accept to speak on your behalf in the event of a catastrophe."

"What's a ca-taz-fee?" Ryan asked curiously.

Brenna patted his shoulder as he stood against her thigh. "Shhh, honey, I'll explain later." When she turned back, Cassidy was studying her and trying to lift her head to see Ryan better. She eventually stopped trying and lay back quietly, holding Brenna's gaze for a long, thoughtful moment.

Pinning Heath again, Cassidy asked, "What do I have to do?"

"There are two documents that offer assurances you will be cared for as you see fit." He waited as Cassidy's gaze returned to Brenna, the look now searching her, delving for something. Brenna swallowed.

"What are they?" Cassidy prompted.

"A Living Will and a Health Proxy." Paul waited for a response. "Would you like to discuss them?"

"She doesn't need to discuss them. She's going to come home like a good girl."

Cassidy bridled at her father's assumption. In a voice more sharp than she probably intended, she asked for clarification. "The documents. What exactly would they do?"

She was tiring already, Brenna saw, leaving her head and neck carefully aligned, facing the ceiling instead of the lawyer.

"The first spells out the way you expect a hospital to proceed with your care. It can't cover all contingencies, though. The Health Proxy designates someone with the right to authorize your care in those instances the LW doesn't cover."

Cassidy closed her eyes and Brenna worried the strain was getting dangerous. "Maybe this should wait," she suggested softly. "You shouldn't do anything that might put extra stress on your heart."

Blue eyes filled with pain found Brenna. "No. I want this settled," Cassidy wheezed. "Do I have to complete both right now?" she asked Paul.

"No."

"I'd like to designate a proxy then," Cassidy said.

"No, Cassidy dear. Please. Give it some thought?" Sylvia asked.

"She's not fit to make these decisions right now, anyhow," Gerry challenged.

Paul had her chart in his hands. "Do you mind?" he asked Cassidy. She shook her head, just barely. "The doctor thinks she can be moved to a regular room by Monday. Her recovery is expected to be slow, but she's not been judged delirious or without clear judgment in any of her lucidity exams."

Brenna breathed a sigh of relief. "Then she's out of danger." Turning to Cassidy, she encouraged, "You don't need these things." She sensed what Cassidy wanted to do—cut her parents as they had cut her. *But does it have to happen right now?*

"There's no one I trust more than you, Bren. I want you to do this for me."

"Wait. No."

"It should be family!" Gerry argued.

"It doesn't have to be someone here right now, does it?" Brenna asked Paul earnestly. He shook his head. "Then pick someone not in the middle of this."

Cassidy shook her head. "I have no other family, Bren. Please?"

Brenna wavered. Cassidy, it seemed, was determined. Brenna was not family, not legally. But Cassidy's statement seemed to be enough for Paul Heath. She looked from the lawyer back to her beloved's face and worried at her bottom lip. Everyone looked at her intently, awaiting her decision.

She could see that Gerry wanted to kill her, figuratively at least, if not literally. Sylvia was afraid of her. When Cassidy gave a small nod, though, the world around Brenna collapsed to just those trusting blue eyes. Swallowing, Brenna nodded back. Her stomach twisted and her head hurt. She could not deny Cassidy her protection. Not now. "I'll do it."

Gerry threw up his hands explosively. "That's it?" He pointed at Brenna. "You're in charge because she says so? Your control is insidious, bitch!" He turned to see Paul withdrawing a pre-typed document from his portfolio. "I will fight this in court! You just see if I don't, you gay-loving bastard!"

Paul paused and looked askance at Gerry, and with utter calm said, "Yes, sir." He gave the older man a faint smile.

"Father, get out."

Brenna spun to see Cassidy, strain drawing her face in heavy lines, pushing herself up higher against the pillows.

"You can't mean that."

"I mean it. You didn't want to see me again until I'd changed my mind. I haven't. And I won't. I am done with you. Get out. Don't come back. The law is on my side."

Though Brenna clearly saw, as everyone else in the room surely did, Gerry Hockman wanted to strangle the first person he could lay his hands on, he managed to contain himself, only stalking from the room. Judiciously, both Brenna and Paul moved out of his way.

"Mom?" When Cassidy had her mother's attention, she continued. "There will be no courts, no lawyers." Sylvia remained at the bedside, searching her daughter's face. Cassidy looked back at her with a plea in her eyes.

"I understand." Eyes reflecting her hurt, Sylvia's gaze shifted to Brenna then drifted sadly over Ryan. Her body screaming resignation, Sylvia Hockman walked from the hospital room.

Paul spoke again, drawing Brenna and Cassidy to him from their individual thoughts. "Hmm. I thought maybe she might serve as the second witness." To Cassidy he said, "Are you ready to do this?"

"Yes."

"All right. I'll find the head of nursing." He left the formulaic document on the small rolling table. "In the meantime, read this."

Cassidy carefully reached for the paper and said, "Thank you."

He nodded briefly, tucked the rest of his papers together and quit the room.

For the longest time, as Cassidy lay quietly reading, the only sounds in the room were the swish of her oxygen pump and the regular echoing beep of the heart monitor. At the end of her bed, Brenna did not move.

Ryan fidgeted. "Mommy?"

Despite being unable to really see him, Cassidy heard and responded to the worry in his voice. "Ryan, come here." She saw Brenna's shoulder move as her hold on Ryan lingered until he tugged his hand free, coming up the window-side of the bed. Brenna's eyes followed Ryan's progress. Meeting Brenna's gaze when it reached her, Cassidy tried to ease Brenna's distress. "You too, Rocky."

Brenna blinked and offered her a puzzled look. "Huh?"

"Of the two of us, I'd definitely say you're the smart, short one," she explained.

"Oh. I thought maybe you meant the boxer," Brenna responded sheepishly, moving up the near side of the bed.

"You needed a smile. Bren, it's over."

"You... Do you really think you should've done that? You really hurt your mother."

Cassidy had seen the signs her mother was not fully in accord with her father. "But he planned to take everything away from me." She exhaled and gestured at the document as she looked back up. "Thank you."

Brenna shook her head and grasped Cassidy's hand. "I don't know what for. If it hadn't been for me, your parents wouldn't have gone off the deep end."

"My parents honestly don't understand, Bren. If he comes at me with a lawyer, I'll fight him." Cassidy took a moment to watch as Ryan pulled himself onto her bed. "My relationship with them has apparently been nothing more than a facade. They say all the right things, but they don't really believe I'm capable of making my own decisions."

"Mommy?"

"Yes?"

"Can we go home now?"

"Not yet, Ryan." Brenna said with a staying hand across Cassidy's waist as she tried to push herself up for a hug. "Mommy may be stronger than she thought, but she's still very delicate." To Cassidy she said earnestly, "You should sleep, you know. We'll do this paperwork later."

Brenna's hand settled for a moment on Cassidy's chest. Through the bandages, Cass felt a sense of security from the gentle reassurance of the touch.

"Why don't you want to do this?"

"Why do you really want me to?"

"Bren, I..." She looked at Ryan and paused, tickling him lightly across the ribs as he sat listening intently. "Ryan, could you...?" She was at a loss what to suggest, but she wanted to talk to Brenna seriously for a moment and she didn't need little ears taking it all in.

Brenna helped. "Ryan, why don't you go and get the pictures you drew?"

"I'll be right back!"

He slid from the bed quickly, causing the mattress to move. Cassidy inhaled and exhaled shallowly to combat the pain, trying to minimize the movement of her jaw.

"Thank you," she gasped.

After he was gone, Brenna settled carefully on the edge of the bed, searching Cassidy's face. The concern and the love shining there told Cassidy she had made the right decision.

"Now tell me—why do you want to do this?"

"In less than four months, you have become closer to me than anyone else in my life. You care for my son as if he was your own. You've charged in on my behalf in situation after situation. I love you. I want you to have the protection of knowing you have the right to be with me when you need to be."

"I don't understand. The Health Proxy is designed to protect you."

"What don't we have that other couples do without question?" Cassidy asked. She saw Brenna fidget at the word "couple", and understood her bashfulness about it. "You think I don't know what you did to get to stay with me here?"

"What?"

"About forty-five minutes ago, before I had the nurse get you. I'd been out of it so long, I asked for the news on the TV to ground myself a little." She paused. "We're the third story on HNN's Entertainment segment."

Brenna sighed. "After the questions I got downstairs, I figured something had come out."

"Yes," Cassidy said gently. "You and me."

With a sad chuckle, Brenna slipped her fingers around Cassidy's. "Are you mad at me?"

"I'm worried for you. And me, a little. You had to hide out in a bathroom. You only got to stay with me because you announced our relationship. It was hard enough on you telling Thomas and James. It won't help with Kevin and your divorce. It shines a very public light on our family." Cassidy laid her bandaged hand on Brenna's thigh. "I liked it when it was sort of our secret."

"I know. Me, too."

Cassidy smiled as Brenna bent forward, lightly brushing her mouth across Cassidy's lips.

There was a knock, interrupting their conversation. Brenna swiveled. "Yes?" She turned back, identifying their visitors to Cassidy. "It's Paul and, I guess, the head nurse." Cassidy nodded; Brenna stood and gestured the lawyer and nurse to the bed.

"Ready to proceed?" Paul asked. "This is Carrie Meeks, R.N., director of the hospital's nursing staff."

"Hello," Brenna greeted with a courteous nod.

From the bed, Cassidy echoed, "Hello. Thank you."

"A lot of people don't think of these things 'til times like this. You're looking like you'll recover, though," Nurse Meeks commented with a generous smile. "So. You're assigning her your Health Proxy?" She looked from Cassidy to Brenna.

"Yes, I am."

Carrie nodded, her tucked back brown hair bouncing lightly. "Sounds pretty definite."

Cassidy looked completely worn out by the time she had signed her last document copy. Brenna took the pen from her and studied her final signature line. "This is more complicated than getting divorced," she remarked idly. "Or married, for that matter."

"If you had been able to do that, you wouldn't need to do this," Paul reminded her, his hand resting gently on her shoulder. Cassidy smiled as Brenna's light eyes met his and accepted his support.

Ryan bounded back in with a sheaf of papers, followed by Cassidy's nurse.

"What trouble did you get into?" Brenna asked as he looked up with a broad, very pleased with himself smile.

"Not much," answered the nurse. "Just a drawer of adhesive bandages," she explained, lifting his shirt. "Seems he wanted to look just like Mom."

Across his stomach and chest, Ryan had haphazardly applied at least a dozen flesh-colored adhesive strips of various shapes and sizes. Brenna laughed, then covered her mouth to hide it. Paul, who was notarizing the documents as Carrie signed them, also chuckled.

"What is it?" Cassidy asked. Hearing his mother's voice and seeing Brenna's laughter, Ryan apparently decided it would be a good thing to show off. He climbed a chair so his mother had a clear view and showed off his bandaged stomach, lifting his shirt over his face.

"Ryan!" Cassidy looked at the nurse sheepishly. "I'm really sorry about this."

"No harm done."

"We won't let him out on the floor alone again," Brenna assured, steadying him with a hand on his arm. "Did you at least bring your mommy's pictures?"

He nodded and jumped down, jumping back up again with the papers in hand. "Here."

While Brenna helped Ryan show off his pictures, Cassidy submitted to the nurse taking her vital signs. "Best recovery I've seen in your kind of case," the woman said. "Fever's almost entirely gone and even your color is looking better." She smiled toward Brenna and Ryan. "Nothing like having family around, hmm?"

She patted Cassidy's good arm and breezed out.

Brenna's flustered expression made Cassidy smile faintly. Laughing would just hurt too much. "Nothing better," she agreed, catching her lover's gaze. "You are my family, Bren."

"I envisioned that," Brenna admitted after a moment. Settling into one of the chairs, she explained. "You and Ryan stood with Thomas and James at—"

"With us where?" a young male voice asked.

Shocked pleasure suffusing her face, Brenna turned. The curtain moved aside and her two sons stood at the side of the bed.

"Hi," Thomas and James greeted together.

Brenna rose quickly and swept her sons into a hard hug, one boy in each arm. She kissed both cheeks before pulling back. "What on earth are you doing here?"

"Well," Thomas started, "we haven't seen you in almost two days. I thought we should." He held up his bus pass. "So, after school we got on the Transit."

Brenna hugged and kissed him again.

"Besides," James added wryly, "there seem to be fifteen zillion reporters who figured out where we live." He looked around. "They can't come up here, right?"

"Oh no." Brenna brushed her fingers over James' cheek. "I'm sorry." She urged the boys closer to Cassidy's bedside. "What did they say to you?"

"What's it like to have a gay mom? Did she date anyone before this? And what do you think of Ms. Hyland?" James shrugged. "You know—the usual stuff."

The usual stuff? She was surprised by his nonchalance. "What did you say?"

James studied Cassidy for a long moment before he answered. "I haven't had one long enough to know. Yeah, guys. And, Ms. Hyland's better'n all of 'em."

"You are amazing." Brenna shook her head in disbelief.

"He shrugged again. No. Man, you are. Mom, I saw the news. That man is enormous, and you just attacked him?" The unspoken "I'm impressed" was clear in James' voice.

"You saw Mitch on the news?" Brenna asked.

"Yeah. He was arraigned this morning. Assault. He was given a fifty thousand dollar bond and a court date next month."

"He's out of jail?" Brenna's voice conveyed the same alarm Cassidy felt. "Only assault!"

Thomas nodded. "Actually, I ... We thought you should know. The police came by as a courtesy to report that he made some threats against you during his release."

"Then why isn't he still behind bars?" Bren asked.

"Apparently making a threat isn't sufficient grounds. You have to go down and press stalking charges before they'll take him in again."

Cassidy watched Brenna sit down hard, hand covering her mouth, her eyes pained. Supportively she squeezed her hand, frustrated the bandage prevented full contact. She cursed Mitch for the shivers she felt from Brenna.

So focused on Brenna, it took Cassidy another minute to feel Thomas' scrutiny. "Yes?"

"What exactly happened? Are you going to be all right?"

"Your mom probably knows more details, but I can tell you I hurt pretty much everywhere." Energized by the concern of people she knew cared, Cassidy tried to shift herself up so she could talk more normally.

Brenna's hands were abruptly on her shoulders. "You better stop moving so much," she chided, easing her back down again. She reached up and pulled Ryan into her arms from the chair. "Come on. Why don't we all go and let Cassidy sleep?"

"Bren, wait." Cassidy turned to the boys. "You go on ahead. She'll be right there."

"What's up?" Brenna asked, leaning close as Cassidy looked up. She could see the shadow of the other woman's attempts to cover her anxiety.

"Please be careful," Cassidy urged. "Mitch is resourceful."

"I'm going to call the studio and request a security detail for you."

"Not me, you. Bren. The news reports... He knows where you live." She gestured toward the silent TV on the opposite wall. Brenna looked up. They both saw the tag line at the same time: KTLA News. Live. The neighborhood's welcome sign was clear in the background.

"Thank God, Thomas and James came here," Brenna breathed.

The captioning revealed the rest of Don Deering's story:

Fantasy took a turn into reality as colleagues became lovers. Ex-husbands, ex-boyfriends, even neighbors and friends are stunned as two stars emerge from the closet.

Deering had obviously done some digging. Cassidy recognized footage from interview sessions the Pinnacle PR Department wouldn't have approved for print, of her and Brenna answering questions, standing casually, even intimately close. Deering had also covered Ryan going missing at the Sports Warehouse. Video rolled of the women and their sons in the parking lot after the ordeal.

Was this the beginning? the caption read.

More recent video followed. For the first time, Cassidy saw the pandemonium surrounding Mitch's attack. The playback froze on a shot of Cassidy's untreated, battered face and Brenna holding her bruised hand just at the edge of the frame.

Will this be the end?

Deering concluded his sensationalist report with a few actual facts, notably their public roles and respective ages.

Brenna groaned. Cassidy brushed her fingertips through the woman's soft hair as Brenna lowered her head. Cassidy whispered, "It doesn't matter to me. I love you."

Despite the bandages and the pin in her jaw, Cassidy judged the tender kiss more than passable. She murmured her appreciation before Brenna pulled away.

Deeply affected, the other woman's voice trembled. "Think you can stay out of trouble until I come back?"

"When?"

"After I've gotten the boys in bed. I don't think I could fall asleep knowing you're here alone."

"Don't," Cassidy said. "Call Rachelle, or Terry. Go to a hotel. Don't go home, Bren, please. Not with Mitch out there."

"He can't scare us if we don't allow it."

"He's apparently not content with just scaring anymore."

Brenna's expression told her she had accepted the warning, as she nodded.

"All right. I'll talk with someone at the lot tonight." She kissed Cassidy's forehead lightly.

Cassidy let the tears from her physical pain fall quietly as she watched Brenna leave with the three boys. Closing her eyes, she adjusted the covers and tried to sleep, despite the worry plaguing her.

CHAPTER SEVENTEEN

DESPITE THE hot afternoon sun, the boulevard that led to Pinnacle's gated entrance was thronged on both sides by picketers. Brenna's Mountaineer crept carefully through the surging crowd and the microphone-waving reporters. Waved to a stop at the guardhouse, she rolled down her window, making the previously unintelligible din clearer and revealing both support and condemnation. Unable to completely ignore the menagerie, Brenna stole a glance to the left, where, from the positive tenor of their signs, the pro camp was gathered. Many shot her a thumbs up and pumped their fists in the air. Signs waved back and forth proclaiming "Grrl Power" and "Lanigan-Hyland: Pinnacle's New Power Duo." There were also "Get Well Soon, Cassidy" and "Best Wishes" placards.

An explosive noise went off behind the Mountaineer, making Brenna jump. Looking in the rear view mirror, she saw a protester running away toward the sea of signs decrying her, Cassidy, and the studio. Sentiments such as "God Decrees Time Trails Time is Up" and "No Gay Jakes" were waved at her. More damning and personal were "Play Gay—Play Dead", and Brenna fumed at the most hateful sign: "Mitch Hyland should finish the job."

"Are the writers planning to write this into the show?"

Brenna turned away from the signs and looked at her younger son.

"No. As a matter of fact, we just did an episode where Hanssen imagines a relationship with Raycreek."

"That's nuts," Thomas said. "Raycreek and Hanssen hardly talk."

"I thought you didn't watch the show," she teased.

He shrugged sheepishly. "I've caught it a few times. Enough to know that storyline definitely doesn't fit the characters."

"Cassidy agreed with you. She asked to rework some of the script and turned it into a delirium. She turned in a very good performance." Brenna held up a hand as the guard came to the window. "What was it?"

"Firecrackers and pop caps, but nothing up your tailpipe. Go on ahead."

"Thanks, Randy. Do you know where Victor Branch is right now?"

"He's been in the main offices with a lot of the production team all day. They're working out story line changes around Ms. Hyland's injury."

She reached out and patted the guard's shoulder. "Thanks. You have a good day."

"When you see Ms. Hyland next, tell we're pulling for her." Brenna smiled. "You be careful, too, ma'am."

Brenna checked her rear view one last time then drove through the opened gate. She guided the car into the authorized vehicles lot, pleased to see a blue-clad officer riding up and down the parking lanes in a golf cart. Security had obviously stepped up since the attack.

Should've been better before, she thought angrily.

"Time to find out how everyone else feels about recent developments," she said, mentally girding herself for the executives' questions. "Stick close, guys," she advised the boys.

Holding Ryan's hand, she led her sons through the foyer. Nodding at another security guard standing in the entry corral, she turned to the Television Division secretary who sat at a desk near a closed door. "Victor Branch around?" Brenna asked, and Cheryl Little wordlessly pointed toward the back offices. Not a good sign. Tensions must have everyone on edge.

In the back corridors, Brenna was self-conscious about the stares she received from open doorways. She drew to a stop at the end of the hallway and knocked firmly on the closed conference room door.

Answering the query from within, she said, "It's Brenna Lanigan."

Lonny Nickel answered the door. Looking harried and disheveled, he combed his fingers through his dark curly hair as he stepped back, gesturing her inside. He balked at the children's presence. "What're they doing here?"

"We're about to head home for some dinner. I thought you'd all—" She gave the room a visual sweep, finding Victor Branch at the far end, flanked by Michael Sassman, Susan Strom, and Cameron Palassis, "like an update on Cassidy's condition."

"Media's doing a fine job of that," Lonny snapped. "A domestic dispute has left one of our stars in Intensive Care, unconscious. Though," he conceded, "Terry did tell us she's awake."

"Off and on since about four-thirty this morning, yes." Brenna settled into a chair and gestured Thomas and James to take a seat on either side of her. Cringing from the sharp tone in Lonny's voice, Ryan pulled himself up in Brenna's lap. She automatically rubbed his back soothingly. "She is still in CCU here, rather than where her parents wanted her moved."

"What?"

"They wanted to move her to Missouri, but it's been worked out."

Cameron cleared his throat. "She's stable now?"

Brenna detected worry in his voice and provided more details. "Surgery went well. The EKG didn't show any lasting damage from her two heart attacks—"

"Two heart attacks!"

"Yes," she replied solemnly. "She had a lot of internal bleeding. Some of it put pressure on her heart. The surgeon spent most of his time plugging holes and draining fluids."

"God," Cameron exhaled, resting his face in his hands.

"I did a lot of praying," Brenna admitted unashamedly.

"But you're here, which must mean her prognosis is good?" Victor prompted.

"They'll probably move her to a general room on Monday. She'll be in the hospital for at least another full week."

"After that?" Lonny asked.

"She's got broken ribs and wears out very quickly. She'll need at least a month of at-home convalescence, and a brace when she comes back to work."

"So, no stunt work, then." Brenna shook her head. "Damn," Lonny fumed. "How are you for work?"

"I'll be taking care of Ryan for her, but I can report."

"Turn the kid over to his grandparents—"

"No!" Ryan exclaimed. "Not going with Grandma and Grandpa." He hugged Brenna hard.

She whispered in his ear, "I promise you'll be safe. I promise." That seemed to soothe him.

"What's wrong with him?" Lonny interjected.

"He witnessed some disturbing arguments between Cassidy and her parents," she explained vaguely. "And not only today."

"Oh." Lonny put his hands in his pockets. "We've moved childcare into an office next to Props. You can leave him there while you work."

"What have you got so far?"

"We're doing all the fill shots first. We gave one of your sequences with Brady—the first apprehension—to Chapman. Will can play it just as well."

"All right."

"Otherwise we're stuck. Could you come in Saturday to work with Brady on your other shots? His contract time was very narrow. We can't get him next week."

Brenna nodded. She had expected that. "Saturday bright and early, I'll be here."

"Are you going back to the hospital?" Cameron asked.

"Tonight." She remembered the most important thing she had to put in place. "I have a request."

"Something you want us to tell the press?"

"I don't want to issue any press releases until after I've talked with Cassidy again and we decide exactly what we want to say." She shook her head. "No, what I need now is someone for Cassidy's protection. Mitch got out of jail on bail this morning. If you don't hire a bodyguard for her, I will."

Victor tapped a folder in his hands against the tabletop. "You think he'll go after her again?"

"I'd bet on it."

Cameron added, "I agree. Before Cassidy's divorce became final, he was always calling, and he does fit the profile of a stalker."

Branch nodded. "All right." Brenna exhaled in relief. "There'll be someone at the hospital by third shift," he assured her. "Now, we need something from you."

The group fell silent as she looked from face to face. Seeing mostly consternation, she grabbed the subject by the proverbial horns. "I don't want to do a press conference."

"You need to give us something," Branch insisted. "The studio's being overrun."

"From what I've been able to piece together, Cassidy went to visit her family in Missouri over the holiday break. We'd begun seeing each other outside work. Her parents found out about it."

Lonny was flabbergasted. "So it's true? You're dating?"

"Wow," said Susan Strom, one of Time Trails set coordinators, who had been sitting quietly in the furthest corner. "This is going to be hot to handle. It crosses that fantasy/reality line fans have a hard time remembering exists anyway."

"I..." She looked at Cameron, who particularly seemed to be trying to ignore her. "We'd have liked it to come out under different circumstances." That was an understatement but these were not close friends, Brenna reminded herself. Details were not required, and in Cameron's case, unwelcome.

Lonny looked at his papers. "We'll help you draft a statement to the press, something to keep them occupied."

"I'll call my agent, and give you something for tomorrow."

Victor Branch shook his head. "Today. Your agent and also Cassidy's are cooling their heels in my office."

"I'm not going to get out of this, am I?" Brenna said with a sigh.

James spoke up. "Why is any of this anyone's business? They chased us out of our house, man."

Brenna put a hand on James' shoulder. "It's all right. He's right; I have to do this."

"All right, let's get the kids to Karen and sit you down with the agents. I'll tell PR they can assemble the press in media room 7."

"Understood." She pushed to her feet. "First I'm going to Cassidy's trailer to collect her appointment book. She needs to have her agent cancel her commitments for the foreseeable future."

"We'll send a runner over to take care of that. Get into my office," Branch snapped.

Brenna had been hoping for at least a short reprieve during which she could marshal her thoughts. She had no idea what she could say in answer to all the press questions. "All right. She's at Pasadena City General, CCU room 408." Brenna scribbled the room number on a scrap of paper and slid it across the table to Branch. "Can I at least talk to the rest of the cast first?"

Victor's expression told her he wasn't sure she wouldn't bolt. Brenna was about to reassure him when Cameron spoke up from across the table.

"I'll walk with her," he volunteered. Turning to Brenna, he repeated, "I'll go with you."

Why on earth would he want to go anywhere with me? Brenna knew she was "the next man" after Cassidy ended her relationship with Cameron. If they were alone, he could say or do a lot of things Brenna was unsure she could deal with right now. Charitably, she did recall he went pale at the news of Cassidy's heart attacks. Maybe he only wanted private confirmation Cassidy was recovering. "All right."

The walk from the executive offices over to the sets for Time Trails had never seemed quite so long. Brenna wanted to both hurry to see the others, and hang back, because she was still trying to piece together where to begin in the press conference. She knew that no matter what prepared statement she gave, the media would harangue her with all the questions she didn't want to address, unless she gave them something else to satisfy them. *Pack of dogs*, she thought uncharitably. *Have to throw them a reasonably tasty bone so that I can jump in the other direction while they're gnawing that to bits.* Cameron shuffled along, his hands shoved in his pockets, his head down. Thomas kept looking from her to the writer, stumbling occasionally as he shortened his strides to avoid tripping over either of them.

Ryan circled, occasionally catching Brenna's hand and asking to see Mrs. Grinaldi. Finally Brenna stopped. "Thomas, do you remember the way to the Prop department?" She caught Ryan's hand and put it in Thomas'.

Thomas nodded. "You're sure?"

"We'll be there shortly, but I think maybe we'll be quicker if Ryan gets some playtime in, instead of crawling on the rigging." Bending over, she hugged Ryan. "You be good." She brushed her palm over his cheek. James held back for a moment, looking from Thomas to Ryan, who he clearly didn't want to spend a lot of time with, and his mother and Cameron. She raised her eyebrow at him in question.

"You need someone with you, though," he said.

Brenna shook her head. "I'll be fine. You don't want to face the press any more than I do."

Cameron stood in silence until James was also gone, having followed after his brother.

"You're pretty good at that," he said. "No wonder Cassidy appreciates you."

"Cameron, don't do this. To me or yourself," she advised kindly.

He tried for nonchalance. "I'm just saying that I... I can see why she loves you." He shook his head. "I don't... I just can't get into kids."

"That isn't why she stopped seeing you," she said quietly.

"How could you know? Have I been the topic of some pillow talk?" he jabbed.

"It isn't like that."

"Damn you," he growled. "One stupid script and she's crawling into your bed." He stabbed a finger at her. Brenna ignored his anger, knowing it stemmed from his hurt. "I used to be the hero. Me. I collected her from that airplane when she was barely able to walk. I saw to it she got treated. She cried on my shoulder every night as I helped her in and out of the brace. Don't you wonder why no one ever saw her out of makeup or out of costume that first month?" He inhaled. "The costumer was the only other person who knew."

Brenna nodded. It all made sense. Ribs took so long to heal. Cassidy never moved much in those early months because she was hampered by the brace. What Brenna had thought a corset had instead been a rigid medical aid.

Cameron was not finished with his rant. "And you! You of all people. You froze her out! Now this—you and her? How does that work?"

Ashamed, Brenna's gaze slid away from his. Cassidy had never mentioned the early days or demanded an apology for Brenna's cold shoulder treatment. She was content to take their relationship forward, leaving the past behind. That seemed to be the way Cassidy lived her life— always in the moment and focused on one thing at a time. Completely. She could be on a set totally in character, to the point that there had been a guest actor who thought Cassidy was a cold fish when she was in "Hanssen mode."

Or she could be totally into you. Brenna recalled being captured by swirling pools of blue eyes on a moonlit mountain night. She inhaled sharply, recalling the last time she and Cassidy had made love. *Was it only two days ago?* It feels more like a lifetime. Her arms suddenly ached with the desire to hold Cassidy again as she cried out in pleasure, the sound making Brenna feel like the queen of the universe.

Hearing Cameron shuffle impatiently beside her, Brenna returned her attention to his question. "You're right. I don't deserve that she should love me, but she does."

"Do you think I could visit her?" Cameron asked. "I know what you said in the office, but..."

"Cameron, I don't know that I would if I were you. She's weak, tired. If she's still upset at you, it might not be the best thing for her to see you." She offered an olive branch. "I can ask her, though."

"She amazed me, taking up with you," he said reflectively, apparently taking her offer to heart. "I thought we were pretty compatible."

"When you treated her like a trophy instead of a person, Cameron, it was over." The look of bewilderment on his face told Brenna that he had no idea what she was talking about. "I don't expect you to understand; you've gotten too used to controlling things. Cassidy has an infectious sense of wonder, and despite her rapid rise in this business, she's not cynical. She's intelligent and insightful. She makes me feel this is all still worth it, that honest love still exists. I'd forgotten."

"Sounds like you had a mid-life crisis," he snorted.

"Maybe I did. But she's worth a crisis."

He still looked completely baffled. They reached the stage door and Cameron pulled open the door to the soundstage. "We'd better make this quick."

With a sigh, Brenna entered ahead of him, then hung back until she heard the director call, "Cut!"

Rachelle stumbled toward her chair. Right behind her, Brady bounced a little and smiled as he looked up. "Hey, Aunt Brenna!"

She held the two chairs as the actors flopped into them. "Hi, Brady."

Rachelle looked up. "Bren!" She glanced beyond Brenna to see Cameron lingering beside a camera. "Cameron?"

"Hi." Brenna smiled and grasped the hands that reached toward her. "Working hard?"

"They rearranged some scenes to free up you and Cassidy, so, here we are," Rachelle explained. "We got our calls at five a.m. I'd barely put my head on my pillow. Will's tickled, though. He got some of your scenes with Brady."

"I heard," she said. "I'll be in on Saturday to finish up my part." She glanced up at Brady. "Are you all right with that?"

"Sure," the young man answered readily.

"Is your dad around?" Brenna asked, thinking about how abruptly Max had left the hospital.

"Came through a little while ago, but haven't seen him since."

"Okay. I'll call him later." Brenna patted Rachelle's shoulders. "I have to run."

"Tell Cassidy we're pulling for her."

"I will. She woke up about four-thirty, actually."

"That's good news. How did the morning go with her parents?"

Brenna frowned. "Her father thinks she deserved it," she revealed quietly.

"Son of a bitch," Rachelle exclaimed with heartfelt emotion.

"They almost got the doctor to agree to move her to Missouri. While Cass was unconscious, they had the medical control. I argued long enough for Cassidy to wake up and take control of things herself."

"What did she do?"

"She named me her health proxy." Brenna caught Rachelle's raised eyebrow. "She'd had another heart attack. I couldn't let her parents do something she clearly didn't want. It's kind of made things more ... permanent between us."

"Sounds like it. What did her parents do?"

"Gerry Hockman fumed, threatened to sue, and then stalked out of the hospital. I have no idea where they are now."

"Where's Ryan?"

"Ryan needed to run off a little steam. It got pretty stormy at the hospital. I think he's nervous and upset, but being around my sons seems to make him feel secure. All three boys are with Mrs. Grinaldi right now."

"So the home front is weathering the press storm?"

"James says there's crowds around our house, which is why they came to the hospital—to get away for a while."

"Shall I tell you what we've been doing to help?"

"Don't tell me. I've been painted as the matriarch of the troupe. My concern over Cassidy is no more or less than what I showed to you, or Rich, or anyone else, when you all had troubles of your own."

Rachelle chuckled. "Nobody's buying that."

"I know. Branch has ordered me to do a press conference. Within the next hour."

Rachelle stood up quickly. "I'll ask for a break. We'll be there to support you."

Brenna sighed. "Thank you." She looked at Brady. "If you see your dad..."

"I'll have someone find him. We'll be there too."

"Thank you." Brenna reached out to give Rachelle a hug, but Rachelle grabbed her and kissed her cheek firmly, startling her.

"Keep your chin up. I'll have as many of us there as I can manage."

"I... Thank you, Chelle."

"See you in an hour."

Brenna walked out of the soundstage area, followed by Cameron. "How much of that stuff about her parents are you telling the press?" he asked.

"As little as possible. Her parents don't deserve the fifteen minutes of fame, and I won't do anything to help Mitch's case by airing it in the press. I want us left alone."

Cameron didn't respond. Brenna inhaled the crisp January air and slipped Cassidy's trailer key out of her purse. She mounted the steps quickly, but the key did not easily fit. Bending down, she examined the lock and noticed scoring around the cylinder. A chill skittered down her spine and she took a step back.

The noise of a golf cart approaching startled her. Turning, she saw a young man in bright blue shorts and a white crew shirt—a Pinnacle runner—driving up to the trailer.

"Hey, Ms. Lanigan."

"Hi. What's up?"

"Mr. Branch sent me to get some of the flowers and stuff from Ms. Hyland's trailer to send over to the hospital."

"I'm here to collect some things she might like myself."

"Give me a hand then?" he asked.

Brenna nodded and stepped back as he moved up the steps. He had the same trouble with his key. The rasp of it in the lock, not settling the tumblers, made her nervous. "Maybe you ought not to..."

He bent away from her outstretched hand and peered into the keyhole. "Looks like something's been jammed in there." He tried the knob. "Dang, it's already unlocked." He pulled the door wide. The knob clicked suddenly in his hand and Brenna grabbed his shoulder, yanking him backward. "Hey!"

Brenna peered around the edge of the open doorway. When nothing jumped at her from the dark interior, she shrugged sheepishly. "Sorry. Guess I'm a little jumpy."

"Yeah, guess so." The runner stood, brushed himself off and reached inside for the switch, flooding the interior with light. "Just flowers and cards everywhere."

Everywhere was right. Several arrangements had been knocked to the floor. The pots lay cracked and flower petals were strewn around. "Well, I'll take these," she said, scooping up a stack of postcards and telegrams and dropping them in her purse. "You get the flowers that are still in decent shape; I'm going to grab her appointment book."

"That was one of the things I was told to find. I was delayed getting out here—couldn't find a cart. All the security folks seem to have 'em." The runner was already hefting several arrangements.

Brenna searched Cassidy's desk and found a combination appointment/address book. "I'll be right back." Stepping out into the sunshine again, she spotted someone else coming up the walkway.

"Can I help you?"

He held out an electronic signature pad. "Making a delivery to Cassidy Hyland." he explained. "I was told her trailer was unlocked and just to put it somewhere there's space. Apparently there've been a lot of deliveries?"

"Yeah."

She read the company name, Flowers Unlimited, and his name, Jim, on his lapel.

"I better get the delivery inside." He started to turn away.

"Wait. I'm a friend of Ms. Hyland's. I'm going to take some of the flowers and cards and things to her. Why don't you leave it with me?" As an afterthought, she asked, "Who is it from?"

"Well, Ms. Hyland's supposed to..."

"She's in the hospital. Who is it from?"

He read the delivery information. "Mrs. Gwen Talbot, 1402 Sycamore."

Brenna nodded, familiar with Cassidy's neighbor. "I'll take the flowers directly to Cassidy. She'll enjoy them."

"But the delivery..."

"You've made it." She grasped the electronic pad and signed her name. "Thanks, Jim." She nudged him back around the end of the trailer where he had set down his package.

There were flowers... but Brenna laughed as she identified the logo on the side of the two-foot tall bucket. "God, that'll send her into catatonia!"

"It's our Chocolate Lover's Bouquet." She hefted the arrangement and sniffed the flowers, distinctly overlaid with the blessed scent of rich chocolate. "It's supposed to be for the recipient," he added with a grin.

"Of course." Brenna dropped her chin and shifted the "bouquet" onto one hip, holding out her freed hand to shake his. "Thanks."

As she headed again for the trailer steps carrying the bouquet, Cameron shook his head. "What the hell?"

"Flower delivery." She nodded toward the delivery man who had started back toward the main buildings. She eased a small wrapped piece of chocolate from the side. "Fortification before I face the press." Surprisingly, Cameron laughed.

Chapter Eighteen

Brenna entered Victor Branch's office and saw Ray Aruth sitting primly, his briefcase open on his lap. Next to him sat a woman Brenna didn't recognize. "Hi, Ray." She turned to the woman and held out her hand. "You must be Cassidy's agent. I'm Brenna Lanigan."

The woman shook her hand. "How is Cassidy?"

"Recovering slowly. It'll be several days yet."

Her own agent still hadn't spoken. "Ray?"

"I'm just here to deliver this," he said, tossing a packet of papers toward her.

She caught it with consternation.

"What's this?" She flipped the first page over and was surprised to see the contracts for the English project Celtic Queen staring up at her. "Voided?" She studied the language appended by the production team's legal representative. "But why?" She looked to Ray for an explanation.

"They want a particular type. You are no longer it," he stated bluntly. "I spent the holidays convincing them to wait for you, saying you were going to be perfect for the role. That you were not pigeon-holed in sci-fi, that you were going to give the project the maturity to bring it spectacular reviews." Ray was tense and aggravated, and didn't care if it showed.

"But I am all those things. I'd have given my complete attention to every tiny detail. Cass and I—"

"Cass and you are the problem," he snapped. "When they decided on you for this film, you were a mature married woman with two kids, the epitome of respectability." He snatched the contract and it crumpled in his tight grip. "Now you are a philandering woman with a lesbian following. That is not what this project wanted from you! Your divorce isn't even final and she's living with you!"

"Actually she's still in the hospital," Brenna said slowly. She swallowed her surprise and hurt at Ray's bluntness. "Thanks for asking."

"The agency doesn't care. You threw away a golden opportunity, for what? For sex? People sleep their way into roles, not out of them."

"This is ludicrous. I'm still the same actor," she chafed. Would people now expect her to only play a gay woman, or that she would only draw gay people to her projects? "Who I love doesn't affect what I can do," she said with asperity.

When she looked at Ray, she found not the ally who had helped her continue to find roles when she had hit the "deadly 4-0," but a man who was just as disappointed in her as the industry now appeared to be.

"There has to be some other reason," she insisted. "Did they find they preferred Sarandon or something?"

"No, they have decided to go with an unknown Scottish-born actress who has been circulating in their Royal Shakespeare Company for twenty years."

The information left her nothing with which to salve the wound. The producers really had decided against her, plain and simple. She clasped her hands around her knee to still their shaking. "What did you try to change their minds?"

"Nothing."

"I see." She stood, turned away from him, exhaled and brushed her fingers through her hair. There was really very little to say. Not looking at him, she asked as plainly as he had spoken to her, "Do you wish to terminate our contract, as well?"

Out of the corner of her eye, she saw Ray pull out another document and her heart sank.

"We foresee that any prospects you might have had will now dry up," he said. "The agency has decided to drop its representation of you."

Roll with it, she counseled herself. You've been in more difficult situations in your career. On the heels of that was the abysmal thought that maybe this actually was the worst. She looked at him, but he was looking at the paper he held out rather than at her. "Do you agree with them?" she asked, accepting the paper.

"I thought you were a good investment when we first acquired you," Ray said neutrally.

"Now you don't think so."

"Why didn't you come to us to handle the publicity on this?"

"This what? My personal relationships were changing; it had nothing to do with my career."

Ray was incredulous. "In six months you went from being married to having an affair with a co-star—a woman!—and you didn't think you'd need publicity management?"

Looking at her situation from the outside for a moment, Brenna realized she might feel the same as the agency did. However, she wasn't outside of it. She was inside, and she was happy. But it was true that her divorce was not finalized. Defensive, Brenna said "It wasn't my intention to have my relationship on the front page of every newspaper in the country."

Ray shook his head. "I thought you were more savvy than that." His words were a final indictment.

"Will the agency be... making a public statement?" she asked. How much more could she take?

Ray shook his head. "Embarrassment is not something we desire, either. Our other clients might get antsy."

"Do you represent any... gay clients?" she asked.

Again shaking his head, Ray said, "If we are, none are out, but the Bormanis Agency prefers a stable of mature clientele in any case."

A label for which she apparently no longer qualified. Brenna exhaled. "Right." At least she could be mature about watching her career self-destruct. "My portfolio?" she inquired, as she snatched up a pen from Victor's desk and signed her name to the agency's dismissal papers.

"I will have a courier deliver all your properties to your home address."

He wasn't even going to bring it himself. Ray was washing his hands of her quickly, cleanly, and quietly. Brenna kept her gaze down so he would not see her eyes shining with unshed tears. She pushed the paper back to him, holding out the pen. Taking it, he signed his name below hers.

"Thank you for the time you spent on my behalf."

"You're welcome," Ray said. He would not meet her eyes.

There was a long silence between them. Finally Ray turned, collected up the signed documents and his briefcase, and hurried through the door.

"Ms. Lanigan?"

Brenna turned with a start. She had forgotten the presence of Cassidy's agent. "I'm sorry for that, Ms. ..."

The agent stood and held out her hand. "Natalia Gardner. My friends call me Talia." Brenna took the hand in surprise. "Looks like you need my help."

"I am going to give a press conference in about half an hour. You were here to help with Cass' side of things."

"I think I can help both of you." Talia nudged Brenna into the chair vacated by Ray. "We can manage this exactly the way you and Cass want."

"What does the studio want me to do?"

"The studio told us..." Talia's gesture included the absent Ray. "Well, I'll finish what I was asked to do," she said, resting her hand on Brenna's knee.

"To say whatever it is two formerly straight actresses can say to quiet the damn reporters so they'll leave the set alone except on media day."

As anxious as Brenna was, the statement sounded exactly like Victor Branch. Delivered by this woman, it made her laugh. "That sounds exactly like Victor. All right." She sobered. "Trouble is, Cass isn't out of the woods yet, and I'm pretty frayed around the edges. I am quickly realizing that I had never considered what it means to be gay—until one of our directors made me see that I could become Hollywood's newest poster child."

"So you've considered it for about five seconds." Talia nodded, seemingly completely unfazed. "All right, I can work with that."

Brenna shook her head. "How did Cass find you?"

"She looked in the Yellow Pages under damage control," Talia replied. "I helped her and Cameron Palassis keep her news all positive while she was divorcing Mitch."

"So you knew about her being abused?"

"Yes, and we will get through this new challenge together as well." Talia resumed her seat beside Brenna. "Now, I've got some ideas here about where to start."

"Let's hear them." Brenna scooted her chair closer to Talia's, looking over the woman's arm as she withdrew a yellow legal pad and a pen.

The large auditorium-style room frequently doubled as a full feature screening room for pre-release movie showings for all the big reviewers. Now Brenna stood in the wings, leaning hard on Talia's arm and wishing she had time to call Cassidy to watch their "coming out" on TV. She might have dared to bring their sons to stand with her, but Talia had advised that the boys be kept away. They didn't want to prompt questions about how the new family would go forward, just deal with the disruption to the sets, the beating Cassidy had received from Mitch and its presumed cause, the relationship she and Cassidy had begun.

Looking at the small note cards Talia had carefully printed as they settled on the order and nature of the questions they would answer, Brenna exhaled nervously. Talia had warned her not to perform. "They need to see the real you, Bren. That's the only way they'll believe every word you say and leave you alone."

The media is too damn interested in our lives, Brenna thought angrily. *Why don't they just get their own?* She took a deep, calming breath. She had to get through this, needed to get back to the hospital and see to Cassidy's care. What was important now was to find out what it would take to make Cassidy fully well again. And this press conference was standing in her way. Best get it over with. She straightened her back.

Talia patted Brenna's hand and smiled encouragement. "You handle this the way I know you can, and I'll represent you from here on out."

Brenna felt a small portion of her load lifted from her shoulders. "Thank you."

Standing room only, it seemed every member of the entertainment-interested press, television, radio, and internet were in attendance. There were hand-held recorders, video cameras, production cameras, pens and pads or palm-sized computers in nearly every visible hand. There were still cameras on tripods, a few hanging around the necks of still more reporters edging in around the outskirts of the bucket seating.

"Victor's going to speak first, then I'll go." Talia winked. "Then you can wipe the floor with them."

Brenna laughed and the tension in her back miraculously vanished.

There was suddenly a large hand on her right shoulder, making Brenna jump. Victor looked down as she looked up.

"Ready?" he asked.

"As I'll ever be," Brenna allowed.

"You have the skills to do this," Victor said. "So do it." He stepped forward.

Talia leaned closer. "What was that about?"

"Victor once told me that nothing I ever do is accidental."

"Really?"

"I dumped a bowl of punch on a man who was aggravating Cassidy and made it look like an accident."

"Is the man still alive?"

"Yes."

"Then I'd say 'brava'."

Victor's appearance at the podium raised the noise level momentarily and Brenna calmed herself as the flashes from cameras gradually stopped. Raising his hands, Victor said, "All right, everyone, take a seat. We all know why we're here, and I am finally able to say that we can give you some definitive, accurate information."

Brenna turned at a hand on her shoulder and

Rachelle Cheron smiled. "We're with you." Behind Rachelle stood Sean Durham, Will Chapman, and Terry Brown. A little further back, Brady stood with his father Max. Brenna bit her lip to keep from bursting into tears as her friends all gave her a thumbs up.

She turned back to face the crowd, the show of support putting a little more steel in her spine.

Victor continued,

"...not going to treat being gay as some pariah condition. Far too many people who work in this industry know it isn't. You're here because two presumably straight actresses have revealed they are having a relationship, and a very private grievance harbored by a former spouse landed one of those women in the hospital."

"So let's get on with it!" someone shouted from the gallery.

"Regardless of the imagined reasons for it, there is no excuse for spousal abuse," Victor said. "This studio should have done more to protect Ms. Cassidy Hyland from her ex-husband. That fault we accept, and studio security procedures have been updated as a result of this terrible incident."

"So you're sorry. We get it. Move on!"

Victor's glare could have immolated the man on the spot. He did not rise to the baiting. "Ms. Hyland remains in the hospital. Her condition has been upgraded from critical to serious, and she will likely be moved from CCU to a private room on Monday. We have her agent, Natalia Gardner, to address questions of Ms. Hyland's condition." He stepped away from the podium and Natalia moved up to take his place. "Thank you, Mr. Branch. As Ms. Hyland's representative, let me go on record stating that this studio has handled this terrible situation with as much attention to Ms. Hyland's medical needs as possible. Cassidy sends her thanks, and she promises to be back at work as soon as her doctors allow."

Brenna listened as Talia outlined the extent of Cassidy's injuries, as well as congratulating the studio for immediately bringing her parents in from St. Louis. Brenna could debate how good that action had been, but it played well to build the studio's image of being family-oriented and also a supportive employer for an injured employee.

"Ms. Hyland and Ms. Brenna Lanigan and their colleagues spent more than eighteen months working side by side, long days and often long into the night, to bring Time Trails' dramatic adventures to the American viewing public. The show is a ratings bonanza every time this cast comes on screen." Talia shuffled cards in front of her, signaling her plan to change points. "But their private lives have never played out on that same screen and been held up to public scrutiny."

Brenna was surprised to see Rachelle step forward as Talia turned to the wings. "Ms. Rachelle Cheron's pregnancy last year was hidden from the cameras—for the simple reason that her character was not pregnant."

Rachelle nodded at the crowd as she stepped back past Brenna. She stopped briefly to give Brenna's hand a supportive squeeze, unseen by the gathering. Brenna turned her attention back to Talia, impressed with the woman's quick thinking.

"In this same way, an actress' sexuality is her own private affair." There was a wave of snickering sounds. "Yes, this was an affair," Talia repeated. "And it came as much of a surprise to the two women involved as it has to you now over the last few days."

Sure she was about to be called forward, Brenna cleared her throat and waited.

"Cassidy Hyland is a young beautiful woman, a tempting sexual icon to men everywhere. That was the primary purpose of her being cast in Time

Trails almost two years ago—a key male demographic got juiced every time she appeared." Talia danced quickly to her other point. "Her vivid acting skills made scenes crackle with energy and intelligence."

Talia turned to Brenna. "And women began to fall in love with her too." Brenna stepped forward at the nod from Cassidy's agent. "Competition is the heartbeat of so many in Hollywood, so much so," Talia pointed out, "that Brenna Lanigan and Cassidy Hyland fell in love, and didn't even know it."

Talia grasped her hand and pulled her to the podium. Brenna felt the notecards crumpling in her clenched fists and stood waiting for her eyes to adjust to the white lights that were blinding her. For the first time she was unable to be outside of herself, to see herself do all the right things and walk herself through this event.

Brenna blinked, and then said the first thing that came to mind. "I didn't know it was possible to feel this way." She paused. "About anyone.

"Some women... Me," she corrected. "I grew up like most Midwestern girls, expecting to finish high school, marry a nice man, maybe have a career, definitely have children, and raise them to send them off into the world on their own someday."

Brenna looked at the first card which read, "Expectations." She lifted her gaze back to the reporters. "I wanted the career so badly, I left home at 18, determined to make or break it in New York. The children and the husband could come later. But I understood that they would come."

She looked over her shoulder, wishing to see her sons there, but finding a smile from Talia, and beside her, Rachelle. She lifted her eyes briefly to the ceiling and thought of Cassidy. "It never occurred to me that I would want, or need, anything else."

She looked back at her cards. The second read "Things I want and need." Brenna smiled. "But I did want and need other things. I needed understanding. I wanted the outdoors. I needed to act. I wanted my children's health and happiness. And I wanted to find someone who wanted these things too." She inhaled and exhaled to settle the nerves making her palms damp. "I tried twice but failed at my marriages to two men. Not all of it was their fault; a great deal of it was mine. I hadn't learned how to express what I wanted and needed in ways they could comprehend, and deliver on. I had begun to believe the 'Men are from Mars, and Women are from Venus' claptrap about the differences between the sexes. I had women friends, and I had men as lovers. I was resigned to the fact that I wasn't going to find one person fully capable of being both." She let the smile be born from the warm glowing core of herself, growing and growing until she could only laugh a little to release the full feeling. "But I was dead wrong. There was someone out there for me capable of being both a friend and a lover. I just never expected it to be in a female package."

Looking down at her notes, she saw the next card read "Cassidy." The name said everything to Brenna. "Cassidy," she began, "is beautiful." She shook her head. "I couldn't even look at her for long before my heart was in my throat and I wanted to stammer, feeling completely inadequate next to her. So I never managed to talk to her for any length of time."

"You sound like a teenager!"

Brenna laughed at the characterization from the reporter.

"Yes, I did. Acted like it, too." She shook her head. "Cassidy had her own reasons for trying to reach through that impasse between us." She looked up. "I will be forever grateful that her son turned five.

"I've known many actresses over the years, and this is not a slight to a single one of them," she went on carefully. "When Cassidy looks at Ryan she loves her son. Her home is a child's home. She organizes her life around caring for him. She made the choices she's made because she refused to see anything harm him."

"You fell in love because of children?" came a shouted interruption.

"No. We became friends because of that."

"So how did you fall in love?" someone called.

"It wasn't quite like falling over a log," Brenna chuckled, "but it was just as amazingly unforeseeable and that simple. Think back to when you met your own partner, husband, wife, a boyfriend, a girlfriend. How did you know it was love?" She formed a picture of Cassidy in her mind and spoke to it instead of the crowd before her. "When you have that feeling, there's no mistaking it. Even if you'd never expect it, when she takes you in her arms, there's doesn't even have to be a kiss. Something inside you meets something inside her, and for the first time, everything you touch, everything you say, everything you are... is whole and solid. You're real."

Cassidy's image faded from her mind and Brenna stepped back.

There was a short ring behind her and she turned to see Talia opening her cell phone.

"I think this is for you," Talia said, holding out the phone to Brenna with a smile.

Brenna frowned at the unplanned interruption but took the phone. "Hello?"

"You made me real too."

"Cass?" She turned away from the podium microphone to keep her conversation private.

Cassidy's voice was breathy, strained. "I was watching the news...Saw Victor... Talia... You... You're beautiful, Bren."

Brenna felt her balance steady. "Cass, you sound tired."

"Yeah, I..." Cassidy's voice trailed away and Brenna held the phone tightly, just listening to her lover breathe over the open line. "You...shouldn't be alone."

"I'm not. You're here with me. I'll be back later. You go to sleep."

"'Kay."

"I love you."

Brenna heard nothing over the line for the longest time until finally she heard a click. Either Cassidy had ended the call or given it to a nurse to do so. But the buoyant feeling of knowing Cassidy was coherent stayed with Brenna as she closed the cell phone and handed it back to Talia. "Thank you."

"Any time."

Turning back to the podium, Brenna smiled. "Any questions?"

Hands immediately shot into the air.

CHAPTER NINETEEN

THOMAS SHIFTED a black checker, jumping one of Ryan's red ones. Across from him, Ryan Hyland squirmed in his chair at the folding table. Unable to concentrate on his next move, he realized he couldn't wait any longer.

"Miss Karen," Ryan said, "could I go to the bathroom?" He carefully turned around in his chair to find Mrs. Grinaldi.

The woman with curling black hair and a friendly smile looked up from her magazine and met his gaze. "Do you remember the way?"

He nodded but Thomas offered, "I could take him, Mrs. Grinaldi."

Ryan frowned. As much as he liked Thomas, he knew how to go to the bathroom. "I'm big enough to go by myself," he said.

"He'll be fine, Thomas," Mrs. Grinaldi said. "We're safe here."

Ryan walked out of the room and looked up and down the hallway. To the right was the door out into the sunshine he could see peeking through the window. To the left would be where the bathroom was, around a corner. He walked quickly, finding the door labeled MEN.

He pushed it inward and stepped into the first empty stall, closing the door. A few minutes later he was tucking in his shirt when he heard noises as another door opened.

"Ryan?"

He frowned. That did not sound like Thomas.

"Ryan, are you here, son?"

Leaving the stall, Ryan looked up into the familiar face. "Daddy!"

"Shhh, son." He pulled off the baseball cap that hid much of his face and crouched. Ryan noticed that his shirt label said "Jim." "How are you, buddy?"

"Fine, Daddy." His daddy's face looked scratched up, but he wasn't crying, so Ryan decided the scratches must be makeup. Since Mommy wore costumes and makeup to pretend to be somebody else, maybe his daddy was doing that too. "Are you playing dress up?"

"Something like that," was the answer. "Come on. Let's go." His father looked quickly over his shoulder then down to the end of the stalls. "We don't have a lot of time."

"Are we going home? You didn't come by the hospital and see Mommy."

"No. I had some things to do first," Daddy said.

"I'm gonna tell Miss Karen that you and me are going to see Mommy. I can tell Thomas I got to see my daddy!"

There was a knock at the door. "Ryan?" His daddy stood quickly and backed away from the door. "Ryan," said the voice. "Are you all right?" Ryan reached for the door handle just as it opened inward. "You're taking too long. Mrs. Grinaldi sent me..." Thomas smiled at Ryan. "There you are."

"This is my daddy!" Ryan introduced proudly, stepping back and gesturing. His daddy stepped forward.

Thomas looked startled. "What the...? Holy shit! James!" Thomas stumbled backward through the open door, and Ryan watched his daddy chase after him. "Ow!" Ryan howled when his shoe was caught in the closing door.

"James! Mrs. G!" Thomas bolted, yelling, "He's here! He's here!"

Ryan pushed his foot free and watched his father run for the door leading to the outside. "Daddy! Wait, Daddy!"

Thomas skidded to a halt as he heard the outer door open. He pushed open the door to Miss Karen's room and yelled, "James, he's here!" Then he turned around and spotted Ryan still by the bathroom. "Ryan, are you okay?"

"Why'd you scare off my daddy?" Ryan pouted. "We were going to see Mommy together."

"Ryan, we are going to see your mom again tomorrow. Tonight it's too late."

"That was my DADDY!"

Miss Karen came out into the hall and called him back into the classroom. "We'll wait right here for your mother," she said to Thomas. "I'll call Security." She ushered Ryan and Thomas back into the small room, shut and locked the door. "Come on."

Ryan sat down in a chair in the corner and tried to figure out what was happening. "Will Daddy come back for me?"

There was a sharp banging on the door. Karen looked through the window and quickly unlocked it, letting in James, who said, "He got out through a side door. I couldn't catch him."

"Daddy!" Ryan pulled at the door.

James pulled him away from it. "Ryan, stop!"

"I want my daddy!"

"Ryan, man, your dad is bad news. C'mon." He tugged on Ryan's arm.

Ryan pulled away from him and ran to a table, where he sat down and cried.

Ryan was still sobbing when Brenna arrived with two men from Security, and he would not come to her when she called. "What on earth happened?" she asked.

Thomas frowned. "He saw his father."

"I thought I asked that the news be kept off." She rose to her full height. "I ask you to do one thing—"

"We did what you asked!" James intervened. "Shit, Mom, listen. Mitch Hyland came here. He was going to take Ryan away. What the hell was Thomas or I supposed to do? We weren't going to let him take Ryan."

"Mitch was here?" Bren swallowed hard and her face blanched. "He was here?"

Thomas stepped forward again. "Yeah, caught up with Ryan while he was in the bathroom."

"You confronted him?"

"I didn't plan to," Thomas protested. "Ryan was taking too long and when I went to check on him, I found him with his father."

Brenna studied Thomas for a long moment and noticed a bruise just beginning to discolor his cheek. "He hit you?" she growled, brushing it with her fingertips.

"No. I stumbled backward and hit the wall." Thomas squeezed her hand. "It's all right. He's gone."

She crossed her arms over her chest and muttered, "Now he knows I have Ryan." She shook her head.

"Mom, call the police."

"I know, James," she assured her younger son. "I am going to talk to them, but you all need to be safe first."

Thomas sighed. "Where?"

"With us?"

Brenna turned to see that Will Chapman and Terry Brown had followed her over from the press room when a security guard had alerted her to an "incident" with the children.

"You ran off in a hurry. Is everyone all right?"

"There's been a little excitement," Brenna downplayed. "Hang on."

As Will and Terry talked quietly with Thomas and James, Brenna tried to reach Ryan. He had stopped crying, but he continued to sniffle as he rubbed at his runny nose and eyes.

"Ryan, it's time to go home," she coaxed. She took a box of tissues from Karen. "Come on, let's clean up." He sniffled hard once and rubbed his nose on his arm, looking at her, his eyes narrowed. It was the same furrow his mother had when she concentrated. "Are you tired?" It was well after six o'clock. He shook his head. "Hungry?"

"Yes."

"Well, I've got some food at home. Do you like soup and sandwiches?" He turned up his nose at her. "How about just peanut butter and jelly?" He nodded, but still would not move toward her. "Are you scared?" He nodded. "Because of your dad?" He nodded again. "I'm sorry," she said. "He won't be coming back again."

"Why not? What did I do wrong?" he asked, tears brimming in his eyes.

"You? Ryan, no, you did nothing wrong," she said emphatically.

There was a long silent stretch of time as Ryan thought. Brenna wanted desperately to hug him, but she held back, waiting.

"Did Daddy really hurt Mommy?"

Ryan's voice was filled with an uncertainty and hesitation a five year old should never have. Brenna couldn't help the tears that formed in her eyes.

She swallowed past the lump in her throat. "Yes, he did. I'm sorry."

"Why did he?"

"I don't know why. I just know I don't want the same thing to happen to you. Your mom wouldn't want that either." She could see the upset and confusion in his expression. She had to give him the time to come to grips with his emotions on his own, if he could.

When at last he spoke, his voice was small, but it held a tendril of hope. "Miss Lanigan?"

He stood up and walked to her. Resisting the urge to wrap her arms around him, she responded cautiously, "Yes?"

"Do you love me?"

She kept very still. His father no doubt said he loved him. *Will Ryan believe me or not?* "Yes, I do love you, Ryan. So very, very much."

"Can I see Mommy?"

"Of course you will see her," Brenna soothed.

"Now?"

He obviously wanted to ask his mother who he should be trusting, and Brenna was sorry she had to make him wait. "Not now." He looked up past her and she realized the others in the room had come up behind her. "Do you think you can trust me just a little longer?"

Ryan didn't answer but she held his gaze for a long moment. When she finally broke the connection and looked back over her shoulder, Brenna met Will's eyes. "I'm going to send you to a friend's house for tonight, okay?"

Chapman assented with a nod. "Thomas and James too?" she asked the big man. He nodded again. "Ryan," she smiled at him, "do you have a favorite movie?" The boy nodded. "Do you think my sons would like it?"

"Star Wars: Episode One," he said. "Do they like pod racers?"

Brenna looked up imploringly at Thomas, and he supplied the clincher. "We love the pod race." Ryan beamed. James groaned, and Thomas took Ryan's hand, leaving her watching the three boys head for the door with Terry following close behind.

Will put his hands on his hips. "Are you sure?"

"Mitch is obviously following me. I've got to separate myself from the kids until we get him back under wraps."

"He's certainly bold," Will commented. "I can't believe he came back here."

"He looked pretty bad when I last saw him. You'd think he'd attract attention."

"We're a studio. Hell, maybe he came in with an extras call. Or passed his scratches off as the results of a bar fight."

"Doesn't exactly speak well for our security," Brenna said.

"You can't worry about that now. Security will look for him. What's next for you?"

"Well, we're done with the press for now. I hope it holds them. I want to get back to the hospital."

"You need company."

"No, I don't."

"That wasn't a question." Will lowered his voice. "We have to split up. Get a plainclothes officer, take the studio limo, but don't go into town alone, Bren."

"He's not after me; he's after Ryan."

"As long as he thinks you have Ryan, you're a target."

"Maybe we can use that to our advantage," Brenna mused. "What if I lead him to someplace the police can grab him?"

"How will he find out where you are?"

Despite the seriousness of what she was suggesting Brenna couldn't suppress a chuckle. "That's the easy part. I'll let the press follow my every move."

CHAPTER TWENTY

THE SUBURBAN community where Brenna made her home sloped down from foothills. The single lane streets wended away from a tiny, exclusive business district, ending in loops and cul-de-sacs where driveways departed through tight clutches of trees toward some famous and not-so-famous homes. Built before the age of cookie-cutter construction companies and when land tracts were more generous, each home spoke, if not necessarily of the current resident's character, at least of their tastes in post-modern Spanish art deco or classic European villa, or of some other bygone Hollywood era.

Despite the high concentration of celebrity homes, and the lack of gates at the entrance roads, the paparazzi tended to remain clear of the area. Until this week. Their numbers had swelled from two or three photographers, to dozens of news stations following the single press statement by Pinnacle Pictures two days earlier:

"Cassidy Hyland, accompanied by Brenna Lanigan, both cast members of our Time Trails series, was transported to Pasadena City General for treatment of injuries sustained in an encounter with Hyland's ex-husband. Shooting on the series Time Trails has been temporarily suspended."

Everyone knew the history of the two actresses. If not, it was widely documented in interview archives. Before the public had completely recovered from the revelation that Mitch Hyland's attack had been provoked by a jealous rage, news crews following the women to the hospital caught a juicy sound bite: Lanigan declaring to a desk nurse, "I'm her lover." Now most of the studios were carrying Brenna Lanigan's press conference. Don

Deering wanted a full interview and was determined to get it.

As the KTLA van stopped before the private home, it became just one more amongst the dozens of news vans lining the small street and milling reporters with still cameras. The hospital had been crowded. Don had asked one question, then, getting no answer, he decided to wait until things died down a little, hoping Lanigan would come home. Straightening his tie, he hopped down from the passenger side. His cameraman and driver, Lou Phillips, set the hydraulic on the transmitter and pulled his camera from the back, hooking it into the feed with a quick cable connection.

"Shit, Don." Lou looked around. "I thought you said we'd be first on this."

Don shushed him. "What's going on?" he asked another reporter.

"Studio unit reported Lanigan is on her way here."

"To make a statement?"

"Had a full press conference at the studio. So... not sure," the reporter admitted.

Damn. Don knew he had sensed something when dealing with the two women almost five months ago. He had been covering their mishap in the Sports Warehouse. Now they had admitted they were lovers, and he possessed some of the earliest footage of them intimately close, likely just as their relationship was starting. He wanted to get one or both of them alone for an exclusive perspective piece.

"I'm going to get the lay of the land," Don said to Lou.

"Gotcha."

Lou settled against the side of the van and shot a few minutes of establishing footage, as Don got a feel for the character of the neighborhood and the house he was approaching. It was a cozy, ranch-style home done in hand-hewn stone and wood fascia with a big front picture window. The shutters were stained rosewood, picking up the dark reds in the drapes. Lanigan had a very homey personality, he suspected, imagining there was a fireplace at the end of the stone chimney where she probably curled up. "Nice place," he commented aloud.

He crossed the lawn, peering briefly through slats in the privacy fence, unable to determine the lay of her backyard. He heard an engine and quickly hurried back to the public easement.

A delivery van from Flowers Unlimited pulled up alongside the mailbox, and a delivery man slid out. "What's going on here?" he asked as Deering joined him.

"Waiting for the lady of the house to come home," Don supplied. He was surprised to see scratches and a bandage on the man's nose. "I didn't know the world of flower delivery was so rough."

"What? Oh. Yeah, well a guy didn't like that some other guy wanted flowers delivered to his girl."

Deering shrugged. "I gotcha. Take it out on the messenger. Hope you got in a few good licks."

"Yeah. Well, I've got to deliver this. Can't leave it out here."

The muscular shoulders shrugged. Don couldn't help thinking the man's blue jacket looked just a little tight. Must work out and the company hasn't gotten him a new uniform yet.

Noting the man's name tag, Don offered advice, "Jim, she's not home. But there's word she's on her way." The man shrugged away from him and opened the back of his van, pulling out a bouquet and starting up the front walk. "Where're you going?" Don followed the delivery man up the drive and along the walk to the front door. "We aren't supposed to be up here."

"To deliver this." Another car drove into the cul-de-sac. Don glanced over to see a green Mountaineer garnering all the camera attention. Behind him, he could hear the delivery man trying the knob.

"I told you..." The man's shoulders blocked him and the front door opened. "How in the hell...?" Darkened blue eyes met his and a strong hand wrapped around his throat, dragging him inside the house.

Brenna anxiously studied the news assembly. It seemed every outlet she had left behind at the studio had dispatched a unit to her home. She sat in the back of a studio limo; the driver, however, was from the plainclothes division of the LAPD.

"I'll walk you to the door." He keyed the in-car radio. "This is Unit 1-9. Move in to the Lanigan address," he said into the microphone. "Let's hope our boy took the bait."

He moved the car forward steadily despite the crowding cameras. Once they were inside the Lanigan property line, the press fell back. He stepped out first and opened the door. When she got out of the car, like a sea crashing, everyone surged forward, thrusting microphones and portable recorders and cameras in her face.

"Ms. Lanigan! How did the fight with her husband start?"

She sighed and put her hand up defensively. "It's late. Don't you all watch your own news?"

Not being indulgent sorts, the reporters stayed. "What's next for you?"

"A little sleep. Please."

With the officer watching her back, Brenna turned around and pushed her door open. Distracted by the crowd, it didn't register that she had entered without benefit of the key. Letting the officer in behind her, she shut the door between herself and the press, resting her forehead against it as she set the lock.

"I'm going to check through the house," the officer informed her.

She nodded wearily. "Fine." There had been no sign of Mitch. If he hadn't heard the news reports meant to bait him to her house, he could be anywhere. She wondered if he had headed for Cassidy's home instead. Their children should be safe with Chapman, but maybe she'd better call.

She tingled at the sudden realization that she had included all three boys in her thought. *Our children. Mine and Cassidy's.* Wearing a wide smile, she started toward her bedroom.

There were the sounds of a scuffle ahead and two figures emerged into the hallway from her bedroom. At the sight of her, Mitch struggled against the cuffs behind his back. "Where's Ryan? You were supposed to bring the kids home."

"They're all safe, away from you."

She put her hand on the officer's arm. "Be sure you find out how he got on the studio lot looking like a reject from a fight film."

"Will do, ma'am."

She started past him to her bedroom, but he stopped her. "You shouldn't go in there, ma'am. I'm going to call for the paramedics."

Brenna blinked, then went to her bedroom doorway and looked inside, stifling a gasp at the sight. The reporter, Don Deering, his face black and blue, lay unconscious across her bed.

CHAPTER TWENTY-ONE

BRENNA LANIGAN'S exhausting morning had begun before dawn and now, with the sun high overhead, she had begged off of meeting her coworkers at the commissary in order to spend lunch with someone very precious. She pushed the door closed behind her with a satisfying thud. Walking past the bathrooms which opened onto the corridor, Brenna slipped her arms free of the heavy military-style vest which she wore over a light gray cotton undershirt. Her mood lightened at the sensation of air circulating on her skin.

"How's things today, Ms. Lanigan?"

The guard was seated at the desk in the corridor. Bestowing a warm smile on him, Brenna's eyes brightened from gray to a deep blue as she stopped next to him. To her right was a pair of swinging double doors, a large sign beside them stating "Props". "Great now, Harry," she answered, Behind him was a single door, inset in the wall and painted the same light gray of the walls. She stepped past him and grasped its knob.

"Enjoy your lunch," he said. "I'll keep it quiet out here for you." He wrote her name on a check-in pad and checked his watch before writing her arrival time next to it.

"Thanks." She turned away, pushed inward on the door, and entered the brightly painted room. The sound of her entry did not go unnoticed. As she rounded the edge of the door, a small blur hurtled toward her. Her reflexes, admirable for a woman over forty, allowed her to catch the blond five-year old under his outstretched arms.

"Hi!" followed by a rapid series of questions, and news about his day, assailed Brenna's ears. She pulled Ryan's slender body into her own, instantly even less tired because of his enthusiastic greeting. Small arms wrapped around her shoulders and warm lips pressed a wet kiss on her cheek.

Her eyes grew moist and she pulled back to looking into his glowing eyes. "It's good to see you too," she said, brushing her fingers through his thick hair. He's almost due for a haircut, she thought. "What's for lunch today?" she asked him.

"Mrs. G and I are making peanut butter and jelly sandwiches," he announced with pride. He tugged on her hand as she stood up. "Come on."

"Of course." Walking across the room behind him and carefully moving around the little tables, Brenna saw Karen Grinaldi standing beside a kitchenette counter, complete with undercabinets and a sink. Behind the caregiver was an oven inset in the wall.

"Good afternoon, Bren," Karen said warmly. "Do you have a long break?" She reached out a steadying hand to Ryan's back as the boy stepped up onto a footstool in front of the counter and reached for a jar of grape jelly.

"Long enough for sandwiches and milk."

"And cookies." Karen smiled. "Ryan wanted to bake some this morning."

"They're peanut butter too," Ryan added, glancing away from his task of upending the jelly jar over the bread.

Both women moved to stop the mess before it happened. Karen grasped the bottom of the jar, beginning to turn it upright, while Brenna caught an errant glob of jelly in her cupped hands.

Ryan looked sheepish. Brenna smiled and said quietly, "Oops."

"Sorry," he answered, his smile faltering.

Brenna cleaned her hands at the sink. "No harm done, but remember, when you're working, you can't let yourself be distracted."

"I'll do better," he assured her gravely.

She kissed his cheek. "I know you will."

With renewed determination and the smile returning to his face, Ryan went back to his task. One at a time he put the three sandwiches on the cutting board and Karen cut each in half. Brenna collected three plastic cups in different primary colors and filled each with milk from the refrigerator.

Carrying two plates, with Karen carrying the third, Ryan led the trio over to a child-height table and carefully set one plate in front of each chair.

Brenna set the milk cups down and turned to take a seat, only to find Ryan pulling out the one next to her leg. "For me?" she asked. He nodded. Seating herself, she adjusted to the tiny proportions and watched Karen do the same.

Ryan settled quickly onto his own seat between them.

He looked at Brenna expectantly, waiting for her to taste it first.

She examined her sandwich, the bread lumpy in several places over extra thick globs of jelly. "It looks wonderful," she declared with a smile.

Ryan beamed as she bit into a corner and chewed thoughtfully. "Good?" he asked.

She swallowed and cleared her mouth with a sip of milk. "Delicious."

Ryan giggled and took a bite of his own sandwich. Karen had already consumed half of her own lunch while Brenna played out her ritual with Ryan.

I need this time together as much as he does. Brenna felt her fatigue fading as she ate her sandwich and watched Ryan rush through his. As soon as they finished lunch, they could move on to the next phase of their time together—a phone call to his mother who was still in the hospital, a stay now concluding its second week.

Brenna had taken over caring for Ryan, bringing him with her to and from the set each day for Karen's child care services. But the lack of contact with his mother wore on Ryan, and on Cassidy, as well. So they had arranged to make the midday call to keep mother and son connected.

Ryan was already carrying his plate and cup to the sink as Brenna finished the last bite of her sandwich and the dregs of her milk. "Ready?" she called.

He ran over to the cubbies and pulled out his bright orange backpack, searching through it until he came up with a small cellular phone. The phone was Cassidy's, another connection between mother and son, and the number for the hospital room where Cassidy recuperated was programmed in the quick dial.

"You know how to call," Brenna said.

Ryan quickly pressed the button and put the device to his ear, his face lighting up by degrees as the phone rang. "Hi, Mom!" he said brightly when the call was connected. His face contorted into a frown. "Are you feeling okay, Mommy?" There was a pause, and Brenna wished she could hear the reply. "Oh. Okay. So you've been sleeping?" He nodded, obviously echoing his mother's affirmative reply. "I made Ms. Lanigan lunch again." He smiled. "Yes, she always likes it."

Brenna rolled her eyes as she held out her hand. "Ryan, may I talk to your mother?"

Ryan looked from Brenna's face to her outstretched hand, then informed his mother, "I'm giving you to Ms. Lanigan now."

Brenna smiled at his grown up tone. "Thank you," she said graciously. Ryan cocked his head, as if to listen. She shook her head and he dashed off. She waited until he had grabbed a bucket of toys off of a shelf. "Cass?" As she spoke into the phone, her voice softened with concern. "Rough day?"

"Therapy is a bitch," the woman on the other end admitted, her voice sounding sharp and breathy. While Cassidy Hyland might tell her son everything was fine, she and Brenna had been through too much, learned too much about one another, to ever be able to cover up personal pain for long. "But they are letting me check out today."

"Do you want me to cut out of here now?" Brenna asked. It was atypical of her work ethic to leave the set early for anything other than a catastrophe, but Brenna's priorities had been significantly reordered since the near fatal attack on Cassidy. She would definitely leave early if Cass needed her. There was a moment of silence and Brenna recognized it as Cassidy weighing the pros and cons. "I can settle you at home and come back later," she added as an inducement.

"You can't afford the time away from the set. I've upset the schedule enough." Cassidy exhaled. "What time do you think you'll be done?"

Brenna shook her head. "I can be done now."

"I'm not in any shape now... just took the Percocet."

In the background, Brenna heard the sounds of Cassidy adjusting her position in the bed. Brenna felt a sharp desire to be there to adjust her pillows, anything she needed. Then the television began to buzz in the background.

"Don't depress yourself with the news," Brenna said.

"Look at that," Cassidy remarked at the television. "At least we're no longer the top story every day."

"Maybe midnight is a better check out time. Less press," Brenna pointed out.

"I still can barely walk," Cass grumbled.

"I know. We'll work together on that," Brenna said gently.

"Brenna, I shouldn't go home with you."

"Why not?"

"You've taken so much on with Ryan. I should just get a Home Nurse."

"It's no bother, Cass."

"But you're doing so much. It's not fair."

"I want to do this."

"But—"

"Cass, please. It's all right. You're not going to impose. I'll enjoy having you at home."

"What about the press?"

"Damn the press. Your health comes first."

"All right."

Despite her agreement, Cassidy sounded frustrated.

Brenna could also hear the washed out quality that signaled Cassidy falling under the influence of the strong pain medication. She called Ryan to the phone. "Ryan, time to say bye."

He yelped a cheerful, "See you tonight, Mommy," into the phone and handed it back.

Brenna's smile filtered into her voice as she offered her own sign-off. "Having you home will be wonderful. You'll see. You'll get well much more quickly with me taking care of you than you would with some impersonal home health person. I'll see you tonight. I love you."

"I love you, too." Cassidy's murmur faded and then there was only the click of the connection closing and Brenna pressed the end button on the cellular.

"Is Mommy ever going to get better?"

"Yes, she is," Brenna replied firmly. "We just have to help her a lot."

"Should I stay at home and take care of her?" he asked. "I could. I don't have to come here."

"Darling, you do. As much as your mommy needs help, you can't take care of her."

"I want to help," he declared stubbornly.

Brenna smiled at his endearing expression, so much like his mother's.

"You do. Just by loving her as much as you do." I can speed things along just a little. I can make sure the afternoon filming session goes damn efficiently. "Will you be ready to go when I come at dinner time?" He nodded emphatically. "All right. I'll see you then."

She looked at the wall clock and realized the call would come down soon to report back to the set. "I have to go."

"Wait!" he said suddenly, running to the counter and picking up a small, semi-round lump off of a paper towel. "You forgot your cookie."

She took it and kissed his cheek. "Pack up the rest and we'll give them to your mommy for dessert tonight. I bet they will be the perfect medicine."

Ryan beamed, and Brenna steeled herself for the afternoon's work ahead. As she left the child's haven, she tried to set aside her personal life for her professional one.

Brenna sat waiting for the stagehands to reset the stage after the explosives experts had done their job. There were still two more takes, just for camera angles. It was well after six. It would very quickly be after eight if they didn't get everything on the first try. While she could not always count on others to not miss a cue, or to take it in their heads to initiate a harmless prank, she usually could count on herself to get it right. Two of the first four retakes had been necessary because she missed her blocking, stepping toward the wrong follow-up speaker or turning to look upstage when she should have looked downstage.

It was just too damn hard to concentrate. She heard Cassidy's tired voice over and over in her mind, and her heart and body screamed to be with her lover, soothing away the pain, rather than on set. Besides, she felt Cassidy was still uneasy about staying in Brenna's home for the rest of her recovery.

"Brenna? Bren?"

A voice penetrated the fog.

Uncurling her fist from under her chin and looking up dourly, she met the inquisitive gaze of Terry Brown. She saw her reflection in his dark-as-night eyes and picked up her chin. "Are they ready?"

"Are you?"

She started to push to her feet, but he restrained her with a light push against her shoulder. "What?" she asked.

"Do you want to rehearse the scene again?"

"I know it cold," she said wearily.

"But—"

"Terry, I want to get this done."

"Maybe you shouldn't have come back yet. It has only been two weeks since—"

Brenna whirled on him and growled, "Don't."

Terry's expression grew somber, silently expressing his thoughts.

She spun toward the set. "Let's get this over with."

A reporter stepped up to them. "Do you have a minute?" he asked.

Brenna took in his appearance with a quick top-to-bottom sweep of her eyes. Pen behind his ear, Dockers pants, and a brown polo shirt were fairly typical of the rag reporters, who tried to look like nothing so much as an underpaid stagehand. She tried hard to push a smile onto her lips. "We're due on the set," she said.

"I just wanted to ask Mr. Brown a question. Have you been pleased that the production schedule has spread the work out more evenly amongst the whole ensemble since Cassidy Hyland's injury?"

"More work?"

"Yeah, there were complaints when she first got here that a lot of the screen time was taken away from folks like you and," he nodded toward where Will Chapman and Sean Durham stood, arms crossed, also waiting for the set to be reset, "and those guys."

"We are all a team," Brenna said uneasily, though she suspected where he was going with his question.

"You didn't think so a year ago."

He was looking for a quote, and sniffing hard. "Things change," she said without elaboration.

"Yeah, a starlet getting beaten by her ex doesn't happen every day."

Terry stepped forward abruptly, grasping Brenna's arm which she had almost swung at the reporter. Unobtrusively, she released her fist slowly. "No, it doesn't." *God, this man is an idiot.*

"Work will be waiting for Miss Hyland when she is able to return. Now," Terry said, "we have to get back to filming." Gently laying a hand on

Brenna's arm, he steered her toward Sean and Will, who had stiffened when the reporter broached Brenna and Terry.

The reporter called after them, "Would you take a swing at Mitch Hyland in open court, Ms. Lanigan?"

Yes, I would take a pickaxe to Mitch Hyland if I could. Terry's reassuring squeeze on her elbow encouraged her to clamp her jaw tightly shut.

"What's up?" Sean asked Terry when the two joined them.

"They want me to say something about Cassidy," Brenna said. "All week, if it isn't about the show, it's about whether or not, as her lover, I knew her ex-husband was after her. I wish they'd cut us a break. She's only getting out of the hospital tonight."

"That's good news."

"Yeah, maybe. She's not real happy about it. Her therapy's still going well, but mostly I get the feeling she doesn't want to come home to my place."

"Why not?"

"She has her own."

"Obviously that's still bothering you," Sean ventured. "You need to work it out. Go to the hospital early. Talk. Leave the work behind and tend to your heart's needs for a change."

Brenna shook her head. "I have to finish this first." Squaring her shoulders, she turned and preceded the group to the set.

The scene being taped had as its focus the ensemble's absent member played by Cassidy Hyland, Lieutenant Christine Hanssen. At first, the schedule had been juggled, rotating episodes focusing on other cast members so that they were shot earlier in the schedule. Eventually, the studio had to acknowledge the absence of the Alliance's regular crew member. They were also beginning the arc of episodes leading to the end of the series.

As she tried to be the stalwart Commander Susan Jakes, it was not helping Brenna's concentration to think about why Cassidy was absent, and would remain absent for at least another three to four weeks. Her blood still boiled at the least reference to the incident where Cass had been beaten nearly to death by her ex-husband Mitch Hyland. She was losing her customary control.

She was walking a simple corridor scene with Will Chapman playing Lieutenant Raycreek, her second in command. This was the third take. The first two times her mind had drifted and she had missed cues. On the surface, their exchange was just a discussion of a terrorist conflict which had caused Lieutenant Chris Hanssen to be ordered back to her original fighter squadron. But Brenna could not help but play it deeper, as deeply as her emotions ran, for herself and for Susan Jakes who had been smoothing over her relationship with Christine Hanssen, the rebellious young officer now missing in the disputed territory.

"What does Command say?" Jakes asked.

"Nothing good." Raycreek shook his head. "Neither side is allowing any teams into the area to verify anything."

"What is the latest estimate of casualties?"

"The terrorists detonated a multi-ton device. The tectonic shockwave registered as far as the Gobi. Deaths already number in the hundreds of thousands."

Without looking at Raycreek, she asked, "Were you able to reach Hanssen's wing command about her last known coordinates?" As she waited for potentially bad news, Jakes swallowed hard and stared at her fingers spread against the wall, holding her up.

Raycreek's hand started for her shoulder but her expression narrowed as she looked over at him, and he abandoned the gesture meant to reassure. "Yes," he admitted.

She spun away from him, as much to distance herself from the fatalistic word as to bark her next command. She hit the communication panel on the nearby wall. "Creighton, this is Commander Jakes. Inform HQ that we're planning a mission in aid."

"Yes, Commander," came the voiceover reply from Terry Brown, off-stage as the tactical officer, Lieutenant Creighton.

"Sue," Raycreek started.

Jakes cut him off with a silent glare then turned to the communication console again. "I want every document concerning every ship and troop movement for the last two weeks. We're going to plan this down to the last microsecond." Her chin came up, daring Raycreek to challenge her decision. He didn't.

"I'll alert you when we have the data," he said. As she strode away, he turned to watch her go.

Off camera, Terry Brown and Sean Durham did the same. Brenna went off-camera at the other end of the set with her back to the camera. As she shed her portrayal going around a corner, they could see the instant the sturdy lines of Commander Jakes shattered into the softer lines of Brenna Lanigan.

"Cut and print that!" Mike Landau, the episode's director, yelled from behind Camera 2, which had been tracking down the corridor after Jakes.

"Oh, thank God!"

Brenna's exclamation made everyone chuckle.

"Collect Ryan before you go," Will teased.

She turned and waved her thanks, restraining herself from running away from the set. She would be with Cassidy in less than thirty minutes. And they would be going home together.

CHAPTER TWENTY-TWO

CASSIDY WATCHED with detachment as the nurse checked her vital signs. For the moment she felt relatively pain free. The brace she now wore offered support to her while she sat up in the bed. Her left arm, held in the nurse's hand as she timed her pulse, was only a little chilled. Early in her recovery her fever had fluctuated so often that she wasn't sure she would ever be consistently at normal temperature again. She felt weaker than she wanted, dependent on too many people to do things for her.

She wanted to go home, but at the same time knew that going home required her to be able to handle so much more than simply her own healing: being Ryan's mother, being Brenna's lover, trying to deal with Thomas and James for longer than a few hours. She wondered where she would find the energy for it all.

The door opened and the nurse said automatically, "Visiting hours are over."

Cassidy grinned as Brenna appeared around the edge of the door. "We're here to take her home."

"In the middle of the night?" the nurse objected.

"Yes, actually. I have her release papers right here." Brenna held them out blindly toward the nurse; she only had eyes for Cassidy. "Hi. We're a little early, but I couldn't wait any longer to see you."

"I'm still here," Cassidy said grumpily.

"You're sitting up and everything, though," Brenna praised. She realized the nurse was still standing by the door, and said, "That's all we need, thanks."

Waiting until the nurse was gone, Cassidy admitted, "A combination of the Percocet's residual effects and the brace."

"Mommy?"

Cassidy smiled at him hugging Brenna's leg. "Hi, sweetheart."

Ryan started to leap on the bed, but Brenna caught him before he could move the mattress with his intense forty-five pound body. "We're taking Mommy home. You can do that later," Brenna assured him.

Cassidy nodded her thanks.

"I haven't packed anything yet."

Brenna shook her head. "Don't worry about that. I've got it." She started by fetching the overnight bag from the closet. "What do you want to wear?"

"No belts, ties, heels..." Cassidy shook her head, "but I desperately want out of this backless number." She plucked at the hospital gown.

Brenna chuckled. "All right. How about these?" She held up a pair of Cassidy's sweatpants, trim fit but with a drawstring waist. When Cassidy nodded, Brenna added,

"Doesn't really match, but I brought a button up shirt. Thought maybe we could get it on you without aggravating your chest too badly."

The thoughtfulness made Cassidy regret her earlier carping. "I just don't want to impose on you."

"I do understand your wanting to be on your own, but this isn't... It can be temporary. Though I'd really love it if you... stayed."

"Promise me you'll let me pull my own weight?" Cassidy inched her legs over the side of the bed; her knee still ached but at least her legs mostly worked. She stretched against the strain in her lower back and tried to adjust her position. Her weakened arms and a whirling dizziness made her close her eyes, stemming a seemingly unstoppable tide of tears.

Brenna moved forward, resting her hands on Cassidy's quivering thighs. "When you can lift something more than your own feet without help, we'll talk. All right?"

She slid an arm around Cassidy, who slowly lifted her uninjured right arm and managed to return the embrace. Cassidy's immobilized left arm, with the custom brace around her wrist and hand, was secured with Velco straps to the front of the body brace. The heavy material was lined with hardened plastic ribbing, thwarting her aching need for closeness and comfort.

Awkwardly she rested her cheek against Brenna's shoulder and let the tears fall. Brenna stroked her hair and placed soft kisses against her brow and temple. "I'm sorry for being grumpy. You've done so much for me."

Brenna placed her palm under Cassidy's chin and gently tilted her head upward. "I love you. Nothing, but nothing will ever change that."

As Brenna pushed Cassidy along the corridor in the wheelchair, Ryan walked alongside, holding his mother's hand and talking non-stop. Cassidy tried to shush him a few times, then gave up trying. She frequently reached up over her shoulder to caress Brenna's hand on the handlebar. They said little to one another since they were surrounded by hospital security, two of whom checked outside the door while two waited with them.

"All clear," they reported.

"All right. Let's go home."

"I'm ready," Cassidy murmured. Out on the landing, she waited while Brenna pulled open the doors and buckled Ryan into the car seat in the middle of the center bench seat. When she started to push herself up onto her feet. Brenna was quickly at her side. Cassidy's intention was to push Brenna's hand away, but, muscles shaking, she grasped the strong forearms instead. "Thanks."

"You're welcome."

Brenna supported Cassidy as they slowly walked the few steps to the car. Grasping the frame of the door and bracing her hand on the front passenger seat, with Brenna's assistance Cassidy boosted herself inside. Seated, she reached for the shoulder harness, stopping in only a few inches when she discovered the limits of her mobility. Brenna handed her the buckle from the harness and Cassidy gratefully pulled it across her chest and waist, closing her eyes as she pushed in and heard the buckle snap into place. The effort just to get this far had been exhausting.

Brenna walked around the car and got into the driver's seat. "Thanks, fellas," she called with a wave.

"Thank God there was no press to see that," Cassidy said.

"They're probably all waiting at home." Cassidy groaned. After the car engine started, Brenna's hand slipped over Cassidy's and gave it a reassuring squeeze. "Hang in there. Won't be long now."

Thankfully there were no members of the media lurking around Brenna's home. She pulled Ryan out of the car first, cradling him in her arms as she unlocked the front door. Crossing quickly through the house, she put him down in the spare room, stripping him without waking him, and tucking the sheets around him before she went back out to the car. Cassidy was leaning against the side of the SUV.

"What are you doing?"

"Being stupid," Cassidy muttered. "I got up, hoping I could walk a few steps on my own."

Brenna hugged her, holding her up at the same time. She felt the moment Cassidy gave in to her exhaustion and leaned on Brenna's strength. "All right, let's get you inside."

She helped Cassidy from the car to the wheelchair, shouldered the overnight bag, and moved toward the house. Leaning down to Cassidy, she asked, "Are you still bothered about staying here?"

"I'm not used to being able to depend on anyone but myself, Bren," Cassidy groused. "I guess that's why it's a difficult thing for me to do."

"So, it's just general grumpies. You're no longer upset with me?" Brenna turned the wheelchair around and backed Cassidy into her home.

"I know you're right. I can't take care of myself at home."

"There was always the option of a home nurse."

Cassidy frowned. "You were right about that too. It'd be a stranger."

Brenna smiled. "Besides, I think you'll enjoy the baths I give you."

Cassidy laughed, then clutched her side. "Damn that hurts. But thank you."

"You're welcome." Brenna wheeled Cassidy down the corridor to her bedroom. After pulling the sheet down, she helped Cassidy onto the bed, arranging her feet, and pillows to support her. "How's that?"

"I'm fine."

"Well, let's get your clothes off."

"I'm looking forward to you saying that when I'm well again."

"Trust me, I will." Brenna kissed her, brushing her fingers under Cassidy's chin, lifting her head gently.

Slip on shoes slipped off. The sweatpants had to be worked off over the bandages and brace, but Cassidy was stalwart throughout the process though Brenna cursed herself several times for not being careful enough with this or that movement.

Brenna undid the line of buttons and pushed it back off Cassidy's shoulders. Cassidy then pulled off the Velcro strip securing her left arm to her brace. "What do you want to wear to bed?"

"I usually wear an oversized t-shirt, but I don't think I can get my arm into one."

"Do you want a button up shirt then? A robe?"

"Maybe a robe."

Brenna retrieved a terrycloth robe from the inside of her closet door. "How's this?"

Cassidy nodded, and Brenna eased her up and helped her push her arms through the roomy sleeves. As she tied the belt, Cassidy used her good hand to cover Brenna's on her waist.

"Thank you."

"You're welcome." After stripping off her own clothes, Brenna pulled on a nightgown under Cassidy's appreciative watchful gaze.

As Brenna settled onto the bed far to the other side, Cassidy fingered the strap securing the brace to her left hand and wrist. She was leery of losing the support, but the doctor had assured her it could come off at night. And, God, how she wanted to hold Brenna.

Finally she pulled at the strap and loosened the contraption.

"Are you sure?" Brenna asked.

"I don't want to inadvertently hit you with it in the middle of the night." Cassidy tentatively flexed her fingers, just one at a time. She lifted her arm and placed her hand on Brenna's shoulder, letting her fingers roam the skin, her fingertips warming as she traced Brenna's collarbone and then caressed up her throat to her cheek. "Can we cuddle?" she asked.

"Are you sure we should? I don't want to hurt you."

"You won't. I just need to hold you against me. Please."

"All right." Brenna gingerly arranged herself, and Cassidy, so that their bodies were touching. Her lower leg arranged over Cassidy's thigh, her palm resting on the thick vest fabric encasing Cassidy's chest, just above her heart. Her head settled against Cassidy's shoulder. No weight, just contact. She pressed her lips to Cassidy's clavicle. "How's that?"

Cassidy's right arm lifted carefully behind Brenna's back and she held the bare shoulder, stroking the silky skin around the narrow strip of cloth. "Much better." Cassidy pressed her lips to Brenna's hair. Their eyes met; Cassidy studied her lover's features, seeing that dark circles had formed. "Go to sleep."

"You too."

"I will eventually. Just want to hold you. Let you sleep." Brenna's kiss on her shoulder made Cassidy smile. "Do you want something to help you sleep?"

"You're the only drug I need right now."

Brenna's blush was endearing. "I've never been called a drug before."

"Both a stimulant and a muscle relaxant." Cassidy chuckled. She felt herself losing the struggle to stay awake.

"Love you, Cass."

Chapter Twenty-Three

Brenna exhaled as the directed called, "Cut!" For what seemed like the first time in weeks, she was actually pleased with her performance. She lowered herself into a canvas sling chair, hands folded contemplatively over her stomach.

When Terry Brown reached past her for a small towel that rested on the arm of her chair, Brenna impishly snatched it up, grinning broadly as she ducked under his reach and darted behind the chair.

His eyes were smiling as he gave chase. Dodging one another, they bounced around the small area until she cut left and he intercepted her. Wrapped up in his arms, she patted his face with the towel, grinning all the while.

"Thank you," he said.

She kissed his cheek. "Thanks to you and Will for insisting I leave early the other day to take Cassidy home."

"We didn't want to ask about that. Amazingly, we saw nothing about it on the news. So you had a trouble-free trip home?"

"Yes, the press was mercifully absent. She's settled in at my place. She was as out of sorts as I was about our disagreement. I discovered that I was only listening to what she said, rather than what she meant." She added, "She does want to do more for herself, but that doesn't mean she doesn't want my help at all."

"How's her actual health?"

"She's weak, but her mood's brighter already now that she's out of the hospital. The physical therapist will start coming by on Monday. And today, she asked me to leave Ryan with her when I went home for lunch break."

"Then she's definitely feeling better."

The episode director, Mike Landau joined them. "I'm sure you know we nailed it all today."

Brenna nodded. "Thanks again. Is there something else?"

"No, I was just finishing my notes for editing, and looked up to see the crew had vacated, except for you two. It's after ten. You should go home."

Brenna looked at Terry. "Why don't you come by and see Cassidy this weekend? It'll make her smile."

"You keep her to yourself for a while. I really have to take my mug home to see the wife for the weekend."

"All right."

"But I will visit eventually, I promise." Terry hugged her and left the set.

Turning back to Mike, Brenna said, "I, um, haven't talked to the writers recently. Any word on what's coming?"

"You mean whether they are writing Cass in or out?"

"I know she wants to come back."

"What are her chances of being sufficiently recovered to return before we wrap here?" the director asked. "What does her doctor say?"

"I'll ask Cassidy if I can go with her to her next appointment to get a better idea of his prognosis for the time frame of her recovery," Brenna decided.

"Then let us all know." Mike put a hand on Brenna's shoulder and, though younger than her, looked at her with a fatherly concern that Brenna found somewhat unsettling. "Frankly," Mike said, "I do hope Cass comes back. The two of you are among the best couples I've directed."

Brenna's brow furrowed. "That comes through in the film—that we... Cass and me... we're a couple?"

"I've seen a few in front of the camera who were able to hide that they hated each other's guts. But they were automatons. You and Cass, though, you two had sparks crackling between you right from the start, eighteen months ago. Recently, the sparks became flames and I thought..." When Brenna's gaze slid away from his, he asked, "Did I say something wrong?"

"Just... I'm embarrassed, I guess."

"Don't be. There are a lot of people who envy the passion you display." He tucked his hands into his jean pockets. "Some of us wish we could find something like that for ourselves."

Brenna heard the wistfulness. "Mike?"

"Closest I ever came, I think, was Esteban, a Spaniard I met in '91. Hot bod, great smile..."

Mike's gay? Brenna's eyebrow hitched in surprise.

"Forget it. Anyway, it's great to see someone really making it work. Anytime you and Cass want a place to hang out, I've got a place in

Redondo."

After Mike left, Brenna remained alone on the set for several minutes. Hands on her hips, she tried to figure out why she felt surprised by his revelation.

As far as she knew, no one else on their set knew that Mike Landau was gay. There were members of the crew who were openly gay, like Justin, a stylist in Makeup, or Melody Capstan from Props, who wore their orientation like a badge of honor.

It suddenly hit her that Mike was seeing her as "one of us", a safe person to share his thoughts with. If the stage crew saw her that way, would it be very long before fans had that same perception? Being a gay role model was one role she knew nothing about.

The sound of the front door opening stirred Cassidy awake. Sitting up slowly, she looked around the living room from her reclining position on the couch. Blinking sleep from her eyes, she checked the clock and saw it was just after eleven-thirty.

At first she thought it might be Brenna arriving home, but when James walked in, she realized that having a chance to talk to him alone was probably a good thing.

Around ten o'clock, decidedly late for Ryan, Cassidy had stopped their cathartic snuggling on the couch and had taken her son into Brenna's extra room to put him to sleep on the futon there. What had formerly been the Lanigan boys TV and game room had become Ryan's space almost completely. It was strewn with toys more appropriate to the preschool child than the two high school boys, and so she had leaned against the door jamb watching over him as he tidied up his scattered belongings. Despite being exhausted when he finished, Cassidy had looked on the clean room with pride and praised his effort, then settled him down to sleep.

What was bothering Cassidy was that Ryan had also found a ticket stub for an art show in the downtown district, and she decided that this might be a good opportunity to ask James about it. He was past curfew. She wondered how many nights he had been out so late while his mother was tied up on the set or sitting with her at the hospital.

"Miss Hyland?"

Cassidy looked over the back of the couch to see James depositing his backpack on the floor. "Hi, James. Did you have a good evening?"

Brenna's younger son pushed his hand through his light brown hair. "Yeah. I... was out with some friends."

"Fridays are definitely prime for that," she said easily. "Your mother will be glad to know you're home safe."

"Is she home already?" The thought apparently worried him, if his anxious look toward the bedrooms was any indication.

"No, she's not home yet," Cassidy replied, and he visibly relaxed. "So, did you see another art show?" When he stiffened, she held out the ticket stub. "I came across this when I was putting Ryan to bed."

James took the stub from her and gave it a cursory glance. "Has Mom seen this?"

"No. Is this where you were tonight, too?"

James debated with himself, but apparently her non-confrontational tack was working. A little warily, he answered, "Yeah. I... I, um, have a few pieces showing there."

Cassidy smiled; that was great news. "I saw the portrait you did of your mother." She had even coaxed Brenna into mounting the painting and hanging it on the bedroom wall. She considered it a wonderful view to focus on while lying in bed,.

Warmed by her reaction, James settled on the couch next to her. "These aren't like that."

"Different medium?"

He nodded. "And different subject."

"Are you trying to sell them?"

"Hannah says I could. I guess that's why I go, to see... well, to see who's looking at them and what they're saying."

"Hannah?"

"Hannah Shropshire." He fished in his pockets and Cassidy became aware of his clothes. He was dressed quite sharply, in a pair of black Dockers pants and a slightly large matching black cotton, button-down shirt with a single breast pocket. His typical attire for school would have been a white polo shirt and faded blue jeans. Finally he passed her a small business card. "She's the gallery owner, a friend of my art teacher."

"Your art teacher recommended you for a showing?"

"Along with other kids," he said. "It's an Arts for Education campaign."

"But it's not sponsored by the schools, is it?"

James shook his head. "That's why I've been glad Mom doesn't get home early. She'd have a cow if she knew it was unchaperoned."

"What's the subject matter?"

James dropped his head as he considered his answer. "Teen life," he said finally.

Cassidy looked at the card in her hand, which mentioned not only the gallery but the show title: Sex, Drugs, and the American Teen Experience. She closed her mouth tightly. Oh, boy.

"Am I grounded?"

"I don't have the authority to do that. You should tell your mother, though."

"I'd be grounded faster than an electrical line. I wouldn't get a chance to explain."

"Maybe if you talked to me, you would."

Cassidy looked up, as James turned around abruptly, their gazes settling on Brenna who was just entering the house and taking off her light jacket.

"Hi," James said warily.

"Did things go smoothly on the set?" Cassidy asked quietly.

"The set is fine," Brenna answered briskly, striding forward. "So, where have you been?" she asked her son.

James ducked his head and Cassidy recognized the gesture as one that Brenna often had when she was unsure what would be best to say. "Go on," she encouraged James with a cautious pat to the back of his shoulder.

Standing up, James turned to his mother and said, "I was at the Isis Gallery." His mother's expression didn't change. "It's an art gallery off Simon. I... They're showing a few of my pieces."

Brenna's fingers tapped on the back of the couch, and she looked down at the fabric for a long moment, breathing deeply several times before speaking. "All right. Have you been going there every night?"

"Nobody's been here. I didn't think it would hurt anything," he muttered.

"Not hurt anything! James, what if something happened to you out there? Would anyone know to call us?"

"Bren." Cassidy's initial call went unheard, so she called louder, "Bren!"

"What?"

"I've already talked to him about this. I've handled it."

Brenna turned away but Cassidy clearly saw her anger. She knew that most of it was a result of James' actions, but wasn't sure that some of it wasn't reserved for her intervention.

"Thank you. Tomorrow I want to go see this gallery," Brenna said after a minute. James swallowed, but nodded. "Good night, James."

"Good night, Mom."

Brenna waited until James was out of sight before speaking again. "Cass? Why did you do that?"

"Because I was here. You said "us" when talking to James just now. You want us to be a couple, Bren? I can handle a broken curfew."

"But you're..." Brenna gestured widely.

"Not his mother?"

"I wasn't going to say that. You're still mostly flat on your back."

"All I did was talk to him." She winced a little as she pushed herself into a better sitting position.

"You're supposed to be recuperating." Brenna plunked herself down next to Cassidy on the couch, and Cassidy stretched out an arm, encouraging Brenna to snuggle up against her but Brenna balked. "I don't want to hurt you."

"I'll live. I need a hug as much as you do." Cassidy closed her eyes in contentment as Brenna's body moved against hers. The weight was light, but the solidity of her lover beside her filled her eyes with tears. "I've missed you. Being at the hospital, I frequently had visitors, the nursing staff at least, but I still missed you. Being home and having Ryan to talk to for much of the day was nice, but..." Cassidy lifted Brenna's chin. "I missed you. I haven't hugged you since our first night home."

"We really have to remedy that," Brenna acknowledged. "I miss you constantly. Knowing you're here, though... I have been better able to keep my mind on task."

"So shooting went well?"

"Yeah. Mike Landau's looking forward to us being back on set together."

"Really?"

"Says that when he's watching us together, it gives him hope he'll find his own lover."

"Mike's gay?"

"Seems so."

Cassidy laughed. "We're role models."

"Scares me to death."

"Come on, what's difficult? You just keep loving me and I'll keep loving you. We'll figure out how to parent the kids together and be absolutely model citizens. Maybe we can single-handedly turn the public tide for gay marriage."

"That's not likely."

"We're bound to be asked sooner or later," Cassidy persisted.

"Would you marry me, really? I have a terrible track record."

"Bren, your track record has been for running the wrong race." Feeling Brenna's heartbeat under her palms and the warm flesh through the thin shirt, her mind turned to more immediate interests. With an intent look, she leaned close and brushed her lips against Brenna's. "I'm ready for bed, aren't you?"

Brenna helped Cass up with a hand under her elbow. They walked together down the hall and entered the master bedroom, closing the door behind them with a click.

Chapter Twenty-Four

Cassidy awoke feeling more rested than she had in weeks. She lowered her gaze to the woman lying across her shoulder. Brenna was awake, a peaceful smile on her lips as she traced her fingertip lightly along Cassidy's clavicle. Unable to see the clock, Cassidy wondered how late they had slept.

"What..." she began, stopping as she realized her mouth was dry. She cleared her throat and summoned some moisture. "What time is it?"

Brenna lifted her head from Cassidy's arm and her blue eyes sought out the clock on the nightstand behind her. "Just about seven-thirty. You can go back to sleep." Brenna lowered herself down to snuggle against Cassidy's shoulder. "Most strenuous thing we have today is to spend the day together."

Cassidy turned onto her side and wrapped her arms more snugly around the smaller woman, then nuzzled Brenna's hair.

With Brenna moving faintly against her, their breasts making contact as each breathed, their feet entangled, Cassidy felt her body gradually awakening, a pleasant experience until her bladder became uncomfortable. She reluctantly kissed Brenna on the forehead and pulled her arm free from underneath the other woman. "I'll be right back."

Propping herself up on one elbow, Brenna watched as Cassidy rolled over, located her slippers with her toes, and pushed off the bed. She stopped at Brenna's vanity to take the robe hanging over the back of the chair, removed her brace and put on her robe. Brenna enjoyed the vision of lean, smooth curves, a generous rear, and softly defined shoulder and back muscles. Brenna's fingers itched to explore. "Need a hand?"

"No, I'm fine," Cassidy answered distractedly as she made her way to the bathroom and settled on the toilet, leaving the door ajar so she could hear Brenna.

"Since you've got the brace off, why don't we bathe this morning?" Brenna asked. "You haven't had anything more than a sponge bath in three weeks."

"Sounds divine."

"So what do you want to do today?"

"Didn't you want to go see that art gallery owner?" Cassidy reminded.

"I do, but I can do it later when you're napping."

"A little sunshine would do me good."

"You want to come?"

"I want to know what James is involved in too."

"Wouldn't it be too exhausting?"

"Not if we take the wheelchair."

"You hate that thing."

"I'd hate being out of the loop more."

Brenna stepped into the bathroom and kissed the top of the blonde's head as she passed Cassidy. "All right."

"Thanks for understanding."

"Thanks for sharing."

Closing the bathroom door, Brenna went to the tub and started the water. From underneath the bathroom sink, she retrieved a small jar of crystals and checked the label.

"Are you allergic to any scents?"

Cassidy leaned over her shoulder. "No. Why?"

Rotating, Brenna kissed her. "Aromatherapy," she said, taking a handful of the crystals and bringing them close for Cassidy to sniff. "Lavender," she identified. "It's very relaxing."

After filtering the crystals through her fingers under the running water, Brenna returned to looking under the sink. From a small wire basket, she took a natural sea sponge as large as her fist and a bar of clarifying soap. She placed both in a niche in the wall of the tub and stood. Turning, she offered her hand. "Ready?"

Dropping her robe, Cassidy stepped carefully into the tub and Brenna steadied her as she gingerly lowered herself to a sitting position. "The water temperature is perfect," Cassidy said, swishing her hands and forearms through the silkiness.

Brenna's hands slid along her legs, from thigh to calf and back again, lightly massaging the muscles before lifting each leg out of the water and scrubbing it with the natural sponge.

Cassidy moaned softly in appreciation as her body flowed with energy. The washing was thorough, between toes, over knees and ankles. An excited quiver started low in her abdomen as gentle fingers moved along the inside of her thighs and closer to her sex.

However, Brenna clearly was not working to arouse, only to energize and relax. When her legs were settled back under the water, Cassidy felt like she was floating. When Cassidy opened her eyes, Brenna was pulling her nightgown off over her head. A moment later she stepped into the tub behind Cassidy, bending her knees around Cassidy's hips and cuddling against Cassidy's back as she stretched forward to retrieve the soap and sponge again.

"Now for the top," she said.

Soon Cassidy's stomach, arms, sides, and breasts were tingling from Brenna's detailed attention. She leaned forward, wincing just a little as her stomach muscles tightened.

Standing up, Brenna pulled down the showerhead and Cassidy's shampoo. The scalp massage that accompanied the shampoo and rinse left Cassidy nearly asleep.

"You are so good to me," she murmured, tucking her arms around her knees as she rested her head on top and felt Brenna's hands, slick with soap, begin to knead her back.

She was feeling lighter than air when all motion stopped. Brenna's hands rested on the flare of her hips and Cassidy could feel the other woman's hair and cheek against her back.

"Ready to dry off and have some breakfast?" Brenna's breath caressed the back of Cassidy's neck sending shivers of pleasure chasing up and down Cassidy's spine.

No," Cassidy replied bluntly. "I wish I could do this for you."

"I'm glad you enjoyed it."

Her lips lingered on the base of Cassidy's neck. Brenna rose and helped Cassidy from the tub. Seated atop the toilet lid, Cassidy accepted the thick green fluffy towel and said, "I can do this. You finish your own bath."

Cassidy admired the wet beauty as Brenna scrubbed herself clean. Wiry legs, dainty feet, taut abdomen and smoothly muscled shoulders received the attentions of the sponge. Brenna refused Cassidy's offer to do her back, and soon she had finished shampooing and rinsing her hair, and was rising from the water.

As the damp woman stepped from the tub, Cassidy pulled Brenna toward her and wrapped her arms around Brenna's back, pressing her face into the valley between twin handfuls of breast and licking at the warm beads of water. "I can't wait to make love to you again," Cassidy whispered.

Mindful of Cassidy's limitations, the two shared a kiss of promise and then set about getting dressed. Brenna quickly donned a pair of jeans and a three-quarter-length sleeve, pale violet cotton cling top. Cassidy's supply of clothes was limited, and while the day promised to be sunny, it was still February. Brenna helped her back into a button up shirt, secured the orthotic brace to her left hand, And then helped her step into loose jeans. Lastly she pulled the body brace around Cassidy's stomach and chest.

"I should probably strap this up tight for the support today," Brenna said, suiting action to words. "Do you want a sweater over that?" Cassidy nodded and Brenna found a long, overly large cardigan she wore when she curled up in front of the fireplace.

The two women emerged from the bedroom and Cassidy followed Brenna into the kitchen, where they found Ryan and James finishing a breakfast of cereal. Each accepted a good morning hug from Ryan and a cautious, "Morning," from James.

"Muffin, bagel? Some fruit?" Brenna asked Cassidy, looking through her cupboards and refrigerator.

"Juice and a muffin would be fine." Cassidy reached into a tin and pulled out a blueberry mixed grain muffin. "You?"

"Same." Brenna poured two glasses of apple juice while Cassidy collected two small plates and a second muffin. Together they walked back out to the table and took seats side by side opposite James and Ryan.

James was quietly spooning down his last bite. Ryan, however, noticed there was something different and bubbled over enthusiastically, "You got dressed nice today, Mommy! So we're going home?"

"We're all going downtown," Brenna said. "To see James' work at the art gallery."

"What about Ms. Hyland?" the young artist objected to his mother.

"I can use the wheelchair," Cassidy said. "We need to get out and about, and your mother's right—we should check out the art gallery where you've been spending your time."

"Everyone?" James squeaked.

"Why can't we go home?" Ryan asked. "You're all better."

Brenna said sternly, "Yes, all of us."

"I am feeling better today," Cassidy acknowledged Ryan, "but we can't go home just yet. Why do you want to go home?"

"I want my toys."

"You have toys here," Cassidy pointed out.

"I miss Ranger. Can we bring Ranger here?"

Brenna shook her head. "The Talbots are taking good care of Ranger."

"Why can't he come here?"

"This house isn't set up for a dog," Cassidy explained.

"Can I go stay with Ranger?"

Cassidy wondered where Ryan's distress was coming from. Was it just the dog? He had first asked about his toys, only asking about Ranger when that excuse was challenged. Asking directly, however, probably was not the best approach. Next to her, Brenna was quiet. A dimple had formed in her cheek where the other woman was clearly biting to stay quiet. Under the table, Cassidy reached out and gently squeezed Brenna's thigh.

"We're going to see some artwork that James made," Cassidy said, wondering whether her son could be distracted for the time being.

"Why?"

"Because that's what we've chosen to do," his mother said patiently.

"When can I choose?" he asked.

Cassidy looked over to Brenna. "Tomorrow?" she queried.

"Thomas will be home tomorrow morning," Brenna said. "He's supposed to be at a FIRE session until then."

Nodding, Cassidy offered to Ryan, "How about a trip tomorrow afternoon to see Chance? I can call his mom tonight."

Ryan frowned. "I have to wait 'til tomorrow?"

"Yes," Cassidy said firmly.

Brenna didn't say anything but Cassidy knew her mood had shifted; she seemed upset. The auburn-haired woman tucked her hair behind her ear as she looked down at her wristwatch and pushed away from the table. "I guess it's time to go."

CHAPTER TWENTY-FIVE

FOLLOWING THE directions James gave from the back seat, Brenna drove into an area of Los Angeles that Cassidy was sure she had never seen before. For an "underbelly" of the city, it was pristinely clean, and historic looking.

There were café style eateries mixed in among the storefronts. Each business had its name on a wide canopy, shading the doorways in a variety of colors.

Brenna stepped out of the SUV looking around in curiosity before she assisted Cassidy into the wheelchair. Cassidy noted one place in particular and looked up at Brenna to suggest, "Want to try Mata Hari's Mediterranean for lunch?"

"We may want to placate them with pizza or burgers afterward." Brenna nodded toward the children.

Cassidy noticed Ryan's frown, matched by James' frown beside him, though neither was looking at the other.

James started south down the wide sidewalk and Brenna followed, pushing Cassidy as Ryan skipped between them.

By the time they reached the gallery, Cassidy was grateful that Brenna had paid so much attention to massaging her lower back. While she felt her muscles had tensed during the ride over the uneven sidewalk, the pain was nowhere near the usual levels. I might just manage this, she thought as James stepped back and Brenna wheeled her inside the open door.

The wide open door had a glass inset that was covered with every manner of printed flyers, signs, and business cards, almost obscuring the gallery name etched in the glass—Isis Gallery.

Inside, Brenna lowered her sunglasses from her nose and turned slowly to take in the layout. Cassidy received a warm smile as their gazes intersected, but Brenna's smile immediately vanished into the seriousness she usually reserved for her performance in front of the camera as her gaze continued around the room.

The lighting was track style, selectively placed to illuminate the art pieces—those hanging from the various dividers and walls, as well as the sculptures posed on boxlike stands in the open spaces. The walk areas were mostly in shadow and Cassidy saw a few figures moving among the displays near the back. A person would have to practically be on top of another to make any sort of identification.

Only in the front area was the lighting better, due to the sunlight streaming through the front glass windows.

At a small counter to one side, next to a battered metal cash box stood a young man, probably no more than sixteen, who was dressed like someone out of the Dillinger era of gangsters and Prohibition. His pressed suit pants were midnight black, his vest the same single color, v-points on each side of the vest lining up exactly with the creases on the slacks. He wore shined patent leather shoes.

"How many tickets?" he asked, as Cassidy continued to study him. His voice was young, not quite fully changed. Nodding down at Ryan, he added, "We have an art room for the younger kids. Only thirteen and up can go through the displays with a parent."

Brenna stepped forward and the young man stopped his ticket spiel when her business tone declared, "We would like to see Hannah, please."

He looked confused for a moment then looked up at James shifting from foot to foot behind the woman's shoulder. "Got another piece, Jamie?"

Jamie? Cassidy was surprised. Even his mother did not call him that. Brenna had noticed it too, if the narrowing of her eyes was any indication.

James took a step to the side then forward. "I, uh, don't have another one yet, Micah. I, uh, this is my mother." He gestured awkwardly and somewhat dismissively to Brenna beside him.

Micah looked down from Brenna to Ryan again. "Thought your brother was older," he mused.

James turned red and his expression darkened in anger. Before he could speak, Cassidy interjected, "James' brother is older. This is Ryan, my son." She gestured out to the gallery area. "We're friends of the family and came to look at James' work."

Micah did a double take when he looked at her more closely. Finally, though, he simply nodded. "His work is among the best my mother has ever seen."

"How did his work come to your mother's attention?" Brenna asked, looking relieved to finally have an opening.

"Jamie's art teacher is my partner."

A mellifluous voice reached them all just as the generous figure of a woman blocked the light through an open doorway behind Micah. The woman stood still a moment, holding her hands open against the door jambs as if to give everyone a moment to adjust to her presence. At last she stepped up beside Micah and rested her thick forearms on the counter. "So you're Jamie's mother." Her hazel eyes held a twinkle.

Brenna bristled. "James," she emphasized, "says you want to sell his work. I like to know the people my son deals with."

Brunette ringlets bounced in a dark halo around the woman's head as she nodded and reached out a hand as big and meaty as any man's. "I'm Hannah Shropshire. I own Isis Gallery, and I have collected and sold art for almost twenty-five years."

Brenna did not take the woman's hand. "In L.A.? I've never heard of this place."

"We've only been here since September. Connie, Micah, and I moved to L.A. in August."

Brenna continued to keep her hand to herself, despite Hannah's ready openness, and Cassidy recognized that her lover was determined not to give an inch. "And your 'theme' for this showing?"

"Happenstance," Hannah answered. "Connie's students have been my main resource, though I have shown a couple of featured private artists."

"What happens if something does sell?"

"James would receive the money from the sale. The gallery would take part as a commission. Visitors are constantly asking about several of Jamie's works. Two in particular," she added as she stepped back from the counter.

"He's only 15," Brenna objected. "He paints in his spare time. I've never seen—"

"Your son's work belies his age. The style is a merging of Durban's and Rye's vivid realism with an atmosphere of the fantastic, reminiscent of Vorhees or Pinot."

Hannah Shropshire was tall, Cassidy realized; the woman loomed over Brenna and herself in the wheelchair.

"Are you all right, ma'am?" Hannah asked her.

"Yes, thank you." Despite what sounded like a distinctly English name, Cassidy got the impression from Hannah's dark thick hair, and Mediterranean coloring that she was actually Italian. She had the vaguest accent in her speech.

Hannah was talking again, and gesturing them to follow her.

"Why don't you come with me?"

His voice anxious, James interjected, "Hannah?"

Hannah stopped and studied his face a moment with deep affection and compassion. Finally she said, "Don't worry."

Micah took Ryan into the children's art room while Brenna pushed Cassidy after Hannah and James, catching up to them as they rounded a separator wall which made an alcove of about fifteen square feet of space against the building's back wall.

Each of the three walls held framed oil paintings, eight in all. The middle three caught Cassidy's attention. There were noticeable differences in their style and yet, somehow, the content and complementary nature clearly made them a group.

Brenna stepped around a free-standing statuary and read the identifying placard to the right of the sequence of works: "Jamie Logan, Los Angeles."

He's not even showing his artwork under his given name.

Cassidy studied the first of the three, from right to left, and found a nightmare leaping out at her from the dark heavy layers of paint. The subject of The Animal Man was figuratively human, male genitalia bulging but hidden beneath tight, spandex-looking shorts. The wild feral feeling came from the fact that the eyes, a deep sea green, had the elongated pupils of a cat, and the facial muscles stood out in strained relief from the snarl of lips pulled back from dog-like canines. Bare-chested, the body had the physique of an attacking bear on its haunches, even the arms and hands drawn wide had fingers tensed and extended claw-like.

Cassidy could not look at the entirety very long, moving her gaze over it in pieces, marveling at the sensation of being grabbed and mauled which it evoked.

"It took my breath away when I first saw it as well," Hannah said from behind her. Cassidy's gaze jerked away with relief to look at the gallery owner, catching Brenna doing the same, obviously equally entranced. "I thought the artist who created it must be tormented."

"It certainly seems to be saying that," Brenna said dryly. "James, where did this come from?"

He opened his mouth to say something but Hannah drew their attention to the second painting.

Where the first painting had seemed dark, heavy in the oils, the second was light and airy, the colors spread thin like gossamer. Where the first bespoke hideous nightmare, the second seemed an attempt to put the beauty of heaven itself on display. A hulking shadow lay prone, rays of light defining themselves arrow-like and piercing the body. The figure seemed to block the light to the lower left corner of the canvas, where the shadows deepened around a thin figure with the suggestion of a quiver of arrows on its back.

If the first canvas had made Cassidy hold her breath, this second made her sigh and stare, and search the shadows for the identity of the beast-killer.

She was startled again as Hannah introduced the third painting.

"This one came to us last week," she said.

The angelic and profane styles of the first two seemed to have merged on this canvas. Less stark than The Animal Man and more solid than Pierced, Woman Rise depicted the figure of a woman with sunlight bright hair stepping through shadow, half in light and half in darkness, her back to a figure behind her. Much of her upper body remained in shadow. Her legs stepped out, as though over some threshold, breaking through to a light that captured every detail of the muscles in her legs, the tendons in her feet, the sharp relief of a skirt wind-blown around her hips.

Covering her mouth, Cassidy was surprised to realize the image had moved her to tears, as two tracked down her cheeks and were caught at the corners of her mouth.

Beside her, Brenna had lost her edginess. "James," she glanced to the second and first paintings, then back to the third. "I never expected... this." She gestured helplessly. "You created these." She brushed her hair from her cheeks, discreetly brushing at her eyes.

Cassidy reached for Brenna's hand to say something but lost her thought when Brenna's hand found hers first.

In a steady voice, Brenna asked Hannah, "What offers have you had for them?"

"Mom, you can't buy them," James pleaded.

Brenna regarded him for a long moment of silence. "You want to sell them."

"Not to you."

Hannah shook her head. "I haven't set a price on them. One of the interested parties is an associate docent at COMMA."

Cassidy prevented herself from giving a low, impressed whistle. The California Museum of Modern Art. Brenna's fingers squeezed harder and Cassidy brushed her thumb over the back of Brenna's knuckles. Their eyes met; Brenna nodded, so slightly that it was imperceptible to anyone other than Cassidy

She turned to her son. "James," she said, "do you need me to sign anything?"

His face lost its deep anxiety, shattered by the onslaught of a giddy smile. "Does this mean I can keep coming here?"

Brenna looked to Hannah. "If I can count on you being supervised."

"Anytime he wants to use my workroom, I'd be honored," Hannah replied.

"I will expect you home by ten on school nights," Brenna said, sealing the agreement by sharing a handshake with Hannah. "And you have to keep up with school."

"Since James is under eighteen, I do need your permission to use his name on the sales orders," Hannah said to Brenna. The two started back to the front of the gallery. James reached for Cassidy's wheelchair handles.

"How are you doing?" she asked him.

"I didn't expect this. She really likes them."

"They're amazing, James." She paused then asked, "Will you continue to use the pseudonym?"

"Do you think that bothered Mom?" he asked.

"Maybe a little. But you don't have to hide anymore."

"I like that my paintings are not being hung simply because I'm Brenna Lanigan's son."

"Well then, maybe you should keep the name you're using."

They stopped at the counter, where Micah was waiting for them.

"So, man, what's the word?"

Jamie shrugged, still a little dazed at the unexpected turn of events. "Looks like she's going to let me sell them."

Micah's face split into a wide grin. He offered a high five, which James returned.

Cassidy looked up to see Hannah and Brenna emerging with Ryan. Her son was liberally spotted with a rainbow of colored chalk dust on his face, arms, and hands. Micah had thoughtfully put a small smock on him, though.

"Thank you," Cassidy said as Micah leaned back against the door jamb.

"No problem. Maybe we'll see you around here more often."

CHAPTER TWENTY-SIX

THEY WERE having lunch at a round table inside the Mediterranean café Cassidy had suggested earlier, and James sat next to Brenna, quiet now. He had been so animated with Micah, who was clearly a friend for all the right reasons and not just because his mother was a celebrity. It was clear that Micah and Hannah both considered James someone special because of his talent and for who he was as an artist. Brenna tried not to stare at James with the awe she felt. She had imagined such a different scenario for explaining his late nights. She felt as if she was rushing to catch up with understanding her younger son, and felt guilty about missing the changes he was going through.

He looked up from his menu. "Mom?"

She tried not to smile too widely. "Yes?"

"I'm really going to sell those paintings?"

"Signed, sealed, and soon delivered," she quipped with a smile. "Jamie Logan is off to a grand start."

"Does that bother you?" he asked. "That I used a different name?"

She knew that James had always been the least comfortable with her celebrity. It was no wonder that he presented his work under a pseudonym, though she had been bothered by that revelation at first. "I guess I was surprised as much as hurt, but I know why you did it."

He looked down at his plate then back up at her. "I was worried that would hurt you."

"Before or after you worried the subject matter would shock me?" She resisted the urge to reach over the table and grasp his hand, grasping

Cassidy's instead as the blonde put a hand on her thigh.

"Before. Was it really shocking?"

"That first one was definitely out of a nightmare. Vivid."

James considered that. "Thank you."

"You're welcome." Brenna smiled and squeezed Cassidy's fingers. "So, how do you see this working?" she asked James as the waiter delivered their drinks and a cutting board holding a crusty loaf of bread.

"I've been sticking around after school in Ms. Vetter's room; now I can hitch a ride to the gallery with her."

"Don't impose. It might be out of her way."

"It isn't. Hannah said that James' art teacher is her partner," Cassidy reminded.

Brenna felt embarrassed at the surprise she felt. "Oh. Right."

"Are you ready to order?"

Brenna turned her attention to the waiter attending their table. Wearing pantaloons and an open vest over his bare chest, he looked first at Cassidy and then at Brenna with dark eyes almost black in his olive-toned face. However, his accent was distinctly Southern Californian. She smiled.

"I want a burger and fries," Ryan declared.

"This isn't Mister Burger, Ryan," Brenna corrected gently. "But I think you'll like the braised chicken."

She glanced at Cassidy.

Other than her reminder to Brenna, Cassidy had been quiet since they had left the gallery. Brenna remembered their hands clasping in front of James' third painting, and the sheen of tears she had seen in Cassidy's eyes. She squeezed the captive hand. "Is that all right, Cass?"

The blue eyes that drifted up from the menu obviously had not been focused on the food list. They held the faraway look that Brenna had come to recognize as Cassidy wrestling with something painful.

Cassidy closed her eyes and shook her head. "Excuse me," she said as she struggled to her feet and left the table.

"Hold on, I've got it." Brenna quickly told James, "Two salads. We'll be right back."

In the bathroom, Cassidy was in front of the handicapped accessible sink, instead of in a stall. "Cass?"

Silent, Cassidy cupped her hands under the water flowing from the faucet. Bringing her palms to her face, she dampened it and then her neck. When her gaze intersected with Brenna's in the mirror, she exhaled.

"Cass, why didn't you say you don't feel well?"

Turning away to pull off a paper towel for her hands and face, Cassidy answered, "Because I didn't want to argue with you about going home."

Brenna lifted her hand to Cassidy's shoulder and cupped the muscles gently, feeling the tension holding the blonde tight as a bowstring. "It's your first day out. What's the crime in admitting you're tired?"

Cassidy breathed out against her shoulder. "Now that I'm out of the hospital, it's harder to remember I'm not well," she admitted wryly.

"We'll go home right after lunch."

"We should get back out there." Cassidy lifted her head from Brenna's shoulder and leaned into a comforting caress of fingers brushing over her cheeks. "I'm sure James is tired of making Ryan keep his hands to himself."

"He'll manage."

"He's not Ryan's brother, Bren. Didn't you see his expression when Micah mistook Ryan for Thomas?"

"I think Micah was pulling his leg. They seem pretty close."

Cassidy sat down on the small chair next to the sink. "He looked like he was angry."

"He apparently has an outlet for that now," Brenna mused. "James really surprised me today," she added. "I was sure I'd find something else."

"He has amazing talent," Cassidy agreed. "I remember telling you I thought that portrait he did of you for Christmas was very professional."

"Guess you were right. He's about to get paid for it. That's pretty professional." Brenna crossed her arms over her chest, shaking her head in amazement. "I never noticed it really." She looked at Cassidy. "I almost missed my son growing up."

Cassidy lightly stroked her fingertips over Brenna's cheek just before tilting her head up and capturing Brenna's lips in a tender kiss. The contact was a slice of heaven. Cassidy lifted her chin and deepened the kiss with the tip of her tongue entreating entrance. Brenna gasped and opened her mouth.

"Well, I never!"

Surprised by the interruption, Brenna released Cassidy's lips and turned see the back of a woman leaving the bathroom. "Apparently she was not expecting a show," Brenna said lightly.

Cassidy chuckled, and kissed Brenna's temple before wrapping an arm around Brenna's waist. "Let's get back to our sons."

Returning to the table, Brenna found Ryan making a crumbly paste of his bread and several pats of butter. She sipped her water with studied calm as she caught the disdain on the face of a woman staring at her from another table. When the woman turned to whisper something to her male companion, Brenna put down the glass with a heavy thud.

Cassidy grasped her wrist. "Don't."

"Something wrong?" James asked.

With precise care, Brenna loosened her wrist from Cassidy's grasp, lifted her napkin and patted her lips with it. "Nothing," she told James. Looking over his shoulder, she caught sight of their waiter with a tray balanced on his palm. "Here comes our lunch.

Still, Brenna could not completely dispel her upset at the cutting behavior of the woman in the bathroom.

After lunch, the group stepped outside to the sidewalk. Cassidy slipped her sunglasses from her purse and saw Brenna doing the same. "You want to see what else is around here?" she asked, shifting in the wheelchair,

"No, you need to go home. Thomas is probably due home any minute now, anyway."

CHAPTER TWENTY-SEVEN

HEARING A car's motor, Brenna looked up from her script reading. As she processed that the vehicle was not just passing by on the street, she also realized that it had pulled into her driveway. She looked over to her right to where Cassidy was reclining amid a pile of cushions at the opposite end of the couch.

The blonde's bare feet were tucked up beside Brenna's hip. Brenna had given them, and Cassidy's lower legs, a massage earlier. Ryan lay partially on Cassidy's chest with his head butting up against his mother's chin. Both were sound asleep.

Putting down her pages, Brenna went to the door. Looking through the peephole revealed a blue SUV parked on the driveway and a large African American in a tan uniform walking around the back of it. He was facing away from Brenna, so she could not see his face.

A moment later, the man reappeared, talking to someone who was following behind him. Brenna instantly recognized Thomas, though he was looking down at the ground, concentrating on moving his feet with the precarious aid of crutches. She was out the front door in a flash.

As the door opened and his mother burst through the doorway, Thomas stopped and looked up sheepishly. "Hi, Mom."

Searching down his body, which was dressed in a sleeveless shirt and hiker's shorts, Brenna focused on how he held his left leg slightly bent, keeping the weight off of the foot that bore thick wrappings, though it did not look to be in a cast. "What happened?"

"I took a spill during the hike. My ankle's twisted."

"That's all it is, ma'am. We just came from the hospital."

Brenna looked at Thomas' escort and recalled her manners. "I'm sorry. I'm Brenna Lanigan, Thomas' mother. You are...?" She held out her hand.

"Sergeant Leroy Abernathy," he answered, shaking her hand. "I'm one of Thomas' instructors at FIRE. Nice to meet you."

"The Forestry program?" Brenna clarified.

"Yes, ma'am. We were out on Nativity Ridge studying the game tracks when Thomas fell."

"Leroy helped me wrap up the ankle and we trekked back to town for the x-ray. I decided I wasn't going to be much good to the group with a bum ankle, so I asked him to drive me home."

"Thank you, Sergeant Abernathy," Brenna said.

"No problem. Damn fine man you've got, ma'am. Hurt like a bi—" Leroy cleared his throat and corrected himself before continuing. "Hurt real bad, but he handled it real well."

The man blushed, which surprised Brenna.

She almost told him she had said worse herself, but decided against creating that level of familiarity between them. "Thanks again for bringing him home."

"Yes, ma'am." Abernathy clapped Thomas on the shoulder. Thomas patted the hand in return and the two shared a smile. "Take care, man. See you next weekend."

"I'll be there," Thomas promised.

Brenna remained quiet beside her son as they watched Abernathy back out and drive away.

"Well, I'd better get inside," Thomas said.

Brenna held the door for him. "Cass is asleep on the couch with Ryan. Do you need anything for pain?"

"Whatever they injected in my ankle seems to be taking care of the pain for now."

"Where are the hospital instructions?" she asked.

"In my backpack."

He nodded to his right shoulder and she lifted the bag off, waiting patiently as he shifted his weight so that he could get his arm free of the strap without dropping the crutch.

"Any prescriptions?"

"Said not to use aspirin, but over the counter stuff should be fine if I need anything."

"All right, let's get you settled and then I guess we've got everyone home for dinner for a change."

Inside, Cassidy had awakened. Seeing Thomas' predicament, she moved out from under Ryan and sat up.

"Hey, you're up," Thomas greeted brightly.

"Hey, you're down." Cassidy's nose crinkled as she quirked a smile at him. "What happened?"

"Twisted my ankle." While his mother took away the crutches, Thomas' powerful arms braced against the side and back cushions and he lowered himself to the couch. He looked over at Ryan sleeping. "What'd you do to tucker him out?"

"You first," Brenna requested, leaning over the back of the couch. "The whole story, please."

Thomas shook his head but smiled. "I'm a klutz."

"Really?" Cassidy sat down next on another chair. She was a little surprised. Accidents could happen, but Thomas was one of the more agile and athletic individuals she had met. "So how did it happen?"

Thomas leaned back into the cushions, getting comfortable before he started his tale. His hands illustrated points in the air as he excitedly recounted it all.

"We went up to Nativity Ridge to talk about the animal tracks, habits, and behaviors. There's a loose trail up there. Lindsey Carmichael jumped when one of the guys startled her with a wiggling snakeskin, and she leaped into me. I slipped in the loose rocks, and as I was trying to regain my balance, I landed with my foot half in one of the rat snake holes that dot the trail."

"Snakes?" Brenna repeated with alarm. Cassidy reached over and took her hand.

"Not there at the time, I swear." With a smile, Thomas lifted his hand in a Boy Scout salute. "I just turned the ankle." He thrust his thumb over his shoulder. "Abernathy was right there, practically caught me before I hit the dirt. We wrapped it up, and he and I hiked back down to get it x-rayed."

"You got away without breaking your ankle. You're lucky," Cassidy complimented.

Thomas grinned. "Yep." He shook his head. "I would have liked to impress Lindsey, though."

"I'm sure you did," Brenna said.

"Mom, I fell on my ass in front of everybody."

"But you prevented her from falling too."

Thomas cocked his head in thought. "You're right." His dust-covered face split into a wide grin.

Brenna patted his shoulder and straightened up. "Well, you rest that ankle. I'll start dinner."

"Need some help?" Cassidy asked.

"No. I just thought I'd put together a casserole."

Cassidy pushed to her feet with her uninjured right arm. "Doctor says I have to move around some."

"But you spent all day out."

"You did?" Thomas asked.

"A little sunshine goes a long way," Cassidy said with a smile. To Brenna she added, "I promise I'll sit down if I get tired."

"I'll put a stool from the breakfast bar in the kitchen."

Cassidy sighed. "All right."

After collecting the ingredients, Brenna took down the cutting board. "I'll chop."

Working the can opener for the soup stock, Cassidy sat on the breakfast stool next to Brenna. From their position, they could see Thomas settling back, lifting his foot onto the tabletop. His gaze turned to Ryan, and he was soon lightly rubbing the back of the five year old's calf.

Apparently smelling the aromas of the cooking vegetables when Brenna seared them in a wok, James appeared, smiling at his brother until he noted Thomas' injury with some alarm. "What happened to you?"

"Snake hole," Thomas said. "How's your weekend been?"

Flopping down on the couch, James blurted, "A damn sight better than yours. Mom's agreed to let me sell my paintings."

"That's great!"

Obviously, Thomas was not surprised by the revelation about the gallery showing. Brenna frowned. *What else am I going to be the last to know?*

Cassidy nudged her. When Brenna met her gaze, Cassidy asked quietly, "Are you mad that Thomas already knew?"

"I just thought I knew my sons a little better than I apparently do," she whispered back.

"Well, maybe my convalescence can give you some down time too."

Ryan woke and Cassidy watched Thomas begin wrestling with the boy on the couch. Leapfrogging over Thomas's waist, Ryan slammed into James, and Cassidy held her breath.

"Squirt, I am not a trampoline," James said, easily picking Ryan up. But he only gently tossed him in the air toward his brother. "Here, catch."

Thomas caught Ryan, who laughed. "Wanna go hit some balls outside 'til dinner's ready?"

"I'm not very good," Ryan said.

"We'll teach you."

"Chance says Daddies do that."

"Well," Thomas said, "dads and... almost big brothers."

"Brothers?" Ryan asked.

"Yeah. C'mon, Slugger." James urged Ryan out ahead of them, and Thomas followed after them relying heavily on his crutches.

James picked up the bat and glove from just outside the door, while Ryan grabbed the ball.

Brenna stopped Thomas. "Almost big brothers?"

"Yeah."

Nothing else needed to be said. Brenna stepped back as he shifted his weight, then her gaze followed him outside.

Turning back to the kitchen, Brenna's saw Cassidy leaning on the kitchen wall, her mouth open in surprise. Brenna reached out and caressed Cassidy's chin, then slipped her arm behind Cassidy's head and gently pulled her down for a kiss. Drawing back, she said with a smile, "Hi, Mom."

Cassidy responded happily, "Hi, Mom."

Epilogue

It was a beautiful Saturday, and Cassidy was sitting on the swing by the pool deck in Brenna's back yard. Two weeks had passed, two weeks of Brenna taking Ryan with her to the set while Cassidy continued to recuperate. Today Brenna was out running some errands, and Ryan was working on his batting. Since Thomas and James had taught him how to swing at the baseball while it was resting on a batting tee, Ryan had been practicing diligently ever since.

Gently swaying to and fro, Cassidy sighed deeply. She hadn't heard anything from her parents, not to follow up on her recovery or pursue the legal trouble her father had threatened. Obviously her words had had an impact on him. She suspected it would be some time before she could expect her father's civility, or want to give it to him in return.

As she watched Ryan with pride, occasionally calling out her approval, she felt a surge of relief that Mitch's custody of Ryan would never again be an issue. Her ex-husband had been arraigned on attempted murder charges, for his attack on her and also that of the flower deliveryman he had assaulted and robbed of his clothing and ID in order to camouflage his presence on the set. The battered man had been found unconscious in a bathroom stall near the prop room.

Cassidy shivered at the realization of how close she had come to losing Ryan. She watched him protectively as he ran after another batted ball. He looked stronger to her now. And he was less dependent on her. She realized that in the fall, he would be starting kindergarten, and, she suspected he would be physically and emotionally ready.

Looking into the clear sky, Cassidy realized it was quickly turning into evening. Brenna had said she would be gone only a short while, but had been gone for more than three hours, missing Cassidy's physical therapy session. That was worrying. She usually made it a point to be available during PT in case the therapist had instructions for follow up.

As if on cue, Cassidy heard the sound of an engine cutting off out front. She could hear the sliding door of the SUV opening, and suddenly there was barking.

The side gate to the back yard clattered and opened. Ryan ran to it as Ranger, Cassidy's Dalmatian, bounded inside, pulling Brenna behind him. He stopped as soon as he spotted Ryan, eagerly licking the boy as Brenna released the clip of the leash and secured the back yard gate.

Brenna coiled the leash around her fist and walked across the garden path toward Cassidy. "I'm back," she called.

"I can see that. Are you sure you want to have Ranger here?"

"If my begonias survive, I'll live. But I thought it would be good for Ryan." Brenna sat down on the swing as Cassidy shifted to make room.

"You didn't have to do this."

"I did." Brenna wrapped her arm around Cassidy's shoulders and they melded together. "Ryan was miserable here with all his things at your house."

"After you get off work, you've been stopping there with him and letting him pick something to bring over here every day for a week."

"But it wasn't anything that he really wanted."

Cassidy nodded her recognition of Brenna's perception, and then Brenna kissed her. "And, I have something for you."

"Something for me? You brought over half my closet last week."

Brenna handed over a pamphlet. "It's a birthday present for you."

"My birthday?" Cassidy rubbed her forehead as she considered the revelation for a moment. "I'd forgotten."

"You've been sort of... distracted. Then again, that's what a lover's supposed to remember, right? Birthdays, anniversaries, special occasions."

Cassidy looked at the pamphlet. "So, what's this?"

"A weekend vacation package for your birthday. I haven't booked it yet, I wanted to talk to you first, but... I was remembering back... in January, when we were talking about our plans after Time Trails. I was thinking about a ski weekend."

"Kind of out of the question," Cassidy said, indicating her wrapped ribs.

Brenna kissed her then, indulging them both in the taste and feel of their passion rising. "I don't ski either," she admitted, "but I thought... snowed in in a luxurious lodge... Irish coffees... curled up by a fireplace..." She punctuated her description with breathy kisses down Cassidy's throat.

Cassidy cleared her throat. "Sounds... warm."

"I thought so."

"The doctor did clear me to return to work in another week."

"So, no snuggling by a fireplace until after we're done shooting?"

Cassidy shook her head then kissed Brenna's nose before moving on to taste her lips. "How about when Time Trails is over, we plan another family camping trip?" she suggested.

"Every day will be a vacation with you here," Brenna said, "but going away together would be really nice."

The noise of feet thrashing through flowers caught both women's attention, and they looked over in time to see Ryan go sprawling in a flower bed along the far side of the pool while Ranger bounced enthusiastically around him.

"I'm sorry about the flowers," Cassidy said. She called out to Ryan, "Ryan, bring Ranger out—" Brenna's hand on her arm stopped her.

Brenna teared up. "It's... not important. Please?"

"It is important, Bren. I told you—"

Brenna swallowed and shook her head. "He's just a boy."

"With a big dog!" Cassidy winced as her sharp tone caused Brenna to recoil. "My place is Ranger-proofed. Yours isn't."

"Maybe we can find a doggie daycare—"

"Brenna!"

Brenna burst to her feet and turned around. "I need this to work out!"

Clasping Brenna's hands between her own, Cassidy pulled Brenna back down into the swing. "It will. Be patient. A lot has changed in such a short while; we all need time to adjust. Thomas starts college. Ryan starts kindergarten. We can find a way. Together. But you can't just make the choices, or assume all the responsibility, or suffer quietly when something you love is being trampled." She gestured toward the flowers. "We'll take Ranger back to Gwen and Lou tomorrow." She cupped Brenna's cheek as her lover wiped her eyes.

"Everything's moving so quickly," Brenna said wistfully. "I can't believe Ryan starts school in the fall. Have you decided where you'll enroll him?"

"The school where Gwen teaches serves my neighborhood."

"But that's all the way across town."

Cassidy saw Brenna's hesitation. "It's where we live," Cassidy said quietly, knowing where the conversation was going. "I should go home soon."

"Just because you are able to go doesn't mean you have to move out. I thought we were doing well. We love waking up together. We get Ryan ready together..." With a wince, Brenna resigned herself.

Cassidy rubbed Brenna's shoulder. "It'll be spring soon. I have things I need to do."

Brenna sighed. "It's more practical for you to stay—"

Kissing Brenna's forehead, Cassidy feathered her fingertips through the delicate auburn hairs at Brenna's temple. "Not very romantic, I know." She eased back, drawing Brenna's gaze to her with the earnestness in her tone. "I want to stay with you. Part of me loves how it's been these last weeks too. We are already a family, Bren." Cassidy shook her head. "But I feel...we missed out. This wasn't what either of us planned. I missed out on courting you. I want to have all the romance, all the dating, all the time together that has nothing to do with being practical."

She lifted Brenna's chin. "We'll make all the plans—camping, what our next jobs will be, where Ranger will live—we'll decide those things together. Then..." She kissed Brenna, tasting her mouth with leisurely sweetness. Brenna's soft moan of arousal made her smile against the bow-like lips and Cassidy eased away. "When the time is right, we'll move in together, and I'll make you mine officially."

She softly growled the last words, feeling the shiver of pleasure course through her lover and the pulse pounding in Brenna's throat. Her smile deepened as Brenna's cheeks turned pink and she closed her deep blue eyes, struggling against her emotions. Cassidy wrapped her arms around Brenna's back and tucked her closely against her body.

"I'm already yours," Brenna murmured, her voice husky and her breath brushing Cassidy's collarbone. "Everything about you makes me fall in love a little more deeply each day." Brenna traced the small dimple in Cassidy's chin.

"Talking with Kevin about your divorce today got me thinking about marriage, Bren." Cassidy looked up at the sky. The sunset was beginning to paint the cloud-dotted sky in deepening blues, pinks, and purples. She cupped her hand over Brenna's in her lap. "I intend to have your whole family around you when we marry, and I haven't even met most of them yet."

Brenna's expression, uncertain and briefly panicked, suggested she wasn't as keen as Cassidy on the idea of having a formal ceremony. Cassidy knew she'd guessed right: Brenna had been letting her take the messages from Kevin in order to avoid facing her family.

True to form, Brenna shifted the focus away from herself. "What about your family?"

Cassidy's eyes stung with tears. She closed her eyes and felt Brenna's fingertips brushing the tears away from her cheeks. "That's not fair," she murmured. "You and your sons are the only family that matters to me," Cassidy said earnestly when she opened her eyes.

Brenna moved out of Cassidy's embrace and clasped her hands between her own smaller ones. Planting gentle kisses on the knuckles and into the palms as she gently opened the fists, she said, "And you and Ryan are the only other family that matters to me." The words were spoken like a vow.

"So..." Brenna's inhalation pushed her chest against Cassidy's briefly. She exhaled. "If you want to meet my extended family, we'll plan it..."

"...together." Cassidy smiled. "We can accomplish anything together."

"Together sounds just perfect to me," Brenna sighed. "If I have to wait a little while before we're together all the time, I can do that. I love you, Cass."

"I love you, too, Bren."

Cassidy returned Brenna's kiss and then coaxed her head onto her shoulder as Brenna started the swing moving with a gentle push against the ground. Facing westward, they swung and snuggled, watching the sun slowly setting.

ABOUT THE AUTHOR

Lara Zielinsky is a bisexual married woman and works from home as a writer and fiction editor. She grew up reading, as it was the one thing as an introvert she could do alone in a house full of people. When she realized these stories weren't reflecting the things she thought about, she started writing her own. She discovered romance books in her teens, particularly looking for stories with strong female leads. When she opened up about her orientation, her stories started reflecting bisexuality. She got her start writing fanfic in the Xenaverse and then drifted into other fandoms. Eventually she started writing original fiction. Her first novel *Turning Point* was published in 2007. *We Fit* (2022) is Lara's fourth published novel through Supposed Crimes (Acquitted Books).

Website: http://larazbooks.com

It is now 2013 as I write this. We in the LGBTQ community have come a long way with our struggle for civil rights and legal recognition of our relationships and families. In 2001, when I was first penning the drafts of *Turning Point* and *Turn for Home*, much of what my characters struggle through was very real. Today it is no longer an issue in many parts of the world. Whole generations no longer hold onto a bigotry regarding sexual orientation. However, there are still places today where it remains a struggle to come out and to become who you were meant to be, where a person is denied the right to love and create a family with whomever she chooses. This is Brenna and Cassidy's story – fiction to be sure – but shares their struggle so no one will ever forget what once was reality for so many.

www.ingramcontent.com/pod-product-compliance
Lightning Source LLC
Chambersburg PA
CBHW060552310726
48982CB00008B/1101/J